Oggie Jones is N[...]
unlikeliest matchm[...]
wants peace in his house—and more
grandchildren!—then he had better
get his independent offspring wed....

WAGERED WOMAN

Prim-and-proper Delilah Jones was so ornery
that her father bought her a bridegroom!
Trouble was, Delilah thought Sam Fletcher
rude, crude and loco. Was Sam really the man
to tame the sexy shrew?

MAN OF THE MOUNTAIN

Jared Jones never came to town without
getting in at least one fistfight—and more
likely than not precipitating a brawl.
So what was with do-gooder
Eden Parker living in his house?
Maybe Jared was on his way to paradise....

A HOME FOR THE HUNTER

Tracker Jack Roper always got his man—
but quirky runaway heiress Olivia Larrabee
kept him hopping! Suddenly the cool loner
was experiencing a family—
but was he ready for a wife?

The Jones Gang:

WAGERED WOMAN—
Delilah Jones & Sam Fletcher

MAN OF THE MOUNTAIN—
Jared Jones & Eden Parker

SWEETBRIAR SUMMIT—
Patrick Jones & Regina Black

A HOME FOR THE HUNTER—
Jack Roper & Olivia Larrabee

SUNSHINE AND THE SHADOWMASTER—
Heather Conway & Lucas Drury

THE MAN, THE MOON AND THE MARRIAGE VOW—
Evangeline Jones & Erik Riggins

NO LESS THAN A LIFETIME—
Faith Jones & Price Montgomery

HONEYMOON HOTLINE—
Nevada Jones & Chase McQuaid

A HERO FOR SOPHIE JONES—
Sophie Jones & Sinclair Riker

THE TAMING OF BILLY JONES—
Billy Jones & Prudence Wilding

CHRISTINE RIMMER

Marriage— JONES STYLE!

Silhouette Books

Published by Silhouette Books

America's Publisher of Contemporary Romance

SILHOUETTE BOOKS

ISBN 0-373-20184-2

by Request

MARRIAGE—JONES STYLE!

Copyright © 2001 by Harlequin Books S.A.

The publisher acknowledges the copyright holder of the individual works as follows:

WAGERED WOMAN
Copyright © 1993 by Christine Rimmer

MAN OF THE MOUNTAIN
Copyright © 1994 by Christine Rimmer

A HOME FOR THE HUNTER
Copyright © 1994 by Christine Rimmer

This edition published by arrangement with Harlequin Books S.A.

® and TM are trademarks of Harlequin Books S.A., used under license. Trademarks indicated with ® are registered in the United States Patent and Trademark Office, the Canadian Trade Marks Office and in other countries.

Visit Silhouette at www.eHarlequin.com

Printed in U.S.A.

CONTENTS

Dear Reader,

It's so exciting for me to see these three early JONES GANG stories available at last for a whole new group of readers to enjoy in *Marriage—Jones Style!*

The JONES GANG started out as a stand-alone Silhouette Special Edition. That first story, *Wagered Woman,* is included here. When I got to the end of *Wagered Woman,* I just didn't want to let those Joneses go. I wanted to return to the tiny Gold Country town of North Magdalene. I wanted to write another story about an untamable man and a woman with humor and heart, a story where the family patriarch, matchmaking Oggie Jones, would be up to his old tricks again. So I did. In fact, I've written ten JONES GANG books—so far.

I do hope you like these three stories. I sure had a lot of fun writing them.

All my best,

Christine Rimmer

WAGERED WOMAN

For M.S.R.,
with absolute conviction—and all my love.

Chapter One

"Sam, whatever's eatin' you, I'd like to help." Oggie Jones let out a tired sigh and shifted the cigar he always kept clamped between his teeth to the other side of his mouth. "But it's creeping up on 3:00 a.m. Either spit it out or call it a night."

Sam Fletcher took a pull off the beer that had been sitting in front of him since closing time, only realizing after he had a mouthful of it that it had grown warm. He scowled, swallowed and pushed the mug away.

"It's about a woman." Sam said the words so low that if Oggie hadn't been standing less than two feet away, he would never have heard them.

Oggie leaned closer. "What woman?"

Sam wasn't quite ready to answer that question yet, so he leaned on the bar and pondered aloud instead, "I'm forty years old."

"I *know* how old you are, son."

"I own a store. I own a house. I own a cabin up at Hidden Paradise Lake—"

"You done all right for yourself, no one's arguing there."

"I should be happy."

"Damn straight."

"And I *am* happy."

"'Course you are."

"Almost."

Oggie wiggled his eyebrows again and chewed his cigar but said nothing. One of the jobs of a bartender was to know when to keep his mouth shut, and Oggie Jones had been tending bar for a long, long time. Oggie sensed that he should let Sam proceed at his own pace.

And Oggie sensed right. If Oggie had rushed him right then, Sam would have clammed up. But Oggie gave him a little time, and Sam put off getting to the point for a few minutes more by staring into the mirror over the bar, studying his beard.

Once a pause long enough to drive a train through had elapsed, Oggie did just the right thing: he gave a meaningful cough.

Sam bestirred himself and picked up where he'd left off. "I'm *almost* happy, Oggie. But not quite…"

Oggie dared to prompt, "So somethin's missing, is that what you're getting at, son?"

"Yeah. There's an…empty place in my life."

Oggie picked up Sam's rejected beer, tossed the last of it down the drain and washed the mug. "So this ain't about *a* woman, it's about *the* woman," he sagely suggested.

Sam leveled his gaze on the old man, impressed at the depth of his perception. "That's right."

Oggie nodded. "You got it all—now you need someone to spend it for you." Oggie let out a rheumy cackle.

Sam granted the old codger a wounded frown. "Oggie, this is no joking matter to me."

"All right, all right. No disrespect intended."

"Fine. None taken."

Oggie leaned toward Sam. "So who's the lucky lady? And what's the problem?"

"The lady *is* the problem."

"She's playin' hard to get?"

"She's playing nothing."

"Well, then what—?"

"There *is* no lady. That's the problem." At last Sam had reached the crux of the matter. "I haven't found her yet."

Oggie, clearly gratified that at last they were getting somewhere, breathed, "Ah-ha." Then he slid his thumbs under the frayed suspenders that held up his pants and inquired, "Not even a prospect?"

Sam stared down at the ring on the bar where his beer mug had been. "No. And not because I haven't been looking. I've been dating. Nice women, too."

"And?"

Sam shook his head at the ring. "There's nothing there. Zero. I want fire, you know? I can't even raise a spark." He sighed. "Maybe there's just no one out there for me."

Oggie Jones straightened up at those words. "Don't say that, Sam Fletcher. There's someone out there for everybody."

"You think so?"

"I know so."

Sam smiled. Oggie knew all the bartender's jokes about women, and he was willing to use them just between him and other men. But he believed a man needed the right woman deep down, which was why Sam had decided to go ahead and consult him about this.

Oggie had been married only once, to Bathsheba Riley, who'd given him three big handsome sons and one spiteful little daughter and then died of a stroke at the young age of thirty-seven. To this day, nearly a quarter of a century later,

Oggie would still on occasion wax poetic about "beautiful Bathsheba, the empress of my heart..."

"Okay then, Oggie," Sam said. "I could use your help."

"For what?"

"Finding that woman out there who's right for me."

Oggie beamed. "You got it, son. What do you want to know?"

"Oh, suggestions, I guess. Ways to meet women. And the women here in town who might be right for me. It would be good to find the right woman here at home. Someone who loves this town as much as I do and never wants to leave."

Oggie was cackling again. "This here's North Magdalene, son, in case you ain't noticed. Population 215, er, 219, now that Beatrice Brantley's had those twins, and those two ladies from Oakland moved into the Luntman place over on Pine Street."

"I realize that. But you know how it is. I think I've thought of everyone who could conceivably be right for me. But maybe I've missed someone. It's always a possibility."

"Hmm." Oggie considered this, then said, "By my count, there are seven women in town who might remotely be eligible for a serious relationship with a man your age—I'm discounting anyone married, living with a man, under eighteen or over fifty, as well as those two ladies from Oakland I just mentioned. Rumor is they are in love with each other."

Sam lifted his head. Hope stirred his blood. "Seven? You count seven? I could only come up with six myself. And I've discounted all of them."

Oggie wrinkled up his nose, as if counting once more to make sure. "Yep," he said at last. "Seven. I count seven."

"Who?"

"You want me to name them off?"

"Yeah, if you don't mind."

"Hell. Okay." Oggie began, "Alma Santino?"

"I thought of her. But she's barely twenty. That's way too young for me."

"Regina Black."

"Uh-uh. She's nice, but she's so shy. I've tried to strike up conversations with her more than once." Sam shook his head. "It added up to zero. No, Regina is out."

"Betty Brown."

"No way. She is one bossy woman."

"Angie Leslie?"

"Too flighty. You know she's been divorced three times."

"Now wait a minute here. Jared's been divorced twice. Jared ain't one bit flighty, and you know it."

"Well, I'm not thinking about getting involved with Jared," Sam said of Oggie's eldest son, "so I'll make no judgments about him. But Angie Leslie is not for me."

"All right, all right. So Angie's out."

"Right."

"Too bad. She's a fine lookin' woman."

"No argument there, but looks aren't everything. Where were we?"

"Er, Cathy Quail. Hey, didn't you take her out last month?"

"Yeah."

"And?"

"Nice woman, no spark."

"Okay. Chloe Swan."

Sam shook his head. Everyone knew Chloe would wait until the end of forever for Oggie's second son to pay attention to her. "Chloe's always been in love with Patrick," Sam said. "No, Chloe's not for me. That's the sixth one. Did you miscount?"

"Hell, no. I said seven, and I meant seven."

"Then who else?"

Oggie's crafty smile made Sam a little nervous. Sam understood why when Oggie proudly announced, "Why, my Delilah, a course."

Sam felt the little ember of hope that had glowed warm in his chest wink out and turn cold. Oggie's venomous only daughter was the last person he'd want to curl up with on a cold winter's night.

"That's a real humorous suggestion, Oggie," he muttered dryly, then went on with a sigh. "So all the local ladies are out. I guess I knew that, but you can't blame a guy for hoping."

"Wait a minute." Oggie jerked his mangled cigar out of his mouth, looked at it, and stuck it back in. "My Delilah's no worse a prospect than any of the others."

Sam squinted at his friend and realized he'd hit a nerve by rejecting Delilah out of hand. He'd heard Oggie complain more than once that Delilah should be finding herself a man before she was too old to present her dear old dad with a few grandchildren. But never before had Oggie dared to suggest that Sam might be that man. Of course, Sam had never before confessed he was looking for someone special, either.

Sam decided to smooth the old man's ruffled feathers before going on. "Okay, Oggie. Objectively speaking, Delilah's…" He hesitated. He wasn't in the habit of trying to think of nice things to say about Delilah Jones. "She's fine, just fine," he said at last. "But she's not the woman for me, and you know it. So let's move along to other ideas."

Oggie's feathers were not smoothed. "No, let's the hell not," he growled. "Let's think serious about my girl for just a damn minute here. Let's give her a chance."

Sam decided to try pointing out the obvious. "She hates my guts, Oggie."

"Now, son. She don't hate you. She *despises* you. There is a difference."

"Yeah. If she found me dying in a ditch, she'd step over me instead of finishing me off."

That gave Oggie pause, but only for a minute, during which he thoughtfully chewed his cigar. Then he spoke confidentially. "Try to see her side of it. She lost her mom when she was only eleven, and after that she got nothing but headaches from her rowdy brothers and me. She swore to better herself, and she did. She went to college. Now she's part of a noble profession; she's a teacher of young minds. She ain't got a lot in common with any of us anymore. She can't help looking down on us lowlifes even if we are her family—and she thinks of you as just another one of my boys, you know that damn well. But she's got a true heart. If the time came when any one of us needed her, you know she'd be right there."

In spite of his own personal dislike for Delilah Jones, Sam had to admit that Oggie was right. "Yeah, okay, Delilah's loyal and true-hearted to a fault. I know that. But that still doesn't make her right for me. I'm talking about finding someone sweet to come home to. Delilah is about as sweet as a treed bobcat."

"My girl can be sweet." Oggie's slight wince contradicted his words.

Sam had had enough. "Oggie, this is pointless. I don't want Delilah, and she damn sure doesn't want me. Let it be."

Oggie shook his head, looking rueful but determined. "I just plain *can't* let it be, son. The more I think of it, the more sense it makes."

Sam realized he was becoming uncomfortable. He didn't like that gleam in Oggie's eyes. The old man was looking downright zealous, all of a sudden. It was spooky.

Oggie went on, "It's…" He paused, as if grasping for just the right words to explain some unforeseen and marvelous revelation. "By God, Sam, it's like something that's been in front of my nose all the time but too obvious to notice. You're exactly the man my girl needs, and she's just what you need! And you *did* say you wanted fire. My girl's got fire.''

Sam groaned aloud. ''Damn it, Oggie. Face it. I couldn't get along with her. Never in a million years. She'd as soon sic the sheriff on me as look at me.''

Oggie's little raisin eyes were suddenly red with unshed tears. ''She's my little girl, after all. And she's the only one of my kids who ain't been married at least once. I'd like to see her happy, settled down with the right man, before I meet her mama in the great beyond.''

''I'm not that man, Oggie.'' Sam was getting worried. He was beginning to realize that confiding in Oggie hadn't been such a great idea after all. But hell, it had just never occurred to him that Oggie could stretch things so far—that he could delude himself into believing there could ever be anything between his spinster schoolmarm daughter and the man she'd always hated with all her mean little heart.

''You're like a fourth son to me,'' Oggie wheedled.

''Damn it, Oggie…''

''And you've done yourself proud since you showed up in this town with nothing but a bad attitude and the clothes on your back. Lord, Lord, why didn't I think of this before?''

''Oggie—''

''It's perfect. You even got…artistic leanings, what with the jewelry you make and your whittling. That one boy-friend Delilah had way back in college was an artistic type. I think if anyone will ever get a chance with her, he'll have to be artistic.''

''I've heard enough of this.'' Sam stood up.

''I ain't through, son.''

''Maybe not. But I am.'' Sam turned for the double doors.

''I got a proposition for you, boy!''

"'Night, Oggie."

"Get back here."

But Sam only waved a hand and headed for the doors.

Oggie was forced to voice his proposal to Sam's retreating back. "The day you and Delilah tie the knot is the day I deed over The Mercantile to you!"

Sam hesitated when he heard that. The Mercantile was an ancient brick barn of a building adjacent to the bar, which Oggie had bought forty years ago for a song. It was big enough to house Sam's expansion plans for his gold sales store. But it was also promised to Oggie's second son, Patrick, when Oggie died. Or at least, that was the excuse Oggie had given him for not selling it the last time Sam had made an offer.

"You hear me, Sam Fletcher?"

Sam heard, and he couldn't help considering. He wanted The Mercantile—and it was true what Oggie had said about Delilah and him. The spark was there, all right. He had to admit that the thought of Oggie's little witch of a daughter didn't leave him with that nothing, empty feeling that all the other women he'd considered inspired. Thoughts of Delilah Jones invariably made his temperature rise. Too bad the heat was caused by animosity rather than desire; he couldn't stand her, and she hated him right back.

No, he had to face facts. Even with The Mercantile thrown in to sweeten the deal, he and Delilah Jones would never make a go of it. Sam shrugged and pushed through the doors.

"Got that?" Oggie shouted, as Sam went out into the star-thick night. "You been after me to sell that building for how long now? But I ain't never sellin'. You'll be takin' it for free, Sam Fletcher, the day you make a fulfilled woman of my little girl!"

Chapter Two

Delilah Jones stood outside the small, weathered building at the north end of town that housed Fletcher Gold Sales and wondered if she should even bother going in. She certainly didn't want to go in. Sam Fletcher owned it, and to her that was reason enough never to step inside the place.

But she'd agreed to contact all the merchants in town. She just hadn't thought too carefully before volunteering, or she would have realized that there were only six merchants in all of North Magdalene—and two of them were her rascal of a father and that troublemaking wild man who owned Fletcher Gold Sales.

She'd already acquired pledges from Lily's Cafe, Santino's BB&V—Barber, Beauty and Variety—North Magdalene Grocery, Swan's Motel and finally The Hole in the Wall Tavern, which her father owned and ran.

That had been unpleasant, asking her father for a donation. He had cackled and chomped his smelly cigar and wondered aloud, as he always did, if she'd found herself a man yet. The few local yahoos with their bellies already up to the bar at one in the afternoon had chortled right along with him.

Goodness, how Delilah had longed to be outside again where the clean, spring sun was shining and the mountain lilac was in glorious bloom. Instead, determined to fulfill her obligation, she'd stood there in the stale-smelling dimness, waiting grimly for her father to say yes or no to her request for money toward the renovation of the Community Church's collapsing bell tower.

At last he'd cracked open the till and handed over several grungy bills. "There you go, gal. That oughtta help."

"Thank you, Father." She'd stuffed the bills in the donation envelope, dashed off a receipt and whirled for the exit.

But Ogden Elijah Jones just couldn't let it go there. Oh, no. He'd had to call after her. "I'm serious as a heart attack about you givin' me some grandkids, gal. In fact, I have taken matters in my own hands. Expect a man to come knockin' on your door one of these days soon. Be ready. You hear?"

Delilah had kept right on walking. She had not paused in the least, though the rude laughter of the men in the bar followed her out into the light. She'd walked briskly up Main Street, putting her father's absurd threats right out of her mind.

Now, there was only Sam Fletcher left to approach and her obligation to the Bell Tower Committee would be fulfilled. Delilah brushed at her slim skirt and straightened her collar and then pushed open the door to Sam Fletcher's store.

Overhead, as she entered, a little bell chimed.

"Be right out!" The deep voice came from beyond a door at the back.

Delilah said nothing. She was here to beg for money for the church's sake, after all. If she called out, it was just possible Fletcher might recognize her voice and refuse to speak with her. Who could say ahead of time what that wild man might do?

They hadn't shared two words together in the last ten years that she could recall. Maybe, just maybe, they could manage to be civil with each other now if she handled things right. Nervous, she clutched the donation envelope and receipts and her small handbag, and tried to calm herself by looking around.

What she saw elicited a tiny gasp of disbelief.

Beneath the sun that streamed in the spotless many-paned windows, the old wooden floors gave off a smooth, buffed shine. Glass display cases gleamed, filled with a wide variety of gold samples, jewelry and eye-catching souvenirs. Oils and watercolors of wildlife and the disappearing wilderness—the back country of which, in California at least, so little remained—brightened the walls. The rows of shelves stacked with mining gear were scrupulously neat and free of dust.

There were several excellently carved wooden sculptures: a rearing horse, a bald eagle, a delicate foot-high fawn. Delilah had heard somewhere that Sam Fletcher did beautiful carvings in wood. She wondered if these pieces could possibly be ones he had made himself.

How strange, she thought, bewildered. Could this beautiful little shop actually be crude Sam Fletcher's place of business? He'd had it for—how long now? Eight years or thereabouts, as she remembered. Before that, he'd sold his gold samples and the jewelry he made right out of that beat-up van he used to own.

People had told her that the store was a gem. And she knew tourists came from all over to rent panning and dredging equipment from him. But she hadn't paid much attention to what Sam Fletcher was doing with his life, as long as he kept away from her. And never before had she had the slightest reason to see for herself.

Not that it mattered what his store was like. It didn't matter at all. It just...didn't fit with her idea of him, that was all.

As Delilah stood and stared, the little bell over the door tinkled again. A man and a woman, tourists out for a Saturday drive in the gold country from the look of them, came in.

The woman went immediately to the jewelry cases and began exclaiming over the rings. "Walter, you must look at this one. Please, darling, look. Here."

Delilah backed away, not really thinking that she was moving into the shadows, until she stood in a corner near a tall stand filled with long picks and shovels. The door to the back room opened. She jumped a little, knocking the stand with her elbow and causing it to clatter slightly. At the sound, the man called Walter glanced over and saw her.

But then Delilah forgot all about anyone else, because Sam Fletcher came out of the back room, huge and imposing as always, his lion's mane of red-gold hair bright as fire, his full beard combed and gleaming.

Delilah blinked, recalling, for some strange reason, their first confrontation two decades ago, at her private place by the river.

The memory came at her, swift as a diving hawk. She had no chance to shut it out. She saw Sam Fletcher come out of the back room of his store, and suddenly she was fourteen again and going out the front door of her father's house on her way to her special place by the river where she always went to be alone.

It was early summer, late-morning, and the trees had all their leaves. She was wearing her bathing suit under her jeans, and her hair was braided down her back. The sun was warm on her face when she opened the door.

She let herself out of the house, heaved a little sigh, and felt relief. She was escaping that house, really. Since her mother had died, there was rarely any peace and never any order there. Her father and her brothers thrived on trouble and confusion.

The house, as she left it, was quiet for once. They were all sleeping late as usual. The night before had been pretty bad and each of her brothers had done his part to make it that way.

First, her youngest brother, Brendan, who was thirteen years old, had fallen asleep in his room with a lit cigarette between his lips. Luckily, Delilah had smelled something funny and burst in to find him stretched out on the bed, dead to the world, encased in a greasy cloud of smoke.

Terrified that he might already have suffocated, she tore back to the kitchen, filled the dishpan with water, flew to his room again and threw the water over him. He woke spitting and swearing and calling her terrible names.

But finally he got up and helped her drag the ruined mattress outside where they could douse it thoroughly. Then he stalked back toward his room. She'd followed after him, to insist he not smoke anymore in there.

"Don't lecture me about smoking, Delilah, damn you. You're my sister, not my mom. Mom's dead. Get that through your thick head. I'll smoke if I damn well please!" He'd slammed the door in her face. She'd stood there for a moment, fuming, wanting to pound on the door until he opened it—and then to spit in his mean little face.

But she'd controlled herself. She'd returned to her own room and read for a while, then gone to bed.

She was sound asleep when Patrick, her second brother, came crashing into the house. She woke with a start, and saw that it was almost 2:00 a.m. Patrick kept slamming around out there, so she threw on her robe and went out to see what was the problem.

"What the hell are you sneakin' around about, sis?" Patrick demanded when he saw her. Then he held out his right hand, which had a gash above the knuckles and was dripping blood all over the kitchen floor. "Well, while you're up, find me some bandages, will you, and take care of this?"

She'd gotten him patched up and gone back to bed. But she'd no sooner dropped off to sleep than her oldest brother, Jared, had started beating on the front door.

"Damn it, let me in! Let me in, damn you all to hell!"

Delilah waited for one of her other brothers to do something, but neither of them did. Her father hadn't come home from the bar yet. Jared went on pounding, yelling louder and louder. She knew soon enough he'd go ahead and kick the door in—he'd done it before. So she pulled on her robe once more and went out to let him in.

He shoved the door back violently when she unlocked it, swore something crude under his breath about women and barreled past her and back to his old room, sending the door in there crashing shut behind him. Delilah knew what had happened without having to ask; he was drunk and his wife, Sally, had kicked him out again.

And, she thought, as she walked down the trail to her private place, her father was no better than his sons. Right now, at 11:00 a.m., he was still passed out on the couch, snoring away. He'd stayed out after his bar closed toasting the memory of her three-years-dead mother with his friends.

But she had left all that behind, she reassured herself. At least temporarily. She was on her way to her special place, her secret place, where beauty and tranquility reigned. She thought to find peace.

What she found instead was a greasy-haired giant and a huge, ravaging machine.

She stood there, where the trail ended at the willows near the beach, and stared, unable to believe what she was seeing.

Her place was savaged, the river a swirling pool of mud. Someone had decided that her special place would be a good spot to dredge for gold. The dredger, which floated near the rocks on black inner tubes, pumped and pounded, spewing water and gravel a foot into the air and filling the mountain quiet with hideous hungry gulping sounds.

A man was kneeling among the boulders on the bank in a black wet suit, fiddling with the big hose that nosed into the river. His mask and his rubber diving helmet had been tossed aside, and his long hair, dirty and uncombed, but boasting at the same time a burning, crude vitality, gleamed in the early summer sun.

She recognized him then: her brother Jared's new buddy, Sam Fletcher, who'd shown up in town out of nowhere a few months ago, a rowdy troublemaker, who got drunk every night just like Jared did, and lived out of his van.

Something snapped in her. She started yelling—screaming, really. She leapt across the small beach to his black-suited back and attacked him, pounding him with clenched fists, beating him about the head and shoulders, calling him all the awful names she'd always despised her father and brothers for using, ordering him and his horrible machine to get out of her place.

He froze for a moment. And then he reacted, throwing her off with a rippling shrug of his huge shoulders.

He switched off the pumping mechanical monster and then loomed over her as she lay half-stunned on the sand where he'd thrown her down. "What the hell's the matter with you, you stupid brat? Get your butt off my claim."

That did it. She started screaming again. "Claim! Your claim? This is my place, mine! *You* get out of here, you…dirty, good-for-nothing tramp!"

The insult stung him. "Why, you little—" For a moment

she thought he might actually hurt her. She cowered back. But he seemed to control himself. His eyes narrowed, and he peered at her closely. "You're Jared's little sister, aren't you—Oggie's girl, Delilah Jones?"

She shrank backward some more, wanting only to escape him, but too proud to scramble to her feet and run. "*Miss* Jones, to you," she announced with a bravado that seemed absurd even to her. "Now you get that dredger out of here."

He grunted. "You've got it backward, kid. You're the one who's getting out. Now."

Her rage came back, pure and strong. "No, I'm not, you creep. *You* leave! You've got no right to be here!"

"Go on," he said quietly. "Get lost."

"No, *you* get lost. You get out of here, you bum! Get out right now!" She kept on shouting at him. He must have realized that arguing with her would do him no good. So he didn't say another word.

He lunged at her. She scrambled back, but not fast enough. He caught her by the ankle, dragged her toward him, and slung her over his shoulder like a bag of meal.

Then he started up the trail. He didn't even bother to toss her into his van that waited up by the road, but stomped on bare feet the two miles to her father's house, down Bullfinch Lane to Sweet Spring Way, with her hammering his back and screeching all the way.

He marched right up to the door and pounded on it. All three of her brothers and her father came out, looking as scruffy and disreputable as the black-suited giant who had her slung over his shoulder.

"What the hell, Fletcher?" her father groused. "I was sleepin' real peaceful five minutes ago. I heard you comin'." Delilah screeched again. Her father looked pained. "Delilah, honey. Can't you keep it down?"

So shamed and past caring was she at that moment, that she screamed once more, louder than all the screams that came before. And her father and brothers just stepped back, clearing the way, so that Sam Fletcher could carry her into the house and toss her on the couch.

"Keep her off my claim, Oggie," he said then, and turned and walked back out the door, closing it quietly behind him.

Once he was gone, there was silence. But not for long. Her father and brothers looked at each other. And then they started to laugh.

They laughed and laughed, they thought it was so funny. And she screamed at them to stop. At last, she leapt from the couch and ran to her room and locked herself in for the rest of the day.

Her father came knocking later, to try to make up with her. She pulled herself together and came out and more or less forgave them—her father and her brothers.

But she never forgave Sam Fletcher. He was trouble and she knew it, and as time passed she grew to hate him more and more.

"Can I show you something in that case?" Sam Fletcher, an older, cleaner version of the giant who'd once treated her so intolerably, strode toward the couple bent over the ring display.

"Yes." The woman's voice was eager. "This one. And this one as well, please."

Walter, beside her, coughed politely and tipped his head toward Delilah where she lurked in the shadows. "Anna, there's someone ahead of us, I think."

Anna—and Sam Fletcher—turned to look. Delilah froze, her back pressed against the wall. Sam Fletcher's blue gaze found her, pinning her to the spot.

Delilah, who up to that moment had remained half-lost in a long-ago summer day, wished she could close her eyes and disappear right through the floor. To have him catch her cowering behind a shovel stand like a shoplifter caught in the act was a thousand times worse than having to seek him out in the first place. For a minute that seemed like half a lifetime to Delilah, no one said a word.

Then Fletcher muttered, "Well, I'll be damned."

And the woman at the display case demurred, "Of course, I didn't realize…"

Delilah, who knew something had to be done immediately if she hoped to salvage one shred of her self-respect, forced herself to step out from behind the rack of shovels. She squared her shoulders, straightened her cardigan sweater and said with as much nonchalance as she could muster, "No, no. I'm not here as a customer. You two go ahead. I'd just like a word with…you, Sam." Lands above, she'd addressed him directly in a pleasant voice, and actually called him by his Christian name. When in heaven had she ever done *that* before? His mouth dropped open for a moment, and he looked as stunned as she felt. She made herself go on. "I'd like a moment of your time, when you can spare it.…"

His frown told her that he didn't trust her for a second, but luckily the two customers politely waiting for him to help them kept him from saying whatever rude things might be in his mind. "Fine," he muttered curtly. "Be with you in a minute, then."

"Great." She actually forced her lips into a brittle pretense of a smile.

After that, he turned his back on her and gave his full attention to his customers. When the couple left twenty minutes later, Anna was wearing a new ring and a nugget necklace and Walter was fully outfitted for recreational gold panning.

"Okay, what the hell's going on?" Sam Fletcher demanded without further preamble, before the little bell over the door had even stopped tinkling behind the two tourists.

Delilah, who'd been pretending to study a painting of a

spotted owl on the far wall, suddenly felt as if the small store had grown smaller still—as well as much too warm. She stared at him.

And it came to her in a suffocating rush: this was never going to work. A person did not approach the man she most loathed in all the world to ask him for a donation—even for the sake of her church's collapsing bell tower. Nellie Anderson or Linda Lou Beardsly would have to handle this one, and that was that.

She whirled, in a hurry to get out of there and not caring in the least if he knew it, and made for the door. "Never mind," she said tightly as she rushed past where he stood behind the register counter. "This was a bad idea, that's all. Someone else will be contacting you."

The scoundrel laughed, a low, rolling kind of chuckle, and he stepped out from behind that counter and right into her path. She had to jerk herself back from plowing into him. And then, worst of all, in order to scowl at him, she had to look up. Way up. The rat was well over a foot taller than she was.

"Contact me about what?"

She held on to her temper. She was a grown woman now, not an anguished fourteen-year-old. She made herself answer his question. "Making a donation. For the church bell tower. It's been condemned and has to be rebuilt." The words came out through clenched teeth.

His ice blue gaze froze her to the spot. "That's the only reason you came? For the church tower? You haven't been...talking to your father?"

"What do you mean? Yes, I spoke with my father. He gave two hundred dollars."

"Two hundred dollars." He looked at her sideways. "For the bell tower?"

"Yes. That's what I said."

"He didn't mention...anything else?"

"What *are* you talking about, Sam Fletcher?" she demanded. The temper she was holding onto was doing its best to get away from her. If he kept pushing, she might just let it run free.

"Nothing. Never mind." He smiled then, she could see it, his thin slash of a mouth curling beneath all that mustache and beard. "Just a little coincidence, that's all."

"*What?*"

"Nothing."

They stared at each other, she fuming, he grinning. And then she told him in carefully measured tones, "All right, then. That's all. Will you please step aside?"

His grin faded, as if he remembered they'd always been enemies, and he strove to reestablish the status quo. "Don't you want what you came for?"

She longed to tell him that the church could do without his money just fine. But that wasn't true. So she swallowed her pride and said tightly, "I...certainly. If you'd like to make a contribution, that would be fine."

"All right, then," he said, and stepped away. He went behind the counter and pulled out one of those big commercial checkbooks, and wrote out a donation for five hundred dollars.

She scribbled him a receipt. "Thank you," she said, though the words came out a little strained.

"Anything for a good cause," he told her, accepting her forced pleasantry with more grace than she had shown in giving it.

She turned and got out of there, sure that he watched her go, but determined not to let him know that she felt his gaze on her back, cold as twin icicles, sending dangerous shudders up and down her spine.

And she was right. Sam did watch her go.

Worse than that, once the door closed behind her, he actually pushed aside the Help Wanted sign in the window and observed her progress as she skedaddled down the street. And as he watched, he remembered the offer her father had made him less than forty-eight hours before.

The day you and Delilah tie the knot is the day I deed over The Mercantile to you! The shouted proposition echoed in Sam's mind.

Not that it mattered what the old scoundrel proposed. The old man could offer him everything he owned, and it wouldn't be enough to make him go after a woman who had never had a single agreeable word to say to him in all the time he'd known her.

Still, Sam shook his head in mild perplexity as he realized he hadn't really looked at Oggie's daughter in years. Somehow, in that time, the damned little witch had gone and turned into a good-looking woman.

By God, when he'd stepped out from behind the counter and she'd almost run into him, he'd looked down and seen that she had grown a pair of breasts—and a luscious-looking pair, as well. How long ago had that happened?

And her hips, he observed, sweet heaven if they didn't roll smooth and easy beneath her pencil-thin skirt as she trotted off away from him, fast as those nicely shaped legs would carry her.

Strange. He'd known the woman for two decades, and in his mind he'd always seen her as the scrawny little brat of fourteen who'd jumped on him kicking and biting and calling him a good-for-nothing bum. He shrugged. Oh, well, even if she did seem to be better looking than before, it didn't *mean* anything. He'd noticed she'd grown up now, that was all. It was no big deal. And it *was* only a coincidence that she'd appeared in his store so soon after her father had come up with the outrageous idea that Sam was just the man for her.

He wasn't the man for her. And she certainly was not the

woman for him. He and Delilah Jones couldn't stand each other. It had always been that way, and there was no reason on earth that what had always been should change.

However, he kept on watching her, staring out the window feeling downright dazed, until her tempting little backside had disappeared from view.

Chapter Three

For Sam, the rest of the weekend went by with a minimum of excitement, like most weekends in North Magdalene. The only commotion worthy of even passing mention occurred Saturday night at The Hole in the Wall when Owen Beardsly accused Rocky Collins of moving the eight ball during a pool match. Rocky took immediate offense and dived at Owen right across the pool table. Oggie broke it up straightaway by firing a warning shot into the ceiling with the .38 special he kept behind the bar.

Sam heard the story secondhand on Sunday. He'd decided to keep clear of The Hole in the Wall for awhile. He wasn't in the mood to have Oggie Jones start in on him about Delilah. Sam didn't want to be badgered about Delilah, especially not after having gotten such a close look at her Saturday afternoon.

And that was another thing Sam decided, after considering it way more than he should have. He wasn't going to spend any of his time thinking about Delilah Jones and how good-looking she'd turned out to be all of a sudden. Only a man with a self-destructive streak as big as the San Andreas fault would let himself imagine what might happen in a bedroom alone with her.

And Sam was not self-destructive. Not anymore. The years when he'd been his own worst enemy were over. He went to the store Monday morning firm in his resolve not to think of Delilah Jones.

At nine sharp, Julio Santino's third son, Marty, came in. Marty asked about the Help Wanted sign in the window. Sam, who'd been handling things on his own since he'd had to let Roger McCleb go two weeks before, explained that it was full-time work.

Marty, fresh out of high school last June, said that was just what he was looking for. There was no place for him in the family business, Santino's BB&V. His sister helped his mother with the variety store and the beauty shop, and his father could easily handle the barbering alone. In fact, his two older brothers had long since left town for lack of work.

"There aren't a lot of heads in North Magdalene, Mr. Fletcher," Marty explained glumly. The boy eyed Sam's hair and beard with a rueful expression. "And there's a heck of a lot of longhairs—no offense meant, sir."

Sam, who'd put up with more snide remarks about his grooming over the years than he cared to think about, simply shrugged and got back to business. "You can start right now."

"Gee, great, Mr. Fletcher!"

They shook on it, and Sam began showing Marty his duties. By noon, Marty was handling things just fine. At three-thirty, Sam decided to go across the street and pick up his mail at the post office.

North Magdalene wasn't big enough to support its own

door-to-door carrier. The mail was dropped off at the post office, and the postmistress sorted it into private boxes. For most people in town the process of picking up the mail was a daily ritual.

"No problem, Mr. Fletcher," Marty said brightly when Sam told him of his plans. Sam left the store feeling the next thing to jaunty. He'd come close to giving up on finding good help, and now it looked as if good help had been right next door at Santino's all along.

Once inside the post office, he waved at Melanie Swan, the postmistress, in the counter room beyond an interior door and went to the wall of private boxes in the long main room, which was left open seven days a week for the convenience of the box-holders. He just had his own box opened and was reaching in to get the rolled pile of flyers, cards and bills when he heard the door open and felt the slight, chilly breeze from outside.

He glanced toward the door.

And there was Delilah Jones.

She paused in the doorway when she saw him, and the afternoon sun from behind her made a gold rim around her thick black hair. She wore a gathered skirt today, its swirling colors rich and deep, with a dark red sweater on top. Most likely, he thought, she'd just come from the school that must have let out a few minutes before. He thought, with her inky hair and the strongly colored full skirt, that she looked like a gypsy, slightly wild, a little dangerous. When she spotted him, she froze for a moment.

Then she seemed to shake herself. She nodded, tightly. He nodded back. She swept into the narrow room and went to her own box, beyond his. She passed close to him. He got a whiff of her perfume, woodsy and faintly musky, too. A damned alluring scent. He snatched the envelopes and brochures from the mailbox, slammed the little door without bothering to spin the combination dial, and got the hell out of there.

The rest of the day, he kept catching his mind picturing black hair and dark, turbulent eyes. That was when he decided he was letting his mind get out of hand. And he was going to have to stop it. He just plain wasn't going to think about her anymore. He wasn't even going to think her *name* anymore, and that was all there was to it.

Later, after he'd sent Marty home and was locking up the store, he realized what was wrong with him. He'd been spending too much time without pleasant feminine companionship, and that was causing him to imagine the most ridiculous things about a woman who was as far from what he was looking for as it was possible for a woman to be.

He needed a date, that was all. If he had a pleasurable evening with a nice woman to look forward to, his overactive imagination would settle itself right down.

That evening, when he got home, he called Sarah Landers, a medical technician who lived in Grass Valley and whom he had dated twice before. He asked her to dinner Saturday night. She accepted, sounding pleased that he'd called.

When he hung up, he tried not to remember that the last time he took Sarah out, he'd more or less decided she just wasn't the woman for him. After all, he really did like Sarah. She was everything he'd been looking for in a woman: sweet and gentle, with a soft touch and a quiet voice.

Not like some women he could mention, whom he *wouldn't* mention, whom he'd promised himself he wouldn't even let himself *think* of....

It happened again on Thursday.

Sam was rearranging the main window display while

Marty cleaned the shelves by the side wall. With no warning, *she* drove up in her little hatchback car.

Forgetting every solemn vow he'd made to himself about how he would ignore her, Sam pressed his nose against the edge of the window so he could watch her pull up in front of Santino's next door. She and a passenger, little Emma Riggins, got out of the car. They went together into Santino's store.

"Looks like Emma's won the book."

At the sound of Marty's voice, Sam jumped as if he'd been caught doing something reprehensible. He glanced over to where Marty dusted the shelves, near a side window with an angled view of the street.

"What do you mean, the book?"

"Last Thursday of the month," Marty explained, busily dusting away as he spoke. "Kid with the most book reports turned in gets a book of their choice from my mom's store. Miss Jones buys it herself. She's been doing that forever. She did it when she taught me, and that was almost seven years ago now."

"I didn't know she did that," Sam remarked.

"No offense, but everybody knows that, Mr. Fletcher."

The bell over the door rang, and Sam was spared having to decide whether or not to reply to Marty's comment. Marty rushed to help the customer, and Sam returned to his window display.

Not long after, Oggie's daughter and Emma Riggins emerged from Santino's. Emma clutched a brown bag against her chest. The woman and the child got back in the car and drove away.

"Er, Mr. Fletcher?"

Sam sprang back from the window. Somehow Marty had stepped right up beside him and was looking out the window, too.

"Haven't you got a customer?" Sam challenged.

"He just left, Mr. Fletcher." Marty was grinning all-too-knowingly for an employee, Sam thought.

"Then get back to the shelves."

"Right away, sir." Marty flew to the shelves, and resumed cleaning them with great enthusiasm.

For a few minutes, the young man and the mature one worked without speaking. Then Sam said, "All right, Marty. What's on your mind?"

"Well, sir, no offense, sir…"

"Spit it out, Marty."

"If you got your eye on Miss Jones, sir, you better visit my dad's barbershop before you go asking her out. She's a teacher, sir. She likes a clean-cut look."

Sam looked at Marty for a moment, recalling with a rueful sigh his last short-lived employee, Roger McCleb. Roger never would have noticed if Sam had been staring out the window at Oggie Jones's daughter. Roger had had his hands full trying to remember how to make change. Maybe, Sam found himself thinking, there were a few drawbacks to hiring a go-getter like Marty; Marty saw too damn much.

"Mr. Fletcher—did I say something wrong, sir?" Marty inquired nervously, when Sam had been glowering at him for a while.

"Just finish the shelves, Marty."

"Er, you betcha, Mr. Fletcher."

Saturday evening, Sam drove to Grass Valley for his date with Sarah Landers. They shared a meal, and took in a movie. It was a pleasant evening.

And Sam knew halfway through dinner that calling her again had been pointless.

She invited him in when he took her home, smiling at him sweetly, the light of anticipation shining in her soft hazel eyes. He declined the invitation, knowing for certain this time that he would see her no more. She kept her sweet smile, but he watched the light fade from her eyes.

After he left her, he drove the twisting highway for home, feeling a depressing mixture of sadness and relief—sadness that he was alone, relief that he'd finally faced the fact that Sarah was not the right woman for him.

At the edge of town, he thought for a moment of stopping in at The Hole in the Wall. Maybe Jared would be there, in from the logging camp in the woods where he lived most of the time after his second messy divorce. Though Jared no longer touched liquor, he sometimes hung out in the bar for companionship when he was in town. If Jared were there, Sam would buy him a soda and they could talk about old times…

But Sam vetoed that idea before he let himself act on it. Oggie would be there, and Oggie, next to *she-who-could-not-be-named,* was the last person he could afford to get near right now. Oggie would be after him about *her.* And he didn't want to talk about *her.*

He turned off Main Street and drove home. Once there, he went to the workroom over the garage where he kept his woodworking tools. He labored for a while on a hunk of white pine he'd found, one in which he had recognized the vague shape of an owl waiting in the wood to be set free. He boasted, or roughed out, the basic shape of the bird, finding peace in the concentration, comfort in the feel of his own hands on the wood. Then, his spirit somewhat soothed, he showered and watched some late-night television, eventually falling asleep on the couch.

He dreamed of his first claim, that spot at the bend of the river that Oggie's vindictive little daughter had called hers. He dreamed he was working that four-inch dredge he'd spent his last five hundred dollars to buy, down below the surface of the water with the hose, vacuuming the crevices for placer deposits trapped there. Something stuck in the hose. He surfaced, and as he fiddled with the machine, he felt someone watching him.

He looked up. And *she* was standing there.

He stirred in his sleep, moaning a little, because he was trying, valiantly, even while unconscious, not to think her name. But then it came to him, rolling off the tongue, sweet and tempting as the smell of her: Delilah Jones.

No. Wait a minute. Not Delilah. Lilah. Yeah. Lilah, that's what he would call her if he ever said her name again. Lilah. He muttered it aloud in his sleep, though of course no one heard.

Lilah…smiling at him. She held out her hand. In her palm gleamed the biggest, purest nugget he'd ever seen in his life.

She said, "The gold's over here, Sam. Come on and get it." And she tucked that big nugget down her shirt, right in the sweet valley between her full breasts.…

Sam sat bolt-upright, kicking the coffee table with the leg that was hanging off the side of the couch. He stared blankly at the television he'd left on, watching a giant reptilian bird tear the head off of a man in swim trunks as a pretty woman in a bikini cowered screaming nearby.

Then he groaned, raked his hair back with both hands and switched off the television. Soon enough he staggered grog-gily to his bedroom and fell across the bed, asleep before his head hit the pillow. The next morning, he told himself that he had no memory at all of his dreams the night before.

Around eleven, he dropped in at Lily's Cafe for a late Sunday breakfast.

And there *she* was.

In a booth at the back with Nellie Anderson and Linda Lou Beardsly, in for a snack after church. Sam almost turned around and got out of there. But he couldn't spend his life running from the sight of her.

He slid onto a counter stool, resolutely turning his back

to her, and ordered his usual. But he could see her in the mirror that took up the whole wall behind the counter, and he knew she saw him, too.

Nellie and Linda Lou noticed him as well, though they sat side by side facing the other way. More than once, each of those old biddies turned and shot him a sour glance. He didn't let it bother him. He'd had run-ins with both of them, way back when, as he had with most all of the town's really upstanding types.

Once, after a particulary wild night out with Jared, he'd awakened to find himself in Nellie's flower bed. Nellie herself, out in her robe and slippers to pick up her paper, discovered him right after he realized he was awake. She'd started screaming. He'd thrown up on her slippers. It had not been his most shining hour.

But that had been years ago. Still, he was sure Nellie and Linda Lou continued to think of him as the rowdy young fool he had once been. And he just bet they were having a hell of a time reconciling the young wild man of whom they'd so thoroughly disapproved with the local merchant who'd just given five hundred bucks to help prop up the church bell tower.

But Sam didn't really give a damn what Nellie Anderson and Linda Lou Beardsly thought. He was too busy trying to pay no attention to *her*.

It shouldn't have been so difficult to ignore her. She hardly moved or made a sound, sitting there in the corner in a blue wool dress while the two battle-axes she called friends, Linda Lou and Nellie, jabbered away about the bell tower fund and the declining attendance at church. It should have been a piece of cake, to keep his eyes on his omelet and forget about her.

And maybe, if she'd never moved a muscle, he might have done all right. But suddenly, when she'd been sitting very still for a long time with her hands in her lap beneath the table, she raised her right arm.

For no reason he could fathom, Sam had a crystal clear mental image of her smiling at him, holding out something golden and gleaming. He almost choked on his coffee, and it sloshed in the saucer when he put the cup down. He looked again, furtively, and saw there was nothing at all in her hand. She had only lifted it to smooth her black hair.

His appetite, he realized then, had fled. He paid for his untouched ham omelet and left.

Good God, was there no escaping her? He couldn't go on like this.

He saw her twice in the following week. Both times, mercifully, were at a distance. It was what happened on Saturday that finished him off.

Saturday afternoon, Sam left Marty in charge of the store and drove to Grass Valley to stock up on staples.

He went to the big supermarket on Brunswick Road. He was actually feeling about as contented as he'd ever felt the past two weeks, strolling the wide aisles picking up his flour and his bacon, far away from the never-ending temptations of Oggie Jones's one and only baby girl. Or so he thought.

Until he came around the floral display to the produce section—and there she was, leaning on the handle of a big basket just like his, and chatting with the produce clerk. Sam froze in the aisle and listened as she asked for fresh mushrooms and the clerk pointed to them. She smiled and thanked him. It was a downright gorgeous smile.

Had she always smiled like that? Sam wondered. And if she had, why not for him?

Because she can't stand the sight of me, he reminded himself grimly. *And I've never been able to tolerate her, either. She's a prissy little twit half the time, and mean as a riled rattler the rest, not what I'm looking for at all....*

But he stood there, transfixed, as she wheeled her cart away from him, her beautiful hips swaying provocatively in trim jeans, and rolled down a plastic bag to begin choosing her fresh mushrooms. She selected them with great care, never looking up, and Sam found himself wishing he was one of them, a pale, fresh mushroom in her slender hand.

After the third or fourth irritated shopper murmured a pointed "excuse me" at him, Sam realized he had to get moving again.

Like a thief in the night, he pulled his cart backward, around the floral display and out of her sight. He simply could not make himself stroll past her, have her look up and glare at him, or worse, stare right through him, as if he didn't exist.

He headed for a check-out lane and paid for what he'd already picked out. Then he loaded the bags in his new Bronco and returned to North Magdalene. He took the food home, put it away, and then joined Marty at the store.

He and Marty worked smoothly together until nearly closing time, when he left Marty alone again to pick up the mail. As he entered the long room, he did not let his mind even consider the thought that *she* might be lurking there among the mailboxes, ready to drive him insane with her fierce, frozen glances, with her perfume that mingled a woodland morning with musk.

But everything was fine. There was no sign of her. He spun the dial. The little door swung open, and he took his mail in his hands. He left the long room quickly, not wanting to tempt fate. He made it outside, where the sun was nearing the western hills and all was as it should be. He crossed the street to his store again.

And then he saw her. Getting out of her car up by Lily's Cafe. She shut the car door and began strolling right toward him.

He saw her stride break when she recognized him. She

gave him that tight little nod, like she had in the post office a week before—that nod that, he supposed, was a concession to the fact that they'd spoken more or less civilly Saturday-before-last, when he'd donated five hundred dollars to her bell tower fund.

But the nod was all he got. After that, she kept right on coming, her face blank, like it always was, not acknowledging him further, as if, in reality, he was no longer there at all. He wanted to rush forward to meet her. He wanted to grab her by the arms and shake her, until she looked in his eyes at last, until her mouth went soft and yielding and she held it up to his....

He heard a low growling sound and knew it came from him. And then he ducked into the next doorway, into Santino's store. He went straight to the back, to the little room where Julio Santino presided, with the Naugahyde couch and scarred side table stacked with tattered magazines by one wall, and the barber's chair in the middle of the floor.

"Well, shut my mouth and call me a rug," Julio Santino exclaimed at the sight of him. "I never thought I'd see the day."

Sam sat in the chair. "Just the mustache and beard," he said flatly. "Don't touch the hair."

"Well, it's a start," remarked Julio.

"Shut up and cut."

Chapter Four

That wild man Sam Fletcher was sitting on her front porch when Delilah drove up. It took her a moment to realize it was him. For some inexplicable reason, he'd shaved off his mustache and full beard. He'd also tied back his shoulder-length hair into a ponytail. From the front at least, he almost looked respectable.

But not quite. There was still that troublemaking gleam in his eye and the arrogant way he carried his big, powerful body. Even crouched on her front step, his shoulders hunched over a stick of wood as he worked at it with a knife, he looked alert and ready to pounce at a moment's notice.

Delilah shot him a "get lost" look from behind the wheel. It had absolutely no effect. He didn't budge, but just went on slicing away at the little stick of wood.

For a moment, reluctant to get out of the car and deal with him, Delilah didn't move. What in heaven's name could he be doing here? she wondered. He'd never come to her house. Yet here he was, sitting on her step like he belonged there, causing her stomach to knot in a distressing way.

And that really bothered her—to feel anxious about Sam Fletcher. Seething, furious, indifferent, disgusted, enraged— all those emotions came to mind when she thought of the man. But anxious? Never. Until recently.

Oh yes, there was definitely something going on with him lately. Since the day she'd solicited a donation for the bell tower fund from him, it had seemed like the man dogged her every move.

He watched her in the mirror while she tried to enjoy her Sunday brunch at Lily's Cafe. He stared at her in the post office as if she had her skirt on backward. His icy gaze chilled her when she passed him in the street, and she could swear he peered at her out of the windows of his store every time she passed by.

It just didn't make sense. For over a decade, they'd lived in a perfectly good state of truce. They'd put the battles they'd fought during the years she'd lived with her father behind them. They'd learned to ignore each other; each had developed the habit of pretending the other wasn't there. And it had worked out just fine.

Now, all of a sudden, the rotten rogue was changing the game plan on her. And Delilah didn't like it. Not one little bit. It made her nervous, very nervous. And, worse than that, it made her *think* about him. Which was crazy. She had better things to do with her time than to think about Sam Fletcher.

Well, she thought grimly as she emerged from her car, whatever the incorrigible wretch was doing here, she was going to give him a large piece of her mind for his trouble. She would take this opportunity to tell him in no uncertain terms that she wanted him to stop giving her the eye every time she walked by him. She wanted him to start ignoring her again, and that was that.

Also, he had no business being on her porch, which was the first thing she said to him once she'd marched around the nose of her little car and planted herself at the base of her own front steps.

"Sam Fletcher, you have no business being on my porch."

He shot her something that resembled a grin—a sort of flattening out of his lips. Then he stood up and pocketed his whittling knife. "Good to see you, too, Lilah."

She glared at him, shielding her eyes with her arm because, to the west behind the house, the sun was dropping low. "What do you want?"

He held out the bit of willow that he'd been slicing away at. "For you."

Dropping her shielding arm, Delilah looked down at his outstretched hand where a wooden raccoon sat, balanced on its hind legs, paws up. The little figure was primitive, but utterly charming. She stared at it for a moment, realizing with alarm that she itched to finger the grooves where his knife had shaped it. Then she pointedly looked away.

With a shrug of his muscular shoulders, he stuck the lovely thing in a pocket. Delilah felt a stab of regret for that small object of rough beauty, lost to her because she mistrusted its creator.

"What do you want?" she demanded again, more forcefully than before.

He looked over her shoulder, into the windows of her car. "You've got groceries. I'll bring them on in."

"No, you won't."

Ignoring her words, he took the few steps down to where she stood. She didn't budge.

He feinted around her. She mirrored his step. She wasn't exactly blocking his way; Sam Fletcher was six-five and broad as an oak. She could no more block his way than a gnat could stall a buffalo. But she *was* standing, quite purposefully, in his path.

"Come on, Lilah," he said.

"I don't need your help."

He looked minimally annoyed. "I didn't say you needed it. I just said you're getting it, that's all."

"What for?"

"Why not?"

"You're up to something. I want to know why you're here."

He looked at her for a moment, sighed as if he were the one whose patience was being tried, and then casually took her by the shoulders and moved her out of his way. He'd reached her car before she even had time to sputter her outrage that he'd dared to lay hands on her.

"You have absolutely no right—"

"I want to talk to you." He tossed out the words casually, overriding her budding fury with nonchalance, as he pulled open the hatch at the back of the car and hauled three grocery bags into his powerful arms.

"Stop that," she snapped. "I told you, I didn't want—"

"Settle down, Lilah," he said, sounding weary. "Let's get this stuff inside, and then we can talk."

He mounted her steps again and went to the front door, where he waited quite patiently for her to let him in.

"Oh, all right," she muttered, when a few seconds of vituperative glaring did her no good at all. She had some frozen things in the cooler, and the groceries had been waiting in the car for a while now; she'd had errands to run in town before coming home after her trip to Grass Valley to get them. It would probably be best to get the perishables put away as soon as possible—even if that meant putting up with Sam Fletcher for a few grueling minutes more.

Grabbing up a bag herself, she climbed the steps, slid

around Sam Fletcher's imposing bulk, and unlocked the door. "This way," she instructed. He followed her in.

They set the bags on the kitchen counter. Then he went back for the cooler, which he said he could handle himself. She quickly set about putting the milk and meat in the refrigerator and when he returned she took the frozen vegetables out of the cooler and put them away.

Once that was done, she faced the clean-shaven giant. "Now, what do you want?"

He glanced around at the bags on the counter, almost as if, now the moment had come, he shrank from it. "There's more here to put away."

"It will wait. Talk. Now."

He looked at her, an unnerving look that seemed to drink in the whole of her, though his eyes never moved from staring into hers. "It's Saturday night," he said finally.

"So?"

"Do you have a date?"

She gaped at him. What in the world difference could it make to Sam Fletcher if she had a date or not? "As a matter of fact, no. Though it's none of your business."

"You aren't…seeing anyone, then?"

"What are you getting at?" This was becoming stranger by the second. These were the kinds of questions a man only asked a woman when he was considering…

Heavens, she couldn't even bear to finish the thought. It wasn't possible. Not wild Sam Fletcher who detested her just as much as she loathed him. He couldn't be thinking of asking her for a…

Delilah shook her head. No. She wouldn't think it. It was too appalling. There had to be some other perfectly reasonable explanation for the way he'd been behaving lately.

"Sam." She was so taken aback by her own thoughts that she actually forgot to be hostile for a moment. "Sam, what is going on?'' The pleading note in her voice shocked both of them. They stared at each other.

He was the first to look away, smoothing his already tightly pulled-back hair with his hand. ''Look. I'm thirsty. Could I have—''

Without letting him finish, she whirled, popped open the fridge, and yanked out a can of cola. She shoved it at him. ''Here.''

He looked down at the can, as if he couldn't figure out how it had gotten in his hand. ''Mind if I...sit down?'' Good heavens, he was being so *polite*. There was something the matter with him, no doubt about it now.

She peered at him more closely. He didn't look well. His face was pale, and his breathing seemed rapid. Maybe he was sick, maybe that was what was wrong with him. Maybe he'd been sick for a couple of weeks now, and that was why he'd been behaving so strangely. Yes, that must be it.

Though it made no sense. If a man was sick, why would he show up at the house of a woman he hated just to tell her he was ill? Unless he hoped she'd catch what he had.

''Lilah?''

And why was he calling her Lilah all of a sudden? ''What?''

He looked longingly at the table in the window nook a few feet away. She remembered he'd asked for a seat. ''Oh. Of course. Go ahead.''

He dropped to a chair and popped open the cola. She waited, her heart doing erratic things in her chest, as he took a long drink.

He set the can down. ''That's better. Thank you.''

''It's okay. Now, tell me—''

''I am. I will...Lilah, I—''

Suddenly, she didn't want to hear. ''You know, you're absolutely right.''

He blinked. ''I am? About what?''

"These groceries. I really should put them away."

She sprang to life, peeling herself off the refrigerator where she'd been drooping in dread and flying around the roomy kitchen as if getting the bags unloaded meant life or death.

"Lilah?"

She grabbed a bag full of produce and whirled to yank open the refrigerator door. Then she knelt, the bag beside her, and began frantically piling lettuce and celery, radishes and zucchini, into the crisper drawer.

"Lilah?"

"Won't be a minute..."

"Lilah?"

Slowly, she looked up. He'd left the chair and now loomed above her, looking down. His eyes, always so cold in her every memory of him, shone now with a strange blue fire.

She shot to her feet and confronted him. "You stop. You just stop. I won't, I will not, do you hear?" She backed away, stepping over the half-unloaded bag.

Gently, he closed the refrigerator door. "Lilah."

She shook her head. "It's no. No ahead of time. So don't bother to ask."

He smiled then, a smile that charmed and beguiled her. Stars above, with all that hair gone, his face was downright...handsome.

"Ask what?" he said tenderly and took a step toward her.

Out the window over the sink, the day was going. The sun gleamed on the rim of Sweetbriar Summit, which rose on the other side of Main Street, past the river and the woods. Shadows claimed the edges of the bright room. Oh, she had to get rid of him, she knew it. Before dark, before he could say what he'd come to say.

"I want you to leave. Please," she told him on a mere whisper of sound.

He only shook his head. "Not until I ask you..."

"No. Don't do it. Please."

"I have to."

"Oh, heavens, Sam, don't..."

But it was too late. He said, *"How about a date, Delilah?"*

She turned away and looked out the window, as the sun slid behind the mountain. For a moment the room lay in soft, tempting shadow. She could feel his hopeful, tender gaze.

And then Delilah turned, edged around him swiftly, and went to the wall by the living room arch. She flipped on the light. "No. Never. Forget it. No way."

His gaze was hard now, his big body tense. When he spoke he almost sounded like the rotten scoundrel she'd always known. "Why the hell not? It's only a date."

"Because."

"That's no answer."

She looked past him out the window over the sink again, at the near-darkness where the trees were only dim shapes now and the rim of Sweetbriar Summit shimmered with the very end of day.

"Why not?" he demanded again. "Give me one good reason." He took a step toward her. She slid around him once more and went back to the sink.

"A reason, Delilah."

She said, rather mindlessly, "You want a reason."

"That's what I said."

"Fine. I'll give you a reason." She crossed her arms under her breasts. "I don't go out with jailbirds, for one."

"What the hell do you mean, jailbirds? I'm no jailbird."

She shook her head, feeling self-righteous. "Don't stand there and lie to me. Sheriff Pangborn is always tossing you in the jail, for being drunk and disorderly, for getting in fights.''

"Lilah." He spoke with infinite patience. "I haven't spent the night in jail in fifteen years—and even then, the sheriff was more giving me a place to sleep it off than anything else. Charges were never filed. Not once."

"Sheriff Pangborn's a forgiving soul. Too forgiving, as far as a lot of people in town are concerned."

"That was fifteen years ago, I'm no jailbird now. Let's talk about now, that's fair, don't you think? Why can't you go out with me now?"

"Well…" She glowered a little and bit the inside of her lip. "There are a hundred reasons."

"Fine. Start with one."

"All right—you drink too much."

"I *used* to drink too much. Past tense again, Lilah. We're talking about now."

"Drunk or sober, you're always hanging around my father's bar."

"My friends are there, and I drop in once or twice a week. But that's tops. Lately, I haven't even been stopping in that often."

"You love to gamble. You're a gambling man."

"Lilah. I like a game of poker with the guys every now and then as much as the next man. But that hardly adds up to a dangerous habit."

"Of course you'd say that."

"Because it's the truth."

"Well, it doesn't matter anyway. My answer is still no."

"You still haven't given me one solid reason."

"I…I have the best reason in the world for not dating you. I don't need any others."

"All right, what? What is the reason?"

"Because we've *always* hated each other!"

He looked completely unconcerned. "No reason that can't change."

"It can't. It can't change. It's how it's always been."

"Past tense, Lilah. Give right now a chance."

Delilah uncrossed her arms and recrossed them again. She felt more than uncomfortable now. She felt…like her whole world was fraying at the edges. He sounded so reasonable. She was weakening, and she knew it.

She was actually starting to wonder why she shouldn't say yes to him—a man exactly like her father and brothers, a man she'd always been careful to avoid like the plague. Oh, what was wrong with her? She must be getting desperate, though she'd always believed she was perfectly happy with her single life.

She'd had one love affair, in college. It had not amounted to much in the end. In fact, the physical part of it had been awkward and groping, and had left her secure in her conviction that she could get along just fine without whatever it was that everyone else got so excited about.

But, heavens to Betsy! If she was as completely immune to passion as she'd always thought, why was it that right this minute, she was actually pondering what it might be like to kiss Sam Fletcher on the lips?

Could it be, she wondered, even though she wished she hadn't, that she'd always loathed Sam Fletcher as a defense, because deep down she was *attracted* to him?

Delilah recoiled from such an impossible idea. Frantically, she sought a fresh defense against this forbidden new fascination with a man who would never in a thousand years be the right man for her.

And then it came to her: her father, two weeks ago, tossing off that ludicrous taunt that he'd picked out a man for her. It was crazy to think that he might have really done such a thing. However, if Oggie *had* done it, who better to choose than Sam Fletcher, fellow troublemaker, son of his heart if not of his blood?

And, come to think of it, Sam had begun acting strangely on that very day....

Delilah, who'd felt her bones starting to melt, now stiffened her spine. She glared at the handsome giant across the room from her. "My father put you up to this, didn't he? I know him. He wants to see me married. He doesn't care to whom. He's probably offered to *pay* you if you can put a ring on my finger. Do you actually think I'd have anything to do with a man who was paid by my father to take me out—let alone, if that man was *you*...."

Though Delilah didn't know it, this particular indictment gave Sam a moment's pause. After all, Oggie *had* offered him The Mercantile if he married her.

But then, Sam shrugged. Two weeks ago, there wasn't enough money in the world to bribe him to go after Delilah Jones. And today, there wasn't enough to hold him back.

He answered her accusation with heavy irony. "Why, thank you, Delilah. Your high opinion of me never ceases to amaze me. But you're wrong. I'm not here for money. I'm here for *you*."

Delilah eyed him warily. He sounded grim, but sincere. She found, against all wisdom, that she actually believed him, though to believe he'd only come here because he wanted *her* seemed impossible. Incredible. Downright dangerous.

And yet—Heaven help her—captivating, too.

She stared at him, feeling suddenly bewildered by her own forbidden thoughts.

He smiled, knowing as men have always known, what her dazed look meant. She was softening, giving ground.

"Lilah." His voice was a caress. His gaze spoke of things she knew she shouldn't let herself imagine. He took a step toward her.

"No…" She stepped back and came up short against the sink.

"Lilah…"

"Stay away. I mean it."

He took another step.

She had to stop him. Frantic, she fumbled behind her in the dish rack, and felt the handle of a heavy frying pan. She grabbed it and held it up. "Get back."

He smiled. "God, Lilah. You are something."

His eyes were sea blue mirrors in which she saw herself. Oh, foolish, foolish, she thought vaguely. Never before, in all their years of battles and armed truces, had she let herself be alone with him. Alone in her kitchen after dark.

She should never have let him in. She should have grabbed her groceries from him on the front porch, and refused to let him cross her threshold into her personal space. At the least, she should never have allowed him to tell her why he came. She should have ordered him out the minute he set her groceries on the counter.

Yes, order him out. That was the thing to do. She was going to order him out. Now…

But he took the final step. And she said nothing. Her weapon, the frying pan, grew too heavy to hold high. She let it sink to her side.

He whispered her name again, and she felt the warmth of him, radiating out, enveloping her. His big hand, rough and tender, was on her cheek, stroking, guiding her chin up so her mouth would be ready.

Oh, my gracious, he was going to kiss her. His mouth was going to cover hers, and she was going to know the taste of her enemy on her lips. And she wanted it, *wanted* it, couldn't wait for it. She felt her head droop back on the stem of her neck. His mouth descended….

And the forgotten frying pan in her nerveless hand clattered to the floor.

The jarring sound saved her. With a choked cry, she shoved at his chest. He grabbed her arms. She struggled, briefly, and then she just glared at him, into those seductive blue mirrors that now looked hard, and hungry as well.

Slowly, so she would know he did it by his own will, he released her and stepped back. There was a long silence, which she broke at last by retrieving the frying pan and setting it on the counter beside the remaining grocery bags.

Then he tried that voice on her again—that soft, tempting voice that soothed her and beguiled her into forgetting who he was.

"Lilah…"

"No."

"Lilah."

"I want you to go. Now."

He shook his head, his expression bemused. "I know what you want, Lilah. I saw it in your eyes. Felt it, in the way your body—"

She put up a hand. "No more."

"Aw, Lilah. Why run from it? You can't get away anyway. Believe me. I know." They looked at each other, and she wondered if her own face mirrored the barely restrained longing she saw in his. "Come out with me. Tonight," he said. "We'll drive down to Nevada City. I know this nice, quiet little restaurant there, where we could—"

She couldn't let him continue, it sounded too lovely. "No. Please leave. Now."

"Lilah…"

She looked him level in the eye and spoke with some force. "Get out of my house."

"Come on. It's only dinner."

"No. I mean it, Sam Fletcher. No dates, no nothing— ever—between you and me." He went on looking at her tenderly, and her frustration at his unwillingness to leave loosened her tongue. "I've spent thirty-four years proving that being a Jones doesn't necessarily mean I'm a person who likes to brawl over things that make no difference, and shoot out the lights rather than walk across the room to reach the switch. Do you actually imagine that I'm going to let myself become involved with a man who's more of a Jones than the Joneses?''

"You want me."

"There has to be more than that for me."

"Give it a chance. We can find more."

"No way. Find yourself some other woman."

His eyes glittered at her, the way moonlight reflects on a night pond, in gleaming ribbons. Then he reached in his pocket and took out the willow raccoon she'd refused on the front step. He set it on the table.

"I made it for you. Sitting there, nervous as hell, waiting."

"I don't want it."

He was already on his way to the door. "Fine. Throw it away."

She gave a little gasp at the thought. She didn't want it; to take it would somehow speak of intimacies between them. But beauty like that was rare, however unrefined. She could never toss it away.

She heard the front door close. He was gone. She listened as his booted feet retreated down the porch steps. Then she looked again at the figure on the table. The tiny animal gazed back at her, too appealing to bear, through its roughly etched raccoon mask.

Quickly, Delilah turned away from the tiny creature and finished putting her groceries away. After that, she made herself a simple dinner and sat down to eat.

The raccoon, which she hadn't touched since *he* set it down, watched her every bite. When she could tolerate its fetching glance no longer, she grabbed it up, rushed into the living room and, balanced on a stool, stuck the thing on top of a high bookcase, all the way against the wall, where she wouldn't be able to see it from anywhere in the room unless she stood on a chair. Then she returned to her solitary dinner and enjoyed it very much.

The phone rang at eight, while Delilah was getting a head start on the papers she had to have graded by Monday. It was Nellie Anderson.

Nellie hardly gave Delilah time to say hello before she was off and chattering. "I just spoke with Loulah Bends, and, of course, I had to call right away and let you know."

"What is it, Nellie?"

"Loulah says that Janie Fashland says that Billie Rae Naylor claims she drove by your house before dark and saw that crazy Sam Fletcher sitting on your porch, bold as brass."

"Oh?" Delilah set her papers aside. She'd been expecting Nellie's call—or one just like it from Linda Lou Beardsly. Not a lot went on in North Magdalene that everyone didn't find out about sooner or later. As a child, Delilah had been hurt more than once when the gossip turned on some insane thing that her father or her brothers had done. But when she decided, after college, that she missed her hometown and wanted to return here to live, she also decided how she would handle rumormongering when it came her way. She would listen quietly while it played itself out, and not contribute to it in the least.

"Well…" Nellie had temporarily run out of steam. Delilah's noncommittal *Oh?* had given her pause—just as it always did. But then she got herself going again. "I thought you should know that he was hanging around there earlier."

"Yes. I know."

Nellie's breath caught, a little eager gasp. "You saw him then?"

"Yes. He was here when I drove up."

"And?"

"He helped me with my groceries."

"And?"

She bent the truth just a smidgen, by not telling all. "He left."

"But what was he *doing* there in the first place?"

Delilah considered. She hated to lie. But Nellie would be burning up the phone lines, calling everyone in town with the news, if she admitted Sam Fletcher had asked her for a date.

"Well?" Nellie prompted.

Delilah removed her reading glasses and rubbed the ache at the bridge of her nose. "Nellie, I'm just not at liberty to say. It was a private matter, and now it's settled. And that's all there is to it."

Nellie said nothing for a moment, her disappointment palpable. Then, "Delilah, honey. You know you can trust me."

"Of course I do. But it's all over now."

"*What's* all over?"

"Nellie." Delilah's voice was kind and firm. "It's over. Let it be."

Nellie sighed. "Oh, all right. But if you need a listening ear…"

"Thanks. I'll remember that."

They talked for a few more minutes, but Delilah knew her friend was eager to hang up and burn the wires a little with the small amount of information she'd been able to glean from their conversation. Delilah didn't hold this against Nellie. That would be a little like blaming the wind for blowing.

After Nellie said goodbye, it was a few minutes before Delilah put her reading glasses back on and resumed correcting the stack of papers she'd set aside. She did feel a bit uncomfortable, knowing that tongues would be wagging for a day or so, hypothesizing what might have gone on between her and Sam Fletcher.

But then she told herself the talk would die down soon enough. She kept a very clean profile in North Magdalene. She led a sober, quiet life. She'd been born into a family whose antics gave all the local gossips one thrill after another. And she'd made sure, as soon as she could choose her own way, that she lived the kind of life that put scandalmongers right to sleep.

Yes, give it a day or two, and the gossip would die out. She was sure of this because she intended to give them nothing more to go on. And because she knew that Sam Fletcher would never say a word.

Delilah put her glasses back on and reached for her papers and her red felt pen. She returned to her work, not letting herself think about Sam Fletcher anymore. Or about how she could be so certain that the man she'd always despised had too much integrity to tell a soul what had passed between them in her kitchen earlier that evening.

She worked diligently for half an hour. Then the phone rang again. She almost let it ring. And then, with a sigh, she answered.

"How about *next* Saturday, then?" Sam Fletcher asked in her ear.

"Never," she quietly replied. "Goodbye." She hung up, but not before soft laughter, deep and beguiling, tormented her from the other end of the line.

After that, he called nightly. She learned to have the phone back in its cradle before he'd even finished saying hello.

And that wasn't all. Every morning, a new and charming wooden figure would greet her from an outside windowsill—an owl, a squirrel, a dove. She resolutely ignored them.

Moreover, she discovered that she could no longer walk

on Main Street without seeing him. He popped out of his store and lounged against the wall by the door the moment she set foot in town.

He never tried to speak to her, either. And somehow that made it worse. He just stayed there by his store, not even looking at her, managing maddeningly to respect her privacy at the same time that his very presence telegraphed his unspoken message:

He was not giving up.

So she ended up scurrying for the post office every day, promising herself that she would keep her eyes completely averted as she passed Sam Fletcher's store. She was doing just that on Tuesday, making a dash for the post office door, when a loud diesel honk caught her up short.

She whirled around. It was her brother, Brendan, up behind the wheel of the like-new Long Nose Peterbilt he and his wife Amy had put themselves in hock to buy. Brendan signaled that he'd pull over down the street.

Delilah, still hoping to get her mail and get away before Sam Fletcher appeared, almost shook her head. But then she reconsidered.

Truth was, in recent years, she didn't see much of her brothers. She avoided them because they'd driven her insane during the years she was growing up. But now, in the few seconds before Brendan drove by, she felt a little guilty. Maybe she wasn't really being fair. Almost two decades had passed since they'd all lived at home. Maybe Brendan—and Patrick and Jared as well—had changed.

Unbidden, she recalled a seductive voice suggesting, *Past tense, Lilah. Give right now a chance....*

"Oh, shut up," she muttered under her breath, as if the voice in her head had been real.

Then she nodded at Brendan and waved. After all, she'd never even seen the Peterbilt, Brendan's pride and joy, up close. It seemed only right that she stop and take a look.

That seductive remembered voice had nothing to do with her decision—nothing at all....

Just then, Brendan's truck rolled by, its spotless chrome gleaming. Delilah caught a glimpse of her own face in the deep maroon gloss of the flawless paintwork. Her expression was a beleaguered one.

And why shouldn't she look beleaguered? Sam Fletcher was driving her crazy, after all. Every single thought she had seemed to lead right back to him.

Down the street, Brendan had found a space long enough for the big truck. Delilah hurried to meet him. Brendan jumped down to greet her, explaining how he was off on a run from Sacramento to Phoenix before dawn the next morning.

They talked for a few minutes, exchanging pleasantries. Delilah found herself charmed by Brendan's eagerness—as well as heartened by his obvious happiness. Could this be the sullen baby brother who took up smoking at the age of eleven and displayed an astonishing command of imaginative profanity whenever she asked him to pick up his room?

He and Amy expected their first child in a little over a month. He'd given up smoking, he told Delilah, when he learned about the baby. He spoke with a grateful kind of pride, and said softly that he fell more in love with his wife with each passing day.

And Brendan's adoration for Amy shone on more than his face. The big truck was a rolling personification of his unabashed love. On either side of the matching trailer, Brendan had talked a talented friend into painting portraits of Amy—very vivid portraits, five times life-sized, from which Amy's wide doelike eyes regarded the world with shy allure and her long blonde hair flowed away behind, as if blown by the wind. Beyond that, both the gleaming front grill and the sleeper declared the truck to be the Sweet Amy in fanciful, flowing script.

Brendan insisted Delilah climb into the sleeper to see what a home-away-from-home it was. He gave her a hand up. Inside, there was actually a small section of flooring to stand on as well as a double bed—and a microwave. The colors were a soothing silver-gray. Quite comfortable, Delilah decided, for a man who lived so much of his life on the road.

Brendan, still outside on the sidewalk, explained that once the baby was a few months old, Amy would be riding with him at least part of the time again. He mentioned how difficult it was for her now, with him gone so much and the baby almost due. Then he insisted on shutting the sleeper door, so Delilah could get a feel for how comfy and private it was.

After a moment, Delilah pushed open the door to step down—and found Sam Fletcher grinning up at her. "Let me help you, Lilah...."

Nonplussed, Delilah gaped at him. His red-gold hair, pulled back as always lately, gleamed in the sun. He wore a pale blue ski sweater that hugged the massive contours of his shoulders and emphasized his trim waist. The sweater matched his eyes, which looked at her with humor and understanding and carefully restrained desire.

Something hot and forbidden bloomed in her stomach. He grinned wider, as if he knew just what she felt. She had to resist the ridiculous urge to shrink back into the sleeper and slam the door, to cower there, hiding from her own taboo reactions as much as anything else, until he finally went away—which, of course, he wouldn't do.

Seeking a more viable escape, she looked beyond him. She spotted Brendan a few feet away. Brendan shrugged—as if there was nothing *he* could do about it if Sam Fletcher had a sudden urge to pop up out of nowhere and assist his sister to the ground.

But Brendan's shrug didn't fool Delilah. She recognized

the wayward gleam in his eye. He hadn't changed completely, after all. He might have cleaned up his act for sweet Amy's sake, but he still had enough hell-raiser in him to want to see what would happen when his sis was offered a helping hand by the man she most despised in all the world.

Nothing, Delilah thought. *Absolutely nothing is going to happen, baby brother. So there.*

She composed her face into cordial lines and said sweetly, "Why, thank you, Sam. How kind of you."

She must have sounded convincing, because she saw out of the corner of her eye that Brendan's jaw dropped. Quite pleased with herself, she held out a hand. Sam's huge paw engulfed it. Tempting heat, like that in her stomach, shivered up her arm. With an effort of will, she kept her expression tranquil.

She stepped down, figuring she could handle it since the only contact between them was their clasped hands. But Sam Fletcher knew how to exploit a situation. Just as she stepped free of the sleeper, he released her hand and caught her about the waist. The heat of his touch seemed to spin and close around her as he swung her to the ground.

She came up against his broad chest. He looked down at her, pale eyes alight. "There you go."

Somehow, she smiled. "Yes." She delicately placed her palms on his chest, felt the deep thudding of his heart for an instant, and gave a light shove. "Thanks again."

His hands fell away. She resisted the mad urge to sway back into his arms, to feel her breasts brush against his chest one more time.

He said softly, "I'll talk to you tonight."

She murmured so only he could hear, "Get smart. Give up."

"Never."

"Hey!" Brendan interjected. "What gives between you two?"

Delilah turned her back on Sam. ''Nothing,'' she told her brother calmly. ''Nothing at all.''

That night when Sam called, Delilah hung up even more swiftly than usual.

The next morning, a wooden rabbit looked at her hopefully from beyond the window over the kitchen sink. She closed the curtains on it.

In town that afternoon, as usual, Sam lurked by the door to his store. She ignored him.

He called that night. She hung up.

Thursday, a doe, poised in the moment of scenting possible threat, stood on one of the sills of the windows around the kitchen table.

The doe astonished her. She stood looking out the window at it for a long time. What skill he must have, to shave the wood away from those delicate legs without cutting too deep and destroying the whole.

That night, when he called, she stayed on the line too long, long enough to hear him ask, rather sadly, when she was going to stop being so stubborn. Then she made herself hang up.

Friday, a bear cub waited in the next window over from the doe. It was plump and appealing, rolled over on its back batting the air with its paws. She couldn't help it. She smiled when she saw it.

But then, strangely enough, he failed to materialize by the door to his store when she went to get her mail that afternoon—which was just fine with Delilah; a relief, as a matter of fact.

Then, Friday night...nothing. He failed to call. Delilah felt great about that. It was just what she'd hoped for, that he'd leave her alone.

Saturday morning, the same wooden animals greeted her

when she peeked through the drawn curtains. But no new ones had joined them.

That was just terrific, as far as she was concerned.

That afternoon, after her weekly trip to Grass Valley for groceries, she walked over to Main Street as usual to pick up her mail. She ducked into the post office swiftly, sure that his absence yesterday and the lack of a new wooden creature in the window this morning had been only a fluke to make her let down her guard. She just knew that when she emerged, *he* would be standing there, by the door to his store.

No such thing happened. He wasn't there when she came out.

Saturday evening, after dark had come, she sat in her living room easy chair and read a mystery novel. Tonight, there were no papers to correct. Easter week lay before her, and she looked forward to the break.

Beside her, the phone sat silent. And she was really and truly relieved. She was finally beginning to believe that Sam Fletcher had at last given up. And that was good. That was just what she wanted. She was grateful to have her privacy and peace of mind restored. She was. She really was.

In fact, now that she thought about it, it all made sense. More than likely, he'd called someone else for a date yesterday. He was probably out with that someone tonight. Taking her to that nice restaurant in Nevada City he'd mentioned, and having a wonderful time.

And that was great; that was just great. If some other woman wanted to go out with Sam Fletcher, that was okay with her.

Just then, Delilah realized she'd let her book drop to her lap and she was staring blindly at the far wall. She made a disgruntled little sound, took off her reading glasses and put the book aside. She got up and turned on the television and tried to concentrate on it, though she found her mind still insisted on wandering where it shouldn't go—to thoughts of Sam Fletcher and where he might be tonight....

Chapter Five

Sam hadn't gone out with another woman. He'd gone instead where he knew he shouldn't: to The Hole in the Wall.

Oggie greeted him with a muttered, "It's about damned time," and a cold mug of Sam's favorite brew. "Drink up," he suggested, before Sam even had time to slide onto a stool. "You look like you need it."

Sam grunted, sat down, and lifted the mug.

Oggie leaned on the bar. "Go ahead, son. Tell me all about it."

"What?"

"Whatever's got you lookin' discouraged as a woodpecker in a petrified forest."

"I'm fine, Oggie. Just fine."

Oggie gave Sam a disbelieving wiggle of his eyebrows and then remarked, "Well, one thing I gotta tell you—you shoulda shaved fifteen years ago. Great balls of fire, if I was a woman, I could go for you myself!"

Sam saluted the old rapscallion with his beer before draining the last of it. Oggie leaned closer and pitched his voice low and confidential. "By the way, how you doin' with my little girl?"

Sam set his mug down. "I don't know what you're talking about, Oggie." He pushed the mug toward the other man. "How about a refill?"

Oggie poured out another draft and slid it to Sam. "C'mon. Don't tell me you ain't been givin' my offer some thought. Julio Santino tells me his boy Marty says—"

"Marty's a real self-starter. If he's got a flaw, it's too much imagination."

"Marty's a good, honest kid," Oggie argued.

"I didn't say he wasn't honest."

"Good. So let me tell you what Julio says—"

"If it's true, I already know it, and if it's a lie, I don't want to hear it."

"Sheesh." Oggie shook his head. "You're as testy as Brendan tonight."

Sam looked around. "Brendan's here?"

Oggie tipped his head toward the heavy green curtain at one end of the room. Beyond it was the poker table. "He and Amy had words, from what I could pull out of him. He showed up here a half hour ago, ordered a double whiskey and bought a pack of smokes. Now, if he's lucky, he won't go and lose his shirt to those two slick out-of-towners in there before he gets up the courage to go home. Which is where he oughtta be right now, if anybody asked me. He's a rotten rascal for fightin' with that sweet girl."

"It takes two to make a fight, you know, Oggie," Sam pointed out reasonably.

"It don't matter. That little girl is carrying my grandbaby... And don't go thinkin' I don't know what you're doing, son. I'm old but not that old. I know when a subject's been changed on me."

"What are you talking about, Oggie?"

Oggie grunted. "Good enough. Keep your own council about you and Delilah. For tonight. Just don't you forget this is North Magdalene, son. Secrets around these parts got all the stayin' power of a frozen daiquiri in hell."

Sam knew the wisest thing to do right now would be to set his mug down and leave. He felt edgy and antsy, the way he used to feel in the old days just before doing something crazy. In this kind of mood, there was no telling what he might do. Sheriff Pangborn might end up extending the hospitality of the local jail to him once again—thus proving Delilah's accusations of last week correct.

But hell. Another Saturday night staring at four walls when he knew what he wanted, and what he wanted kept saying no, was enough to make a man do foolish things.

Like show up at The Hole in the Wall when he'd sworn to himself he was going to keep away.

"Sam? Sam, you in there?" Oggie cackled gleefully.

"Lay off, Oggie."

"Well, pardon me for breathin'," Oggie groused, looking much less hurt than he was trying to sound. In fact, if anything, Oggie Jones was looking downright delighted.

"Hey, Oggie. 'Nother round down here," someone called from the end of the bar.

"Keep your pants up. I'm comin'." Oggie moved down the bar.

Sam, relieved to have the interrogation at least temporarily suspended, turned and sat, facing out, sipping his beer and staring at the room.

At the pool table nearby, Chloe Swan, who ran Swan's Motel, was playing eight-ball with some guy Sam had never seen before—and beating the pants off him, too. But the guy didn't seem to mind. He looked gone on her, grinning in frank appreciation of her ability every time she made a shot. And she was nice to him. She joked and she was friendly. Probably the poor guy didn't have the faintest idea that he didn't have a chance. No one really had a chance with Chloe. She was Patrick Jones's to the core, even though the whole town had started to doubt that Patrick would ever get smart and claim her.

Sam shook his head. Who could figure the things that went on between women and men? Not him, that was for sure. Take Delilah—which he'd love to do, but which wasn't damn likely, the way things were stacking up. Sam had been absolutely positive, after what he'd seen in her eyes last Saturday, that with a combination of persistence and patience on his part, she'd drop right into his arms.

But it was not happening. She left his carvings, the gifts of hand and heart, outside in the cold and damp. And she hung up every time he called. Persistence and patience, with Delilah Jones, at least, were getting Sam exactly nowhere. He'd given up on them yesterday.

He was still foolish enough to hope that just maybe she was sitting home tonight, longing for his call. But if she was, he knew it was for only one reason—so she could hang up on him again.

He was just going to have to get real about this, Sam admitted. He was going to have to forget all about the hard-hearted little witch and start looking around again.

He rubbed at his jaw. Maybe he'd grow his beard back. Hell, yes. Then he'd go out looking for a woman who could appreciate him just the way he was.

At the pool table, Chloe sank the eight ball. The stranger applauded. Chloe laughed and began racking the balls for another game.

Oggie approached once more. Sam, who in recent years always limited himself to two a night, signaled for a third beer, and soon after that, another. Five minutes later, he was signaling again.

"That's your fifth," Oggie pointed out.

"Don't worry. I'll make this one last awhile."

Oggie, looking doubtful, filled the mug once more. When he set it down, Sam picked it up and carried it to the end of the room and through the split in the green curtain to the poker table beyond.

In the smoky recess on the other side of the curtain, eight men were playing: the two strangers Oggie had mentioned and six locals, including Brendan Jones. Brendan, a cigarette hanging from one side of his mouth and an empty drink at his elbow, looked like a man who'd lost his best friend.

Brendan's mental state didn't seem to have hurt his card playing, though. The stack of bills in front of him was triple the size of any other stack on the table.

In fact, the game itself appeared to have gotten pretty serious. Some real money was changing hands.

One of the strangers, a rangy character with a black mustache, made a tight comment about Brendan's playing style just as Sam slid through the curtain.

Brendan's smile was humorless. "I may not have your style. But I do have a lot of your money, my friend."

"That'll change," the stranger said.

Brendan gave a mirthless laugh. "Ante up."

Owen Beardsly, across the table from where Sam had entered, looked up. "Sam. You want in? This table's too rich for my blood."

Sam considered. "What's the game?"

"Texas Hold'em."

Sam rubbed his chin. Texas Hold'em was a chancy game to get involved in. Two cards were dealt to each player, with five cards in the center, face down. The betting commenced as the dealer flipped the center cards, two first, then one at a time. Each player built a five-card hand from the two he held and the five cards in the center. The problem was that a player saw too much. It was easy to assume the hand the other guy was building. And too often, it was easy to assume wrong.

But Sam had purposely brought along a wad of cash. He'd been thinking a good game might be just what he needed on a lonely night like this, that maybe a few hands of cards would settle down the reckless feeling that was eating at his nerves.

"Bump limit?" Sam asked.

"Nope."

"Betting limit?"

"Fifty."

"Hell, why not?" Sam said. He took the chair Owen Beardsly vacated and laid his money down.

The game resumed.

Sam more or less held his own, winning a hand now and then only to lose several times soon after that. He was down a few hundred by eleven o'clock. But he didn't really care. Keeping his mind on the cards was working. The edgy feeling that could get him in trouble stayed in control.

The real game was between the black-mustached stranger, who called himself Parnell, and Brendan. Tension grew higher between them as the hours ticked by. Brendan, apparently suffering over whatever had happened with his wife, took his frustration out on the thin stranger.

Whenever Brendan won a hand—which was often—he'd haul in the pot with a big, smug grin on his face—a grin directed at Parnell. Parnell would remark that, where he came from, only fools gloated while they were still sitting at the table.

And Brendan would chuckle. "I'd rather be a fool than a loser, that's for sure."

There would be a charged moment of silence, where every man wondered if Parnell would go flying across the table to grab Brendan by the throat. But then the next dealer would mutter "Ante up," and there would be another round of play.

As the hours went by, though, Brendan's playing became reckless. He started losing. The pile of bills in front of him shrank. He then became morose, sipping steadily at his double whiskeys, his handsome face growing more sullen with each hand. Parnell, cold-eyed and quiet, seemed to radiate a wintry satisfaction as his own stack of winnings grew.

Sam, who'd finally started to win himself, considered advising Brendan to go home. But he knew if he did that he would have found the trouble he'd been trying to stay out of. You didn't give a Jones advice when he'd had a fight with his wife and was losing at poker—unless you wanted your face rearranged.

Maybe, Sam thought, Brendan's luck would turn again. But it didn't. Brendan Jones continued to lose.

At a little past one, Parnell suggested in a toneless voice that they play a hand with no betting limit. Brendan, grown even more reckless with frustration, agreed. And Rocky Collins, who'd always had more nerve than sense, said that was just fine with him. Three men opted to sit out the hand, including the other out-of-towner, Bernie Flack.

Tim Brown, to Sam's left, dealt. When all the cards were out, Tim flipped over the first two center cards: deuce of diamonds, Ace of diamonds.

Parnell, first to bet, shoved two hundred dollars into the center of the table. Brendan, whose pile was dangerously low, saw it and raised a hundred. Rocky Collins, Sam and Parnell all stayed in. Tim Brown dropped, and then turned over the next card: five of hearts.

Parnell shoved another two hundred into the center of the table. Brendan pushed out two hundred to match it, and raised a hundred once more.

Rocky sighed and shook his head. "I'm out." Glances were exchanged around the table. Who could tell what in the hell Rocky Collins had in his head for brains? He'd stay in for no reason anyone could see—and drop out the same way.

Now, as the game continued, there were only three players left: Sam, Parnell and Brendan. Sam and Parnell shoved out their money to stay in.

The next card was a Queen of diamonds. Parnell, who must have got what he was hoping for with that, shoved out five hundred dollars. Brendan was forced to do a little counting, but he had it and covered the bet. Sam, whose hand was also looking good, stayed in, but played it safe and didn't raise. He stole a glance at Brendan, who now had nothing but bare table in front of him. What the hell was Oggie's youngest son planning to use for money on the final round?

Tim flipped the last card: the black lady, Queen of spades.

Parnell calmly pushed another five hundred dollars into the center.

Brendan looked at the pile of money for a long while. Then he turned to face Parnell and stated the obvious in a flat voice. "I don't have it on me."

Parnell replied, "Then you're out."

Brendan stared at the other man, his black eyes burning. And then he took the ring of keys that always hung at his waist and threw them on the table.

Rocky Collins shook his head and muttered something disbelieving under his breath.

Brendan said, "That's to my truck. She's a beauty, and she's worth eighty grand. I've got over fifteen thousand in her. Will you take that as a guarantee—say, for a thousand?"

Parnell turned to Sam. "What do you think?"

Sam thought Brendan Jones was acting like an idiot. But he didn't say that. He considered his own hand and came to a decision. Better let him do it, he thought. Give him a good scare, then make sure everything worked out okay.

"I've seen the truck," Sam said. "I'll allow it as collateral on a thousand."

Parnell shrugged. "All right, then. If it's okay with you, it's okay with me."

Brendan spoke right up. "Agreed then. That's your five hundred—and a five hundred raise."

Sam looked at his two cards, and thought about making a little mischief himself. But no. He was getting soft and sentimental in his old age. If he raised, who knew what the hell Brendan would throw in next. He'd give Brendan a break, because right now Brendan was very close to the edge of a cliff as far as Sam could see. Sam shrugged, and he pushed a thousand into the center of the table.

Parnell kicked in his own five hundred to call. Then he laid his cards on the table: a three and jack of diamonds. With the cards in the center, his best hand was an Ace-high flush.

Brendan smiled. He laid his cards down: a pair of deuces. with the other deuce and the two queens on the table, he beat Parnell. "Full house," he said.

Sam almost felt guilty laying down his hand, but he did it. He laid down his two queens. "Four of a kind," he said gently and glanced at the huge stack of bills with the keys to the Sweet Amy right there on top. "I guess that's all mine."

After that, it was all over but the goodbyes.

Parnell, none too happy, but not as incensed as he might have been had Brendan cleaned him out, gathered up his remaining winnings and left. One by one, the others stood and went out through the green curtain, too. In minutes, only Brendan and Sam remained, looking at each other over the pile of booty in the center.

Now the other men were gone, Brendan had the grace to look sheepish. "Amy will have my hide on a stretcher," he muttered grimly.

Sam grunted. "Then why'd you do it?"

Brendan shrugged. "That crazy Jones blood, I guess. Amy accused me tonight of not loving her. And after that, nothin' meant anything anyway. And I did think I could take that sucker. Hell, I *did* take him. It was you I couldn't beat." Brendan fell silent for a moment, staring at the keys in the center of the table. Then he went on, "Truth to tell, I haven't got the faintest idea where I'm going to come up with your thousand, Sam. I just made the monthly payment, so I'm a little short. I was playing tonight on just about all I got left. Will you give me a day or two to work it out?"

Sam looked at the other man, thinking. He'd planned to simply give the fool back the keys and be satisfied with the tall stack of bills. But he'd just had an idea.

In his mind, he saw Delilah, the way she'd looked that night in her kitchen, just before she dropped that damn frying pan and shoved him away. Her mouth had been turned up to his, soft as a full-blown rose, her body had been pliant to his touch. She'd been ready, he was sure, to fall into his arms. She did want him, he knew it. All he needed was some time alone with her, some time to make that flicker of desire he'd seen in her eyes burst into a hungry flame.

Brendan was standing up, casting a rueful glance at the keys he'd just lost. "I guess no answer is answer enough. You'll be wanting to keep the keys, and I don't blame you. Just think about giving an old friend a few days before you do anything with her, okay?" Brendan waited. Sam still didn't speak. Then Brendan shrugged. "Well, I suppose I better head on home. I got the feelin' I'm gonna be doing some serious crawlin' before the night is through. I've not only got to soothe Amy down for the harsh words we shared, but now I've got to tell her I've lost our livelihood as well.'' He laughed mirthlessly. ''Hell, maybe this solves all our problems, now I think about it. Amy was on me because I've got a run out of Marysville at six Sunday night. She was upset because I'm never home. But now, unless I find me a thousand bucks under a rock somewhere, it looks like I'll be home a lot.''

''Maybe not,'' Sam said.

''What do you mean?''

''Sit back down a minute, Brendan. Maybe we can both get what we want out of this deal.''

Chapter Six

Delilah, sound asleep, stirred and tried to block out the knocking that kept intruding on her dreams. But then it came again, urgent and demanding. She turned over and wrapped her pillow over her head.

"Go away," she mumbled at the mattress.

But talking to the bed did no good. The knocking continued—along with some idiot calling her name.

Finally, she surrendered to wakefulness. She sat up and listened.

More pounding. On the front door. "Delilah. Hey, sis!"

Delilah grabbed the little bedside clock and glared at it. 2:30. One of her insane brothers was pounding on her door at 2:30 a.m.

"All right, all right," she muttered. Then she called out, "Put a lid on it! I'm coming!"

She grabbed her robe and shoved her arms into it, belting it as she strode through the short hall and the living room to reach the front door. She flung it back.

Brendan stood there, looking horrible. Delilah gaped at him for a moment, worry replacing vexation. Had something terrible happened? Had their father breathed his last? Were Amy and the baby okay?

But then she noticed that he was smiling that smarmy smile that all three of her brothers used to bestow on her whenever they wanted something out of her. A warning buzzer went off in Delilah's head. She closed the door most of the way, and peered around it suspiciously.

"Brendan." She made his name an accusation.

"Sis." The smarmy smile widened.

"What do you want?"

"Well..."

"Is there an emergency?"

"Well..."

"Is there?"

"Well, sort of."

"*Sort of* does not cut it at 2:30 in the morning, Brendan Jones."

"Look, I'm sorry to bother you—"

"Don't be sorry. Just don't." She tried to close the door on him. He stuck his foot in it.

Grudgingly, she pulled it open once more. "All right. What do you want?"

"I have to talk to you."

"Now? Can't it wait till morning?"

"No, it can't wait. Look, I really am sorry, but I don't have much of a choice. I can't go home to Amy until—"

Delilah looked beyond his shoulder at the darkness, which smelled of coming rain, at the black sky where the clouds were gathering, and at her neighbors' houses across the road. She was a respectable citizen, not the type to conduct urgent conversations through a crack in her front door. She reached out, grabbed Brendan by the collar, and yanked him into her living room.

"Hey, back off, " he complained, swatting her hand away.

They stood facing each other by the door. She could smell him now—he reeked of cigarettes and whiskey.

"You can't go home to Amy until what?" Delilah demanded.

Brendan rubbed his eyes. "Can you spare a cup of coffee? It's been a hell of a night."

"All right. Come on." She led him into the kitchen, told him to sit at the table, and then quickly set about spooning grounds into the filter basket and setting the maker up to brew. When the coffee had dripped, she plunked a full mug in front of him and allowed him a few fortifying sips.

Then she said, "Talk."

He looked at the table, at his own fingers wrapped around the handle of the mug. "Amy and I had a big fight tonight." Brendan winced, at the painful memory no doubt. Then he tossed back more coffee, until he'd emptied the mug. After that, he got up and poured himself a refill.

"Brendan," Delilah said, her patience hanging by a thread.

"I'm getting to it. I am." Brendan returned to the chair and sat down again. "Okay, now. Where was I?"

"You and Amy had a fight..."

"Right. And I slammed out of the house and went over to Dad's bar."

"How surprising."

He gave her a look that only brothers give sisters. "Delilah, if you're going to make sarcastic comments, I could start getting crude. You remember how I used to swear. I still know how."

"Sorry. Go on."

He looked at her for a moment more, as if to press home his threat. Then he acquiesced to continue. "I went over to The Hole in the Wall, and I got into a poker game—"

"Very bright," she remarked. He glared. She mouthed another "Sorry."

He went on, "And for quite awhile I was rakin' it in. And then…"

"You started to lose."

He gave her a quelling look. "Who's telling this?"

She sighed. "Keep talking."

"I'd had a few hundred on me, and I'd built it up to near four thousand at one point."

"That's a high stakes game," Delilah couldn't help but point out in obvious disapproval. "Father is always swearing that the games that go on at The Hole in the Wall are just friendly little—"

"Delilah. If you want to start preaching the evils of gambling, will you do it in church tomorrow, and let me get on with this?"

"Well, I'm only saying that this just goes to prove what Nellie and Linda Lou and I have always claimed. Gambling is a dangerous pastime—not to mention the fact that it's illegal in California."

"*Organized* gambling is illegal in California, Delilah. Not a friendly game of cards with the guys."

"*Friendly?* You call losing thousands of dollars on a Saturday night *friendly?*" Brendan just looked at her. "All right. I'm sorry. You're right. I've interrupted."

"Thank you." Brendan dragged in a big breath. "Anyway, I started to lose, and I kept on losing. And before you know it, I had this hand I *knew* I could win with—and not a red cent for the final bet. So I threw in the keys to the Sweet Amy."

"Oh my heavens," Delilah muttered, knowing exactly what her brother would say next.

"And I lost."

In the grim silence that followed, Delilah stared at her

brother, unable to comprehend how he could have done such a harebrained thing.

Brendan looked up. "Okay. It was about the stupidest thing I've ever done in my life."

"No comment." Delilah stuck her hands in the pockets of her robe. "Now what's this got to do with me?"

Brendan swallowed. "Well, see. There *is* some good news here."

"Oh, really. What's that?"

"*You* can make everything all right."

"Me?"

He nodded, looking earnest.

"How?" The faint warning buzzer inside Delilah's mind that had started when she saw his smile at the front door was reaching full volume now.

"If you do me one little teeny favor," Brendan said, "I get the truck back and I can go home to Amy down only five hundred or so—not good, but not the end of the world, if you know what I mean."

"What is the favor?"

Brendan swallowed again. "Well, see. It's who won the truck that makes this all possible...."

"Who won the truck..." Delilah repeated the words blankly. Then she asked, with some force, "Well, who was it?"

Brendan raked back his black hair with both hands. "Well..."

"Who?" she asked again, and then suddenly she knew. She uttered the rotten scoundrel's name. "Fletcher." Delilah closed her eyes and groaned. Then she forced herself to look again at her brother. "Sam Fletcher."

"Now, sis—"

Very quietly, she asked. "What does he want?"

"It's really hardly anything."

"What?"

"I mean, compared with the Sweet Amy…"

"*What?*"

"Just…"

"Yes?"

"…a date with you."

For a moment, Delilah stared at him, as his words sunk in. And then she hit the roof.

"You wagered your own sister in a poker game!?"

Wincing, Brendan put out his hands in a fruitless plea for reason. "Settle down, sis. How're we supposed to work this out when you get like this? I already explained. I didn't bet *you*. I bet my rig—or at least, I put down my rig as guarantee on a thousand. But I haven't got the thousand, so Sam would be completely within his right to take the Sweet Amy. But he said he'd be willing to take you instead."

Delilah felt like the top of her head was going to pop off when he said that. She managed to keep from shouting, barely, as she asked, "Do you realize what you're telling me? That my person will do as a substitute for a truck and trailer?"

"Sis, you got that look you used to get back in the old days when me and the other boys would pull a harmless little joke on you. It worries me, it truly does. I thought we were beyond all that now."

Delilah felt like she might explode. "You are not listening to me, Brendan Jones. I asked if you comprehend what you've done? You've…you've offered me up like a sacrifice to the man I most despise in all the world so that you can keep your truck."

Now Brendan was the one to look offended. "That isn't so. And you know it. Sam never asked for you. Just a date with you. You know…dinner, drinks and a show? Lord, sis. This isn't your *virtue* we're talking about. It's a few hours of your time…to save me and Amy and the baby from ruin." He looked at her with a kind of defensive self-righteousness that set her teeth on edge. "And besides that, you two seemed downright friendly in town last week. You were smiling at him and saying 'why, thank you, Sam,' when he helped you down from the sleeper. It seems to me it couldn't be *that* horrible for you to spend an evening with the guy...."

Delilah longed to box her brother's ears. "Oh, what do you know, Brendan Jones? What do you know about anything?"

Brendan had sense enough not to answer that one. He was quiet for a moment, having said all he imagined he could get away with right then. Then he resumed, looking doleful, "Okay, sis. This is a free country. I can't make you do it." Now his voice dripped resigned nobility. "And I suppose it *is* way out of line. To ask you to do such a disgusting thing just so Amy and the baby will have food on the table and a roof over their heads."

"You are pushing it, Brendan."

"I'm only stating the facts."

"Fine." She recrossed her arms. Her brother went on looking at her as if she held the lives of his wife and unborn child in her hands. Finally, she couldn't stand it anymore.

"Stay here." She headed for her bedroom where she could change into jeans and a sweater. "I'll deal with you as soon as I get through with *him!*"

In less than ten minutes, Delilah pulled up in front of the new house Sam Fletcher had recently built.

The house stood, framed by cedars and birches, on four acres near the end of Bullfinch Lane. Though there were few homes nearby as of yet, there would be soon enough. Bullfinch Lane was a neatly paved road now, and little resembled the dirt trail down which Sam, barefoot in a wetsuit, had carried the kicking and screaming teenaged Delilah twenty years before.

As she sat in her car after turning the engine off, bolstering her courage to do what must be done, Delilah noted that the porch light was on. The rest of the house appeared unlit. But *his* room could be at the back, after all. And he could be asleep. Though, the way she'd always heard it, the devil never slept.

Maybe he wasn't there. Maybe she should come back in the morning.

Delilah banished the cowardly thought the moment it took form. If she had to wait all night, she wasn't going away until she'd told the rotten rascal just what she thought of him. She'd yell at him so long and so loud that he'd give her the keys to the Sweet Amy just to get her to stop.

With that idea firmly in mind, Delilah bolted from her car and gave the door a slam. Then she hesitated for a moment, as she breathed in the moisture on the cold air. The crescent moon had already gone down. The sky was a mass of turbulent shadows as the clouds that obscured the stars churned, black and heavy with rain. A spring storm was on the way.

That's the truth, Delilah thought grimly, a doozy of a storm. And it's hitting Sam Fletcher's house right about now....

She marched up the front steps. Once at the entrance, she began alternately pounding on the front door and leaning on the bell, discovering great satisfaction in making such a ruckus—especially considering that he lived far enough out that no one else in town was likely to hear her at this hour of the night. Or rather morning...

"Sam Fletcher!" she shouted. Ah, what gratification to holler out his name with all the loathing she was feeling for the rogue right then.

Normally, she liked to think of herself as a very calm person, a self-controlled person, a no-nonsense person, level-headed and reasonable above all. The passion and tumult of her painful childhood and adolescence had passed, she always told herself, and she had grown into a mature, rational woman, who never went in for rash displays.

But tonight was an exception. Sam Fletcher had finally pushed her one step beyond rationality. She was a one-woman storm, to match the one in the sky.

She bellowed, "I know you're in there! You come out this instant! I want to talk to you!"

She pounded on the doorbell in several sharp bursts, and then hit the door some more with a tightly clenched fist.

"Sam Fletcher, I warn you! I'm not leaving this spot until you come out here and—"

The door was pulled back, suddenly, cutting her off in mid-tirade and nearly causing her to go sprawling into the small foyer beyond. Delilah gasped, and pulled herself up. And then she fell back a little, her mouth dropping open in surprise.

It was her nemesis, all right, standing there with that knowing grin spread over his too-handsome face. He was soaking wet. And wearing only a towel.

"Why, Lilah," he murmured cordially. "How nice of you to drop by. I was just cleaning up and getting ready for bed."

She blinked, and licked her lips and struggled desperately to match his composure, though her heart pounded like jungle drums in her ears and her face felt aflame from within. He had...why, he had silky reddish hair on his chest, and his little nipples were hard, from the chilly night air. In fact, his golden skin, beneath which the hard muscles rippled and bulged, had goose bumps all over it. He stood with one powerful arm fisted on a hip. The reddish hair on that arm was matted with moisture, as was the hair on his chest. The hair on his head looked darker, all wet like it was. It was loose, too, falling on his shoulders in snaky water-weighted curls. He looked—primitive and magnificent, like a viking or some feral barbarian from a lost, untamed age.

Her insides, as they had on the street the other day, bloomed with heat once again. And she saw herself stepping forward, her lips parting, pressing herself up against him, running her hungry hands over his huge shoulders as she licked him dry with her tongue.

He chuckled. "I'm glad to see you too, sweetheart," he said softly, as if in response to a greeting she had never— she was sure—uttered. "Why don't you come in?"

She stepped forward in a kind of daze, and was beyond the threshold before she really let herself decide if such a move was wise. He gently pushed the door shut behind her. And there she was, alone with him in his house....

He was standing behind her after shutting the door. She turned, too quickly, like a small frightened animal cornered by a large beast. She retreated a step, though that brought her backside in contact with the wall.

She realized she was staring. And from the look in his eyes, she knew there must be way too much of the sensual longing she didn't want to feel written clearly on her flaming face.

She forced herself to croak, "I want to talk to you."

"Okay. Talk."

She sucked in a breath. In the closed space, so near him, she was having great difficulty deciding what to say next. He smelled of soap and water and man, a delicious, arousing scent, one that messed up her thought processes, short-circuited her synapses.

She had to get control of herself, she knew it. Otherwise this encounter was going to end up a rout. Silently, she castigated herself for a fool. She'd indulged in a stormy scene by pounding on his door and yelling as she had. And stormy scenes were something she never allowed herself since she'd matured. And now she was paying the price.

She'd been caught off guard, with her adrenaline flowing, when he'd pulled back the door—off guard and vulnerable in the worst and most dangerous way.

She decided a little retrenchment was in order. She drew herself up.

"Go put something on first," she instructed in the same tone she used when one of her students dared to misbehave. She poked her head around the corner and saw a living room. "I'll wait in here." She flew out of the foyer and into the larger space.

He chuckled behind her. "Yes, ma'am," he said softly, and then left her alone.

She ignored him as he padded up a switchback staircase. Then, while she waited for him to return decently covered, she pretended to study the angled ceilings and the full book-cases and the gray leather furniture accented with bright-colored pillows and throws.

But even looking around worked against her. As she had in his store three weeks ago, she couldn't help but notice how different this was than what she would have imag-ined—if she'd ever felt like imagining where Sam Fletcher made his home. The room was attractive and inviting. The books, both hardbound and paperback, looked as if he might even have read a lot of them, and the prints and paintings on the walls were ones she herself might have chosen.

Oh, it was all just too...disorienting. She'd rushed over here without stopping to consider, caught him in the alto-gether, and now she was wandering around waiting for him to cover himself, thinking that she liked his house better than her own.

"Do you like that table?"

Her head shot up, and she spotted him, barefoot but oth-erwise decent, dressed in faded jeans and that blue sweater he'd been wearing the other day. His long hair, still wet, lay in coils on his shoulders. A key ring—the keys to the

Sweet Amy, Delilah had no doubt—dangled from one hand. He came down the stairs toward her.

Delilah, positive the keys constituted an outright taunt, decided to ignore them for the moment. She'd already put herself in enough trouble by reacting without stopping to think.

Keeping her expression composed, she looked down again at the huge table to which he'd referred. It was of some pale wood, perhaps white pine. It was very beautiful in its simplicity.

She said, "Yes, I like it."

He smiled, and then went on, as if she'd come here at 3:00 a.m. for the express purpose of learning more about him and his woodworking skills, "I saw it in my mind, just what I wanted. And since I couldn't find it anywhere, I made it. I don't go in much for furniture making. I mostly sculpt in wood. But you already know that."

She thought of the figures, so perfect and fine, abandoned by her on her various windowsills, and she felt a sharp stab of something like shame, to have left such beauty outside in the elements to fend for itself.

Oh, she thought desperately, it had been a mistake to come here. She should have let Brendan go on home, and confronted this beguiling, continually surprising knave someplace tomorrow, in the bright, safe light of day.

He dropped to one of the gray leather couches, and casually tossed the ring of keys on a table beside him. The sound of them dropping made her stiffen. He saw that, and the ghost of a grin lifted a corner of his mouth.

"Sit down," he suggested.

She swallowed and gathered herself. "No. Thank you. I'll stand."

"Suit yourself."

They looked at each other. And, in this graceful room where the paintings intrigued her and the man on the couch watched her with an interested air, this whole melodramatic mess seemed suddenly silly and pointless. A man who'd read Shakespeare and seemed to enjoy John Le Carre for light entertainment, who fashioned incredible sculptures out of wood in his spare time, surely couldn't be serious about forcing her to go out with him by stealing her baby brother's Long Nose Peterbilt.

And that, she decided with some relief, was how she would approach this. As a silly, pointless misunderstanding that two mature adults could easily clear up.

She said, "I really appreciate this."

He frowned, momentarily, and then his brow smoothed out. "You do?" he asked casually.

She smiled, a smile she hoped appeared midway between embarrassed and grateful. "Yes. And I'm sorry things got so out of hand. But I see now that you've made the wisest decision."

"I have?"

"Yes. And, as I said, I'm grateful."

"You are?" He watched her with great interest.

Boldly, she approached. She reached for the keys...

Before she could grab them, his hand shot out and closed on hers.

The familiar hot shivers quivered up her arm. She forced herself to ignore them, to keep on smiling, though her instinct was to jerk away as if she'd been burned.

She said, faking bewilderment, "But you *have* changed your mind, haven't you? Otherwise, why would you bring me the keys?"

Slowly, he released her. "No, I haven't changed my mind. Brendan told you the terms. They stand. And you know damn well why I brought the keys to you. So you can give them to your brother once you've agreed to hold up your end of the deal." He was grinning again. "Nice try,

Lilah. But you didn't really believe it would work, did you?''

Delilah glared at him, dropping her pose of civility since it had done so little good. She said, ''I despise you, Sam Fletcher.''

He answered, ''Why doesn't that surprise me?''

''You're a low-down, mean, rotten scoundrel, and I was right about you all these years.''

''Why, thank you, sweetheart.''

''I am not your sweetheart.''

''Allow a poor fool his fantasies.''

''You have left me no choice.''

''That was the idea.''

''And I *hate* you for that.''

''So you say now.''

''And a night out with me isn't going to do you one bit of good.''

''It's not?''

''No. It is not. But if that's the price for Brendan's rig…'' Oh, it almost choked her to say it, but she did. ''I'll pay it. You'll have your pointless date. Next Saturday, all right? You can pick me up at seven. And you will have me home by eleven, and that will be that.''

''Oh, will it?''

''Most definitely. Now, give me those keys.'' She reached again, he caught her arm. This time, she didn't even try to pretend his touch didn't affect her. She yanked away and jumped back. ''What now?'' she fairly shouted. ''I said I'd do what you want.''

''You're a hardheaded woman, Delilah Jones.''

''What is that supposed to mean?''

''I think you've made a real point here.''

''What? What point?''

Casually, he picked up the key ring and spun it on a finger. The keys tinkled with nerve-shattering cheerfulness.

"Next Saturday night. Seven to eleven. That's what? Four hours? How can even the most persistent of men get through to a woman like you in four hours? It's my guess that if it could have been done, it would have been done already."

"What in heaven's name are you babbling about?" she challenged tightly. She clenched her fists and ground her teeth—because what she longed to do was fly at him and claw his glittering eyes out.

"I mean," he said pleasantly, "if I only get one chance at you, I'd be wise to make it a damn good one."

She didn't like this, not one bit. Something unbearable was coming, and she didn't want to know what it was. She said, "A date. That's what you told Brendan. Those were your terms, dinner, drinks and a show—"

He spun the keys again. "I said a date. That's all. Brendan assumed what kind of date it would be."

"A date's a date. Saturday night, seven to eleven is a perfectly reasonable—"

"From your point of view, yes. But from my point of view, it's a bust."

"What do you mean, a bust?"

"I lose what I won fair and square—either a thousand cash or fifteen thousand equity in a great little piece of equipment. And what I get is you, for exactly four hours, glaring at me across a table and telling me you hate my guts."

Delilah clenched her fists so hard, her nails bit into her palms. She had to keep her temper, she just *had* to.

She pointed out, through lips pale with her effort to keep from screaming out loud, "It's not your truck, anyway, not really. It's Brendan's. And you took it from him by gambling—which you swore to me a week ago was something you never did any more. You came to my house and you told me you'd changed, and I... well, I started to believe that maybe you had. But you have not changed one bit, Sam

Fletcher, and now I know that with certainty. And no matter what you do, I will never in my life spend a willing hour in your company. Do you understand?''

"Completely," he replied. "I understand completely."

"Good."

He rubbed his chin thoughtfully, as his gaze moved over her, caressing and bold. "And since I *do* understand, these are my terms—"

"We've already named the terms. And I agreed to them, I—"

He waved the keys. She fell silent. "These are the terms. I want a week."

"A *week?*" she croaked.

He went on as if she hadn't made a sound. "This week, to be exact. It's Easter Vacation for you, so you're free. Marty can handle things at my store. We're going away together, you and I. Go home and pack for a camping trip. There's a cabin where we're going, but expect low temperatures, it's still the tail end of winter there. We're leaving at dawn."

"You are insane...."

"You'll be my *date* for a week, Sunday to Sunday. You'll give me seven days, and Brendan can go home to Amy with the keys to his rig in his pocket where they belong."

Chapter Seven

Delilah stared at the rotten rat who sat on the gray couch, grinning and holding the keys to the Sweet Amy in his big hand. Oh, how she longed to call him a name so foul it would burn her own ears to utter it.

A week. He wanted a week, for those keys.

And she might as well face it. Her own temper had gotten her into this mess. She should have left well enough alone. If she'd only kept her mouth shut and sweetly agreed to his original terms, she'd be looking forward to a grim Saturday night—and no more.

Instead, she was doomed to spend a week at his side— or let Brendan stew in his own pot. Letting Brendan stew would have been quite easy. But unfortunately, a pregnant woman and an unborn child would be stewing right along with him. Delilah just didn't think she could stand by and let that happen, not when it was in her power to stop it.

Stars above. Now she knew all over again why she always

kept herself out of her brothers' lives. Getting involved with them meant trouble. Pure and simple. And being grown up wouldn't change them, they would always be that way: The Jones Gang, wild, crazy and nothing but trouble for any woman foolish enough to get close to them, be she wife, mother, girlfriend, or sister....

Fletcher hefted the keys again, so they clinked together on the ring. "Well?"

She looked at him sideways. *Think fast,* she told herself. There just had to be a way to get out of this mess. Camping. He said they were going camping. Lots of people hated camping. Maybe he would believe she hated it, too.

"I can't go camping with you," she said. "I hate camping. Ugh. There's nothing worse, as far as I'm concerned."

"Oh, no?" He didn't look convinced.

She elaborated. "No, absolutely nothing. Who in the world would consciously choose to sit around a smelly open fire, swatting at biting insects, eating things out of cans? And don't forget about hygiene."

"What about it?"

"That's just it. When you camp, there isn't any. 'Facilities' consist of disappearing behind a boulder with a wad of paper towels. And there's never, ever a place to take a real bath." She shook her head emphatically. "No way. Give me indoor plumbing, and somewhere to plug in my hot rollers."

Sam chuckled. "Nice try, Lilah. But I'm not buying."

She tried to look guileless. "What do you mean?"

"I mean, even if you hate camping, you seem to do it three or four times every summer."

"I never—"

"Yes, you do. You go camping with your church group. And you're usually the one in charge, as far as I can remember. At least, it's always your name and phone number that are plastered all over the flyer." He granted her a superior smirk. "You know what flyer I mean, don't you? The one Owen Beardsly always brings in and asks if he can put up in the front window of my store?"

Delilah resisted the urge to slap his smug face. The blasted flyer, she thought heatedly. How was she supposed to remember that—let alone imagine that a heathen like him would ever bother to read anything with the church logo on it?

He went on looking at her, still smug, still waiting.

She considered telling him she suddenly felt ill—too ill to go *anywhere* for at least a week. But then she knew what he'd do: send her home to recover *without* Brendan's keys.

He asked, "Well?" again.

The sinking feeling in her stomach told her that this dreaded trip was inevitable. But before she gave in and agreed to his terms, she intended to make one thing crystal clear.

She stared him straight in the eye. "All I have to do is go, right? I don't have to like it. And I don't have to...be intimate with you."

He went on looking smug, the misbegotten cad. "Why, Lilah? What are you implying?"

"I'm not *implying* anything, I'm saying it straight out."

"What?"

Oh heavens, she loathed him. She forced herself to speak even more plainly. "I'm not going to...go to bed with you."

He shrugged. "That's fine with me. You can threaten me with a frying pan any time I dare to come within two feet of you."

He was still smiling. She knew just what he thought. That all he needed was time, and she'd be sure to change her mind about intimacy with him. And the hideous truth was, she wasn't absolutely positive that he was wrong.

Well, there was no point in dwelling on how long she'd

be able to keep her forbidden desires at bay. She would manage, one way or another. Maybe, if she was lucky, she could stall for a little while before the grueling ordeal began....

She said flatly. "All right. You win."

He nodded. "Be ready to leave in three hours."

Trying for breezy indifference, she suggested, "I'd like to leave Monday morning instead of today, if that's all right. I do need some rest, and I'll need time to find someone to, um, water my plants."

"Your plants will survive. I'll pick you up in three hours."

"But I—"

He shook his head. "Three hours. Don't argue."

She almost told him again exactly what she thought of him, but then resigned herself to the fact that he already knew.

"The keys," she said.

He tossed them to her. She caught them neatly, and then got out of there.

At her house, she found Brendan in the kitchen making another pot of coffee.

He turned from the counter where the coffee was dripping when he heard her come in. "Well?"

He looked so downtrodden, his black hair a tangled thatch, his eyes red and tired, that she almost felt sorry for him, though she tried to remind herself that her sympathy was the last thing he deserved.

"How'd it go?" he asked.

She remembered how she'd planned to tell Brendan exactly what she thought of him once she was through with Sam Fletcher. But now it was settled, yammering at her brother seemed pointless; a waste of good energy. She said, "It's all taken care of," and held out the keys.

Brendan took them. Then he just stood there for a moment, looking at her, his brows drawn together, as if he were trying to decide what exactly to say. At last, he shrugged. "Thanks, sis. I owe you one."

Delilah nodded. "It's okay."

It wasn't, of course. But she supposed she had to admit that things could have been worse. Brendan could have lost the truck to someone who wasn't willing to give up his winnings for the privilege of hauling Delilah off to the wilds for a week.

And she had to remember that even a week wouldn't last forever. In seven days, the debt would be paid. She could go back to her life. Everything would be as it had always been once again.

Or would it? After a week alone with Sam Fletcher, would anything ever be the same?

Delilah sank into a chair. She remembered Sam Fletcher's broad chest, the reddish hair there, the beads of water that had clung to his skin, the clean, moist scent of him, the blue mirrors of his eyes...

"Sis? You okay?"

Delilah blinked. "What? Yes, fine. Just tired, that's all."

Brendan looked chagrined. "Well, I...suppose I oughtta head on home now, get it all worked out with Amy and everything...if you're sure you're okay."

Delilah stood up. "Yes. I'm fine. You go on." She went to the coffee pot and poured herself a cup. "And give Amy my best."

"You bet," Brendan promised. His voice came from behind her, near the door to the living room. "'Night, then."

Delilah glanced over her shoulder at him, waved, and then turned back to the counter to sip from the coffee.

"Sis?"

Delilah looked around again. Brendan was still standing there. "What?"

"You're a hell of a sister, you know?"

"Yes." She sighed. "I'm wonderful."

"In a pinch, you always come through."

She turned around to face him. "Brendan. I said it's okay. You can spare the testimonial."

"But I..." Brendan raked his hair back.

"What?"

"I...well, I'm sorry, damn it. For being a horse's ass. I don't deserve a sister like you, any more than I deserve a wife like Amy...."

Delilah didn't know what to say. He was right, of course, he didn't deserve her or Amy, but that had never seemed to bother him before. Now, however, he seemed honestly moved by what she had sacrificed for him. His frank apology struck a chord in her. She didn't know how to react.

"Brendan, I...It's all right. Really..." Delilah's voice trailed off as she stared doubtfully at her brother, who looked sweet suddenly, so flustered and unsure.

Then, out of nowhere, he muttered something ear-burning and strode the few steps to where she stood. He took the coffee from her, set it on the counter, yanked her up against him and hugged her so hard it knocked the breath out of her.

"Brendan!" Startled, she shoved at his shoulders.

He held on. "Thanks. Just thanks," he whispered fiercely in her ear. With that, he released her just the way he'd grabbed her, in an instant. She fell back against the counter, nearly knocking over her full coffee cup. She grabbed it and steadied it.

And when she looked up he was gone.

Delilah stared after him for a moment before she returned to the table and sat down again. He *was* different than the mean little boy he'd been, even if trouble still followed him around. She realized she was glad now that she hadn't had the energy to tell him he was exactly the horse's behind he'd called himself, let alone inform him that his *dinner, drinks and a show* had become a week-long ordeal in the woods.

And where? In what woods? Delilah realized with increasing exhaustion that she hadn't the faintest idea. But she'd be finding out soon enough, since she was leaving right away.

She sat down, but only long enough to drink the coffee. And then she plodded to her room to start packing.

In a way, it was soothing to her frazzled nerves to prepare for the trip. She concentrated on packing and tried not to think that at dawn she would be off for a week in the wilds with her worst enemy for a companion. As Sam Fletcher had already deduced, she had all the necessary gear.

She set out long underwear, sturdy pants, bulky sweaters and flannel shirts, a down vest and jacket, hiking boots, heavy socks and a good sleeping bag. She also took along her little vanity pack which contained the bare necessities for grooming and hygiene.

It was while she was fumbling in the back of a bathroom drawer for that special small bottle of shampoo which just fit in the pack, that her groping fingers found the little foil pouches she'd stuck there two years ago.

Delilah pulled out one of the condoms and looked at it. She'd bought them after she'd taken that required course for teachers in sex education. She supposed they were still usable…

Delilah looked up from the small pouch to her own face in the mirror. What, really, was she thinking?

Nothing but the truth, she thought grimly. Because the attraction she felt for Sam Fletcher was powerful. It was just possible, given the long days together, and the longer nights…

No. She shook her head. It was not going to happen. She

wasn't going to surrender to this...pull he exerted. And there was absolutely no need to be prepared.

She tossed the condom back where it had come from and firmly shut the drawer.

Then she went to the service porch off the kitchen, where she stored a pack full of basic, sturdy cooking equipment— things like tin plates, flatware, a cup, a saucepan and a frying pan.

She smiled for the first time in hours when she found the frying pan. He'd suggested she have it ready in case he got near her. She would—though unfortunately it was only aluminum and wouldn't be near as threatening as her nice cast iron one had been.

She also kept plenty of high-energy snacks and freeze-dried food on hand for camping trips. She filled another pack with these items, since she had no idea what kind of cooking setup they'd have or how much he would bring. Basically, she assumed he would be taking care of the food problem. But she didn't intend to starve if she was wrong.

After that, she straightened her house.

She considered, for about half a second, calling Nellie and asking her to look after the plants. But dealing with Nellie and her passion for other people's business was more than Delilah felt she could handle right then. It was going to be rough enough when she returned next Sunday. By then, she had no doubt, the whole town would be buzzing. She and Sam Fletcher were going to be grist for the gossip mill, she was certain.

Delilah almost felt like crying when she realized that. Her spotless reputation as the only Jones in North Magdalene who led a civilized life was not long for this world. Everyone would be saying that she was just as wild as the rest of them after all.

Well, Delilah told herself firmly, she'd lived through it when she was little, and she could live through it again.

And besides, there was no point in borrowing anguish anyway. She had a whole week with the wild man to get through before she worried about the gauntlet of whispering and rumors that would come next.

Pushing concern about what hadn't happened yet to the back of her mind, Delilah set a tray of water under each of the plants to keep them going until her return.

After that she was ready—a full hour before Sam Fletcher was due to pick her up.

She tried lying down, thinking a little rest would probably do her good. But her eyes stayed wide open and her body wouldn't relax. So she got up and wandered around her little house, checking the back door and the window locks.

The sky lit up beyond Sweetbriar Summit as she lifted the curtain over the sink. The rabbit beyond the glass stood out for a moment in sharp relief. Its wide eyes seemed to look at her, startled, full of reproach and dumb entreaty. Then the sky went dark, thunder rolled, and Delilah was looking at her own tired reflection and the first rain drops blown against the glass.

For a frozen moment, she remained there, poised with the kitchen curtain raised, staring at her own shadowed face. Then the sky lit up again, the rabbit flashed and disappeared as the thunder crashed once more.

Delilah Jones, who despised foul language as much as she loathed gambling and mind-altering chemicals, swore roundly. Then she whirled from the window and stomped outside in the rain to gather up the wooden figures one by one.

She would have left them, she reassured herself, she really would, if only the rain hadn't come. But they were simply too fine to leave to be destroyed by the storm. In spite of who had made them, they were beautiful and deserved to be treasured.

But not by Delilah, of course. Oh, no. She would never

keep them. She would insist that he take them back, that was all, once the wagered week was over. And if he wouldn't, why she'd return them to him the same way he'd brought them, by stealth. She'd wait for a time when he wasn't at home, and she'd drop them off, and that would be the end of it.

Back inside, she set them on the kitchen table. They appeared undamaged, as far as she could tell, and seemed to have been coated with a thin layer of shellac or varnish which had protected them quite well. But they were wet from the rain.

She found a clean cotton cloth and wiped each one carefully. Sweet heavens, they were marvelous to touch, the wood smooth as tumbled stone, only warmer, more alive. She palmed the plump stomach of the bear cub, and stroked the long legs of the doe. And then she thought of the little raccoon, stuck up there in the shadows of her tallest bookcase.

She found a stool and brought the raccoon down and set it on the table with the others and thought that it was as beautiful in its unfinished roughness as the others were in their smooth and varnished splendor.

She sat down at the table, still holding the little raccoon. She smiled at it.

And then, beneath the pinging of the rain in the gutters, she heard the sound of a vehicle pulling up out in front.

Good gracious, it was Sam! A frantic glance at her watch told her she'd been mooning over the wooden animals he'd carved for the best part of an hour.

Swiftly, she pushed the figures toward the far side of the table, near the windows. That way he couldn't possibly see them from the front door—which was as far as he was going to get this time. She'd learned enough after what had happened last time never to let him into her house again.

But then, as soon as she pushed the animals out of sight,

she felt foolish. Why shouldn't he know she'd brought them in, after all? Leaving them outside had been childish anyway. And she wasn't going to keep them. She could make that perfectly clear.

She heard his boots on her step, followed by his knock at the door. She went to answer.

He smiled when she opened the door, and for a crazy moment, she almost felt like they were partners—longtime companions heading off on some grand adventure.

Behind him, in the east, the orange glow of the rising sun bled through a space in the heavy cover of clouds, creating the most miraculous of effects, a quarter of a rainbow arch, glimpsed for the briefest of seconds, and then gone as the clouds rolled and reformed once more.

His hair, pulled back tidily now, was dewed with water, and he smelled of the rain, as did the whole brightening, glorious, cold world.

He said, "Where's your gear? Let's get loaded up." And he stepped forward, gaining entrance as she'd sworn he wouldn't, because she was too busy thinking forbidden thoughts to remember her intention to keep him on the porch.

"I..." She stepped back, and then decided that ordering him out would be ridiculous. They should get her things together and they'd be out of there soon enough. "I have two packs out on the service porch—cooking utensils and some food."

"We probably won't need the utensils. The cabin has all that, or at least it's supposed to. But I haven't been there in a year, and someone could have helped themselves. You never know these days. How about if we go ahead and take your cooking gear, just in case?"

"Sounds fine."

"Okay. Now what kind of food?"

"Some canned meat and snacks and some freeze-dried entrées and fruits and vegetables, too."

"Great. We can take that for backup, just in case. What else?"

She gestured toward the hall that led to her room. "My clothes and sleeping bag."

"Fine. You get your clothes." He headed for the kitchen, beyond which lay the service porch.

She remembered about the carvings at the same moment that he saw them. He paused, his huge frame filling the kitchen doorway. Then he turned and looked at her, one sandy eyebrow raised.

She just stared back for a moment, since her voice had somehow become hung up in her throat. Then she managed to mutter defensively, "Well, it was raining. So I brought them in."

"I see." He went on looking at her, his expression different than ever before. It was a rather soft expression, actually. A rather vulnerable one....

Delilah swallowed. "I'll get my things."

"Good idea."

Neither of them moved.

"Well..." she said.

"Right." He turned and headed for the service porch.

She shook herself and went to her bedroom where her sleeping bag and clothes pack waited.

When she slid into the passenger seat of the shiny Bronco 4×4, he handed her a notepad and a pencil. She shot him a questioning look.

"We'll drive down to Grass Valley first, to shop for food," he explained. "We can plan the menus on the way, so we'll know just what to buy."

"Where *are* we going, anyway?"

"Hidden Paradise Lake."

"Where's that?"

"You'll see." He started up the engine and turned on the wipers and lights.

She shot him a grim look as he pulled out of her driveway and onto her street. "Gee whiz." Her voice dripped sarcasm. "Here we go, on our way to who knows where. Maybe we'll get lost, and *never* find our way back."

"Don't worry." Sam reassured her, "I called Marty Santino and had him meet me at the store so I could show him how to handle the receipts while I'm gone. I also drew him a map. He knows where to send the search party if we don't return Sunday."

"Terrific," Delilah said, thinking exactly the opposite. Marty still lived at home, with Julio and Maria and their only daughter, Alma. In her mind's eye, she could see all the bleary-eyed Santinos, awakened by the departure of Marty in the middle of the night, waiting up for him to come home and tell them all about how Sam Fletcher was running off with Delilah Jones for a week. Delilah stared out at the pouring rain and beat the pencil on her knee for a moment. "Did you...tell Marty that I was going with you?"

"No."

She stilled the pencil from its nervous tattoo. "Oh." She felt a sweet wash of relief.

Sam swung the Bronco onto Pine Street, and then from there onto Main. In a few hundred yards, Main became the highway. In the rearview mirror, North Magdalene, gleaming in the rain, disappeared around a turn.

They drove for a few moments in weighted silence, and then Sam swore softly. "Damn it, Lilah. Someone in town *will* put two and two together, you know. If not Marty, then Brendan. Or your father. Or your pal, Nellie Anderson—"

"Look. Let's drop it, okay?"

He gave her a narrow look. "Did you tell *anyone* you were leaving?"

She shook her head. "I'm a single, self-sufficient adult. I can go where I please, and I'm accountable to no one— during my vacations from school, anyway."

Sam muttered a few more choice expletives.

"Will you please stop swearing?"

"Nellie and Linda Lou are a couple of nosy bit...er, cows, as far as I'm concerned," he said. "But they do care about you. Did it ever occur to you that they'll worry when you don't show up at church this morning?"

It hadn't, Delilah realized. She'd been too busy dreading the way their tongues would wag when they heard where she'd been. "That is my business."

"Fine." He shook his head in an I-give-up sort of way, and gave all his attention to the twisting road.

Delilah raised the pencil. Suddenly planning the menu seemed very attractive. "Does this cabin have a stove and refrigerator?"

"Yes."

"Okay, then, we can have real meals. We can get some steaks, and some hamburger, a few vegetables, salad stuff. Not to mention eggs, bread, milk—all the staples." She cast a glance at Sam. He was glaring at the road. "Sam?"

He waved a hand. "Fine. Whatever you say."

She lowered the note pad to her lap. "Sam. What do you want from me?"

He shot her a look that sent a bolt of heat right down to her core, but all he said was, "Honesty. And a little plain sense."

"What is that supposed to mean?"

"You are a schoolteacher. A highly respected and ad-mired member of your community. If you disappear into thin air for a week, there will be hell to pay."

Delilah felt her temper rising. She grimly reminded her-self that it had gotten her nothing but trouble the last time she let it loose. She said, through clenched teeth, "You are absolutely right. So why don't you turn this vehicle around and take me back home?''

He slowly shook his head, never taking his eyes from the twisting, rain-slicked road. ''I paid well for this week. By God, I'll have what I paid for. And you agreed to it—including whatever inconvenience it might cause you.''

''Inconvenience?'' She breathed the word in restrained fury. ''You force me to go away with you against my will, and you think all it will be is *inconvenient* for me?''

''Nobody forced anybody. It was your choice.''

She gripped the pencil in a tight fist and stared at the streaming windshield. ''I am not even going to dignify that remark with a reply.''

''Glad to hear it.''

There was a seething silence. Delilah reminded herself that they had a week to get through. She was going to have to watch herself, or she'd murder him before the day was out.

After a few minutes, when her adrenaline had settled down and she thought she could look at him without leaping across the stick shift and scratching his eyes out, she said, ''Now. What else do we need?''

''Gasoline. There's a generator to run.''

''Gasoline. Fine. What else?''

''*You* need to decide who you're going to call.''

''Call? What do you mean, call?''

He spoke with steady patience. ''When we get to Grass Valley, you are going to call *someone* and explain that you've gone camping for a week and will return sometime next Sunday.''

''I loathe and despise you, Sam Fletcher.''

''Tell me something new. Who will you call?''

She slapped her knee with the note pad. The sound was sharp and final in the enclosed space. ''All right. I'll call someone. Will that satisfy you?''

He shrugged. "It's a start."

When they reached the big supermarket on Brunswick Road, Sam went inside while Delilah trudged to the phone kiosks by the newspaper racks.

She had no trouble finding a phone that was not in use. Delilah picked up the headset and sighed.

Whom to call?

She knew she should probably contact Nellie or Linda Lou, but she just couldn't bring herself to do it. Right now, on her way to who knew where with Sam Fletcher, she didn't think she could bear to hear another woman gasping in shock and then palpitating to get off the line so she could spread the news.

She decided to call Brendan, since he knew the basic background of the situation anyway. Delilah found his number through information and grimly punched the buttons.

A soft, feminine voice answered. "Hello?"

"Amy. It's Delilah."

"Oh. Hi." Amy panted a little, as very pregnant women often did. "Gee, Delilah. Brendan told me. About everything that happened. I can't thank you enough."

"It's okay. How's the baby?"

"Fine. The baby's fine."

"May I talk to Brendan?"

There was a silence. "Well, sure," Amy said at last. "Give me a minute. I'll have to wake him up."

"Wait. Amy?"

"Yes?"

"Does he have to be on the road again soon?"

"Yes, tonight."

"Well, then, maybe you'd better let him sleep. I can just as well tell you."

"What?" Worry crept into the soft voice. "Are you okay? Is everything—?"

"Fine. Nothing's wrong. Um, Brendan told you everything, right?"

"Yes, he did."

"That I'd agreed to go on a date with Sam Fletcher, to get back the Sweet Amy."

"Yes, and that was wonderful of you, Delilah. I can't tell you—"

"It's okay. Really. But I'm calling because I...didn't explain, about the date."

"You didn't?"

"No. You see, it wasn't just for an evening."

"It wasn't?"

"It was for a week. This week, to be exact."

Amy gasped, and then began panting harder than before. "Maybe you *should* talk to Brendan. You just hang on. I'll get him—"

"No. No, Amy. Listen. Don't wake him. Just, please, listen. Okay?"

"But a week? A week *where?*"

"I don't know. Camping. At someplace called Hidden Paradise Lake."

"Never heard of it."

"Neither have I. But Marty Santino knows where it is, if for some reason somebody has to know. I just...realized I should let someone know, just in case. That's all."

"But, Delilah..."

"Really, Amy. I know what I'm doing. I'll be fine."

"You're sure?"

"Positive."

"Delilah?"

"Yes? What is it?"

"That Sam Fletcher must really be gone on you, huh? I mean, it's awfully *romantic,* don't you think? Him givin' up the Sweet Amy for a week alone with you?"

"Amy."

"Okay, okay. I know you two are famous around here for how much you hate each other. And I should mind my own business. I know. But maybe you ought to give a guy like that a chance...."

Delilah wanted to scream. Just what she needed. Advice from a hopelessly romantic pregnant twenty-two-year-old—one who'd married a Jones, to boot.

"Amy," Delilah said in her best no-nonsense tone. "I am going camping with Sam Fletcher. I'll be back next Sunday. Marty Santino knows where we are. I would appreciate it if you wouldn't spread it all over town. That's all I called to say."

"Okay." Amy's voice was softer than ever. She sounded hurt.

Delilah felt like a bully. "Look, um, you take care of that baby—and that brother of mine."

"I will." A pause. "I promise. And you take care...of yourself."

"It's a deal."

"Bye."

Delilah hung up.

"Good. That's handled," Sam Fletcher said from behind her.

She whirled from the phone kiosk to confront him. "I thought you said you'd go on into the store."

"Well, on second thought, I decided to make sure you went through with it."

"What did you do with yourself before you had my life to control?"

"Ah, Delilah. Relax. Take things easy. We have a whole week to go."

"Don't I know it."

"Come on." He gestured out at the parking lot, beyond the overhang which protected them. "Cheer up. Before you know it, it'll be a gorgeous day."

She looked where he pointed and saw he was right. The rain had eased up quite a bit. The clouds were thinning. It was just possible that in an hour or two, they'd be enjoying a sunny spring day. Yet Delilah felt far from sunny. She gestured toward the glass doors. "Let's just get the food."

He gave a mock bow. "After you."

Chapter Eight

Within an hour, they were back on the road. A half hour after that, as Sam had predicted, the storm had passed. The sky was a flawless blue overhead, the road was a winding ribbon lined with tall conifers, and they were climbing ever higher into a sea of cedar and pine.

Eventually they left the highway, switching back onto a road that was paved at first, and then became a bed of moist pine needles splotched with patches of melting snow. They crossed a wooden bridge over a creek swift with spring run-off, and then the road became so rutted and rough that they had to proceed much more slowly. After a while, Sam switched to four-wheel drive.

They came to more than one crossroads, and Sam always seemed to know which raw, half-frozen route to take. Once or twice, Delilah spied small lakes or ponds through the tall trees, like huge puddles of sapphire, reflecting the smooth perfection of the sky. She also saw the occasional cabin nestled among the tall cedars.

Then the land opened up. The far mountains became rolling carpets of fir, spiked now and then with rugged rock faces, still heavily bearded with snow. Nearer, moraine from an aeons-ago glacier dotted the low hills.

For some time they drove up and down the moraine-dotted hills, where melting snow lay in the cracks and crevasses between the giant stones. Then once more they left the open country behind and entered the tall, silent trees where the snow lay on the banks of the rutted road, growing thicker with each mile that passed.

They went on, into the dark tunnel of the trees, through which, now and then, the sun would find its way in bright, stunning shafts, cutting the shadows like a heaven-sent spotlight and picking up jewel-like gleams in the white drifts of the snow.

At last, up ahead Delilah saw a patch of blue. It glimmered through the trees, then disappeared, then winked at her again. Finally they trundled around a curve, and the trees opened up to a clearing where most of the snow had melted away. The clearing ended at her teasing patch of blue: a small lake.

The lake glittered in the sun and reflected back the blue bowl of the pristine sky, as well as the mountain that rose on the other side, high and craggy, a moonscape of granite rock and glistening, wind-crested snow.

Sam pulled the Bronco to a stop and turned off the engine. Delilah, seduced by the beauty of the scene, only sat and stared. Heaven help her, faced with splendor like this, she could almost forget that the man beside her had held her brother's livelihood hostage to get her here.

Delilah glanced at Sam. He smiled at her. She smiled back. Right at that moment, it was simply impossible for her to do otherwise.

He gestured at a spot out her passenger window, and she

saw a log cabin, at the edge of the trees. "That's where we'll be staying."

She found she couldn't hide her excitement. "How did you find this? Whose is it?"

"Ten acres, back into the trees, including the cabin and up to the lakefront, are mine. The rest is national forest."

"Ten acres?" She was awestruck. Land like this was rare now in overpopulated California. "But how did you ever convince anyone to sell a place like this?"

"I didn't," he said flatly. "It was my father's."

Delilah blinked. His *father's*...

The idea that Sam Fletcher had once had a father struck her as terribly strange. But then, everyone did have a father, after all. So she supposed Sam would be likely to have had one as well.

She'd just never thought of his having parents or a family. He'd shown up in town alone twenty years ago, and no evidence of a family had surfaced since. Until now.

She said, puzzled, "Your father? But Sam, I didn't even know you had a father..."

"I don't," he replied in that same flat tone. "He's dead."

"But—"

"Let's go inside," he said, suddenly brisk. "We have work to do getting settled in." He leaned on his door and got down from the Bronco before she could demand to hear more about this father she'd never known he had.

And then, when she thought about it, she decided she would only be asking for trouble to hear too much about Sam Fletcher anyway. Hearing his life history would be getting to know him better. And getting to know Sam Fletcher better was exactly what she'd sworn *not* to do.

In fact, she determined, the wisest course over this entire week would probably be to keep conversation to a minimum whenever possible. The less they talked, the smaller the chance she'd be drawn into the intimacy she'd sworn to resist. Also, every time they talked, things seemed to get out of hand. He either stirred her temper or her senses—two equally dangerous occurrences.

Yes, she thought, pleased with herself. As much as possible, she would keep her mouth shut. She'd be reasonable and helpful in getting things done. She'd be...polite. She'd do her best not to cross him. And just maybe she'd get through this week without killing him—or dropping right into his waiting arms.

That decided, she got out and joined him at the back of the Bronco, where he handed her a box of groceries. Then he took the other two boxes of food and led the way to the cabin. There, he balanced the stacked boxes in his arms against the door frame as he fitted a key into the padlock on the rough wooden door. The lock fell open.

He pushed the door inward and led the way into a single room with natural log walls and an unfinished plank floor on which their steps echoed when they walked.

He crossed the room and set the boxes down on a section of counter next to a stained sink. Delilah followed suit, pausing to glance out a rather large, many-paned window above the sink which granted a stunning view of the butte across the lake.

"Nice, huh?" Sam said. The window framed the craggy peak like a picture. "I put that window in myself two years ago. It was pretty dark in here without it."

Delilah, recalling her resolve to keep unnecessary conversation to a minimum, only nodded. Then Sam began inspecting the place. Delilah took the few moments while Sam was poking in cupboards and peering into cabinets to take stock of her surroundings.

The accommodations were far from deluxe, but the cabin appeared sound and dry. Settling in here would be a great improvement over sleeping outside on the half-frozen ground.

She noted most of the basic amenities including a simple pine table with two straight chairs and a fireplace of natural stone before which a pair of battered easy chairs huddled. The walls were lined with rough-hewn shelves and cabinets. There was even a scarred dresser into which they could unpack their clothes.

Also, in one corner, there was an old-fashioned iron bedstead. Its tired-looking mattress was levered up against the wall.

Delilah sighed. One bed. That was it. She glanced resignedly at the braided rug rolled up by the hearth, and realized where she'd be laying down her sleeping bag that night.

There was no sign of a bathroom. "Facilities," as she had predicted, would consist of a roll of tissue and one of those big trees out there to duck behind.

Sam, who'd been looking around himself, announced, "The good news is it looks like the rat bait I put out last time did the trick. The bad news is the dust is pretty thick, and we'll need to do some washing up. But I can't get the water pump going until I start the generator. So maybe I ought to do that right away."

Delilah agreed with him.

"Don't bring anything else in until I get this taken care of. Otherwise you'll only be stirring up dust."

"Okay."

He turned and left her standing alone in the cabin, gazing at the wood stove and the ancient refrigerator. The refrigerator actually had one of those old-fashioned coils on top of it.

In a few minutes she heard a motor start up several hundred yards away. She glanced out the tiny window on the west wall and saw an electric cable leading into the trees. She thought it clever of him to put the generator away from the cabin, where the sound would be less noticeable.

A bare lightbulb dangled from the middle of the ceiling. Delilah pulled the chain on it. The bulb shone brightly. Too brightly, she decided, and switched it off. The light from the big south-facing window would do until the shadows came.

The ancient refrigerator, whose door was held open by a towel for airing, began to hum. She removed the towel so the door would close.

Then she realized that there was only one spigot in the sink fixture, which meant no hot water. She decided to get the fire started. After checking to see that the tap was open, so there would be no pressure backup when the water began to flow, she found kindling, an old newspaper and a couple of logs in the basket by the stove. She started the fire.

As if on cue, the water in the sink began to run. It was the color of the hair on Sam's chest at first: rusty brown. But in a few minutes, it ran crystal clear. She found a big pot and put some on to heat.

After that, she looked in the cabinets for the cleaning supplies, and she started to work. In a few minutes, Sam joined her.

They worked without pausing for an hour, getting things in shape, dusting and wiping down counters and sweeping up the floor. They pulled the mattress flat on the springs and clouds of thick dust flew up, so they coaxed the thing out to the small front step and beat it awhile with the broom.

All this time, they hardly spoke, except to give verbal clues to facilitate the job at hand. Besides the fact that not speaking fell right in with her plans, Delilah found it very soothing to work so smoothly and purposefully.

She remembered, as she hadn't in years, the hardrock mine her mother's brother, Uncle Cleve, had owned, way up in the hills above North Magdalene. When Delilah was little, they all used to pack up and go camping up there, where the cabin was cruder than this one, and everyone had to pitch in to make things livable.

She remembered the starry summer nights, when they'd build a campfire outside, and make *S'mores,* sweet sandwiches of graham crackers, roasted marshmallows and chocolate bars. She remembered her mother, Bathsheba, tall and graceful in her frayed jeans and plaid shirt, her thick dark hair in a bouncing braid down her back, dancing a polka in her father's arms around the open fire as uncle Cleve beat out a tune on his old guitar.

Funny, in that memory, all her brothers were smiling, clapping their hands and cheering the reeling couple on....

"Lilah?"

She realized, with some chagrin, that she'd been wiping the same clean shelf for several minutes now. She stopped, and looked at Sam. "What?"

He stared at her strangely for a minute, as if he wondered what she'd been woolgathering about, but he didn't ask. Instead, he said with frank admiration, "You're a hard worker."

She was pleased at his praise, in spite of herself. "I like to do my share."

"We work the same."

Now what in the world was that supposed to mean? "So?"

"So that's good."

She peered at him warily for a moment, considering asking him just what was so good about it. But she was afraid she already knew the answer, which would have something to do with how two people who could work so smoothly together would probably do other things smoothly together as well. She didn't need to hear anything like that!

He chuckled, as if he could read her thoughts on her face. Then he pointed out, "Things are in pretty good shape now. I'll get the rest of the stuff from the truck."

She tossed her cleaning cloth in the bucket and followed him out. Together, they brought in everything else and put it away.

Delilah was careful to set her bedroll in the corner by the fireplace. But Sam, without a word, went over and picked it up and carried it to the bed. She opened her mouth to order him to put it back. But then he carried his own bag to the corner where hers had been and pointedly dropped it there. She decided not to argue. She could be foolish when it came to Sam Fletcher, but not foolish enough to complain about getting the only bed in the place.

By then, it was well past lunchtime. They made sandwiches and poured cups of milk, and took them out by the lake where they sat on a fallen log and watched the shadows grow longer on the north-facing butte across the water. Delilah found it very pleasant, actually, just sitting there by the lake, filling her growling stomach, feeling no urge to say a word.

It wasn't till the simple meal was through that she began to wonder if she was finding all this a little *too* pleasant. Once or twice, Sam had glanced her way and smiled and she had smiled back without thinking, as if she were here with him of her own free will, as if she were *enjoying* herself.

When they'd taken the empty cups back inside and straightened up the counter, Sam decided to replenish their supply of usable wood. Delilah, who had sense enough not to hang around and watch him flex his muscles, decided on a nice, long walk. She headed off into the woods without saying a word to him.

She followed a trail around the lake to the foot of the big butte. She walked slowly, enjoying the stillness of the woods, which was broken only by the occasional cry of an unseen bird or the scrabblings of small animals off the trail in the trees. She found herself relaxing a little, and was grateful for the time alone, away from Sam and the forbidden temptations he represented.

When she returned, it was nearing evening. She found wood stacked high against the side of the cabin, and Sam inside at the sink.

It was warm in the cabin; he had both the stove and the fireplace going. The bare bulb glared from above, its light necessary now. She hung her heavy jacket on a peg by the door, and looked at Sam's massive back, his narrow waist and tight buttocks. Suddenly, the tension inside her that had eased during her walk began building once again.

"Nice walk?" he asked over his shoulder. His voice was very casual. Too casual, in fact. "Well?" He set down the carrot he was slicing and turned to face her.

"Yes," she said carefully. "I had a nice walk."

"You didn't tell me you were leaving."

"I...didn't stop to think," she said, though what she longed to tell him was it was none of his business where she went or how she got there.

He lifted an eyebrow at her. "It's stupid to head off alone into country you don't know without telling anyone where you've gone."

"I'm aware of that," she said, feeling her temperature rise a notch, and reminding herself grimly that he was right; it *was* stupid. Delilah knew very well that in unknown territory, going off alone could be foolish. But if she'd told him she was leaving, he might have argued with her. And she'd already decided she must avoid arguing with him at all costs.

"Then why did you do it?"

"I just wanted to get away for a while, that's all. I didn't think."

"Well, you'd better *start* thinking."

"All right!" She realized she'd raised her voice. She reminded herself to keep calm. Things would be getting out of hand. She took a deep breath, and said levelly, "It won't happen again."

"Good." He turned back to the sink, seemingly satisfied with her word that she would not go off alone another time. Then he asked with a backward glance, "Where did you go?"

"Does it matter?"

He glanced at her once more, and she realized she'd been too curt. Oh, this was like walking a tightrope—as the handsome cad across the room no doubt knew very well.

She made another stab at being civil. "Well, if you really want to know, I walked to the base of that mountain around the lake."

"That's a pretty trail," he said, his tone as innocuous as the statement.

"Yes, it was lovely." Much better, she thought. He's innocuous, I'm insipid. We'll get through this week alive yet.

"But next time, take the handgun." He'd brought along a revolver for routine protection in the woods.

She looked at his broad back for a moment as he continued scrubbing and slicing the carrots, knowing she should agree. But when she opened her mouth, agreement didn't come out.

"Why?"

He shot her a look. "Come on, Delilah. You know why." He went on to explain anyway, in a gratingly patient tone. "If you get in trouble, you can fire a couple of shots. I'll hear them and come for you—as long as I know where to look. Also, if you come face to face with a mountain lion or a bear, believe me, you'll feel a lot better with a gun in your hand."

He was right, of course. She knew she should simply agree to take the gun and let the subject drop, but somehow her mouth just didn't want to take orders from her brain. She said, "I'll be fine without a gun."

He said, "You won't *go* without a gun."

"Oh, really. And just how do you intend to stop me?"

"That's an interesting question. I'll have to give it some serious thought." He cast her a grin, and she realized he was winning this silly argument simply by refusing to take it seriously.

She reminded herself once more that her intention was to avoid strife, not stir it up. She said, exerting great effort not to sound surly, "All right. To be on the safe side, I'll take the gun next time."

"Good."

There was a silence. Delilah actually dared to hope that she'd managed to pull herself back from the brink of a full-blown confrontation.

Cautiously, she crossed the room to stand by the table, not too close to him, but near enough that she could see his ponytail was wet; he must have washed in the sink, after chopping the wood.

She felt her skin pinkening, thinking of that, of him stripping down and soaping himself standing in front of the big window in the fading light of day. Of him hanging his head over the sink, and ladling water over his thick red-gold hair...

He glanced at her. Something as hot and intense as the fire in the stove arced between them. She thought of the way his big body had looked when he answered the door the night before, of the water drops left from his shower, which she'd wanted to lick off with her tongue.

They were staring at each other. She saw the hunger on his face and the question in his eyes. She knew her own eyes were answering....

Swiftly, she looked away. She stared blankly at the scarred surface of the old table, waiting until her heart found its normal rhythm again and her breath came more evenly into her chest.

When her yearnings were under control and she sensed he'd gone back to cutting the vegetables, she turned to him again.

"So," she asked, absurdly bright, "What's for dinner?"

"Steak, carrots and salad." His voice sounded as falsely cheerful as her own. "Want to help?"

"You bet."

They cooked. They ate. They cleared the table and washed the dishes. When the meal was done, it was dark outside, though the hour was far from late.

Sam suggested, "Come out with me. I'll show you the stars from Hidden Paradise Lake."

Delilah decided that wouldn't be wise. "No, thanks."

"Lilah—"

"I said no."

He looked at her for a moment, and she thought she saw a hint of real frustration in his blue eyes. But then he shrugged. He went to his gear and took out a soft cloth. He unrolled the cloth on the table, and she saw a basic set of woodworking tools tucked into the pouch inside. He then produced some stones of different shapes, a leather strop, and a can of oil and set about the involved process of sharpening the tools.

Delilah watched the whole procedure until it became clear what he was doing. She was curious about his wood carving, and wanted to ask questions. But questions meant conversation and conversation wasn't a good idea.

Suddenly feeling at a loss, Delilah cast about for something to occupy herself. She knew she ought to be exhausted. She'd had perhaps four hours' sleep the night before, cleaned a cabin and hiked around Hidden Paradise Lake that day. But she didn't feel tired. Not the least bit. In fact, her whole body seemed to thrum with unspent energy.

Oh, she just had to do something with herself, instead of standing in the shadows watching Sam Fletcher sharpen his chisels and picks—or whatever the blasted things were called.

Delilah thought of the books she'd brought. She went to her pack and took them out and lined them up on the dresser by the bed. Then she chose one—the one she'd been trying read last night, as a matter of fact—found her glasses and sat in one of the easy chairs to read.

Even with the soft hum of the generator outside, and the occasional far away cry of a nocturnal creature, the night was very quiet. She could hear every stroke Sam made of metal on stone.

She forced herself to look at the page in front of her, but it didn't help. She kept forgetting what she'd just read, so she'd read the same paragraph over and still the book seemed to make no sense at all.

After an interval that seemed to last forever, Sam put the tools and the stones away, took his jacket off the hook and went outside. Since he said nothing, Delilah assumed he was answering the call of nature.

But the minutes dragged by, and he didn't return.

She should have been grateful, she knew, for a few minutes alone. The fire crackled cheerfully in the grate; it was cozy and warm. She had a full stomach and a good book—even if she still hadn't the faintest idea what the thing was about. Now that her nemesis had taken a hike, she should be able to relax and enjoy the moment.

But where could he have gone? It couldn't have taken this long for him to see to his needs, could it?

She thought of hungry mountain lions, suddenly. Of big brown bears awakened and grouchy after their long winter's nap. She remembered that she hadn't seen him take the handgun when he left. He was out there unarmed, against the dangers of the night....

"Oh, this is ridiculous," she muttered aloud. It was so quiet out there, she would have heard any yowling or roaring that went on within a half mile of the cabin. She was letting her imagination get away with her, and that was going to stop now.

He knew how to handle himself in the woods. There was no reason to worry. And she *wouldn't* worry, that was all. She would read her book and enjoy her solitude.

Five minutes later, he was still gone.

She found she just couldn't sit there another moment. She set her book and glasses aside and went to the big window over the sink. She peered out, pressing her face near the glass so she could see beyond the reflected glare from the bulb hanging overhead.

Out in the night, the moon, a thickening crescent, hung over the rugged spires of the mountain across the lake. The sky was cloudless, thick with stars. A dark shape, hunched against the cold, was sitting on the fallen log beside the lake.

It was Sam.

He didn't look like there was anything wrong, she decided. Maybe, as she had, he'd just wanted a little time alone. The forbidden thought came that she might join him—and was as quickly banished. That was probably just what he hoped for, that she'd grow lonely, and come to find him. She was giving him nothing of what he hoped for.

Delilah turned from the window. Even though she loathed and despised Sam Fletcher, she felt better knowing where he was and that he was okay.

She found her vanity pack and cleaned her face and brushed her teeth. Then she went outside herself—staying well away from the lake, of course.

When she came back in, she pulled the curtains over the big window so that, should Sam turn around from his contemplation of the lake, he wouldn't see her undressed. Quickly, she shimmied out of her clothes and put on her long underwear, which would do well for pajamas. Then she rolled out her sleeping bag and climbed in.

She'd just snuggled down when the door opened.

"Lilah?"

She decided not to answer, to let him think she was asleep. It was easier that way; it saved another exchange that could only invite one kind of trouble or another.

She heard nothing for a moment, though she sensed him listening. She tried to make her breathing even. At last, she could almost feel his shrug.

He began quietly moving about. She heard the water run briefly as he brushed his teeth. And then he rolled out his bag on the rug. Then his boots dropped, and she knew he must be taking off his clothes. After that, he pulled the chain on the light, and the room, lit only by the fire now, grew dim. She heard him crawl into the bag.

There was a silence. Far away outside in the darkness, a coyote howled at the almost-half-moon. Sam shifted in his hard bed. Delilah curled into a ball with her back to the room and resolutely waited for sleep. She was actually beginning to think it might find her, when Sam spoke.

"Lilah?"

She said nothing.

"I know you're awake."

She tried to keep breathing evenly. How could he know for sure whether she slept or not, if she simply refused to answer? She waited, trying not to go rigid and give herself away, dreading the moment he'd climb out of his sleeping bag and approach her to see for himself if she slept.

But he didn't get up. She heard him shift again, and thought that perhaps he was now sitting up, maybe staring into the fire, contemplating...what?

"This afternoon," he said at last, "you asked about my father..."

It was a mistake. Pretend I didn't, she thought, but of course didn't say.

He went on, "And I cut you off." He shifted again, and the fire popped. "I'm sorry about that. Since then, I've given it some thought. And I've decided to tell you whatever you want to know about my father, and about my life before I came to North Magdalene."

Delilah debated the feasibility of sitting bolt upright and ordering him to keep his life story to himself. But she'd already pretended she was asleep, and even if he knew she wasn't, admitting her deception now would only put her at a disadvantage.

"Lilah?"

She almost said *What?* and let him know she was awake. But then he chuckled—the rat. And that did it. She pressed her eyes closed and determined not to listen.

"You are the most stubborn woman I have ever known." He actually had the nerve to say it fondly. Then he fell silent.

Delilah fumed and waited and wondered what he was doing, over there by the fire where she couldn't turn to see without admitting she was awake.

Just when she thought he was going to show a little mercy and keep his past to himself, he began, "My father. Whew." He paused, thinking. "My father was...a man with a mission. His mission was to save the world from the sin and degradation he was absolutely positive lurked around every corner."

He fell silent. Delilah waited, forgetting to breathe for a moment.

Then he went on, "He was a preacher, a nondenominational preacher." Delilah stifled a gasp. Could he actually be telling the truth? Mad, bad Sam Fletcher had been a minister's son? Sam continued. "By the time I was five, we'd settled down in a little farm town just north of Fresno, and my father had his own church—the Valley Bible Church.''

He paused again, a long pause. And suddenly, Delilah understood that he was just trying to get a rise out of her. He expected her to pipe up and stop him before he revealed too much.

Well, she wouldn't, that was all. He should have thought twice before he started telling things he really didn't want to tell. She would say not a word and move not a muscle and he could just go ahead and lay out all the secrets of his heart—and then wonder if she'd heard him at all.

The silence stretched out. Then she heard the poker shoving the logs around in the fireplace and realized he must be stirring the fire. After that came the sound of the poker clinking on the hearth as he propped it back in place.

Sam remained quiet. She pictured him, staring into the flames he'd just stirred. Then he said, ''This is your last chance, Lilah. Say something, or hear it all.'' He sounded tired—and even a little bit sad.

Delilah realized she couldn't do it—lie here unmoving and listen to the man she'd always loathed tell her all about the little boy he'd been, the hurts he'd known, the setbacks he'd suffered. It wouldn't be wise. She could hear too much, *feel* too much. And that would put her in worse jeopardy than she was already in.

''Lilah?''

''I hate you, Sam Fletcher.''

He laughed.

''You are lower than low,'' she muttered through clenched teeth.

''That's my Lilah.''

Delilah let out a furious groan. Then she sat up, wrapped her arms around her blanketed knees and glared at him as hard as she could.

"I am not, nor will I ever be, your Lilah. Is that understood?"

He only grinned. He was sitting up, too, his bare torso gleaming in the light from the fire. His lower body was covered by the sleeping bag. He watched her. His smile was tender, his eyes promised delights she'd never known.

"I asked you a question," she demanded, when he went on grinning and didn't say a word.

He still didn't answer her question, but he did point out in a gentle whisper, "So you weren't asleep."

Something inside her snapped. "You are a—"

He wiggled a finger at her. "Lilah. You are about to say something you'll regret. Think twice, now."

She brought herself back from the brink, and then explained tightly, "I don't want you to tell me about your father. I don't want you to tell me anything about where you've been or what you've done. I know all I'll ever need to know about you, so get that through your thick head."

"That's not true, Lilah. You'll end up needing to know more, much more, before this is through."

"You are wrong. I don't need or want to know a thing more than I do now—not that my needs and wants have ever mattered in the least to you."

His eyes changed, lost their teasing look. Now his gaze penetrated, burned. "You want *me*. That matters. It matters a hell of a lot. I'm only trying to get you to admit what you want."

"Oh, are you?"

"Yes."

"Well," she fumed, "here's a hot bulletin for you—I don't want to want you. I don't need to want you. And even if I *do* want you, I won't be doing a thing about it. Ever. So learn to live with it."

He smiled again. "Give yourself time."

"Time won't matter."

"We'll see about that."

"Sam Fletcher—"

Before she could go on, he stood up. His big body emerged from the sleeping bag with a power and grace that shut her mouth and took her breath. She stared at him long enough to register the heartstopping fact that he was utterly naked and achingly magnificent.

Then she gasped and looked away, her face burning, her body flaming with responses she hated herself for feeling. She heard him toss a log on the fire and prod it into place with the poker.

After a few moments he said in a teasing voice, "You can look now."

She dared a glance; he was back in the sleeping bag, covered to the waist and looking smug as a cat who'd cornered a plump mouse.

She said, "I will make one last effort to appeal to any tiny kernel of decency that just might be waiting, undiscovered, somewhere deep down inside you."

"Please do."

"Take me home in the morning."

"No way."

"This will be a totally wasted week for you. Realize that. I will never ever give you what you're after."

"Ah, Lilah. Do you really even know what I'm after?"

"I have a general idea."

"Say it, then."

"Why not? Attention. Affection. Companionship. Sex."

"Not a bad estimation."

"The point is, you are not getting any of those things from me. Ever."

"So you keep telling me."

"I am never going to be your woman. I have learned my lesson the long, hard way, about what a woman gets with a man like you. With a man like you, I'd have just what my mother had, what each of my brothers' long-suffering wives and girlfriends have had—endless nights waiting up to learn what trouble you've got yourself into now."

"You're not being fair, Lilah."

"Fair? Fair! What does any of this have to do with being fair? You used totally *unfair* means to get me here. And I told you from the first that I didn't like it, that I'd *never* like it. But I have tried to be civil about it, thinking that if you would just leave me alone while I'm here, maybe we can get through this with a minimum of conflict. But you will not leave me alone."

"Lilah." His voice was like rough velvet. "I didn't bring you here to leave you alone."

"I have finally come to fully accept that fact. And that is why I am through even attempting to be civil. You do not deserve civility. I despise you and I loathe being here alone with you and I'm through telling myself the best way to get through this week is to avoid confrontation with you. I intend to make you miserable, as miserable as you're making me. Do you understand?"

He looked at her for a moment, his eyes hooded.

"Do you understand?" she demanded again.

"Perfectly," he said at last.

Chapter Nine

Delilah went about making Sam miserable with a vengeance.

For the next two days, Monday and Tuesday, she never said a single pleasant word. Most of the time, she didn't talk at all. She did her share of the work, and when there was no work to do, she would read or walk off by herself.

She was meticulous, also, in never giving him a single reason to engage her by questioning her actions. She always informed him in clipped tones of exactly where she was going. And she'd always take the handgun just in case, so he couldn't even argue with her that she wouldn't be safe out there alone.

Sam, alert to every possible angle for getting through to her, did the best he could over the issue of the gun. The first time she went off alone on Monday, he challenged her about her ability with it, though he suspected that, growing up with the Jones Gang, she'd probably learned at least the basics of how to shoot.

Still, he'd indulged in a brief fantasy of showing her how to use the gun, of explaining how to load it and handle it, and then of stepping behind her, feeling her supple back and soft bottom caressing the length of him as he wrapped his arms around her and steadied her hand.

She quickly demolished his little fantasy. "Do you doubt my competence with this weapon," she buzzed like an angry hornet, "is that it?"

"Sweetheart…"

"Don't call me sweetheart, you manipulative snake."

"Sweetheart," he said again, slowly and very clearly. She held her tongue, but her eyes spit fire. "I'm just suggesting that a .357 is only as useful as the person who's carrying it. And I wouldn't be responsible if I simply gave it to you without making sure you know what to do with it."

"Fine." She left him there in the cabin where they'd been arguing and went outside. He heard her at the west wall, fooling with the garbage and recycling bins, which he kept strapped shut with bungee cords to discourage the raccoons. She got the lid off of one. He heard the sound of empty cans rattling against each other, then silence as she apparently found what she was looking for. Her boots crunched on pine needles, headed in the direction of the lake.

He glanced out the south window. She was bending over the fallen log they'd shared their lunch on the day before, setting out three empty beverage cans in a row. Her round little bottom was a captivating sight to see. He watched, smiling in spite of himself, as she stalked back toward him. She disappeared for a moment around the side of the house, and then poked her head in the door.

"Bring the gun, and the cartridges."

He brought the revolver down from its high shelf, grabbed the box of cartridges and did as he was told.

Outside, she took the gun from him, broke it open, shoved the cartridges in and slapped it closed. In one seamless motion, she whirled on the cans and fired off three shots. All three cans went flying.

She turned to Sam. "Satisfied?"

He could do nothing but nod. She was magnificent. Too bad she was also so damn mean. She replaced the cartridges she'd fired, handed him the rest, and demanded the holster he'd left inside.

"You know where it is."

She went and got it and stalked off for her walk with the gun strapped around her waist.

Their every encounter was like that, Sam came to realize quickly enough: pure hell. She wore a sour expression at all times; her attitude varied between impatient and downright nasty.

Sam tried to bear with her, to wait her out. He set up a vise on the table in the cabin, and created his own miniature wood carving shop, which he dismantled for meals. Monday, he began carving a coyote sitting on its haunches, howling at the moon.

As she continued to torment him, he found himself immeasurably grateful for his hobby. When he was working with wood, he could almost forget Delilah's spitefulness. Whenever the slightest opportunity arose, she made sure he suffered endless indignities for daring to want her and then having the absolute gall to go after what he wanted.

She would alternate long spells of silent seething with periods when she would argue about anything. Sam would hardly have believed, until those two days of her crusade to make his life miserable, how many subjects in the world there were to be argued about. Things he would swear made no difference at all, she could make an issue of.

And she didn't seem to care which side of an argument she took—as long as it was the opposite side from the one he was on.

Monday at dinner, he mentioned that he'd seen Chloe

Swan out with a stranger Saturday night, and she snapped that that was preposterous, everyone knew Chloe Swan would never look at any man but Patrick, even if Patrick refused for the rest of his life to give her so much as the time of day.

"Well, Lilah, I'm just telling you what I saw."

"You're either lying or mistaken, Sam Fletcher—either way, you're wrong."

"I'm not lying, Lilah. And I know what I saw."

"You know nothing."

"Fine, Lilah. Have it your way."

"You admit you know nothing?"

"I admit this is a ridiculous argument, and I can't wait to find out what you'll accuse me of next."

"Take me home," she suggested. "The ridiculous arguments will stop."

"Not on your life."

She gave him a look meant to freeze his blood in his veins and fell seethingly silent once more.

After they'd cleaned up the meal, he picked up the latest issue of the *North Magdalene News,* which he'd brought along on the trip. He made himself comfortable in one of the chairs before the fire. She sat at the table with that same mystery novel she'd been reading the day before.

He read the front page of the paper and then turned to the Over a Hundred Years Ago section on page three. There, he discovered a piece by Mark Twain. He began reading it with relish, found it as full of humorous irony as he'd expected, and was soon chuckling aloud.

"What is so funny?" she demanded, as if there were something inherently distasteful about people who indulged in a good laugh now and then.

"Mark Twain."

"What about Mark Twain?" She took off her reading glasses in order to be able to glare at him more effectively.

He read her a little of the article, wherein the author had visited a San Francisco prison and been appalled to find a sweet-looking sixteen-year-old girl doing time there—until he heard her talking to the other inmates and learned she'd done worse than murder in her day.

When he'd finished Delilah demanded, "What's so funny about that?"

He glanced at her, then turned back to the paper. It was obvious she was on the warpath again, and he decided the best response was no response at all. "Never mind."

"I asked what is so funny about a sixteen-year-old girl who's been used and abused all her life by men?"

Sam lowered the paper and, against his own better judgment, decided to hold his own. "I think the point was that the girl had done a little using and abusing of her own."

"She was sixteen. She was only a child."

"She may have been sixteen. But she was far from being a child."

"And whose fault was that, do you think?"

"All right, Delilah. It was all the fault of men. Horrible, wicked men."

"Don't you patronize me."

"I'm not patronizing you. I'm being ironic, just like Twain."

"Ironic." She gave him a sour frown. "What do *you* know about irony?"

He considered the question. "What do I know about irony? Hmm." He stood up. Her eyes widened; she sat bolt upright in her chair. He couldn't help enjoying her obvious apprehensiveness just a little. He pressed on, though he was careful to keep his voice light. "I know plenty about irony, since I've been spending so much time with you." He took the few steps to her side and stood looking down into her flushed face. "And I find a sense of irony very comforting.

Especially since you've gotten so far out of hand with this project of yours to drive me right up the wall.''

She glared defiantly up at him. ''You deserve to be driven up the wall.''

''So you've explained to me.''

''And I'm not out of hand.''

''Oh, no?''

''Absolutely not. Every rotten thing I do to you, I do on purpose.''

''How reassuring.'' He loomed a little nearer, suppressing a smile as he watched her breasts rise and fall in growing agitation.

She was trying her damnedest to pretend that his nearness didn't bother her in the least. Her mouth quivered; she pressed it into a grim line to make the quivering stop.

''Ah, Lilah,'' he murmured.

''Don't you 'ah, Lilah,' me.''

He longed to reach out and touch her. But he knew better. Instead, he dropped to a crouch by her chair. She gasped at the suddenness of the move, and then contained herself.

''What are you up to?'' Sitting as far back in the chair as it was possible to sit, she peered down at him.

He faked an ardent sincerity. ''I'm *begging* you, Lilah...''

''For what?'' she asked, then realized the question could only bring her trouble. ''On second thought, don't tell me.''

He chuckled. ''Too late. You already asked.''

''Get up off the floor. I mean it. I'm warning you...''

''Give me a chance, sweetheart—''

''I told you not to call me that.''

''Give *us* a chance.''

''Not on your life. Now get up from there.''

''You're a hard-hearted woman, Delilah Jones.''

''Right. So take me home tomorrow.''

''Uh-uh. We had a deal.''

''A rotten deal. One you forced on me.''

"A deal's a deal."

"Fine. Have it your way."

"I plan to."

"Just don't ever delude yourself that you'll get anything from me but the misery you deserve."

"Oh, no?"

"No."

He moved then, so swiftly she had no hint of what he intended. He grabbed her hand. She gasped, her whole body tensed. And then she sighed.

Sam relished that sigh. He turned her hand, swiftly, and placed a kiss in the heart of her palm. He barely accomplished his goal, before she tried to jerk away.

He didn't let her. Instead, he rose to his full height, and pulled her along with him.

She came up against his chest. He wrapped his arms around her and held her there. He looked down at her stunned face and saw the hunger there, a hunger he recognized, since it was a mirror of his own.

He smelled the woodsy, sweet scent of her, saw the softening of her lips that meant they waited for his kiss. Her breasts were pressed against him, ripe and ready for his caress. He cupped her face, holding her still.

And then she managed to whisper, "Please don't..."

He almost hated her for that. Because if she'd said anything else, if she hadn't looked so crushed and vulnerable, he would have gone ahead and kissed her, and who could say where things might have gone from there?

Instead, with a muttered curse, he dropped his arms and stepped back. His whole body protested at the loss of her softness. He silently called himself ten kinds of fool. Then he turned and grabbed his coat and got the hell out of there.

When he returned a half hour later, she was already in bed with her face to the wall.

* * *

After that, things grew worse. She must have decided that arguing with him wasn't a good idea, because she refused to be drawn into any disagreements with him from then on. She seethed and glared and spoke only when spoken to.

Sam spent every spare minute on his carving. He worked on the coyote till afternoon. Then he put it aside for a while and glued three pieces of poplar together, thinking that Wednesday he would begin the fine, strong head of a mountain lion, its sharp teeth bared in a warning snarl.

But by Tuesday night at bedtime, Sam had begun to wonder what the point of this was. If he was going to spend all his time carving away at hunks of wood to keep from fighting with Delilah, he might as well go on home where he could carve in his own shop—and not have to look up from his work and find her glaring at him as if she longed to shoot him dead with his own gun.

That night, as the two previous nights, she got ready for bed early and then lay down with her face to the wall, leaving him to stare at the fire. It was then, as he leaned his head back in the old armchair and watched the flame shadows dance in the beams of the ceiling that he finally admitted to himself that this hadn't been such a hot idea after all. He'd told himself Saturday night, before he won Brendan's truck and got the brainstorm to take Delilah instead, that she was never going to give him a break. And he'd been right.

It was driving him crazy having to be around her night and day, and keep hands off. He just couldn't take it anymore. Her never ending meanness had broken him down—and his own frustrated desire had done the rest. He was ready to give up.

"Lilah?" he said quietly, thinking that if she would only turn, and say one reasonably pleasant word—a plain *What?* would do, as long as it was lacking in animosity—he would tell her she'd been right all along, this wasn't working. They were going back to North Magdalene at dawn.

But she didn't turn over. She did nothing at all but continue to lie still as a stick facing the wall.

Fine, he thought wearily. He'd tell her tomorrow. He'd had it with her as much as she had with him. They were going back.

His mind made up, he prepared for bed himself, settled down in his own bag and waited for sleep.

He woke at dawn to the sound of her stomping around the cabin.

He groaned and opened his eyes, noticing first that four pans were steaming on the stove. He glanced around, looking for her. He found her standing by the sink, fully dressed, her arms folded beneath that pair of breasts which belonged on a much more amenable female than she'd ever be.

"Good. You're awake." Her voice was colder than the frozen morning mists obscuring the butte that could be seen out the window behind her head.

He sat up and raked his loose hair back from his face. He didn't miss the way she averted her eyes from the sight of his bare torso. He felt anger—and a hot flare of desire—and realized that maybe he wasn't as resigned to giving her up as he'd thought.

She deigned to speak to him again. "I want to take a sponge bath. Get out, and give me twenty minutes before you come back."

Beneath the sleeping bag, his desire increased as he glanced at the steaming pots again and realized she intended to use their contents to bathe. She would strip down, and wet her body with a cloth, then she'd work up a lather, over those beautiful breasts, that flat belly, the soft flare of those hips…

He swallowed, then said gruffly, "It's freezing outside. It's barely dawn."

"Wear your coat."

He remembered he'd decided last night that they were leaving. He should tell her that, tell her to forget the bath, she could take it when she got home.

But lust—and her endless orneriness—made him contrary. He wasn't telling her that she'd won, finally broken him down with pure nastiness, while he was sitting bucknaked in his sleeping bag, wondering how he was going to stand up without her knowing just exactly how he felt about her.

She was glaring at him, waiting for him to agree to do her will—or to risk her viper's tongue by refusing. He considered standing up suddenly, as he'd done the other night, shocking her into an uncontrolled response.

But then he knew she'd only act appalled. And he could do without that.

He said, "Fine," and shifted enough in the sleeping bag that she saw he intended to rise.

She turned around and faced the window. He got up and shoved his legs in his pants, then quickly pulled on a thermal shirt and heavy sweater.

"It's safe now," he told her with some sarcasm, and then sat in one of the easy chairs to put on his socks and boots. He winced a little when he sat down. His lust was still not fully under control.

Then he stood up and stalked to the sink. She slid swiftly out of his way. He rinsed his face and brushed his hair and anchored it back in a ponytail. Then he got his coat and wool hat and gloves. He put them on and opened the door, not saying a word.

"Wait." She handed him his watch. "I mean it. Twenty minutes." She went back to the sink and yanked the curtains shut to keep out prying eyes—*his* eyes, he was perfectly aware.

He left, barely restraining himself from slamming the door.

Outside, the morning was cold and misty, as it had been yesterday and the day before. When the mist burned off, the day would be clear and gorgeous—as long as those clouds he could see to the west didn't thicken and move in.

He stomped out into the trees and took care of nature's call. After that, there were a good fourteen minutes left before he could return to the warmth of the cabin. He spent them walking in circles around the clearing, watching his own breath come out as freezing mist, getting madder and madder as each second passed.

Just who the hell did she think she was, anyway? All right, maybe it had been a fool's dream, for him to imagine he could win her by hijacking her off into the woods. But damn it, he hadn't done a thing but treat her with courtesy and respect this whole time. The one time he'd almost kissed her, she'd asked him to stop and he had—in spite of his raging desire to do otherwise.

They'd had a deal: a week of her time for Brendan's rig. He'd turned over the rig before the week even began as a gesture of good faith. And now here he was, waiting out in the freezing cold for her to finish washing that gorgeous body of hers so he could take her back home halfway through the week she'd sworn to give him.

He stopped in mid-pace in the middle of the clearing and stared at the mist-shrouded mountain across the lake. When he'd planned this ill-fated trip, in the wee hours of Sunday morning, he'd pictured them climbing that butte—Ladyslipper Peak, his father had always called it—together. It was a challenging hike, but not dangerous, with a clearly delineated trail around the south side most of the way to the top.

Sam glanced at his watch. Five minutes to go. She'd be

finishing up rinsing now, dribbling clear warm water over her shoulders, her neck, the tender valley between her breasts...

Sam glared up at the mountain again—and decided he was not going to go meekly back inside and tell her she was getting what she wanted.

No, by God. They weren't leaving today. They'd leave when he was damn good and ready.

Yes. Absolutely. He could see now that the mistake he'd made was to meekly hang around the cabin, hoping and praying for a kind word or a soft look from a woman who wouldn't call an ambulance if she found him bleeding in the road.

He'd been here to the lake ten times by himself in as many years. And he'd always, up until now, found his own company plenty to satisfy him.

And it would be plenty now. He'd arranged this week for rest and recreation. And he wasn't leaving without getting what he'd come for, whether the mean little witch inside the cabin joined him or not.

Sam glanced at his watch again. Time was up. He turned from the lake and headed for the cabin, noticing that she'd pulled the curtains open once again.

She was completely dressed, her wet hair in a braid down her back, and making coffee when he entered. He could smell her shampoo in the steamy air. He carried the wood he'd brought in over to the bin by the stove and dropped it in. Then he took off his coat, gloves and hat and put them away.

Next, he went to the refrigerator, took out bacon, an egg and some milk, got the biscuit mix from a shelf and started whipping up a batch of pancakes. She saw what he was doing and fell into step with him, getting down the plates and fixing up the table, putting out the milk and sugar he

liked for his coffee, as well as the margarine and syrup for
the pancakes.

It was almost spooky, really, the way they worked together. From the first day, when they cleaned the cabin from
top to bottom without sharing more than ten words the
whole time, it had been like that. They were like two parts
of a well-oiled machine when they tackled a task. He'd mentioned it the first day, but she hadn't wanted to hear it. She'd
known, of course, that he was thinking of the other things
they might do well together.

He was still thinking of those other things. All the time.
It was driving him crazy, if the truth were told.

As they sat down to the breakfast table and ate the crisp
bacon and fragrant griddle cakes without speaking, he
looked longingly out the window at Ladyslipper Peak. Yes,
it would be good to get out and take that mountain, a long,
hard hike. He would do it today.

Maybe, if she decided to follow along, the view from the
summit would soften her hard heart. In any case, the exer-
cise would work off a little of the tension that kept coiling
tighter and tighter, like a snake readying to spring, inside
him.

They finished the silent meal. Then they got up as one
and cleaned the table.

After that, it was near eight. He decided to work for an
hour on the carving of the coyote, to give the mountain a
chance to warm up a little before he tackled it. He got out
his tools and set to work, feeling better than he had in two
days.

Though he did his best to pay no attention to her, he
couldn't help but notice that she seemed restless. She went
out and came in again, settled down with a book, then put
it away.

He wondered if she sensed a change in him, if she had a

feeling that something between them had shifted, though he'd said not a word about anything at all.

Things *had* changed, he realized. She'd had him on the run, and now he'd decided he wasn't running anymore. She refused to want him. Fine. He was through trying to get her to change her mind.

But she still had her end of their bargain to keep. She was here for the rest of the week, if he wanted it that way. And, the more he thought about it, the more he knew he did want it that way.

At nine, he put his tools away and found the small day pack he used for hikes. He got out a few of the snacks and drink boxes she'd brought from home and loaded them in the pack. Then he found his canteen and filled it. Though he never glanced her way, he knew she watched his every move.

When the pack was ready, he loaded the handgun—she always conscientiously removed the cartridges every time she put it away—strapped it on and pulled a sweatshirt over his sweater. Then he put on his down vest and pulled on his gloves.

He could feel her eyes on him the whole while, and he knew the only thing that kept her from asking what was up was the knowledge that he was bound by the laws of safety and common sense not to head out without saying where he was going and how long he'd be gone.

He waited, enjoying the upper hand for a change, until he was sliding his arms in the day pack and slipping his canteen on his belt hook, before he said, "I'm hiking up Ladyslipper Peak—the mountain across the lake. There's a trail around the other side that goes to the summit. It's a couple of hours up, and less coming down. I should be back by one or two this afternoon."

She just stared at him, her dark eyes smoldering with all that pent-up resentment—and repudiated desire.

He knew a perverse stab of satisfaction. It was obvious she hadn't the faintest idea what to do about this development. She'd gotten used to him tiptoeing around, waiting for her to make a move so he could react to it. She didn't know how to handle it when he acted of his own accord.

He grabbed his hat and stuck it on his head and turned for the door.

"Wait!" she said at the last minute.

He turned, lifting an eyebrow. "Is there a problem?"

She blinked, her expression bewildered. He had to stifle a smug grin as he watched her furiously casting about for some reason why he should stay here where she could abuse him at her leisure.

"Wh-what if you have an accident or something?"

"We've been through this. I'll fire two shots."

"But I haven't the faintest idea where that trail starts. I don't know the terrain. I would have hiked up that mountain myself if I thought it was safe to go alone."

"It's safe."

"You've done it before?"

"Yes."

"You never mentioned that."

He said nothing in reply. He just gave her a look intended to remind her of everything she'd put him through in the past few days.

She glanced away—rather defensively, he thought. Then she pointed out, "And anyway, if something happened to you, I'd have trouble finding you. That wouldn't be good."

It was an absurdly weak argument, one he demolished without missing a beat. "*If* you hear shots—which you won't—then take the truck back the way we came in, to the last crossroads. Go right. Go right again when you come to the next fork. Go about two miles and you're at paved road. Turn left. From there it's four miles to the ranger's station." He turned around and reached for the door.

He heard her stand up. "Sam..."

"What?"

"I...I think I'd better go with you."

He felt a hot surge of triumph, a delicious sensation, one he savored fully before turning at last and giving her an unconcerned look. "What for?"

Her face was flushed. She looked confused and adorable and he had to remind himself that just the slightest hint of weakness on his part and she'd be on him unmercifully once again.

"It's...well, it's just better if we stick together."

He shrugged. "Nothing is going to happen. And if by some weird chance it did, you know what to do."

"But I—"

"You what?"

For a moment, she didn't speak. He stared at her, at her flushed face, at the wisps of dark hair that had escaped her braid and now kissed her temples, at her stormy dark eyes and her sweet red mouth. He liked staring at her, especially now, when she was at a disadvantage. She looked vulnerable now, which didn't happen often—he could testify in court to that.

"I...just think I should go," she said at last.

"No," he said flatly.

Her black brows drew together. That sweet, vulnerable look was fading. She'd be spitting and scratching again in a moment, if he didn't stay ahead of her.

"Unless..." He let the word wander off into nowhere.

Her brows smoothed out a little. "Unless what?"

"Unless you just plain *want* to go."

She gaped at him. "Excuse me?"

"You can go if you *want* to go. Do you...*want* to go?"

"Well, I—"

"Yes or no? This is not a trick question."

"Well, I...yes! Yes, of course." Then she added, unwilling to completely concede to him even on this small issue, "but only because I don't think you should go off alone."

He studied her for a moment, and considered telling her that that wasn't good enough. She either wanted to go or she didn't. But then he decided he'd pushed things far enough.

He looked down at the soft moccasins she was wearing. "Fine. Get your boots on, and get ready. I'll wait outside." With more satisfaction than he'd felt in days, he flung open the cabin door and stepped out into the bright morning.

Delilah, even more at a loss than Sam realized, stared at the closed door for several seconds after he was gone. She knew she should stick her head out the door, right now, and tell him to head on up that mountain without her.

What she'd done, making all those absurdly weak excuses for keeping him here, and then, in the end, virtually begging him to let her come, was a grave lapse. She was supposed to be staying as clear of him as the circumstances would allow, not chasing him willingly up the side of a cliff.

But good grief, she was just so...confused. Not to mention at the end of a very frayed rope when it came to her emotions.

Making Sam's life miserable twenty-four hours a day had not turned out to be an easy task for her. True, she'd had a lot of practice in her life at being mean; a girl didn't grow up in the Jones Gang and live to tell about it unless she learned to get tough when she had to. Yet since she'd grown up, it hadn't been necessary for her to be mean with any consistency. She was out of practice.

Being mean to Sam for two days running had practically worn her out. It took fortitude and stamina to be consistently vicious, she was learning. And it was even harder in this situation, since he'd seemed to get nicer the meaner she became.

It was driving her right out of her mind, to be honest. To be here alone with him, and have to look at him and *feel* his presence every hour of the day—and constantly remember that he was not the man for her, that he'd brought her here as the payoff on a wager, and that she'd only be asking for heartache if she softened toward him one bit.

Sam Fletcher was forty years old. He'd never married, and she doubted he ever would. Not that she wanted to marry a man like him, anyway. No, whatever might happen between them would take place right here, in the next few days, and be over as soon as they went home.

And she didn't want that, a temporary fling. She wasn't the type for a temporary fling.

"So nothing is going to happen," Delilah announced to the empty cabin, and then went to get her heavy socks and boots.

Well, she decided, as she laced up the boots, she *did* want to go with him, and she was going to do what she wanted. She'd go stone cold bonkers, sitting here alone for four hours, staring at the lake and trying to keep from thinking about Sam.

Yes. Going with him was the better option. If nothing else, the heavy exertion would work off a little of the strain that kept building between them, worse every hour.

Delilah stood up and put on a sweater and a sweatshirt and a padded vest, just as Sam had. The layers were efficient for hiking; they could be peeled off and tied at her waist as she grew warmer. She got more food, her canteen and her own hat and gloves and went out to join him where he waited on the log by the lake, taking the key and locking the door behind her.

He stood up when she approached, and saw the extra juice boxes and snack bars she carried. He turned around, without saying a word, so she could add the food to that already in the pack.

"Okay," she said, when the food was packed.

He glanced over his shoulder. "Ready?"

"Yes."

He headed for the trail that she'd taken alone the first day they arrived. She fell in step behind him, glad to be moving, to be going somewhere.

Yes, the hike would be good for her, she was sure. And the lapse of voluntarily going along with something he wanted to do meant nothing. What could possibly happen between them while they were climbing a cliff, for heaven's sake?

But then she glanced up, at the craggy face of the cliff they would be scaling. It looked stark and uncompromising, like the powerful frame of the man in front of her.

A frisson of taboo excitement skittered through her body. She felt reckless and daring, eager for whatever might lie ahead.

And then she froze, her face flaming.

Recklessness. Daring. Such emotions were not for her. Growing up a Jones, she'd seen well enough what happened to people who gave in to their every wild urge.

They got in big trouble. Frequently.

In her mind, the voice of caution advised, *Go back right now. You're playing with fire to go with him. You're breaking your own rules. You're on hazardous ground....*

Delilah shook her head. There was nothing to worry about. She was being plain paranoid. What could possibly happen? It was a hike up a mountain, and nothing more.

She realized she'd stopped moving for a moment, and Sam was getting way ahead of her. She hastened to follow him into the trees.

Chapter Ten

They walked briskly for a half hour, following the trail through the trees east of the lake. But when they came to the place where the path veered to lakeside, Sam went the other way. He strode cross-country for awhile until he reached a different trail. Delilah followed his lead, keeping her eyes open, noticing everything from the occasional deer tracks to the hot pink head of a snow plant poking through the mulchy ground.

It was good, she decided, to be out, moving around, *going* somewhere. It had been the right decision to follow him. She felt better with every step she took. Her fears *had* been groundless after all.

The new trail snaked around to the base of the mountain on the other side. There, it began to ascend on a series of switchbacks that took them ever higher, up the south slope of Ladyslipper Peak. As they climbed, the morning mists faded. An hour after they'd left the cabin, the day had warmed considerably and both of them had tied their sweat shirts and sweaters at their waists.

Delilah, no slouch when it came to hiking, found she had to push herself constantly to keep up with Sam. At one point, they took two steep grades in a row, up which Sam maintained a killing pace. Near the top of the second one Delilah stopped for a moment to nurse a stitch in her side By chance, she paused at a gap in the tall stands of ever greens which until then had blocked out a clear view of the sky.

Breathing hard, she rubbed her side. She glanced up— and saw the gray clouds rearing up in the sky to the west The freshening wind blew in her face—from the same direction as the rising clouds.

Sam, who must have become aware that she had stopped turned back to check on her. She called, "Wait up!"

He remained unmoving, waiting, as she hustled up the trail to join him. She hurried, not paying as much attention to the trail as she should have. She slipped on some loose shale just as she reached him. She teetered.

He warned, "Watch it," as he reached out and grabbed her.

She fell against him.

"Easy," he muttered, steadying her.

She gasped and gaped up at him, witnessing the swift heat that leapt in his eyes, knowing the answering fire inside herself—a flash fire, racing along every nerve, searing her down to pure desire in an instant.

The whole world surged into sharp focus. She was aware right then of *everything* at once—from the scent of dust and pine that surrounded them, to the call of a hawk in the distance, to the loose strands of her own hair, which the rough wind had whipped against her mouth.

His eyes seared through her. Time spun out. She continued to gaze up at him, so stunned by her own sudden, complete arousal that she couldn't move. The wind sang in the pines to the same wild tune as the blood roaring in her ears.

At last, she remembered herself. She put her hands on his chest. "S-sorry." She pushed, feeling the warmth of him, the strength, the call of his hips against her own....

He let her go. Her body, had it a voice, would have wailed in yearning protest. She looked down at the loose earth that had tripped her, and waited for some degree of composure to return.

When it did, she dared to look at him again. He watched her, through eyes that gave away nothing. She noticed that he had stepped away from her while she collected herself.

She gestured at the incoming clouds and raised her voice so he could hear her against the wind. "Storm coming."

"I know."

"Maybe we should go back."

He shrugged. "It's not cold enough to snow. And a few drops of rain won't kill us."

"It looks like more than a few drops of rain, Sam."

He didn't immediately reply but only stared at her. She saw the look in his eyes, a look turbulent as the wind that whipped all around them. She knew what he was thinking. He didn't want to go back to the cabin, be locked in there with her, until he absolutely had to. She couldn't blame him. She felt the same way.

"I'm going on," he said. "If you want to go back, fine. You know the way now."

She thought about that, as he went on watching her. About returning to the cabin alone, to wait for him. About sitting there by the fire through the storm, wondering when he would return, trying to read that book she'd been trying to read since Saturday night.

No way, she thought grimly. She looked up at the sky again and decided he was right; it wasn't that cold. If they kept moving, they'd get wet—but nothing much worse.

"I'll go on with you!" she shouted into the wind.

"Why?"

Her gaze did not waver. "I *want* to."

He gave a slight nod. "Fair enough."

He took his canteen from the hook at his waist and drank from it. Then, wiping his mouth with the back of his hand, he held it out to her. She should refuse, she knew it. She had her own canteen. But her hand was reaching out of its own accord. She took the canteen, put her mouth where his had been, and felt the sweet water slide down her dry throat. Then she screwed the lid on and handed it back.

"Let's go," he said.

They went on as the wind swirled around them and the clouds rolled closer still.

The trees thinned visibly as they climbed, and the trail got rougher. There were places where erosion had worn it completely away. There, they clung to whatever rocks or hardy branches were handy and inched their way across. Often Sam, after crossing a rough spot first, would hold out a hand to her.

The first time she almost refused it, but he gave her a look that promised dire consequences should she spurn his aid and get herself in a bind as a result. She could almost believe that he might leave her there, and not help her climb out, should she go sliding down the hillside after scorning his assistance.

She took the hand he offered and felt the heat between them as if it were an electric current, shooting from his palm to hers, right up her arm, through her pounding heart—and down into her most private parts where it pooled and roiled and clamored for release.

More than once, she had that nagging feeling that she should go back. She ignored it.

There was no going back. Not now.

Something had happened. She wasn't sure what, exactly.

All she knew for certain was that now the whole world shimmered with life and beauty and a vibrant intensity. She felt truly free. It was glorious. She never wanted it to end.

The wind howled, as they came out into the open, above the thick close-growing belt of evergreens. Now, the carpet of fir and pine lay all around on the surrounding hills. But they climbed above the trees, in a place of stark, granite beauty, free of snow on this, the south side, because the springtime sun had done its work. Gradually, the only trees that grew were juniper and white pine, their gaunt pale branches twisted and gnarled by the unrelenting force of frequent winds.

Overhead, now, the once-blue sky was obscured by the agitated clouds. Sam and Delilah had been working their way up the granite shelves for perhaps fifteen minutes when the sky lit up, the thunder boomed, and the black sky above opened up with a hard, wet vengeance.

Delilah was crossing a rough spot when the rain began. She glanced up for a moment, and the water beat on her face, whipping and pelting at her with the aid of the torturous wind.

She opened her mouth. The heavy drops were cool and sweet. She smiled, glad with a fierceness that made her breath catch in her throat that she'd come, glad, as the rain rapidly soaked her to the skin, that she was whole and strong and climbing a mountain beneath a turbulent sky.

She looked down again, seeking a foothold to continue. Sam was waiting, arm outstretched.

She put her hand in his. The now-familiar shaft of heat and hunger arrowed up her arm and seared down to the core of her, building the growing need there higher still.

He pulled her across the slick space. She found her footing quickly. He released her and stepped back.

"This is crazy." His low words carried easily; the wind was at his back. "You were right. Let's turn around."

She was silent for a moment, within the rush and swirl of the wind. She felt a sinking feeling—of disappointment bordering on despair.

All her life, she'd been so careful, done nothing reckless, taken no crazy chances. Because she knew what crazy chances got a person: trouble. Her whole family was living proof of that.

But then her lifelong enemy had decided to pursue her. He'd chased. She'd run. As fast and hard as she could. But still he stayed on her tail. He'd forced her to come here— away from her carefully managed life where he'd had no chance of getting through to her—and he'd done his best to break her down.

Well, he hadn't done it. She had held out against him. But the stress had been torture. And now, here they were, on top of a mountain in a pounding gale.

And she felt free and strong and full of energy and heat. She felt gloriously, utterly, completely *alive*.

And she didn't want to go back down, not without reaching the top, going over the crest to lakeside, and witnessing the panorama of the lake and the wild land laid out before her while the wind tore her hair and the rain beat down upon her.

"How far is it?" she shouted.

"Not far."

"Let's finish it."

He shook his head. "It's foolish. We'll be drenched."

"We already are." For the first time, of her own accord, with no reason other than to communicate, she touched him. She laid her hand on his arm.

"Lilah…" He stiffened.

"Please, Sam. I want to reach the top."

He met her eyes. And he saw what had happened to her, the wildness in her, that she'd at last let come to the fore.

She let him see it, *wanted* him to see it, to share her excitement, catch it like a fever and be willing to go on.

"You're crazy," he breathed.

"Yes. Yes, at last."

"All the way to the top?"

"Yes. You said it wasn't far."

"No. Not far. Not too far..." He touched her face. His rough thumb slid across her lips, back and forth.

"The top," she barely whispered the words, but he caught them, in spite of the wind and the din it made.

"The top," he said back to her.

She released his arm; his warm hand left her face. He turned to the upward trail. They went on.

He'd spoken truly; it wasn't far. Fifteen minutes at most, minutes that burned away to nothing beneath their clambering boots. They cut back to the east, then scrambled up a gully that already ran with water, drenching their boots.

After that, it was bare rock faces, and blasted trees. They struggled up the last of it, on all fours much of the way.

And finally, he hoisted himself over the top, and reached down a hand. She took it, he hauled her up—and into his arms.

She landed against the hard wall of his chest. She looked up. His eyes burned into hers. The world was a wild, wet maelstrom. All rational thought had fled.

He saw what he sought—call it surrender, call it the triumph of her own secret, reckless heart. His arms closed more tightly, stealing her breath and searing her senses. Her breasts grew tender, aching, and full. She boldly thrust them forward, and his big hand came up and cupped one.

He groaned. She sighed. He held her gaze captive, as he thumbed her nipple, teasing it thoroughly through the wet cloth of her nubby thermal shirt.

She said his name. He told her yes.

She reached up, grabbed his big head, and hauled it down so she could taste him, know him, as she had dreamed of knowing him in these last agonizing nights when he lay so close and yet a thousand miles away.

The rain beat down on them. His mouth, hot and hungry, so long evaded, finally sought, closed over hers.

They moaned in sensual glee, as one. His tongue teased her lips, she let it in eagerly, as he rubbed himself against her, and she rubbed back.

The kiss, wild as the storm, went on forever. Delilah, who had never known such delight, gloried in it. He kissed her mouth for a long, drugging eternity. Then he cupped her head in his big hands, and he kissed her cheeks, her nose, her temples, the wet coils of hair that had long ago pulled out of her braid and now lay plastered against her streaming face. He sipped the raindrops from her chin, and kissed her closed eyelids and the soft corners of her mouth.

And Delilah touched him, as he kissed her. She ran her questing hands over his shoulders, found the straps of the pack and slipped it off. It fell to the rock at their feet. Neither of them noticed. She stroked his back through his soaking shirt, loving his hardness, his strength, the bulk of him that seemed such a complement to her slender suppleness.

She was bold—fearlessly sensual. She felt the narrowness of his waist, the tight curve of his buttocks. She cupped his face as he did hers, and matched him, kiss for kiss.

At last, he whispered against her mouth. "Turn. Look."

She stilled, looked in his eyes, her arousal creating a sweet, heavy languor even beneath the fury of the storm.

He smiled down at her, a smile that said everything—what he would show her, the delights they would share.

"Kiss me some more, Sam. Like that. Like you just did."

"You're greedy."

She felt a quick flush of embarrassment.

He chuckled. "It's okay. I like you greedy."

"Oh..." She looked down.

"Don't."

She gazed at him once more.

"Better. Much better." He glanced up, at the angry, streaming sky. "We're going to have to head down soon. If this keeps up, we could actually end up in trouble."

She nodded gravely. She remembered that gully they'd climbed, already running with its own overflowing stream. The dirt sections of the trail would turn to mud, and mud meant the possibility of slides.

"But first..." He let his voice trail off.

"What?"

He took her by the shoulders and turned her so she fitted back against his body. "Look."

Delilah blinked away the rain and did as he bid her.

"We're in the slipper," he said in her ear. "Ladyslipper Peak, remember?" She nodded, against his shoulder, liking the feel of his body, behind her, along the length of her, caressing every inch. He explained, "From down by the lake, if you look closely, you can see where we're standing. It looks like a lady's high heeled shoe."

"You'll have to show me."

He chuckled. "Don't worry, I will. If we ever get back down there."

She smiled, and armed away the water from her eyes. Then she gazed down over the glorious panorama spread out below.

On this side, the cliff beneath them tumbled away to nothing in a series of escarpments that eventually widened out at the base to huge boulders that were lapped by the waters of the now-turbulent lake. Across the lake, she could see the clearing, but mistily, through the rain. The cabin was barely visible, and even that was mostly because she knew where to look for it.

The whole scene appeared mysterious and magical, a universe of lake and tall trees—and tucked within it, a tiny fairy glen. The veil created by the rain made the clearing seem incorporeal, as if, should she blink, she might look again to find it gone.

Lightning glared in the sky and the loud crash of thunder came after. "Sweetheart. We have to go."

"I know." She accepted his judgment, and the endearment, without debate. Somewhere on the rocky cliffs of Ladyslipper Peak, the long pitched battle had ended. He had won—or had her wilder self?

For a time at least, in this place, she was his; he was hers.

She bent and took up the pack, helped him slip it on. They turned as one and started down.

Chapter Eleven

The rock faces ran with miniature streams, the dirt turned to slippery mud, and the wind seemed to grow to gale force, screaming like a banshee through the trees.

But somehow, they struggled down the unforgiving granite ridges, into the cover of the trees, and finally down to the base of the mountain, where they followed the trails that at last led to the clearing by the lake.

Nearly two hours after leaving the crest, they fell into the cabin, shivering uncontrollably and covered with water and mud. They pulled off their boots and shrugged out of their drenched outerwear right away, and then worked together to build up the fires, Delilah replenishing the stove and filling the pots with water to boil for bathing, and Sam laying and lighting the fire in the hearth. Soon enough, the cabin was filled with soothing heat.

Delilah, by the stove, looked over at Sam. He knelt by the fireplace on the rag rug, staring into the flames. Overhead, the rain pounded on the roof, a loud, hollow drone. But Delilah thought of silence, of the waiting stillness between them, beneath the roar of the storm outside and the crackle of the fires in the room.

She stood very still, in her muddy clothes, looking at his back as he bent before the fire. And then she went to him.

He looked up at her, his gaze taking in the whole of her. She knew he could see the pebbling of her nipples beneath her clinging shirt. The thought excited her, and she found, incredibly, that she could let herself feel that excitement, accept it, even revel in it.

The excitement had a taste to it, a sweet taste, like the taste of Sam's mouth on hers....

He said, "You want me, Lilah."

It was the same challenge he'd tossed at her more than once before. Now, strangely, it didn't even occur to her to try to deny its truth.

"Yes."

He reached up, hooked a finger through her belt loop, and slowly pulled her down, so she kneeled, as he did, before the fire. They faced each other.

His hand fell away. "As soon as the sun goes, the temperature will drop."

"I know."

"By morning, there'll be snow."

"Yes, probably."

"If we leave now, we could get out. Otherwise, we'll probably be stuck in here for a few more days."

"Yes."

"Yes, what?"

"Yes. I understand."

"Do you?" He reached out again, as if he couldn't help himself, and he brushed the tightened nipples of her breasts. She tensed, then relaxed, and let the pleasant, teasing sensation have its way with her body. It felt as if—the finest thread connected her breasts to her secret feminine heart. His touch tugged the thread. The feminine heart of her opened, bloomed....

With a small shrug of regret, he let his hand fall away.

"I'll take you back now," he said quietly, "if you want to go. The bargain we had is met."

She frowned, confused. "Met?"

"The deal. The bargain. I'm...satisfied. I'll take you home now, if you want."

She understood. She allowed herself a secret smile. "You'll take me home. Now."

"Yes."

"And Brendan can keep his truck."

"That's what I said." He sounded impatient; she suspected he was afraid she would leap eagerly to her feet and start packing up her gear.

She shook her head slowly, letting her secret smile show. "You have no mercy."

He didn't move. "You called me a manipulative snake the other day. And maybe I have been. But not anymore. If this goes any further, you'll never say you didn't have a choice."

She took in a shaky breath. "Okay."

He glared at her. "Okay. Okay? What does that mean?"

"Okay. Yes. I want to stay."

He made a low sound in his throat. And then he grabbed her and pulled her to him. He cupped her head in an unyielding hand. Right then, she couldn't have pulled away if she'd wanted to. His mouth claimed hers, hard and hot. She answered the kiss in kind. He touched her breast again, a knowing, maddening touch, and she moaned in delight.

But then he restrained himself. He pulled back, and turned her, so she lay between his thighs. For a long moment, they stared into the hungry flames of the fire he'd built.

She thought, then, of the little pouches she'd left in the

drawer at home. She murmured, "I have nothing…for contraception."

He kissed her temple, smoothed the moist hair there. Then he helped her to sit, slipped out from behind her and padded on stocking feet to his gear. He fumbled in a pocket of one of the packs and returned to her, his hand outstretched. "It's okay. I do."

She looked at the pouches that were like the ones she'd left at home.

He chuckled ruefully. "You can't blame a guy for wanting to be prepared. Just in case his dream comes true…"

"No, Sam. I can't blame a guy for that…." She reached for him, he came down to her, turning her toward the fire again.

She leaned back, so she lay across his lap. He cradled her head and began kissing her all over again, working her braid loose as his lips played with hers, then combing the wet strands with his fingers until they lay in snaky tendrils across his big thighs.

Then, very gently, he worked her clinging, still-moist shirt from the waistband of her jeans. He slid his rough and tender hand under there, and caressed her skin. Delilah sighed, and wriggled a little, eager as she had never imagined she would be to have a man stroke and touch her, and ready her for ecstasy.

He took the wet shirt and pulled it up and over her head. She raised her arms for him, so it would easily slide away. He took a moment to pull his own shirt off and away. Then he looked down at her once more.

He said, "Beautiful…" as he unhooked her bra and tossed it aside. Once she was bare for him, he lowered his mouth and kissed her, taking her breast into his mouth, sucking first gently and then more strongly, until she writhed and moaned for more.

Delilah lay stunned with delight as his hungry mouth be-

gan to wander, tasting her, knowing her. He nuzzled beneath
the low curve of a breast, a place revealed now since she
lay on her back across his thighs. He licked the bottom swell
of that breast; his lips trailed up, and he took her nipple in
his mouth once more.

Delilah groaned and clutched his head, her fingers thread-
ing through his long, wet hair, pulling out the band that held
it back, combing through it, feeling it trail in heavy, moist
strands over her belly and breasts, teasing the nipple he
wasn't sucking on until his hand cupped it and tormented it
the more.

Then he raised his head and spanned her waist with his
hands. He stood her up, before him. Kneeling in front of
her, his light eyes holding hers, his wild mane of hair falling
on his bare shoulders so he looked more primitive and feral
than ever, he unhooked her belt and unzipped her pants and
then slowly, taking her panties as well, he skimmed down
her jeans. She stepped out of them. He tossed them aside.

She stood before him in her socks alone. His gaze
branded her.

"Sam?"

"Shh..."

He leaned forward a fraction. And he nuzzled her belly.

"Oh!" she gasped in delighted shock.

He kissed her there, then lower, parting her, and touching
her most secret place with his hungry lips. She let him do
that, *wanted* him to do that. She clutched his shoulders and
pressed herself toward him, and he went on kissing the
womanly heart of her until she thought she would die of
pure pleasure. She flung her head back and cried her ecstasy
at the rafters, where the flameshadows danced and the rain
beat in hard flurries with each wild gust of wind.

And then, in an instant, he was pulling her down. She
lost the dizzying torment of his intimate kiss, only to find
herself beneath him. She forced her heavy lids to open.

He looked down at her, his hair touched her breast. She saw his hunger. She saw what he wanted. And she wanted it, too. She reached for his belt, slipped the tip from the loop, the tongue from the hole. She had it undone in seconds. Then she undid his heavy corduroy jeans, pulling the fly apart quickly, shoving the jeans down his hard thighs and pushing his briefs away, too.

He sprang free. She touched him.

"Lilah..." He groaned the word at the ceiling, the tendons in his powerful neck standing out with the strain.

"Yes, Sam. Yes, now..."

He looked down at her again, and grabbed up one of the condoms waiting nearby. He slid it on, with her help.

Then she wrapped her legs around him. He thrust into her.

She let out a long, ecstatic cry.

"Look at me, Lilah." The command was low, weighted with heat.

She looked at him, into his light eyes that seared through her, knowing her, in a way no other human being ever had.

He moved out. She whimpered, a wordless plea for his return. He slowly filled her once more. Then he pulled back again. Her body yearned for his. He gave her what she was longing for.

And all the time, his eyes held hers, so there could never ever be a doubt of what they did with their bodies, here in the center of the storm.

"I've wanted this," he muttered, "dreamed of this..."

"Yes, oh, yes, I know..."

A squall of seeking wind hammered the rain against the little window on the west wall. Lightning crashed and thunder rolled.

Sam took her slowly, watching her build to a shattering fulfillment, holding himself on the brink until she thrust herself against him so hungrily that he knew she was nearing her final spiraling climb to ecstasy.

He levered himself up a little, and held still, so she could find her own rhythm, set her own pace. And when she pressed herself wildly against him, rubbed her soft body all over his, he knew he wouldn't last unless he did something quick.

He rolled, then, so swiftly that she cried out. And then she was on top.

"Oh, my!" She looked down at him, her hair curling in riotous coils all around her face. She looked wild and utterly free, her lips full and red from his kisses, her eyes glazed with her own need. "What is this?"

"Ride me," he instructed.

"Oh, my!" she murmured again. Then she raised herself up, experimentally. "My, my, my..." Slowly, she sank upon him again.

She let her head roll back; her wild hair fell away to expose the column of her neck. She moaned. He felt himself inside of her, sheathed by her—the most incredible creature he'd ever seen, something mythic and too beautiful to tame or possess.

And he knew, down in the deepest part of his being, that no one had ever seen her like this before. And, if he had a damn thing to say about it, no one else ever would.

This was the Lilah he had sought to free. His Lilah. His woman. Now. And from now on...

He thrust his hips upward, to give her more of him, and he gloried in the way she responded, moaning louder, thrusting back. Then she braced her hands on his chest, and she moved against him, faster and faster. Her dark eyes branded him, held him, a willing captive in her erotic spell.

She said, "Oh, Sam, I never thought, I never imagined..." and she couldn't finish. There were no more words.

Her eyes, drugged at last with her own mounting, ex-

panding bliss, drooped shut. Her head fell back. She cried
out something feral, something triumphant. Her body rose
and fell in wild crescendo, gleaming in the fireglow.

He held her hips to stay with her and found he himself
was caught up, rising, going over the edge of the world
along with her. They cried out in unison. He thrust the final
time into her and felt himself spilling, releasing, a last eternity of pleasure that went on and on, as her softness held
him, took everything he had and gave it back to him ten-
thousandfold.

She fell across him, spent, her magnificent soft breasts
crushed against his chest, her breath sliding over his skin,
warm and sweet, one hand unconsciously stroking him at
first, then lying limp as a fallen flower in the crook of his
shoulder and his neck.

He touched her hair, a black tangle all around her head,
smoothing it, and then idly caressing it, as he slowly came
back to the world.

For a while he merely lay and memorized the feel of her
body, limp and satisfied, on his. He heard the rain on the
roof and the wind blowing wild outside. And then, lazily,
he rolled his head toward the bubbling sound coming from
the stove. The pots she'd set out were boiling. The big window, he noticed, was covered over with steam.

He chuckled then. "Sweetheart, we've really fogged up
the place."

"Hmm?" She began caressing him again, touching his
arm in long, trailing strokes. And then burrowing her fingers
in the hair on his chest, making little cooing sounds.

Sam chuckled.

She asked, softly, "What?"

"Nothing. You."

She sat up on him, then. And she was smiling. "What
about me, Sam Fletcher?"

"I just never thought I'd see the day, that's all." He

grinned back at her, thinking that he'd wanted her to smile for him for how long now? And now she had.

"The day that what?" she prompted. Her full breasts tempted him. He touched one, a feather-light caress. She hitched in a kindled breath.

"This day," he explained. "You and me, together."

She bent and kissed him. "Well, Sam Fletcher. You *have* seen it. And guess what?"

"Yeah?"

"So have I."

"Surprised?"

She tipped her head, considering. "A month ago, I never would have believed it. But lately..."

"What?"

"It started to seem..."

"Yeah?"

"Inevitable, I guess." Her expression changed. The firelight licked across her skin, picking up the sheen from the sweat of their lovemaking. Her hair foamed out around her face, a veil of tangled ebony. She looked wild and pagan— and far away from him.

Sam, watching her, found he didn't like that faraway look. He didn't like it at all. "What's wrong?" he demanded. "What is it?"

"Nothing." The look was gone. She smiled down at him once more. She bent her head and kissed him, a sweet, soft brushing of her lips on his.

Then she slid to the side. He sat up for a moment, to get rid of the condom. Once that was taken care of, he went to the bed and came back with the spare blanket. After that, he opened his sleeping bag and laid it out on the rug for them to lie on. He stretched out again. She lay beside him, between him and the fire and he settled the blanket over them. For a while, neither spoke. There was the rain and the fire and the occasional caress, a smile and an answering look.

Finally, across the room, a pot bubbled over, the water hissing and popping as it hit the scorching stove top.

"We can have our baths," she remarked. "The water's boiling."

He reached for her. "The water's not the only thing that's hot. Come here."

Eventually, they got up from the floor and went to bathe, a wholly enjoyable process now that there was no need for either of them to go outside in the storm and wait until the other was through.

They mixed the boiling water with cold, and took turns washing each other, a marvelously sensual experience—not to mention revitalizing.

After that, they both realized they were starving. They prepared dinner, and sat down to eat in a shared mood of quiet congeniality. They cleaned up afterwards, as darkness fell. They turned on the light and Sam set up his improvised woodworking shop and began boasting the head of the mountain lion.

Delilah at last allowed herself to ask the thousand and one questions about his woodworking tools and the whole process of carving that she'd been dying to ask these three days. He answered them all.

And then, later, as they spread his sleeping bag on the bed for a sheet and laid hers over it as a blanket, Sam suddenly went still.

"What is it?" she asked.

"Listen…"

"I don't hear anything," she said, and realized it was true. The wind had died down, and the rain seemed to have stopped some time ago. She couldn't have said when exactly.

He prompted, "Yes. Yes, you do. Listen."

She listened—and she heard it. Like a whisper, like a coat made of feathers, drifting slowly down…

"Snow."

He smiled and held out his hand.

They went to the big window together. Sam took a towel and wiped away the steam and like eager children they pressed their faces to the glass.

Delilah saw it, falling steady and thick.

Sam turned to her. He spoke with great solemnity. "Miss Jones, we are being snowed in."

She turned to him. "We might never get out."

"Oh, we'll get out. Eventually."

She looked at him from under her lashes. "But what will we do with ourselves…until then?"

He reached out and ran a finger down her neck, over the collar of the clean shirt she'd put on after their shared bath, to the soft swell of a breast. "I have an idea or two of how to pass the time."

"You do? Show me…"

"I'll be glad to." And he did.

They woke the next morning to a world of white, and found it no hardship to remain in the cabin—except for necessary sojourns into the trees—the entire day, and all of Friday as well.

They ate and slept and made love when they felt like it. Sam worked on his carvings. Delilah whipped through that mystery novel which previously hadn't been able to hold her interest at all.

They avoided, by tacit agreement, talk of what would happen when they returned to North Magdalene. They talked instead of their pasts, of what had shaped them, made them each who they were.

Sam *had* been a preacher's son, the rebel of his family,

the black sheep who left home the day he graduated from high school and never went back. His father had been dead for fifteen years, but he still had a mother and a sister somewhere down around San Diego.

Delilah confided what it was like for her, to lose her mother at eleven and be left with a houseful of troublesome males.

She confessed that things had not gotten really bad until her mother died. Before her mother died, the boys smiled a lot. They'd always made trouble, of course—that was bred into the Jones boys from their rapscallion father. But somehow, Bathsheba could always work the troubles out.

That was what Bathsheba Jones had been: a miracle-worker. Doing wonders daily that no one ever knew about—until she was gone. Oggie had always been a borderline case, but somehow Bathsheba made their lives work. And then she died. And nothing was the same. Delilah had tried in vain to take her place. But she'd only botched things up, ending up in screaming battles with her brothers, who weren't about to be told what to do by *anyone,* let alone their bossy sister.

Sam interrupted then. "Your brothers worship you." He chuckled. "Usually from afar, since you won't let them get near you anymore."

"Well, what can they expect? Look what happens when I *do* get near them—I end up wagered to you for a week." She playfully punched his shoulder.

He grabbed her and wrestled her to the rug. Then he kissed her and she kissed him back, and neither of them felt much like talking for a while.

They did the chores together smoothly, as they'd done before, but now they both wore smiles and the words they shared were tender ones. And they each took pleasure in doing little things for the other. She repaired the rag rug that had come partly unbraided. He gave her the coyote and the mountain lion to add to what they'd both started to think of as her "menagerie."

Delilah admired both carvings and stroked them with loving hands. She marveled that less than a week ago she'd told herself she wouldn't keep the wooden creatures he'd left on her windowsills. It seemed impossible to imagine such a thing now. She would never give those beautiful animals up. Never in a million years....

Saturday morning dawned crystal clear. By noon, the temperature was in the high sixties in the sun, and most of the snow from Wednesday's storm had melted away.

Though neither of them spoke of it, their looming departure seemed to hang in the air between them. Tomorrow was Sunday, and they would be heading home.

After lunch, Delilah washed Sam's hair for him, trickling the water gently over his scalp, working up a good lather, and then rinsing it thoroughly and rubbing it dry.

She teased him, as she combed it out. "I don't know, Sam Fletcher..."

"*What* don't you know?"

"I don't know if I could ever get too serious about a man with longer hair than mine." She bent over and nuzzled his ear. "I'm a conservative woman."

He caught her arm, and kissed her, a kiss that lingered so long she almost forgot what she'd been saying by the time she went back to work on him with the comb.

His next words reminded her. "There are certain things a man won't do, sweetheart. Even to snare the woman of his dreams."

Delilah's heart leapt at that. To think that he—once her worst enemy—now called her his dream woman. And more amazing, that she delighted in hearing it. She teased him some more. "Right. As if getting a haircut were some major concession."

"For me it is."

"But why?"

"My hair's my freedom. I grew it long when I left home and it's been that way ever since."

"Because?"

"My father used to shave my head."

Her comb paused in midstroke. "Come on. You're exaggerating."

"No." His voice was flat. "He shaved it. With an electric razor, like they do to recruits in boot camp. He thought long hair was the devil's business. Once I pointed out to him that Jesus had long hair. I didn't sit down for a week after that, let me tell you."

"Oh, Sam. I'm sorry...."

"Why? It's not your fault." He said nothing for a moment. Then he seemed to shake himself and added, "Anyway, I left there as soon as I had my eighteenth birthday and a high school diploma."

She didn't want him to stop. "And then what?"

"I went to L.A., got a job as a janitor."

"And?"

"I worked for two years, living in a residence hotel in East Hollywood, taking classes at City College and saving every penny I could."

"What did you study? At college?"

"Shakespeare and jewelry making—with a lot of time out for partying hearty on cheap wine that wouldn't deplete my slowly growing nest egg." He chuckled. "I wasn't a real ambitious guy. I realize now I was suffering from a whopping case of low self-esteem. But back then, we didn't know a lot about self-esteem. Back then, they called guys like me losers—at least that was what my old man had been telling me I was for eighteen years. A bad boy, with Satan in his heart."

Sam's hair now lay smoothly on his broad shoulders. Delilah set down the comb and sat across from him at the table. He smiled at her.

She said, "You were twenty when you showed up in North Magdalene."

"Yeah."

"So. What happened. How did you get there?"

"Well..."

"Honestly, Sam. Don't tease me. I want to know."

"It's nothing exciting."

"Just tell me. Please."

"I never could say no to you when you say please. You say it so seldom...."

"Sam!"

"All right, all right. I bought myself a present for my twentieth birthday—you remember that old van?"

Delilah nodded.

"Well, I bought the van, and I took what was left of the money I'd saved from working, and I got in that van, and I started driving. I drove north. And ten hours later, I came to this little bend-in-the-road town."

"North Magdalene."

"You got it. I parked on the side of the road and I went in the bar, where I met an old geezer named Oggie Jones." He gave her a telling look. "He did ask for my ID, by the way. And when I gave him a phony story, he threw me out. But. As luck would have it, I met a guy on the sidewalk right away, a guy named Jared Jones, the bar owner's son. Poor Jared. He was depressed because his wife had just kicked him out—"

"For the umpteenth time," Delilah couldn't resist pointing out.

"Jared had a bottle," Sam went on without missing a beat. "He *didn't* ask for ID. And he was willing to share."

"How heartwarming."

"Ah, Delilah. You have no idea what it's like when a lonely man at last finds a friend."

"I can imagine.... So you remained in North Magdalene."

He nodded. "Why would I leave? I found my substitute family in your dad and your brothers. And I found my dream."

"And exactly what was your dream?"

"Well, first it was gold. I got a taste of gold fever."

Delilah made a scoffing noise. Except for college and her stint as a student teacher, she'd lived in the gold country all her life. She knew that gold fever was mostly an affliction of greenhorns. Men who hung around the hills a little knew better. Few people got rich anymore mining for gold.

He smiled, and shrugged. "Hell, I was a kid," he said, in explanation of his own innocence then. "And it was damn good to have a dream at last. I bought my dredger—"

"And staked your claim at *my* special place."

"I know." He looked appropriately contrite. "I never gave the tender feelings of a motherless fourteen-year-old a thought. I was obsessed with the idea that I was going to make my fortune. And by the time I realized I wasn't going to find any nuggets the size of my fist, I was already making jewelry and selling it out of the van."

"You found another dream," she said softly.

"That's right. One I could really live with. I opened my store eventually, and I built myself a house. It is a fact that for a few years, I drank a lot. And I got in fights. I made trouble."

He reached across the gouged surface of the rough table and took her hand. He gave it a squeeze. Delilah squeezed back. He continued, "But slowly, as the years passed, as I built my business and started to feel like I belonged where I was, I began to believe my father just might have been wrong. I wasn't a loser, and the devil had no permanent claim on me after all.'' He paused then. ''You hear what I'm saying, Lilah?''

She nodded, wondering why he suddenly seemed so intent.

''I own a store and a house and this ten acres by the lake that my father left to me when he died—along with a note saying I was still his son, in spite of my devil ways.''

''Oh, Sam...''

''I'm a man of property, a respected member of my community.''

''You are. I know you are.''

''I'm not a bad catch, if you know what I mean.''

Delilah looked at him, at his handsome face and his long red-gold hair, at his powerful torso and his muscular bare arm that was stretched across the table to her. And she knew, with equal parts joy and despair, exactly what was coming.

''I'm good enough for the schoolmarm.''

''Sam...''

His hand tightened on hers, until his grip was almost painful.

She winced. He held tighter.

''So marry me, Lilah. Marry me tonight.''

Chapter Twelve

Delilah stared at him, across the table. She hadn't expected this, she hadn't expected *anything,* really. She'd been pur- posely living for the moment only, not letting herself think what might happen next week—or even tomorrow.

"Well?" he demanded, still crushing her hand.

"Oh, Sam…"

"What?"

"Well, Sam, I…"

He waited, his fervent expression fading.

"Sam, I just think…"

"You think what?" He released her hand, then, and pulled his own back to his side of the table.

She faltered on. "This is so sudden.…"

"It isn't sudden to me."

"Well, I mean, we haven't talked about marriage be- fore."

"I know. So let's talk about it now. Marry me. Tonight.

We can pack up and head out right away, be in Reno before sunset. We'll get married, spend our wedding night in a good hotel, and then go back to North Magdalene in the afternoon tomorrow just like we planned so you won't have to miss even a day of school.''

Delilah bit the inside of her lip, as it came home to her that the wagered week really was coming to an end. She'd be behind her teacher's desk at school just forty-eight hours from now.

Of course, she'd known they were going back tomorrow, but she'd purposely not been thinking about it. Her life back home seemed far away, almost unreal, eclipsed by the immediate reality of the special and secluded world she and Sam had created since the day on the mountain.

She winced as she thought of home, of what it would be like, when they returned to North Magdalene together—that crazy Sam Fletcher and the schoolmarm, Miss Jones. Of Nellie and Linda Lou, and how they loved to burn up the phone lines at even the slightest hint of scandal.

Sam said, ''Forget about them. Think about us.''

Delilah blinked. ''What do you mean?''

''You know what I mean. You're thinking about home. About what people will say. I can see it in your face.''

She shook her head, and felt the guilty flush that turned her cheeks hot. ''No...''

His gaze was level. ''Don't lie to me, Lilah. We don't need lies between us. We've got something better than lies.''

Delilah looked down at her hands, ashamed. ''All right. Yes. I was thinking of what it will be like, going home.''

''Look at me.''

She lifted her head and met his eyes.

He said, ''You'll find that out when we get there.''

She forced a brave smile. ''I know.''

''Then let it go for now.''

"All right."

"Let it go and answer my question. Will you marry me?"

"Oh, Sam…"

"You said that already."

Delilah couldn't sit still. She got up and went to the big window and looked out at the mountain. Most of the snow had melted away in the last few days, but near the crest, glittery fingers of white still filled every gully and crevasse.

She heard Sam rise from the table and approach her. Then his arms came around her. With a sigh, she leaned back in them.

"You never showed me the slipper," she said.

He chuckled, the sound low and good against her back. She felt him relax a little, and was glad. He spoke softly, close to her ear. "See the big round boulder balanced on the ledge about three-quarters of the way to the top?"

She nodded.

"Pretend there's a line straight up from there." He pointed then and she drew a bead on the summit using his finger for a sight. "See it?"

"Yes—yes, I do." She smiled. It was so clear, now she'd found it, the sharp shelf that looked like a pointy toe, the spike in the rock that could have been the high heel, the sloping ridge that formed the instep.

She saw the place where they'd stood in the storm, that high spot that made the cradle where the heel of the lady's foot would rest. It was there that she'd kissed him for the first time, and accepted what would happen when they reached the haven of the cabin once more.

Sam made his demand again. "Marry me."

With him so close, pressed up against her, it was hard to think of anything but him, and what they'd shared, and could go on sharing—for the rest of their lives. Of his hands on her body, his smile across a room, of the way they got in and took care of what needed to be done, side-by-side.

Considered in the light of their commonality, his proposal was more than tempting. But he was pushing her so hard and so abruptly; that bothered her. And there was another thing that disturbed her, too.

He said he wanted to marry her right away—but he hadn't said a thing about love.

But then, to be fair, neither had she.

And, now she was down to it, *did* she love Sam?

He growled in her ear. "Say yes."

"I'm thinking."

"You think too much."

"If you wanted some brainless fool, you wouldn't have gone after me."

"Point taken. Now tell me you'll marry me."

She turned in his arms. "Why?"

That gave him pause. "Hell and damnation, Delilah."

She pushed him away. "Don't swear at me, answer me. Why do you want to marry me?"

He dragged in a breath. "Because we're good together. And I want us to go on being good together, from now on."

"Fine. What else?" She waited, refusing to simply ask the question, Do you love me? and be done with it. She was like any other woman. She wanted words of love, and she wanted them because he chose to say them—not because she'd asked for them.

But he looked totally flummoxed. "What do you mean, what else? What else is there?"

"Oh for heaven's sake, Sam."

"You're mine," he said flatly. "I want the whole damn world to know it."

Delilah felt like screaming. This was getting worse instead of better. "Great. 'You're mine,'" she imitated his possessive words. "You sound like one of my brothers, talking to one of their wives."

"I *am* like your brothers. I've never denied it. I've read

a few more books than any of them, maybe, spent a little more time figuring out what I want from life and then going after it. But make no mistake. In the ways that really matter, Jared and Patrick and Brendan and I are all brothers under the skin. We've all got our wild sides. And we've all been looking for the right woman—and scared to death we'd find her.''

He came at her again, his jaw set, his eyes lit with a reckless light. She backed up, and felt the sink rim behind her. He put his hands on either side of her, imprisoning her there. ''There's nowhere to run, sweetheart. For either of us. I've found the right woman for me—you. And you scare the hell out of me. That's a pure fact. But I won't let you go.''

She looked up at him, trying to understand. ''*I* scare *you?*''

He nodded. ''You bet, sweetheart. I said you were mine. But you didn't let me finish…''

''Y-yes?''

''I'm also yours. At your mercy. You could really hurt me, if you wanted. Because I'm open to you.''

''Oh, Sam…'' She reached up, touched his lips, felt his breath on her skin. ''I would never hurt you. I swear. I…I love you.''

The words passed her lips on a sigh. And she had no wish whatsoever to call them back. Because she knew they were true. Of all the sweet, gentle men she might have chosen, it was this wild, troublesome one she would have. She was his, he was hers. She loved him. That was that.

''Then marry me,'' he said.

She lifted her chin. ''All right.''

He didn't move for a moment. Then he loosed a triumphant shout that echoed to the rafters. And after that, he pulled her close for one of those kisses that always obliterated rational thought.

She held back. "But not tonight."

He tensed. "When?"

She laid down her terms. "We will be married in the North Magdalene Community Church—and my scamp of a father will give me away."

He looked pained. "Lilah, I have not set foot in a church in twenty-two years."

"It is not God's fault that your father was…misguided. But be that as it may, you are allowed your own beliefs, and you may wrestle with them on your own. However, this is my wedding, too. And I will have it in my church."

"Lilah—"

"I'm not finished. Let me see. I'm sure we can arrange the small ceremony for some time in the next few weeks. And during that time, you can contact your sister and mother and see if they want to attend."

"But I haven't spoken to either of them in years."

"Precisely my point. They're your family. And *my* family too, once we're married. I want to get to know them, if they want to know me at all."

"All right," he said. "Fine."

"What does that mean?"

"It means I agree to your terms. Though it would be a hell of a lot simpler to—"

She touched his mouth again. "Life is not always simple, Sam Fletcher."

His gaze was hot and intense. "It's settled then. You've promised to marry me. You won't find some way to back out once we get home?"

She felt uneasy again. He really did seem to be pushing awfully hard about this. "Do you think I won't keep my word?"

"I think lots of things can happen between now and a church wedding."

"They won't. I've promised. We'll be married."

"Good. Now let me show you what else you can do with those lips, besides giving orders."

"Oh, Sam…"

He grinned. "Oh, Lilah…" The teasing words were husky.

He pulled her close then, and she knew he would not be denied or put off this time. That was okay with her; she didn't want to put him off.

His mouth covered hers with a hot, rash intensity that stole all thought away. Delilah surrendered to his touch, eagerly tangling her clutching fingers in his hair.

He groaned into her mouth, and began tugging her shirt open. After that, he made short work of her bra. He kissed her breasts, one and then the other, standing there before the window, with the afternoon sun slanting in to bathe them in its glow.

And Delilah gloried in it, giving back his hungry touch in kind, feeling his hardness against the cove of her womanhood, rubbing her body against his, driving his passion higher still.

He muttered her name against her heated skin, and then began working at the clasp of her belt. She understood, and helped him, and then set to work on his clothes as well.

Soon enough, they stood before the window naked. He left, and came back with a condom. She slid it on. He lifted her. Her legs clasped his hips and then he was inside her, thrusting, demanding every bit of her.

And she gave herself up willingly, crying his name, as he moved first slowly and deeply, and then faster and faster within her. She held him, as he held her, deep and fast and hard. She cried out his name as she went over the edge and then stayed with him, as he found his release as well.

Sweating, satiated, they remained upright for endless moments, holding onto each other for dear life. And then at last he carried her, staggering a little, to the bed. They fell across the mattress, arms wrapped around each other. He held her close against him. She closed her eyes and buried her head against his neck. He nuzzled her hair and whispered her name.

She could *feel* his love, she told herself, beyond his desire and the commonality they shared. True, he had not actually said the words. But he'd said other words that amounted to the same thing.

She was sure he loved her. Why else would he want to marry her? Of course he loved her. She would allow no doubt in her heart. It was just a matter of time before he told her so.

He moved then, to remove the condom and then flip the blanket over them. She snuggled up against him and let the sweet languor that came after lovemaking draw her down toward the edge of sleep.

She hovered at the rim of consciousness for a timeless while, thinking that soon they would get up, maybe go out for a walk, then come in and make dinner. Then he'd work on his carving for awhile; she might read.

They'd go to bed, make love again, slowly and tenderly. And then go to sleep.

And when they woke up, it would be time to get ready to go home to the real world, where she would start planning her wedding—to wild Sam Fletcher....

Feeling suddenly restless, she rolled over.

"Lilah?" Sam muttered groggily, reaching for her. "You all right?"

"Fine," she told him softly. "Go to sleep."

He snuggled up against her. She held him and lay still. But she found she wasn't sleepy; her sweet lassitude had fled.

They spent the next morning packing up and closing up the cabin, and they were ready to leave at noon. Delilah climbed into the Bronco beside Sam and spared a last, misty glance across the lake at Ladyslipper Peak before they drove away.

"Sorry to leave?" Sam asked from the driver's seat.

"Yes," she confessed. "I guess I am."

"Don't worry. We'll be back."

She smiled. "I'll keep that in mind."

He shifted the truck into gear and turned around, then headed into the trees the way they had come seven days ago.

It was a pleasant, companionable ride home. Delilah looked out the window at the trees and the mountains and gave Sam a warm smile each time he glanced her way. She wondered a little about how her plants had held up, how things had worked out between Brendan and Amy, but she carefully avoided thinking about anything else.

Things would work out. She and Sam would take it all one step at a time.

They stopped in Grass Valley on the way, and bought groceries. Sam suggested they fill either her refrigerator or his. No need to stock two kitchens, since they were together now.

Delilah stopped dead in the aisle. It hadn't occurred to her that they'd be *living* together before the wedding. But apparently, he assumed they would.

He was pushing the cart, and had rolled on to the canned tomatoes before he realized that she was still back with the green beans.

He turned. "Lilah? What's the matter?"

She had a painfully clear image of Nellie, of the way her face would look when she heard the news that Delilah and Sam Fletcher were cohabitating.

It shouldn't matter. Delilah knew it. It was small-minded of her that she *let* it matter. But it did.

"Lilah?" Sam was looking worried.

She hurried to catch up with him. "Sam..." A lady with a toddler in her cart rolled by. Delilah waited until she had passed.

"What? What is it?"

"Sam. I just can't do it. I just can't."

"What?" His eyes bored into her. "*What* can't you do?"

"Live with you before we're married. I know it's old-fashioned. And hypocritical, too. But I'm the schoolteacher, and I—"

"You're right," he said. "It is hypocritical."

"Sam, please—"

"But I understand your position."

She gaped at him. "You *do?*"

"You think you have a certain image to uphold."

"Well, I do. I *do* have an image."

"An image you'd have no problem with whatsoever if you'd only marry me right now."

"Oh, Sam..."

"So let's go to Reno."

"Sam..."

"All right, all right. Have it your way. We'll buy food for *both* houses...and that wedding better be coming up pretty damn quick."

She reached up and kissed him, paying no attention to other passing shoppers who eyed them with knowing smiles. "Thank you."

"Come on. Let's get the milk and eggs."

They pulled up in front of her house at around four. Her little hatchback waited on the sidewalk, looking dusty from its week without use.

Her house had been built in the twenties, without a garage. Delilah found herself thinking of how she'd always planned one day to add one. It occurred to her right then that she probably never would. Sam's house was newer, nicer and bigger than hers. They'd be more likely to end up living there. The thought made her feel sad, somehow, that the dreams of her single life no longer amounted to much.

"Lilah?" Sam was smiling at her, leaning an arm on the steering wheel. "Why the glum look?"

She shook her head. "It's nothing. Really."

"You sure?"

"Yes. Really. I'm sure." She opened her door and stepped down from the truck.

The afternoon sun was warm on her back. Here, in North Magdalene, true spring had come. The grass was vibrant green, the trees had most of their leaves. Her roses, in the small plot in front of the porch, were in full bloom, some of the petals fallen and curling on the grass, since she hadn't been here to rake them up.

At the lake, it had been different. There, the winter was only just coming to an end. The world had seemed an intimate, closed-in place. Just Sam and herself and the cabin, the mountain and the lake and the tall, silent trees that whispered their windy secrets to each other, secrets no other ears could hear.

She realized Sam had gotten out on his side and was at the rear of the truck. He'd opened the back end, and was watching her.

She caught his look, a waiting kind of look. Though she saw a question in his eyes, he asked nothing this time.

He said, "Let's get your things inside."

"Right. Good idea."

Within minutes, they had all her gear and groceries out of the truck and into the house. Then Sam said he ought to go on into town, check with Marty to see how the store had fared in his absence, take his things to his house and maybe pick up the mail.

They were in the kitchen by then, and Delilah was busy putting the groceries away.

Sam said, "That is one fine-looking chicken," of the bird she was just pulling out of the grocery bag.

She gave him a look. "Translation—you want chicken, this chicken. You want it tonight, and you're hoping I'll volunteer to cook it."

"No woman has ever read my mind as well as you do, sweetheart."

She grunted. "Dinner's at six-thirty. Be here or be sorry."

"Yes, ma'am." He grabbed her and kissed her.

"Get my mail, too, would you?" She gave him the combination to her mailbox.

He kissed her nose, hugged her close once more, and then he was gone.

Delilah put the rest of the food away, then unpacked her gear. She spared a moment to add the mountain lion and coyote to the menagerie on the kitchen table, telling herself that later she'd move them, perhaps put a few in each room, so she could enjoy Sam's beautiful gifts to her all over her house. After that, she took the now-dry water trays out from under her plants, which all appeared to have survived their week without care just fine. Next, she indulged in a hot shower and changed into fresh clothes.

By then, it was five, and time to get the chicken started. So she washed it off, patted it dry, stuck some vegetables in the cavity along with spices and a little salt, and put it in the oven to roast.

The phone rang just as she was assembling the ingredients for a salad. Delilah froze, with a bunch of radishes in one hand, and a head of redleaf lettuce in the other. The phone went on ringing.

Not many times in her life had she *not* wanted to do something as much as she didn't want to answer that phone. She knew who it would be: Nellie, or Linda Lou, or someone else wondering where in the world she'd been for a week. Or worse, *knowing* where she'd been, and dying to hear all about it.

The phone rang again. And again. And Delilah knew that, while she could refuse to answer this time, she couldn't go on not answering forever.

She was going to marry Sam. The truth would come out. Might as well be open and aboveboard from the start.

Delilah set down the lettuce and radishes and went to the phone in the living room.

"Hello?"

"Delilah? You're home. At last." The breathless voice belonged to—who else?—Nellie.

"Yes, I'm home."

"Are you all right? Did he…hurt you in any way?"

"Who, Nellie?"

"Why, that wild man, Sam Fletcher."

"So you know I was with Sam."

Nellie drew in a sharp breath. "Sam? You call him *Sam* now?"

Delilah sighed. "Nellie? Are you my friend?"

"Well, of *course* I'm your friend.…"

"Then will you stop making shocked little noises and tell me what is going on?"

Nellie was silent for a moment. Then she complained, "You could have said something, you know. You could have *confided* in me. What are friends for, after all?" Nellie paused, but not long enough for Delilah to actually answer her. "And why should I tell you what's happened since you left, you haven't told me a single thing about *anything*. And I was worried sick about you, too. Linda Lou and I didn't know what to do when you didn't show up for church and then didn't answer your phone for two days. I finally had to see Sheriff Pangborn—and you know how *he* is."

After a quick gulp of air, Nellie imitated the Sheriff's laid-back manner. "'Now, Miss Anderson, don't you go havin' a coronary on me there. I'm sure Miss Jones just forgot to mention she was going out of town for awhile, that's all. She'll turn up.' Can you believe that? 'Turn up,' he said, like you were something missing from a kitchen drawer or something. I vow, I have no idea who keeps electing that man. But I stood firm. And finally he agreed to check with those brothers of yours and your father and see if they knew anything."

Nellie paused, but only for breath. "And he did. And it turned out that little Amy knew exactly where you were, though she asked the sheriff not to tell *me,* only to say you were okay, because *you* had asked that she say nothing unless she had to. I was never so hurt in my life."

"Nellie..."

But Nellie was not through. "And then, of course, it ended up being spread all over town anyway. I think the sheriff told his wife, Leona, and Leona just couldn't resist whispering it to Marcella Crane, and, well, you know how these things are. Now everyone knows, about the card game and the wager of that truck of Brendan's, and how Sam Fletcher said he'd take a date with you instead. But then that rotten rascal wasn't satisfied with only a date, oh no, he had to sweep you away to some...wilderness area, I think everyone said and—"

Nellie went on talking, but Delilah missed what came next, because someone knocked on the front door. Delilah knew a massive feeling of relief. No matter who it was, it couldn't be worse than this.

"Nellie..."

"—and everyone over at that bar of your father's has gone—"

"Nellie."

"—insane over this. You won't believe—"

"Nellie!"

She must have finally gotten through. Nellie hitched in a breath. "Yes? What? What is it?"

"There's someone at the door. I'll have to call you back."

"But—"

"Talk to you soon."

Nellie's voice babbled on as Delilah quietly cut off the connection.

The knock came again, more insistent this time. The blinds were drawn across the big window by the door, so Delilah, standing in the middle of the living room, had no idea who it could be. It was too early for Sam to be back. And besides, the door was unlocked. She had little doubt that Sam wouldn't hesitate to walk right in.

It was probably Linda Lou, she thought grimly, come to express her outrage at Delilah's actions right to her face. Oh well, she decided, straightening her shoulders and smoothing back her hair, she had never kidded herself that this was going to be easy.

The knock came again. "I'm coming!" she called. She strode across the room and pulled open the door.

Her second brother, Patrick, stood on the other side. He looked like he'd just lost a best friend.

"Sis, I've got to talk to you."

Chapter Thirteen

Delilah peered at her brother suspiciously. A week ago, in the middle of the night, she'd opened this door to find Brendan standing where Patrick stood now. Brendan, too, had said he *had* to talk. And later she'd promised herself she wouldn't get involved in her brothers' problems ever again.

But Patrick really did look miserable.

She asked in a wary tone, "What is this about?"

He looked around. "C'mon, sis. Have a heart. Not on the front porch. Let me in."

Delilah, still undecided, did nothing for a moment.

"Please, sis…"

"Oh, all right." She stepped back and he entered.

Then he just stood there, looking glum. Finally he wondered, "Got a beer?"

"I might, somewhere. Come on." She led the way into the kitchen, gestured at the table for him to sit, and then found a bottle of light beer in the back of the refrigerator. "Do you want a glass?"

He shook his head. "That's fine." He took the beer from her and had himself a long swallow. Then he set it down. "Thanks."

"It's okay. Now what's going on?"

He was staring at the carved figures, which still waited on the table. "Sam made those for you?" In spite of the rising inflection at the end, it was a statement requiring verification, not a question.

Delilah realized that, whatever rumors were flying around town, Patrick had heard at least a few of them. She began to suspect that this visit had something to do with Sam. The thought increased her uneasiness.

"Yes," she said cautiously of the carvings, "they're from Sam."

Patrick took another drink, then shook his head. "Hot damn. Everything changes, and that's a fact." He stretched his booted feet out in front of him and stared at the beat-up toes. Then he looked up at Delilah, his blue eyes—their mother's eyes—full of bewildered sadness. "A man can't count on anything to stay the same. Things I always would have sworn were impossible are actually happening. Things like you running off with Sam Fletcher, and Chloe dating some stranger...."

Delilah felt her uneasiness fade a little when he mentioned Chloe. Maybe this visit had nothing to do with her and Sam after all. Maybe Patrick had just decided he needed to talk about Chloe Swan and had chosen Delilah for a confidante. It didn't make a lot of sense; Patrick had never confided in her in their lives. But it was possible.

She volunteered, "Sam told me he saw Chloe at The Hole in the Wall with a man he'd never seen before."

Patrick nodded and took another drink of beer. "That was a week ago. She's been out with him twice since."

Delilah hid a knowing smile. "You're keeping an eye on her, are you?"

"Of course not. Chloe and I are...friends, everyone knows that. It's nothing more. It's never been anything more. I just, well, I just hope she knows what she's doing with that guy, that's all." Patrick began peeling the label off the beer bottle.

"You came here to talk about Chloe, then?"

"No. Not exactly. Chloe's just...on my mind, that's all. Like all the things lately that can't be counted on to stay like they were. Like my ex-wife moving to Arkansas and taking our two girls along with her."

That bit of news shocked Delilah. "She isn't."

"She is."

"But Patrick, I'm sure that has to be illegal, for her to take your children out of the state without your consent."

"So what am I going to do? Sue her from two thousand miles away? And is that going to be good for the girls, anyway? And besides," he confessed, "Marybeth said if I wasn't careful, she'd just ship those girls right back to me. And I could raise them on my own."

Delilah thought about that. Patrick's daughters were eight and ten. She couldn't in a million years see Patrick raising them alone. She decided to give no more free advice on this subject. She said, "I'm sorry, Patrick," and meant it.

"Hell," he replied. "It's all just part of what I was talking about. Nothing can be counted on anymore to stay the same."

Delilah sighed, knowing what he meant. She felt cast adrift herself, after that abortive phone conversation with Nellie. She realized more and more all the time that, with Sam in her life, things would not be as they had been. She felt sympathy with her brother; she could see he was suffering from the way things were changing, too.

"Yes," she agreed softly, "things do change."

Patrick spoke to the beer bottle. "Like my sister, going

off for a week with a man she's hated since the first day she met him.''

Delilah heard the disapproval in his voice and did not like it. "Did you come here to lecture me, is that it? A heck of a lot of room you've got for lecturing *me,* Patrick Jones. You've hardly led a blameless life."

Patrick looked up sharply. "Look. This is no lecture. I just want to know…" He paused. His face went beet red. "I mean, he *forced* you to go, didn't he? What choice did you have? It was either that, or Brendan and Amy lost everything."

Delilah suddenly decided she should get going on the salad. She turned to the sink, and started washing her hands.

"Delilah?" her brother demanded. "You gonna give me an answer or not?"

She squirted out the liquid soap and began furiously lathering, as if she could wash Patrick's question away with a good scrub.

"Delilah?"

She knew she should just agree with him. What he'd said was only what she'd told herself; that she'd had no choice, for Brendan's family's sake.

But in her head she kept hearing Sam's voice. *If this goes any further, you'll never say you didn't have a choice….*

She pinned her brother with a piercing look, "He didn't drag me off. I agreed to go. I *had* a choice."

"Well. Fine. But you never would have gone if it hadn't been for the bind Brendan was in."

"That's true."

Patrick nodded, broke the hold of her gaze and stared at his beer bottle some more. "Are you glad you went, now it's over?"

Delilah ripped off a paper towel and dried her hands. "What are you getting at here, Patrick?"

"Well, sis, I don't rightly know how to say this…"

"I can see that."

"People are talking, about you two."

"So I've heard."

"And, over at The Hole in the Wall…"

"What?"

"Well, there have been bets placed."

Delilah's throat went dry. She tried clearing it, and when that didn't work, she stuck a glass under the tap and took a quick drink. When she felt she could speak, she said, "Bets? About me and Sam?"

Patrick looked out the window, at her liquidambar tree, with such avid concentration she would almost have thought he'd never seen a tree before. "Yeah. About you and Sam."

"Wh-What kind of bets?"

Patrick kept ogling the tree. "I put my money on you. I figured, if there was one thing that would never change in this world, it would be the way you hate Sam Fletcher."

"How many bets, Patrick?" Delilah's voice had acquired an edge. "And on what?"

Patrick glanced at her, winced, and then swiftly looked away again. "Two bets."

She waited.

He shot her another pained look, then began, "One on whether Sam would…" Patrick faltered and then forced himself to go on. "…get you in the sack, if you know what I mean."

Delilah stared out at the liquidambar tree herself for a while, until she thought she could speak without shrieking in mortified fury. Then she said in measured tones, "And the other?"

"Whether or not he's talked you into marrying him." Patrick sat up a little, probably feeling better now the bad news was out. "I put my money on you, like I said. I bet that you'd hold out. On both counts."

Delilah felt sick to her stomach. She'd known people

would talk, but this was worse than her wildest nightmares. They'd actually been *betting* on the outcome of her wagered week with Sam.

And beyond her dismay, she was confused. The bets didn't add up, or at least not the second one. She could understand the wager on whether or not she and Sam had slept together. It was the kind of thing over which the yahoos at the bar would love to lay their money down. But the other bet, the bet on whether she'd said she'd marry him...who could have known that Sam was after marriage? She certainly hadn't, not until he'd asked her. And even then, she'd been surprised.

"I don't understand," she said carefully. "Who came up with the idea that Sam wanted to marry me?"

"Dad."

"Father?"

Patrick shot her a condescending glance. "Aw, c'mon, sis. You know how Dad hates it that you've never got yourself a man."

"So?"

"So he and Sam had a long talk about a month ago, one night after closing. He convinced Sam to go after you and get himself married to you. He's bet a thousand dollars that Sam proposed, and got you to say yes."

Delilah stared at her brother, thinking the best thing to do right now would be to tell him to leave. She was just asking for hurt to continue with this. But somehow, she couldn't stop. She demanded, "And just how is Father supposed to have convinced Sam Fletcher to go after me?"

Patrick granted her a pitying look. "You don't know, then? That bastard didn't tell you?"

"If I knew," she pointed out with great reasonableness, "would I be asking you?"

Now Patrick looked guilty. "No, no. Of course you wouldn't. Aw, sis. I'm sorry."

"You have as yet failed to answer my question, Patrick."

"Sis…"

"Answer. Now."

"Well." Patrick also appeared suddenly to have a dry throat. He coughed. Then he muttered, "It was a damn bribe, that's what."

"Father bribed Sam to marry me?" Her own voice sounded hollow, far away.

"You got it."

"With what?"

"The Mercantile."

"Father said Sam could have The Mercantile if he'd—"

"—Marry you. Right. Can you believe it? The Mercantile. *My* inheritance. *I* couldn't believe it. But when I asked our dear old Dad what the hell he was doing breaking his word to me, he winked and said 'Don't worry about that, boy, I always take care of my own. You'll get yours. You just sit tight.'" Patrick lowered his voice to a growl. "The lying old coot. I don't buy his promises for a New York minute. And that's why I'm here. Because I want you to know that I'm not putting up with this. I may have to stand by and watch Chloe wreck her life with some out-of-town stranger. I may decide it wouldn't benefit anyone to sue Marybeth about the girls. But you can be damn sure I'll sue my father if he thinks he can take back what he's promised me all my life just to buy a man for you!"

At last, Patrick fell silent. Delilah stood at the sink, gaping at him, realizing it was time to tell him that she'd heard enough. He could leave now. But her fickle voice had deserted her again.

"Sis?" Patrick was at last looking at her—staring at her, actually. "Sis, you all right?"

She managed to murmur, "I'm fine." She wasn't, of course. But no way would she admit that to Patrick.

"Aw, sis. You really do love that wild man, don't you?"

The question was rhetorical and anyway, Delilah wouldn't for the life of her have answered it right then. Patrick continued, "Haven't you figured out that a guy like that is no good?" He gave a wry chuckle. "Especially after growing up with three brothers just like him?" Delilah turned away. Her brother said, "Aw, sis. I really messed up here, didn't I? You poor kid. I'm sorry...."

She didn't want that. She didn't want anybody feeling sorry for her. She drew on all her reserves and said, "Thank you for the information, Patrick. You can be sure I'll make use of it. And now you may go."

"But, sis..." Patrick had started to look sheepish. "Look. I guess I went a little far there with that remark about Dad buying you a man and I—"

"Stop it, Patrick. That's enough."

"Oh, hell."

"Would you please go?"

"But—"

She took a few steps in his direction, to let him know she meant business. "Just go, Patrick." She had her arms tightly folded under her breasts and she gestured with her chin in the direction of the door. "Now."

"Okay, okay..." He stood up and backed out of the kitchen toward the living room. "Sheesh," he said as he reached the front door. "Lately, I can't open my mouth without sticking my size ten in it..."

"Goodbye, Patrick."

At last, he opened the door and went through it, closing it soundlessly behind him.

When he was finally gone, Delilah hadn't the faintest idea what to do with herself, so she just stood there, between the counter and the kitchen table, staring into space and trying, though her heart balked at the prospect, to come to grips with the information her brother had just provided.

The thought she kept having, the really hurtful thought,

was that if what Patrick claimed was true, then all the strange contradictions in Sam's behavior would finally make sense. From the abrupt and relentless way he had pursued her, to his insistence that she marry him in Reno—before they came home and she had a chance to learn that it was more than a lifetime of love he was after from her.

In fact, she could see now, love had had nothing at all to do with any of it. Sam had never said he loved her. And at last she was beginning to understand the real reason for that.

But then, with a rush of emotional pain that felt as real as a blow to the stomach, she thought of his kisses, of his tenderness, and his light eyes looking into hers, as he said, *We don't need lies between us.... You could really hurt me, because I'm open to you....*

All that, all they'd shared, had been true, she was sure of it. Okay, perhaps her experience with loving a man had been limited. But her instincts about what was truth and what was a lie couldn't be that bad.

Or could they?

For twenty years she'd had sense enough to keep clear of Sam Fletcher. She hadn't trusted him an inch. Over the last month, she'd changed her mind about him, since he'd kept after her constantly until she finally broke down.

But which perception of him was the true one? The one she'd held for twenty years, or the one he'd *forced* on her in the last few weeks?

Another arrow of hurt pierced her right to the heart, doubling her over. She dropped to the chair Patrick had vacated. She had to wait, till he came back, she knew it. She had to wait and be fair and ask him if what Patrick said was true.

She reached out and picked up the exquisite wooden doe he'd left on her windowsill. She stroked its smooth flanks.

No, she decided. He couldn't have taken a bribe from her

father to marry her. Sam would never, ever do something like that.

Or would he?

Chapter Fourteen

Something was bothering Marty.

Sam sensed it the minute Marty joined him at the store, which had been closed to the public for the holiday. But Marty didn't say what was bothering him until forty-five minutes later, when the two of them were sitting side by side on folding chairs going over the receipts.

After several injured glances, Marty finally came out with it. "Mr. Fletcher, how come you didn't tell me you were going off with Miss Jones?"

Sam eyed his clerk uneasily. "Who says I did?"

"Come on, Mr. Fletcher. It's all anybody in town has talked about since the middle of the week."

Sam shook his head. He supposed he'd expected as much. "What are you complaining about, then? You found out soon enough."

"Well." Marty really sounded hurt. "It would have been nice to have been told by you. It would have been nice to know you trusted me."

"Look, Marty. It was between Miss Jones and me. I didn't think it was any of your concern."

"Well, you were wrong. It did concern me."

"How?"

"Have you talked to Jared Jones yet?"

"No." Sam closed the ledger; it was in fine shape anyway. "Jared's in town?"

"He was, as of yesterday morning."

"And?"

"He came looking for you."

Sam smiled, thinking of his old friend. "Jared and I go way back."

Marty shook his head. "Mr. Fletcher, you're not getting my drift here. Jared Jones wasn't behaving like he wanted to talk over old times. In fact, he grabbed me by my shirt and lifted me off the floor and said if I knew where the hell you'd headed out to with his sister, I'd better say now, or I'd never be a father in this lifetime."

Sam was quiet, digesting this. Then he asked, "Did you tell him?"

"Hell no. I *like* this job."

"Still got your manhood?"

"So far, yes, sir, I do."

"Thanks, Marty," Sam said, wincing at the thought of what might have happened if Jared Jones had appeared at the cabin in a rage. He realized he probably should have expected this. Of the three Jones boys, Jared had always seen himself as the protector of his sister's virtue. Just because Sam and Jared had always been close friends, didn't mean Jared would think Sam good enough to get near Delilah.

"What will you do now?" Marty asked.

Sam considered the question and couldn't immediately come up with anything too satisfying. In the old days Sam and Jared, side-by-side, had taken on ten fools in a bar in

Redding over some minor insult that Sam couldn't even remember now. When the dust cleared, Sam and Jared had been the ones still standing. Sam wasn't sure who'd end up upright if the two of them went at each other. He fervently hoped he wasn't about to find out.

Marty coughed nervously. "Er, Mr Fletcher?"

Sam remembered he'd been asked a question. "Look. Don't worry, Marty. Everything will be all right."

Marty didn't consider that any kind of an answer. "But what will you *do?*" he demanded again.

"If I can get him calmed down, I'll talk to him. The problem will be that Jared's not a very good listener when he's mad." This was the understatement of the year, Sam admitted to himself. He decided not to dwell on that, though. He finished on an upbeat note. "But as soon as Jared sees what's really going on, he'll settle down."

Marty just couldn't help but ask, "And what *is* really going on, Mr. Fletcher?"

"Nothing. Everything is fine."

"Er, could you be a little more specific, Mr. Fletcher?"

"Hell, Marty."

"C'mon. For the guy who risked future generations of Santinos just to keep your whereabouts a secret..."

"Hell."

"Yeah?"

"We're getting married."

Marty's brown eyes grew wide. "No kidding? You and Miss Jones." He settled back in his folding chair. "Well, ain't that a kick in the pants.... When's the wedding?"

"In a few weeks, over at the Community Church."

"Well, what do you know."

Sam allowed himself a smile. "Yeah. It's a crazy world, isn't it?"

Marty grinned right back, and then moved a little closer. "Mr. Fletcher?"

"Yeah, what?"

Marty lowered his voice, his eyes on Sam's hair. "You want to really thrill Miss Jones, you know what to do."

Sam gave the boy a forbearing look. "What is it with you, Marty? You think just because your father's the barber you can't rest until every guy in town's got a buzz cut?"

"Look how far you got with her once you got rid of that beard."

"She likes my hair," Sam muttered, remembering the feel of her tender hands, massaging his scalp when she gave him that shampoo, and of the way she combed through it with her fingers when they made love. At the same time he tried to forget how she'd teased him about cutting it, saying she'd never take him seriously while he had hair longer than hers.

Marty wore a sagacious expression. "Yeah, but if you're gonna end up having to beat up her brother, it's better if you got an ace up your sleeve. Some way to show her how much you really care. You just think about it, okay?"

"All right, all right." Sam pushed the ledger aside. "We're finished here." He grabbed the checkbook and wrote Marty out a check. "Thanks." He tore it off and handed it over. "A little bonus. For a job well done."

Marty's eyes grew big again as he looked at the amount. "Like I said, I like this job. And I think I better get on home. Mom's got dinner on." He got up. "See you tomorrow, then."

Sam waved him out the door.

After that, he locked up and went across the street for the mail, thinking that maybe he ought to go looking for Jared to tell the poor fool what was going on. But then, he had no doubt Jared would find him soon enough.

He opened his mailbox and had to virtually pry the stuffed-in circulars and bills out. Next time he and Lilah left town, he'd have Melanie Swan hold his mail—or have Marty take care of it.

Once he'd liberated his mail from the box, he spent several minutes sorting the junk and tossing it out. Then, setting everything else on the little counter that was provided in one of the corners, he went to Delilah's box. He had it open and was trying to pry her mail out, when Linda Lou Beardsly came in.

She saw what Sam was doing and gasped, "Stop that this instant, Sam Fletcher!"

Sam turned. Linda Lou was a tall, big-boned woman, with a long face. Sam couldn't help thinking that she looked, right then, like an outraged mule.

Sam decided to try for lightness. "Got a problem, Mrs. Beardsly?"

"I certainly do, Mr. Fletcher. That is Delilah Jones's box you've just broken open."

"I know that," he replied, the soul of calm rationality. "And I haven't broken it open. She asked me to pick up her mail."

Linda Lou heaved a massive breath. "I find that difficult to believe."

Lord, Sam thought, she was a steel safe of a woman. It was said she was good with children, and that all the little kids she taught until they got old enough to graduate to Delilah's class adored her. But right then, Sam couldn't help thinking it was no mystery why her husband, Owen, spent so much time in The Hole in the Wall's back room.

"Believe it," Sam suggested, his voice dripping patience. "It's true. How else would I get the combination, unless she gave it to me?"

"I could think of ways. I know how you are."

Sam sighed. He knew he should probably advise Linda Lou to check with Delilah and find out the truth. But Lilah had been on edge when he left her, he'd seen that well enough. She'd been nervous about their relationship, and about how people in town would take it. There was no telling what damage an outraged call from Linda Lou would do to her equilibrium right now. Old Nellie Anderson had probably given her a call already, if he knew Nellie at all.

Linda Lou was still sticking out her chest and pinching her thin lips together. "You have already done enough, I'll have you know. It's disgusting, that's what. A man like you abducting a sweet, good person like Delilah. But then everyone's always known how much you've always hated her, that you were out to destroy her life if you ever got the chance."

"Look. Mrs. Beardsly..."

Mrs. Beardsly wasn't finished. "It is unforgivable what you've done to her—"

"Mrs. Beardsly, she's fine. She's home right now, cooking a chicken for our dinner."

"Cooking a chicken for your dinner! What kind of fool do you take me for, Sam Fletcher? Delilah Jones would never willingly cook a chicken for you."

Sam realized he was getting nowhere. "Mrs. Beardsly, this is really none of your business."

"None of my business!" She couldn't seem to stop repeating what he said. "I'll have you know that Delilah Jones is my dear, dear, friend. And we all know that she never would have gone away with you of her own free will, that she only went to save one of her no-good brothers from ruin."

"Everybody seems to know just about everything around here," Sam managed to interject.

"This is North Magdalene. It's everyone's *business* to know. Where was I? Oh, yes.... But now her ordeal is over. She's paid her brother's debt to you. And I want you to leave her alone."

Sam eyed the old battle-ax, wondering what to do now.

He was beginning to think that she'd go after him with tooth and claw if he actually dared to reach in Delilah's mail box and extract the contents.

Sam felt weary suddenly. He thought of Jared, threatening his clerk to find out where he and Lilah had gone. And now this confrontation with Linda Lou. No wonder Lilah was anxious about what people would think.

And beyond weariness, he experienced disappointment. Since he'd risen above his father's tainted image of him, he'd let himself imagine that most people were basically open-minded. He'd begun to believe that not only could people change, but that other people could learn to accept those changes—or at least that they'd take the time to ask what was going on before assuming the worst. Right now, though, looking at Linda Lou Beardsly's outraged, mulish face, he was beginning to doubt his own hard-won beliefs.

Linda Lou jabbered on. "But *this* is the pinnacle, the summit, the crowning glory of contemptibility. For you to steal her mail.... I tell you, I am *speechless*—"

"Good," Sam said. "Then shut up."

"I beg your par—"

"Shut up!"

Linda Lou sputtered for a moment, and then actually held her tongue.

Sam said, "Thank you."

He paused before he went on, giving her a threatening stare that kept her quiet—probably in fear for what that evil Sam Fletcher might possibly do to a poor woman alone in the deserted post office on Easter Sunday afternoon. He considered telling her that he and Lilah were getting married. But he doubted there was even the smallest chance she'd believe him. The news would have to come from Lilah.

And the mail would have to wait. He and Lilah could come here after dinner and pick it up together. He really did believe that if he tried to take it now, Linda Lou would either physically attack him, or run out the door screaming "Thief!"

"Look, I'll leave the mail." He turned quickly, shut the little door and spun the lock. "See?"

Linda Lou folded her arms. "Hmph."

"Delilah will come over for it herself later."

"You had better believe she will, Sam Fletcher."

He edged around Linda Lou and collected his own mail, wondering grimly how he would explain this confrontation to Delilah without her getting all upset.

He was worried, he realized, worried for the first time since she'd agreed to marry him about how all this was going to work out.

Sam burst out of the dim post office like a prisoner busting out of jail—fast, with a lot of relief at the sight of the clear, early-evening sky. He started walking fast, too, wanting to hurry back to Lilah, even though it was still an hour before he was due at her house. He wanted to touch her and kiss her and be reassured that, even if most everyone else in town was up in arms about wild Sam Fletcher running off with the schoolmarm, what the two of them shared remained the same.

Unfortunately, he had to pass The Hole in the Wall to get to Pine Street, which led to her street. And he was on foot, since he'd left his truck at home; it was a beautiful spring afternoon and he'd thought the walk would be agreeable. He hadn't stopped to consider that being on foot would leave him vulnerable to greetings—and questions—from anyone he happened to pass on the street.

As he went by the bar, Rocky Collins was just coming out through the double doors.

Rocky, who looked as if he'd been celebrating Easter Sunday by knocking back some serious shots of his favorite tequila, crowed at the sight of him, "Whoa, Lordy! What have we here! It's the man of the hour, or I'm a ring-tailed raccoon.''

Sam didn't much care for the greeting—and had no desire to hang around and find out exactly what it meant. He said, ''Back off, Rocky,'' and kept on walking.

But Rocky had never had sense enough to come in out of the rain, let alone not bother a man who didn't want to be bothered. ''Hey, c'mon Sam!'' he called. ''I want to ask you somethin'!''

Sam heard Rocky's lurching footsteps, dogging his own. With a muttered oath, he turned. ''What do you want? Make it fast.''

Even Rocky, not famous for his brains, finally understood that it probably wouldn't be such a good idea to trifle with Sam right then. And Sam was one of the few men in town that Rocky, who always seemed to end up in a fight, never chose to mess with. Still, Rocky wanted more than anything to be the first of the guys in the bar to know the answers to the burning questions of the day.

So he smiled his friendliest smile and asked real politely, ''Well, what I'd really like to know, Sam, that is, if you don't mind my askin'—''

''Get to it, Rocky.''

''What we're all wonderin' is—''

''Yeah?''

''How'd it go with the schoolmarm?''

Sam looked at Rocky for a long time, long enough that Rocky was already backing away when he answered, ''None of your damn business.''

''Well, sure, yeah, I knew that....''

''Then why'd you ask?''

''I dunno. Plum stupid, I suppose.''

''Get lost, Rocky.''

''Yeah. Right. I am gone.'' Rocky turned and hurried off up the street, as fast as his unsteady legs would carry him.

Sam watched him go, and wondered if everyone in town had gone crazy since he and Delilah headed off for Hidden Paradise Lake. He'd left Lilah at her house less than two hours ago. In that short time, everyone he'd run into had had something to say about the two of them. If this was the kind of reaction he was getting from people, what must she have heard in the time since he'd walked out of her house?

He realized he was nervous. Nervous as a kid about going back to her. And scared. He had pushed her, he knew it, forced a commitment from her before she was really ready to give it.

Because he'd been afraid of precisely this: that they'd get home and everyone would start in on them, and she wouldn't be able to take it. She'd tell him she just wasn't cut out to be the wife of wild Sam Fletcher. She'd break it off with him.

But she was a woman whose word a man could trust. A promise that she'd marry him would be a binding thing to her. He'd been certain it would be enough to keep her with him, until the talk died down, until she was as sure as he was that what they had at the lake could be theirs for a lifetime—if they'd only reach out together and claim it.

But now…now, damn it, he just didn't know. He'd expected there to be talk. But not what this was beginning to look like. Hell, he'd hazard a guess that everyone in town was in on this.

And he wondered if a mere promise, and a hesitantly granted one at that, was going to hold up against the wagging tongues and the sly, knowing winks, against Jared's misguided protectiveness and Linda Lou Beardsly's upright outrage.

He didn't know.

God—if there was a God—help him. He just didn't know.

He wanted to run to her.

But he also needed to be sure she would still know, when she saw him, that she'd made the right choice with him.

He wanted to give her something, a talisman, a proof of his regard.

So he turned and went back to his store. He dropped off his mail there and picked out a ring, a diamond solitaire that he thought might please her. He put the velvet case in his pocket and let himself out again, and then he stood by the door for a time, knowing that jewelry just wasn't enough.

Not for her, not for Lilah, who was fire and laughter, beauty and strength. There had to be something *more* he could give her, so that she'd know without another doubt that her promise had been wise.

And then he knew what he would do.

He took the few steps to the store next to his, Santino's BB&V, and he pounded on the door.

He kept on pounding until Julio appeared, with a napkin stuck in his collar and a half-full glass of red wine in his hand. "What's this?" Julio demanded. "A man can't enjoy his Easter dinner in peace around here?"

Maria, his wife, peered over his shoulder. "Come in, come in, Sam. Join us upstairs for our Easter feast."

"No, thanks. I, well, Delilah's cooking dinner for me."

Both Maria and Julio grinned at each other the way married couples do when something they've discussed is confirmed. Then Maria asked, "Well then, what is it? What can we do for you?"

Sam shrugged. "Well, I was hoping for a haircut. But I didn't stop to think that Easter Sunday at dinnertime is probably not the right time to visit the barber."

Maria and Julio looked at each other again. And then both of them laughed, sounds of pure delight. "I'll send Marty down with another glass of wine for you," Maria said to her husband. "And one for you, too, Sam."

Sam gave them one more chance to back out. "You're

sure you don't mind...?'' He hoped they wouldn't take it. He wanted that haircut.

He needn't have worried. Julio was so tickled at the idea of giving a good cut to one of North Magdalene's staunchest longhairs, that he couldn't have cared less right then if his food was stone cold when he finally returned to it.

"Let's go, Sam." Julio turned and led Sam to the back room.

Sam sat in the chair and Julio set to work. They were interrupted once, when Marty brought them the wine and gave Sam a high sign that signified his enthusiastic approval. After that, Julio went about his work with calm concentration. When he was done, and the long, shining swatches of hair lay all around Sam's chair, he turned Sam to the big mirror.

Sam grunted. It wasn't as bad as he'd thought. From the front, it didn't look much different than when he'd pulled it back in a ponytail.

Julio gave him the hand mirror so he could see the back.

Sam laughed.

"Something wrong?" Julio, who took pride in his work, looked apprehensive.

"Hell, no," Sam replied. "I was just thinking that, after twenty years of fighting it, I now look respectable both coming...and going.''

"I think it looks fine," said Julio.

"I do, too. And thanks."

Julio removed the big apron and brushed off Sam's nape. "That's it then," he announced.

Sam thanked him again and paid him enough to make up for interrupting his dinner. Then he went out the front door and headed for Lilah's with the ring making a reassuring bulge in his pocket and his head feeling lighter than it had in a long, long time.

He was still early, but not by too much. And he was still

nervous about how she might have handled whatever had come up since they parted.

But he felt much better now that he had concrete ways to show her how he felt.

And he was relieved, too, that he made it past the post office and the bar without being accosted by any scandal-mongering citizens. He turned onto Pine and walked briskly to the corner of Rambling Lane, where he turned again. He was mounting Delilah's front step in no time.

The door was unlocked. He went on in. The house was warm and cozy. He realized how much he liked her house. And it smelled of savory roast chicken. Sam's stomach growled. He was suddenly starving.

He caught a glimpse of her, in the kitchen by the sink. He stood for a moment, just inside the door, thinking how good it was, to be here, where she was, in the warmth of her house, with the smells of the food she'd cooked for him fragrant on the air. He noticed that she'd pulled all the carvings he'd made for her away from the window, to the near side of the table; he could see them from where he stood now.

He smiled. It looked as if she'd sat down with them, and just looked at them for awhile. The thought touched him.

However, the chicken, most likely, was ready by now. It smelled ready. And the table wasn't set. That was something he could do while she put the finishing touches on the meal.

He moved forward, into the heart of the room and beyond, through the doorless arch to the kitchen. She was standing in front of the sink, with her back to him. She appeared to be just staring out the window.

He glanced toward the stove. The chicken, still in its roasting pan, sat on top. It looked done.

But nothing else was. Greens for the salad lay in their plastic bags on the counter. Raw broccoli and potatoes waited there, too. All of this, he perceived in an instant.

And he also knew it was all strange. Wrong. Not good.

Still, he tried not to know. He went up behind her and put his arms around her. She stiffened.

"Hey. It's only me." He nuzzled her neck.

She didn't move, didn't sigh, didn't relax in the slightest. She could have been a mannequin, one made of flesh and blood, but lifeless all the same.

"Lilah?" He took her by the shoulders, turned her, stiff but not really resisting, until she faced him. "What's the matter? What's wrong?"

She moved then, to get away from him. She went and she sat at the table, in front of the wooden menagerie.

"Lilah? Talk to me."

She picked up the raccoon, the rough willow piece he'd carved for her that first night, when he'd come here hoping and praying she might agree to go out on a date with him. She looked at it, and then she turned to him, still holding the wooden creature in her hand.

"I've been wondering, Sam." Her eyes were flat, like unpolished black stones. "I've been wondering—do you love me? Do you love me at all?"

He felt fear. Was she all right? He pleaded tenderly, "Lilah, what's wrong? Talk to me, sweetheart."

She chuckled. The chuckle was ice-cold. "Oh, come on, Sam. Just answer the question. Just answer it straight. I asked you if you loved me. It doesn't take a college education to answer that. All I want is a yes or a no."

"Yes," he said flatly, feeling irritation rise and trying to remember that they couldn't both go off the deep end or disaster would follow. "Now what the hell is going on? Has Nellie Anderson been jabbering at you? Or did Linda Lou give you a call?"

She totally ignored his question. She set the raccoon on the table.

"Lilah, talk to me…"

She shrugged. "Somehow that *yes* was not totally convincing." Her voice was light, hollow at the core.

"Lilah, will you please, for godsake, look at me?"

She didn't, but she did volunteer, "Patrick was here."

"And?"

"And he said the bets are flying fast and furious over at The Hole in the Wall."

"Bets about what?"

"About us. One, whether you'll get me to go to bed with you."

Sam swore softly.

"That's not all. The other's whether you'll get me to say I'll marry you."

"Lilah—"

She waved a hand over her shoulder at where he stood by the sink. She still conscientiously refused to look at him. "I thought that was strange," she continued. "That they'd bet on whether *you* got *me* to agree to get married. That's not the kind of bet men make, as a general rule. Men always think of women as the ones who want to make it legal—though I can tell you that there are a lot of women out there who'd like nothing better than to just be left alone by men."

"Lilah." Sam was really trying to hold on to his patience now. "What is this? Get to the point."

"I thought it was strange, that's all, that they'd bet *you'd* get *me* to marry you. But then Patrick explained the rest to me, and it all made perfect sense. He said that you'd discussed me with Father a month ago, and that Father had told you he'd give you The Mercantile if you'd take me for a wife." She cast him a quick look over her shoulder, as if checking to make sure he'd heard that she was on to him at last.

"Lilah."

She waved him silent again, a jerky, pained movement. "I told myself I would wait, and talk to you, and find out if it was true, before I started thinking too much about all the…contradictions in everything you've done. But then, I couldn't stop my mind from thinking, and I couldn't help but remember that day I went collecting donations for the bell tower. My father told me that day that he was tired of waiting for me to get married, that he'd found a man for me and I should expect that man to come calling soon.'' She laughed, a choked sound that was really more like a barely contained sob. "Of course, I thought that was so totally ridiculous, I didn't give it a second thought. But then, when I went into your store, you asked me if I'd been talking to my father. Remember?''

"Yes."

"And then, it was after that, that you started…looking at me strangely every time I saw you. And then soon enough, you showed up here to ask for a date. I asked you then if my father put you up to it. And you denied it. But you lied.''

"Lilah—"

"Wait. Just wait. Let me finish. I'll be finished soon enough.'' She sucked in a breath, and then her words picked up speed, until they tumbled over each other, accusation following accusation, "You wanted that building, and you were willing to go after me to get it. You never said you loved me. Because you *don't* love me. You told me how you and I didn't need lies between us, we had something better than lies. But that was a lie, it was all, all lies. All the time, all of this, nothing but a great, big whopping lie!'' She pounded the table with a tight fist. The wooden animals jumped, wobbled, and then righted themselves.

After that, she was quiet. Standing very still behind her, Sam waited, listening to her breathing as she controlled herself, made it even and slow.

The silence was never ending. At last, she couldn't stand it anymore. She twisted in the chair and looked at him—or at least aimed a frozen glare at where he was standing. But she wasn't really looking at him, she wasn't looking at him at all.

"Well?" she demanded, all injury and outrage.

"Well, what?"

"Do you have a single thing to say for yourself?"

He shrugged. "Why should I? It appears to me you've said it all."

For an instant, the real Lilah peered at him through the mask of affronted pride. She said in a small voice, "Say...it's not true..." She stopped, and the rage and belligerence took over once more. "Say *something!*" she demanded then.

"All right." He folded his arms across his chest, mostly because he'd caught himself in the act of stroking the back of his neck. He didn't want to do that now. She'd been too caught up in her own wounded rage to notice that his ponytail was gone. And now, he wanted to get out of here without her finding out. He didn't want her to see the ridiculous grand gesture he'd made for her. Not now, when he knew at last how little she believed in him.

He had to come to grips with reality here. It was never going to work between them. He'd been living a fool's dream to think that a woman who'd hated him enthusiastically for two decades was ever going to become his best friend and his wife.

He'd always known he'd lose her when they returned to North Magdalene. And he had been right.

She was biting her lip in frustration at his extended silence. He took pity on her and spoke. "Why should I argue with you? You've already made up your mind about everything."

She said through clenched teeth, in a parody of reasonableness, "*Did* my father offer you that building if you'd marry me?"

He shrugged. "Yes." He knew he should just let her go ahead and think what she wanted, but some idiot part of him still hoped she might understand. "But—"

"But what?"

"But that isn't why I went after you."

"It isn't?"

"No, it isn't."

"Oh, really?" She looked at him, narrow-eyed, not giving him an inch.

Sam's anger kindled and grew hot. Not only had she already judged him, she wanted him to try to defend himself after the fact. Well, to hell with that.

He inquired with leashed fury, "You want to call it off, is that it?"

She said nothing, she just glared at him, her eyes brimming, her chin high and haughty.

He went on. "Well, fine. You call it off. But don't try to tell me any lies, all right? Let's have it out on the table like it really is."

"Don't call me a liar," she sneered. "Don't you dare call me a liar. We both know who tells the lies around here!" She gripped the back of the chair, as if she were restraining herself from leaping up and jumping on him the way she'd done at the river all those years and years ago.

He looked right at her as he said, slowly and softly, "I call you a liar because you are one, Lilah. And what's more, I think somewhere inside you, you know that you're lying." She gasped. He went on before she could gather herself for more denials. "Deep in your heart, you know what you're doing. And it's not the fact that you never got fancy words of love from me that bothers you now. And it's not your father promising me The Mercantile if I'll marry you, either. What's really bothering you is who you are and who I am. Or at least who you've told yourself for twenty years I am—without ever bothering to make sure."

Her face wore a stricken look. He hardened himself against it and continued, "I thought maybe, after this week, that you *did* see the real me now. But you don't. Or you won't. Any more than you see yourself as you really are—"

Right then, she managed to mutter, "No...that's not true...."

He overrode her weak objections without effort. "It is true. You have an...idea of yourself, of the person you've made of yourself in spite of your rowdy relatives. You came back here after college when you could have gone anywhere, started from scratch. But you had something to prove to this town, didn't you? You came home and you taught at the school and you never got near a man and you purposely made friends with the most upright, narrow-minded citizens you could find. You *created* yourself from scratch. A Jones who wasn't a Jones, who led a quiet, uneventful life, a dedicated teacher who went to church every Sunday and spent Saturday night watering her plants. You made yourself up. And the person you made up would *never* go for a man like me."

"No, I—"

"I'm not finished." He gave her a look that silenced her completely. Then he went on, "You swore you'd never fall for me. But you *did* fall for me. And you loved it. From that day on the mountain until you got home. But now you've probably had a few choice words with Nellie or Linda Lou. You've heard about the bets on us over at the bar. You see how it's going to be, the way people will talk about the schoolmarm hooking up with that wild Sam Fletcher. And you're embarrassed. You want to go back to who you *think* you are. And you want *me* to be the rat you always *knew* I was."

"No—"

"Yes." He dropped his folded arms to his sides and took the two steps that placed him right behind her chair. She remained twisted from the waist, facing him. He looked down into those dark eyes, the eyes he'd dared to dream he might look into every day for the rest of their lives. "Well, fine," he said flatly. "Tell yourself lies. Have it your way."

She looked up at him, speechless, stunned, and he saw the slow realization come over her fine, strong face. He saw the precise moment when she understood that every word he'd just uttered was true. She had lied, the worst kind of lie…she had lied to herself.

She whispered, "Oh, Sam…" She reached out for him.

He stepped back. It was too late. And not enough. He couldn't trust her now. Hell, he'd never be able to leave her alone without wondering what he'd be accused of when he got home.

She'd always doubt him. He saw that now. A whisper in her ear might sway her against him. He wouldn't spend his life convincing his woman that she could trust him.

He raised his arm, so full of hurt and rage—and thwarted longing—that he wanted to strike out.

"No, Sam!" She grabbed for him.

He shook her off—and he swiped the carved figures off the table. The wooden animals went flying, some arrested by her chair, others sailing halfway to the stove, before they clattered to the floor. Then, when the last wooden figure had landed and fallen still, they stared at each other, over a chasm of inches that might as well have been ten thousand miles.

He said, very quietly, "Goodbye."

And then he walked past her, through the living room, and out the front door.

Chapter Fifteen

Delilah couldn't bear to watch him leave. She closed her eyes as he swept past her, and didn't open them again until she heard the closing of the door. The tears, unchecked now, ran down her cheeks and onto the hands that lay limp in her lap.

Sam was gone. And the unbearable fact, the horrible truth, was that she herself had sent him away.

At her feet, the little raccoon lay, staring brightly up. She slid off the chair and took him in her hands, setting him carefully back on the table. Then she crawled around the room, collecting each of the wooden treasures, her heart breaking anew when she saw the crack in the doe's slender foreleg, the chip in the beak of the owl.

She tried, as she assessed the damage, not to think at all, to close off her mind for awhile, until she could stop crying and look at what had happened from a more balanced frame of reference.

But her mind would not shut off. Everything, *everything* Sam had said to her was brutally, horribly true. Her carefully constructed image of herself had had no room in it for Sam; she had been subconsciously waiting for any excuse to send him on his way. The issue of The Mercantile had been just what she'd been waiting for.

Delilah sat in the chair again, still holding the wounded doe. Slowly, she ran a finger over the cracked leg. She could feel the sharpness of the break. A fresh onslaught of tears ensued.

And then the doorbell rang.

Delilah looked up, and swiped away the tears with the back of her hand. But then she only sobbed again.

"Oh, to heck with it," she muttered. The last time she'd answered the door, she'd had to deal with Patrick.

Who could say what would be next? She just wasn't up to it, not today. Whoever it was could just keep ringing until they tired of it. And then they could go away.

There was a silence. Then another ring.

Delilah waited to be left in peace.

But then, the door slowly swung inward. "Delilah?" It was Nellie's voice.

Oh, no! Delilah wished she could just shrink down to nothing and disappear into thin air. Nellie was the last person she wanted to see right then. She considered sliding off the chair and running out the back door.

But she didn't act quickly enough. Nellie was already peering cautiously around the edge of the door. She spotted Delilah and her little eyes widened. "Oh!" Nellie said, surprised for a moment. Then she saw the tears and the abject misery on Delilah's face. Nellie sighed and her own eyes filled with sympathetic tears, "Oh, honey. What has he done to you?" Nellie pushed the door all the way open.

And that was when Delilah saw that Linda Lou was with her.

Delilah opened her mouth to tell them to go away, she wanted to be alone. But the two of them swept in like a pair of oversized mother hens, clucking in sympathy and ready to take charge.

They fluttered across the living room and right into the kitchen, where they swept her up and engulfed her against their bosoms and clucked in her ear not to worry, not to worry at all, nothing was that awful that it couldn't be made right.

"You just come on in the living room, honey. Yes, you sit here on the couch...."

"Better, much better. Here's a tissue...."

"That's right. You just cry...."

"You just let yourself go...."

"I'll put on some hot water, a nice cup of tea...."

"Yes, tea. Nellie will make us a nice cup of tea...."

Nellie got up then, and went back into the kitchen. Linda Lou stayed with Delilah, patting her hand, smoothing her hair and clucking all the while.

"There, there," Linda Lou said, "you've had a traumatic experience, but it's all right, you'll be fine in the end, just you wait, you'll see...I swear, that man ought to be shot, and that's the Lord's truth."

Delilah, who'd been rather enjoying all the clucking and stroking from her female friends, made herself pull away from Linda Lou. She'd already betrayed Sam in her heart. No matter if he could never trust her, she would not betray him with others ever again. "No," she managed on a sob. "You don't understand...."

"There, there. I certainly do. I understand well enough. That Sam Fletcher is crazy—"

"No, no. Oh, Linda Lou, you just don't understand."

"Of course I do. I understand. We all understand. And everyone in town admires you, Delilah, they truly do, for sacrificing yourself for your brother, for going off with that horrible man for an entire week just to—''

"Stop," Delilah said. "Just stop right there." She blew her nose and then sat up tall. "You're my dear friend, Linda Lou, and I think the world of you. But I won't have you saying things against Sam."

Linda Lou blinked. And then she started clucking again. "You are a truly noble soul, I must say. After everything he's done, to refuse to disparage him—''

"Oh, come on, Linda Lou," Delilah objected, and paused to blow her nose again. "Listen to yourself. What you're saying makes no sense at all. Have I ever refused to disparage Sam Fletcher before?"

Linda Lou thought about that. "Well, no. I can't say as you have."

"Of course I haven't. In fact, I've always been the one most willing to explain in detail what a low-down, mean, rotten rat he is."

"Well, yes," Linda Lou allowed, "I suppose, now you point it out, that that is true."

"You'd better believe it's true."

"And you were right," Linda Lou announced staunchly.

"No. I was wrong."

Linda Lou blinked again. "Wrong?" The word was disbelief personified.

Delilah nodded. "Yes, wrong."

Linda Lou did not take this information well. Her browless eyes were all scrunched up, her mouth pursed tight. But then her long face softened, and she looked pitying again. She started patting Delilah's hand once more. "Now, now, dear. It's going to be all right. You just need a little rest, that's all. You can take some time off from school and have a long talk with Pastor Johnson...."

Delilah batted the soothing hand away. "Stop it, Linda Lou."

Linda Lou remained undaunted. "You've been under a lot of strain, dear. Just try to—"

"There is nothing wrong with me."

"—relax. The hysterics will pass, and you'll feel much better very soon."

"I am not having hysterics."

Linda Lou shook her head. "Fine, fine, dear. Whatever you say."

The patronizing tone was too much. Delilah stood up. "Look at me, Linda Lou. Look at me real well. Do I look crazy to you?"

A terribly pained expression crossed Linda Lou's face. "Now, dear…"

"I do? I look crazy, is that what you're thinking?"

Linda Lou blinked again and looked away.

This was too much. Delilah shouted. "Nellie!"

"Yes, honey?"

"Nellie, get in here!"

"But the tea—"

"Forget the tea. In here. Now!"

Nellie flitted in. "What in the world is the matter?"

"Sit down," Delilah commanded. "There. Next to Linda Lou."

Nellie looked at Linda Lou. "Is she all right?"

Linda Lou went on looking pained, but wisely refrained from answering.

"Nellie." Delilah's tone gave clear warning. "Sit."

"All right, I'm sitting." She dropped down next to Linda Lou.

"Now," Delilah said. Two pairs of eyes watched her, wide and wary. "You two are my very dear friends, and it is my hope that you will both remain that way. But it has recently come to my attention, through personal and intimate experience—" Delilah paused, irritated no end as she watched her friends share a shudder and a significant look

"—that I have been cruel and nasty and completely off-base about a certain man we all know. And you both know who I mean. I mean Sam Fletcher."

"Oh, no, you haven't been," Linda Lou protested.

"Not for a minute," Nellie declared.

"Yes." Delilah held firm. "It's true. I've misjudged him for years. But not anymore. And I've made other gross errors in behavior as well. I've been…dishonest, with myself and with everyone I care about. I've pretended for years to be less than my whole self. Because really, deep down, I'm a lot like Sam is. I've got wildness in me, just like he does, a wildness I've denied for years."

"No," Nellie breathed, as Linda Lou murmured simultaneously, "It's not so."

"It is so." Delilah looked right at Nellie. "Nellie, he asked me out the night you called two weeks ago."

Nellie gasped. "I knew it. I knew something was going on even then—"

"You were right. And I wanted to go out with him then—"

"No!"

"Yes. But I was too foolish and full of myself to admit it. He was forced to resort to desperate means to get my attention."

"The wager," Linda Lou breathed.

"Exactly. And now he *has* my attention."

Nellie rose up and then sat down again. "Delilah, what are you saying?"

"He asked me to marry him."

"He didn't." Linda Lou spoke with awe.

"He did. I said yes."

Nellie sputtered, "You never—"

"I did."

"Oh, my heavens!" Linda Lou put a hand to her heaving breast.

"But then, I didn't really believe in him, not deep down, and I've hurt him very deeply, I'm afraid. I'm afraid, to be honest, that he's never going to forgive me, no matter what I do...."

Nellie longed for the details. "But what *happened?*"

"It's too involved to explain right now."

Both women sighed in mutual disappointment.

"But the point is," Delilah went on. "I love him."

Nellie and Linda Lou gasped in unison at that.

"It's true. I love Sam Fletcher. And you can call me crazy, you can shake your heads in pity and say I should visit Pastor Johnson. You can do and say whatever you please. It doesn't matter. Because Sam Fletcher is the man for me. He's *always* been the man for me, whether he ever lets me near him again or not. And anyone who says *anything* against him will not be someone with whom I choose to associate on a regular basis. Is that understood?"

Both Nellie and Linda Lou stared at her with their mouths hanging open.

"Is that understood?" she repeated once more.

"But, honey—" Nellie began.

"But, dear—" said Linda Lou.

And then both of them fell silent at the sound of heavy, hurried footsteps on the porch. They stared past Delilah. Delilah turned just as her baby brother appeared in the open front door.

"Brendan," Delilah muttered. "What now?"

"Sis..." Brendan gulped in air. His hair was windblown, and his face was flushed. He looked like he'd just run a hard mile. "I have to talk to you!"

"Come in," she told him. "Don't just stand there. And for heaven's sake, close that door."

Brendan stepped over the threshold and shut the door as he'd been told. He nodded at the wide-eyed pair on the couch. "Ladies..."

"Good evening."

"Hello, Brendan."

"All right," Delilah cut through the pleasantries. "What's happened now?"

"It's Jared…" He eyed the women on the couch. "Sis, could we talk alone?"

"What for? Whatever it is, they'll find out soon enough anyway. This is North Magdalene. We have to face facts." Delilah approached her brother and looked at him closely. "What's this?"

"What's it look like? A black eye." He winced. "Hey. Hands off."

"You and Jared got into it?"

Brendan nodded. "He got on me for my part in you going off with Sam. And sis, he's—"

Delilah shook her head. "Jared's always been trouble looking for somewhere to happen."

"That's what I'm trying to tell you—"

"So tell me. I'm listening."

"That's what you say, and then you interrupt."

"Brendan, get to the point."

"Okay, okay. It's like this…Jared's been looking all over for Sam, swearing he's going to beat the bejesus out of him, for taking you off against your will, even though Dad has been trying to get him to see that Sam really only wants to put a ring on your finger—"

"So?"

"So Jared finally found him. Just now. Over at The Hole in the Wall. And Sam, instead of being reasonable, is acting crazy as Jared, like he was even *looking* for a fight himself, you know what I mean?"

Delilah's heart sank. She knew exactly why Sam was in such a troublemaking mood. "They're beating each other up," she said grimly.

"Are they ever!" Brendan replied. "And since you went

off with Sam for my sake, when I saw the trouble happening, I thought just in case you *did* care for Sam, I should tell you—''

But Delilah was already moving. She flew into the kitchen and grabbed her keys from the peg there, then rushed back to the living room, shot around her dumbstruck brother and flung open the door.

As she went by, Brendan asked, ''But what are you gonna do, sis?''

''I'll figure that out when the time comes.'' She rushed out into the twilight and slid behind the wheel of her car.

She no sooner had the door shut than Brendan was dropping into the passenger seat and Nellie and Linda Lou were piling in the back.

''What are you two doing?'' Delilah demanded over her shoulder, as she pumped the pedal and turned the key.

''Well, if you love him, dear—'' Linda Lou said.

Nellie finished. ''We *are* your friends, after all.''

''Things could get pretty rough,'' Delilah warned.

''We can take it,'' Nellie vowed. Her eyes were shining— just like Linda Lou's. It occurred to Delilah that this was probably more excitement than either of them normally saw in a month of Sundays.

And then there was no more time to think of Nellie and Linda Lou. The engine sputtered to life. Delilah switched on the lights and shoved it into gear. The tires squealed as she swung around. She peeled rubber down the street and almost ran into Roger McCleb who was crossing the street at the intersection of Pine and Main. Luckily, she missed Roger and made it onto Main.

She found a free space across the street from the bar, and slammed into it, missing the car in the space in front by mere inches. She was out of the car and striding across the street for the bar within seconds.

She paid no attention to whether her brother and two

friends were following. Her concentration was on the double
doors, on the sounds of cursing and crashing from beyond
them. She thought for a moment that maybe she ought to
call Sheriff Pangborn, but then she realized the odds were
ten to one someone already had. He'd be there eventually—
when the fighting got loud enough.

Her toe touched the sidewalk in front of the doors—and
the doors burst open. From inside, unmuffled now, came the
sound of a splintering table, the crashing of a chair. A loud
splat followed by a man's groan.

Two locked bodies rolled out, tussled briefly at her feet,
and then struggled upright and forged back in again. The
doors swung shut.

"Sis," Brendan warned as he came up behind her. "This
is entirely out of hand. It's no place for a woman."

"Shut up," Delilah told him. "And come on."

She put her shoulder against the door, and encountered
some resistance as someone fell against it on the other side.
She shoved again, harder. The door swung in. She went
through.

She faced pure chaos. Swiftly, she tried to assess the situation—no mean feat, as she kept having to duck flung beer
mugs and flying furniture. Still, she managed to scan the
room—and spotted Jared and Sam going at it like a couple
of pit bulls in the center of the fray. Both of them, at this
point, looked bloody, dogged and determined, the way men
get when they're evenly matched and neither of them has
the good sense to give it up.

She saw her father, then, beyond them, trapped across the
room from the bar where he'd probably been when the trouble broke out, trying to convince them the fight wasn't necessary, and then, when that didn't work, ordering them to
take it outside.

That's what he was still shouting now. "You hooligans!
You get your butts out the door! You're wreckin' my place!

Get it out, get it outside now!'' He kept yelling orders, with only an occasional pause to punch any fool who got close enough to make him nervous. Then he'd start in shouting again.

The situation assessed, Delilah wasted no time. She dropped to her knees and scurried to the bar. She ducked behind it just as a pool cue soared tip-first into the big mirror on the wall over the register. The mirror cracked, the way ice does on a frozen pond, in sharp splintering fingers. But miraculously, it stayed stuck to the wall while the pool cue clattered to the register counter, knocking over bottles, which shattered and spilled their contents all over the counter and down to the floor.

Delilah crept along behind the bar, trying to avoid the puddles of peppermint schnapps and orange liqueur, looking up at the underside of the bar and the counters, watching for what her father had always kept somewhere back here, since she was a child.

She found it, at last, right next to the seltzer fountain. Her father's .38 special, strapped under the bar in a tacked-up beltless holster, where he could easily yank it out whenever things got out of hand—as long as he had sense enough to stay behind the bar.

Still crouched where no flying objects could reach her, she drew the gun. She broke it open. The gun was fully loaded, just as she'd expected.

Over her head, a chair came sailing, hitting the mirror squarely and sending the splintered pieces flying.

Now, she thought resolutely, was as good a time as any.

So she rose up, quick as a cat, and leapt onto the bar. Below and all around her, the fighting continued unabated. Over by the door, she spotted Linda Lou, sticking out her foot to trip a brawler who dared to get too close. When he got up and came at her, Nellie brained him with a beer bottle. Across the room, Owen Beardsly spotted his wife. "Linda Lou!" he shouted, "My God, Linda Lou!"

"Oh, settle down, Owen!" Linda Lou advised and gave another man a shove who came flying out of the fray and got too close to her for comfort.

In the center of the floor, Sam, swaying on his feet, aimed a punch at Jared. It connected, Jared went down, and doggedly rose up once more.

"Gentlemen!" Delilah shouted, "Gentlemen! Please!"

She might as well have tried to stop a stampede with a feather duster. No one even paused to look her way.

Resigned, she aimed the gun at the big light fixture that hung over the center of the room. She fired off four shots, until each of the bulbs in the fixture was no more than splinters and dust.

Somewhere around the destruction of the third light bulb, the battling patrons ceased trading blows and dived for cover—all except for Jared and Sam, who simply stopped fighting and stared at her, their mouths hanging open.

When all four light bulbs were no more, she announced, "That's enough, gentlemen!" She was gratified to discover she had everyone's attention. "Wrap it up. This fight has reached its conclusion."

"Delilah!" said her father, scratching his head. "Delilah, you shot out the lights!"

She gave him an infinitely patient glance. "Someone had to do something."

"Well, I know that gal. But I swear I never thought I'd see the day…"

"Don't worry, I'll replace them." Slowly, around the battered barroom, the men were picking themselves up and checking themselves for damages. Delilah, too terrified that Sam might reject her to look at him, aimed a glare at her oldest brother. "And just what in the world do you think you're doing, Jared Jones?"

Jared, never known for his sweet disposition, swiped the blood out of his eyes and glared right back at her. "Sticking up for you, sis. What the hell do you think?"

A murmur of agreement went up from the crowd.

"Yeah, right on, Jared..."

"A man's gotta do what a man's gotta do...."

"Stick up for your sister, whatever it takes!"

Linda Lou cut them short. "Hush up, you roughnecks! Let Delilah talk."

The man she'd tripped turned on her. "Hey, you're the old bitch who hit me with that beer bottle...."

Near the curtain to the back room, Owen Beardsly spoke up. "You watch how you talk to my wife, mister!"

"Yes, you watch it, young man," Nellie piped up. "And she didn't hit you with that bottle anyway, that was me. Want to make something of it?"

The man muttered another insult and took a step toward Nellie.

Owen was already elbowing his way across the room. "You leave her alone. You want to fight with someone, you fight with me!"

"Don't trouble yourself, Owen!" Nellie called. "We can handle this moron!"

"Moron!" The man was furious now. "Who you callin' a moron, you old—"

It was obvious to Delilah that another brawl was in the offing. So she aimed the gun at the ceiling and fired it again. Plaster flew and rained down. All fell silent once more.

"I have one more shot, Gentlemen," Delilah announced. "Don't make me use it."

A sea of subdued male faces stared up at her expectantly. But Delilah was aware of only one pair of eyes. She could feel those eyes watching her; she just didn't have the nerve to look into them yet.

She focused on her brother once more. "I appreciate your efforts on my behalf, Jared, but next time see me first."

Jared totally ignored her real point and took issue with the sincerity of her thankfulness for all he'd done. "Yeah, well, you don't seem too damn grateful. In fact, you don't seem grateful at all."

Oggie cut in. "And why should she be grateful, you idiot? You're beating up her fiancé!"

Jared glowered at his father. "He never said so. I asked him straight out, 'You gonna marry my sister?' and he never said yes. You heard it. You were here. He said what he and sis were gonna do was nobody's business but theirs. And when a man won't answer if he's gonna do the right thing by a woman straight out, then as far as I'm concerned, it's a done deal. He's got what he wanted, and he's out the door."

Oggie turned to Sam. "Tell him, Sam. Tell him right now. Tell him you and my little girl are walking down the aisle side by side. Shut this blockhead up, and make me the happiest old man on earth."

The time had come, Delilah knew it. She had to face Sam now. She forced herself to look at him, at his bloody face and his ice blue eyes. He was looking right at her, as she'd known he would be, staring right through her, right down into her heart.

She said to her father, to Jared, to everyone in the bar, to the town, to the whole wide world, and most of all to Sam, "Yes, we're getting married. We love each other more than anyone else can know. We've had our...difficulties, but we'll come through them, side by side." She kept looking at Sam, willing him to know, to understand, to give her one more chance to show him she was a woman he could trust forevermore. He looked back but said nothing. Her heart sank. She asked, "Aren't we, Sam?" And a pleading note crept in.

"Answer her," Oggie hissed.

"Shut up, Oggie," Sam said softly. And he started moving forward. The crowd melted out of his way, leaving a clear path to Delilah where she stood up on the bar. Sam came on, closer and closer.

And then he was there, at her feet. She stared down at him—and at last she saw what had heretofore escaped her notice.

"Sam! Oh, Sam...." Her voice said everything. It was the voice of a woman long-gone in love. "Sam Fletcher, you went and cut your hair!"

So deeply moved was she, that she forgot momentarily that she was still holding a gun. It fell from her suddenly limp fingers. Several quick-thinking patrons hit the floor once more. But luck was with them. Brendan, who'd moved behind the bar when Delilah leapt up on it, caught the gun before it could go off and actually hurt someone.

A collective sigh of relief went up from the awestruck crowd.

And it was as the sigh faded that Delilah Jones leapt from the bar and into Sam Fletcher's waiting arms. He caught her without effort. His lips came down on hers.

Neither of them noticed the cheers and catcalls. They were lovers, loving, and the rest of the world meant less than nothing at all for a time.

Eventually, though, they came up for air. And that was when Sam said, "I love you, Delilah Jones."

And Delilah, hearing those precious words at last, felt her heart rise up, light as a sunbeam, carrying her with it, into an infinity of bliss. She said, "And I love you, Sam Fletcher. Till death do us part."

"So what does this mean?" Jared was still demanding. "He still hasn't said he'll marry her."

"He's marrying me," Delilah told her brother, never taking her eyes from the man who held her in his arms. There was a cut over his left eye. She gently wiped the blood away, clucking, "Oh, Sam...."

Oggie cleared his throat, "Uh, Sam, I gotta ask you. About The Mercantile..."

Delilah looked at Sam with appeal in her eyes.

"Keep it," Sam Fletcher growled, smoothing Delilah's hair. "I got everything I wanted out of you, Oggie Jones."

Oggie winked at Patrick, who stood over near Owen Beardsly, by the curtain to the back room.

Delilah said, "I have everything I ever wanted, too. Now Sam, may we please go home?"

"Which home?"

"It doesn't matter. Your house or mine. Home is either one of them, as long as you're there."

With a deep, joyful laugh, Sam Fletcher hoisted his woman high in his arms. He turned for the double doors.

"He gave up The Mercantile and that fine truck of Brendan's just to get him the schoolmarm," Rocky Collins declared in total bafflement, as Sam pushed through the double doors.

"Was she worth it?" some smart aleck nearby inquired.

"You better believe it, bud," Sam tossed the words over his shoulder as he kicked open the door.

Delilah sighed and laid her head against his heart as the man she loved carried her out of The Hole in the Wall and into a magnificent starry spring night.

* * * * *

MAN OF THE MOUNTAIN

For my dear cousin, Gail Clemo,
who looked out for me when I started out—
and when I started over

Chapter One

Eden had no idea what woke her. Perhaps a strange sound. Or maybe just a feeling that something wasn't right.

She stirred and turned over, then fitfully turned over again. But changing positions did no good. Sleep had fled. With a little moan, she rolled to her back and slowly opened her eyes.

A man stood at the foot of her bed.

Eden gasped.

And then she realized what must be happening. She must still be asleep. She *thought* she saw a man. But it was only the shadows, only the last after-image of an already forgotten dream.

She closed her eyes again, sure that the man would be gone on a second look.

When she opened her eyes the man was still there.

He murmured something.

Eden made no sense of his words. Her heart had just

kicked into overdrive. It seemed to expand in her chest. Her mouth tasted like old pennies. Her blood roared in her ears.

She sat up, rubbed her eyes, looked again.

He was still there. Oh God, still there…

This couldn't be happening. Not here, not in her darling little cabin by the river in lovely, safe North Magdalene.

Disoriented, terrified, Eden glanced down and beheld her own long legs gleaming palely in the darkness. It had been a hot night, and she'd drifted off without pulling up the sheet. Now her legs were visible all the way to the hip because her sleep shirt had ridden up. And *he* could see exactly what she could see—which was way too much.

Yanking down the hem of her shirt, Eden scuttled back against the headboard, tucking her legs up under her, trying vainly to hide them from his view.

Cowering there among the pillows, shaking all over, she demanded, "Wh-who are you? What do you want?"

"An answer." He stepped around the end of the bed.

"Don't you come any closer!"

He swore softly. "What the hell's your problem? Settle down." He took another step toward her.

Frantic, she stuck out a hand for the night table, groping for something—anything—to use in her own defense. Her fingers found the hard, firm shape of her old-fashioned windup alarm clock. She grabbed it and raised it high.

"You get back from me. Don't come any closer. I mean it!"

"Put that damn thing down."

Her heart was pounding way too fast. Adrenaline slammed through her system, beckoning her to give in to pure hysteria. She was trying desperately to keep her head, not to let herself admit how far away she was from the next house and how unlikely the chance that her cries for help might be heard.

The intruder gave a low, disgusted grunt. "Put it down, I'm warning you." He took another step.

That did it. For Eden, it was either take action, or start shrieking like some helpless victim in a bad horror film. Eden was no victim. She hurled the clock.

And then, not pausing to see if she'd actually hit her target, she shot off the bed on the other side and headed for the door.

She didn't make it.

She heard the clock bounce on the little throw rug by the bed and then something snared her sleep shirt. The shirt stretched like a huge rubber band. She prayed it would tear. It didn't.

Grunting, the intruder hauled her in with a jerk, wrapping an arm that felt like a steel band around her the minute he had her close enough. She spun and found herself plastered against a hard, broad chest.

"Why you little—"

"Let me go, you creep! Let go!" She pounded his chest and kicked at his shins.

"What the hell is the matter with you? You're crazy—oof!"

There. She'd done it, kneed him close enough to his privates that he flinched. She tore backward.

But the man was an octopus. He held on. They toppled to the floor in a tangle of arms and legs. Her sleep shirt slithered up. She could feel the hard length of him, all along every inch of her struggling body. Once or twice, she felt the harsh scrape of his boot. She fought on and she fought hard, scratching and punching and squirming with all her might.

But the intruder was as hard as tempered steel, as lean and sinuous as a snake. And Eden Parker, slim and strong as she was, was simply no match for him.

With unfailing, unswerving determination, he subdued

her. He redirected her. He slithered out of her way. And yet somehow he managed never to let go of her.

How long she fought him, Eden didn't know. Time lost all meaning in the battle for survival, for self-protection.

But eventually, she felt herself weakening. Her blows had less and less effect. He managed to capture both her wrists, forcing them over her head and pinning them to the floor.

His body was like a lead weight on top of hers, pressing her down. Exhausted, she panted and squirmed, hating her own lesser strength. She knew she had to keep her mind clear. She had to be ready for any slightest chance he might give her to get free.

Her cruel captor panted, too, his hard chest moving in and out against her own. "Are you done?" he muttered in a harsh growl.

"I'll never be done. Never," she managed to say between painful gulps for air.

Then, unable to look at the shadow of him, her unknown attacker, so close above her, she turned her head so her cheek touched the floor. She shut her eyes. She wasn't giving up, oh no. All she needed was a few more good breaths and she'd be ready to fight again.

But then, just as she closed her eyes to concentrate on regrouping, she felt it. She felt *him* down there, where the placket of his jeans was pressed so unmercifully against her womanhood. He was growing hard....

"Oh, no," she moaned in desperation.

He swore, crudely and succinctly.

And then he reared back on his knees.

Eden blinked, not understanding his withdrawal when she had feared the worst. And then she realized that right now was the chance she'd hoped for.

She rolled, then scrambled to her knees.

"Oh, no, you don't," he muttered grimly. He grabbed her arm and yanked her to her feet. Then he groped with his free arm for a moment, until he found her brass-backed vanity chair. He spun it around and shoved her down in it, flicking on the vanity table light at the same time.

For a moment, now that they could both see more than mere shadows and shapes, they stared at each other. To Eden, he looked just as she'd expected him to look: hard and mean and dangerous. His grim slash of a mouth was set in an ungiving line. His steel gray eyes were slits.

She saw with bleak satisfaction that her makeshift weapon had actually hit its mark. A trickle of blood dripped down above his left eye. As she watched, he swiped the blood away with a forearm. She stared at that arm, noticing the ropy tendons in it, the complete lack of any softness to it.

She thought how lean he was, too lean. There wasn't an ounce of fat on him. He was all tendon and muscle and bone. Like a wolf or a junkyard dog, he looked hungry, ready for anything—and not an animal that should be let in the house.

He muttered another invective, then demanded, "Don't you have a robe or something?"

The question totally bewildered her. "Huh?"

"A robe." He looked at her as if he wondered what she used for brains. "Do you have a robe?"

"Yes, I...on the back of the door."

He whirled and saw it. Then he strode to it, grabbed it off the hook behind the door and tossed it at her. "Now for godsakes, cover yourself."

Eden just gaped at him for a moment. If he intended to rape her, then why would he—?

"Do what I said. Put on that robe."

"O-okay. I will. Sure." Swiftly, gratefully, she stuck her hands into the sleeves of the robe and gathered it close about her.

"Now talk," he demanded in that low, sibilant voice of his.

"A-about what?"

"Answer the questions I asked you before."

"Y-you didn't ask me any questions."

He drew in a long breath and then he spoke very slowly, very patiently, the way a man does when he's trying to hold himself back from doing something he'll regret. "Yes, I did. I asked you two questions when you first woke up. Before you attacked me with that damn clock."

Eden frowned. "What questions?"

"I asked who you are—and what the hell you're doing in my house."

Chapter Two

"*Your* house?"

Eden's dazed mind struggled to comprehend what he was telling her. That he was no rapist, that he wasn't even really an intruder. That he *owned* the cabin.

She stammered out, "But if this is your house, then you must be..."

She peered at him more closely. Yes, she could see it. A little of sweet old Oggie around the mouth and something of Heather, who had rented Eden the cabin, in the determined set of the jaw. She swallowed.

"Er...Mr. Jones?"

His gunmetal eyes stayed narrowed. His mouth remained grim. But he did grant her a slow nod. "Right."

"You're...Heather's dad, Jared Jones?"

He grunted in acknowledgment.

Eden just couldn't believe it. Relief that he was not what she'd feared, coupled with embarrassment at what had just happened between them, loosened her tongue.

"But you live out in the woods. By yourself. You hardly ever come to town. You're a *hermit*..."

As soon as the word was out, Eden regretted her own tactlessness. It seemed rude to call a man a hermit to his face, even if it was the truth.

She felt her cheeks flushing, looked away and then added defensively, "Heather said the last time you came to North Magdalene was four months ago. When your sister, Delilah, married Sam Fletcher."

"So?"

She faced him again. "So what in the world are you doing here now?"

He gave another grunt. "You ask too many damn questions." Then he was the one looking away.

"I think I have a right to ask some questions. After all, you broke into my house—"

"*My* house."

"—in the middle of the night. And you—"

"Look. Could you just put a lid on it for a few minutes here?" He rubbed the back of his neck. "Give a man a chance to think."

She stared at him, frustrated and bewildered. "Think. You want to *think*...."

"Yeah."

"Great. Fine." She raked her hair back from her face. "You just think."

He made another of those grunting sounds and sank to the edge of the bed. Wincing, he prodded the tender spot over his eye.

She watched him, feeling a slight twinge of guilt and hoping she hadn't hurt him too badly. Reluctantly she decided she probably should apologize for smacking him with the clock, though there was no doubt that what had happened was more his fault than hers.

She offered, "I'm sorry that I hit you."

He granted her a doubting glance. "You still haven't told me who the hell you are."

She tucked her robe more closely around her and made herself sit straighter. "I'm Eden Parker, a friend of Laurie's."

He said nothing, but just looked at her with that strange flat expression.

She heard herself reminding him, "You know, your second cousin, Laurie Riley?"

"I know who Laurie is. Where do you come in?"

"I told you. I'm Laurie's friend."

"I mean, how do you know her?"

"Laurie and I met in Sacramento, where she goes to college." He went on staring. She elaborated, "You did know Laurie's going to college in Sacramento?"

He nodded. He was peering at her mouth. One corner of *his* mouth was lifted just slightly, in a sort of wary, silent snarl. She thought again of hungry wolves and wild dogs.

Though she was no longer exactly afraid of him, the way he kept watching her made her nervous.

"Look. It's very simple, really. We met because Laurie needed a part-time job." Eden found that the sound of her own voice soothed her nervousness a little, made this whole bizarre situation seem a little less strange. She prattled on. "I'm sure you know how expensive college is in California these days. Even though her folks are paying the tuition and basic expenses, Laurie couldn't get by on that alone. So she applied at La Cantina. That's a Mexican restaurant on Howe Avenue."

"So?"

"So that's where we met. I was the manager there and I hired her. And we just hit it off from the very beginning. Right away, we became best friends." She forced what she hoped was a cheerful smile.

"So you're just visiting here, then?"

"No, I live here."

"Since when?"

"A few months ago. Laurie brought me up here for a visit. And I just…fell in love with this place. And with your family, too. You really do have a terrific family. And I was looking for a change in my life. So I decided to leave my job in Sacramento and move up here. I needed a place to stay and Laurie said you told Heather to rent this cabin if she could find a trustworthy tenant. So I met with Heather and—"

"That was two years ago."

"Excuse me?"

"It was two years ago, when I told Heather to rent this place."

"Well, I know but—"

"I've been back half a dozen times since then and my place is always right here, waiting for me. Until now."

Eden looked at him sideways. It was becoming painfully clear that Jared Jones was not happy with the news that he had a tenant.

Well, if he didn't like it, then *he* had a problem. She had a signed agreement that said she had every right to be here.

Eden drew herself up. "Mr. Jones. From what I understand, most of the time you're not an easy man to find. I'm sure Heather intended to tell you that she'd found you a tenant as soon as you gave her the chance."

"Yeah, great. But that doesn't do me a hell of a lot of good right now."

"What do you mean?"

He gave her another of those brooding, snarly looks of his.

She prompted, "Well?"

Instead of answering, he looked away.

Eden had the impression he was deciding how to proceed from here, and that until he *had* decided what he was going

to do, she'd be lucky to get even one more surly grunt out
of him.

"Oh, never mind," she supplied unnecessarily.

Then *she* fell silent. And since Jared Jones wasn't much
of a talker, the room was suddenly deathly quiet.

In the soft light from her vanity table lamp, Eden stared
at his rugged profile. As she stared she realized she still had
no idea what this man had thought he was doing, appearing
at the foot of her bed in the middle of the night, scaring
several years off her life.

She said pointedly, "So now you know all about what
I'm doing here. But you haven't said a word about what
you thought *you* were doing, a total stranger to me, appearing at the foot of my bed in the middle of the night. I have
to tell you, I've never been so terrified in my life. What was
going through your mind? You must have realized that when
I woke up I would be frightened out of my wits, but still
you—"

He pinned her with those piercing eyes again and waved
a hand for silence.

Generously Eden held her tongue for a moment, waiting
for him to explain himself. But he didn't explain a thing.
He just sat there on the bed, glaring at her as if *she* were
the intruder instead of him. Then he poked at the cut over
his eye again.

Right then, it occurred to her that after bopping her landlord on the head, she probably ought to patch him up. Even
if she had only thrown the clock in what she'd honestly
believed was self-defense.

"You should put some ice on that," she suggested, trying
for a sympathetic tone and somehow ending up sounding
abrasively cheerful.

He shot her a pained look. "Never mind. It's fine."

She said nothing for a moment. And then she made up

her mind to do what *she* thought was best, not what *he* told her to do.

"I'll get the ice." She stood up.

"I said forget it."

It was a simple thing to pretend she hadn't heard him, since she was already out of the chair and halfway to the door. She marched through the big living area, around the end of the stairs that led up to an open sleeping loft and straight to the kitchen. There, she flipped on the light and set right to work knocking ice cubes from a tray to wrap in a hand towel. As she was arranging the ice on the towel, she noticed a flicker of movement out of the corner of her eye. It was him.

She glanced his way, thinking that it was the next thing to creepy, how quietly he could move around. She hadn't *heard* him follow her at all. She'd simply happened to turn her head when he came in the room.

Small surprise, after all, that he had been able to enter the cabin, find his way to her bedroom and stand at the foot of her bed for heaven knew how long without her even knowing it. And actually, the more she thought about it, the way he'd entered the house *and* her bedroom without her knowledge really did aggravate her.

She spoke a bit harshly. "Sit down at the table. I'll be right back."

"Look, I said I—"

"Sit down," she told him and swept past him, not deigning to check to see if he did as she ordered. She strode to the cabin's one bathroom and found the first-aid kit she kept in the medicine cabinet. Then she returned to the kitchen.

He'd done as she'd told him and was sitting at the end of the table. His expression was no longer quite so stony as before. Now, if she had to define his look, she'd probably call it glum.

Well, she decided, it didn't matter how he looked. She

was going to patch him up and find out what, precisely, he was doing here and then send him on his way. To that end, she set down the first-aid kit on the table and then crossed to the sink to collect her makeshift ice pack.

"What did you do with my stuff?" he said in a flat voice as she returned to him.

Eden was instantly defensive. "What stuff?"

"You know, my furniture. The clothes in the closets. My pots and pans."

"*I* didn't do anything with it. Oggie took care of all that before I moved in. I understood he was going to store everything for you." She held out the ice pack.

He ignored it. "You're on a first-name basis with my dad?" He looked up at her, both eyes slitted and one of them swelling perceptibly because of the injury she'd inflicted.

Eden's irritation with him increased, partly because he wouldn't take the darn ice pack. And partly because he was right. She most definitely was on a first-name basis with Oggie Jones. And she suspected that Jared Jones was not going to be pleased to hear the exact nature of her relationship with his father.

"Your dad is my friend. He's about the sweetest old guy I've ever met."

Jared Jones snorted in response to that, then looked away. Her irritation at him increasing, Eden slapped the ice pack down on the table. He glanced at her again, a very superior glance.

Eden seriously considered turning on her heel, striding to her bedroom and locking herself in for the rest of the night. But that would solve nothing. Judging by his behavior so far, Jared Jones would probably still be here at dawn if she did something like that. She'd emerge from the bedroom to find him snoring on the couch. After all, he'd entered without even bothering to knock. And even when he'd found out who she was and that she was a legal tenant, he still hadn't left. It was going to take more than walking away from him, she feared, to get him out of the cabin so she could get back to sleep.

But before she got rid of him, she was going to disinfect that wound. She'd caused it and she would treat it, whether he welcomed her efforts at nursing or not.

Resolutely she opened the first-aid kit and took out a sterile pad. She doused the pad with hydrogen peroxide.

He was slouched in the chair, his legs aggressively spread. She pointedly slid around him, moved to his left side and nudged his thigh with her knee. He had the grace to pull his legs together so she could get near without stepping between his thighs.

She began swabbing the wound. Up close, she could see that the cut was only minor. The bleeding had almost stopped. But he was going to have a real shiner by tomorrow. Already, the swelling flesh was turning the color of a ripe plum.

"There. All clean," she murmured.

He gave a small shrug. "Fine." He started to duck away from her.

She caught his shoulder. "Wait."

He looked up at her. All at once, she was acutely aware of the feel of his shoulder beneath her hand: lean, sharply contoured, as strong as tempered steel. She picked up the scent of him, an outdoorsy scent, like evergreen and leather and dust.

His expression was very strange. She couldn't read it at all, but suddenly she was pondering things that, until that moment, she'd been very careful not to consider in any depth.

This man had watched her as she slept. He had wrestled her to the floor of her bedroom and subdued her. He had been pressed against her intimately. And he had become physically aroused.

She let go of his shoulder as if the heat of it burned her.

He was still looking in her eyes. "What?" he asked.

She frowned at him, feeling a slow warmth creeping up over her cheeks. She hadn't the faintest idea what he was asking her.

He reminded her. "You said to wait. What for?"

"Oh. Right." She glanced away, then back, hoping he hadn't noticed her blush. She made her tone very business-like. "Because I have some antibiotic ointment. I'll put a little on the scratch."

"Not necessary. It's fine."

"It'll only take a second." She edged around his knees and took a little foil pouch from the kit. Then she moved back into place at his side and squeezed the contents of the pouch onto the cut.

In spite of his protests, he allowed this final ministration, remaining very still and seeming to look off toward a far corner of the room as she bent over him. One of her fingers touched his cheekbone. His skin there had a rough, new-beard feel. Her knee accidentally brushed his thigh. It was as solid as granite. She felt bewildered suddenly, to be so very conscious of this rough stranger, of the scent of him, of his hardness and his strength.

"All right. Is that it?"

She stepped back, conflicting emotions playing leapfrog inside her. "Unless you'd like a bandage."

"No."

"Well, okay then. that's all." She swiftly gathered up the contents of the first-aid kit and took it back to the bathroom, where she put it away.

When she returned, he was still sitting in the kitchen chair where she'd left him.

She stood in the doorway and sighed. What to do now?

The clock on the kitchen wall said it was 2:15 a.m. She wanted to return to her bed. Yet Jared Jones was infuriatingly unforthcoming about what he was doing here. And he was showing no inclination whatsoever to be on his way.

Eden decided to take one more crack at polite inquiry. "Does...anyone else know you're in town, Mr. Jones?"

He tore his gaze away from the far wall to give her another of those expressionless stares of his. "You talk a lot."

She took a deep breath, released it slowly and kept her voice calm and unchallenging. "Yes, I do talk a lot when I'm nervous, Mr. Jones. And, in this situation, you really can't blame me for being nervous. After all, you—"

He waved a preemptive hand. "Look. Let's cut through the chitchat here. I don't know any other way around this situation but to tell it to you straight. It's like this. Things have changed. I don't want to rent this place after all. You'll have to move out."

Chapter Three

Eden rubbed her eyes. She'd suspected this was coming, when he'd seemed so annoyed at the news that he had a tenant. But still, to hear him actually say the words made her very, very tired.

She slumped against the doorjamb, feeling put-upon. First, he'd terrified her half to death, then he'd wrestled her into exhausted submission, and now he was telling her that she was evicted.

Well, he had another thing coming, and that was all there was to it.

She was the soul of reason when she spoke. "I'm sorry, Mr. Jones. But you can't just order me to leave."

"What do you mean? I'm doing it, aren't I?"

"I have a signed rental agreement."

"So?"

"So you are required by the terms of that agreement to give me sixty days notice to vacate the premises."

"Lady, it's only a piece of paper."

"It has your own signature on it, as well as mine. Heather said you gave it to her when you told her to look for a tenant."

"That was then. I've changed my mind since then."

"Well, apparently you never bothered to inform your daughter."

"Look. I need a place to live."

Eden blinked, confused by what his words implied. Was this more than a visit? Did he actually plan to live here? Jared Jones was supposed to be through with towns and people, from what everyone in his family said. But he was talking as if he intended to return here to stay.

Well, if he is moving back to town, Eden thought, he'll have to find another house. She remained firm. "I need a place to live, too."

He stood up. "You can move out tomorrow."

"How generous of you." She folded her arms across her breasts. "Forget it. I'm staying. I get sixty days notice to vacate, and I intend to use them to find another place."

He took a step toward her, his lip curling in that mean-dog snarl again. "You keep jabbering about that damn contract. What do you think you are, a lawyer?"

Eden eyed him warily, but refused to back down. "No, I'm no lawyer. But I do have a legal right to be here. For at least another two months."

"I want my house back."

"Well, that's just too bad."

"I oughtta…"

"You ought to what?" she challenged, keeping her chin up and her shoulders back. "Spy on me in the middle of the night? Terrify me out of my mind? Tackle me and knock me down and…sit on me and fight with me until I'm too tired to fight anymore?"

"I did not sit on you."

"Right. But you did everything else. We both know what you did. And you *still* haven't said why you came in my room and just stood there. And I'd also like to know, exactly how long *were* you standing there?"

"Not long. A minute or two. Hardly any time at all."

"Right. I'll bet."

"You are a damned irritating woman."

"Fine. So answer my questions. Or get out of my house."

"*My* house."

"Okay, *your* house that *I'm* renting. *Your* house that I don't have to leave until sixty—count 'em—*six-o* days after you serve me formal, written notice to vacate."

He was less than two feet from her now, glaring and snarling and looking like he could snap her neck with his bare hands and not think twice about it. For several seconds, they stared each other down.

And then, with a low, enraged growl, he whirled around and stomped out the kitchen door.

Eden stood where she was and stared at the place where he had been and didn't know whether she felt shaken or triumphant.

Jared Jones had a reputation as a hot-tempered man. It was said of him that he never came to town without getting in at least one good fistfight—and more likely than not, precipitating a brawl. Of course, it was also said that he would never hit a child or a woman and that he was as protective of women as he was distrustful of them. So it was probably unlikely that he would have actually hurt Eden, no matter how much she had goaded him. Still, after witnessing the seething rage in those pewter eyes, she knew she'd been taking a chance to taunt him like that.

But it had been worth it, she told herself. Because she had made him so mad, he left. Now she could go back to her bedroom, crawl beneath the covers and get what was left of a decent night's sleep. Outside, Eden heard a vehicle door slam.

Over on the table, her homemade ice pack had begun to drip. She went and got it and emptied the melting ice cubes in the sink, then she wrung out the towel and laid it over the counter rim to dry. While she did all this, she was listening, waiting to hear the engine start up and the crunching of tires on gravel that would mean Jared Jones was driving away.

Those sounds never came.

Instead, moments later, the kitchen door was thrown back and he strode in once again. This time, he was carrying a backpack in one hand and a sleeping bag slung over his shoulder.

Eden longed to scream. But she didn't. She asked, "Just what do you think you're doing?"

"I'm beat. I'll sleep in the loft."

"But you can't just—"

"I won't bother you at all. Go back to bed."

He brushed past her and headed through the door that went to the living area and the stairs that led up to the loft. Eden stared after him with her mouth hanging open, thinking she ought to chase after him and *demand* he leave the cabin this instant.

But then she reconsidered. It *was* late. And it wouldn't really put her out at all for him to roll out his sleeping bag on the guest bed in the loft. Beyond that, this *was* his house, even if she had a legal claim to stay in it. And he *had* returned here thinking he would find it vacant. And he was Laurie's second cousin. And Oggie's son…

He had already disappeared in the shadows overhead before she collected herself enough to march to the foot of the stairs and call up to him, "All right! But just for tonight!" He didn't bother to answer. She had no idea what he was doing up there. Perhaps laying out his sleeping bag—or peering down at her from the shadows with a smug grin on his face. She added, "And if you want to use the bathroom, please do so right now!"

That got a response. "Fine, I will!"

"Well, good night, then!"

"Good night!"

Not knowing what else to do, Eden returned to her room. She was careful to engage the privacy locks on both the door to the hall and the one to the bathroom. She found her alarm clock on the floor and checked it for dents. There were none. Then she reset it for an hour later than usual and put it back on the little table by her bed. She took off her robe and climbed in beneath the covers.

A few minutes later, she heard water running in the bathroom, which had another entrance in the main part of the cabin. She also heard the toilet flush.

And then there was silence.

A pair of squirrels jabbering and chasing each other up and down the big fir tree outside her open window woke Eden the next morning. Then the alarm chimed in.

Eden reached out and silenced the clock. After that, she got up on her knees at the head of the bed and leaned on her brass headboard to watch the squirrels for a while. The squirrels scampered like furry trapeze artists, following each other from limb to limb, letting out their urgent, breathy squirrel noises, sounds that made Eden smile.

Overhead, the sky was pale blue and clear. And though it was only nine o'clock, the air was already warm. Today would be another scorcher, by North Magdalene standards. It might even hit a hundred at the height of the afternoon.

But Eden wouldn't suffer from the heat, nor would her customers over at The Hole in the Wall Saloon. Since June, thanks to Eden, The Hole in the Wall had boasted air-conditioning.

She'd been insistent about putting in central air, explaining to her new partner, "Oggie, it's an important investment. People have to be comfortable. Especially if we want to draw in a wider range of clientele."

Oggie had let out one of his cackling laughs. "You mean less lowlifes, more regular folks."

"Well, Oggie. I mean, since we're the only game in town, if we spiff things up a little, appeal to the ladies as well as the gentlemen—"

"Gentlemen?" Oggie cackled again. "What gentlemen? We ain't never had no gentlemen around this joint."

Eden grinned to herself, thinking of Oggie. The cagey old charmer was just such a sweetheart. He was crotchety and crude and full of naughty jokes. Yet his heart was as big as the whole Sierra Nevada mountain range. Eden had adored him from the first.

"Hell," Oggie had said. "It's your money, gal. If you wanna spend it on air-conditioning, then you go right ahead."

Eden had begun collecting estimates that very day. And now, when the mercury got near the triple figures, people in town often came into the tavern just to cool off a little from the heat of the day.

Yes, The Hole In The Wall was a lot different than it used to be. Eden was proud of the improvements she'd made there. She'd done a lot in a very short time.

Outside, the squirrels dashed out of sight. From the bathroom Eden heard water running, the shower this time.

With a sigh, she fell back on the bed and closed her eyes.

For a few moments, she'd succeeded in forgetting about Jared Jones. But the respite was over.

This morning, one way or another, she had to deal with him. She had to get his agreement that he'd let her have the cabin for sixty days. Or at least until she could find somewhere else to live.

She also knew she should break the news to him about her partnership with his father. But that was something she wasn't looking forward to at all. In fact, it got her heart going a little too fast just thinking about telling him.

She'd been informed by more than one person in town that Oggie had promised to leave The Hole in the Wall to Jared when he died. Of course, she'd gone right to Oggie when she heard about that. And Oggie had given her several reasons why she shouldn't worry about Jared. So she *hadn't* worried about Jared.

Until now.

"Relax, Parker," she muttered to herself. She reminded herself firmly that she had no reason to feel guilty. She had done nothing wrong.

"So why do I feel so…reprehensible?" Eden asked her own reflection in her vanity table mirror.

She had no answer for herself. So she pulled on her robe and went out to turn on the coffeemaker, so the coffee would be ready whenever her uninvited visitor wanted a cup.

Eden took a quick shower after Jared left the bathroom. She dressed swiftly for work in black slacks, a man-tailored white shirt with a string tie and a black vest. She slid her feet into low-heeled black shoes. Then she pinned up her chin-length strawberry-blond hair. For work, she wore it off her neck, but loose and curly around her face.

After that, she went out to the kitchen and set about making breakfast. She fried bacon and toasted bread. She set the table for two and mixed up a can of frozen orange juice. Judging by the level of the coffee in the pot, Jared had already been into the kitchen once or twice. She was counting on the smell of frying bacon to bring him downstairs again.

He came just as she began cracking the eggs in the pan.

Again, she caught a glimpse of him coming through the door before she heard a sound. It was really amazing how silently he could move around.

She beamed him a smile. Today was a new day, after all. Maybe they could start it off by being pleasant with each other.

"How do you like your eggs?"

He didn't smile back. "Cooked."

She refused to be less than cheerful. "Over easy is fine, then?"

He grunted.

She decided that would have to do for a yes. "How many would you like?"

He went to the coffeemaker and refilled his cup. Then he turned and leaned against the counter with a kind of rangy, ready grace that made her distinctly uncomfortable. The eye she'd smacked with the clock was swollen shut and the color of burgundy wine. His good eye, though, could see just fine. It made a slow, roving pass from the top of her curly head to her trim black flats and then back up again. "What kind of getup is that?"

"I'm dressed for work."

"What kind of work?"

As soon as she told him, she'd have to explain about the partnership. She evaded his query. "Do you want eggs or not?"

"Yeah."

"How many, three? Four?"

He sipped from his coffee again. "Sure. Four." She set about frying the eggs, all the while waiting grimly for him to quiz her more about the work she did. But he seemed to have become more interested in the meal she'd prepared than in her job.

He looked at the table, at the two place settings, the carafe of orange juice, the tall stack of toast and the bacon, crisp and brown on a serving plate. "What are you up to?"

"Look." She pointed her spatula at him. "Do you want these eggs I'm cooking or not?" This time, she didn't bother to keep the edge from her voice.

He considered. Then he shrugged. "Yeah, sure. I want those eggs."

"Fine, then." She gestured at the chair across from the one where she liked to sit. "Sit down there."

He slid in where she'd told him to and got right to work pouring himself a big glass of juice and piling bacon slices on his plate. Then he grabbed the jam and slathered some on a slice of toast. He shoved the toast into his mouth and stuck a couple of slices of bacon in right after it. Then he grunted in satisfied pleasure as he chewed with stolid concentration, grabbing more toast to pile with jam at the same time.

To Eden, he looked just like what she knew he was: a logger who'd been out in the woods too long, a man who ate most of his meals off of a tin plate with a bunch of other snorting, grunting loggers for company.

She wrapped the pot holder around the handle of the frying pan and carried the pan to the table, where she dished up her single egg first. Then she moved around to his side of the table.

"Excuse me," she said.

He looked up at her in midchew, his mouth so full he looked like an huge, greedy chipmunk—with a black eye. "Ungh?"

Eden sighed and shook her head. "Mr. Jones, what would your mama say?"

The effect of her words was immediate. Jared swallowed, wiped his mouth and hands on his napkin and then smoothed his napkin over his lap. Then he sat up very straight.

"Uh, pardon me," he said sheepishly.

Eden smiled sweetly down at him. "That's quite all right."

It was amazing, really, what mentioning his mother could accomplish. It was that way with the other two Jones boys, Patrick and Brendan, too. Oggie and the boys had worshiped Bathsheba Riley Jones and though she'd been dead for almost a quarter of a century now, one still had only to refer to her in passing to elicit mannerly behavior from any one of her rowdy sons—or her widowed husband, for that matter.

Carefully, Eden slid Jared's four eggs onto his plate.

"Thank you," he said, when she was done.

"You're very welcome."

Eden carried the pan back to the stove and then, after pouring herself a fresh cup of coffee, joined Jared at the table. They ate in silence for a few minutes. And then Eden decided to make another attempt at reaching some sort of understanding with him.

"Jared?"

"Yeah?" He was spreading more jam on yet another piece of toast. He did it slowly and with great care.

"You know, you really did, um, surprise me last night."

"Yeah."

"And, I really would appreciate knowing…"

"What?"

"Well, for one thing, why, exactly, did you arrive so late?"

Jared bit into the toast and chewed with extreme conscientiousness. Then he swallowed. Then he answered, "Decompression time," before he took another careful bite.

"What do you mean?"

Jared shot her an impatient scowl. But as soon as he finished chewing, he explained, "I wanted to get in and get settled before I had to deal with any people. And the only way to do that in North Magdalene is to sneak in after midnight with your headlights off.'' He put the last of the toast into his mouth and patiently began chewing again.

Eden watched him for a moment. Truth to tell, she was longing to remind him of how frightening it had been for her to wake to the sight of him looming over her bed. However, she wanted him to be reasonable about the cabin. And she wanted him to be in a good mood when she told him about her business arrangement with his father. So as far as last night went, she'd probably better let bygones be bygones.

She continued with her tactful inquiry. ''So then, you're planning to move back to North Magdalene?''

Jared narrowed his good eye at her. ''Haven't we already been through this?''

''Well, yes. But I'm still trying to understand. Why would someone like you suddenly decide to live in town again?''

Jared shook his head and wiped his mouth with his napkin. Then he stood. ''Lady, there's a question mark coming at me every time you open your mouth.'' He picked up his plate and carried it to the sink.

Eden turned in her chair. ''I just feel it would be good for us to come to some sort of agreement about—''

His dish and juice glass clattered into the sink. He turned on her. ''Get this straight. It's my business why I do things. What matters to you is I'm back and I'm staying. Here. In *my* house.''

Eden sighed. So much for trying to get along with him. She took her napkin from her lap and tucked it beneath the rim of her plate. Then she pushed back her chair and stood.

''Where the hell do you think you're going?'' Jared Jones demanded.

Eden said nothing. She calmly strode from the room and straight to her little desk by the big window in the living area. From the desk, she took her copy of the rental agreement. Then she returned to the kitchen, where Jared Jones stood, glowering hatefully, by the sink.

She marched right up to him and waved the agreement under his nose. "Not until my sixty days are up, you're not," she said.

"I could rip that thing to pieces right now."

"But you won't. I know you Joneses. You can be mean and rough, but you're not cheats." She gave the agreement another taunting wave in front of his face.

He grabbed her wrist. "You *think* you know us Joneses."

Eden blinked. His grip seemed to burn her. His palm was rough, scratchy against the tender flesh of her wrist. One side of his mouth had lifted, in that half snarl of his.

"L-let me go," she said, the command sounding shaky and breathy and not convincing at all.

He exerted a little more pressure on her captured wrist, enough to bring her up closer, so he could warn in a too-soft hiss, "You oughtta watch yourself, Miss Parker. You wave a red cape in front of an angry bull, you just might get gored."

She could smell the coffee on his breath, and the soap he must have used when he showered. His face was smoother than last night. He must have shaved....

"You listening to me?"

"Y-yes." She swallowed. "I heard every word you said."

"Good." He breathed the word almost tenderly.

His mouth was very close. She had no idea where the thought came from, but it was there: just the slightest lift of her chin, and their lips would meet....

She asked, "Jared?"

And he blinked. Then he seemed to shake himself. He let go of her wrist. That broke the spell. She was able to step back.

They regarded each other. Eden was trembling. She

wanted to order him out. She wanted to throw herself against him.

Again, she recalled the way he had lain on top of her last night. This time, it was more than a recollection of her own terror and, later, her embarrassment, more than the knowledge that he had physically responded to her. This time, she pinpointed her own reaction.

She could desire this man.

Could desire him? Sweet Lord. She *did* desire him, right now.

And it was crazy. It was totally inappropriate. Completely out of line.

He said, in that voice of his that was as soft and deadly as the hiss of a rattlesnake, "I don't like this. I don't like it one damn bit."

She didn't need to ask him what he meant. She knew exactly what he meant. He didn't like this…magnetism between them any more than she did.

She said, "I agree. Look. Forget the rental contract." She crumpled it into a ball and tossed it in the sink. "Give me the rest of the month, okay? Two and a half weeks. I'll find another place and be out by September first."

He measured her with his undamaged eye, as if trying to decide whether he should trust her. "Let me think about it."

Then, without another word, he turned for the door.

Eden stared after him for a moment, as her baffled mind registered the fact that he was walking out, just like he had last night, abruptly and without so much as a "See you around."

"Hey, wait! Where are you going?"

He opened the door and went through it.

"Take your things with you!"

He didn't even pause. Instead, he closed the door behind

him. Outside, she heard the slamming of a vehicle door. Shortly after that, she heard the vehicle start up and drive away.

Chapter Four

Fifteen minutes after he walked out on Eden, Jared Jones shoved back the door of Lily's Café. He was looking for his daughter, who had worked the morning shift at the café five days a week for the past year and half.

Heather was there, all right, standing over by the cook's window, buttering toast fresh from the toaster. Jared's heart swelled a little at the sight of her. More and more every time he saw her, she resembled her mother, Sally, who had been dead for seven years now.

Right then, as he was thinking how much his daughter looked like her mother, Heather turned with a plate of toast in her hand and saw him. Her hazel eyes—Sally's eyes— lit up. Her smile was Sally's smile.

"Dad!" She tossed the toast on the counter in front of Rocky Collins. Rocky, who spent most of his waking hours at The Hole in the Wall, gasped in pain at the slight clattering sound that the dish made. Jared guessed he was nursing a hangover, as usual.

Heather bounced around the end of the counter, arms out-stretched. "Dad, this is great. It's been too darn long."

Jared hugged his daughter, moved as he always was each time he saw her. She had turned out to be such a nice, warm, open person.

Heather was twenty-one now. She was married to Jason Lee Conley, her high school sweetheart, and she was about the happiest person Jared had ever know. Around town people called her Sunshine, because she always had a smile on her face. Jared knew lots of people marveled that a kind, sweet young woman like Heather could have had a malcontent like himself for her dad. After Sally died, he'd finished raising her himself. And the way she had turned out was about the only thing in his life of which he was truly proud.

Jared pulled back enough to look down at Heather. "Got a minute?"

"For you, anything." She was still smiling, but the smile wavered now. She was getting a good look at what Eden Parker had done to his eye. She called over her shoulder, "Lily, I'm going outside! I'll only be a moment!"

From beyond the cook's window, Lily shouted, "Don't be all day!"

"Five minutes, max, I promise!" And then Heather was grabbing his hand and towing him through the swinging doors that led to the kitchen and the rear entrance.

There was a bench right outside the back door, in the bright morning sun. Heather sat down on it and pulled coax-ingly on Jared's hand so he would join her. He dropped down beside her.

Right next door to the café was Santino's BBV—Barber, Beauty and Variety. Jared said nothing for a moment as he watched Maria Santino, who ran both the *Beauty* and the *Variety* parts of the store, lean out an upstairs window and shake the dust from a throw rug. The Santino family lived on the upper floor. Mrs. Santino spotted Jared and Heather and gave them a wave. Jared nodded.

Heather called, ''Hi!'' and then tactfully waited until Mrs. Santino had disappeared inside. Then she asked quietly, ''Dad, are you okay?''

''Fine.''

''But you've…had a fight, right?''

He gave his eye a careful tap. ''You mean this?''

She nodded, looking subdued and concerned.

''No, not a fight. Not exactly, anyway.''

''Then what?''

''Look. It wasn't a fight. And no one else was hurt, so you don't need to worry.''

''You mean you don't want to talk about it?''

''You got it.''

''Okay, Dad.'' Heather closed her eyes, turned her face up to the sun and waited. She was a hell of a girl, his Heather. She knew when to keep her mouth shut—unlike some people he could think of.

Jared remembered she had to return to work in a few minutes, so he went straight to the point. ''I hear you rented my cabin.''

Heather's eyes popped open and she looked at him. ''Did I do wrong?''

''Well…''

Heather was all contrition. ''Oh, I *knew* I should have waited to talk to you first.''

''Then why didn't you?''

''Oh, Dad. A lot of reasons. I never know when you'll show up, for one thing. And Eden's such a terrific lady. And Grandpa and Laurie—heck, everyone in the family, really—thought it was a great idea. And Grandpa made it so easy. He stored your things. He also insisted that there's no reason you can't stay with him whenever you come to town. And also, I thought you'd like the extra money.''

Heather sighed. "But I should have waited, I can see that now."

Awkwardly Jared patted her hand. "It's okay, honey. You only did what you thought I wanted. Don't worry. I'll work it out."

"Dad?" Heather peered at him anxiously. "You didn't...scare Eden, did you? You didn't show up at the cabin in the middle of the night and order her out or anything...did you?"

He coughed. "What do you mean, *scare*?"

Heather looked at him for a moment more, then shook her head. "Oh, Dad. Is she okay?"

Jared snorted. "More okay than I am."

He watched Heather's face and saw understanding dawn. "Oh, my goodness. *She* punched you in the eye?"

"Not really. She threw a clock at me."

Heather clucked her tongue. "That Eden. She's something."

Jared leaned his head back against the wall of the café and wondered why he couldn't get more sympathy from his own flesh and blood.

Heather asked, "Dad, I know this is a crazy notion. But since you aren't happy about having a tenant at the cabin, is it possible that you're thinking of moving back to town?"

He took a minute before he answered. "Yeah."

She stared at him. "Really? You're moving back to town?"

"Right."

"Oh," his daughter said.

That *oh* told Jared everything. When he'd left for the woods two years ago, he'd sworn it was for good. He'd vowed he was through with towns and people, that an occasional visit to civilization was about all that he could take. Judging by his daughter's shock at the news that he was coming home to stay, he realized he must have been very convincing back then.

But that had been a rough time for him. It was right after Belle, his second wife, had taken her two sons and returned to her first husband. He'd had to get away from people then, because he'd been as sensitive as a skinned rattler and every bit as mean. It had gotten so he could hardly walk down the street without ending up in a fight. And he'd been tempted—God, how he'd been tempted—to go back on the booze again.

But things were different now. He was ready now to try once more to get along with the rest of the world.

Beside him, Heather slowly smiled. "Well, okay. Now that I've had a minute to consider the idea, I think it's great, Dad. I'm glad. I've missed not having you around."

Jared squeezed her shoulder. "I've missed you, too. And besides, I've been thinking a lot about your grandpa lately. The past few times I've been to town, he's done nothing but complain that he's overworked running The Hole in the Wall alone. I think it's about time I helped him out a little. After all, the tavern will be mine someday. And he needs to start taking it easy. He's not getting any younger, you know."

Heather was looking at him strangely. "But Dad, I…" She seemed to run out of words.

"What?"

"Er…nobody's told you yet?"

"Told me what?"

Lily chose that moment to stick her head out the back door. "Heather, are you here to work or yak?"

"Be right in." Heather stood up. "Look, Dad, I—"

"I mean it, Heather," Lily insisted. "You got two new couples in the booths and three singles at the counter. They're all gettin' seriously irritated that they ain't even got coffee yet."

"But I—"

Jared took his daughter by the shoulders and turned her toward the door. "Don't be losing you job over me, Sunshine. We can talk later."

"Yeah," Lily said. "Like after her shift's over."

"Okay, Lil," Heather said just a tad curtly, "I will be there in one minute."

"You better," Lily growled, but she did leave them alone.

Heather turned back to Jared. "Dad, I—"

He cut her off. "It's okay. Whatever it is, it can wait a few hours."

"Sure. I guess so." Heather looked doubtful. "Just…um, stay calm, okay."

"Yeah. No problem."

She was smiling again, somewhat ruefully. And then she was going up on tiptoe to kiss his cheek. "Love you. Come for dinner tonight. Six sharp. I'll get Jason Lee to barbecue us some ribs."

"Sounds like a great idea."

"Does that mean yes?"

"You bet."

Jared watched as Heather disappeared through the door into the café, wondering what it could have been that she thought he should know yet was nervous about telling him.

Well, whatever she was afraid to tell him, he'd find out soon enough. This was North Magdalene, after all. And in North Magdalene, secrets lasted about as long as an ice cube in a forest fire.

Jared lifted his wrist to find out what time it was and realized he'd run off without his watch, an oversight he blamed on the redhead who'd stolen his house. Because of her, he'd been in a hell of hurry to get out of there. Grabbing his watch had been the last thing on his mind.

He shaded his eyes and checked the position of the sun:

around ten. His father, still a night owl even now in his seventies, would be unlikely to show up at The Hole in the Wall until at least noon. Ten to one, the old coot was still sprawled on his bed, snoring away.

Jared decided it was time Oggie woke up. So he walked around the side of the café, climbed into his pickup and headed down Main Street.

He had to pass The Hole in the Wall before he made the turn that would take him to his father's house. One look at the bar his father had owned since before Jared was born, and Jared knew something really strange was going on.

The tavern was transformed. There was a fancy sign out front that announced The Hole in the Wall in lariat script. Red café curtains hung in the spic-and-span windows. And the several layers of paint that had been peeling off the exterior of the building the last time Jared had seen it were now completely camouflaged by new wood shingles.

Jared swore roundly under his breath and managed to swerve just in time to avoid hitting the fire hydrant on the corner. He was damned anxious to have a few words with the old man now. Something was definitely going on. More and more, it looked as if Oggie would be the one who could tell him just what it was.

When he pulled up in front of the house where he'd grown up, he wasted no time. He jumped out of the pickup and marched up to the door, which he banged on for a good minute to give the old man a chance to get his butt out of bed. Then he waited, expecting a rumpled, grouchy Oggie to fling back the door and swear at him for disturbing an old man's slumber. But that didn't happen.

He tried the door. It was open so he went on in.

A quick pass through all the rooms proved that Oggie wasn't there. So Jared went out back to check the garage. Not counting the usual clutter, he found it empty. Oggie's ancient Eldorado was nowhere to be seen.

Jared stood in the driveway and rubbed his chin. Then he climbed back in his pickup and headed for Main Street once more.

At exactly ten-thirty, Eden parked her car in the small lot behind The Hole in the Wall. She got out of the car and did *not* lock it behind her. That was another thing she loved about North Magdalene. You never had to lock up anything. No one ever stole anything here. It simply was not done. She let herself in the back way with her own key and set about getting ready to open up at eleven.

Inside, the tavern was as dim and shadowy as most bars, but much cleaner and more welcoming than it had been before Eden became Oggie's partner. Eden smiled to herself in satisfaction at the scrubbed-clean bar and tables and the deep shine she herself had waxed into the hardwood floor. She glanced up in approval at the new molded ceiling. She'd paid for it and had it installed not too long ago. The old one had been riddled with bullet holes. Oggie used to be forever shooting holes in it with his .38 special, trying to get his customers' attention long enough that they'd break up whatever brawl happened to be going on at the time.

Since Eden had become Oggie's partner, there had been no brawls.

Yes, Eden had done a heck of a job with the place. And next spring, when she opened up The Mercantile Grill in the vacant landmark building next door, people would be coming from the small towns all around the area to enjoy an evening of good food and good times in the charming gold rush town of North Magdalene. Feeling quite satisfied with herself and her plans, Eden went about counting the take from last night and setting up the cash drawer for the day and evening ahead. She had the drawer in order and was sliding it back into the register, when she thought she heard the back door squeak.

She turned around and peered into the shadows of the hall that led to the door. But she saw no one, so she shrugged and went out to the main floor to take the chairs off the tables, where Oggie left them each night after mopping up.

A moment later, she turned around again and came face-to-face with Jared Jones.

Eden gasped in frightened surprise. And then she realized who it was.

"What is the matter with you?" She exerted great effort to keep her voice calm. "Can't you enter a room like a normal human being?"

"Sorry." He didn't look sorry at all. He immediately demanded, "And just what the hell are you doing here?"

Eden glared at him. She was getting tired of the way he kept popping up out of nowhere every time she turned around. Also, she was not looking forward to his reaction when she told him why she was here. She wished she had told him earlier, as she'd meant to, right after he'd finished that nice breakfast she'd cooked for him. Now, in the dimness of the deserted tavern, with him scowling and fuming at her, seemed altogether a bad time.

Well, to be honest, anytime was probably a bad time.

She decided to put off answering him, though she knew that in the end there was no escaping his finding out. She turned her back on him again and continued taking down the chairs.

Jared wasn't about to be stalled. He grabbed her elbow. "Answer me, damn it." He whirled her around to face him.

And their eyes met.

And it was happening again. The exact same way it had happened this morning, only more intense. As sudden as a flash fire and every bit as hot, it arced between them. A searing burst of sexual heat.

"Damn," he muttered darkly. He tugged her up closer, so her breasts just grazed his hard chest.

Eden felt her nipples tightening, a sweetly agonizing sensation that set off an answering awareness in her most private place.

"Oh, no," she whispered on a breath.

"Damn," he said again.

Then, heaven knew how, she found the strength to pull away. He didn't try to stop her. In fact, he let go and quickly stepped back from her.

Shaken, weak-kneed, she patted her hair, which he'd never even touched. Then she pulled herself together and forced herself to take down the last of chairs.

She was careful, as she did this, not to look at him. And anyway, she didn't *need* to look at him. She knew exactly what he was doing. It was just what she was doing. He was trying to put that instant of hunger and desire they'd just shared completely out of his mind.

At last he demanded, "Where's my father?"

Lord, she thought, this is an effort. This man is rude and crude. He doesn't even have a good sense of humor. And still I wish he'd grab me and hold me close and put his lips on mine and...oh, I can't let myself even *think* what else.

She wanted to tell him to take a hike—almost as much as she longed to move closer to him and see if he'd grab more than her arm this time.

Somehow, she kept her distance and spoke civilly. "If he's not at his house, he's probably fishing. But I don't really know. He's not due in here until seven tonight."

He scanned the large, shadowy room, obviously ticking off the changes she'd made. "How long have you been working for my father?"

"Three months." Eden drew herself up. Then she said the words that she regretted almost before they were fully out of her mouth. "And I don't work *for* him, I work *with* him. We're partners."

The pause that ensued lasted a very long time. Eden stared at his stunned face and accepted the grim fact that she'd really put her foot in it. She truly had meant to tell him about the partnership in a more tactful manner. But a woman would have to be a saint to stay diplomatic around this barbarian.

"Partners?" Jared's dismay was painful to look at.

"Yes." From the way he was looking at her, Eden decided maybe she'd be better off to put a little distance between them. She trotted purposefully to the end of the bar. The flap there was up, so she darted through the opening, flipping it shut behind her.

Once she had the bar between them, she dared to face him. He was watching her the way a cat looks at a canary. If he'd had a tail, it would have been twitching. She was acutely aware that the bar would be no barrier at all if he really wanted to get to her.

Jared spoke, his voice low and icy cold. "I suppose you have some damn piece of paper that says you own half this place, just like you've got one that says you can stay in my house."

She knew it would do no good to hedge. She looked him square in the eye. "I've spent most of my savings, between what I paid your father outright to become his partner and the improvements I've made since then. You can be sure I have a contract that says what I *get* in return for what I've spent." Then she added without pausing to consider what the words would imply. "I am not a fool."

Jared leapt over the bar. He did it so swiftly and gracefully that, to Eden, it was as if he never moved, as if he dematerialized in one place and reappeared right in front of her.

"Oh!" she managed to murmur in surprise, before he

grabbed her by the arms and yanked her up against his chest. "Are you calling *me* a fool, Miss Parker?" His voice was soft—too soft.

And all those awful, wonderful feelings that seemed to occur whenever he touched her were occurring again.

Eden's last trace of reckless bravado fled. She gaped at him. "No. No, I'm not. I swear to you..."

He breathed the next words into her upturned face. "But you know damn well this place is supposed to be mine someday. You know that it's promised to me when my old man dies, don't you?"

Eden blinked. She was totally disoriented. First, there was the feel of him, so close, his hard chest against her breasts. And then there was his claim about The Hole in the Wall, a claim that she knew had at least some validity to it. "B-but I was told you never cared about the place..."

"By who?"

"By Laurie. And your father. By your brothers and your sister Delilah. By everybody. They all said you would never come back to live in town and if you did, the last thing you'd want to do was run the bar. After all, you're an..." Eden gulped as the sentence trailed off unfinished.

Talk about tactless! What she had been about to say was way out of line. It was not something any considerate person would throw in a man's face after having known him less than twenty-four hours. Somehow, Jared Jones brought out her most insensitive side.

"I'm what?"

"Jared, look..."

He released her then, setting her away from him carefully—as if she were some sort of human detonating device, dangerous to touch, to be handled with extreme caution.

He stepped back. "No. Say what you were about to say."

"Jared—"

"All right. *I'll* say it." He spoke with great precision. "I am an alcoholic. That is why I do not drink. I haven't had a drink in over fifteen years now. And I have no trouble at all being in a bar for long periods of time without *taking* a drink. In fact, that's exactly what I do every time I come to town. I come here, where most of the bad actors like me hang out. I drink cola. And I manage, in my own low-class way, to have a helluva time.''

"Jared, I—"

"I'm not through talking yet."

"O-okay."

"So, my point is, my being an alcoholic wouldn't stop me from running this place. And my old man knows it, too.''

"I see. I—"

"And as for that other feeble excuse you just threw at me, that I don't *care* about this bar. Well, Miss Parker, get this. Whether I care or not doesn't matter a damn. What matters is that my father had three sons and one daughter, and he made a promise to each one of us. He promised that when he dies, his house goes to Brendan, the house our mother got from *her* father to Delilah, The Mercantile building next door to Patrick and *this bar to me*.''

Eden swallowed hard and then forced what she hoped was a coaxing smile. "B-but you'll still get *half* of it someday.'' As she said that, she silently prayed that Oggie would live a long, long time. Being partners with Jared Jones was not her idea of something to look forward to. Jared continued to scowl at her. She babbled on, "I swear, Oggie said it would be okay with you, that you'd be glad to hear he found himself some help.''

"And naturally you just took his word for it.''

Eden did feel awful. And she knew her guilt could be heard in her voice as she trotted out more justifications. "Your father said you'd understand. I guess I really wanted to believe him. And since there was no trust agreement involved, I didn't question him too much about it. And everybody really did say you wouldn't mind, that as soon as you saw what a good thing this was for Oggie, you'd go along…''

"They all said I'd go along." He repeated her words as if testing their veracity.

"Yes." She lifted her chin. "They did."

Jared peered at her. She felt that he was trying to see into her mind, to ferret out whether she was telling him anything close to the truth.

At last he said, "All right. That makes sense."

"You believe me?" She tried not to sound as amazed as she felt.

"I said it makes sense. And I can see you're not at fault here."

Eden released a long sigh of relief.

But she realized she'd sighed too soon when Jared added, "My father's the one to blame. That old coot, I'll wrap his damn fishing pole around his neck."

Visions of poor Oggie, strangled to death by his own son, flashed through her mind. "Oh, you wouldn't. Not really."

Jared didn't answer. Instead, he jumped over the bar again and headed out the way he'd come in.

"Wait! He's an old man. You won't really hurt him, will you?"

But all she got in reply was the squeak of the back door as it swung shut behind him.

Chapter Five

At the end of Bullfinch Lane, right where he thought it might be, Jared found his father's Cadillac. He pulled in beside the dusty old boat of a car. Then he got out of his pickup and started down the steep path that led to the river below.

When he reached the river's edge he didn't have to look far. To the right of the trail, where the rocks petered out to dirt ground, a big, gnarled oak grew close to the stream. There Oggie sat, his back propped against the oak, his fishing line bobbing on the current a few yards away. The old cheat appeared to be sound asleep.

"Dad?"

Oggie snorted a little at the sound of his son's voice, but he didn't wake up.

"Dad?"

In his sleep, Oggie turned his head away from Jared and his fishing pole sank a little closer to the surface of the stream. Jared started to shake him, but then something made him hesitate.

Jared gazed down at the top of his father's head. He couldn't help noticing that what was left of the old scoundrel's hair was all white now. The wispy strands framed a bald crown dusted with age spots. Oggie's chin drooped on his chest, the loose skin of his neck hanging wattles. His hands, folded on his slightly protruding belly, looked as wrinkled and gnarled as the aged oak he was leaning against, now Jared could see them in repose. Strange, for all of Jared's life, his father's hands had always seemed so swift and sure. No one could mix a drink with the style and grace of Oggie Jones....

"What the hell you gawkin' at, boy?" Oggie turned his head and winked at him. His face was a road map of a long, hard-lived life.

Jared shook himself. He'd almost started to feel sorry for his father. And the last thing a swindler deserved was sympathy.

"You old bastard," Jared accused. "You were awake the whole time."

Oggie chortled. "Ah son, it's good to see your ugly mug. Whoa. That's quite a shiner you got there."

Jared didn't want to talk about the black eye Eden had given him. "I ran into a door."

"Yeah. Right. Where you been keepin' yourself, anyway?" Oggie patted the ground beside him.

But Jared wasn't about to sit down. He wanted the truth. "Why'd you screw me over, Dad?"

"Screw you over?" Oggie yanked his line out of the water and set his pole on the ground. He sat up straighter and assumed an expression of outraged dignity. "Who says I screwed you over? You give it to me straight. I'll beat the livin' daylights out of whoever thought he could—"

"Cut the malarkey, Dad. You took on a partner over at

The Hole in the Wall. I know it. You know it. Everybody knows it. You also pushed Heather into renting out my place.''

"Now you listen here, Jared Jones, *you're* the one who told Heather to find a tenant and—"

"She wouldn't have done it without you pushing her into it. She would have waited to talk to me."

"Yeah. Sure. And when exactly would that have been? We never know when the hell you'll show up anymore. If we waited to do what needs doin' until after consultin' you, nothin'd get done around here, and that's a plain fact."

"You always promised that bar to me, old man."

"And you'll still get half of it."

Jared snorted. "Half. Thanks a lot. What you did wasn't right."

"I did what I had to do."

"Yeah. What you had to do. Sure. Without even a word to me. When we both know I've got rights to that place, that I've put my own good money in on that place—from the card room at the back to the plumbing to the wiring to that new pool table you just had to have last summer."

Oggie sniffed. "Well, it's right you should put in on what will someday be yours."

"Exactly. Mine. *All* mine." Jared turned from his father, looked out over the river and concentrated hard on staying calm. Right then, his hands were just itching to close around the old fraud's neck.

Behind him, he heard Oggie haul himself, grunting, to his feet. Then he felt his father's hand on his shoulder. "Okay, son. I admit. I acted out of line. I oughtta be gutted and skinned and hung up for quartering."

Jared pulled away from his father's touch. "Damn you, old man. You could have at least let me know what you were planning. You didn't have to let me find it out like this."

"Now listen to yourself, will you?" Oggie pulled a stubby cigar from his shirt pocket. He studied the cigar for a moment, then bit off the end and spit it into the river. "Just think about what you're asking here. How exactly was I to let you know? When you disappear into the woods, no one can find you for months." Oggie gestured grandly with the cigar as he pulled out a book of matches. "You're with a crew up by Tahoe, then you're over near Hayfork. The only way we know you're alive is when a check comes for Heather in the mail. I knew you'd find out when you finally showed up. It's all worked out fine." Oggie stuck the cigar in his mouth and put a match to it. Then he puffed until the end of it glowed red.

Jared stuck his hands into his pockets—to keep from picking up his father and tossing him into the river in front of them. "If you weren't my father, I'd—"

Oggie blew a cloud of smoke and let loose with that watery cackle of his. "Settle down, boy. I always take care of my own, and you know it. You're still gonna get half of that bar. And that little gal I partnered up with has got one fine head for business. By the time I go to be with your mama, the half you get will be worth twice what the whole shebang was before Eden Parker came along. I'm gettin' old, and I'm gettin' tired. I needed a little help around that place. And then Eden showed up. It was like the answer to a prayer."

Now that he had his cigar going, Oggie clamped it between his teeth, picked up his fishing pole and reeled in his line. Then he set about gathering up his gear, pausing only to glance at his son and explain, "You know, this year is the first year since I was knee-high to a horsefly that I've gone fishing. I never had the time before. And I'd like to try to get me a buck this deer season. Truth is, I'm headin' home right now to get down my old huntin' rifle and clean it up nice."

"Damn it, Dad…"

"C'mon boy, what's done is done. And maybe it'll turn out just fine in the end anyway. In any case, you'll know your old man's gettin' a little time to himself in his wanin' years."

Hearing his father put it that way, Jared felt all the fight go out of him. Hell, the old man was right. Oggie had needed someone to work with him. He'd said so more than once. Jared had never been quite willing to provide that help. And then Eden Parker had come along.

The simple fact was, Jared had returned too late.

Slowly Jared sank to the ground in the space his father had left and leaned his back against the old tree. He closed his eyes. For a few minutes, there was only the sighing of the wind in the pines and the soft rush of the river flowing past.

Then Oggie asked, "What's happened, son?"

Jared didn't even open his eyes. "The company's shutting down. I've been laid off. I'm through running logging crews. The damn spotted owls are getting their revenge."

Oggie heard his father huffing as he sank beside him. "Hell, son. Tough break."

"Yeah."

"So what'll you do?"

"I'll get by."

"You bet you will."

"And besides…"

"Yeah, son?"

Jared picked up a flat rock and skipped it across the river. "Well, just lately I've been thinking it's time I got over what happened with Belle. Time I stopped hiding out and feeling sorry for myself."

Oggie lit up like a light bulb. "Are you sayin' what I hope you're sayin'?"

Jared looked at his father sideways. "What's that?"

"That you're ready to try again at findin' the right woman for you?"

Jared stood up. "Stop it, old man. Stop it before you even get started. Two out of four of your kids are happily married. Be satisfied with that. I'm back because I think it's time I learned to get along with people, in general. But I'm through with *women*. And that means love and marriage and all that bunk. I'm just no good at that stuff, and that's a proven fact."

"You worked things out with Sally in the end, didn't you?"

"Yeah. I did. But we had a damn rough time doing it."

"But the point is, you *did* do it."

"Look, Dad. Let's drop this subject, okay?"

"I'm only saying that you've married two women and you did okay with one of 'em, when all was said and done. In this day and age, one out of two ain't half-bad. And, if you ask me—"

"I'm *not* asking you, Dad."

"Don't interrupt. If you ask me, the problem with Belle was that you jumped right to the wedding, without stopping to, um, smell the flowers first."

"Dad. Drop it."

"No, it's time you thought about this. Maybe part of your problem is you always thought you should be married to a woman before you—"

Jared picked up his father's tackle box and the wicker basket in which the old man's catch was stored and started for the trail to the road.

Oggie, grabbing up his pole, hustled after him. "Wait up. And I don't see why we can't talk about this. I'm only sayin' that if you'd a slept with Belle first, you might have found out—"

Jared turned on his father. "Did *you* sleep with Ma before you married her?"

Oggie's beady black eyes went wide. He stopped on the trail. "What's got into you son, askin' questions like that about your sainted mother?"

"Just giving you a taste of what it feels like to have another man pry into your private life."

"All right, all right." Oggie puffed on his cigar and waved at Jared to move on up the trail. They walked the rest of the way to the Cadillac without speaking.

Then Oggie went to the trunk and opened it. "You're home to stay, then?"

Jared tossed the tackle box and the basket of fish into the trunk. "I thought so. But I also thought I'd go in with you at the bar. Now, I don't know. Maybe I'll head down to Sacramento, see if I can find something there."

Oggie took his pole apart and tucked the two sections in next to the tackle box. "The hell you will. You'll stay right here." He closed the trunk. "You'll take over your half of The Hole in the Wall now. I got my nest egg put aside. I'm more than ready to retire."

Jared shook his head. "Thanks, Dad. But it would never work."

"Why not?"

"You've got a partner. You don't need me."

"Hell yes, I need you. I'm seventy-five. I need all the help I can get. You got a problem with Eden, is that what we're talkin' about here?"

"No," Jared muttered. "She's fine. I've got no problem with her." He leaned against the dusty back door of the Cadillac and looked away toward the trail they'd just come up.

"Good," Oggie said. "'Cause truth to tell, son, I got a soft spot for Eden. That sweet little gal kinda reminds me of your mother."

Jared's head snapped around. "My God, Dad. What are

you talking about? She's nothing like Ma. Ma didn't have orange hair.''

Oggie actually looked kind of dreamy. ''That hair of hers is strawberry-blond, boy. Strawberry-blond. And I was talkin' more about her smile, that wide, sweet mouth she's got. And those legs. Why, that gal's got legs longer than—''

Jared wasn't about to hear any more of this. He'd seen Eden's legs. He gave his father a stern look. ''For godsakes, Dad. You're old enough to be her *grandfather*. Hell, you could be her *great*-grandfather. You have to be aware of that!''

Oggie let out one of his raspy cackles. ''You always was a bit of a prude, boy. A hell of a temper and a mean man to cross. But more scruples than an old maid, yessiree.''

Jared knew he shouldn't ask, but somehow the words were out of his mouth all by themselves. ''Have you got something…going with her? Is that what you're telling me?''

Oggie looked wounded. ''You know me better than that, son. If I had something going with a woman, you wouldn't need to ask me about it. Everyone in town would know it. I'm a Jones, after all.''

Jared clamped his mouth shut. He wanted to demand the truth of his father. He wanted to know for certain if Oggie was more than a business partner to Eden Parker. But that was none of his concern and Jared knew it damned well.

And then Oggie volunteered, ''Naw, there's nothin' between her and me, son. She thinks of me as a second father. But an old man can dream, can't he?''

Jared sighed. He felt relief, and he had no intention whatsoever of examining why. He clapped his father on the shoulder. ''Hell, Dad. Sure. Why not?''

Oggie got into his car and then rolled down the window. ''Look. Give yourself a few days before you head out of town. Think it over, 'cause I really am ready to retire.''

"I've made up my mind, Dad."

Oggie started up the car. "We'll see. Tell you what. Follow me home. I'll fry you up some fresh trout."

Jared was halfway to his father's house, tagging obediently along behind the Cadillac, before he realized that he didn't trust the way his father had given in so easily, or the sound of the old rascal's voice when he had said, "We'll see…"

But then he shrugged. It really didn't matter what Oggie Jones had up his sleeve. Jared had made up his mind. Miss Eden Parker could have his house after all. He'd be moving on.

Chapter Six

It was well past midnight when Eden arrived back at the cabin. Friday nights were always busy at The Hole in the Wall. Eden always stayed as late as Oggie needed her. She did the same on Saturday nights and any other night when things were jumping. It didn't bother her in the least that she occasionally worked as many as sixteen hours in a day. Eden liked to work, especially since she'd joined forces with Oggie and she was working for herself. Usually a mere thirteen or fourteen hours on her feet didn't daunt her in the least.

But tonight Eden felt distinctly droopy as she got out of her car and trudged toward the natural stone steps that led up to the kitchen door. The events of late Thursday night and Friday morning had gotten to her. And realizing that she was going to have to find another place to live, even though she loved it right here, only increased her weariness.

Her mood was not improved when she saw the pickup

truck that was parked, as if it belonged there, beneath a fir tree that grew right by the front deck. It didn't take any serious mental gymnastics to guess whose pickup truck it might be. Eden dropped her key into her purse, since she was sure she was going to find her door unlocked.

But she was wrong. The door *was* locked, just as she'd left it when she went out the previous morning. She'd been careful, as she rarely was anymore, to lock it behind her. Which, now that she thought about it, was pretty silly. After all, the only person who would want to break in had a key of his own. Judging by the pickup under the tree, he'd used it, too. And then added insult to injury by locking Eden out.

All the lights inside seemed to be off. The rat was probably asleep up in the loft. She considered pounding on the door until he answered. But after measuring the paltry satisfaction of disturbing his slumber against the real trial it was to deal with him, Eden decided to let him sleep.

She had to fumble in her bag to retrieve the key. And then, since he hadn't bothered to leave on the light by the kitchen door, she had to fumble some more to get the key into the lock.

Once inside, she half expected him to leap on her from the shadows, demanding to know what the hell she thought she was doing in *his* house. But that didn't happen. She flipped on the kitchen light and saw that everything was pretty much as she'd left it, except for the single glass on the drainboard. Apparently Jared Jones had helped himself to a drink of water before turning in for the night.

Eden turned off the kitchen light behind her and went out into the main room. She started to flick on the wall switch to light her way to her room, but then she hesitated. If he really was asleep up there, which it seemed all but certain that he was, then the light might wake him. And if he woke, they'd only end up in another unpleasant scene. They could have one of those in the morning, after she'd had a good night's sleep. She turned from the stairs and started to make her way to her room in the dark.

But then she hesitated. She just plain wasn't comfortable with the idea of going off to her room not even knowing for sure whether there was someone else in the house. She'd never get to sleep, wondering if he was there, or if he wasn't there.

Better, she decided, to simply find out for sure. If she was very quiet and very careful, she was confident she could put her mind at ease without waking the brute and having to deal with him.

Gently she set down her purse and slipped out of her flats. And then, on tiptoe, she crept up the stairs.

At the top, she paused and peered through the shadows at the bed, which was up in the corner, on a diagonal from where she stood.

He was there, all right. There was no missing him. The moon was shining in the window nearby, bathing him in its silvery glow.

Eden didn't know she did it, but she sighed. When she should have turned around and crept back the way she'd come, she only stared, transfixed.

He was sprawled faceup, one muscled arm thrown across his face. His body was covered with his sleeping bag to the waist. His bare, powerful torso gleamed alabaster in the pale light from outside. Her gaze took in everything, from the ridged hardness of his belly, to the whorling trail of hair down his solar plexus to the soft shadow of the tuft beneath his arm.

Something…strange was taking form down inside her, a little bud of need, hot and tender.

Slowly, only half-aware that she was doing it, she approached him.

Far off, way back in her mind where reason was sequestered, there was a voice calling to her, *ordering* her to turn around and descend the stairs and go immediately to her room. But the voice was very far away. It added up to nothing when compared with the sweet siren's call of her own blood.

Before she knew how it had happened, she was standing right beside the bed, looking down at him.

He lay there so still and splendid. Yes, splendid was the word for him, lying there in a spill of moonbeams, looking like a statue of masculine perfection come to life and then fallen asleep on her spare bed.

His hard chest rose and fell evenly. Beneath the arm he'd thrown over his eyes, the grim line of his lips was softened now with sleep. Hardly daring to breathe, knowing she shouldn't, yet unable to stop herself, Eden bent nearer to those tenderly parted lips.

And that was when he reached out with the arm not thrown across his eyes and grabbed her wrist.

Eden shrieked and jumped back. But she didn't get far, because he didn't let go.

Jared dropped the arm that shielded his face. His eyes were open. "Something I can do for you?"

"Let go of me!"

He instantly released her wrist and then actually made a placating gesture. "Look. Settle down. It was only a joke."

"Your sense of humor eludes me. You *scared* me. You're *always* scaring me."

"Sorry. Okay? Finesse is not my strong suit. But I don't want to fight with you. I swear it."

She backed toward the stairs, bewildered by how decently he was acting about this. Not to mention chagrined at her own behavior. After all, he never would have had the chance to grab her and scare her again if she hadn't been sneaking around trying to get a closer look at him while he was supposedly sound asleep.

She clutched desperately for the original issue. And miraculously remembered it. "I told you to leave. You have no right to be here."

"Will you just settle down? Just...take it easy, okay?" He sat up. She tried not to look as the sleeping bag fell away a little. "Busy night at The Hole in the Wall?"

"Yes. Very busy." She hitched in a tight breath and forced herself to speak evenly. "And you really must leave tomorrow."

He surprised her by allowing in a perfectly reasonable tone, "I know."

"Y-you do?"

"Yeah. I spoke with my old man. Everything's worked out."

"What do you mean?"

"You're his partner. That's how he wants it. That's good enough for me."

"Oh. I see. Well, good then."

"And you can forget moving out. I've had a little time to think this afternoon and I decided that Heather and Jason Lee can use the money every month for their house payment. From now on, you just make out the rent checks to Heather, all right?"

"To Heather? Well, I—"

He let out a disgusted grunt. "Oh. Right. I forgot. You gotta have a legal document before you'll agree on the time of day."

"That's not it. I—"

"Well, don't worry. We'll write something up tomorrow, before I leave. Fair enough?"

"Sure. Fine. But—"

"But what?"

"Well, I mean, what about you? Where will you live?"

His sculpted, moonlit shoulders lifted in a shrug. "It's not a problem. I won't be staying in town after all."

Eden absorbed this information with a truly ridiculous

mingling of guilt and sadness. She had his house and half his inheritance. And now he'd have to go elsewhere to find a place for himself. Good Lord. She almost felt like crying.

"Where will you go?"

He shrugged again. "I don't know yet. Maybe down in the valley. Sacramento, Stockton. I'll work it out."

"You don't have any plan?"

He actually smiled. It was the first time she'd ever seen him do that. The little bud of tender need inside her began to bloom. "Don't worry about me, Miss Parker. I'm a tough customer. I'll get by. And you're right. I shouldn't be here. I came back here after a nice dinner with my daughter and her husband, and I really was planning to take my things and go. But then I couldn't resist getting one more rise out of you before I pulled up stakes. I can stay with my father until I'm ready to leave town. I'll be out of here tomorrow morning."

"Oh." She felt terrible, all achy and crestfallen. What in heaven's name was the matter with her? She heard her own voice weakly proposing, "I'll make you breakfast. Before you go."

"You're on."

"O-okay, then. Good night…"

"Good night, Miss Parker."

She backed halfway down the stairs before she turned and fled to her own room, not even pausing to pick up her purse and her shoes. Then she undressed in a daze and lay down on her bed and tried not to think how much she was going to miss a man she hardly even knew.

"Have you seen baby Bathsheba yet?" Eden asked as she watched Jared pour half a bottle of syrup on his second helping of pancakes. Baby Bathsheba was the two-month-old daughter of Brendan, Jared's brother.

"Yeah." Jared set the syrup down and sipped from his

coffee. This morning, she hadn't had to remind him of his manners. He was eating enough for a small army, but he was doing it slowly and with great care.

He was also back to being his old taciturn self. Unlike those few moments in the moonlight last night, he was revealing nothing that she didn't pry out of him first.

Eden, on the other hand, was feeling nervous. Edgy. So naturally, she wanted to talk.

And she did.

"When did you see her?"

"Who?"

"Baby Bathsheba."

"Last night."

"Isn't she beautiful? Did Amy bring her over to Heather's, then?" Amy was Brendan's wife.

"Yes."

"I think Amy looks terrific, don't you? I mean, it's only two months since the baby came and you can hardly tell she was ever pregnant. Brendan is so proud, of both his beautiful daughter and his gorgeous wife. Well, we all know how Brendan is about Amy anyway. But it seems like he's just more in love with her every day. Honestly, it's just incredible to see." Eden pushed back her chair and went to the coffeepot to refill her cup. Still standing at the counter, she held the pot out to Jared. "More?"

"Sure."

She cheerfully trotted over and poured him a cup. "There."

He looked up at her. "Thanks."

"You're welcome." Standing right above him like this, she could smell the shaving cream he must have used when he shaved. She liked it. And his hair, which she hadn't really paid a huge amount of attention to before, was very silky-looking, a rich brown color, threaded very lightly with silver. Also, she could really look at the eye she'd clobbered.

It seemed a little better this morning. The swelling seemed to have receded a tiny bit, though it was still a lurid purple.

He was still looking at her, so she ventured, "Jared?"

"Yeah?"

"I'm really sorry. About your eye."

He shrugged. "I'll live."

She realized she'd been standing there, gaping down at him for an inordinate amount of time. So she shook herself and took the coffeepot back to the warming plate. Then she returned to her chair.

For a while, since he volunteered nothing, she managed to sip her coffee and finish her breakfast and be quiet. But soon enough, the silence was too much for her.

"Did Oggie tell you about my plans for the restaurant?"

Jared was just mopping up the last of his pancakes. He looked up. "No."

"Well, it's pretty exciting, actually. Next spring, we're opening a restaurant next door to the tavern. In The Mercantile building? It'll be called The Mercantile Grill, and we'll knock out the walls between the tavern and the restaurant, make them a joint venture, if you know what I mean. Oh, and you don't have to worry about Patrick being cheated out of *his* inheritance, because he's going in with Oggie and me on this particular project."

Jared actually said something of his own accord then. "Patrick, opening a *restaurant?*"

Eden understood his disbelief. Patrick, Oggie's second son, had worked on the county roads, done a stint in construction and was an excellent mechanic. Though he could tend bar when forced to, he was not the kind of man one pictured as a restaurateur. Still, Eden was sure it would work out, because she intended to see that it did.

"I know, it sounds incredible. But don't worry. Patrick won't be doing it alone. In fact, I'm the one who'll really be running things."

"I'll bet."

"Do I detect a note of sarcasm there?"

Jared rolled his eyes a little, but said nothing more.

Eden babbled on. "Well, Mr. Jones. You just wait and see. You come for dinner on the house at The Mercantile Grill. Say, the Fourth of July next year."

Jared stood up. "Fair enough, Miss Parker." He picked up his plate and flatware and carried it to the counter by the sink. Then he stuck in the drain stopper and filled up the sink, adding dishwashing liquid as the water ran.

Eden watched him for a moment before she realized that he intended to do the dishes. She almost told him not to bother, she'd take care of them. But then she decided that his cleaning up after she cooked was a nice gesture. No reason for her to spoil it.

So instead of objecting, she helped him a little, carrying her own dishes over, clearing the table and wiping down the counters. She kept up a pretty steady stream of chatter as the work was done. He said little, only replying when she asked him something directly.

Eden knew she should probably just be quiet. But as the minutes ticked by and the time for him to leave loomed ever closer, she found she felt sadder and sadder. Talking helped her deny the sadness somewhat.

After the dishes were put away, he insisted she write up a short addendum to the rental agreement. It said she was to make out the rent checks to Heather from now on. They both signed it.

Then Jared went upstairs to collect his things. He was back in nothing flat, his sleeping bag slung over his shoulder and his pack in his fist.

Eden was waiting for him at the foot of the stairs. "Have you got everything?"

"Yeah." His voice was gruff. "This is it."

She stood back. He walked past her, into the kitchen and

over to the kitchen door. She trailed after him, feeling absurdly bereft.

And then, before she knew it, they were standing at the door facing each other. It was time to say goodbye.

Eden swallowed and started talking. "Well, then. I...suppose I'll see you again, before you leave. I mean, it's a small town. And I'm sure you'll be back, now and then, since your family's here and all...." He was standing very close. She was smelling him again—soap and shaving cream and man. She kept talking. "You'll want to visit Oggie. And Heather and Jason Lee, not to mention all of—"

"Miss Parker—"

"—your friends. You know, I heard you and Delilah's husband, Sam, used to be real drinking buddies. But, of course, as we discussed yesterday, you don't drink anymore, though. I heard you gave it up after, well, after your first divorce, because you loved your wife, Sally, and you wanted to get back with her. And then, you two did work things out, and you got married for the second time, to each other and everything was fine. But then poor Sally got squashed flat by that runaway logging truck and—"

"Miss Parker?"

"Um. Yes?"

"Do you ever shut up?"

"Well, I—"

"I can think of much better uses for that mouth of yours than talking."

Eden blinked at him and the mouth he was referring to dropped open. "Ex-excuse me?"

"I said, there are other things to do with your mouth than talking."

"Oh. I see." She was staring at *his* mouth, which, strangely, seemed to be almost as soft and tempting as it had been last night, during those forbidden moments when she'd spied on him in the moonlight.

"Other things," she echoed idiotically.

"You want me to show you?"

Did she nod? She wasn't sure. If she did, she shouldn't have. Yet if she didn't, she wanted to.

But whether she nodded or not, it happened anyway.

His mouth descended and closed over hers.

Eden gasped. And then softly sighed. She heard a pair of thuds, dimly, in the distance, as his pack and sleeping bag hit the floor. She expected him to reach out, then, and haul her hard and close against him.

But he didn't. He just went on kissing her, his body straining toward her, and his mouth…oh, sweet heaven, his mouth…

His mouth tasted her, and stroked her and worked gently, nudging, coaxing, until her own lips were parting, and his tongue was teasing, playing, mating with hers.

Eden groaned. And then she was the one reaching out, twining her arms around his neck and pressing herself hungrily, shamelessly into his heat and hardness. Her breasts flattened against his chest and the cradle of her hips rubbed against his. She could feel how much he wanted her, then, and she groaned again.

That did it. He groaned back. His arms went around her.

Eden sighed her appreciation at being held by him, so tight and close. It was wonderful. It was heaven. It was the kind of thing that only happened in sexy novels and it was happening to her. She wanted it never to end.

But of course, it did.

Jared ended it. He did it very tenderly, sliding his hands to her shoulders, gripping them gently and then slowly, reluctantly, lifting his head.

Her eyes fluttered open and she looked first at his mouth. It was swollen a little, from the kiss. Hesitantly she raised her glance. She saw that his injured lid was opened now to a slit. He watched her through that slit and she felt that his gaze set off sparks where it touched her.

Eden lifted a hand and laid the pads of two fingers on her own lips. Were they swollen like his? They'd have to be, wouldn't they? After what they'd just been through.

Still dazed, she watched as he bent and retrieved his gear. When their eyes met again, she could read nothing in his. The fire had been banked. She looked into cold steel.

"That was a damn fool thing for me to do," he said. "But I've always been a damn fool. Goodbye, Miss Parker."

"Bye..." she said in a croak.

He pulled back the door and went out.

Eden stood in the doorway and watched him drive off.

She was still standing there several minutes after his pickup had disappeared from sight.

She was trying, befuddled as her poor mind was right then, to comprehend the enormity of what had just transpired between herself and her surly landlord. She was trying to fathom the unfathomable: the meaning of a kiss.

She was unsuccessful in her efforts.

All she knew was that the foundations of her reality had suddenly shifted, leaving her perched on an emotional precipice and foolishly longing to fling herself into the chasm below. She yearned with all her heart to chase after his pickup and beg him to come back. At the same time she knew such an action would be totally foolish.

The man was forty years old—she'd learned that last night by asking Oggie a few subtle questions. Jared had always had trouble getting along with people. He'd been married three times—though, to be fair, two of those times were to the same person—and he thought nothing of sneaking into a woman's room in the middle of the night and scaring her to death. Eden could never get anything meaningful going with a man like that. She just *couldn't*. No way...

And, in the end, it didn't matter if she could *or* if she couldn't. Because Jared Jones wasn't going to be around for long. Within a day or two, he'd be heading out of town.

Sighing, Eden went back inside and finished getting ready for work. When her hair was pinned up and her makeup applied, she got into her car and drove into town and parked behind The Hole in the Wall.

Eden went inside and tackled her morning duties. For some reason, though, the mundane satisfaction she usually attained from the simple series of chores was missing today.

She had the chairs on the floor and was proceeding to get the popcorn popping and the cocktail mix set out when Rocky Collins pressed his hangdog face against one of the front windows, in the split between the red café curtains.

Eden glanced up at the big clock over the hall to the back door: 10:48. She really shouldn't let him in, though she knew that Oggie always used to, back when he ran the place himself.

Right from the first, she'd made the rule that the front double doors were unlocked at eleven sharp six days a week, never earlier and never later. Eden believed that starting things off punctually every day gave people an impression that here was a place they could count on. Besides, Eden didn't like to encourage poor Rocky, who spent way too much time here as it was.

But she *was* feeling just a little bit low today. And seeing Rocky looking lower than she felt, Eden's sympathies were aroused.

Against her own better judgment, she went and let him in.

"Gee darn, Eden. Thanks a million."

"Have a seat." She gestured at his favorite stool. "But I'm not serving until eleven sharp."

"Hey. I hear you. No problem, I swear." Rocky sat down and gave a luxurious sigh. He was a man who never felt quite at home if he wasn't leaning against a bar. "Hey, Eden?"

Eden measured the oil into the popper. "What is it, Rocky?"

"You got any aspirins?"

"Coming right up." She poured in the correct amount of popcorn kernels, flipped the metal lid closed and then pulled her hand out of the glass enclosure. She closed the glass doors and then she found Rocky his aspirin.

"Hey, thanks. You're okay," Rocky said.

"You're welcome." Eden started scooping cocktail mix into wooden bowls.

Right then, the phone beneath the bar rang.

"I'll get it," Rocky announced.

Before Eden could tell him she preferred to do it herself, he was standing on the rungs of his stool and hoisting the phone up onto the bar. He picked up the receiver.

"Yeah, hullo?" he grumbled into the mouthpiece, causing Eden to cringe. Proper telephone etiquette was another thing she insisted on at the new, improved Hole in the Wall. "Hey, howzitgoin', Jared, my man?"

Eden's heart suddenly rose and stuck somewhere near her throat. And while it was stuck there, it beat out his name.

Jared, Jared, Jared, Jared...

Settle down, she told her heart silently. *Settle down. He's probably just looking for Oggie....*

Rocky held out the handset. "'S for you, Eden."

Eden swallowed, to get her heart back where it belonged, and set down the bowl she was just about to fill. Then she took the phone from Rocky.

"Yes?"

His wonderful, low, sibilant voice hissed in her ear. "Bad news."

"What?"

"The old man."

"Oggie?"

"Yeah. He was cleaning his hunting rifle and—"

Eden felt numb, suddenly. There was a stool right beside her. She sank onto it. "Yes? Tell me."

"He shot himself in the foot."

Relief, as cool and soothing as clear water, coursed through her. She had thought for a moment that Jared would say the dear old coot was dead. "Is he all right?"

"As all right as he can be with a big hole in his foot. I'm at the hospital in Grass Valley now. They're patching him up."

"But is he—"

"Relax. He's going to be fine. Eventually."

"Oh, thank God."

"But he won't be standing up for a while."

"Well, of course."

"And he sure as hell won't be tending bar. In fact, he won't even be leaving the hospital for a day or two. Because of his age, they want to monitor him for a while."

"I understand. And tell him not to worry about The Hole in the Wall. I'll manage things here."

"Well, that's the other thing I called to tell you."

"What?"

"See, the gun went off just as I pulled up in front of his house."

"Yes. And?"

"And I ran in there, and it was—hell, it was a damn messy sight."

"So?"

"So I tried to pick him up, to carry him to my truck and get him here to the hospital."

"Yes?"

"But he wouldn't go."

"He wouldn't?"

"No. Not until I promised him that I'd take over for him at The Hole in the Wall until he was on his feet again."

Eden was silent, a rare thing.

Jared said, "So, I'm just calling to tell you. I'll be in at seven, same time as the old man always is."

"I—"

"We're just going to have to make the best of this, Eden."

Eden. He'd called her Eden. She was positive that was the first time she'd heard her given name on his lips. "Yes, I—"

"And after we shut down tonight, we'll talk. If that's convenient for you."

"Talk?"

"We'll come to an understanding. About how it's going to be."

"Oh."

"What does that mean, 'Oh'?"

"Nothing. Oh. That's all. Just oh."

"You understand, then?"

"About what?"

"About us coming to an understanding."

"Oh. Yes. I do. I understand. About an understanding."

"Tonight, then? After we close."

"Yes. All right."

And then she heard the click at the other end of the line. He had hung up. She took the receiver away from her ear and looked at it.

"Eden? You okay?"

"Why yes, Rocky. I'm just fine." She handed him the receiver. "Here. Hang this up for me, will you?"

"Be my pleasure. But, er, you'll have to give me the phone first."

Eden realized she was clutching the thing against her

chest. She coughed. "Certainly," she said, and shoved it at
him. He took it, grinning.

Eden turned quickly. With great purpose and dignity, she
returned to the other end of the bar where she recommenced
filling little wooden bowls with pretzels and nuts and small
toasted squares of salty cereal.

Chapter Seven

Jared arrived promptly at seven. He wore a new-looking pair of jeans, a tooled leather belt, a black vest and a black long-sleeved shirt. The shirt was open at the neck, the sleeves rolled neatly to below the elbows. His boots were dress boots. Eden's silly heart tried to jump out of her mouth at the sight of him.

And even beyond her personal response to him, Eden was thoroughly impressed. From a purely business standpoint, except for his black eye, he looked just great. Casual but professional, wearing a Western costume that was almost, but not quite, a uniform. It was exactly the image she was trying to cultivate at The Hole in the Wall. An image that Oggie, in his wrinkled shirts and grimy suspenders, had never managed to achieve.

Which was okay, she quickly told herself, feeling a little guilty for being critical of her partner, especially now, when the poor old dear was flat on his back with a hole in his foot. Oggie, after all, was Oggie. He brought a certain color and spontaneity to the tavern that would be sorely missed in his absence.

Everyone at the bar seemed happy to see Jared.

"Jared. Hey, heard you were in town."

"Goldurned, where'd you get that shiner, m'man?"

"Hey, Jared. What's the word?"

Jared greeted them all with a wave, as he flipped the hinged counter up and went through, joining Eden on the business side of the bar.

"You look great," Eden told him, meaning it.

The corners of his grim mouth twitched. She knew he was pleased. "Since you seem to be upgrading the image around here, I went through some of the stuff my father's storing at his place and came up with this." He gestured at his outfit.

"That was—" she sought the right word "—thoughtful."

"Yeah. I'm one damn thoughtful guy."

They just stared at each other. Eden knew she was grinning like a borderline idiot, but somehow she couldn't seem to stop herself. Here they were, forced by her partner's injury to work together very closely for the next several weeks.

It was probably going to be sheer hell.

So why was she so glad to see him? And why couldn't she stop smiling?

Down the bar, one of the regulars by the name of Tim Brown groused, "Who do you have to shoot to get a drink around here?"

Someone else piped up, "Anyone but Oggie. He's already down."

A ripple of laughter flowed over the room. By now, of course, everyone knew about what had happened to Oggie.

Tyler Conley, a cousin of Heather's husband, chimed in with, "Yeah, Jared. Tell us. How's Oggie doing?"

Jared went to the wells and poured a whiskey and soda. "Oggie's in Prospector's Hospital for a day or two more. And he is hurting," Jared said, neatly setting the drink on a coaster in front of Tim Brown. "But he'll get over it. He's a Jones, after all." He told Tim the price of the drink.

Eden watched him, amazed. He mixed a drink like a true pro. Quickly and effortlessly, with only the slightest bit of flash and dazzle when it came to squirting in the soda. Also, he'd known Tim's drink without having to ask what it was. That was pretty good, considering Jared hadn't even been in town since early May.

Jared turned then and saw her watching him. "You don't have to look so stunned, Miss Parker. I've been helping out at this bar for longer than I care to remember."

"Well, of course. I can see that now. I just didn't realize, I mean, I thought—" She was babbling.

He knew it, so he saved her by interrupting. "So do I pass muster as your substitute bartender?"

She nodded. "I think you'll work out fine."

"Good. Then how about if you play cocktail waitress, and I'll handle the bar?"

Eden had no argument with his plan. It was the way she and Oggie always did it, unless things piled up, in which case Eden helped with the fancier drinks. "Fair enough."

The night was a busy one and it seemed to fly by. Jared wasn't like Oggie, who kept everybody laughing and who would sometimes talk more than the most loquacious of his customers. Jared was cool and businesslike and never missed an order. Working with him, Eden found that she herself became more outgoing.

With Oggie, Eden was the one who kept things running smoothly, while the old man supplied the personality. But with Jared, if there was going to be any personality supplied, Eden had to deliver it. Jared worked, and he worked hard, but he was simply not the kind of man who kept people in stitches with the latest traveling salesman joke.

So Eden spent more time with the customers. And, all in all, it worked out just fine.

She also stayed right through until closing time, partly because it was Saturday night and so busy. And also because of the *understanding* Jared had said they must reach together once they'd closed the doors.

At two-fifteen, Eden escorted the last customer, Rocky Collins, to the door. There, Eden stood for a moment and watched as Rocky tottered down the street. She was relieved when he made it safely to the North Magdalene Grocery Store, above which he rented a small apartment. He grasped the railing to the stairs that ran up the side of the building and pulled himself toward the floor above. When he reached the top, he swayed in front of his own door for a few moments. At last, he succeeded in getting out his key and fitting it into the lock. He disappeared through the door.

"Kind of sad, isn't it?" the low voice said from behind her.

Eden didn't turn to look at him. She was afraid that if she did, he would walk away. She asked, carefully offhand, "Sad? Rocky, you mean?"

"Yeah. He wasn't always like that."

Eden looked up at the tall pine trees on the surrounding hills. It was cooling off now. She breathed deeply of the fresh air, which still seemed warm, and sweet too, after the air-conditioned smokiness in the bar. "What made him change?"

"Hell. What makes anybody change? Life. One too many busted dreams."

Eden folded her arms over her breasts and leaned against the shingled outside wall. She wanted to ask, Were *you* ever different, Jared? And if so, what made *you* change? But she didn't. She had heard from everyone in Jared's family that he had always been a hot-tempered, unapproachable kind of guy. And more than that, such a personal question would probably put a quick end to this lovely moment of peace and near-companionship they seemed to be sharing.

He said, "You're very quiet, Miss Parker."

"Enjoy it while it lasts."

He chuckled then, a kind of rusty-sounding chuckle. She thought that chuckling was something he probably didn't do often. And then he leaned against the building, too, and looked up at the shadowed trees. They were quiet together. Eden thought it was a friendly silence and didn't mind it at all.

Eventually he spoke. "Sometimes, when the people around here are driving me up the wall, I forget what a nice little town this is."

She closed her eyes for a moment. "North Magdalene's much more than nice. It's the home I've always dreamed of."

"It is, huh?"

"Oh, yes. I knew it the first day Laurie brought me here." Eden smiled to herself, remembering. "It was late spring and everything was still green. There were poppies along the road and the locust trees were in bloom. And people were friendly. It was like I was never a stranger."

Jared made a low noise in his throat. "There's a flip side to how friendly folks are, you know. They can also be nosy and interfering as hell. That's why I like this town best in the middle of the night, when the streets are empty and there's not a soul in sight."

"Oh, come on, Jared."

"Oh, come on, what?"

"Well, I mean. Saying you like this town best in the middle of the night is like when a mother says she likes her kids best when they're asleep. Everyone knows mothers are only joking when they say things like that."

"Wrong. Everyone wants to *believe* a mother is only joking when she says things like that."

"You are such a cynic. And besides, loving North Magdalene in the middle of the night is so *limiting*. There are only four streetlights, so you can hardly even *see* it in the middle of the night."

"I don't need to see it. I've got it memorized."

"Is that why you don't miss it when you're gone, because you've got it memorized?"

"Who says I don't miss it?" There was an edge to his voice. Then he said, "Come on. We're wasting time. Let's get things cleaned up. Then we can talk."

Eden sighed. She would have remarked, "I thought we *were* talking," but he didn't give her the chance. He had already ducked back in through the double doors.

Jared cleaned up as efficiently as he tended bar. They were ready to head out the back door in twenty minutes flat.

Then he asked, "You want a drink or something?"

She found she dreaded what was coming, so she tried to keep things light. "Will I need one?"

But that one rusty chuckle he'd given her earlier had apparently been about all the humor he could deal with in one night. He answered without even a trace of a smile, "That's up to you."

"Well, no then. I'll...take it straight."

"Suit yourself."

He took down two of the chairs they'd already put up and sat backward in one. She took the other, though she didn't really feel like sitting. He looked at her for a moment.

Then he began, "Er, Miss Parker..."

It was too much. She felt edgy and awful again, like she had last night—or was it night before last, by now?—when she'd realized he was actually leaving town.

She snapped, "Look. Could you just call me Eden?

Please?'' She couldn't sit still for another second, so she stood up and looked down at him. "I mean it's too strange, your calling me Miss Parker. Face it. We're going to be tending this bar together for the next several weeks." She threw out both her arms. "You can at least call me by my given name." She realized how widely she had gestured and dropped her arms. Then, feeling totally foolish, she sat back down again. "Okay?" she asked meekly.

"Fine," he said, his good eye looking wary. "Eden."

"Thanks a lot."

"You're welcome. Where was I?"

"Not very far," she said tartly. "I think you got to 'Er, Miss Parker' and that was about it."

"Hell." He raked through his hair with his fingers and then rubbed the back of his neck.

Eden decided that waiting around for him to figure out what to say was worse than having him actually say it. "Oh, for heaven's sake. I can't stand this. Let's just...get it over with."

"I'm trying." He really did look miserable. He was gazing off toward the pool table.

"Oh, why is this happening to me?" Eden muttered. "Shall I help you? Is that what you want?"

Now he actually turned those bullet gray eyes on her. His expression was nervous, but hopeful. "Well, I—"

Eden wished she hadn't volunteered. But it was too late now. "It *is* what you want, right?"

"Hell."

"All right. Fine." She stood up again. This was not a task she wanted to tackle sitting down.

She began, "Let's see. *You* want *me* to be aware that you are not in the market for any kind of relationship with a woman. You are through with women, forever. And, even though you kissed me recently and both of us liked it *a lot,* we have to learn to put that behind us and just be...what?

Friendly colleagues? Is that right? I mean, to work together and be nice to each other but only in a very professional way?''

Slowly he nodded.

"Okay. So we're going to be buddies on the job and nothing else, until Oggie gets over shooting himself in the foot and you can do what you really want to do and leave town again.'' She took a breath. "Is that it?''

He looked up at her from his chair. "Right on the money, Miss —er, Eden.''

"Okay.'' For some completely incomprehensible reason, she wanted to cry. But she was not going to cry. "Fine with me,'' she said brightly. "I mean, it's pretty obvious you and I are hardly a match made in heaven, right?''

"Exactly.''

"Shake on it?'' Eden stuck out her hand. He stared at it for a moment, then his own engulfed it. She resolutely ignored the heat that shot up her arm. After a couple of teeth-rattling pumps, he let go.

"See you tomorrow night, then. Seven sharp,'' she said.

"You bet.''

Eden turned and got out of there.

At home, she went right to bed. Her dreams were sad dreams, in which she wandered, feeling lost and alone.

She woke at seven when her alarm went off and wished she could simply throw the darn thing across the room and go back to sleep. But she wanted to see Oggie before she went to the tavern, to make sure he was okay and find out if there was anything she could do for him.

So she dragged herself from her bed and stood for several minutes under the cold spray of the shower. After a good breakfast and some heavy-duty primping to disguise the circles under her eyes, she began to feel as if she just might make it through the day and night to come after all.

At a little before nine, Eden pulled into a parking space in the Prospector's Hospital lot. Inside, the front desk clerk gave her directions to Oggie's room.

When she peeked around the door at the old darling, he was sitting up in the adjustable bed. His right foot was propped in front of him, wrapped in what looked like a small mountain of gauze bandaging. His seamed face lit up at the sight of her.

"Well, what's that there? A ray of sunshine on a damn gloomy day! Get on in her', gal." He waved her into the room.

Eden smiled widely and scooted around the doorframe. She held up the flower arrangement she'd brought with her.

"Not bad," he said. "'Course, I woulda preferred a case of whiskey."

"I'll bet. Where should I put it?"

"Aw, hell. How 'bout over there?"

Eden set the flowers on the windowsill and then took the chair by his bed. She looked at him for a moment before she said anything. Then she squeezed his bony shoulder. "Oh, Oggie. Are you all right?"

He snorted. "Hell, no. I'm wounded for life. And in the worst possible place, too—my pride."

"Jared said you were cleaning your hunting rifle and—"

"Yep. It went off. *Blam.* Right through the foot."

Eden thought about this as he described it and something odd occurred to her. "But, Oggie, I thought people cleaned guns with the barrel up. I mean, when you hear about gun-cleaning accidents, you always hear about injuries to the upper part of the body."

Oggie looked chagrined. "Well, see, like I've explained to Sheriff Pangborn and just about every other damn person who's come in this room, I thought I'd taken out all the shells. I had the rifle pointed down at the floor and I was... Aw, hell. It don't matter how I explain, I still come out a damn fool. At least if I *had* shot myself in the head, I might not have to live through the razzing I'm gonna take when I get back on my feet.''

"No one's going to razz you, Oggie." She patted his hand. "I won't let them."

Oggie chortled. "I feel better already, knowin' you'll stand up for me—since I myself ain't gonna be standin' up at all for quite a while."

"How long will it be until you're really over this?"

"Too long, like I said. The doctor says I'm lucky the bullet only snapped one little bone and went on through, but still it's gonna take weeks and weeks to heal."

Eden thought of that, of weeks and weeks of laboring side-by-side with Jared. Some foolish part of her was disgustingly gleeful at the prospect, while her wiser self knew the best she was going to get out of this deal would be a tension-filled work environment.

"Eden? Something on your mind, gal?"

"No, no. I was just wishing you were over this, that's all."

Oggie's grizzled brows drew together. "Did my boy, Jared, leave you alone to handle things all on your own last night? Is that it? If he did, I'll—"

"No, no, Oggie. He showed up right on time and he…he was great. You know, actually, he's an excellent bartender."

"Damn straights. Who d'ya think taught him everything he knows?"

Eden smiled and nodded. She was thinking that she'd like to ask her partner a few questions about the way he'd misled her when it came to his oldest son—in saying that Jared wanted nothing to do with the bar, and swearing that Jared wouldn't be the least upset to hear his father had taken on a partner.

But right now, she was looking at an old man with a painful injury. And somehow, now didn't seem the time to take him to task. She'd have it out with him later, when his wrinkled face didn't look quite so gray with pain and tiredness.

"I can't stay long, you know," she told him.

"Lucky you," he muttered dryly. "This place is a prison, don't let anyone tell you different. One more day, maybe two, and I'm outta here. 'Course, then I gotta go stay with Delilah for a while. That'll be a trial. But it can't be helped. Since school's out now, she's got time to take care of me." Oggie's only daughter was a teacher. "On second thought, maybe I'll just stay here in prison for a while."

"Oh, come on, Oggie. Delilah will take wonderful care of you."

Oggie looked at her from under his brows. "You ain't known Delilah for too long, Eden. And besides, since she married Sam, she comes across a lot different than she used to. Fulfillment will do that to even the most hard-hearted of women. But there was a time, and it wasn't too long ago, when I'd a shot myself in more than the foot before I'd ever let myself be put helpless into Delilah's hands."

"Oh, Oggie. You're exaggerating."

"You go ahead and believe that, Eden. You're a sweet, bighearted gal. A gentle woman like you don't even want to consider the bloodthirsty inclinations of her less civilized sisters."

Eden couldn't help laughing. "Whatever you say, Oggie."

"This ain't no laughing matter, Eden."

"All right, all right."

"Damn. What I wouldn't give for a smoke."

"Oggie, listen. What I really came for is to see if there's anything I can do for you. You know, anything I can bring you, or any errands I can run?"

"Yeah, hustle over to my house and bring me that box of cigars I left on the coffee table in the living room."

"Now, now, Mr. Jones." A nurse bustled into the room just as Oggie finished talking. "We already told you there is no smoking in the hospital. And besides, you're old enough to know what smoking does to you."

"Yeah, if I'd a known I was gonna live this long, I mighta taken better care of myself."

The nurse winked at Eden. "Isn't he a card?"

Eden nodded. "Yep."

"Now, Mr. Jones. The doctor will be coming by shortly and I think we should remove the dressing on that foot, so he can have a look at it."

"How 'bout you just remove it by yourself?" Oggie asked.

The nurse looked puzzled. "Yes. That's what I said."

Oggie cackled, pleased with himself to be one step ahead of his nurse. "What'd I tell you, Eden? It's hell here."

"I can see they're really making you suffer." Eden stood up. "I'll leave you two alone. But before I go, Oggie, I want you to tell me seriously. What can I do to help out?"

"Aw, hell. I told you what I want. A good cigar. And a six-pack would be nice. And maybe a couple of blondes to help me drink the beer." He looked hopefully at the nurse. She only shook her head. "See? What I want, they won't let me have. So just don't be a stranger while I'm down and out and I'll be happy."

"You're sure?"

"Yep. And take care of business."

"You know I always do."

He spoke to the nurse. "And she ain't foolin' neither. It was my lucky day, when Miss Eden Parker came to town."

The nurse nodded and smiled.

Though she should have known better, Eden still found her heart melting a little at the old flatterer's words. "Thanks, Oggie." She bent over and placed a kiss on his grizzled cheek. "You take care, now."

Oggie made a face at the nurse. "See? With a business partner like this, what the hell do I need with a couple of blondes, anyway?" Oggie grabbed Eden's hand and gave it a squeeze. "Work hard. Make us lots of money."

"I will. I promise."

"And be patient with poor Jared. He ain't had an easy life, you know."

Eden forced a cheerful smile, thinking that only Oggie could get away with bemoaning the troubled life Jared had led, when the old man himself was at least partly to blame for Jared's current problems. She promised, "I'll do my best."

Oggie cackled. "That's just what I'm depending on." As he spoke, Eden thought she detected a crafty glint in her partner's eyes. But if she did, it disappeared as fast as it had come. She hesitated, thinking maybe she should ask him exactly what was going through that scheming mind of his.

But then the nurse coughed and Eden realized that Oggie probably preferred privacy for the unbandaging of his mangled foot.

Eden moved toward the door. "Okay, then. You call me if you need me. Otherwise, I'll drop in tomorrow, and stay a little longer." Tomorrow was Monday, and The Hole in the Wall would be closed, leaving Eden more time for visiting.

Oggie placed a hand over his heart. "I'll be countin' the hours." Then he spoke to the nurse. "Okay, gorgeous, I'm all yours."

To Eden's surprise, things went pretty well at The Hole in the Wall that night. Jared arrived, looking sharp, promptly at seven. At first, when he moved behind the bar and their eyes met, Eden had an awful, sinking feeling in her stomach. Why *him?* she thought desperately. Out of all the nice, openhearted guys there are in the big, wide world, why did it have to be *him?* I can't do this, I simply cannot do this.

But, somehow, she *did* do it. She waited on the customers and bantered with the regulars while Jared mixed the drinks and kept the bar looking shipshape. And within an hour or so, she found she was *almost* able to forget what he'd looked like, magnificent in the moonlight, as he feigned sleep in her spare bed just two nights ago. Not to mention the shameless way she'd responded the next morning when he kissed her at the kitchen door.

And since it was Sunday and a little slower than the night before, Eden was able to turn the place over to Jared at eleven and go home. That spared them those moments alone together that couldn't be avoided when she stayed to the very end.

The next day was Monday and she didn't have to work. Eden puttered around the cabin in the morning and then drove to Grass Valley to make the bank deposit. Since Oggie had been released from the hospital, she stopped by Delilah's house to see him in the afternoon. The old dear was as sweet and amusing as ever.

But she was nervous through the whole visit, fearing that Jared might drop in. She would have felt so awkward, having to sit and make conversation with Oggie, while Jared stood there and glowered, or acted impatient for her to be gone, or worst of all, behaved as if he couldn't care less whether she was there or not.

When Amy appeared with baby Bathsheba to say hi to Grandpa Oggie, Eden took her chance to make a quick getaway. She went home, where she did her laundry and cleaned up the cabin.

Laurie, who was working full-time for the summer at the restaurant where she and Eden had met, called from Sacramento in the evening.

"Hey, pal. I just talked to Heather. She says Great-uncle Oggie shot himself in the foot."

Eden, who'd been feeling a little down, perked up at the sound of her friend's voice. "Yes. It's true. The poor old dear."

"Have you seen him yet?"

"Oggie? Um-hmm. Yesterday and today. He's doing fine. Driving everyone nuts, of course. But that's to be expected."

"Yeah. I'll bet. I've got a day off Wednesday, so I figure I'll drive up and drop in on him."

"He'll love that."

"Heather also said her dad wasn't too thrilled to hear his cabin was rented."

"You could say that."

"So. What do you think of him?"

"Who?"

"C'mon, Eden. Heather's wild-man father. I know you're stuck working with him until Oggie's better. Heather told me that, too."

Eden felt her spirits sinking again. There was just no escaping Jared Jones. Either she was working with him, dreaming about him, or discussing him with one of his relatives. In fact, now that she thought about it, she realized what a bind she was in. The friends she'd made over the past several months were wonderful. But unfortunately, they all seemed to be related to the man she was trying not to think about.

"Eden?"

"What?"

"I asked what you think of Cousin Jared."

"Of Jared?"

"Are you feeling all right?"

"Fine. I'm just fine. And I think your cousin takes some getting used to."

"Oh, Eden. You really are a sweetheart. He's driving you up the wall, right? But you're determined to make the best of the situation, for Oggie's sake."

"Well…"

"Hey. Say no more. I know cousin Jared. He's just one of those guys who was born about a century too late. He should be out fighting mountain lions with his bare hands, building log cabins with only an ax, settling the west. You know, stuff like that."

"Right. It's so limiting for him, to have to act like a reasonable human being."

"Oh, wow. You *are* having a rough time with him."

Eden sighed. "Oh, I'll get through it. One way or another."

"Eden?"

"What?"

"Is there something…going on here?"

Eden could have kicked herself. Laurie wasn't her best friend for nothing. Laurie *sensed* things. Eden should have been more circumspect. Venting her frustrations about Jared had been foolish.

"Eden?"

"Hmm?"

"Did you hear my question?"

"Yes. I heard you." Eden swallowed. "And what do you mean, going on?"

"Honestly." Laurie sounded mildly annoyed. "I mean, is there something romantic going on between you and Jared?"

"Who said that?"

"Nobody. You just seem…"

"What? I seem what?"

"A little defensive about him."

"Defensive? I am not defensive. I'm really not. Not at all."

"Okay, okay."

Eden knew she should change the subject right there, but she wanted to make certain Laurie got her point loud and clear. "How could there be anything going on between your cousin and me?"

"Well, I was only—"

"He's old enough to be my father."

"Well, not quite. I mean, you're twenty-six and he's forty. That's fourteen years. I suppose technically, a guy can be a father at fourteen, but that would have meant he'd have been about thirteen when he—"

"Why are we talking about this?"

"Well, Eden. You said—"

"I said there's nothing whatsoever going on between your cousin and me. He's too old for me and he has a terminal bad attitude."

"He *is* kind of surly." Laurie was trying to be fair.

"And he's been divorced twice."

"Oh, come on," Laurie said. Eden could tell by her friend's tone that she shouldn't have brought up both divorces. "That's not fair. His first divorce doesn't count and you know it. He and Sally remarried and things were going just fine between them when—"

"Laurie. Why are we talking about this? I don't want to talk about this."

"Eden, I—"

"I mean it. I really don't."

"Sheesh. I've never heard you like this. You've never been one to let a man bother you. I mean, let's be frank here. You hardly even *date*."

"I'm a businesswoman," Eden said, as if that explained everything. "I've been busy all my life, making a place for myself. I don't have time for *casual* relationships with men. I've told you that."

"Okay, fine. All I'm saying is, this is *me*. Your best

friend. If I'm nosing around where I shouldn't be, I'm sorry. But please remember I'm here, if you need me. And I really *can* keep my mouth shut in terms of the family, if that's what's worrying you.''

Eden felt contrite. Laurie was right. If Eden couldn't trust her own best friend, where did that leave her? ''Thanks, pal,'' she said. ''I'll remember that.''

''Good.''

''And, the truth is…''

''Yeah?''

''The *sad* truth is, there's nothing to tell.''

''What's *nothing*, exactly?''

''Zero. Zip. Jared and I have an *understanding*.''

''Yuk. Sounds grim.''

''We work together a few hours a night. And that's all.''

''But *you* want more?''

''Oh, Laurie.''

''I'm listening.''

''I'm attracted to him.…''

''But?''

''But he's not the kind of man I pictured myself falling for. I always thought I'd find someone friendly and easygoing. A nice, good-natured, hardworking guy.''

''Well, you're okay on the hardworking part. Cousin Jared's always been a hardworking man.''

''Great. But what about friendly, easygoing, nice and good-natured?''

''No comment.''

''My point precisely.''

''So what will you *do*?''

''Grin and bear it.''

''What fun.''

''What else can I do?''

For a moment there was silence on the line. Then Laurie asked, ''Do you really want to know?''

Eden shrugged. "Sure. Hit me with it."

"Well, it seems to me you've got a golden opportunity here."

"Oh, a golden opportunity. Right."

"Do you want to hear what I have to say? Or would you prefer to just go on being sarcastic?"

"Sorry. I want to hear, I really do."

"Then let me finish, please."

"All right."

"Okay. You've got a golden opportunity. You're working with the guy every day but Monday for the next several weeks. And then, unless something happens to make him change his mind, he's outta here. Right?"

"So?"

"So it's perfect. If things don't work out, he's going to be gone anyway."

"Well, they *haven't* worked out, that's what I'm telling you. And he *isn't* gone. Not for weeks yet. And I've got to see him every night until then."

"Okay, so don't waste the time you have left."

"What do you mean, waste? What is there to waste? It's over before it even started."

"I mean, why don't you take advantage of the situation? Since you're thrown together every night, make it your business to get to know the man better. Just in case he *is* the one you've been waiting for."

"Get to *know* him. Please. He's *your* cousin. How can you say that? You know how he is. The master of the one-syllable response."

"Was I finished? I didn't think I was finished."

"Sorry. All right. Go on."

"Fine. So I'm not sure *how* you do it, but you do it. Become *friends* with him. Don't push, just be receptive, any time he's willing to open up a little. Slowly you'll get to know more about what makes him tick."

"Yeah?"

"And then..."

"Yeah?"

Laurie sighed. "Oh, never mind."

"What do you mean, never mind?"

"Oh, well."

"Oh, well *what?*"

"It would never work."

"What are you saying?"

"That you're right."

Eden gave a little groan. "About what?"

"About my cousin Jared. I mean, no matter how positive I try to be about this, I can't help remembering who we're talking about here. And cousin Jared never opened up to anybody in his life. You really want the advice of a friend?"

Eden didn't, not really. But it was too late to say so now. She bleakly conceded, "I said I did, didn't I?"

"Okay, then here it is. Forget him. Keep it strictly business for the next few weeks. And be waiting at the door to help him into his coat when he heads out of town."

Eden felt like a pricked balloon. But she knew her friend was right. "Yeah." The word was glumness personified. "You said it. And I know it."

"So do it."

"I will."

And Eden fully intended to. At least consciously, anyway.

But deep in her secret heart, she still nourished a futile longing for the man she knew she ought to forget. Thus, it was Laurie's original advice that stuck with her.

Later, as she lay in bed, she couldn't help wondering just how a person would go about getting someone like Jared Jones to open up a little....

Chapter Eight

Jared didn't know how the hell it happened, but after he and Eden had been working together for a while, he began telling her things. About himself. About his life. About his *feelings,* for godsakes.

It started out as a sort of joking remark she made, during a lull on that first Tuesday night after Oggie's injury. That night had been pretty quiet to begin with. And at about nine the place emptied out, except for a few real die-hards at the card table in back.

Eden went out to the tables and began gathering the empties on a tray. Then she trotted over to the bar and set the tray down.

"Okay, Jared," she said out of nowhere, as soon as the glasses and empty beer bottles stopped clinking together. "We've got a spare five minutes here. Why don't you tell me your life story?"

He gave her a look, a look he'd practiced a lot in his life. The look said, *"Back off."*

Eden shrugged and came around to join him behind the bar. Then she began washing the glasses. He assumed he'd shut her up.

He assumed wrong.

She said, very offhandedly, "Okay, forget your life story. After all, if this keeps up, I'll head on home. So you'd better save your life story for some night when I'm trapped here."

He'd grunted then. Though he was really watching it with her, keeping strictly to the terms of their understanding not to get involved, it was hard not to respond to her.

She was so tall and sparkly and full of the oddest, gawky grace. A damn gorgeous flamingo of a woman, with those neverending legs and that flame-gold hair and that mouth that could smile like no mouth he'd ever seen before.

Then she asked, "But how about...the happiest day of your life? So far."

And he said, "The day Heather was born," before he even realized that he'd opened his mouth to speak.

She swooped the pair of rocks glasses she was washing through the rinse water and turned to give him a quick, melting look from those Kahlúa-colored eyes of hers. "I can understand that."

And that was all. She didn't make too much of it. She didn't say, like a lot of women would, *So tell me all about it, every itsy-bitsy detail of how you felt and what you felt and why you felt it.* Just that soft look and *I can understand that* and that was all.

It surprised the hell out of him, to tell the truth. He'd never thought that she could back off like that, that she could hear what he'd said and let it be, because most of the time Eden Parker was such a damn motor-mouth. And also because he'd assumed she was just like any other woman, that she'd fall all over herself at the slightest opportunity to get him to "communicate."

In Jared's experience, most women said they adored a

man who was strong and silent and self-contained. And then they were somehow always after him, nagging him, because he wouldn't "open up" with them.

But Eden Parker never urged him to "open up," and she never nagged because he didn't. She just…invited him to. And damned if he didn't find himself accepting her invitations, as often as not.

"I've got a moment here, Jared," she'd announce. "Name your favorite song of all time."

And he'd be answering some idiotic thing, like "Blue Velvet," before he even realized that he *had* a favorite song.

She'd say, "Well, that's not bad. Not bad at all." And he'd want to ask her, *"Not bad compared to what?"* But by then he would have remembered that he was supposed to be keeping things distant and professional when it came to her. So he'd say nothing. Until later, when she'd pop out another harmless question and he'd answer it before even stopping to think.

"What's your favorite color?"

"Something that doesn't show the dirt."

She'd chuckled when he said that.

Then, later, she demanded, "Favorite kind of movie?"

And he hadn't missed a beat. "One with lots of action and not too much talk."

She asked, "Favorite card game?"

He answered, "Seven card draw."

"Favorite food?"

He grunted at that. "Whatever's in front of me."

She laughed. And then she wondered, "If you could take back one thing you said or did during your life so far, what would it be?"

He told the truth. "Hell. There's no way I can pick just one."

She moved on. "Name an exotic place you'd like to visit."

"How 'bout Tahiti?"

"Fine with me. Name something in this world that you love, not including people."

He thought about that one and then told her, "Peace and quiet. A hawk soaring. The way the wind makes ripples on a mountain pond."

"Hmm," she said after that and walked away with that soft smile on her face.

Later she asked, "What do you hate, Jared? I mean *really* hate?"

"The national debt. A broken promise."

"Got any enemies?"

"Sure. But my enemies don't worry me."

"Why not?"

"A man knows where he stands with his enemies and his friends. It's everyone else you have to watch out for."

When did the questions become less than harmless?

Be damned if he knew.

Maybe it was that night she knocked a glass off one of the tables and he went out with the broom to sweep up the pieces for her.

She was kneeling, her bright head bent, carefully picking up the larger shards. She looked up at him, her wide mouth as soft as a flower in full bloom, her brown eyes like velvet. "Were you scared as well as happy the day Heather was born?"

He stared down at her and hardly realized he was answering until he'd already said, "You bet. Scared as they come."

"Yes. I believe that."

He found he wanted to elaborate. So he did.

"Sally had a hard time of it—with the birth, I mean." His voice sounded gruff, unpracticed. But still he wanted to say more. He continued, "And I was a drinking man in those days. Nineteen years old and a stone alcoholic. Sally and me were having our problems because of that. But not that day.''

''You were sober that day?''

''Yeah. I don't remember now how I managed that. Maybe that was during one of those times when I promised Sally I'd quit. Who the hell knows? What matters is, I was sober and they let me be there, at the end, to see my daughter born.''

Jared leaned on the broom and shook his head. ''Damn, she was ugly. It's hard to believe sometimes, when I look at her now, but Heather Jane was about the ugliest baby I ever saw in my life. I remember I mentioned how plug-ugly she was. And Sally said, 'You wouldn't look that great, either, if you'd just been through what *she's* been through.' And we laughed together. Then I said to Sally, 'I'm real proud.' And she kinda whispered back, 'Me too.'''

Jared flexed his fingers around the broom handle, wondering where the hell all those words had just come from. ''It was a good day,'' he finished. And since he didn't know what else to do, he held out the dustpan.

Eden Parker didn't say anything. She only smiled and took what he offered her.

He told her about Belle and the boys a few nights later, when they were a week and a half or so into their temporary partnership.

She asked what was the *worst* day of his life.

And he said, ''There have been many.''

''Worst of the worst?''

He answered, ''I suppose there were two of those.''

''And they were?''

''The day Sally died. And the day I came home from work to find an empty house and a note from Belle saying she was taking the two boys and going back to the man she loved—that was her first husband, Dale.''

"Taking the two boys," Eden repeated his words in a quiet voice. "Your stepsons, right?"

"My stepsons, T.J. and Lucas. Right."

Right then, a man and a woman, strangers in town, came in separately. They took places at either end of the bar. They each ordered a rum and cola. And then the man looked at the woman and she looked back.

The woman smiled.

The man said, "Put the lady's drink on my tab." And he moved to her end of the bar.

Jared and Eden settled in at the other end. Jared was drying glasses. Eden was tidying up, consolidating bowls of cocktail mix, wiping down the bar, things like that.

Jared didn't know what made him say it. But it was inside him, just itching to get out.

He told her, in a voice low enough that the other couple couldn't hear, "The truth is, stepfathers have got no damn rights at all."

"They don't?"

"No, they don't."

"Why not?"

"If the kids aren't yours by birth and you didn't manage to adopt them, then it doesn't matter what you've done for them." Jared turned and started putting the glasses away on a shelf, one at a time. As he set each glass down, he heard his own voice listing the little things, the everyday things, that make a man a father.

"So what if you walked the floor the nights they were sick? Or drove them to the dentist every time they had to go? Or made sure they got to their T-ball practice on time twice a week? Or fed them, or paid for the clothes on their backs?" He set the final glass on the shelf and then turned to pull the plug so the dirty water in the sink would drain.

He watched the murky water disappear and went on with his list, with all the little things that, in the end, had counted for nothing at all. "And who cares if you were the one to teach them how to tie their shoes? So what if you were tough when you had to be and said 'no' sometimes, because you knew it was the best thing for them, even though it damn sure didn't get you any points with them."

Jared rinsed the last of the dirty soapsuds down the drain. "You could have loved them with everything that's in you. And it doesn't mean squat, it doesn't mean a thing. If their mother wants to take them back to be with their *real* father, well, she can just go ahead. No court in this land will allow you a claim on them. They're nothing of yours. Just step-kids. That's all." Jared dragged in a deep breath and flipped on the faucet to refill the sink.

The room seemed very quiet then. The other couple wasn't talking, they were just staring into each other's eyes. And even the guys in the back room seemed to be keeping it down.

In that silence, Jared knew himself to be a fool. The worst kind of fool, one who talks too damn much. He started to turn away.

But then Eden asked, keeping her voice low, "Do you know where they are now?"

He felt the strangest thing. A kind of sweet relief. She wasn't going to say how sorry she was for him. She had only listened to him, accepted both his self-indulgence and his pain and then moved on from there.

He answered her. "Yeah. I know where they are."

"Did you ever try to see them?"

"Yeah. It was a mistake."

"Why?"

"Because Belle didn't want me around. And Dale didn't, either. And it confused the kids. It only caused problems. From what I understand, they're working things out as a family. And I...I wish them well." Miraculously, as he said the words, Jared realized they were true. The crippling bitterness he'd known for too long really was fading. He volunteered, "They teach about letting go, you know. In Alcoholics Anonymous?"

"Yes."

"So I'm learning. To let go. In this case, I think it's the best thing. Hell. Maybe it's the only thing I *can* do. Because like I said, I've got no damn rights with those kids anyway." He thought about Heather then, about how she was all grown up now and had her own life.

His expression must have told Eden something, because she asked, "What?"

"Just thinking. About raising kids."

"What about it?"

"If there's anyplace you have to let go, it's when you're raising kids. Maybe I just had to let go of Lucas and T.J. a little sooner than usual, that's all."

"Maybe," she said. She looked thoughtful. Then she asked, "So you married Belle because you liked her children?"

Jared actually laughed then. He had a lousy laugh and he knew it. He hadn't had a lot of practice at laughing during his life. "No, liking the boys came later."

Down the bar, the man and woman stopped staring at each other and glanced their way.

"'Nother round," the man said.

"Coming right up."

Jared went and mixed their drinks while Eden wiped down the tables and re-racked the pool cues. Then she went into the back room to check on the poker players there. She returned with four orders, including the usual tequila shooter for Rocky Collins and a whiskey and soda for Tim Brown. She set them up and Jared poured out.

Eden was leaning on the bar, waiting for him to finish, her chin in her hand. "Then why did you marry Belle, if not because of the kids?"

He didn't even hesitate. He said, careful only to keep his voice down so no one else would hear, "Because I wanted to have sex with her." He set the drinks on the tray.

Eden said, softly, "Hmm," and nodded, the way she did sometimes when he told her things, as if she were just storing them away, but making no judgments at this time. He watched her long, slender fingers with their pink-tipped nails as she moved the drinks around so the tray would balance. Then she slid the tray onto her left hand.

He heard himself adding before she could leave him, "I don't believe in sex outside of marriage. I've never had sex with a woman I wasn't married to first."

He expected her to laugh. Hell, he *wanted* her to laugh, to think he was joking, which he was not. If she had only laughed, it would have put some much-needed distance between them. It would have been a proof of a sort that she was not as sensitive nor as keen as he was beginning to believe.

But she didn't laugh. She only nodded again. "I see," she said and smiled the sweetest, most understanding smile. And then she turned to give the guys in the back room the drinks they had asked for.

And when she came back, she asked if he would mind if she called it a night. It was after ten and things were quiet. "Of course," she added, "I'll stay if you want me to."

And he realized he wanted more than anything right then to tell her to stay. But he remembered their understanding—the understanding that, as the nights went by, was getting harder and harder to keep in mind.

"Sure. Go on home," he said.

And she did.

It was after that night that the tension began to build between them again.

Jared tried to figure out exactly how it all came about,

but he couldn't get it straight in his mind. He just knew that they'd come to an understanding, and there had been a time when they'd been careful of each other, distant with each other.

And then there had been a week or so when some connection beyond the way she turned him on had been forged. That connection happened when she got him talking. God knows, he still had no idea how she did that. Even his sweet Sally had never been able to get him to talk. But Eden did it. And once she got him talking, she just listened, or said only what needed to be said to *keep* him talking.

But whatever the hell she had done, whatever had happened between them as he talked and she listened, it somehow made the denial of his desire for her all the harder to bear. Because he started to see her as an equal, as a contemporary. It got harder and harder to remember that she was closer to his daughter's age than his own, that he didn't have a damn thing to offer her, that he never intended to marry again anyway. And that he still held to his belief that it was wrong to have sex with a woman who wasn't his wife.

Not only did he want her more, on more levels than before, he also began to feel more protective of her. Objectively he knew this new protectiveness was uncalled-for. She didn't need or want his protection. She could handle herself.

But wanting her so damn much and knowing he was not going to have her was putting more and more pressure on him as each night crawled by. And it just didn't help his attitude at all when other men would look her over.

He found himself realizing that it was very damn possible that some night a man could come strolling into The Hole in the Wall and walk out with Eden on his arm. Hell, it might be a perfectly suitable man. A decent, unattached man with a good job and a shining future. A real winner of a guy. And if this prize of a fellow liked Eden, and she liked him back, then there would be nothing to stand in the way of the two of them getting together. And that would be good; it would be for the best.

Eden was just what his father had said: a great gal. A hardworking woman with a good attitude and a terrific head for business. She deserved to hook up with a winner.

Jared just prayed to holy heaven that Mr. Terrific didn't dare show his face in North Magdalene until after Oggie was back on his feet and he was long gone. Jared wanted the best for Eden. And the best would be someone else, he understood that. He just didn't want to have to watch it happening.

In truth, he feared that if he *were* forced to watch it happening, he wouldn't be watching for long. He'd be leaping over the bar and beating the daylights out of some poor fool whose only fault was that he was just the kind of sharp, successful guy that Eden Parker deserved to fall in love with.

And then, on top of everything else, there was Oggie, driving Jared right up the wall with his never-ending questions and his sly remarks.

"How's Eden?" Oggie would ask the minute Jared arrived at Delilah's to visit him. "You treatin' her right? You ain't lettin' her work too hard, are you? That gal is a workin' fool, you know. It wouldn't do for you to take advantage of that."

"I won't take advantage of her, Dad."

Then came that damn cackling laugh. "Hell, son. I didn't say don't take advantage of her personally, just don't let her work too hard. If you want to take advantage of *her,* well, you are two adults and there's nothing that I can do to—"

"Drop it, Dad."

"I got a right to have my say."

"Sure you do. And I got a right to turn around and walk right out of here."

"You don't like Eden?"

"I like Eden just fine."

"Then what's the big deal if I ask you how she's doing?"

"No big deal, Dad."

"Good, then." And there'd be more of the same.

Somehow, Jared never seemed to be able to pay his father a visit that the old fool didn't ask him how Eden was doing, or how Eden was feeling, or how he and Eden were managing together. As if Oggie didn't know exactly how Eden was, since she went to visit him nearly every day.

Yeah, Oggie was driving Jared crazy, all right. It was beginning to seem like a toss-up to Jared as to where he'd be more likely to lose his temper first: while watching some punk put the make on Eden, or while listening to his father go on about how damn wonderful she was.

Jared knew he was getting close to the brink. And he did not want to go over. One of the things he'd told himself when he came in from the woods this time was that he was *not* going to get in any fights. His goal was to make peace with the world, not beat the holy hell out of it. Too bad that when he set that goal he hadn't known about Eden Parker. If he'd known about her and her long legs and wide mouth and those big brown eyes that lately seemed to be looking at him even in his dreams, he might have just stayed in the woods.

But it was too late now. He was here. And he was stuck here until his old man could walk again. And, by God, he was going to keep himself under iron control, if it killed him to do it.

But by Saturday night, two weeks after Oggie shot himself in the foot, Jared was ready to snap.

There was a hotheaded street fighter down inside Oggie Jones's oldest son. Jared had battled that troublemaker all of his life. And now, because of Eden, the battle with his own violent self was worse than it had ever been. He was determined to win out over it.

But he was losing.

The sad truth was that it wouldn't take much, now, for the street fighter to rule the day once more. He was only waiting. Waiting for the right excuse to take on any idiot who made the crucial error of looking at Jared—or Eden Parker—cross-eyed.

Chapter Nine

The final Saturday night in August started out the same as the two previous ones. The place was humming when Jared came in at seven.

He went right to work mixing drinks so Eden could concentrate on playing waitress. They worked smoothly and swiftly for an hour or so, which was just fine with Jared.

Jared liked it when business was brisk. Not only did they bring in more money, but time went by faster. Even better, when things were hopping, Jared found that it was *almost* possible not to think for a while about how much he wanted Eden.

And tonight, all the trade they were getting really was a lifesaver. Because tonight it was even harder than usual not to think about Eden. She'd worn something different, a sort of Annie Oakley outfit, a Western shirt and fringed skirt and vest, along with a pair of white cowboy boots. The skirt wasn't that short. It ended just above her knees. But on

Eden, a skirt didn't have to be short. Her legs were so damn gorgeous a man found himself staring at them even when all he could see was the little stretch of calf between her boot tops and her kneecaps.

Jared reminded himself to talk to her later. He'd tell her to stick with the black slacks and white shirt from now on— or else. And then he silently admitted that he'd do no such thing, because there was nothing wrong with the cowgirl outfit except that she looked great in it. He couldn't fault her for looking great, unless he was prepared to admit exactly why it bothered him. And no way was he going to do that.

So he worked fast and hard and told himself to be grateful it was a busy night.

At around eight, Rocky Collins, who was sitting on his favorite stool right by the little rubber mat where Jared poured the drinks, suddenly announced, "Well, lookit who's coming. Ain't that a sight?"

Jared glanced toward the window in time to see his sister Delilah and her husband, Sam, approaching the double doors to the bar. Sam was pushing Oggie in a wheelchair.

"Oggie!" Eden cried out. "Jared, look. It's Oggie."

Jared grunted. What a thrill, he thought.

He couldn't see what she was getting so excited about. After all, it wasn't as if they never saw the old geezer. Jared had visited his father at Sam and Delilah's house that very day and got a slew of unwanted questions and advice for his trouble. The questions, as usual, had been all about Eden. And the advice had been disgustingly personal.

"A man like you really needs a woman, son," Oggie had suggested. "'Cause sexual frustration can be a hell of a problem for a man in his prime. Matter of fact, sexual frustration can make a man a real trial to everyone who cares about him."

"Who the hell gave you the right to lecture me about my sex life, Dad?"

"*Your* sex life? Who said I was talkin' about *your* sex life. I said a man *like* you."

"Right."

"And as for the rest of it, well, that was scientific fact and that is all. When a man goes too long without sex, a pressure begins to build up, a pressure that has been proven by science to have to be let loose somewhere, and—"

"I never hit a man in a wheelchair, Dad. But there's a first time for everything."

Oggie cackled gleefully then. "See what I mean? Something's got to give, son, or before you know it, *ka-blam!* You're just gonna explode."

Jared had left soon after that. He figured he'd seen about enough of his old man for one day.

And Eden saw plenty of Oggie also. She visited him at Delilah's whenever she got the chance—or so Oggie and his sister were always telling him. Jared himself had never run into her there. And he knew why. She was being careful to go at times when she thought she wouldn't meet up with him.

North Magdalene was a dinky little town. However, since he and Eden had reached their *understanding,* Jared hadn't run into her even once outside of the hours they were forced to work together.

At first, he'd been grateful that she gave him a wide berth whenever possible. But recently, as she'd drawn him out and got him talking during business hours, the way she avoided him the rest of the time had begun to irritate him. He knew his irritation was unreasonable. It was his own fault that she was staying out of his way. He had no right at all to be bugged about it.

But he was. He was damned annoyed.

Right that minute, she further annoyed him by clapping

her serving tray on the end of the bar and rushing to prop open the double doors as if royalty had come to call. Oggie, with his bad foot leading the way, was then wheeled in with a lot of clucking and fluttering from Eden and Delilah, and with Sam doing most of the work of getting the old man's chair over the doorjamb.

"Hey, Jared." Sam saluted him. "How goes it, buddy?"

"It's been worse," Jared answered. He even attempted a smile for Sam's sake, in spite of his dark mood.

Jared and Sam went back a long ways. And beyond that, Jared couldn't help feeling respect for the man who had married his sister. Jared knew Delilah, after all. And he had a pretty good idea what kind of a man it would take to sleep with Delilah at night and still walk around smiling in the daytime the way Sam did. So Sam got a real greeting from Jared.

On the other hand, when Oggie called out, "Good to see you workin' so hard, son," Jared felt hard put to spare him a wave.

Once he was inside, Oggie was set up at the best table in the house. He ordered a whiskey on the rocks. Sam wanted a beer and Delilah asked for a vodka tonic. Then every damn customer in the place had to have a fresh drink so they could all propose toasts to Oggie's recovery and make bad jokes about people who shoot themselves in the foot.

Personally Jared thought the whole routine was a pain in the butt. But he gutted it out anyway, even raising his cola can once or twice at the toasts.

And then, just when things started to settle down a little, in came Brendan and Amy. They explained that they'd left the baby with Amy's teenage sister for the evening, so the grown-ups could have a little fun.

More chairs were pulled up at Oggie's table. Amy wanted a cherry cola and Brendan asked for his usual whiskey straight up.

When Eden came over to the bar to get the drinks for them, her eyes were shining so bright she looked like a kid on Christmas Eve. Eden was just nuts about the family and Jared hadn't the faintest idea why. If you asked him, he thought they were all more trouble than they were worth.

But then, no one was asking him.

As soon as Amy and Brendan were settled in with their drinks in front of them, some damn fool dropped a quarter in the jukebox and there was Patsy Cline singing "Crazy." And then what? Brendan pulled Amy to her feet. Sam grabbed Delilah. The two couples went swaying out onto the little square of floor by the curtain to the card room.

Jared was careful not to look at them. It was enough to make a man sick. No four people had a right to look that happy in a screwed-up world like this one.

A few minutes later, Jared's middle brother, Patrick, came in. Thankfully, as far as Jared was concerned, Patrick was alone. Jared didn't think he could stand looking at another happy couple right then. Patrick joined the family table and ordered a drink to be sociable, but Jared thought he looked a little down.

Which made sense. Patrick's ex-wife had recently taken their two daughters and moved out of state. Also, Chloe Swan, who'd been in love with Patrick for years, had run off a couple of months ago with a stranger. Since their messy breakup a decade ago, Patrick had kept Chloe at a distance, insisting she and he were no more than friends. But ever since she'd gone, everyone said Patrick had been mooning around like a motherless calf.

For a few minutes after the glum Patrick's arrival, Jared felt a little better about things. It was a welcome relief to see another man without an ear-to-ear grin on his face.

But then Oggie and Eden got to talking about the restaurant they were going to open next door come spring, and Patrick perked up. Apparently, as Eden had mentioned a couple of weeks ago, Patrick was in on the restaurant deal and enthusiastic about it as well.

Jared's spirits grew darker.

More customers came in. It was turning into one of the busiest nights Jared could remember. And there were almost as many women in the place as there were men. The Hole in the Wall was now the kind of bar where a man could bring his lady and not worry if he'd end up having to protect her honor from some yahoo who'd had one drink too many. That was due to Eden's influence, of course.

Yeah, Eden was a damn wonder, all right. Jared scowled and mixed more drinks.

Around ten, when the atmosphere was more like that of a large, successful party than a busy night at a bar, three single men came in together. They were all big and young— college buddies out in the sticks on a camping trip from the look of them. Jared knew their type on sight. Their bulging muscles and good-natured arrogance gave them away. Jocks. Probably football players from the size of them.

Over near the curtain to the back room, three single women were sitting together, sharing a girls' night out and seeming to be having a pretty good time. The three jocks homed in on the women and had them surrounded in seconds flat.

The ladies put up not even token resistance. They smiled and flirted and helped the jocks find three spare chairs— precious commodities in the filled-to-capacity bar.

Eden slipped through the crowd to take orders from the newcomers. Jared, who was mixing more drinks right then, watched her out of the corner of his eye. He knew how careful she was about getting ID from anyone who looked to be under thirty, and he was a little uneasy about how she was going to handle these guys. You just never knew about jocks, especially when they'd just found themselves some women to impress. They might get hostile about having to show they were old enough to drink.

But Eden proved equal to her task. From that distance, Jared couldn't hear what was said. But he saw that she smiled and made some kind of joke, because both the jocks and the women laughed. Then the three men were whipping out their wallets and handing her their ID's. She gave each one of the ID's a good look before she handed them back in the order she'd collected them.

As Eden returned the final ID, its owner grabbed her hand, turned it over and planted a kiss in the heart of her palm. He looked up at her and said something. Eden's slim back stiffened.

Jared set down the shaker of margaritas he was mixing. His gut was clenching, his whole body gathering...

And then Eden pulled her hand away and made some light remark that sent another wave of laughter over the group at the table. The big jock who'd kissed Eden's hand laughed the loudest. The woman sitting next to him, the most attractive of the women, didn't laugh at all.

Eden turned and left the table. The big jock watched her go. Jared knew just what that college boy was looking at. For the last two weeks, he himself had looked at exactly the same thing whenever he forgot to stop himself.

Jared remembered his job. He picked up the shaker of margaritas and poured them out swiftly into salt-rimmed glasses. "Hey Jared, what about *my* drink?" Rocky complained.

Jared poured out a straight shot of tequila, grabbed the salt and a wedge of lime and put it all down in front of Rocky. "There you go, Rock," he said in a voice so patient and low that poor Rocky, cringing back, almost fell off his favorite stool. "Will that take care of it?"

"Er, uh, yeah. That's it. You bet. Thanks a bunch. That's great—"

Jared turned away before Rocky could finish groveling. He set the margaritas before the customers who'd ordered them and watched as Eden approached him.

She smiled. "A pitcher of the dark stuff for the all-Americans back there. And another round for the ladies. Plus two tall ones for the guys at the pool table." She was already setting up the glassware for him to use. The woman was so damned efficient it set his teeth on edge sometimes.

He poured the drinks. He told himself he was not going to ask, "What'd he say to you?" But somehow, he did.

"What did *who* say?" She was busily arranging the drinks on the tray, looking extremely unconcerned. But she gave herself away when her hand hit one of the drinks and it nearly spilled.

Jared steadied the drink and captured Eden's evasive gaze. "Don't play dumb. Just tell me what he said."

She looked at him for a moment. Then she gave up her pretense that she didn't know who he was talking about. Her wide mouth pursed. She spoke very quietly. "Stop it. I handled it."

His voice was equally soft. "What did he say?"

"Let it go."

"Tell me. Now."

Eden said nothing.

Over at the family's table, Oggie was in the middle of a long, involved joke about a salesman and a pair of silk stockings. Down the bar, someone called for a refill. Behind the curtain to the back room, a winner at the poker table crowed in triumph. The jukebox droned on, a sad song about a desperado who would not surrender to love.

Neither Jared nor Eden noticed any of this. The boisterous crowd all around them had spun away. There was only the two of them, will to will.

They had an *understanding*. They were temporary business partners and no more. Yet he wanted to know what the other man had said to her. And she would not tell him, for fear of a fight.

Then Eden said in a low, even whisper, "Please, Jared. It honestly was not that bad. And it's over. It's done. Don't make trouble. Please."

Jared's fist, clenched on the bar, slowly and reluctantly relaxed.

Damn her, he thought. She *would* have to go and ask him so nicely. What the devil could a man do when a woman said please, except give her what she wanted?

And hell, in spite of how tight he was wound up, he really didn't want to spoil things for her. He knew she was as proud as a peacock over the way the place was cooking tonight. And she had a right to be proud. It was her triumph, her proof that she'd done real wonders with his father's dingy saloon. A fight would spoil everything, and he knew it damn well.

"All right," he said.

"Thank you." Her smile was tremulous, brimming with silent gratitude. Jared drank in her shining eyes, her petal-soft mouth and sweetly flushed cheeks—and that heated, hungry longing down inside him almost took control.

The urge was on him to reach across the bar that separated them and wrap his hand around her soft nape. To pull her toward him, just enough that he could put his lips against hers.

One quick, hard kiss. That was all it would take. And every man in the place would know who she belonged to. And anyone else who messed with her would do it at his own risk.

"Jared?" Her smile had changed. Her sweet mouth was slightly parted.

Damn her. She *knew*.

And she *wanted* him to do it, to stake his claim on her.

He thought of Sally, who had died and left him. And of

Belle, who'd betrayed him and then taken the two boys he loved from him without a single backward glance.

He reminded himself, as damn near impossible as that was to do while he was looking at Eden, that he was never going to put his heart and soul in a woman's frail hands again. And besides, he had to remember that he had nothing left to offer a woman anyway. His heart was a dried-up husk, and he was an unemployed lumberjack, his prospects dim at best.

"Serve the drinks," he told her. Then he turned to take an order from a man who'd just slid onto the only vacant stool down at the far end of the bar.

He knew she stared after him, for the briefest of moments. But Eden Parker was a pro. Before he could mutter "What'll it be?" to the man at the end of the bar, she had hoisted her tray of drinks up high and was off to weave her way between the full tables.

Jared kept an eye out as she served the six at the back table. He didn't miss the speculative sideways looks that the biggest of the three men kept giving her. But the college boy said nothing this time, and Eden was careful never to look at him. And then the woman beside him, not pleased at all with the interest he was showing in their waitress, tugged on his arm. The big jock turned to the woman with a slow, sexy grin, and Eden slipped away.

Oggie caught her as she passed the table where he still held forth, keeping everyone in stitches. "Give us all another drink, gal. And make it snappy."

Eden laughed, a bright, sparkly sound that seemed to prod at Jared's empty shell of a heart. "Watch it, partner. You are in no position to get pushy."

Sam advised, "She's right, Oggie. You get pushy, and I'll be pushing you…right out the door."

"All right, all right. Jeez. What's the damn world coming to? A man can't even be an s.o.b. in his own damn bar."

He pretended to look sorry. "Could we all have another drink. Please?"

Eden agreed that they could.

Midnight approached and went on by. Everyone was having a hell of a time. Brendan and Sam pushed the tables back a little more from the small section of cleared floor, and more couples ventured out to dance to the jukebox. Eden moved, swift and sure, between the tables, stopping to take an order, or to laugh at a joke. And Jared waited on the people at the bar and mixed the drinks and made sure there was plenty of cocktail mix and fresh popcorn.

At the back table, three romances appeared to be in bloom. The all-Americans and their new girlfriends danced and laughed and drank a bit more than was good for them. Jared almost quit keeping tabs on them. The one who'd tried to make a move on Eden was plenty busy as the night went by. He seemed thoroughly absorbed in the woman who had pulled him down next to her when he and his buddies first entered the bar.

She was a pistol, that woman. Small and slim, with a pretty, catlike face and short brown hair. She'd set her sights on the big blond college boy and she wasn't letting him slip through her paws. She pulled him onto the little section of dance floor and she plastered her trim little body up against him. As the jukebox played on, she clung to him like a new coat of paint.

Jared actually had to suppress a grin when he watched that little pussycat of a woman stalk her all-American prey. His opinion, the more he watched the two of them, was that the college boy didn't stand a chance.

In fact, seeing that the catwoman was going to keep the college boy from getting anywhere near Eden, Jared felt his mood improve marginally. He began to believe that he might make it through this night without busting anybody's teeth after all.

But then Eden dropped off her tray, grabbed her purse from behind the bar and made the high sign that told him she was taking a bathroom break. She disappeared down the back hall to the ladies' room, which was all the way out back, through an outside door off the parking lot.

Not five minutes later, he noticed that the catwoman was sitting at her table all alone.

Eden was too flushed with the success of the evening to pay any attention to who might be watching when she went outside. And she was also in a hurry. She was the only waitress on a very busy floor. She wanted to relieve her bladder and run a quick comb through her hair and get back to work.

She gave a little grateful sigh when she got out to the parking lot and saw that there wasn't a line. Even better, the door to the ladies' room opened right then. Angie Leslie, a beautiful brunette who lived across the street from Sam and Delilah, stepped out.

Angie smiled. "Be my guest." She held the door.

"Thanks." Eden smiled back.

Then she slid around Angie into the ladies' room and latched the door behind her. Quickly she relieved herself, washed her hands and straightened her hair. She glanced at her watch. Only four minutes since she'd left Jared alone in there.

Thinking of Jared, she couldn't help smiling. Her face in the mirror blushed as pink as a strawberry daiquiri. He'd wanted to beat some sense into that smug jerk at the back table, for her sake. And he hadn't done it, also for her sake.

Even better, she had seen the look in his eyes after he'd agreed to leave well enough alone. He'd come *that* close to grabbing her and kissing her. She knew it.

Soon enough, he *would* kiss her. She knew that as well.

And, oh, how she was longing for it to be sooner rather than later.

The fact was that over the past two weeks, Eden Parker had come a long way in admitting to herself what she wanted.

"Okay, okay," she said to her own reflection in the mirror. "Settle down there, girl. So you're in love. With an absolutely impossible man. Love finds a way. Give it time. Let it happen."

She glanced at her watch again and realized she'd wasted two minutes grinning like a lovestruck fool and talking to herself in the mirror. She fumbled in her purse until she found her lipstick. After freshening her lips, she hooked her bag over her shoulder and pulled open the door.

There was another woman waiting her turn outside. Eden exchanged a quick smile with her and the woman disappeared inside, latching the door behind her as Eden had done.

And then Eden turned for the back door to the bar, only to be brought up short when she collided with a man coming out.

"Hey, baby. Been looking for you. Where're you going in such a big hurry?"

It was the big all-American jerk. The floodlight over the door to the bar clearly illuminated his chiseled features.

Eden didn't bother to suppress her groan of annoyance. "It's none of your business where I'm going."

She slid to the side to go around him. He moved to block her path. "My name is Lew. What's yours?"

"Get out of my way," she instructed wearily. Eden had spent a lot of years tap-dancing away from overly amorous creeps. Since she'd come to North Magdalene, it hardly happened anymore. She suspected that was because of her connection with the Jones Gang. Generally, in North Magdalene, it was considered downright foolish to invite the wrath of any one of the Joneses. People just didn't do that.

But Lew hadn't been in town long. He waxed poetic. "God, you are gorgeous. I've got a thing for leggy redheads, you know."

"Look. I'm not interested. Step aside, please."

"Call me Lew. And like I said inside, I'd like to find out if you're a redhead everywhere…" He reached out.

Eden stepped back and avoided his grasp. "I said I'm not interested." She was stalling, thinking she only had to hold him off for a moment or two. Someone was bound to come outside.

And she was right. Eden had barely finished thinking someone would come, when someone did. The back door to the bar swung open on a long squeak.

Eden started to breathe a sigh of relief. But her sigh caught in her throat.

Beyond the threshold stood the one person she didn't want to see right then: Jared. His eyes were as cold as steel, his mouth set and grim.

Suddenly the fight she'd managed to avert earlier seemed distressingly imminent all over again.

Chapter Ten

Eden was sure the big jock would turn to see who was standing in the open door.

But right at that moment, the man was oblivious to all but the object of his desire. "My name's Lew. Say it. And give me a kiss. And then *maybe* I'll let you go."

Had she still been alone with Lew, Eden might have become nervous at that point. But Jared was there. Suddenly dealing with Lew seemed the least of her problems.

Right then, in that unnerving way that Jared sometimes had, he vanished from beyond the door and reappeared directly behind the big man. Jared tapped him on the shoulder.

Lew's amorous expression became one of mild surprise. He turned. "Huh?" He looked Jared up and down. "What's your problem, barkeep? Can't you see the lady and I are having a little talk?"

Jared spoke to Eden. "You have anything more you want to say to Lew, here?"

The relief Eden felt was lovely. Jared was being reasonable after all. "No," she said quietly. "I've got nothing more to say to him."

Lew's square jaw clenched. "So what? I've got plenty to say to you."

Jared cut in. "You're not getting the message, Lew. What *you've* got to say doesn't matter, if the lady's not interested."

Lew's face grew flushed. "She's interested. She's just not admitting it yet. And besides, it's no business of yours. You stay out of this, barkeep, or I'll…" Lew left his threat unfinished, as if to emphasize the gravity of it.

Eden suggested, "Look, fellas, if we could just—"

Jared waved a hand at her for silence. "You'll what, Lew?"

Lew threw back his big shoulders and stuck out his already imposing chest. "I'll be forced to adjust your attitude for you."

"Jared, let it go, I—"

Jared didn't even acknowledge that Eden had spoken. He asked Lew, "Oh? And how will you do that, exactly?"

"You want me to show you?"

"Showing's better than telling any day of the week."

Lew grinned, displaying an alarming expanse of big white teeth. "All right, barkeep. You asked for it."

"No. Stop this, I mean it…" Eden insisted.

Neither of the men listened. Lew drew back his huge fist and sent it rocketing toward Jared's jaw.

Unfortunately for Lew, Jared didn't wait around for the blow to connect. Instead, moving so fast that what he actually did seemed invisible, he managed simultaneously to block the punch *and* kick Lew's legs out from under him.

Eden heard her own voice demanding once more, "No, Jared, don't!" as the big man went down.

Jared gave her his frozen gunmetal glare. "Go inside," he instructed in that hissing whisper of his. "Now."

"No, I will not. I want this to stop, and I—"

"Damn it, Eden..."

Jared's curse trailed off as he glanced down at his opponent. Lew had pulled himself to his knees. He was rubbing his scraped hands together and shaking his head.

"Go, Eden. I mean it," Jared said.

But Eden remained firm. "Forget it. I'm not moving."

"What the hell?" Lew seemed unable to fathom how he'd ended up on the ground. He looked up at Jared and asked, "What are you, crazy?"

Jared said, "Around here we don't like it when a man forces himself on a woman."

"You *kicked* me," Lew complained.

"Jared—" Eden began, but got no farther.

"Damn straight I kicked you," Jared said to Lew. "Your manners suck." He shot Eden a grim look. "And since the lady won't go inside like I told her to, I want you to apologize to her. Now."

"Huh?"

"I said, say you're sorry. Now."

Lew looked from Eden to Jared and back again. He let out a kind of low, bellowing noise. It seemed he had decided that he was the one who had been wronged. Then he snarled at Jared, "Why you..." and he sprang upward, straight for Jared, aiming his head at Jared's midsection.

Jared feinted back and kicked sideways, nicking the side of Lew's head with his boot. Lew grunted, but didn't go down this time. He reassessed his target and charged at Jared like a bull at a red cape. Jared moved aside.

Lew didn't notice that his target had shifted. He ended up ramming his head into the front grill of Owen Beardsly's Ford Explorer.

That stopped him for a moment.

But only for a moment. He shook his head to clear it, turned and charged again, snorting like the bull he resembled.

Eden watched, hopping from one foot to the other, trying to decide which one of them she should grab to stop this insanity.

Just then, the woman inside the rest room pushed the door open. She took one look at Jared, crouched and waiting, and Lew barreling toward him headfirst, and let out a piercing scream, pulling the door closed on herself again.

Eden tried once more to inject a plea for reason. "Jared! Stop it. I mean it, stop this right now!"

The only answer Eden got was a sickening thud and an agonized "Oof!" as Jared jumped back and kicked Lew a good one right in the breadbasket. Lew crumpled, holding his stomach. Jared stepped in, hit him on top of the head and then kicked him in the chin with a knee.

The woman hiding in the ladies' room peeked out and screamed again as Lew fell over backward and Jared jumped on top of him. There was a tangle of legs and arms and fists and a lot of awful grunting and groaning.

And then, somehow, Brendan and Patrick and Sam were there, pulling Jared off the other man. And then Lew's friends were there, too, hauling Lew to his feet. A small group of spectators had appeared out of nowhere as well.

Jared cursed his brothers and demanded they let him go. But the Jones boys held on.

Then Sam said to the strangers, "Get him out. And don't let him come back. Understand?"

The other two were not nearly as aggressive as their friend. They nodded and dragged Lew away.

Lew struggled and protested, but Eden thought it was more for pride's sake than anything else. He was staggering, his nose was bleeding and his lip was cut, whereas the worst thing about Jared's face was the scowl on it—and the last

fading remnant of the black eye Eden had inflicted on him
over two weeks before.

After Lew and his buddies had disappeared around the
side of the building, the woman in the bathroom slid out
and made a quick getaway of her own.

Then Sam asked, "Is it going to be safe to let go of you
now, Jared?"

Jared made a low, growling sound.

Patrick and Brendan and Sam exchanged looks. Brendan
suggested, "You just tell us when."

For a few moments they all stood there, Eden glaring at
Jared, while Brendan, Sam and Patrick held him still. The
small crowd that had gathered muttered quietly to each
other. And then Jared grunted.

"All right. Let me go."

Slowly, warily, the other three released him. They stood
back from him.

"Go on inside, folks," Sam said to the spectators. "The
show's over."

The onlookers began filing back into the bar.

Meanwhile, Jared brushed the dust from his sleeves,
tucked in his shirt and rubbed his chin, which, Eden saw
now, had been cut. It was bleeding. She took a handkerchief
from her purse and stepped up to him.

He gave her his narrow-eyed scowl.

"Oh, for heaven's sake. Take this and wipe it up," she
said. She was thoroughly disgusted with him—and very glad
that he hadn't been badly hurt.

He took the handkerchief from her hand and blotted his
chin with it, while she glared at him and he glowered back.

"What the hell's going on out there?" Oggie called from
inside.

"We'd better go on in," Sam said, "Or he'll be wheeling
himself out here, even if he has to batter down the walls in
the hallway to do it."

Brendan and Patrick made sounds of agreement. Jared and Eden, each glaring at the other, paid no mind to Sam's advice. "Don't be long," Sam warned, as he led the other men back in. "You've still got a full house in there."

"We'll be right in," Eden promised, though she kept her eyes locked with Jared's.

When the door had closed behind the brothers, Eden opened her mouth to tell Jared Jones exactly what she thought of his behavior. But then she realized that if she once started telling him off, she might never be able to stop.

She glanced at her watch: a few minutes shy of one. Just a little over an hour to go and they could close the doors on the most successful night they'd seen since Eden became half owner of The Hole in the Wall.

Okay, so she hadn't managed to prevent a fight. But it could have been worse. Much worse. If they went right inside now and picked up where they'd left off, everything would work out just fine from a business point of view, anyway.

She could give Jared Jones the dressing-down he deserved after hours.

Jared, who was watching her expression, chose that moment to let out a rare chuckle. "Are those dollar signs I see shining in your eyes?"

She stuck out her chin at him. "Don't push me, Jared. You're just lucky I'm a businesswoman first."

He was smiling. She didn't like it. He *never* smiled. He held out her handkerchief, which was now stained a vivid crimson in more than one spot. "I think I ruined it."

She didn't care about that. She took the cloth from him without looking at it. "You could have been hurt."

"I'll be hurting all right. Tomorrow. I'm too old to be getting in fights."

She wanted to demand, *Then why did you?* But she held her tongue. She'd demand a lot of things. Later.

She went and pulled back the door. "We've got work to do."

Docile as a lamb, he preceded her inside.

He didn't stay docile for long. Within a half an hour, he was scowling again and glaring at anybody who got too pushy about wanting a drink.

Part of his ill humor was probably caused by the unpleasant incident that occurred shortly after he and Eden went back inside.

They'd gone straight to work, filling drink orders and trying to get back on top of things. In her rush, Eden still managed to spare a glance for the back table. The three women who'd been sitting with Lew and his friends were gone.

Eden had barely had time to notice their absence, when one of them, the petite brunette who'd been after Lew all night, was back.

She came storming through the front door like a mini-hurricane, stomped right up to the bar and pointed a red-nailed finger at Jared.

"You." She poked the finger at the bar. "Right here. Now."

Hesitantly Jared approached.

The little brunette jabbed the bar once more.

Jared moved into place.

The brunette stuck her pert nose right into his scowling face. "You are an animal," she told him. "And you leave Lew alone from now on, or you will answer to me. Understood?"

Jared went on scowling.

"Understood?"

Grimly he nodded.

"Good," the brunette announced. And then she whirled on her pointy-toed high heels and got out of there.

Over at his table, Oggie let out a loud guffaw. "And they try to tell us that *men* run the world!" Then he added, "A round on the house!"

After that, Jared's mood grew progressively darker. To Eden, it seemed as if there had been pressure building in him all night. The fight with Lew had worked like a safety valve, releasing enough steam that Jared had actually relaxed for a minute or two out there in the parking lot, when he'd teased her about the dollar signs in her eyes. But the reprieve had been short. The brunette came in and gave him a hard time and the pressure started building all over again.

By the time Sam finally wheeled Oggie out the door and everyone else went home, Jared was spoiling for a fight all over again.

By then, the only one left to fight with was Eden. And that was just fine with her. She was fed up with him anyway. And now that the big night was over, she had every intention of telling him so.

At first, in the silence after everyone was gone, they ignored each other. Eden cleared all the tables and wiped them down, while Jared cleaned the bar and washed the glassware. Then Eden took the register drawer into the card room and counted what they'd earned that night. It was a stunning amount. She should have been thrilled.

But she was so preoccupied with what she was going to say to Jared that she couldn't even appreciate what a triumph the night had been. She blamed Jared for that, too, for stealing her pleasure in their success.

She set up the drawer for the next day and went back to the main room to return the drawer to the register where it belonged. Jared, she noticed, was already mopping up by then. She pointedly didn't speak to him, but instead took the rest of the money next door to the deserted Mercantile building, where she locked it in the safe that was hidden behind a false cabinet there.

She came back to find him sitting at the counter with a drink in front of him.

He must have taken note of the way her eyes widened when she saw the tall glass, and realized she was thinking that the night had driven him to drink. He toasted her with the sweating glass and then took a long swallow.

After that, he admitted, "Relax, it's only tonic water," before polishing off the rest. Then he stood up. "About time to call it a night, wouldn't you say?"

To Eden, his words amounted to an outright taunt. "No," she said, pushing the single syllable out through her clenched teeth. "I wouldn't say that at all."

The flap was up at the end of the bar. He went through there and tossed his ice cubes into the steel sink. They clattered loudly. "Well, then. What *would* you say?" He set the glass in the sink to be washed tomorrow.

She hardly knew where to begin. But she managed. "You were way out of line, out there in the parking lot tonight."

Idly, as if he were wandering aimlessly rather than moving with absolute purpose, he came back around to her side of the bar. "Oh, was I?"

"Yes. You were."

He flipped over the stool he'd been sitting on and placed it on the bar with the rest of the stools. "That's not how I saw it."

Eden reminded herself to stay calm. She wanted to explain to him very reasonably just what an overbearing oaf he'd been. She took in a long breath. "I have worked very hard, Jared, to make this bar the kind of place where everyone can come and have a good time without worrying that they'll get their heads bashed in. *Anyone* who starts a fight here is sabotaging all the progress that's been made. I believe that you understand that."

He looked away, then looked back at her. Then he said, very patiently, "I didn't start that fight. And you know it."

"Right. Because *he* threw the first punch, *you're* not to blame."

"That's about the size of it. And anyway, nothing happened in your precious bar. We took it outside, so it didn't hurt your business one damn bit."

"It was totally unnecessary."

"Wrong."

She gaped at him. "What do you mean, wrong?"

"I mean it *was* necessary. Both you and I bent over backward giving that bastard a chance to get lost. But he wouldn't take a hint. He needed a lesson in how to behave."

Eden couldn't believe what she was hearing. "You have all the reasoning abilities of a Neanderthal, Jared Jones."

"Call me names if you want. But that's one fool who won't be bothering you again."

"You aren't listening. I said it was completely uncalled-for. Picking a fight with that guy was like…putting out a trash fire with a nuclear warhead."

He folded his arms over his chest. "It was necessary."

"It *was not.* I did not need your help. I had everything under control. All it required was for me to stall him until someone came out."

"Someone did come out. Me."

This was not going as Eden had planned at all. The man actually *refused* to admit that he was the one in the wrong. She put her hands on her hips and moved closer to him. "I was doing fine handling that guy, admit it."

He just looked at her, his eyes like flint, his thin lip slightly curled.

She took another step, until she stood nose to nose with him. "It's my job to deal with people. I've been doing it since I was sixteen years old. And I've been handling creeps in bars since I was old enough to serve alcoholic beverages. I was in no danger from that jerk, and you know it. You're just *jealous,* that's all…."

The minute she said the word, *jealous,* Eden wished she could bite her tongue. It was a taunt, pure and simple. And taunting was beneath her, since she considered herself to be the righteous one here.

But what was done could not be undone. Jared dropped his crossed arms to his sides.

Eden backed up a step. "Um, Jared, I—"

Now he was the one moving in. He closed the distance she'd created. His eyes had changed, gone from flint to curling smoke. "Jealous, am I?"

"Never mind. Really. I shouldn't have said that." She backed up again and started to turn away.

But something had happened to Jared. Something had finally snapped.

"But you did say it." He reached out and wrapped his hand around the back of her neck. Her skin tingled. His touch was electric.

"I—"

"And why the hell shouldn't you say it? It's only the damn truth."

She licked her lips. It was so hard to think, when his hand was there, warm and rough, cupping the back of her neck. "Jared, I..."

He pulled her toward him, so there was no more than a hairbreadth between their bodies. Then he lowered his mouth until it almost touched hers.

"You can bet those sweet, long legs of yours that I'm jealous." His rough whisper slid along her nerves like a physical caress. "As jealous as they come. And that's why it was necessary, what I did to that fool. Because I don't want *anyone* to touch you. Not anyone but *me.*"

Eden gave a small, sharp gasp. Though what she'd just heard was only what she'd been waiting, *longing* to hear, it still stunned her to have him actually say the words at last.

She stared into his eyes like a woman mesmerized. How

long had she waited for him to admit that he wanted her? It seemed like forever.

At last, the waiting was over. He had confessed his desire.

And in the space of an instant, the whole world had changed. The fight with Lew, the threat to her business, none of that mattered.

What mattered—*all* that mattered—was that, at last, he was going to kiss her again. She knew it with every fiber of her being. He'd confessed his desire. And the kiss would come next.

She longed for that kiss.

And yet she feared it, too. Now that it was really here, the exact moment when...

With a low groan, Jared put his mouth on hers.

Eden stood stock-still at the shock. And the wonder. And then she sighed.

He pulled her toward him, into his hard, muscled length.

He murmured something against her lips, some sort of denial, a low, harsh, "This is wrong...."

"Don't stop," she begged, and wrapped her arms around his neck.

He groaned again, a hushed, hungry sort of sound. His tongue traced her lips.

She opened, sighing once more. And then his tongue was inside her mouth, roving, until it found hers and twined with it, in a secret, sparring dance as old as time. Eden gloried in it. This kiss was something she'd waited for her whole life.

His hands moved down her back, stroking, learning every curve as his mouth kissed her with a hunger and a need that stole her breath and left her gasping, overwhelmed, wanting more.

Before, on that aeons-ago morning, when he kissed her at the door of the cabin, he had been careful with her. His hands had been mannerly.

But his hands were not mannerly now.

I want more. More. Her blood seemed to beat the word through her veins. She groaned, as he cupped her buttocks and pulled her up even tighter against him, so she felt him, and knew exactly what he wanted of her. He muttered her name, chanting it, into her mouth, as he went on kissing her and pressing her against him.

And then he was turning her, as he shoved the upturned stools on the bar out of his way. He lifted her, a fleet, seamless movement, so she sat on the bar. Her skirt billowed out around her. He moved, swiftly, before she could grow shy and close her legs against him, and he stood between her knees.

And then he cupped her face in his big, rough hands and kissed her so sweet and long that she feared she would die with the pure, carnal beauty of it.

And then, miracle of miracles, his hands were sliding downward, over her neck, which she arched for him. His lips followed his hands lower...lower. She braced her own hands on the bar, and leaned back on them.

"Eden." He kissed her name into the soft hollow at the base of her throat, at the place where her collar gaped open. He nibbled at her skin there, causing her to release a long, shuddering sigh.

"Jared. Yes..." Was that husky, hungry murmur her own?

His hands slid lower then, nudging aside the little fringed vest she wore, until they found the shape of her breasts. He cupped them gently. Her nipples, through the layers of her shirt and bra, hardened for him. She knew that he must be able to feel them, firm with yearning, wanting more.

He put his head there, between her breasts, and nuzzled her. She brought one hand forward and held his head, pulling him against her, cooing "Yes..." as she stroked his silky brown hair.

And then he kissed her, through her shirt and her bra, a moist, suckling kiss. His mouth sought and found her nipple, closing on it through her clothing, taunting it, arousing it, until it ached and yearned for even more.

His hands strayed down, stroking, seeking, first gliding over her skirt, then caressing her bare knees. And then— she gasped and moaned—sliding up, to the hem of her panties, tracing the elastic there....

And then he froze.

"Jared?" She forced her heavy eyelids to flutter open.

He was watching her, desire still there in his eyes, making them look slightly glazed.

"This is wrong." He was pulling back, smoothing down her skirt over her knees. "I don't believe in—"

She threw her arms around his neck, brought her face right up to his and made no effort to hide the desperation she was feeling. "Take me home, Jared. Take me to the cabin. And make love to me. Please."

He put his hands on her waist in a distancing gesture. "Damn it, Eden, you don't know what—"

"I know exactly what. I want you. You want me. And we...like each other, don't we?"

"Damn it, Eden."

"Don't we? Don't you...like me, Jared?"

He let out a shuddering breath. "Yes."

She hurried on. "I knew it. And I...feel for you. So let's give it a chance. That's all people get in this world, Jared. A chance."

"There's no point. And it's wrong."

She took his face between her hands. "No, it is not wrong. It is *not*. It's never wrong, when there's love."

He blinked. "Love? What the hell are you saying, Eden?"

Eden looked into his eyes. This was it. The moment when

she could play safe and lie, or tell the truth and put her poor heart at his feet.

She chose truth. She lifted her chin. "I'm saying that I love you, Jared."

He swore low and feelingly and pulled loose of her gentle grasp. He turned away.

"Oh, Jared, please. Look at me."

He faced her again, but what he said was not encouraging. "You're crazy. You know about me. I'm not the kind of guy a woman like you should waste her love on."

Eden refused to waver. She kept her chin high. "That's my decision."

"I'm through with love, Eden."

That hurt. That really hurt. But still, she did not let her shoulders slump. "I'm not asking for your love. Did I ask for your love?"

His gray gaze was wary. "No."

"Okay, then. I'm just telling you how it is for me. You don't have to do a thing about it, Jared. That's okay. But you do admit you like me. And want me. Right?"

"Right." The word was a low growl.

"And this really isn't working out—our *understanding,* I mean. Is it?"

"Hell. All right. No, it's not."

"So maybe we'd be better off to go about this a different way."

"What way?"

Eden opened her mouth to tell him.

But a flood of agonized embarrassment overcame her. No. She couldn't. Wouldn't. It was bad enough that she'd revealed her love to him, only to be told it would never be returned. But to baldly suggest that they become lovers until he left town again...

It was too much. That far she would not go.

Looking away from him, she jumped down from the bar

and smoothed her skirt. Then she turned to straighten the stools that he'd pushed every which way in those few glorious moments of passion they had shared.

From behind her, he demanded again, "I asked you, what way?"

She went on fixing the stools. "Never mind. Let it go. We'll sleep on it tonight, and—"

He touched her shoulder. "No."

She froze. "Excuse me?"

"I said no." He turned her to face him, wrapping his hands around her upper arms. He looked hard into her eyes. "All my damn life I've tried to do the right thing. Do you understand?"

His grip was so warm and strong. Ah, how she longed to...

"Eden. Do you understand?"

She nodded.

"And somehow," he continued, "the right thing just about always went wrong."

She nodded again.

"In A.A., they have a saying. *One day at a time.* Have you heard that?"

"Yes."

"So maybe that's how you and I should take it. One day at a time. Starting with tonight."

"What are you telling me, Jared?"

The flinty eyes were turning once more to smoke. "I'm not telling. I'm asking."

"Asking what?"

"Asking if we could go back to a few minutes ago, to what you asked me a few minutes ago."

"What I asked you—?"

"To take you home to the cabin and—"

Eden felt hope glowing warm in her heart. It was a start. A rocky one maybe, but a start nonetheless.

She said, "Take me home to the cabin, Jared. And make love to me. Please."

His warm hands slid up over her shoulders. He cupped her face. "Damn. What's a man to do when a woman says *please?*"

Chapter Eleven

They drove the short distance together, in Jared's pickup. Eden sat close to him, her head on his shoulder, her hand resting on his hard thigh.

At the cabin, he parked where he'd parked before, beneath the fir tree by the front deck. After he stopped the truck, he sat for a moment, looking at her through the gloom of the cab.

"Do you want to back out?"

She couldn't see his eyes in the darkness, but she could feel his gaze nonetheless. "No. Why? Do you?"

"Hell, no." He chuckled. Eden relished the sound. His chuckles were so rare. "I never wanted to go through with anything as much as I want to go through with this. You're sure you don't plan to get smart and call this off?"

She leaned toward him and breathed in the manly scent of him. "No way." She kissed him, on the side of his chin, near the place where he'd been cut in the fight with Lew.

He made a little growling noise, and his arms went around her. His mouth sought hers.

Outside, a slight wind came up, causing a low, sweet sighing in the trees. But the sound was not nearly as sweet as the sighing that went on in the cab of Jared's pickup right then.

Reluctantly he pulled away. "Let's go in."

"Okay."

They walked up the stone steps to the kitchen door with their arms around each other.

Eden flipped on the overhead light once they were inside, regretting the action the moment it was accomplished. After the soft darkness, she had to squint just to get her bearings in the sudden, harsh brightness. She almost flicked the light off again, but then restrained herself. She should probably offer him some refreshment—didn't a woman always offer a man a drink first?—and she'd look pretty silly stumbling around in the dark trying to get him a cola.

She turned to Jared and pasted on a smile. "I'm not, um, really experienced with this." It was the understatement of the year, but he would find that out soon enough.

He took the words at face value. "That makes two of us."

She realized exactly what he meant. Jared Jones had only made love with two women, both of them his wives. He was strict with himself, in terms of his beliefs. Eden liked that. She didn't want a man who held lovemaking cheap.

She felt her stiff smile relax a little. She even dared to brush at a lock of his hair that had fallen over his forehead. "Should I offer you a soda or something?"

He smiled back. His smile was a wonder to her, unpracticed and so very real. "If you offered, should I take it?"

She looked down. "Never mind. Let's skip the soda."

"Good idea." He flipped off the harsh light, casting the room once more into night shadow.

They stood facing each other. And then he asked through the darkness, "Where the hell were we?"

"Excuse me?" She had no idea what he meant.

And then she felt his finger, very lightly, hooking under her purse strap and sliding it off her arm. He whisked it away and set it on the floor somewhere nearby. She didn't notice where. And she didn't much care, either.

She felt his touch again, on her shoulder, right where the purse had hung. The touch trailed down. He took one small piece of her vest's fringe between his fingers and he gave a tug. She swayed against him, sighing.

"I said, where were we?" He guided the vest off her shoulders and set it aside. She heard it land on a chair by the table not two feet away.

She swallowed, thinking, *Here I am in the dark with this man I've grown to love, this man I want so much—and yet fear a little, too....*

Her body felt strangely languorous. And weightless as well. As if she were floating upright in some deep, warm pool.

His strong hands were at her waist. He waltzed her backward, quickly, effortlessly. Until she came up short against the kitchen counter.

"I think we were right about—" he lifted her "—here."

She found herself sitting on the counter, just as she'd been on the bar earlier. Her skirt billowed out again. Jared moved swiftly into the same place he'd been before, close up against her, between her parted knees.

He captured her mouth then.

"Oh, yes," she heard herself sigh against his parted lips. "Right about...here."

His lips played on hers in a long, lovely kiss, while she stroked his hard shoulders and kissed him joyfully in return. He pulled her even closer, so that she could feel his heart beating, strong and swift, against her own.

Then down below, his hands closed on her thighs beneath her skirt. His touch was warm, both a promise and a demand. Eden drew in a long, shaky breath as he guided her legs, gently, inexorably, wider. And then his palms slid around to cup her buttocks and pull her even tighter against him, so that her womanhood was pressed to his hardness.

Her senses heated even more than before. Her whole body knew only one yearning, to be closer to him, to be one with him. Not even realizing she did it, she wrapped her legs around his hips, hooking her boots together.

His hands slid under her thighs.

She moaned as he lifted her. She held on for dear life, still lost in his kiss, as he reeled backward from the counter. She could feel him fully, as she settled onto him, once the counter no longer supported her. He was so hard, pressed against her at her most secret place. His hands cupped her thighs, and his mouth demanded everything from hers.

He carried her like that, kissing her, holding her tight and high against him. Out of the kitchen, through the main room and into her own bedroom they went. And then he turned. She felt her back come in contact with something solid. Her heavy eyelids opened a little. He held her pressed against the wall, in the small space between one of the two windows and her vanity table.

Slowly he let her legs down, until she was standing again. Then he put his hands on the wall to either side of her head and he kissed her some more, his whole body caressing her, just as she pressed and rubbed against him.

Eden was in ecstasy. And when he reached up and cupped her chin and then tenderly stroked her cheek, she took his hand and guided it down, until it was between her breasts.

She forced herself to look at him. The soft glow of starlight from the window showed his eyes to her. His eyes were pure smoke right then. A woman could lose herself forever in eyes like those.

At her breasts, she felt his hand moving, doing as she'd prayed he might, slipping the buttons of her shirt from their holes. He smoothed the shirt open, sweetly, gently, and guided it off her shoulders and away.

Then he stood back a little and he took off his own shirt and vest, tossing them aside as soon as he was out of them. She saw the hard, sculptured planes of his upper body, the little trail of hair that ran down his belly into his jeans. She remembered the night she'd watched him sleep. That night, she had almost let herself imagine doing just what they were doing now....

He bent, never letting go of her gaze, and he pulled off his boots and socks. Then he stood. From his back pocket, he took three condoms. He turned, walked to the bed and set them on the little table there.

Eden watched him, unmoving. She'd known about the condoms, of course. Before they left the tavern, he'd acquired them from the machine in the men's room. That machine was another of Eden's improvements. She'd seen enough in her life to have come to believe in safe sex.

Jared returned to her. Looking in her eyes once more, he unbuttoned his jeans and slipped out of both them and his briefs at the same time.

Then he straightened and stood naked before her. Eden thought he was beautiful, as a man can be beautiful, lean-muscled, sculptured, poised for displays of power and grace. His manhood stood out rigidly, proof of his desire.

Eden knew a slight apprehension when she saw that most private part of him. She thought of what would happen, very soon. But she believed in her love, and she believed this night would be magic for her. She drew in a deep breath and pushed her anxiety aside.

She reached behind her to unclasp her bra. It came undone easily, the cups falling loose from her breasts. But somehow, just to toss the thing away seemed more than she could manage. In a last gesture of shy modesty, she held the scrap of lacy fabric close to her chest.

A knowing, tender smile played on Jared's lips. He lifted a hand. Then, his eyes still locked with hers, he slid the straps, one at a time, from her shoulders. He gave a tug.

She released the bra. It fell away. And she was naked before him from the waist up.

With the same hand, he caressed the side of her face, just a whisper of a touch. And then his fingers strayed behind her head. He pulled out the comb that held her chin-length hair up in the back. The soft, short curls fell around her cheeks.

He put both hands on her shoulders and slowly brought them down, over the swells of her breasts. He cupped her breasts, one in each hand. With a low moan, he lowered his head. He licked a nipple, then blew on it.

Eden sighed and squirmed in delight. He took the nipple fully into his mouth. She groaned. And then he lavished the same attention on the other waiting breast.

His hands, meanwhile, drifted down, over her waist and then around to the little hook and the zipper at the back of her skirt. The hook came open, the zipper parted. The skirt slid to the floor. Her half-slip quickly followed it.

Eden felt the night air on her skin and knew she was standing, naked but for her panties and cowboy boots, in front of Jared Jones. His roving hand dipped into the waistband of her panties. She gasped. He eased the panties off and helped her to stand while he got them over her boots. After that, he knelt to remove her boots and socks, too.

And then he was pressing himself against her again. His hand returned to the vulnerable center of her, dipping in, feeling her readiness and making her more ready still.

Eden, lost in wonder, rolled her head back and forth against the wall and let the sensations his touch aroused have their way with her. He said something low and unintelligible.

She said, "Yes," in return. It didn't matter to Eden what he said. Her answer would always be, forever, "Yes..."

She felt him then, kissing his way down her stomach. She stiffened.

He pleaded, "Eden, don't hold back. Let me..."

And she let him. How could she not let him? She *wanted* to let him, though the kiss he gave her then was a kiss she'd never known before.

It was the most intimate of kisses. She gloried in it. She opened for him and pushed herself against him as he knelt before her, put his mouth on her and drove her higher and higher, to the top of some magical, mythical cliff.

She hovered there, moaning. And then she fell, a falling that was also a soaring, out and over, higher and higher, into an explosion of heat and light. She cried out once, a long, keening sound.

And then she slowly relaxed, feeling that the whole, beautiful world lay beneath her, ready to fold her against its heart as she drifted slowly, sweetly down.

Jared stood, kissing his way back up her body, as she returned to the real world. He pressed himself against her. She felt the wiry roughness of his chest hairs, the heat of his skin, the hardness pushing at the juncture of her thighs. He smelled of that soap of his that she liked and of the smoke from the bar, and of himself, a man-scent, slightly musky with desire.

His mouth covered hers. She tasted herself. She was boneless and liquid, hardly knowing how she remained upright, except that his hard body held her there against the wall.

He said against her lips, "I want you now. You're ready for me now. Open and soft. Now, Eden. Now..."

She said the only word she knew right then. "Yes."

He cupped her bottom and brought her up against him again. She wrapped her legs around his hips and she felt him, against her entrance, straining at her with his own readiness. He carried her that way, over to the bed.

He laid her down, then came down quickly with her. Then he fumbled for a moment with a condom. When that was done, he poised himself above her.

Eden lay beneath him, grateful for the sweet lassitude that had stolen over her limbs after the fulfillment he had just given her. She looked up into his face. This was what she'd wanted, what she'd waited for. She was doing the right thing, she was sure of it.

She could see the glaze of hunger and desire in his eyes. He was far gone in it. And she was glad. Because she wanted him to claim her. And if he knew her secret too soon, she feared he'd call a halt.

He said her name, braced above her on his extended arms.

She gave him her answer, her only answer, "Yes…" Then she brazenly wrapped her legs around him and pulled him down to her.

She felt him, there, at the entrance to her womanhood. He moved, finding the right angle.

And then he thrust into her.

Crying out at the sharp, burning pain, Eden drove upward to meet him, gripping his hard buttocks, taking him fully inside, though her eyes teared and her untried body protested such a sharp invasion.

Jared froze. And then he bucked up onto his arms once more. His lips drew away from his teeth. He glared down at her.

"What the…?"

Eden whimpered a little—both at the way it burned down there, where he felt so very large, buried in the tender heart of her—and in response to the look in Jared's eyes.

"You're a *virgin*..." It was an accusation.

She bit her lip and forced herself to answer. "Not... anymore."

Chapter Twelve

Jared threw back his head and groaned at the ceiling.

He poised himself to withdraw.

And then Eden moved, a slow, sweet rolling motion, beneath him.

He groaned again, before he could stifle the sound. He tossed his head and gritted his teeth. He knew he must break this off now. He jerked back.

She held on and pressed herself closer against him.

"No, Eden…"

"Yes, Jared…"

"I should…"

"…never stop…"

He swore then, a poignant oath.

"Please never stop…"

He glared down at her.

"Please…"

He felt himself weakening. "Eden…"

"Yes. Please..."

He hovered there, as if on a precipice, clinging in fading hope to what he knew he should do, while bewitching desire lured him down.

Her soft, final "Please..." finished him off. Jared, enveloped by her, sheathed in her, admitted that the moment for withdrawal had slipped away.

He let go of what he *should* have done. Desire took him down.

She moved again. He moaned in response.

She whispered, "Yes," once more. He drank the word from her sweet, wide mouth.

He didn't deserve her, not even for the limited alliance they'd agreed upon. He shouldn't have taken her. But he couldn't, in the end, refuse the heat and wonder she offered him so freely, with no holding back.

In all his life, bound by duty, lured by violence, he had never known such a woman as this. Who talked too much and listened too well, and whose smile pierced him in a place he hadn't really known he possessed.

He surrendered.

With a low, hoarse cry, he submitted to his own feral nature. He plunged into her hard and fast, pushing himself ever deeper, into the center of her sweetness, calling out her name.

She held him to her, opened herself wider, letting him claim all of her, though he knew it must hurt her, virgin that she was.

But Jared couldn't control himself by then. He was lost. Gone. Finished. He bucked up, and then surged into her, deeper than all the thrusts that went before. He felt his seed spilling, pumping out of him in that culminating ecstasy that turned a man inside-out.

And then, with a long, shuddering sigh, he sank upon her.

Relaxing along the smooth, satiny length of her, he tangled his fingers in the bright spill of her hair.

It seemed to him that a sweet eternity passed as he lay there, listening to her breathing and his own, feeling the wonderful softness of her, idly stroking her hair. The skin of his hand felt rough against the short, silky strands. He wrapped a lock around his index finger.

And then he allowed his touch to roam the little distance to her neck. He caressed the soft flesh there and put his thumb, possessively, on the deep pulse of her throat.

She was lying very still. He sensed an apprehension in her. A slight tension.

Well, she *should* be tense. She had lied to him. If not with words, then with what she'd *failed* to say.

She was what? Twenty-six, he thought she'd said once. In this day and age, there weren't a lot of twenty-six-year-old virgins around. She must have known he would assume she'd been with a man before.

And she'd probably also known that there was no way he would have taken her if she'd told him the truth. To bed an *innocent*, let alone a woman who was not his wife, was the kind of thing only a womanizer would do. And Jared Jones was no womanizer. A troublemaking unemployed over-the-hill alcoholic, maybe. But a seducer of innocent women?

Never. No way.

Which was why she *hadn't* told him.

So if she was worried he might be mad, well, she *ought* to be worried.

But *was* he mad?

He nuzzled her neck, ran a hand down the slim curve of her ribs to her waist.

How the hell could he be mad? She'd just given him all he'd ever known of heaven. A man couldn't be mad at a woman for that.

"Jared?" Her voice sounded hesitant, a little scared.

"Yeah?"

"Are you…angry at me?"

He smiled to himself and rolled slightly to the side. As he did that, he slipped out of her. He felt the wetness along his thigh and looked down.

The starry light from the window above the bed shone down on her bare thighs. There was a dark trail across them: blood.

"Oh," she said softly, looking at the blood, too.

"I'll be back." He rose from the bed.

He went to the bathroom, got rid of the condom and moistened a towel with warm water. Then he returned.

She'd slipped beneath the sheet while he was gone. Modestly covered, she was peering at him, her brown eyes wary. He thought she looked more like a virgin, right now when she was no longer one, than she ever had waltzing around The Hole in the Wall acting as if she knew everything there was to know about men and their ways.

He approached her, carrying the towel. Her eyes widened. He smiled, reassuringly he hoped, though he'd never been very good at smiling.

He carefully kept eye contact with her as he took the hem of the sheet and pulled it back, revealing her slender, pink body. She allowed him to uncover her, biting her lip the whole time.

He knew exactly why she was keeping that poor lip caught between her teeth. To keep from babbling. She was nervous as hell now. And when Eden was nervous, her jaws started flapping like crazy, as a rule.

And, oh, she was beautiful. As long and slim as a willow wand. With high, firm breasts and a waist made for a man's hands. The curls on her mound were darker than those on her head. He couldn't see in the dim room if they were auburn or light brown, but he knew how silky they were.

He'd felt that for himself. His gaze drifted lower, to her legs. They were a damn poem, those legs of Eden's. He was getting hard again, even at his age, just looking at them.

Carefully he put one knee on the bed and half knelt there beside her. Then he gently began to use the moistened towel, to wipe the traces of blood from her thighs.

He concentrated on what he was doing and didn't glance at her face, both because he enjoyed it and because he wanted to give her a moment of privacy, a moment when he wasn't looking in her eyes. He felt her body relaxing as she realized that he only meant to tend to her comfort. Her legs parted slightly. He tenderly stroked the blood away there, too.

And while he stroked the signs of her lost innocence away, he tried his damnedest not to think that no other man would have that of her. That in this at least, he would always be the only one. He had no right to think that, because his whole intention, as they both knew, was to get out of her life as soon as his father was back on his feet.

When he was done, he took the towel back to the bathroom. And then he returned to her and slid under the sheet that she'd once again pulled up.

"Jared?" she asked, once he was settled in, with his arm beneath her head and one hand cupping her breast.

"Um?"

"You didn't answer me. *Are* you angry?"

"No. I'm not angry." He toyed with her breast a little, felt the nipple grow in quick response. He liked that, the way she responded to him. Her breathing had changed a little. It was quicker, shallower.

He thought of taking her again, but then realized how sore she probably was. He could wait. They had time.

Yeah, but not forever...

He blocked out the taunting voice. This was just for now. One day at a time. As they'd agreed.

"I thought you wouldn't...make love to me, if you knew." She arched a little toward his teasing hand.

"You were right, I wouldn't have." He shifted, pulling his arm from beneath her head and canting up on an elbow. He stroked her hair again. "And hell. I guess I'm glad you tricked me."

She smiled then, a burst of sunlight in the moon-dark room. "Oh, Jared. I'm so *glad* you're glad."

He smiled back, the third or fourth time tonight. Damn. He was turning into a grinning fool. He'd never smiled as much in a year as he had in the last two weeks, since this tall, enchanting creature had taken over his house and half of his inheritance.

He looked at the clock on the bed stand, the clock she'd clobbered him with that first night. It was late. Very late.

She read his mind. "Um. Snuggle down." She fitted herself against him as if she's been sleeping with him for years.

He closed his eyes and thought of how he really did want to ask her about how she could look the way she looked, handle herself as she did, and yet still have been a virgin a few hours ago.

He wrapped an arm and a leg around her. She snuggled even closer.

It was late, he decided. He could ask those questions later. They had time.

But not forever, the taunting voice in his head whispered.

Jared pretended not to hear the voice. He was wrapped up in his woman's arms and halfway off to sleep.

Morning came too soon.

Eden hadn't remembered to set the alarm, but she'd left all the curtains and windows open. The gradual lightening of the room did the trick. That and the incessant squawking of a group of mouthy blue jays outside the window.

Jared awoke looking at the clock. It was eight-fifteen.

Groaning, he brought up an arm and covered his eyes. And then, as the events of last night stole into his mind, he smiled. He turned his head toward Eden's side of the bed and raised his arm enough to look at her.

She wasn't there.

He realized then that there was water running in the bathroom. She must be having her shower.

He dropped his arm and sat up.

And every muscle in his body shouted at him never to move again.

"Ugh," Jared grunted, rubbing the small of his back and shaking his head.

He thought of the fight with Lew and felt some regret. He was still young enough to come up with the moves when he had to. Unfortunately he was also old enough now to have to pay the price later on.

Carefully he eased his legs over the side of the bed and put his feet on the little woven rug there. He rubbed his jaw, feeling the tender place where Lew had clipped him a good one. Then, cautiously, he stood up.

He felt as stiff as an untanned hide. Slowly he stretched, forcing his muscles to stir and respond, though they seemed to be screaming at him to get back into bed and not move for a week. He knew he'd done more damage to Lew than Lew had done to him, but he couldn't console himself with thoughts of how Lew must be feeling right now.

Lew, the lucky stiff, was twenty-five at most. At that age, Jared could have taken on ten idiots, slept the night in a ditch and still arisen in the morning ready to fight again.

Jared forced himself to bend at the waist. It was pure agony. He cursed Lew and his youthful resilience, as he felt each of his vertebrae crack in agonizing turn.

This getting old, Jared decided, was *not* the most fun he'd ever had. On a morning like this, he could *almost* feel sympathy for his father, who was constantly complaining that his aging bones didn't work the way they used to.

Jared was so concerned with getting his body loosened up a little, that he hardly noticed when the shower stopped running. Had he noticed, he would have slipped into his jeans before Eden could emerge from her shower and see him in the altogether by the bright light of day. Jared was a modest man by nature. Besides that, last night had been Eden's first experience with to-the-limit lovemaking. He would have put on some clothes in consideration for her tender sensibilities.

But he didn't notice. And so when Eden opened the bathroom door she found herself staring at a naked man doing push-ups on her bedroom floor.

Her first reaction was more of appreciation than embarrassment. Jared was a marvelously put-together specimen of a man. There really wasn't an ounce of fat on him. Eden watched the muscles of his arms and back flex and release as he raised and lowered his entire body. She thought that it was really a delightful plus that she'd ended up loving a man who was so very nice to look at. She blushed a little, as her roving gaze traveled lower and she was looking at the rocklike hardness of his buttocks and his strong, hair-dusted thighs. Also, she could see his manhood. It looked much different than it had the night before when he'd been making love to her.

Right then, he caught sight of her, out of the corner of his eye. He fairly leapt to his feet.

"Good God, woman!" He flew to the little chair, where he'd tossed his jeans last night. He shook out the jeans and shoved his legs into them, buttoning them up as if his life depended on it. Once he was covered, he barked out gruffly, "You surprised the hell out of me."

Eden felt her slight blush turn to crimson. She gathered her robe closer around her. "Oh. I'm sorry. I..." She gestured, rather ineffectually. And then she started babbling. "I went ahead and took my shower first. But I was careful not to use all the hot water. There's plenty left. So you can go ahead, if you want. And take yours. And I'll go get breakfast started. I thought maybe French toast. Do you like French toast? Because if you don't, I can just make eggs and bacon, or whatever you—"

"Eden."

She hitched in a breath. "Huh?"

A slow smile was curling his mouth. Oh, she really did like it when he smiled. And then he was coming toward her, soundlessly on his bare feet. She looked at his chest, at the beautiful, sculptured hardness of it, at that little tempting trail of hair that went down toward his jeans.

He tipped her chin up with a finger. She saw that there was a bruise on his jaw, beneath the place where Lew had broken the skin.

"French toast is great. Whatever you make is great." His eyes looked into hers, seeing everything, *knowing* everything.

She looked at his mouth. For a man who'd only made love with two women before her, he really knew how to kiss. But then, he could have done a lot of kissing, couldn't he? He could have been a kissing fool, kissed every woman he met, and not have made love all the way with them. Just because you kissed someone didn't mean you had to sleep with them, after all.

"What are you thinking?" he asked softly.

"You have a bad bruise on your chin."

Well, it was the truth. She *had* been thinking that. Before the other about how many women he might have kissed.

"That bruise is the least of my problems. You should feel the rest of me."

I have. You felt wonderful, she thought but didn't say.

"Serves you right. For fighting. Nothing ever gets solved by fighting." She tried to sound reproving.

"I know."

"You do?"

"You bet. I *oughtta* know, if anybody does. I've been in enough fights."

"So why did you get in a fight last night?"

"Haven't we covered this ground already?"

"Yes," she agreed. "I guess so."

"Then can we leave it behind?"

"Yes. All right. That's fine."

"Good." He gave her one of those smiles that she enjoyed more each time he bestowed one on her. "But I will say this much."

"Yes?"

"I'm really working on it—staying out of fights, I mean."

"I'm glad."

His mouth covered hers then, his hands slipping down to wrap around the collar of her robe and pull her closer. Eden let out a long sigh as his tongue slipped beyond her lips.

She let her neck relax. His hand left her collar to cradle her head, holding her still for more of his arousing, blood-heating kisses.

Then, just when she was thinking how close the bed was, he drew slightly away. "If I don't take that shower now, I'll probably never take it."

She smiled up at him. She knew her eyes were shining and that he'd felt her arousal in the way she'd melted like butter in the sun when his lips touched hers. She didn't mind that he knew what she felt for him. It was obvious that he wanted her, too. And beyond that, she was giving all of herself to him, unashamed, in the brave hope that her love and her passion would be enough to make him surrender his wounded, hardened heart.

She kissed him once more, a swift, sweet peck on the lips. "Well, go on, then. I'll make breakfast." She turned him around and pointed him toward the bathroom door. Then she hurried to get dressed.

He joined her in the kitchen twenty minutes later and helped her put the finishing touches on their breakfast. They sat down and ate. Then together they cleaned up after the meal.

Eden felt that there was a certain tension in the air through all of this. Jared was quiet, though whenever she looked up, she found him watching her. And she was constantly on guard against talking too much, so it was a silent breakfast, for the most part.

By the time they got to washing up, Eden had begun to wonder if something was wrong.

She was putting the final dish away as Jared finished rinsing out the sink. She turned to find him drying his hands, looking at her.

"What time do you have to be at work?"

"Ten-thirty."

He shot a glance over his shoulder, at the clock on the wall behind him. "Not for over an hour, then?" He was looking at her again.

Suddenly she knew what was making him so quiet.

She felt a kind of warming, a lovely weakening down in her lower belly. He wanted to…make love again, that was it. Before she left.

He hung the towel up and then he took the few steps to where she stood. Slowly he ran the back of a finger down the side of her cheek.

"Are you sore?" He asked the question gently. "From last night?"

She swallowed and nodded.

"How sore?"

"A little. Not too much."

His hand was sliding back, clasping her nape, creating those lovely, tingling sensations. He bent close, yet he kept his body slightly away from hers.

"I should leave you alone now." His lips brushed hers, insistent, yet restrained.

"Jared..." She dared to touch him, to put her hands on his shoulders and massage the hard muscles there.

He went on kissing her, a tormenting, teasing, promising kiss. And he spoke against her lips as he kissed them. "I want you. And it'll be a long day without touching you. Say no now, or..."

"Jared..."

"That's not no."

"Jared..."

"Say it, damn it. Say it now."

"But Jared. I...I want you, too."

He let out a low, eager sound. And he took the comb from her hair as he had last night. She heard the clatter it made as he tossed it on the counter. Her hair curled around her face. He smoothed it with his hands. And then he slid one arm behind her knees, wrapped the other around her shoulders and swung her high against his chest.

He carried her to the bedroom and laid her down on the bed.

She stared up at him, dazed, as he stripped off his clothes with such swiftness that it seemed one minute he was fully dressed—and the next he was wearing nothing at all. Then he came down beside her and began helping her out of her own clothes.

They were naked in no time. And he was guiding her down and kissing her until she felt her whole body was on fire, a flame of pure longing. For him.

The slight burning from the loss of her virginity faded to no more than a memory as he touched her and kissed her,

making her ready for loving once more. His fingers did
things, wonderful things. And then he kissed her there, at
her feminine center as he had last night, so that she was
open and receptive, longing to have him fill her.

Then, pausing only to slide on protection, he rose above
her. She took him inside her easily this time, in one smooth,
slow stroke.

And when he was in, he lay there for a while above her,
joined with her but absolutely still. His breathing was careful as he let her feel him and know him and get used to
having him there.

She stroked his back and cooed wordless things in his
ear. And he kissed her, his lips so warm and good against
her mouth, whispering how much he wanted her, how much
he wanted *this*....

And then he began to move.

She knew what heaven felt like, when he began to move.

Eden moved with him, at first slowly, then faster, then
slowly once more.

"Oh!" Eden cried out. Her eyes flew open in surprise.
This was different than last night. Last night she had not
felt her body rising toward completion while he was inside
her.

Jared was watching her, knowing what was happening to
her. He lifted his hips and brought them to meet hers once
more.

"Oh, yes..." Her eyes drifted closed.

Their bodies rose and fell as one. Soon, Eden felt herself
spinning out and away, shattering into a thousand tiny stars
of delight. She tossed her head back on the pillows and felt
her body closing around him, milking him, as fulfillment
shimmered through her.

He found his own satisfaction just as hers began to fade
to afterglow. He drove into her, insistent, lost to all thought.

"Eden..."

"Yes..."

She opened herself utterly to him, meeting his every hungry, wild thrust. He drove deep. He groaned.

And then, with a long sigh, his muscular body relaxed on top of hers.

She held him gently, stroking his back as his breathing found its regular rhythm. As he'd done last night, he combed her hair with his hands.

Eden, who'd been seeking a true home all her life, found herself thinking that she'd found her home at last. Her home was right here, in this man's arms.

And then the phone rang.

Jared muttered a low curse against her ear. "Don't answer it."

She pushed at his shoulders a little, so she could meet his gaze. "Why not?"

"It'll only be my father. Or some busybody or other. I'm not up to dealing with any of them now."

"But Jared—"

"Fine." He slid to the side and landed on his feet by the bed. Eden looked at him, stunned as usual at the lithe splendor of his body and also bewildered by his abruptness. The mood had been so lazy and lovely until just a few seconds ago.

"Jared, wait...."

The phone went on ringing.

"If you're going to answer it, then do it," Jared said over his shoulder. He was already halfway through the bathroom door, his jeans in one hand.

The phone rang again and Jared closed the door.

Eden stared at the door he'd shut on her, wondering how a moment so beautiful could have vanished so quickly. Then she picked up the phone.

"Ha. I caught you. I know you're probably just heading out the door, but—"

"Laurie." Eden pulled the sheet over herself and combed her tangled hair with her free hand. "Hi. Look, it's okay. I'm…running a little behind today."

"Well, I won't keep you. But it turns out I've got a day off tomorrow. I thought I'd come up, see my folks and Great-uncle Oggie. The usual, you know." Sacramento, where Laurie lived, was an hour and a half away. She went on. "And I was thinking, since tomorrow's Monday, that you'd be off, too. We could go to dinner in Nevada City or something. What do you say?"

Eden's mind balked. Since last night, her whole life had changed. Now Jared seemed to fill every corner of it. And yet they had agreed to take things one day at a time. And they hadn't discussed what they'd tell everybody, about the two of them.

"Eden? You still with me?"

"Yes, I'm here. Just thinking. Listen, why don't you come here to the cabin for dinner? I'll fire up the barbecue and toss us a salad and we'll split a bottle of wine."

Eden could hear Laurie's smile. "How you do read my mind. I'll bring the wine."

"Done."

"About six?"

"Perfect."

"Bye, then."

"See ya."

Eden hung up the phone.

"Who was it?" Jared stood in the doorway to the bathroom, wearing his jeans and a scowl.

"Laurie."

"Did you tell her about us?"

"No, I—"

"What did she want?"

"She's coming to town tomorrow. I invited her for dinner

here." Eden gave him her warmest, most open smile. "I hope you'll join us, of course."

He didn't smile back. "I didn't think about this, last night. About everyone knowing."

She spoke gently. "I know. Neither did I, really. But it's okay."

"What do you mean, okay? The whole damn town will be buzzing."

"Oh, Jared. Come on. It can't be that big a deal."

"Oh, can't it?"

"No."

He sauntered into the room and dropped into the little chair by her vanity table. He stared off toward the wall, rubbing the bruise on his chin.

"I've gotta think," he said.

"About what?"

"This is no good. I should have considered this. There'll be nothing but talk, if I start staying here with you."

Eden blinked. "Is that what you were thinking of—staying here?"

He stopped staring at the wall and looked at her. "You don't like the idea?"

She looked down at the sheet she was clutching to her breasts and then back up at him. "No—I mean, yes. I do like it. I just, well, you hadn't said anything, before now."

He looked at the wall again. "I know. It was a bad idea."

Eden felt crestfallen. Now she'd had a moment to consider it, she liked the thought of him staying with her. She liked it a lot. Yet he was already saying he wouldn't. "But why?"

He cast her a patronizing look. "I just told you. Because people will talk. It's not so bad for me. I'm used to it. But it won't be good for you. Your reputation will be ruined."

Eden rolled her eyes. "Oh, Jared, please. This is not

1950, for goodness' sake. A woman's private life is her own business.''

"Not in North Magdalene, it's not."

"Jared—"

He stood and began gathering the rest of his strewn clothing. "Look. I should get my truck out of here before someone sees it. And you'd better get moving if you want to be at The Hole in the Wall by ten-thirty. We'll talk about this. Tonight, after closing time. Or tomorrow, when we both have a day off."

"But—"

He was already headed for the door. But before he went through, he turned and pointed a boot at her. "And don't tell anyone about the two of us, until we settle this."

"But Jared, I—"

"Where are your car keys?"

"In my purse, but—"

"Where's your purse?"

"In the kitchen, I think. But I—"

"I'll get your car here in the next half hour. I'll leave the keys in the ignition."

"Jared, why don't you just—"

"Drive you to work? No way. Someone might see."

"Jared—"

"I mean it, keep your mouth shut," he warned again.

And then he was gone.

Chapter Thirteen

As Jared had promised, her car was waiting when Eden went outside a half an hour later.

She was ten minutes late for work, but she hurried to get set up and managed to open the doors on time anyway. And then, once she had the place opened, time slowed to a crawl.

It was Sunday, and Sundays were always quiet. However, today seemed even worse than usual.

Eden tried to make the time go faster by cleaning everything in sight. She wiped the dust from the bottles on the highest shelves, bottles containing obscure liqueurs and other spirits with weird names that people rarely ordered. She cleaned the popcorn machine. She even took an old knife to the undersurface of the bar itself, in an effort to scrape free the numberless wads of chewing gum that thoughtless customers were always sticking there.

Owen Beardsly, whose wife taught school with Delilah, was sitting at the far end of the bar when Eden started in on the chewing gum. "Aw, come on, Eden," Owen complained. "Everyone in town admires you for what you've done with this place. But there's such a thing as a step too far. Scraping the gum from under the lip of the bar falls in that category."

Eden looked up. "I want to keep busy." Each time she stopped working, she thought of Jared and the way he'd left her this morning. Everything was so up in the air. She wouldn't see him again until seven tonight. She missed him already.

"So do something that matters and give me another shot," Rocky suggested from his usual spot on his favorite stool.

"Yeah," Owen chimed in. "I'm ready for another drink, too. And I mean it. Put that knife away. Please? Watching you do that is making my ulcer act up."

Eden wanted to tell Owen that he shouldn't be drinking anyway, if he had an ulcer. Also, it was Sunday morning and why wasn't he in church? His wife, Linda Lou, was probably fit to be tied that he was hanging around the bar at this time of day.

But Eden kept her mouth shut. She knew she was just feeling edgy about Jared. It would be bad business to take her personal frustrations out on her customers.

She put the knife away, washed her hands and served Rocky and Owen their drinks.

Somehow, she got through the day.

But, as Jared had warned her, people certainly did talk. The fight in the parking lot the night before seemed to be common knowledge today. Everyone had a remark or a question about it.

"Hey, Eden. Heard about the fight last night. What exactly was that all about?"

Eden knew how to handle such talk. She turned it right

back on the questioner. "Oh, you heard that, did you? From who?"

"It's all over town, I'm telling you. The word is that Jared Jones and some big blond kid beat the hell out of each other."

"Oh, really?"

"Yeah, really. And you still didn't tell me. What was it about?"

"Well, I wasn't in the fight. You ought to ask Jared. Or that big blond kid."

"But I heard you were there. I heard they were fighting over you."

"You heard that, did you?"

"Yeah. Is it true?"

"No. It was about common courtesy. That big blond kid had no manners."

"Aw, come on, Eden. Tell the truth. It was over you."

"Is that what you think?"

"Yeah. That's what I think."

"Well, what goes on in your head is up to you. Here, have some cocktail mix. And take this half-dollar and play something good on the jukebox. It's too quiet in here."

All the prying questions and knowing grins did get a little old after a while. But Eden was handling it fine, all in all. Maybe it would be harder to take if they knew that Jared had gone home with her last night. But she doubted it. A love affair between her and Jared Jones would be more likely to be discussed in whispers, behind her back.

And Eden couldn't have cared less what people said behind her back. She was perfectly capable of just ignoring such stuff. But she feared Jared wasn't.

And she feared right.

When he came in at seven, he was scowling. Eden felt a quick thrill all through her body at the sight of him. She couldn't help remembering what had passed between them in the dark last night *and* today in the bright morning light.

But the grim set to his jaw and the flinty look in his eyes was distinctly unloverlike. She greeted him. He grunted in return. They switched places. He came behind the bar, she moved out on the floor.

They had enough business the first hour that it was bearable, but more than one man asked Jared about the fight with Lew. Jared answered in terse syllables.

"He needed a lesson. That's all I want to say." Or, "Drop it. You want a refill?"

By eight-thirty, his scowl seemed worse than when he'd come in. Eden bore such surly behavior for as long as she could take it.

Then, when there was a lull, she went around behind the bar and whispered to him, "Please meet me in the back room. Now."

She trotted through the door behind the bar itself, to the little hall that led to the storeroom. She half expected him to ignore her demand, to leave her waiting back there with the cases of whiskey and gin until she gave up and returned to the main room. She sat down to wait on the little stool that they used to reach the supplies on the top shelves.

A moment later, she looked up and he was there, standing in the doorway to the hall.

"What is it?" His voice was low and gruff. "We've got people out there, you know."

She stood up and immediately wished she hadn't. Her knees actually felt weak at the sight of him.

He seemed to be keeping a careful distance from her, staying there in the doorway, where he could turn and bolt at a whim. "Well?"

"I...just wanted to talk to you for a moment. Because you've seemed so angry, ever since you came in tonight. What's wrong?"

He looked at her—a piercing look. She thought he was going to be frank with her, but then he seemed to change his mind.

"We can talk about this later." He started to turn away.

She reached out and grabbed his arm. "Wait."

He froze. He looked down at the hand that was clutching his arm and then back into her eyes. Eden felt his look, burning all through her body. She realized then that, whatever was bothering him, he still wanted her. She suspected that he was exerting iron control over himself to keep from grabbing her.

"What?" His eyes were molten.

"Tell me." She licked her lips because they suddenly felt so dry. "What's making you angry?"

He looked down at her hand on his arm again, a pointed look, one that clearly said, *"Let go."*

Her hand fell away. He started to leave again.

She insisted, "Please, Jared. What is it?"

He stopped and turned to pin her with another look.

She met his gaze, unwavering.

At last he gave out grudgingly, "It's just what I knew was going to happen. The damn story of the fight last night is all anybody's talking about."

"So?"

"And I made the mistake of visiting my father today. He said he called his house this morning early, the house where *I'm* supposed to be staying, and I wasn't there."

"Oh, Jared. You're making a big deal out of nothing."

"The old geezer did a lot of chortling and leering about where in the world I could have been at seven this morning. It was disgusting. He's on to us. I'm sure of it."

"So what?"

"It's not right. Not good for you. You're...a pure woman. And I've ruined you."

"Jared. You really have some seriously outdated ideas here. You have to get over this. Get past it. It's—"

She didn't get a chance to finish. In one of those lightning-swift moves of his, he reached out and grabbed her. She suddenly found herself pressed against his chest. She gasped, then blinked and stared up at him.

"Jared? What *is* it?"

"I should marry you," he said into her upturned face.

"You...you should?" Eden's mind, dulled by the pull his body exerted on her senses, struggled to comprehend his words. They were words she'd been secretly longing to hear for a while now. "Do you mean that?"

Staring at her lips as if he yearned to devour them, and seeming not to have heard either of the questions she'd asked, he continued, "But that would be a rotten thing to do to you. You could have any man. And soon enough you'll realize that. And then you'll hate me, for taking advantage of you in your moment of weakness."

Please, take advantage of me, her heart cried. But she tried to make what she actually said more rational. "I'm a grown woman, Jared. I'm old enough to know who I love and to make my own decision about who I want to marry."

"You say that now."

"Because it's the truth!"

"You don't know what the truth is now. You're confused by this *thing* between us."

"No, Jared. *I'm* not the one who's confused. I know exactly what I want and I'm—"

"Yoo-hoo! Anybody back there?" The voice came from down the hall. Someone was shouting from out in the bar.

"We're getting thirsty out here!" a different voice called in a syrupy singsong.

Jared let go of her. "We have to go. Now." He turned.

"But, Jared—"

"We are parched out here!" It was a chorus of voices now.

"Can it! I'm coming!" Jared shouted back.

"Oh, Jared—"

But as usual, she was speaking to thin air.

Things stayed reasonably busy until eleven, and then the place pretty much cleared out. Jared, by that time, was so withdrawn and uncommunicative that Eden felt a bottomless weariness every time she glanced his way. He seemed farther away from her now than he had two weeks ago, when they'd made that futile agreement to steer clear of each other.

She had no idea what to do to get through to him.

And, for tonight anyway, she decided she was just plain tired of trying. A good night's sleep would probably be the best thing for her right now. And they didn't have to work tomorrow. There would be time to hash out this whole mess then.

Since Rocky and a few other diehards were still hanging around, she spoke in an offhand way, "Jared, if you don't need me, I think I'll go on home."

He turned and looked at her, searing her, as he always did, with his gaze. But his answer was as casual as her request. "Sure. Go ahead. I can handle this."

She wiped the tables and washed up the dirty glasses and took one more round of orders from the boys in the back room. By eleven-thirty she was waving goodbye.

Ten minute later, she pulled into the little garage by the cabin. She left the car, trudged up the stone steps and went straight to the bedroom, shedding her clothes as she went.

She took a long, relaxing bath. And then she put on her sleep shirt and crawled into the bed she hadn't even had time to make that morning.

It was a warm night, though not as warm as that first

night, when Jared had sneaked into her room and frightened her so badly. She pulled up the sheet and a light blanket to cover her.

The sheet smelled of their lovemaking. And her pillow smelled of Jared.

Eden snuggled down and put her arms around the pillow. She was fast asleep in minutes.

When Jared left The Hole in the Wall at 2:23 a.m., he knew very well what he *should* do. He should drive straight to his father's house and go right to bed in the spare bedroom. That was where he belonged while he was staying in North Magdalene.

But Jared wasn't doing much of what he *should* do lately.

And tonight—hell, this *morning* by now—was no exception. He found that his damn pickup suddenly had some kind of a magnet attached to it. The magnet pulled him, relentlessly, to the cabin by the river.

He stopped underneath the fir tree, which seemed to have become his parking space now, since her car was in the garage. He shut off the engine and lights and just sat there in the dark for a while, staring at the shadow of the cabin beneath the star-dusted sky.

This was bad. This was hell. He wanted to throw back his head and howl his longing at the moon.

But there was no moon. It had gone down hours ago. And he'd been through enough in his life that he should have known better than to let this happen to him.

But some men, evidently, were fools their whole lives long. They never learned their lesson. And Jared was becoming more and more certain that he was one of the fools.

He had loved his first wife. Sally had been his high school sweetheart. He'd married her right after they graduated. Loving Sally had been like breathing, the kind of love he never even questioned. With Sally, he was doing what a man did: find his woman and marry her and provide for the children he got from her. Both his mother, bless her soul, and his rogue of a father had taught him that.

If he'd had resentments at the way duty ruled his life, he had conquered them, when he conquered drinking with the help of A.A. and regained his wife and child. Things had been fine.

Then he'd lost Sally to cold death.

He'd gone on. And he'd met Belle.

He'd wanted Belle. And he'd married her to have her, because that was what a man did. Marry. And provide.

He'd lost Belle—and the boys—to another man.

And he'd sworn he was done with women and the traps they laid.

But now there was Eden.

And he was captured, thoroughly ensnared. And he knew, in spite of his own prejudices, that she was a good woman, a woman who would stand by him, as Sally couldn't and Belle wouldn't.

Eden Parker was a woman who would keep any promise she made. Even after the magic of desire melted away and she found she was married to a man who was too old for her, a man with nothing to offer her but a pair of hard-working hands, she would keep any vow she had made to him.

And that was the problem. He'd managed somehow to survive losing Sally and Belle. But to have Eden look at him one day as nothing more than a promise she must keep would be the end of him. His dry husk of a heart would shrivel up and blow away.

Jared straightened in the seat and put his hand on the ignition key. He had to get out of there. He started the truck and flicked on the lights and drove as if demons pursued him back to his father's deserted house.

But he'd no sooner stepped down and slammed the door

than he realized that the magnet he'd thought was attached
to his truck, was in reality inside himself. And it was pulling
him....

He didn't even bother to get back in the truck. He didn't
want to park it at her place anyway, where someone might
see it, and know what was going on between them. In this,
at least, he could protect her, though he'd taken her innocence when he'd had no right at all to do such a thing.

Jared ran into the dark trees, not even bothering to stick
to the roads. This was the country of his childhood, after
all. He knew every hillock, every rise and gully. He covered
the distance between Sweet Spring Way and Bullfinch Lane
without breaking a sweat, burst out of the bushes near Sam
and Delilah's place, and then crossed the road and plunged
into the shadowed trees once more.

He followed the meandering curve of the river until he
reached the end of Middle Fork Lane. Breathing hard, he
emerged at last from the trees into the cleared space around
the cabin.

He let himself into the dark kitchen, stopping to find a
glass and take a long drink before moving soundlessly
through the main room to the door of her bedroom. He
paused there, in the doorway, looking toward the bed.

She lay beneath the covers, her cheek resting on an arm.
Her strawberry-blond hair seemed silvery in the starlight.
Her skin shone like the inside of one the fancy china cups
his Grandma Riley used to display in a glass cabinet in her
dining room. Dire consequences had always been threatened
if any unruly boy dared to get too near those precious cups.

Jared thought of the first night he'd seen Eden, when he'd
come into his cabin and found her asleep in the same place
she lay now. She'd been sleeping without a cover. Jared had
stood and stared at her, at her long, incredible legs and the
china-cup beauty of her skin. He shouldn't have done that,
stared at a woman he didn't even know while she was help-

less, fast asleep, unaware of him. But he'd somehow been unable to stop himself.

He'd approached the bed hardly knowing that he moved. And he'd stood there for a long while, endless minutes, just watching her sleep.

The strangest thing had come into his mind, standing there, staring in forbidden longing at a woman he didn't even know. He'd heard his own voice, inside his head, clear as if he'd spoken aloud.

The voice said, *Too late. You've found her too late....*

And for the first time since Sally died, Jared Jones had felt the thick heat of tears in the back of his throat. In the middle of the night in his own bedroom, while he watched a strange woman sleeping, he'd nearly broken down and cried.

And then she'd awakened and thrown a clock at him.

He'd managed, for a couple of weeks to push those moments when he watched her from his mind. But now, they were back with him, as he watched her once more.

Too late. You've found her too late....

On the bed, Eden stirred.

"Jared?" She sighed and turned over and then she sat up. "Jared, is that you?" She pushed her hair back from her forehead by combing her fingers through it. And then she focused on him, in the doorway. "Jared. Come to bed." Though the light from the window was behind her, he knew she was smiling.

"I shouldn't—"

She cut him off. "Jared, just for now, could you please stop talking about what you *shouldn't* do?" She yawned and stretched, as contented as a well-rested cat.

"Hell."

She reached out a willowy arm and beckoned him. "Come here. Come on."

He felt like a boy, suddenly. His mother used to do that—

reach out to him when something was bothering him. And he'd go and she'd pull him against the side of her tall, slim body and kiss the top of his head. She'd tell him that she loved him, not to take life so seriously, that everything would be all right. Bathsheba Riley Jones had been a steadying influence on the whole crazy Jones gang. It was too bad for all of them that she'd died so young.

"Jared." Eden's voice was infinitely patient. She didn't drop her arm.

He left the doorway and went to her. She slid over a little, making room for him. He dropped to the side of the bed. Suddenly nervous, she plucked at the sheet a little, her eyes focused on his face.

"I tried not to come here," he said.

She said nothing, something of a rarity for her.

He hitched a leg up on the bed, so he could face her more fully. "I couldn't stay away."

"Good." She nodded, a satisfied little nod. "I'm glad you couldn't."

"It's just going to get worse, the more we go on with this."

Eden sighed. "But we *will* go on with this. Won't we?"

He looked at her for a moment, then said, "Yeah. Until one of us has the sense to break it off."

She sat up straighter, as if she'd come to some sort of decision within herself. "Okay, then. Can we make a deal, for as long as we're together?"

"What deal?" He peered at her sideways. He was a man who expected to pay full price for things. He was wary of *deals*.

"Can we please *enjoy* it while it lasts? Can you quit walking around with a frown on your face, mumbling about my reputation and acting as if someone is going to carve a scarlet letter on my forehead if they ever find out about us?"

He considered her request. "All right," he said after giving the matter the serious thought it deserved. Then he added a condition of his own. "But we're going to keep it low-key."

"What does that mean?"

"It means we won't tell anyone. About us."

Eden shook her head. "No. I won't do that. I won't pretend I don't...care for you." He didn't miss the way she hesitated over the word *care*. He knew the word she'd wanted to use, but hadn't. And he despised himself a little for yearning, once more, to hear that word from her lips.

"Oh, Jared." She put her hand on the side of his face in a tender caress. "Don't ask me to lie about how I feel. Please. Don't expect me to work side by side with you every night and act as if you're nothing at all to me. I couldn't bear that."

He caught her hand. "Damn it, Eden."

"Please. Can't we compromise on this?"

"What kind of compromise?" He wasn't sure he liked the sound of this.

"Well. Could we let people know we're together, but just not let on *how* together?"

He frowned. He was beginning to get the picture.

She hastened to clarify what he already suspected. "I mean, let them think we're dating, but keep it to ourselves that we're...lovers."

He thought about that. It just might work. The cabin was off to itself, at least a quarter of a mile from the nearest house. As long as his truck wasn't parked there all night, who would guess what went on inside?

"Personally," Eden added in a tart tone, "I think you're making a big thing out of nothing."

"You didn't grow up here."

"No, I didn't. And I respect your feelings. I do. If it's so important to you to keep our private lives private—"

"It is." When he left, he wanted her to be totally free of

him, which she'd never be in North Magdalene once everyone knew he'd slept with her.

"Then, okay," she said. "I'd be willing not to tell anyone exactly how *together* we are, as long as you don't treat me like a stranger when you come to work at night. Agreed?" She stuck out her hand, to shake on it, as she had that night they'd agreed to stay away from each other.

He looked at her hand, his thoughts bleak. What made her think that this agreement would fare any better than the last one they'd made?

"Jared, please…"

Her voice was so soft, so full of hope and tender concern. How could he ever refuse her, even for her own good?

"Jared…"

"All right, Eden. Agreed." He took the hand she offered him.

Chapter Fourteen

"**W**hoa. Can this really be happening? It's time for one serious reality check here." Laurie, who was stretched out on a lounge chair on Eden's deck, took a fortifying sip from her glass of wine and looked probingly at Eden through the gathering darkness. Dinner had been cleared off a half an hour before. Jared had just left them, saying he wanted to go over to Delilah's and check on his father.

Laurie went on. "Now tell it to me slowly. You and my cousin Jared—"

"Are dating. That's all." Eden gave her best imitation of an unconcerned shrug.

"That's *all?*" Laurie wasn't buying. "I gotta tell you, pal. The air sizzles when you two look at each other."

"We're dating," Eden said again, and knew there was a slight edge to her voice. "Period."

Laurie put up a hand in a pacifying gesture. "Okay, okay. Whatever you say."

Eden looked away.

There was a silence, one that flooded quickly with th sounds of twilight in the mountains: the chirruping of crick ets, the croaking of frogs, the warning whine of biting in sects. A wind set the trees to whispering.

As the silence drew out, Laurie got up from her loung chair and went to the patio table in the corner, where sh poured herself another glass of wine from the bottle she' brought.

As she poured, Laurie ventured, "I thought you said yo two had an agreement...."

Eden tried her best to keep her tone offhand and casua "We did. And it wasn't working. So we decided to, um spend a little time together, to let things sort of...evolve...."

Laurie sipped from her glass. "I see."

"What does that does that mean, 'I see...'?"

"Wow. You *are* defensive about this."

"I'd just like to know what you meant when you said ' see,' that's all."

"Well, Eden, I meant just what I said, that I understan But—"

"But what?"

"Well, I guess that letting things *evolve* just doesn' sound like something anyone could do with cousin Jared." Laurie gestured with her glass. "He's sort of an all-o nothing kind of guy, if you know what I mean."

"No, I don't know what you mean," Eden lied. She wa finding she already hated her new agreement with Jared. Sh wanted so badly to confide all the wonder of what she wa feeling to her friend. But that was denied her, because n one was to know the true nature of what she and Jare shared.

"I mean—" Laurie dropped into her chair again "—he' sort of a caveman, cousin Jared is. You know, *Me-Tarzar you-Jane.* It seems like he'd either be with a woman or no

Letting things *evolve* would be a little subtle for a man like him.''

"Maybe you don't know him that well."

Laurie ran her finger around the rim of her glass. "You're right about that. I mean, I mostly think of him as Heather's wild-man dad. And then, there are all the family stories about him. But he's not the kind of person too many people ever really get to know." Laurie took another sip and then added, "Of course, Heather says he's a big pussycat, that he's really just a good man whose life didn't work out the way it should have."

Hearing what Heather thought of Jared, Eden felt a little better. It was reassuring to think that her opinion of the man she loved was also held by his only child.

Laurie snared Eden's glance. "So I've read things all wrong here, then?"

"What do you mean, all wrong?"

"I mean, it's just a casual thing."

"What do you mean, casual?"

"I mean, no grand passion?"

Eden, who was leaning against the railing, picked up a pine needle that had fallen near her elbow and pulled it in two.

"Oh, wow," Laurie said softly. She sipped again from her glass. "You told him you wouldn't talk about it, right?"

Eden nodded, staring down at the two sections of pine needle as if she didn't know how they'd gotten into her hands.

"You love him?" her friend asked. It wasn't really a question.

Eden nodded again.

"Does he love you back?"

"I believe he does. He's just...fighting it."

Laurie said quietly, "If he hurts you, I'll murder him. The rest of the family will help me."

That made Eden laugh.

"Believe it," Laurie told her. "It's true. If he breaks your heart, he's done for."

"Heather's right about him, Laurie. He's a good man. He really is."

"Nobody said he wasn't."

"But he's absolutely sure he's through with women and with love."

"So what's he doing with you, then?"

"He's confused. He's attracted to me. But he thinks he'd be bad for me, in the long run."

Laurie set her glass on the small deck table near her chair. "Eden, I have to tell you. When it comes to running a restaurant or a tavern there's no one as savvy as you are. But in romance, we both know you're no expert. And cousin Jared is not The Hole in the Wall. You can't…renovate a broken-down heart."

Eden forced a smile and slapped at a mosquito that had landed on her arm. "It'll work out. I'm sure of it." She straightened from the railing and went to pick up the wine bottle. "And let's go inside, okay? Before we get eaten alive out here."

"Wait."

"What?"

"I'll say it again. If you need someone to talk to…"

"I know, and thanks. But really. Everything will be fine."

When Laurie left at a little after ten, Jared still had not returned. Eden walked her friend out to the driveway and then stood waving goodbye as Laurie drove away.

When Laurie's taillights had disappeared around the first bend in the road, Eden turned for the cabin. Her breath caught as she saw Jared, standing at the top of the stone steps, silhouetted in the light from the kitchen door.

Her blood quickened in her veins. He must have been waiting, out in the trees, for Laurie to be gone.

Eden hurried to meet him, all her worries and doubts about where this thing between them might be going submerged in her joy that he had come back to her once more.

At the top of the steps, they embraced. When Jared's arms went around her, Eden sighed in pure happiness. He kissed her. She felt, once again, that she'd found her true home at last.

They went in through the door together and paused, just inside, to share another kiss.

And then he was waltzing her backward, through the main room to her bedroom. Eden went joyfully, unhesitating, grateful for every moment they might share.

He undressed her swiftly and brought her down upon the sheets. Eden cried out as he entered her. And then she forgot everything but the feel of him inside her. The world whirled away to nothing. There was bliss, and that was all.

The next several days were happy ones for Eden. It was a golden time. She and Jared were together night and day. She felt that they grew closer as each hour passed.

He never parked his truck under her tree again. Also, he was careful, though he virtually lived at the cabin with her, never to answer the phone or leave signs of his presence where a casual visitor might detect them. But it wasn't as unpleasant as Eden had thought it might be, because the cabin was isolated anyway. They didn't have to be too sneaky to keep what they shared a secret.

As they grew more comfortable with each other, he began to ask her questions about the life she'd known before she'd come to North Magdalene. He asked about her parents.

"They divorced when I was four," she explained. "And both of them remarried, my father once, my mother twice. I have six half sisters and four half brothers, not to mention all the stepbrothers and sisters from my stepmother's and stepfathers' previous marriages. I spent most of my growing up years bouncing between my mother and father. Whichever one of them could handle an extra kid right then, got me.''

"It was tough, huh?" Jared tenderly smoothed her hair with his hand. They were lying in bed early on Friday morning, just a week after they'd become lovers, snuggling and talking softly together as they had yesterday and the day before that. To Eden, sharing these precious moments at the very start of the day seemed like something they'd been doing for years.

She cuddled up closer to him. "Not that tough," she mused. "I mean, they really did do their job of raising me. I was never hungry, and I was never abused. And I knew that they loved me. I just…never felt like I really *belonged,* you know?"

He made a low noise of understanding.

She continued, "And because no one paid much attention to me, I learned the habit of independence early. I realized that if I wanted to get anywhere in this life, I'd have to get there on my own steam. No one was going to do it for me. I think that's an important thing to learn."

He grunted. Her head was on his chest right then, and she heard the sound as a low, agreeable rumble against her ear. Then he asked, "What held you back, from men, until now?"

Eden smiled to herself, touched by how tactfully he was asking her why she'd stayed a virgin until she met him. "Well, it's partly because I've had plenty to do. There's hardly been time for romance. I worked long hours to save my money, so I would be ready to move, or invest, or whatever was required of me when I finally found what I was looking for."

He chuckled then, a warm, rumbling sound. Eden basked

in it and told herself he was a much happier, friendlier person now he had found her.

"What you were looking for," he playfully scoffed. "To live in North Magdalene and partner up with my father in his tumbledown saloon?"

She kissed him on the chest, reveling in the way the wiry hairs there tickled her nose. "Exactly. North Magdalene and The Hole in the Wall are just what I'd been looking for. And when I found them, I was ready...."

"...because you hadn't wasted any of your young life on falling in love, right?"

"Right. I'd earned the money I needed. And when your father offered me a partnership, I jumped at the chance." Jared's outside arm rested on her waist. She stroked the hard muscles with an idle hand. "Also, in this day and age, a woman has to be careful. Working in restaurants and bars, I've really seen firsthand what not being responsible about romance can lead to. That's why I put the condom machine in the men's room, even though your father ribbed me about it unmercifully. I like to hope that somebody will be saved from an unwanted pregnancy—or much worse—because that machine is there. You see?"

She felt his nod against the top of her head. "And what else?" he asked. His voice was slightly gruff.

She knew what he meant. *What else had kept her a virgin until the age of twenty-six?*

The answer, of course, was quite simple. He must already know it. Because she'd never found a man she loved before.

But somehow, her heart balked at giving him the words outright. She'd told him of her love that first night they spent together, but had not said the words since.

The truth was, she was keeping them back. Somewhere deep in her heart she was waiting, longing to hear the words from him before she uttered them again herself.

She sighed, thinking that to give all of herself to him in

the hope that he could give himself fully to her must include the precious words of love as well. Especially now, when he'd as much as asked to hear them.

She began, "Because I never—"

And he cut her off. "Shh." He lifted her chin with a tender hand, and she found herself looking into his steel-and-smoke eyes. "Never mind. I've got no right to ask," he said in a slightly ragged whisper. "Forgive me."

"But—"

She got no further. His mouth covered hers. His hand found her breast. She moaned. The kiss deepened.

She let her body express what she hadn't managed to say in words.

Later, as she was rushing to finish her hair and makeup so she could get to The Hole in the Wall on time, she decided that she wasn't going to let it bother her that he had stopped her just before she could tell him again of her love.

They were making progress. She was sure of it. Everything was going just fine. Soon, he would come to her and tell her they didn't need their silly agreement anymore. He would admit that he was through trying to keep their love a secret. He'd want to shout it from the rooftops, just as she had all along.

Eden realized she was frowning at herself in the mirror. She ordered her face to relax. But inside, she couldn't help feeling anxious.

She had visited Oggie yesterday. The sweet old coot was getting around part of the time on crutches now.

True, it would be weeks yet before her partner could work again. But when that time came, if Jared hadn't decided that what he and Eden shared could last a lifetime, then Jared would leave, as he'd always sworn to do. And his going was something she couldn't bear to consider.

Eden had believed, until Jared came, that she'd found her home in this lovely little town. But now she knew better.

Home was where Jared was. And if he left, well, somehow she'd live through it. She was a strong woman, after all. But if he was gone, she'd have to start all over again to find the place she'd sought her whole life: the place where she belonged.

Eden caught her thoughts up short. What was the matter with her this morning? Nothing had changed since yesterday. She and Jared were doing just fine.

But for some reason, she kept remembering the haunted look in his eyes when he'd stopped her from saying she loved him. She kept recalling the ragged harshness of his whisper when he'd said, *"Never mind, I have no right to ask."* And she kept having the strangest feeling that what she and Jared shared would soon be coming to an end.

Which was silly. Everything was going along just fine. She just had to stop letting negative thoughts control her, that was all. She smoothed her hair one more time and quickly applied her lipstick. Then she rushed out through the main room to the kitchen.

Jared was sitting at the table there, drinking his second cup of coffee and reading the *North Magdalene News*.

He glanced up as she flew toward the door. "Hey. Don't I rate a kiss goodbye?"

She went to him and bent to swiftly press her lips to his. As so often happened between them, the brief kiss drew out. Eden sighed and felt his smile against her softly parted lips.

After a moment, she straightened up and gazed fondly down at him. Her lipstick was on his mouth. She wiped it away with a caressing thumb. "If you keep that up, I'll just have to stay home for the day."

"You'd never forgive yourself if you did that," he teased, putting his big hands at her waist and looking up at her, his silver eyes gleaming. "You'd lose a day's income, not to mention give customers the idea that they can't depend on you."

"You're right," she agreed, enjoying the feel of his hands spanning her waist. She idly combed his hair with her fingers. "Consistency is everything."

He chuckled. "So you're always telling me." He turned back to his newspaper, though he kept an arm loosely draped around her waist.

"Which is why I'd better get going." She started to edge out of the circle of his arm.

He pulled her a fraction closer. "Hold on just a second. I want to show you something. Look at this." He pointed at the newspaper, which was spread out on the table in front of them.

"Jared, I really have to—"

"Come on, this won't take a minute. Read."

Eden quelled her impatience to be gone and did as he asked.

He was pointing to an ad in the *News*'s scanty Classified section.

Position Sought
I am dependable, hardworking, 23 years old. Seeking entry-level job in any local company. Fast learner, flexible, will work any hours. Inquire at SANTINO'S BB&V 555-2435. Ask for Nick.

Jared explained, "I know the Santinos. They're all good workers. Sam hired their youngest son, Marty, over at his gold sales store. He says Marty's the best clerk he's ever had. Now, Nick would be the Santinos' middle son. He's been out of town for a few years, as best I can remember. But it looks like he's back now and looking for a job."

"So?"

"So I'll bet he'd make a damn good bartender. And we could really use one more pair of hands around The Hole in the Wall."

Eden backed away from him just enough that he dropped his arm from around her waist. "We're managing."

"Just barely," he reminded her gently. "Come on, Eden. You're overworked. You're at that bar up to eighty hours a week sometimes."

"I like to work, especially when I'm working for myself."

"I know, but—"

"Jared, your father handled the place alone for years."

"Right. And you remember what it was like when you became his partner. Half the time, he was so worn-out, he didn't even bother to go in until late afternoon. He was barely getting by. And look what happened when he shot himself in the foot. If I hadn't been around to cover for him—"

"I would have managed." Eden really didn't want to hear anymore. The truth was, she'd been planning to hire another bartender next spring, when the busy season started again. And she probably would have hired someone when Oggie hurt himself, if Jared hadn't been there to fill the gap so perfectly.

With her shrewd head for business, Eden knew that what Jared was suggesting made complete sense. They were bringing in nearly three times the money that Oggie had made alone. And they were often busy four or five nights of the week now. They did need someone to take up the slack. The way it was now, if either she or Jared—or Oggie, once he was back on his feet—got sick, the business was bound to suffer.

But Eden knew very well what having someone else to help out would mean. That Jared could leave even sooner than she'd thought. And she didn't want him to be free to leave until *after* he'd decided he wasn't going anywhere.

"Eden," Jared said quietly. "Just talk to Nick, okay? I

know you won't want to pass up the chance to hire someone like him."

She turned for the door. "I'm late."

"I'm calling him as soon as you leave. And I'll bring him in around noon if he's willing, so you can meet him. The weekend's coming up, and Monday is Labor Day." They'd already decided to stay open on their usual day off this week, to take advantage of the heavy holiday trade on the last big weekend of the summer season.

"Unless we interview him today," Jared went on, "we won't have another chance until Tuesday. And if there's anyone else in town who's looking for good help, he'll be unavailable by then. I think we should move on this now."

"I have to go, Jared."

He grabbed her hand. "Say yes."

No, her heart cried. *Never! Not until you swear you'll love me forever, and never ever go away....*

"I have to go."

"Say yes."

What could she say? He was right. And her heart was breaking in two.

"All right, fine. Call him, and I'll talk to him today."

Chapter Fifteen

Jared brought Nick Santino into The Hole in the Wall at twelve-fifteen that very day. Eden saw immediately that the young man was just what she'd hoped to find when she started interviewing for a helper. He was big and bright and handsome, with a ready smile and a steady hand. And there was a calm levelheadedness about him that Eden found instantly reassuring.

She told him that the pay would be low to start out, but that they were planning on adding a restaurant in The Mercantile building in the spring. Nick could "grow" with them if he found he liked the work. If he learned about both the bar and restaurant ends of the business, there could very well be a manager's job for him eventually.

Eden didn't say so, but she had big plans for farther into the future. Grass Valley and Nevada City were nearby, after all. Eventually she intended to open more restaurants in those larger neighboring towns.

Nick, who'd returned to North Magdalene with the hope of settling down permanently, was eager to start as soon as Eden thought she could use him. They agreed on a salary and that he would begin work right after the holiday. He'd be taught how to open the place first, get his initial training during the day, when things were generally less hectic.

"I'll meet you right outside the back door then, ten-thirty Tuesday morning." Nick stood up from the table where Eden had led him to conduct the interview.

"Sounds good." Eden reached across to take the hand he offered. "See you then."

Nick gave her a nod and turned to go. Eden stared after him until the doors swung shut behind him. She felt strangely at a loss. She knew she'd made a sound business decision.

And yet she wanted to cry.

"Hey."

Eden blinked and smiled at Jared, who had taken over the bar so she could talk to Nick. "Hey, what?"

"Take a break, that's what. Go on over to Lily's, why don't you, and get yourself some lunch? I'll handle things here."

Eden never ate lunch out. She'd either bring it to work with her, or call down to the café and have something delivered. She started to decline Jared's suggestion without even stopping to consider it. But then she decided that getting outside on her own for a little while might be an excellent idea right now.

"Thanks, I think I'll do that." She got up and started to go behind the bar to get her purse.

Jared got it for her. He picked it up and plunked it right down in front of her. "Get lost."

She took the purse and made a mock-sour face at him. "Yes, sir."

Out on the street, she made herself walk slowly. She

looked around and reminded herself how much she loved this little town.

Since she was being purposely observant to keep her mind off her vacillating emotions, she found herself noticing the maples that lined Main Street. They looked different than they had just a few days ago. Their leaves weren't quite as green as they had been. They weren't changing yet, so much as fading, like summer, a little at a time.

Thinking back to last night, she recalled how she'd wanted her sweater the minute the shadows came. Strange, in the space of the week that she and Jared had been lovers, summer seemed to have found its apex and to be fading now toward the autumn of the year.

The thought saddened her, brought the tears that she was keeping down a little nearer to the surface.

Oh, what was the matter with her? Somehow, today, everything seemed to speak of changes.

It was ridiculous. Very little had really changed. She'd hired a much-needed employee. So what? It was something that was bound to happen sooner or later. And it didn't mean that Jared would be packing up his gear and heading out of town tomorrow.

And yet Oggie was on crutches now. Autumn was on its way. And Jared had stopped her from declaring her love. He'd said he had *no right* to hear the words from her....

"Allow me, Miss Parker."

Eden shook herself and realized that she'd reached the café and then stood there, absorbed in her thoughts, blocking the door.

She pushed back her self-pitying tears and murmured "Thank you," to Sheriff Pangborn. He pulled back the door.

Eden sat down in the first empty booth she came to. Heather was there before she even had a chance to look at the menu.

"Hi, Eden. What are you doing here this time of day?"

"Your father kicked me out of The Hole in the Wall. He made me take a break."

Heather laughed. "Well, good. Want coffee?"

"How about iced tea?"

"You got it." Heather bounced cheerily over to the beverage station and poured the iced tea, pausing to call out Sheriff Pangborn's order through the cook's window on the way. Heather returned with the tea. "There you go."

"Thanks."

"You want a few minutes?"

"No, I'm ready." Eden ordered a sandwich and coleslaw.

Heather wrote down the order and then stuck her pencil behind her ear. "Say, Eden…" She leaned in closer.

"Hmm?"

"You know, I've been thinking…"

Eden smiled at Jared's daughter. "What?"

"Maybe you and Dad could come over for dinner. Maybe this Monday night, on your day off?"

Eden felt the tears come again. She held them back by smiling wider. She was touched. She knew exactly what this invitation meant. It was Heather's way of telling Eden that she approved of the idea of her father and Eden together. It also meant that people in town were starting to see the two of them as a couple. And that was good, as far as Eden was concerned. That was just wonderful.

Eden drew in a breath. "That would be great. As long as Jared says yes, too. But it would have to be the Monday after this one. We're staying open for the holiday."

"Okay, then, Monday after the one coming up. Say, six o'clock?"

"Sound's fine. As long as Jared—"

"Eden. Do me a favor."

"Anything."

"Don't *ask* my dad. *Tell* him. You'll save yourself a lot of grief."

Eden laughed at that. "Okay, okay. We'll be there."

"Great. I'll put in your order."

Eden, her sagging spirits lifted a little by Heather's invitation, ate a leisurely lunch and returned to The Hole in the Wall much refreshed.

She didn't get a chance to tell Jared about the invitation until three the next morning, after he'd appeared at her doorstep as he always did, materializing out of the trees once he'd left his pickup at Oggie's place.

She opened the door to him and he came into her waiting arms. For a time, as always when he touched her, she forgot the rest of the world in the beauty of his kiss.

At last, he pulled back enough to look at her. "What a night, huh?" It had been just as busy as they'd anticipated. From seven o'clock on, Eden had felt like she'd never stopped moving.

"Yes. I'm beat." She sighed. "I want a bath and then I want to fall into bed. With you."

"Well, let's get to it." He took her hand and started to tug her toward the bedroom.

She hung back. "Wait. I have to tell you before I forget."

"Yeah?"

"Monday, the fourteenth. We're going to dinner at Heather's house."

"We're what?" His voice was perfectly level. Yet for some reason, the sound of it had her wanting to cry again.

She pasted on a cheerful smile. "Your daughter invited us to dinner, Monday the fourteenth. It's okay, isn't it?" She loathed the slightly pleading note she could hear in her voice.

He rubbed the back of his neck. "Eden…"

"What?"

He looked so sad and strained. She *hated* to see him looking like that. He seemed to choose his next words with great care. "That's more than a week away."

"So?"

"Who knows what could be happening in a week."

"What are you getting at, Jared?"

He looked at her. His whole lean body seemed full of tension. And weariness, too. If she could have read minds, she would have cried in earnest at his thoughts right then.

Right then, the longing in Jared was very bad.

He wanted what he'd wanted since the night he first made love with her. He wanted to make her his true wife before the world.

But Jared knew he must not forget all the things that would forever stand between them. He was forty years old. Eden was only five years older than his own daughter. He was virtually unemployed. He'd been divorced and he had a rotten disposition.

Hell, he could hardly imagine a worse prospect for a husband than himself. Even if Eden said yes, he would never let her marry someone like him.

That was why he had to set her free of him. And the only way he was going to be able to do that was to get away from her, to go somewhere where he wouldn't have to see her anymore.

The morning just past, when they lay in bed together and he found himself longing to hear her tell him she loved him, he had finally realized that he had to put a stop to this. He had to end this sweet torture and get out of her life, once and for all.

The hiring of Nick Santino was a step toward that aim. Nick was smart and quick. Jared's plan was to have the young man trained and ready to fill his own shoes within a week, two at the most. And then he would leave town, not to return for a long, long time. He would get away and he would get over her.

Eventually, when she found a more suitable man, she would remember him with fondness. Hell, she'd probably even be grateful to him for keeping her from wasting her life.

"Jared, I asked you a question. Are you going to answer me or not?"

"What question?" His grim thoughts had made him lose completely the thread of their conversation.

"What are you getting at when you say 'Who knows what could be happening in a week'?"

He knew he should probably tell her now. But that would only make the remaining days they had together all the sadder. No, the best way was to keep quiet until the end, and then cut it clean.

"Forget that," he said.

"But, Jared—"

"We'll go to dinner at Heather's, okay?"

"But Jared, I think—"

"Stop thinking." He pulled her against him. "Kiss me."

"But—"

He covered her sweet lips with his own and there was no more discussion that night, or the rest of the weekend for that matter. By the time they got home Saturday, Sunday and Monday nights, they had little energy for anything but a quick bath and bed.

Nick Santino began work, as agreed, on the day after Labor Day.

From the first, he proved to be everything Jared and Eden had hoped he might be. When it came to any task, he only had to have it explained to him once and he was ready to perform it on a regular basis. And there was no job too menial for him. He bused tables and scrubbed floors with the same meticulous care he brought to mixing a fancy drink. He did what he was told to do, and he never sat around on the job.

By his third day of work, the Thursday after Labor Day, Eden decided Nick was ready to open up the bar on his own. She told him that tomorrow, Friday, she wouldn't be coming in until two or three in the afternoon.

Nick gave her a proud smile and an enthusiastic "Yes, ma'am" in response.

So the next morning, Eden and Jared slept late. They shared a leisurely brunch at around eleven and then found their way back to the bedroom to make use of the bed one more time. At a little after one Eden decided she probably ought to get ready to put in her appearance at work.

Jared had a different idea. "Let me go in early, why don't you? You can take the whole day off."

Eden tried to protest. "It's Friday, and it'll probably be busy. I can't—"

"Yes, you can. I have a hunch things won't be too heavy tonight, anyway. The summer's over. It's been quieter all week, you've said so yourself."

"But I—"

"Come on. Nick and I will do fine. Give yourself a break." He reached for his pants, which were on the floor by his side of the bed and pulled some money from a pocket. He rolled back to face her and held out the bills. "Go down to Grass Valley and buy yourself a new dress or something."

"Jared, I don't think—"

"Right." He wrapped her hands around the money. "Don't think. Just have a good day. And be waiting in this bed for me tonight."

Eden considered. The idea was tempting. She hadn't had a break from work in ten days, after all. She might as well enjoy the benefits of having a dependable employee. And Jared could take some time off, too. This Sunday, if all went as expected, she'd insist that he skip a whole day's work as well.

"All right. I'll do it." She waved his money under his nose and grinned at him.

"Good."

An hour later, he left her to enjoy her day off.

Eden took Jared's suggestion and drove to Grass Valley. After a trip to the bank, she stopped at Brunswick Plaza, where there just happened to be a bridal shop. She only went in the bridal shop to look around. But once she was there, she found she wanted to try on some of the gowns. The saleslady was very helpful.

Before she knew what was happening, Eden did the craziest thing. She took the money Jared had given her, plus quite a bit of money of her own, and she bought a floor-length ivory wedding dress.

It was just nuts of her to do such a thing, she knew, but she couldn't resist that dress. She loved the old-fashioned basque waistline, which dipped to a point in front. The portrait collar framed her smooth shoulders and long neck and the skirt was a filmy wonder, chiffon over satin. Venise lace and tiny seed pearls decorated the fitted point sleeves and adorned the hem.

After choosing an ivory-colored fingertip-length veil, Eden walked out of the bridal shop with the dream of a dress laid carefully across her outstretched arms. She wondered how she would explain to Jared what she'd done.

She decided she wouldn't tell him, at least not right away. She'd give him back the amount of money he'd given her and say she hadn't found a dress she liked after all.

Fantasizing shamelessly about the day she would wear the beautiful dress, Eden shopped for groceries. She stocked up on the brand of cola that Jared liked, and she stacked the cart high with steaks, pot roasts, and racks of country-style ribs. Jared, after all, was a meat-and-potatoes kind of man. Last, she stopped at a bar and restaurant supply house to order some new beer mugs and a case of champagne flutes.

She returned to North Magdalene and drove straight to the cabin to put all her purchases away. She was already feeling a little foolish about the wedding dress, so she stuck it in the back of her closet, thinking she'd surprise Jared when he asked her to become his wife by telling him how she'd found it in Grass Valley that day he'd told her to buy herself a dress.

Eden fixed herself a light dinner, and then she went to see Oggie at Delilah's house. She found the old man alone. He was sitting in the living room watching a game show on TV.

"Come in, come in, gal. I been wantin' a word with you anyway." He pointed the remote at the television, and the big box went silent. "What the hell are you doing out and about at this time of the evening? Shouldn't you be over at The Hole in the Wall makin' us rich?"

"Well, Oggie, I—"

"Say no more. I know the answer already. It's that Santino kid you hired, am I right?"

"Yes, he's turned out to be quite a find."

"All the Santinos are a find. Those kids were well brought up. Julio and Maria had 'em all workin' from the time they were knee-high to a gnat's behind." He felt in his shirt pocket, and didn't find what he was looking for. "Damn. I could use me a good cigar. But Delilah's after me night and day not to smoke in the house."

"Well, I suppose it won't be long until you're back at your own house again, anyway."

Oggie shrugged. "Who knows? Even if I'm dyin' half the time for a smoke, it ain't so bad to have my breakfast and dinner cooked up for me, not to mention my clothes kept clean. And Sam and Delilah swear I can stay as long as I want to. So we'll see, we'll just see...." He shot her an oblique glance, and Eden realized he was working up to saying what was really on his mind.

She prompted, "Oggie, is something wrong?"

"Well, I gotta tell you, I been wonderin'..."

"What? Say it."

"Hell. The truth is, I been wonderin' how come you went and hired you a helper without consultin' your partner?"

Eden felt instantly contrite. The hiring of Nick Santino had come about so swiftly, she'd hardly had a moment to stop and think. And she should have consulted Oggie, she knew, though she was also sure he would have told her to go ahead and do what needed to be done.

"I'm sorry," Eden said. "I really am. It all happened kind of quickly. Jared felt we had to get right on it, or we'd miss out on the chance to hire him. I hope it's all right with you. But if for some reason, it's not—"

"So it was Jared's idea, eh?"

"Well, yes. He said that we really needed a relief person. And it's true, we do."

Oggie looked at her sideways. "Now really ain't the time of year to be hiring someone new."

"Business has just been great, Oggie. You know that. There's plenty of work for another pair of hands."

"Yeah." Oggie grunted. "I guess so. Especially if one pair of hands is walkin' out the door."

Eden frowned. "What does that mean?"

"Nothin' much. Just that it looks like Jared's gone and hired his replacement."

Eden, who'd perched on the end of the couch, found she was too anxious, suddenly, to sit still. She stood up. "No, that can't be."

"Why not?"

"Well, he promised you he'd stay until you could work again, didn't he?"

"He's stayed to find someone to *do* the work. He knows damn well no one would fault him for that."

"But…but *you* would, wouldn't you?"

Oggie's beady brown eyes were infinitely patient. "Eden, honey. If he wants to be a damn fool, who am I to roll my wheelchair in his path?"

Behind the couch, a big window looked out on a group of white-barked birch trees. Eden stared at those trees, thinking that their leaves were noticeably turning to gold.

Autumn. Autumn was in the air. Everything was changing. And Jared *was* setting things up so that he could leave her.

"Eden, you okay?" Oggie's voice came through to her as if from a long way away.

"Yes, fine. Just fine."

"You don't sound so fine. Matter of fact, you look kind of green around the gills."

He was right, of course. She was not fine. It took her a moment before she realized exactly what she felt right then.

Anger.

It was moving through her in a slow, expanding, engulfing wave.

Her six half sisters and four half brothers and myriad stepsiblings had known the truth about Eden. They all said, "It's almost impossible to make Edie mad. But when it happens, watch out!"

It was happening now.

She was simmering now, and in a few minutes, her rage would reach a rolling boil.

She seethed.

How could she have been so blind? Jared had not only coaxed her into hiring his own replacement, he hadn't even had the consideration to tell her honestly what he was doing.

Nick was already good enough at his new job that he and Eden could manage alone if they had to. If Nick worked this whole weekend, he would no doubt be capable of either opening the place *or* closing it up come the slower midweek days. Jared could head out of town Monday and know that The Hole in the Wall would get along just fine without him.

How Eden was going to get along without him clearly didn't concern him.

Oh, she knew what he had told himself. That he was doing the right thing. So what if he was breaking her heart? After all, he was leaving her for her own good.

She'd given him everything, all that was in her. Her love. Her body. And every ounce of patience she possessed. She'd agreed to keep their passion a secret and to take things one day at a time. Though their deceit had chafed her sorely, she had kept their love a shadowed thing. For him.

And he was leaving anyway, without warning, as soon as Nick was ready to take his place at The Hole in the Wall.

Well, he had another think coming if he thought he was going to get away so easily. She was going to have a word with him on the subject.

And she was going to do it now, at The Hole in the Wall. She was through sneaking around. She was going to tell him what she thought of him, and she didn't care who heard what she said.

Eden turned from the view of the changing birch trees and pointed herself at the front door.

She was stopped halfway there by Oggie, who had moved with surprising swiftness, spinning his wheelchair right into her path.

She looked down at him. "Get out of my way."

"Er, Eden? Eden, maybe you oughtta sit down."

"No, Oggie. I ought not. I have to go now."

"Eden, I gotta tell you. You got that look. That rageful woman look. It's a dangerous look to be wearin' on the street. Stay here for a bit."

"No."

"Eden—"

She darted around him and flew out the door.

Chapter Sixteen

Eden descended on The Hole in the Wall about five minutes later. She found a free space on the street, so she entered from the front.

She shoved back the double doors and stepped inside.

That small hush happened, as it always does whenever someone new arrives at a bar. Everyone turned to look at her, and then turned back to what they'd been doing before.

Rocky waved. "Hey, there, Eden. We been askin' where you were."

Eden nodded at Rocky and spared a moment to look around the room. There was a game of pool in progress, and several of the tables were full. There was only one free stool at the bar itself.

Nick was behind the bar, in Jared's place.

If Eden had cherished the slightest doubt that Jared planned to leave her within days, it vanished the moment she saw Nick standing at the little rubber mat where Jared always stood. Tonight, since it was Nick's first night, he should have been doing the footwork while Jared took the money and mixed the drinks. But Jared had put the younger man right into the main job. He was training him as fast as he could.

Eden perceived one of the finer points of Jared's deceit. He'd pushed her to take the day off so that he could speed up Nick's training without her witnessing what he did. And she, fool that she was, had gone out and bought a wedding dress. It was hanging in her closet even now, proof positive that she was a blind, hopeless idiot who refused to see the truth until Oggie laid it out for her in so many words.

Eden clenched her hands at her sides. If she didn't watch herself, she was going to grab the one free bar stool in the place and send it hurtling into the big mirror above the bar. She didn't want to destroy the mirror. She'd paid for it herself, after all. The one before it had been shattered in a brawl.

Oh, yes, Eden most definitely was going to have a word or two with Jared Jones.

Just as she savagely imagined the grim satisfaction she'd feel when she told him exactly what was in her mind, he appeared through the split in the curtain that led to the card room, carrying her service tray stacked high with empties. He saw her at once and froze where he stood.

They confronted each other across the length of the room.

His face was utterly expressionless, his eyes like twin pieces of slate. Yet she knew that *he* knew exactly why she had come.

A hush fell over the crowded room. Every eye in the place looked from Jared to Eden and back again.

Someone muttered, "Woo-ee, this don't look good, boys. She's gonna murder him for sure."

"What's he done?"

"Hell if I know, but you can bet your mama's britches that whatever it was, he's gonna pay in spades."

Eden ignored the whispers. She held her chin high and demanded of the man across the room from her, "When?"

He drug in a breath. "Eden, I—"

"*When* are you leaving? Tell me. Tell me now."

"This isn't the place to talk about this."

"Oh, isn't it?"

"No."

She threw back her head and laughed.

Every man in the room shivered at the sound.

She said, "*You* think it isn't the place. But I can see no reason in the world that *I* should be ruled by what *you* think."

"Eden—"

"*I* think it's time we got everything out in the open. That's what *I* think. *I* think everyone in this bar should know exactly what's been going on between you and me."

"Damn it, Eden…" He dropped the full tray on the nearest table. The bottles and glasses on it rocked and clinked.

"I want them all to know what you are to me, what we are to each other, that we've been—"

He didn't let her finish. She'd never seen even *him* move that fast before. It was spectacular. He literally leapt across the room.

A unified gasp went up.

And then Jared had his hand over her mouth and was dragging her backward out the door, shouting, "Take care of business, will you, Nick?"

"No problem, Mr. Jones."

Eden kicked and struggled. She wiggled and flailed her arms. She even tried to bite the hand that was clamped over her mouth. But it did no good. Jared held her in a grip of steel. He hauled her outside, then dragged her around to the driver's side of her car. He flung open the door and pushed her in ahead of him, not letting up until she scrambled over the console. Then he thrust her down in the passenger seat.

She had made the mistake of leaving the key in the ignition. He held her in the seat with one hand and started the car with the other. She made it as hard for him as she could, squirming and punching him and calling him terrible things.

He pulled away from the curb and swung immediately into a U-turn, which he barely made. He missed a light pole and Sheriff Pangborn's big four-by-four by mere inches. He also left half of the rubber of her tires on the pavement. But somehow, he avoided an actual collision.

He sped off up the street and burned more rubber at the corner, where he turned onto Middle Fork Lane.

By the time he pulled up in front of the cabin, Eden had stopped struggling. She sat there, absolutely rigid, her arms crossed tightly over her breasts, staring straight ahead.

He stopped the engine and then turned to look at her.

She said nothing. She flung open her door, swung her feet to the ground and marched up the steps to the kitchen door. She went in and strode straight to the big living area. She sat on the couch, which faced a stone mantel that served as a mounting place for a large black wood stove.

Jared followed her inside, but stopped in the kitchen to make a phone call. She heard him talking to his brother Patrick, asking Patrick to go over to The Hole in the Wall and give Nick a hand.

"Something's come up," Jared said. "So see that the place gets closed up right tonight, will you?"

Apparently Patrick agreed, because Eden heard Jared say, "Thanks, brother," and that was all.

Soon enough, Jared came and stood in the doorway between the main room where she sat and the kitchen. His eyes found her. They looked at each other.

At last, Eden quietly demanded, "When are you leaving?"

He said nothing.

"When?"

He let out a long breath. "As soon as possible. In the morning, I think."

As she heard him say what she already knew in her heart, she realized that the hot wave of her anger had peaked and receded. She felt drained. But at least she could think clearly now.

She wanted some answers. And she intended to have them.

"Why didn't you tell me the truth?"

"It's better this way."

"Is it?" She stared at him. "Then why do I feel like you've cheated me?"

"Someday you'll thank me."

She shook her head. "You have me all figured out, don't you? You have *everything* all figured out. It's all...for my own good, right?"

"You can sneer all you want. But yes, that's exactly what it is."

"You're doing me one gigantic favor by forcing me to live without you for the rest of my life."

"Yes, I am."

She stood up. "Well, it doesn't feel like a favor. And I don't want to live without you."

"You'll feel differently. Someday."

"I will not."

"I'm too old for you."

"Only in your own mind."

"I don't even have a damn job."

"Yes, you do. You know you do. Oggie would step aside for you in a minute, and be glad to do it." She walked slowly toward him. "And we could be happy together, our life could be good and full together, if you'd only—"

He put up a hand. She stopped where she was.

"My mind's made up, Eden. I'm leaving. Let it be."

"Just like that?" Eden felt the pressure of tears again, thickening her throat, pushing to get free behind her eyes. Oh, how she wished for the wave of anger to come back. Anger was so much better than this sadness, this soul-deep despair.

"Yes. Just like that," he said flatly.

"Oh, Jared..." She took another step. And another.

His body tightened in defense against her approach. "Don't..." The single word was a plea.

She ignored it. She reached out and wrapped her arms around him and brought her body against him with one long, yearning sigh. She laid her head against his hard chest.

"I love you, Jared," she said against his heart. "Now. Tomorrow. For the rest of my life."

He stood rigid for endless, excruciating seconds. Then he grabbed her against him with a hollow groan. She lifted her face, wet now with unashamed tears, and he took her mouth in a kiss that seared her to the bottom of her soul.

And then he swung her up against his chest. He went on kissing her as he carried her across the space she'd covered to reach him, to the couch. He laid her down and knelt on the floor next to her.

He waited, there on his knees, until she opened her eyes and looked at him. Then he wiped the shining tracks of her tears with a tender thumb and combed his fingers, soothingly, through her hair.

"Make love with me." The whispered words had trouble finding their way through the tightness of her throat. "One more time. And don't leave until I'm asleep. I think it might kill me, if I had to watch you go."

"Eden..."

"Shh. Don't say we shouldn't. It was one of our agreements, remember? That you'd stop saying we shouldn't."

"Eden..."

She touched his lips with a tender hand. "Please."

That did it. His mouth descended. With an eager, grateful sigh, Eden raised her arms and wrapped them around his neck.

He kissed her for a long time. Then he lifted his mouth, swollen from loving hers, and slanted it the other way. Eden idly stroked his shoulders at first, reveling in the bliss he could bring her, accepting the drugging wonder of his kiss.

But then an urgency came on her, to touch him, to feel his body, naked, against hers.

Still kissing him, she sat up and struggled quickly out of her blouse and bra. And then she slid the black vest off his shoulders. She unbuttoned his shirt, pushing it free of his hard chest as she kissed a trail down his throat.

She planted a thousand hungry kisses on his chest and shoulders and she stroked his skin as she kissed him. She wanted to touch him everywhere, with all of herself. She had to memorize him, after all, because tonight was the end of all that they shared.

Her lips moved, soft, tender, insistent like her love for him, down the trail of hair at his belly. She laid her hand on him, through his black jeans. He threw back his head and moaned.

Swiftly she slipped off his belt and parted the placket of his jeans. He sprung free into her hand.

She kissed him then, as he had kissed her that first night, a kiss shattering in its utter intimacy. She took him into her mouth, stroking him, finding the rhythm that his body sought, until he cried out and clutched her bare shoulders.

He tried to hold back, she knew it. But she didn't allow him to hold back. At last, he surrendered. His body tightened in that final ecstatic agony. He found his release.

When it was done, he dropped back, his knees folded beneath him, his head bowed. She lay down once more and languorously reached out to comb his hair with her hand.

For a long time they remained that way, Jared on his folded knees before her, Eden stretched out on the couch.

And then, without a word, he lifted his head and looked at her. His eyes branded her. He stood, not even bothering to button his jeans, and he scooped her up in his strong arms.

He carried her to the bedroom, put her on the bed and quickly got rid of the rest of his clothes. Then he removed what was left of hers as well.

He stood looking down at her. She knew what he was doing, because she did the same. They were memorizing each other. Every line, every curve, every last splendid inch.

She lifted her arms to him. He went down to her. He felt so strong and good, all along the length of her.

The kisses began again.

It all began again.

Eden gave herself up to it utterly. It was their last time.

At three-thirty the next morning, Jared rose from the bed.

Silently he dressed and gathered up his things. When he was ready to go, he couldn't resist one last look at her, dreaming there, in the bed where he'd loved her once, and then again, not wanting to leave her though he knew that he must.

She was so beautiful, her hair tangled and soft all around her sweet face, her skin pale and lustrous.

*Oh, how I wish…*he caught himself thinking.

But then he made himself turn from her. She had a whole life to live. And the best thing he could do for her was what he was doing now.

Jared left the bedroom and went through the quiet house on silent feet. He let himself out into the night and disappeared into the shadowed trees.

Chapter Seventeen

Eden woke at dawn. The blue jays and squirrels were chattering away outside the window, but the thought of pausing to watch their silly escapades held no appeal at all.

She felt infinitely weary, yet she forced herself to rise and strip the sheets from the bed and carry them out to the ancient washing machine in the garage. She washed the sheets and changed the bed. She knew it was the right thing to do, to erase the scent of their lovemaking from the sheets, to help her forget.

Once the bed was made she took a long, hot shower, because her body, too, carried the scent of passion on it. When she was done, she smelled like soap and bath powder and her own perfume.

Next, she went through the cabin, looking for the slightest sign of Jared. She found very little. It saddened her all the more to find how little he had left of himself for her to clear away. There was a disposable razor to toss out, and a nearly empty tube of toothpaste. She took the case of cola she'd bought for him yesterday out to her car. She'd take it to work with her. They always needed cola at the bar.

She remembered the wedding dress, but decided not to deal with it today. Someday soon, on a day off, she'd take it back down to Grass Valley and try to get her money back. That decided, she went out to the garage and put the newly washed sheets into the dryer.

She went in and had her breakfast. Then she called Nick Santino and asked him how he'd managed the night before.

"Patrick Jones came in and helped me. It all went just fine," Nick told her.

"Good. Nick, I know it's asking a lot, since you worked late last night, but do you think you could handle opening up today? The closing shift is always tougher on weekends, so I think I should take that one."

"Er...what about Jared?"

Eden swallowed the knot that had suddenly formed in her throat. "He won't be helping out anymore. He was only...filling in until we could find someone like you, anyway."

"Well, okay. I'd be glad to go in early. I'm happy to get the hours, I've gotta say."

"Great. And next week we can talk about raising your pay. Your training time is over, from the way it looks now."

"Hey. Terrific." Before he hung up, he asked cautiously, "Er, everything all right then, Miss Parker?"

"Everything is just fine," she lied. "And for heaven's sake, call me Eden, okay?"

"Sure. Well, okay then. Eden. I'll see you at—"

"I'll be in by five, just to make sure you're doing all right. And call me if it gets too busy. I'll be right over."

"No problem. See you at five, then."

Eden hung up. And then she realized that she had eight

hours ahead of her with nothing to do. It might be better to keep busy.

Maybe she ought to call Nick back and tell him she'd decided to work both shifts, have him come in around seven to help at the busiest time.

But then she reconsidered. Just the thought of getting ready for work right away made her feel totally exhausted. It was strange, really, because Eden usually felt energized at the idea of work.

But not today. Today, she was tired to the bone. She'd go in at five as she'd promised Nick, and that would be good enough.

She called Patrick next and thanked him for helping out the night before. He asked her cautiously about Jared.

She told him the truth. "He's gone."

Patrick was silent for a moment. Then he muttered, "The damn fool. Look, Eden. If there's anything I can do—"

"There's not. But thanks."

After she told Patrick goodbye, she got up with a sigh and wandered back to the bedroom. She lay down on the bed and closed her eyes and took a long nap.

Strangely, when she woke, she didn't feel at all refreshed.

Laurie called about three.

"Hey, pal. It seems we never get together anymore. I was just thinking, maybe I could take a few days off and—"

"Laurie, didn't your new semester just start?"

"Look. I can manage it, don't worry."

It didn't take a genius to figure out what Laurie was up to. Eden cut through the well-meaning subterfuge. "All right. Come clean. Did Patrick call you?"

"No. Honestly, I haven't spoken with him."

"Then who *have* you spoken with?"

"What do you mean?"

"Laurie. Don't lie to me, please."

"Oh, all right. Evidently Patrick called Oggie and Oggie

called just about everyone, including Heather. It was Heather who called me.''

''And told you what?''

''Oh, Eden…''

''Just say it.''

Laurie sighed. ''Heather says that Jared has left town again.''

''So.'' Eden dragged in a deep breath. ''Everyone in the family knows, right?''

''Well, I guess, more or less.''

''It sounds like more, not less, to me.''

''Eden, I know you need a friend right now.''

''I'm fine. Really. I'll survive. I'm just…a little tired, you know?''

''Oh, Eden. It's bad, isn't it?''

''Please. I will call you. When I'm ready to…have a good cry. Okay?''

''Or if you don't want to be alone. Whatever. I'll come.''

''I know you will. And thanks. But listen, I have to go…''

''But, Eden—''

Eden gently hung up the phone.

Oggie called at four.

''I'm gonna find out where that damned idiot went and bust his head in for him.''

''Oh, Oggie. Please just let it go.''

''Good God, gal. I'm a Jones. I ain't never let nothin' go.''

''Oggie, I have to hang up now. I'll call you, I will…''

She could hear him huffing and puffing his outrage into the phone even as she laid it back in its cradle.

It was time to get ready for work. She put on her black slacks and her white shirt and trim little vest and then drove over to The Hole in the Wall.

The sly winks and knowing grins started as soon as she walked in the door. Eden got right to work and tried to ignore the veiled questions concerning herself and Jared and if they'd "worked things out yet."

If she hadn't felt so numb and listless, she would have been pleased at the way Nick reacted to the ribbing she received. He stepped in consistently whenever the teasing comments got too extreme, either redirecting the jibes, or else quietly suggesting that he and Eden had heard about enough.

At six, Patrick came in, and the teasing mysteriously stopped. He sat at the bar the rest of the night, nursing watered-down drinks and giving measuring looks to anyone who spoke to Eden.

It was a good night, in terms of business, but not near as busy as those last hectic Saturday nights of the summer had been. Eden was glad when it was through and she could go home and go to bed at last.

She decided to open the tavern on Sunday, Tuesday and Wednesday, because those nights were generally slower nights and she thought Nick could handle taking the closing shift.

Sunday, when she opened the doors, Delilah's husband, Sam, was waiting there with Rocky to get himself a stool. Sam stayed until Eden left at 11:00 p.m. Not a soul that whole day or evening mentioned the name Jared Jones. By then, Eden had figured out that the Jones men were intent on protecting her from gossip and verbal abuse.

She told Sam it wasn't necessary. "It's not a big deal to me, Sam. I can take it, I really can."

Sam just shrugged. "There's no damn reason why you should have to take it, and that's the plain truth." Sam had beautiful pale blue eyes, infinitely gentle eyes, Eden thought. She could see, looking into those eyes, why Delilah seemed to be such a happy woman.

Eden glanced away from Sam. When she looked at him, she kept thinking about the contentment he and Delilah obviously shared. Some couples had all the luck. They found each other, and they both accepted that what was between them was meant to be. Everyone in town said that Sam and Delilah had once been archenemies. Eden just knew that had to be pure bunk.

"Let us stand by you, Eden." Sam went on. "If not for your sake, then for ours. It'll make us feel better to know you're not getting a rough time from any of the hooligans around here."

"But—"

"Please?"

How could she resist the appeal in those kind eyes? She agreed that they could all waste their time if they wanted to.

Monday, she didn't have to work. The first thing she thought of in the morning was that she and Jared were supposed to have gone to Heather's for dinner that night. But now that wasn't going to happen. She thought, to be polite, that maybe she should call Heather and formally express her regrets. But somehow, she just couldn't go through with it. And Heather knew what was going on anyway.

Eden wandered out to the kitchen, considered making coffee, and then returned to bed instead. She slept most of the day. Laurie called, waking her, about two in the afternoon. Eden's friend suggested that they meet in Grass Valley for a girls' night out. Eden said that she was very tired, some other time maybe. Laurie asked if Eden was sick.

"No, really. I'm fine. Listen, I have to go now."

She hung up and went back to sleep. She was sleeping a lot; she knew it. But somehow, her tiredness just wouldn't go away.

Tuesday, Brendan sat at the bar through Eden's whole shift. And Wednesday, it was Patrick once again.

Thursday morning, Eden had to drag herself out of bed. She really was just terribly tired.

Everything seemed so very…dull lately. As if there were a dirty window between herself and the rest of the world. Her wonderful life in North Magdalene seemed to have lost all of its luster. Somehow, with Jared's leaving, her whole existence had become tedious and drab.

Far back in her mind somewhere, she felt that her real, vital self was an unwilling captive to this deadness, this numbness that had completely claimed her life. She could almost hear a faint voice inside her soul calling her, chiding her to put away her sorrow and get on with living once again.

She understood that she'd have to pull herself together sooner or later. She'd have to spend more time at work. Also, she really should clean up the cabin, which had somehow become a real mess. Her dirty clothes seemed to be everywhere, and the kitchen was a disaster area.

But just thinking about tackling the dishes that seemed to have piled up so high in the sink made her so tired she could hardly stand up. If she couldn't even face the dishes, how was she going to face getting on with her life?

Really, all she wanted was to be allowed to climb back into bed. Come to think of it, she was too tired to work today at all.

She thought of Patrick. Maybe he'd be willing to help out if she called him.

She did call him. When she asked if he'd cover for her, he acted surprised and apprehensive.

"Eden, are you sick or something?"

"No, no. I'm fine. I just…I need a little rest, that's all. And since Nick will be taking the opening shift, if you would just help me out by closing up tonight, well, I'd really appreciate it. I just don't feel like working today."

Patrick didn't answer for a moment. Then he said, "Eden, I'd be glad to close up for you."

"Great. Thanks."

"But maybe you ought to—"

"Look, Patrick. I have to go now."

"Eden, I—"

"Thanks again. I mean it."

Eden hung up and dragged herself back to bed. She lay down and pulled the sheet over herself and closed her eyes.

The phone rang. She ignored it. She just wanted to be left alone to sleep. At last, the ringing stopped. Eden let out a long breath of relief and settled deeper into her bed.

She wasn't sure how much later the pounding started. She groaned a little in her sleep and wrapped her pillow around her head.

"Eden! Eden, gal, you answer this damn door!"

Eden gritted her teeth and tuned out the shouting. If she refused to get up and answer the door, the racket would stop eventually, she was sure.

She sighed in relief and relaxed a little when the pounding and shouting finally did stop. She even put her pillow back *under* her head where it belonged.

And then she heard the kitchen door slam. And someone stumping—there was no other word for it—through the kitchen.

She felt no fear. She knew who it was by the way he was moving, and the shouting voice had been quite familiar. All she wished was that she'd had sense enough to lock the door before going back to bed.

But it was too late now. Oggie was in her house, and he was going to find her.

"Eden! Where the hell are you, gal?"

Eden moaned and pulled the blankets over her head.

"Eden? I ain't foolin' around here. If you ain't decent, you better make it known now, 'cause I ain't leavin' until we've had us a talk." Oggie paused, listening, no doubt, for her response. When he got none, he announced, "All right, then. Have it your way. I'm comin' in."

The stumping started again, slow, loud and determined. She heard every last thump of his laborious approach. Finally he halted with a hard thud of his crutches in the open doorway to her room. She could hear him panting from his exertion and settling himself a little against the door frame.

She stayed burrowed under the covers. Though she knew her behavior was thoroughly childish, she still hoped that if she refused to even push the blanket off her head and look at him, he might just go away.

No such luck. He had caught his breath and he was ready to tell her exactly what was on his mind.

"Pitiful," he said with utter disgust. "Purely pathetic, that's what you are."

She resolutely did not respond.

"This place looks like *my* place, for godsakes, gal. It's a disgraceful mess. And look at you, hidin' like some silly, wimpy little twit under them covers. What the hell's wrong with you?"

Through her numb exhaustion, she felt a twinge of irritation at him. He'd always been a pushy old goat. Who did he think he was to come bursting into her house like this? Hadn't she made it perfectly clear to him—and to everyone—that all she wanted was to be left alone?

"You answer me, gal!"

Oh, why wouldn't he just leave?

"I mean it. Answer, or by God, I'll—"

She didn't want to hear what. "Go away," she whined, though she had told herself she wasn't going to say a single word.

"Not on your life," Oggie intoned. "Now, get out from under those covers, and face me like the real, strong, gutsy woman you used to be!" He struck the wall with something, probably a crutch.

"Leave me alone." Eden pulled the blanket tighter over her head.

Oggie grunted and mumbled. Then she heard the thud of his crutches as he started walking again.

She heard him approach the bed and then stop right beside her head. There was a nerve-racking silence and then a bunch of clattering, then silence again. Eden, still cowering beneath the blanket, surmised that Oggie had just thrown his crutches to the floor.

Eden clutched the covers tighter and gritted her teeth and refused to peek out and make sure that the old fool was okay. He could just pick up those crutches himself and toddle on out of here, whenever he got tired of standing there staring at the lump her body made under the covers. She was not going to talk to him. She was not going to talk to anyone, and that was that.

But then, out of nowhere, she felt the blanket yanked away, ripped free of her hands.

Eden let out a yelp of pure outrage, closed her eyes and turned away. "Go away, Oggie. I mean it. I don't want to talk to you."

He grabbed her shoulder and forced her to .turn back to him. "Look at me, Eden Parker. Look at me now."

His voice was so compelling that her eyes popped open. "What?"

"Hear what I have to say."

"I don't feel like it."

"Do you think I give a damn whether you feel like it or not? I ain't leavin' till you've heard me out."

Eden groaned. There was just no escaping Oggie Jones once he had his mind made up about something.

"You listenin'?"

"Oggie, you've got no right…"

"Just answer. Are you listenin'?"

"This is not fair."

"What part of *'Are you listenin'?'* didn't you understand?"

She glared at him. "Oh, all right."

"All right, what?"

"All right, I'm listening."

"Good."

Grumbling to herself, Eden sat up and pushed her tangled hair out of her eyes. "Okay. Get it over with. Say what you came to say."

"I will." He was holding on to her night table, trying to brace himself there while he hopped a little to keep his balance on his good foot.

Eden found it hard to watch his struggle to stay upright. It had to be painful. As exasperated as she was with Oggie right that moment, there was no denying the facts: the man was seventy-five years old, and still barely able to get around without a wheelchair. It would be cruel to make him totter there in front of her much longer.

"Oh, wait a minute," she said sourly. She reached for her robe that was thrown across the foot of the bed, pulled it over her sleep shirt and then slid off the bed on the other side.

Then she went to him, picked up his fallen crutches and took him out to the big main room. She led him to the most comfortable chair and helped him get seated, propping up his bad foot on a hassock.

"That's better," he said when he was settled back. "Now. You got coffee?"

She put her hands on her hips and cast her gaze toward the beamed ceiling. "Honestly, Oggie."

"Well, I ain't had but one cup this morning," he said with a mildly affronted snort. "I got up a little late, and I got me one cup, and then Patrick calls and tells me you don't *feel* like working today. I mean, what the hell's the world coming to when Eden Parker don't *feel* like goin' to work?''

"I've been...very tired."

"Tired, my rosy-red behind," Oggie muttered. "Anyway, I started callin' and you wouldn't answer, so I got Sam to drop me off on his way over to the store. I towed these old bones all the way up those damn stone steps out there. I deserve a second cup of coffee if any man ever did. I'll say what I came here to say only after I have been sufficiently fortified with caffeine." He pulled a cigar from his pocket. "Mind if I smoke?"

"Would it make any difference if I did?"

His beady eyes gleamed. "Hell, no." He struck a match.

She grabbed an ashtray from the mantel and put it at his elbow. "All right. I'll make the coffee," she grudgingly agreed.

"Three sugars," he instructed, as she went through the door to the kitchen.

Fifteen minutes later, Eden returned carrying a tray with the coffee and sugar, spoons and cups on it. She'd had to wash the cups and spoons, since almost every eating utensil she owned was dirty. She set down the tray on the coffee table and served Oggie his coffee while he sat there, thoroughly pleased with himself, puffing on his smelly cigar.

At last, having served herself, too, she took the seat across from him. "Okay, Oggie. What do you want to say?" She realized with some surprise that she actually wanted to know.

It also occurred to her that bickering with her partner had done her a world of good. She felt more lively than she had since the morning she woke to find Jared gone.

Oggie said, "You are actin' like a quitter, Eden Parker. And that has got to stop."

Eden looked down at her coffee cup. "I know," she said softly, and realized that the dirty window between herself and the world seemed to have been wiped clean. She felt sad, still, it was true. And just the thought of Jared's name caused an aching in her heart. But the numbness was fading.

Her partner was right. She *was* acting like a quitter, and she did have to stop.

Oggie hadn't finished yet. "I didn't partner up with no quitter."

"I know."

"And I'm sorry that my fool son left you. When I find him, I'll break his face. But even if it really was over between the two of you—"

"It *is* over, Oggie."

"We'll get to that." Oggie shifted his cigar to the other side of his mouth. "Where was I? Oh, yeah. Even if the two of you never work things out, you got to pick yourself up and go on."

"I know, I—"

Oggie's eyes grew moist. "Believe me, I know what it is. That dead-numb feelin' when your love is gone. When my beautiful Bathsheba passed on, I thought more than once about takin' the shortcut to her side. But I held on. And I learned to live again, though a part of me will grieve for her for all my born days." A single tear trickled down Oggie's wrinkled cheek.

Eden, feeling as if she intruded on something very private, looked away. And then she heard Oggie's quick sniff and saw in her peripheral vision that he wiped the tear away.

"Well, I do digress," he said, and puffed some more on his cigar. "The point is, you got to get on with your life. You of all people oughtta know that, 'cause like I said before, you are not a quitter. That's why I picked you out for my Jared in the first place. 'Cause you got real stamina, gal. Not to mention one great pair of legs."

Eden gaped at him. "Excuse me?"

Oggie actually blushed. "Well, now, gal. It ain't no secret about them legs of yours."

Eden wasn't asking about her legs. "No. I mean what you said about *choosing* me. For Jared."

"What about it?"

"I could have sworn you said that you *picked me out* for Jared."

"You got it."

"You mean…when I first came to town with Laurie, when Jared was nowhere around, when I didn't even *know* him? You're saying you *selected* me for him *then?*"

"You're damn straight I did. You think I would have given away half my boy's inheritance to anyone but the woman destined by fate to become his wife?"

In spite of her shock at what Oggie seemed to be saying, Eden felt it only fair to point out, "You hardly *gave* it away to me, Oggie."

"Hell. You know what I mean. And you *are* just right for my Jared. You got the patience and the good sense and, until lately, you never took things too serious. Besides that, you're nice to look at. My boys all deserve pretty women, 'cause my boys stay true until death. A true man deserves someone nice to look at for the rest of his life, don't you think?"

"Well, I—"

"Yessiree, I knew you was the one for Jared the first night Laurie brought you into The Hole in the Wall."

"Oggie, you can't really be serious."

"Oh, but I am. Just look at me, gal. Look at me good. I'm an old man. And an old man *knows* things. Otherwise, what's the point of gettin' slow and stooped and all wrinkled up?"

"But, Oggie, I—"

"You purely talk too much, gal. Anybody ever tell you that?"

"Well, I—"

"But that ain't the end of the world. My beautiful Bathsheba, she never could shut her yap, either."

"She couldn't?"

"Hell, no. And still, she was and always will be the empress of my heart."

"Yes, I think you've mentioned that before." Actually, Oggie had rhapsodized about his dead wife more than once since Eden had met him. And he never failed to refer to the woman at least once each time as *the empress of his heart.*

"But enough about an old man's memories," Oggie decided. "We've got some serious plannin' to do. If you're through hidin' in your bedroom, that is."

"What do you mean, planning?"

"Are you through bein' *tired?*"

"Well, yes, I—"

"Listen. You put some clothes on and drive me back to Delilah's now. And then you clean up this place. And then, when you're sure you don't want to crawl back in bed and hide some more, you and me will have a talk."

"But, Oggie—"

"Nope. I am firm. You gotta be strong in your heart to do what I'm thinkin' of. I gotta be sure you're ready to face the world alone again, before we even *consider* how we're gonna get that troublesome man of yours back home where he belongs."

"Oggie—"

"Go. Get some clothes on."

Though she coaxed him for several minutes more, the old man would not tell her what he was thinking of.

At last, Eden got dressed and drove him to Delilah's.

"You call Patrick and tell him you'll be goin' in tonight after all," Oggie said, when she helped him out of the car and got him propped up on his crutches.

"Oggie, you are pushing it," Eden told him tartly.

He cackled. "That's what I like to see. A little fire and indignation. What good is any woman without fire and indignation? Anyway, you work your shift tonight, and you and me will talk after you close up."

"You want me to visit you here at Delilah's?"

"Hell, no. I told you I can't smoke in her house. And I got a feelin' I'm gonna need a good cigar between my teeth in order to explain this to you right."

"Is it bad, is that it?"

He only winked at her. "I'll be waitin' at your place when you come home tonight. Someone will drive me."

"But—"

"Just leave the door unlocked."

Chapter Eighteen

Oggie took his cigar from his mouth, looked at it and stuck it back in. "So whaddaya say? You think you're up for it?"

Eden rose from her chair and went to the big window that looked out on the deck. It was a little after three in the morning, so she saw nothing in the glass but a shadowed reflection of herself and the main room of the cabin behind her. Outside, it was pitch-black.

"Well?" Oggie prompted.

Eden was thinking. His plan was a crazy one. She doubted it would work. But even though she realized now that she *could* go on without Jared, she didn't want to live her life without him if there was any possible way she could draw him to her side.

And even if Oggie's plan was crazy, what else was there? Nothing that she could think of. While Jared was with her, she'd tried everything she could imagine to get him to give their love a chance. She'd slowly coaxed him into telling her about himself. After they'd become lovers, she'd shown him what they might share. At the end, she'd pleaded and even fought with him outright to try to get him to see the light. None of it had worked. She was fresh out of ways to convince Jared to return to her.

Oggie's plan, on the other hand, was a totally different approach than any of the ones Eden had used. It was clever and outrageous—not to mention devious and manipulative.

As a general rule, Eden despised deviousness and manipulation. But Oggie seemed so certain that what he had in mind would work. His confidence, as always, was contagious.

And besides, at the very least, the plan might draw Jared out, bring him to her. Then she'd have a chance to try once more to make him see that she wanted nothing so much as to spend her life at his side.

"But how will he find out what we're doing?" She turned from the window to face the old man. "We don't even know where he is."

Oggie was ready for that. "The other boys'll find him. You wait and see. If you got the style to pull this off so it looks real, they're all gonna be purely outraged. Every one of them believes you and Jared are a match made in God's heaven. They're practically as brokenhearted as you are at the problems you're havin'. But they're not beatin' the bushes for Jared, because they think there's no big rush for him to get back here. All we're gonna do is provide that big rush." Oggie puffed on his cigar and then sighed in contentment. He went on. "They'll all be howlin' mad when they get an earful of what you and me are gonna do. They'll be sure I took advantage of you on the rebound. Hell, when my girl Delilah hears what we're plannin', she'll be breathin' fire. After she tells the two of us off good and proper, she'll go lookin' for Jared, too. And nobody hides from Delilah when she's riled."

"You think she'll be able to find him?"

"I ain't got a doubt in my mind about it."

"Well, if you're sure…"

Oggie chortled. "Trust me, gal. I know what I'm doin'." He granted himself a generous sip of the whiskey Eden had poured for him. Then he cautioned, "We have to make it look real, though. First, we get a license, and then I'll have me a little talk with Reverend Johnson.…"

Oggie's black-haired daughter knocked on Eden's door at eight Saturday morning.

Eden, still in her robe, had just finished making coffee.

"Um, good morning Delilah. Won't you…come in?" Eden held open the door and Delilah stepped in inside. "Would you like some coffee?"

"No, thank you." Delilah folded her slim arms over her rather magnificent breasts. "Eden, last night I spoke with my friend Nellie Anderson. Nellie works as a volunteer secretary over at the Community Church."

"I see," Eden replied. She didn't really know what else to say. She had a pretty good idea where this was leading, but there wasn't much to do but let it play itself out. Delilah continued with some delicacy, "Nellie had some interesting news for me concerning a *wedding*."

Eden swallowed. "Oh," she heard herself say.

"After hearing this news, I said several very rude things to my father. And then I decided that it was time you and I had a talk."

"Yes. All right." Eden gestured toward the living room. "Why don't we sit in there?"

In the living room, Delilah sat on one end of the couch. She wasted no time getting to the point. "All of us in the family are certain that you're in love with Jared. Is that true?"

Eden, who felt unable right then to sit down, responded with an evasion. "Why do you want to know?"

Delilah's black eyes bored through her. "That's an absurd question if I ever heard one. But, for the sake of form, I'll answer it. I want to know if you love my brother, because if you *do* love him, then you really should *not* be marrying my father in a week."

I'm not marrying your father, Eden thought. *It's only a trick, to get Jared to come back to me.*

But she couldn't say that, of course. Part of the plan was that the rest of the family must believe she really intended to marry Oggie.

What could she say? She bravely threw herself into the deception. "Oggie and I get along well. We're quite fond of each other. And I believe we'll have a good marriage."

When Eden finished speaking Delilah gaped at her for a moment. And then Oggie's daughter tossed back her head and laughed, a wild laugh that made Eden think of what a strange woman Delilah was, a prim schoolteacher one moment, a wild gypsy creature the next.

"What is so funny?" Eden asked tightly, when Delilah was through laughing.

"Nothing." Delilah wiped away a few mirthful tears. "I just figured this out, that's all."

"What do you mean?"

"This is one of my father's brilliant schemes, right?"

"I don't know what you're talking about."

"You are an appallingly bad liar."

"Honestly, I—"

Delilah waved away Eden's protests. "Are you sure you know what you're doing?"

Eden felt lost. "About what?"

"Listen, all I'm saying is that my father's schemes can be dangerous. And more often than not, he has some hidden agenda. As his partner, you ought to have learned by now that you've got to watch all the angles when Oggie Jones is around. Because you can be sure *he'll* be watching them. You must be very careful, or you could end up doing what *he* wants, rather than what you thought he'd agreed you *both* wanted.''

''What are you saying?''

''My father has a crush on you, did you know that?''

Eden frowned. ''He does?''

''Yes, I'm sure of it. But he's also downright fanatic about seeing all his children married and settled down. So, in addition to having a crush on you, I believe he really does want to see you and Jared work things out. The question is, what is my father's underlying objective here? Luring Jared back into town? Or is it actually that my father wants to marry you himself, and he thinks he can trick you into it by arranging this wedding and convincing you it isn't really going to happen?''

Eden could hardly believe what she was hearing. ''Oggie wouldn't—''

''You'd be surprised what my father would do. But tell me. What will *you* do, if Jared still refuses to come back, even after he learns that you plan to marry his father?''

''Well, I—''

''Never mind. Don't tell me. It doesn't matter if I know, so long as *you* know what you'll do.'' Delilah's smooth brow furrowed. ''You do know what you'll do, don't you?''

Eden's head was spinning. ''Truly, Delilah, right this minute, I haven't the faintest idea.''

''Then think about it.''

''Yes. I certainly will.''

''And I suppose you should go and talk to Jared. It's going to be pretty hard for him to stop you from marrying my father if he doesn't even know you're doing it.''

''Well yes, exactly. And I'd love to go talk with him. If

I only knew where he went. As a matter of fact, Oggie said he thought that *you* might be able to find him.''

Delilah let out an exasperated groan. ''I *do* have a life, you know? And I probably shouldn't even have come to talk to you about this. I always end up in trouble myself whenever I get involved in my brothers' problems. I could tell you stories....'' She sighed. ''But never mind. Yes, I do have an idea where he is.''

''You do?'' Eden's heart picked up a faster rhythm. ''Where?''

''Look. This is just a hunch. I'm not guaranteeing he'll be there. And I'm only going to show you the way. You can go after him yourself. After all, he's your man, not mine.''

Chapter Nineteen

Though anticipation kept her nerves on a razor's edge, Eden waited until Monday to use the map Delilah had drawn for her. She worked both Saturday night and the early shift Sunday. She wanted an entire free day in which to seek Jared out. And she didn't want to ask anyone to cover for her at work. For one thing, she didn't want to explain where she was going. Also, she'd slighted her business enough during those grim days right after Jared left her. Whenever possible, she wasn't going to do that anymore.

Thus, on Monday morning, she got in the Bronco four-by-four that Delilah had told her she might borrow, and headed out of town. She turned off the highway at the place Delilah had described to her.

She drove what seemed to her like forever. Most of the ride was through shady forest of oak and evergreen. The road clung to the side of the mountain, winding upward.

At last, soon after the road grew rutted, and she was

forced to switch over to four-wheel-drive, she came out onto an open place of manzanita and close-growing buckbrush. There the sky was a splendid expanse of blue and the sun beat down, friendly and warm with just a hint of autumn's chilly bite in it.

A mile or two later, she came to the turnoff and the crude gate Delilah had described to her: a thick cablelike wire strung between two pine trees and secured with a heavy padlock. She got out of the Bronco and used the key Delilah had lent her.

She crested the mountain soon after that and began driving down into a small valley. The hillsides of manzanita and brush were left behind and she was back among the trees again. Sunlight came down through the branches in ribbons and shafts, creating natural spotlights that pointed out the iridescent green of a mossy rock, or the sparkle of natural crystal within a quartz boulder.

Eden took in the wild beauty around her. Concentrating on the scenery helped her to ignore the tension that kept coiling tighter in her stomach. Very soon, she might be coming face-to-face once again with the man she loved.

She reached the valley floor, crossed a pair of narrow streams and found herself on a plain of baked-dry red dirt, within a sea of willow bushes on which clung leaves that had already turned gold. To her left, red dirt hills rose, steep and absolutely naked of all greenery until the very top, where the forest started again, ragged at the edges like a torn carpet. Eden knew what the blasted hills signified. Once, hydraulic mining had been done here.

Eden stared at the stripped hills and marveled at what she saw. She'd heard that they called the huge hoses that had done this thing "water cannons." Now she understood why. For almost a century, mining for gold by ripping through to ancient riverbeds with powerful jets of water had been illegal. And yet still the blasted hills remained flayed bare, even after decade upon decade had come and gone. The damage was long-lasting. And spectacular to see.

Eden turned her gaze ahead once more and saw the cabin.

As Delilah had warned her, the place was very crude, a tar-paper shack where Jared's Uncle Cleve and his partners used to stay while they worked the hard-rock mine across the ravine for gold. The shack sat on the edge of the valley of willows, with the ravine at its back. The red hills loomed over all. Opposite the hills, the faraway mountains seemed to go on forever beneath their verdant blanket of evergreen.

The shack had a door with two wooden steps leading up to it and what looked like a deck on one side. The deck had long ago collapsed and was slowly in the process of tumbling piecemeal down the ravine.

A tin chimney stuck out of the cabin's roof. From it, smoke drifted lazily toward the pristine sky. In front of the cabin there was a small ring of stones with a rusted grate over it: a barbecue pit. Jared's truck was parked on the far side of the barbecue pit, right below the rise that led up to the outhouse.

Eden stopped the engine. She got out of the Bronco. She shut the door firmly. The sound was like the crack of a rifle in the stillness. Ordering her suddenly racing heart to slow down, she marched up to the shack and pounded on the door.

Nothing happened.

So she took the cracked porcelain knob in her trembling hand and turned it. The door opened toward her with a long slow groan. She peered beyond the threshold into a rough room with one small window, plank shelves lining the walls, an ancient wood stove and a sink with a pump faucet. There was a rickety table and two chairs. And an old brass bed against one wall.

Jared was sitting on the bed, his feet stretched out in front of him, using the wall for a backrest. He was fully dressed.

In fact, it looked as if he might have stayed fully dressed in the same clothes for the past couple of days at least. He hadn't bothered to shave for a while either, and his dark beard was rough and random on his scowling face.

He held a half-empty bottle of whiskey in one hand.

For a moment, he blinked and stared at Eden. She knew he was wondering if what he saw was real.

And then he must have decided he wasn't quite drunk enough to be seeing things.

"Get the hell out," he said.

Eden didn't move. She wanted to cry. She wanted to rant and rail at him. But most of all, she ached for him.

The sink was full of dishes, the table displayed the remains of a number of meals. There were clothes strewn on the chairs and thrown across the foot of the bed. The place was a mess. He was going through exactly what she'd gone through in trying to forget what they'd shared. But it was worse for him, because he'd hidden himself away where it took a four-by-four to get to him. And because he'd embraced his old demon, alcohol, to try to drive her from his heart.

"Oh, Jared…"

"Get out."

"Jared, I—"

He turned his head toward the wall.

"Please come back to me," she pleaded softly. "I miss you so."

He said nothing.

"Jared—"

"You heard me. I said get out."

"Once you told me that you always tried to do the right thing, remember?"

"I said—"

"But the right thing always backfired."

"—Get out."

"Well, look at you now, Jared. Is sitting here drunk in this filthy shack the answer to anything? Why can't you believe I know my own mind, Jared? Why can't you believe that when I say you're the man for me, I mean what I'm saying? Why can't you trust just one more time, Jared? Reach out your hand to love just one more time?"

He raised the bottle of whiskey, put it to his mouth and swallowed deeply. Then he grimaced as it burned its way down his throat. "Give it up, Eden," he said. "Give it up and go."

She stepped beyond the threshold and pulled the door closed behind her.

He turned away again, muttering under his breath.

She could think of nothing more to say to him, no new way to tell him of her love. She had hoped, yearned really, for a tender reunion. But she'd known Jared's stubbornness well enough that she hadn't actually expected one.

And he'd armed himself doubly against her with alcohol, she knew. She'd worked in bars long enough to have learned that it never did a bit of good to reason with a drunk. It was pointless to try to get through to him now.

Eden realized there was nothing left to do but hit him with the news of what she and Oggie planned and then go. Either he'd take it from there, or he wouldn't.

She went and stood beside him, though he resolutely refused to look at her again. "All right. I'll go. But I wanted you to know that your father's made me an offer. And I've accepted. I came here hoping that you'd ask me to change my mind, but it appears I was living in a fool's dream on that score."

She had his attention now. He rolled his head and pinned her to the spot with his bloodshot gaze. "What offer?"

She didn't waver. "He's asked me to marry him. I said yes. We'll be married in the North Magdalene Community

Church in five days' time, this coming Saturday at 2:00 p.m.''

Jared went on glaring at her. Then he muttered an obscenity and turned away again. ''I don't believe you.''

''Fine. That's up to you.'' She started to turn away.

He demanded, ''Why the hell would you want to wreck your life? What for?''

Eden felt a tiny surge of hope. Maybe they were getting somewhere after all.

But before she could answer, he waved his own outburst away. ''Forget it. Never mind. What you do with your life is your own damned business. If you want to ruin it to get even with me, you can go ahead and be a fool. I'm not involved. Now go away.''

Eden, wounded to the core and also truly disgusted with him, felt tears of total frustration rising to her eyes. She looked away from him. She didn't want to give him the satisfaction of seeing her cry. That was when she noticed the rifle, on a wall rack by the door.

It took her five giant steps to get to it. She reached up and ripped it from the wall. Then she checked to see if it was loaded; it was.

Jared commanded, ''Put that damn thing back where it belongs.''

Eden looked at him. She was not crying now. She marched back to his side and held the gun out to him. ''Here. It's loaded. Why don't you go ahead and shoot yourself, Jared Jones, instead of killing yourself slowly with whiskey this way? Because I know and you know that you love me. As long as you're breathing, you'll love me. And if you don't reach out and take me, you'll have to stay drunk the rest of your life to stand the pain of what you threw away yourself. That's how the men in your family are when they find the right woman for them. And if that's not *involved,* I don't know what is!''

Jared, whose mouth was hanging open, carefully accepted the rifle from her hands and set it on his other side, where she would be unlikely to be able to reach it again.

Eden wasn't finished. "You think about it, Jared. You consider carefully if you can afford to just sit out here in the woods with a whiskey bottle for company and let everything you ever wanted slip right out of your hands. Because I'm not in love with your father, but I do care for him. And I believe he and I could have a good life together. I truly do. You see, I'm not obsessed with how old a man is the way you are, Jared. It's the heart and the mind that matter. And as long as two people are both adults, how may years lie between them doesn't make too much difference to me." She bent down to him and put her face right up to his. "On the day you left me, I took the money you gave me and I bought a wedding dress. I dreamed then that I would wear it when I became your wife. But whether you're there or not, Jared, I'll be wearing it next Saturday. Do you hear me in there? Have I made myself clear?"

Slowly Jared nodded.

Eden drew herself up. "Good."

Without another word, she strode to the door, flung it open and walked out into the fall sunshine. She never looked back.

Jared stared at the door for a long time after Eden went through it. Then he blinked and lifted the bottle of whiskey slowly to his thirsty lips.

But, as luck would have it, just before he tipped back his head and drank, he had a vision.

He saw Eden in a wedding dress. And he saw his father slipping a ring onto her slender hand and then gathering her into his gnarled old arms and pulling her close for a vow-sealing kiss.

With a curse so foul it was a good thing no one else heard it, Jared threw the bottle across the room. It shattered, splattering whiskey all over the wall.

Chapter Twenty

"It's certainly a beautiful day for a wedding, Edie." Eden's mother, Julia, lowered the bridal veil over Eden's face and smoothed it on her shoulders so that it didn't bunch or gather.

Eden smiled through the veil. Julia and Eden's stepfather had come from Bakersfield for the ceremony. And Eden's father and stepmother were here from Fresno. Also, two of her half brothers and three half sisters, one stepsister and two stepbrothers, plus a number of spouses and children had all seen fit to drive to Eden's new home on very short notice to watch her walk down the aisle.

There was one motel in North Magdalene. It was full to capacity with the members of Eden's family. Some of them were also staying at the cabin and some with Laurie's parents. It did Eden's heart good to see them all. She had cried happy tears when so many of them called and said they wouldn't miss her wedding for the world. All her life, she had felt a little like an outsider in her own family. But now, on her wedding day, she knew she was loved and included by them all.

"Yes, it is a good day for a wedding, Mom," Eden said. "And I'm glad you all came."

They stood in a small room right off the narthex of the North Magdalene Community Church. Through the tall, double-hung window, the sky was clear blue. The flame-leaf maple right beyond the glass displayed the brilliant red fall leaves for which it was named.

From the chapel, Eden could hear piano music. The sound was lovely, lyrical and tender, though Eden didn't know the name of the song. She'd spoken only briefly with Regina Black, who was the church's volunteer pianist. Eden had asked Regina to use her own judgment about the music, and she was glad she had.

Julia went on, "And this is a charming little town. I can see why you'd want to make your life here."

"Yes, I do love it."

"And your fiancé is…quite a character."

The catch in her mother's voice was not lost on Eden. "Yes. There's no one quite like him. Everyone in town says so."

"Are you sure—" Julia coughed delicately into her hand "—that this is what you want, Edie?"

Eden kept her smile. "Yes, Mom. I'm sure."

"Because, you know, it isn't too late to—"

"Mom. I know what I'm doing. I'm going to marry the man I love. Be happy for me, please?"

"I will." Her mother smoothed the lace of Eden's sleeve. "But there hasn't been much time for us to talk. And I would never forgive myself if I didn't tell you what's in my heart."

"Oh, Mom." Eden took Julia's hands. "I know. You think he's not right for me."

Julia nodded. Eden saw there were tears in her eyes. "Yes. That's what I think."

"Just trust me, Mom." Eden gave the hands she held a squeeze. "Everything will work out all right." Someone had thoughtfully set a box of tissues on a small credenza beneath the window. Eden took one and gave it to her mother.

Julia delicately dabbed at her eyes. "Well. It's your life, of course."

"Yes, Mom. It is."

"And at least I've told you about my doubts."

"Yes. And thank you. For being honest."

"I just wish—"

Eden raised a hand. "Please. No more."

"Yes, of course. I understand."

The door opened and Laurie, the maid of honor, came in. She wore the tea-length autumn-gold dress she and Eden had chosen together at the bridal shop in Grass Valley only a few days before. Her honey-brown hair had been swept up into a smooth French twist. Laurie's smile was determinedly bright. "All ready?"

Eden nodded. "How long until we start?"

"Soon."

The door opened once more and Nellie Anderson, Delilah's friend and the church secretary, appeared. Nellie had a rather pinched face, but she was doing her best, like everyone else, to keep a smile on it.

"The pastor has asked me to find out when you'd like to sign the license," Nellie said.

"Would after the ceremony be all right?"

"It's your wedding," Nellie said, in much the tone one might say, *It's your funeral.* And then she seemed to realize that her attitude was slipping. She hastened to add in a too-solicitous voice, "And I believe that signing the papers after the ceremony is traditional, now I think of it. A wise decision."

"Great, then, we'll sign them after," Eden said.

"Fine." Nellie resolutely kept smiling. "I'll be back in a few moments to give you the signal to start."

"Thank you," Eden said.

And then Nellie was gone.

Laurie came close. "Oh, Eden. Are you sure that you—"

Eden didn't let her finish. "Shh. Not a word. This is exactly what I want." She lifted her veil and gave her friend a reassuring peck on the cheek.

Laurie looked as if she might burst into tears any moment.

To distract her friend, Eden asked brightly, "How many people came?"

"The church is packed," Laurie answered. "There are as many folks out there as when Sam and Delilah got married."

Eden was surprised. Since the word had gotten out about the wedding, she'd had nothing but dire warnings. Everyone she talked to begged her to change her mind. She'd felt sure the people in town would demonstrate their concern by failing to attend.

"I wonder why the crowd," she mused.

Laurie had found the box of tissues and was making use of it. She blew her nose. "Nobody's happy about this, Eden. But no one would miss it for the world, either. You haven't lived here long enough to understand that yet, but someday you will."

Eden just shook her head.

Julia handed Eden her bouquet. Then for a few moments, the three women stood silently, sharing an occasional reassuring smile or a quick squeeze of a hand.

And then Nellie stuck her head into the room. "All right. Mrs. Lumley," she said to Julia, "it's time for Brendan to escort you to your seat. And Laurie, you'll follow on Sam's arm shortly after. The bride—" Nellie nodded at Eden "—will wait here until her father comes for her."

Within seconds, Eden found herself alone in the room. The lovely, unknown music ended. The wedding march began.

Eden clutched her bouquet and stared out at the burning brilliance of the flame-leaf maple. As she stared, her lips moved in a litany, a chant so softly spoken, that she couldn't even hear the words herself. "It will be all right. It will be fine. I'm doing the right thing. It's not too late. He could still come. He *will* come. I know it. I believe it. He will..."

"Eden?"

Eden turned and forced a wide smile for her father.

"You look beautiful, Edie."

"Oh, Dad. Thanks."

"It's time. Are you ready?"

Eden nodded. He backed out of the doorway and she walked toward him, into the narthex. The wedding march seemed to swell in her ears as she moved closer to the sound. Her father held out his arm. Eden took it. They stood in the inner door to the chapel. Eden saw how full the small church was. There was not a single empty space in any of the pews. People sat in folding chairs along the sides and at the front. They stood by the windows, too.

Regina Black caught sight of the bride. She played even louder. Heads turned and everyone gaped. No one liked it, but no one wanted to miss it, either. It was a moment that would be whispered about in the lore of North Magdalene for years and years to come, the moment Eden Parker walked down the aisle to marry the father of the man she loved.

Reverend Johnson was at the altar. The maid of honor and the best man stood to the side. The groom, propped up on his crutches and dressed in an ill-fitting outdated suit, waited, grinning slyly, for his young bride.

Eden and her father began the long walk up the aisle.

With every step, Eden felt her heart breaking, shattering like her hope.

But she didn't falter. She maintained her smile. And in her mind, she didn't give up. She kept up the chant.

He will come. He does love me. This will work out. It will....

Eden reached Oggie's side. Her father stepped away.

Pastor Johnson intoned, "If the bride and the groom will please join hands, we will begin."

Oggie grunted a little as he readjusted himself on his crutches so he could stick out a hand. Eden took it.

"Dearly beloved," Reverend Johnson began.

And all hell broke loose.

The big doors at the back of the church were suddenly flung wide.

The guests begun murmuring.

"What the—"

"Who is it?"

"It can't be—"

"It is!"

Eden turned, hope, fear and finally blazing joy searing their way through every inch of her body.

Oggie tossed back his head and crowed with glee, then announced, "You had me a little worried there, boy!"

But Jared didn't hear him. He was looking at Eden. He marched up the aisle and stepped between the bride and groom.

With slow, careful fingers, he lifted Eden's veil. She saw that his eyes were clear. His breath was sweet on her up-turned face.

"You're the most beautiful thing I've ever seen in my life," he said softly. "And I spent way too much money on this damn suit."

She glanced down and saw that he was, indeed, dressed like a man might dress on his wedding day. She opened her mouth to tell him she thought it was a fine suit and that he looked splendid in it. But somehow, no sound would come out.

It was okay, though, because he had more to say.

"I thought about what you told me, when you found me at my uncle's cabin. And I decided every last word was true." His voice was grim, but his gray eyes were shining. "You're the woman I've been looking for all my life. And if you're so damned sure it's not too late for us, then who am I to say different? I love you. And I suppose I'll have to marry you, to save you from my dad."

Eden opened her mouth again. But for once in her life, she found she really was totally speechless. She stared up at him, still not fully daring to believe that he had really come, that he was truly here.

She *had* known it would happen. She had not allowed herself to even imagine that he would not come for her. But still, it overwhelmed her, that he was actually here. That he was smiling at her with all the love she'd always known was in him gleaming in his silver eyes.

Jared looked worried. "Honey? Are you okay?"

She nodded.

"And will you marry me?"

She nodded once more.

He glanced at his father. "Step aside, old man."

"You betcha." Oggie braced his crutches up under him and stomped to the first row on the groom's side, where Patrick got up and gave him his seat.

Jared turned to Pastor Johnson. "Okay, Reverend, get on with it."

Pastor Johnson coughed and clutched his bible against his chest. "Er, Mr. Jones, this is highly irregular."

"Do it anyway, Reverend!" Rocky Collins shouted from a middle pew.

"Yeah, for Pete's sake, yer worship," someone else said, "don't mess things up now."

The ripple of agreement rolled over the packed church.

"Yeah, marry them!"

"It's how it's supposed to be!"

"Do it!"

"Yeah, do it now!"

The reverend cast a nervous glance around the room and came to the decision that a volatile crowd like this should probably be appeased.

He opened his bible.

A prayerful hush swept the chapel into instant silence. Jared tenderly smoothed down Eden's veil and took her hand in his. They turned to the minister and the ceremony began.

At the end, Eden barely managed to whisper, "I do."

Jared's voice, however, was firm and clear as he promised to love, honor and cherish Eden Parker for the rest of their lives.

Epilogue

It was remarked in later years that there was never a man so changed as Jared Jones, after the day he stole Eden Parker from his own father. From that day, Jared went through life with a smile on his rugged face and a good word for everyone on his lips.

Oggie Jones smiled a lot, too. He'd gone to great lengths to see Jared hooked up with Eden. After all, for a man to point a 30-30 at his own foot and pull the trigger on purpose takes more than a little grit. Not to mention the fact that he'd nearly had to marry Jared's bride himself.

But even though Oggie's old flesh healed slowly and there were some in town who smirked that he'd been jilted at the altar, Oggie was content. At last, he could retire. And he knew that in heaven, his beautiful Bathsheba was smiling.

Hell, the real truth was, he'd do it all again in a New York minute if it meant another one of his children would find true love at last.

* * * * * *

A HOME FOR THE HUNTER

For Gail Chasan,
who thought I ought to write a few books
about the Jones boys.

Chapter One

Olivia Larrabee looked up from the blackjack table—right into the piercing midnight eyes of the most compelling man she'd ever seen.

Something happened in her stomach—that down-too-fast-in-an-elevator feeling. If she hadn't had the high felt-topped table to lean against, she very well might have fallen off her stool.

Olivia's face burned. She knew that to allow herself to be so strongly affected by the mere glance of a strange man at this juncture of her life said terrible things about her character. After what she'd endured just twenty-four hours ago, she certainly ought to know better.

Oh, but he was so…mesmerizing. So completely a *man*. There was humor in the lift of his mouth, strength in the jut of his jaw and danger in his eyes. And there was absolutely no doubt about it. He was looking right at *her*.

"Wake up, dearie." The blue-haired lady with the rhinestone-studded glasses who had the seat next to Olivia's nudged her in the ribs.

Olivia stiffened and blinked. "Oh. Um. Yes." She forced herself to break the hold of the stranger's hypnotic glance and to sneak another peek at the six of hearts and the seven of clubs that she'd been dealt. She beamed a smile at the dealer. "Umm. Hit me."

The dealer peeled off another card. A king. Just what she *didn't* want to see:

"Bust." Olivia said the word she'd heard the other players say when their cards totaled more than twenty-one. She turned her cards over.

The blue-haired lady clucked her tongue. "Bad night, eh, dearie?"

Olivia sighed. Then, trying her best to appear cool and unconcerned, she glanced up and scanned the busy casino, seeking again that incredible pair of consuming dark eyes.

But the stranger was nowhere in sight. She felt ridiculously bereft, more solid proof of the meagerness of her character.

The blue-haired lady was peering at her sympathetically. "You all right, honey?"

"Yes, I'm fine." Olivia forced a polite smile. "Thanks." She gathered up what was left of her chips and slid off her stool. Then she headed straight for the change cage to get coins to play the slot machines.

Half an hour later, her arm was tired from pulling levers. She'd failed to hit even one jackpot, though she'd put more than two hundred dollars in quarters into the machines.

She was feeling glum—and not because she was losing. But because she knew that when her jumbo cup of quarters was empty, all she had to do was get more. All Olivia *ever* had to do was get more. In fact, it was probably silly for her to be playing the quarter slots. The least she could do, rich as she was, was to go and waste her money in the dollar machines. She could be down over a thousand now, instead of a mere two hundred. She could feel more like something was at *stake* here, even though she knew it wasn't.

To the only daughter of Lawrence Larrabee, owner of Larrabee Brewing Company, a thousand hardly rated as pocket change.

It was awful to be rich. Especially when it was your father, not you, who had earned all the money. Olivia didn't know how other undeservedly wealthy people felt. But she herself felt a little guilty all the time. A little wasteful, just on principle. Which was why she'd come to Las Vegas, to learn to lighten up a little.

Or at least lightening up was part of it.

But, of course, there was more.

The brutal truth was, she'd discovered her fiancé naked in the arms of another woman and known she had to get away. The alternative was too dreary: to spend weeks wandering around her beach house in a bathrobe, feeling like it was just too much trouble to wash her hair.

No, she'd decided. She was *not* going to sink into some dismally predictable depression. What she needed was a visit to the gaudiest, most gloriously wasteful place in the United States. In the crowds and excitement, she would forget all about Cameron Cain and the way he'd betrayed her.

And maybe a little of the glitter would rub off on her. She'd pictured herself wearing red velvet and throwing around some of the money she hadn't earned. In her mind had been the idea that such profligate spending would not only help her to forget how empty her existence was, but would also teach her to take life more as it came.

But so far she wasn't doing very well. She was wearing red velvet all right. By Kamali. But every time she caught a glimpse of herself in one of the casino's gold-veined mirrors, she thought of Fantine in *Les Misérables*. She was just one of those women who looked like a refugee from a used-clothing store, no matter what she wore.

Beyond her disappointing appearance, everything she played, she lost. And losing wouldn't have been so bad, really. If she only could have lost *largely*. But Olivia was too naturally frugal to bet large. And even all the tension and excitement around her wasn't helping to change that. If anything, it was only making her failure to do anything on a grand scale seem all the more evident.

The single bright spot in this whole questionable enterprise had been that shared glance with a stranger half an hour ago.

"Pitiful," Olivia mumbled to herself. "Utterly pathetic."

"You using this machine, sweetheart?" *another* blue lady inquired.

Olivia wondered morosely what it could be about her that made older ladies call her things like "dearie" and "sweetheart." Olivia suspected that, though she was a grown woman and had been for years, other people did not consider her fully mature.

"Well, hon?" the lady prompted.

"No. I'm done. You go right ahead." Olivia took the lady's veiny, zircon-encrusted hand and pressed her full cup of quarters into it. "Win a jackpot on me."

The lady's rather faded blue eyes lit up. "Well, thanks, hon. You're a doll."

The woman's obvious pleasure at such an unexpected windfall cheered Olivia. "Think nothing of it, sweetie." She tossed the words over her shoulder as she flicked her crimson skirt out of her way and headed for the craps tables.

There, she stood to the side and watched for a while, thinking that craps was a very fast game. Olivia had heard somewhere that it was the true gambler's game. She didn't know about that, but it certainly was confusing.

Still, she wanted to try it. So once she had the general

idea of how it was played, she dared to join in. She put her chips on the numbers and listened to everyone shouting and chattering and watched the man at the money box rake in her chips every time the dice were thrown. She was losing, she could figure that out.

But when the dice came around to her and she tossed them, the other players made appreciative noises. Apparently Olivia had won for *them*.

After she'd thrown the dice twice, everyone else at the table passed up their turns to roll. The dice kept coming back to her. And she threw them, paying no attention to her own bets. The other people at the table cheered her on and threw chips at her. It was actually sort of exciting. And it was nice to have everyone thinking she was wonderful and shouting at her to "do it one more time, baby!"

For a few minutes Olivia almost felt expansive. She tossed her head and laughed and talked to the dice before she threw them. She could have sworn she was actually starting to forget her troubles and have a good time.

But then she was assailed. There was no other word for it. Olivia was assailed by the feeling that someone was watching her. It was eerie. And it broke her concentration on having a good time.

Soon enough she found herself casting frequent furtive glances all around. She saw no one looking at her but the money man, the man with the stick, and the people around the table. And they all had good reason to look at her. They were wondering if she was going to throw the dice or not.

Olivia threw the dice again. But in the very act of tossing them, she couldn't help speculating if it might be *he* who was watching her—he of the mesmerizing midnight eyes.

The very thought that he might be observing her now, during her little moment of glory as the darling of the craps table, sent a sweet shiver all through her. She had a fleeting moment of absurd fancy in which she actually dared to imagine that he'd taken one look at her and known he'd never forget her. Now he was following her around the casino, stalking her, awaiting just the right moment to—

Around the table there rose a collective groan.

It appeared she'd rolled a bad one.

Olivia put her ridiculous fantasies about a man she didn't even know completely from her mind and concentrated on winning more money for her new friends at the table.

But it was too late. Her lucky streak with the dice was over. When she rolled the next time, everyone groaned again. The man beside her grumbled something rude about her under his breath and rolled the dice himself instead of passing them. Suddenly craps wasn't any fun at all.

With a sigh Olivia departed the table. She trudged through the casino, looking for the next diversion. But nothing caught her eye.

So she went out the main doors and stood on the sidewalk for a moment and stared up and down the Strip. She saw bright lights and huge marquees that advertised the ever-popular game of Keno and progressive slots and the most famous entertainers in the world.

And she saw neon, a river of neon. Flashing and flowing. More neon than in Times Square in New York. It pulsed and whirled against the desert night sky. It awed her. And in a strange way it soothed her.

She wondered what time it was. She wasn't wearing a watch, and in the casino there seemed to be no clocks anywhere. As if time were not allowed in Vegas.

She thought of moving on, to the MGM Grand or the Tropicana. She could see what another pleasure palace had to offer. But then again, wasn't one casino like another in all the ways that mattered?

Oh, that was a bad attitude to have. She knew it. How was she going to forget her problems and learn to take life as it comes with an attitude like that?

Determined not to give up yet, she started down the sidewalk. And then she realized she was hungry. The casino where she was staying—the one she'd just left—advertised lobster with drawn butter for $9.95. A bargain.

And, though she knew from long experience that really fine food rarely came cheap, Olivia Larrabee had never been able to resist a bargain. She turned so suddenly that she bumped right into a rather portly urban cowboy who just happened to be walking behind her. He grunted as she stepped on his snakeskin boots.

"Oh, I am so sorry, I—"

"Think nothing of it, little lady." The man was tipping his Stetson at her.

But she hardly noticed what the stout cowboy was doing. Because just past his beefy shoulder, she saw *him*—the compelling stranger who had watched her at the blackjack table.

The stranger had just come out of the casino behind her. And she knew, from the way his eyes narrowed as she spotted him, that he'd left the casino because he was following her.

"Er, miss…you okay?" the beefy cowboy was asking.

She smiled vaguely without looking at him. She was not taking her eyes off the stranger this time. This time, if he turned and disappeared, she would be watching as he did it. She wouldn't be left with the eerie feeling that he had vanished into thin air. "I'm fine. Just fine."

The cowboy grunted and moved on. Olivia stood on the sidewalk and stared at the stranger. He returned her stare for a moment, his look both defiant and knowing. And then he started to turn away.

"Wait!" The plea was out of her mouth before she had time to tell herself that the last thing she needed in her life right now was to go chasing after some man she didn't even know.

The man in question froze where he was, just outside the gilt-framed glass doors to the casino. Around him and between him and Olivia, people jostled and shifted, flowing like so much flesh-and-blood neon in and out of the big doors.

"Don't go." She only mouthed the words.

But he heard them, she was sure he did. He knew what she had said.

Through those deep-set dark eyes he regarded her with extreme wariness. In the garish yellow light of the casino entrance, his pale hair and brows had a gilded look. His skin was rich bronze against the white of his dress shirt. On his tanned cheeks, there was the shadow of a beard. He managed somehow to look both rumpled and lazily elegant.

There was something feral about him. He was like those lions that survive in the African deserts. A little too lean, dangerously hungry. But no less king of the beasts for all that.

Olivia decided all over again that he was the most thoroughly masculine man she had ever seen.

And just as she reached that decision he shrugged and began walking toward her.

Chapter Two

As she watched him stride toward her, Olivia knew very well that she was behaving most unwisely. If she had any sense at all, she would turn quickly and walk away.

But she didn't turn. Somehow, she *couldn't* turn.

He reached her. They stood regarding each other. People going by shot them curious glances, even bumped them once or twice. But they paid no attention.

"Give me a reason why not." His voice, pitched low, was like a long, gentle stroke from a knowing hand.

The desert wind swept up the street, blowing the bloodred velvet in a swirl around her ankles, causing his tie to flip up and over his shoulder. With a boldness she hadn't known she possessed, Olivia caught the tie and smoothed it back into place, then quickly snatched her hand away.

"Well?" He lifted a brow.

"Well, what?"

"Give me a reason why I shouldn't go."

She looked past his shoulder and then back at him once more. "Because…" A few strands of her hair blew across her mouth. She caught them, smoothed them away.

"Yeah?"

She couldn't think of a thing except, *Because I don't want you to go.* And yet that would sound so obvious, so dull. She didn't want him to think her dull. She stared up at him, suddenly tongue-tied, her unaccustomed boldness blown away with the wind. She felt her skin begin to flood with agonized color.

"I, um…"

"Tell you what…" He smiled; a strange smile. Ironic and yet so tender. "*I'll* give *you* a reason. You just say yes or no. And I'll be gone. Or I won't."

She coughed, feeling nervous now. "What reason?"

He actually chuckled. It was a warm, teasing sound, one that enticed and intrigued her as much as his speaking voice had done. Then he asked, without preamble, "Scared?"

The truth was all that came to her, so she gave it. "Yes." Then she asked, "Was that the reason?"

"No. I just wanted to know. And don't be."

"What?"

"Scared. I would never hurt you."

"Oh."

"But take my advice."

"What?"

"Never trust a man who says he'll never hurt you."

She stared at him for a moment. And then she burst into laughter. He laughed with her, standing there on the street, buffeted by the crowds and the night wind. Several people passing by stopped to look at them. Those who stopped smiled knowing smiles. But Olivia didn't notice. She saw only the stranger.

Then he said, "Have dinner with me. Now."

She hesitated. "Is *that* the reason?"

He nodded. "If you have dinner with me, then I've got a reason not to go."

She confessed, "Well, I am a little hungry."

"Is that a yes?"

"I shouldn't."

"Yes? Or no?"

"I..."

"Think about it. Take a minute. I can wait." There was a gold pillar behind him, one of the six that adorned the porte cochere of the casino. He backed up and leaned against it. "No rush."

She laughed again, then composed herself and asked, "What's your name?"

He answered after a brief pause, "Jack Roper."

Jack, she turned the name over in her mind and decided she liked it. It was hard and direct and no-frills masculine.

She volunteered her own. "I'm Olivia." But then she hesitated. She dreaded giving him her last name.

Whenever she said her last name, people would ask, "Larrabee, as in Larrabee Lager?" She hated when people asked that. She didn't want Jack Roper to ask that. For once, she just wanted to be a woman, talking to a man who found her attractive. Not the heiress to the third-largest brewing company in the western United States.

So she picked a last name from a marquee across the street, the last name of a certain country and western singer. "Loveless," she told Jack. "I'm Olivia Loveless."

He grinned. "*Loveless?* You're kidding."

"No, I'm perfectly serious."

She gave him what she hoped was a no-nonsense frown. And as she frowned, she was thinking that really, she shouldn't be lying to him about who she was.

But then again it was so nice, for once, not to have to go into all that.

And besides, who was *he* really, anyway? She knew nothing about him or why he seemed to be following her.

Because he thinks I'm beautiful.

Oh, right. Sure, a more reasonable voice seemed to say.

Okay, fine. If not beautiful, at least appealing. He finds me appealing.

And that's supposed to be reason enough that you should have dinner with him, a total stranger?

Given how many fabulous men like him have even bothered to look twice at me so far in my life, you're darn right.

It's dangerous. Downright dangerous, said her wiser self. *Picking up a man on the sidewalk in front of a casino is just asking for trouble.*

I wouldn't be picking him up. I'm not going to his room with him, for heaven's sake. Only out to eat.

Oh, get real.

I need this, I really do. My ego's been decimated by what happened yesterday.

Pitiful. Purely pathetic.

And I've never done anything like this in my life. I never take chances. It's time I took a chance.

Time you acted like a complete idiot, you mean.

So? She threw caution to the desert wind. *I'm doing it.*

Though her wiser self was still calling her a fool, she granted the incredible stranger a nod. "Okay, Jack. I'll have dinner with you. On one condition."

He came away from the pillar. "Name it."

"That it will be my treat."

He gave her that odd smile again. Ironically tender. "Fair enough."

A little flustered by the intense look in his eyes, she cleared her throat and tried to think what to do next. "I, um, don't know Las Vegas very well. In fact, I arrived this morning and I'm staying right here, in this hotel and casino.

This is the first time I've been outside of it since I got here. Where are *you* staying?''

"Right here, too."

"Oh, well. Isn't that a coincidence?"

He shrugged.

She forged on. "Anyway, just now I was going to go back inside and try the lobster. But if you—"

He took her arm, causing a pleasant little shiver to course through her. "I'm no native, but I know a couple of good places. Come on. We'll take my car."

She reminded herself that she was not going to get carried away with this. She looked at him levelly and refused to be pulled along. "Jack, I hardly know you. I will not get into your car with you right now."

His expression was rueful as he released her arm. "Sorry. So it'll be the lobster, I suppose."

"Is the lobster that bad?"

"Hell, I don't know. As a matter of fact, I'm not much on seafood."

"I'm sure there are other things on the menu. Choose one of them."

"I will. Let's go."

The lobster, while it didn't compare with what Olivia enjoyed at her favorite restaurant in Malibu, was certainly acceptable. Neither stringy nor rubbery, it had enough flavor that Olivia was sure the crustacean had been alive not *too* long ago. She hadn't been allowed to choose one from a tank, but for the price what could she expect?

And anyway, it was the man across the table, not the quality of the food, that interested her. Not surprisingly he ordered rare steak and seemed quite happy with it when it arrived.

He watched her as she expertly cracked the claws and removed the sweet meat.

"Amazing."

She glanced up from her work. "What?"

"That's a damn messy job. But somehow, you do it—" he sought the right word "—so tidily."

"Yes. I'm a tidy eater, all right."

He must have picked up on her ambivalence because he asked, "You don't like being tidy?"

"I'm not tidy, in general." She sucked the last shred of meat from a claw without making a sound. "I'm tidy when I eat. But in most everything else, I'm a mess."

"What do you mean?"

"I don't pick up after myself."

"You mean you're not a good housekeeper?"

"To put it bluntly—" she picked up her glass of Chardonnay and toasted him with it "—I'm a slob."

He sat back in his chair and regarded her.

She waited for him to tell her in some charming way that it was all right to be a slob. After all, if he wanted to please her, that would be the next thing for him to say. It was certainly what her ex-fiancé-as-of-yesterday would have said. Cameron had been a real pro at telling her how wonderful, how charmingly quixotic, how terrific she was in every way.

But Jack Roper only shrugged, as if whether Olivia "Loveless" was a slob or not was her own problem, not his.

She suddenly felt a little ashamed that she'd never had to pick up after herself, so she added, as if it mattered, "But I'm neat in the kitchen. And I'm quite frugal, as well."

"Why the kitchen?"

"I once took an expensive cooking class."

Very expensive. Olivia had spent six months in Paris studying the art of French cooking. In fact, her dream had once been to become a professional chef. But in the end she hadn't been good enough to get a job in any of the really fine restaurants. And eventually her father had convinced her that it was patently absurd for a woman of her means to be cooking in the kind of restaurants where, as a rule, she would never deign to eat. He'd suggested she buy a restaurant of her own to cook in, which somehow had felt like it would have been cheating. So she'd refused.

She told Jack, "I have a great respect for the art and the science of meal preparation."

They looked at each other for a moment over the candle in the middle of their table. She was aware, once again, of how very dark and deep his eyes were, especially in contrast to his pale gold hair. And of how much he attracted her—and how little she knew about him.

She sipped from her wine again. It was kind of nice, really, she thought. Not knowing him. Like one of those lovely old romantic movies. A movie with the word "stranger" in the title. *Strangers in Las Vegas,* perhaps.

He suggested quietly, "Tell me more. About yourself. About Olivia *Loveless.*"

The stress he put on the phony name made her wonder. Did he know it wasn't hers? She looked down at the white tablecloth and back up into his eyes just as the busser cleared her dishes away.

"I'm..."

"Yeah?"

She squared her shoulders. If he knew, he knew, she decided. And if he wanted to confront her with her lie, he could just go ahead and do it. She told him, "I'm just an ordinary woman."

He lifted a white-gold eyebrow but didn't say anything.

"I'm from Los Angeles." It wasn't much of a lie. She lived in Malibu. Her house was right on the beach. Her father had bought it for her as a Christmas present, a few years ago, from a movie star who'd needed a lot of money fast. "I'm here for a few days while I'm between jobs."

That was the truth. Technically. She'd quit her job as a "regional representative" for Larrabee Brewing Company only the day before. It hadn't been a *real* job anyway, just a meaningless position created by her father to ease her guilt about all the money he'd given her that she'd never earned.

"So while I'm in Las Vegas, I want to forget my troubles," she said, "and have a good time."

"And are you?"

"Forgetting my troubles?"

He nodded. "And having a good time."

She gave him a slow-spreading grin. "Now I am."

"Good."

"Dessert?" the waiter asked.

They agreed they'd have coffee.

Once the coffee was served, Olivia asked the question she'd been trying to form all through dinner. "When I turned around and saw you outside the casino, were you following me?"

His eyes seemed even darker than before, and fathoms deep. "Yes, I was." He sipped from his coffee. "I'd been following you for a while by then."

"You had?"

"Yeah. I was watching you at the blackjack table."

"I know." She stirred her coffee, though there was no reason to. She took it black. "I saw you."

"I felt like an idiot."

She looked up. "Why?"

"No one ever catches me staring." She detected a hint of a smile on his lips. "If I'm looking at all, they don't know it. But there's something different about you."

"Different?"

He shrugged. "Yeah. Different. Unusual."

She frowned. "I'm *unusual*?"

"Yeah. You say that you're ordinary, but you're not."

"How do you mean, *unusual?*"

"Well, it's partly that you're so small boned and pale. And then there's that dress."

"What? You don't like my dress?"

"It's different, that's all."

Olivia looked down and stirred her coffee some more, paying great attention to the unnecessary task. She was thinking that maybe the things Jack was saying about her weren't exactly flattering. But somehow, the way he said them, they made her feel complimented, anyway.

"I watched you at the craps table." His voice was low, caressing.

The surge of feminine pleasure she felt was instant and utterly shameless. She remembered the absurd little fantasy she'd indulged in right before she'd thrown the dice and her lucky streak had ended. She'd imagined him watching her. And now it turned out that he had been.

He added, "But you didn't catch me that time."

"No," she murmured softly, watching the coffee swirl in her cup. "I didn't catch you."

"Stop stirring that coffee."

Her hand went still.

"Look at me."

Slowly she raised her head and met his eyes.

"But you spotted me out on the sidewalk."

"Yes, I did."

"You turned around so fast, I didn't have a chance to disappear."

"Umm-hmm."

"That's twice you caught me."

"That's right."

"Nobody catches me." His gaze was so strange. Unreadable. Far away and yet probing.

Olivia had a sudden, disorienting sensation. A feeling of being utterly, completely, out of her depth. She pushed the feeling away and forced a rather brittle laugh. "Well. Should I be sorry?"

"Probably."

"That's too bad. Because I'm not." She took a sip from her overstirred coffee. "I think it's time to change the subject."

"To what?"

"We could talk about what brings you to Las Vegas."

He considered for a moment. "Business."

"What kind of business?"

"Do you really want to know?"

Now she was the one considering. At last she said, "I thought I did, when I asked."

"But?"

"Well, now that I think twice, I'm not so sure. Is it something that's bothering you, this business of yours?"

He didn't answer right away, but then he said, "Yeah, I guess it is bothering me. Just a little."

"I mean, you don't really want to talk about it, do you?"

"No." His eyes were wary again. "To be honest, I'd rather not get into it."

She knew just what he meant. She had no urge at all to tell him what had brought her to Vegas. Now that she was finally having a nice time, the last thing she wanted to talk about was how she'd caught her fiancé with another woman and run off to Nevada to keep from suffering a major depression.

An idea came to her. "Tell you what."

"What?"

"We hardly know each other."

"So?"

"So let's keep it that way. For now."

He looked flummoxed. "What the hell is that supposed to mean?"

She laughed, pleased that she'd managed to catch Jack

Roper off guard for once. In general, Jack struck her as a man who rarely allowed himself to be caught off guard. And he'd already confessed that he'd been unable to stop staring at her earlier in the evening.

Because she was so *unusual*.

Her heart, which up until a little while ago had felt like a lead weight in her chest, was starting to seem as light as spun sugar. Maybe this spontaneous trip to Vegas had been the right idea after all.

It was only a little more than twenty-four hours from the moment she'd discovered her fiancé in the arms of his executive assistant. And yet here she was, having dinner with a mysterious and compelling man and somehow actually managing to hold her own with him. The momentary feeling of being out of her depth was long gone.

"Are you going to answer my question?" he asked.

"What question?"

"You said we hardly know each other and that you wanted to keep it that way. What did you mean?"

"Oh, that." She gave an airy wave.

"Yes. That."

"Well—" she sat forward "—what I meant was, let's not talk about the ordinary things, the mundane things. Not tonight, anyway. We're strangers in Las Vegas. And let's enjoy being just that."

He took a sip of coffee. "It's an interesting idea."

"Does that mean you agree?"

He seemed to study her. "If I did, what would we talk about?"

She put her forearms on the table and leaned on them. She was warming to the idea. "Oh, everything. What we think. What we like. What we don't like. Opinions and observations. But no personal facts. Nothing about what you do or what I do or what our everyday lives are like. Nothing about our family problems or any of that stuff. We could save all that for later.'' She found she was blushing. She sat back a little and added, ''I mean, if there *is* a later, of course.''

''Of course.''

''So what do you think?'' She was so pleased with the idea that she bounced a little in her chair.

He chuckled. ''Hell. Why not?''

''We have a deal?'' She stuck out her hand.

He took it and gave it a firm shake. ''You bet we do, Ms. Loveless.''

''Brussels sprouts,'' he said much later. They were sitting in a pair of wing chairs next to an areca palm in a little alcove they'd discovered right off the lobby.

''Brussels sprouts.'' She pondered a moment. ''In any form?''

''Yeah. It doesn't matter how you serve 'em up. I hate 'em.''

She didn't realize that what she was thinking must be showing on her face until he said, ''I mean it. There is no way you can serve me a Brussels sprout that I would eat.''

''I know this little place on Sunset in L.A.,'' she told him. ''They make a Brussels sprout quiche that is out of this world.''

He looked at her sideways. He was clearly disgusted. ''Quiche?'' he asked. ''*Quiche?* Next to Brussels sprouts, I hate quiche worst of all.''

''A macho and ridiculous prejudice,'' she informed him.

''Get that nose of yours out of the air.'' He reached from his chair to hers and brushed her nose with a forefinger. Then he peered more closely at her. ''You have freckles, you know.''

''I know. I've always had them.''

''They're cute. *You're* cute, to tell you the truth.''

He sounded like it pained him to admit this, which Olivia found funny. She laughed.

"What is so funny?" He looked noble and wounded.

"Nothing. Everything."

"Start with everything and go on from there."

"It seemed like it almost killed you to say you thought I was cute. I've noticed that about you, Jack."

"Oh, right. You're some big expert on me already.... You've noticed *what?*"

"That you're not exactly lavish with compliments."

He sat back in his chair and sipped the drink that a cocktail waitress had just served him. In the casinos there were cocktail waitresses everywhere. "I should be more lavish, is that what I'm hearing here?"

She smiled softly. "No. You shouldn't. You should be just like you are. A little too blunt. An honest man."

He looked away. She knew at that moment that he hadn't been completely honest with her. But she wasn't really bothered by whatever he was holding back. She'd had a magical evening, made all the more enchanting by its very unexpectedness. They'd talked of so many things. From football to favorite movies. But they'd held to their agreement to keep their real lives out of it. So Jack Roper had a right to a secret or two.

He was looking at her again. "It's late."

She knew he was right. "Yes. So late, it's practically early."

He set his still-full drink aside and stood. "Come on." He reached down. "I'll take you to your room."

She twined her fingers with his and let him pull her to her feet. His touch was warm, his grip strong. Her heart beat faster. She relished the little tingle she felt all through her body, when all she'd done was take his hand.

In the elevator she pushed the button for her floor. They rode up together in silence, fingers still entwined. She was careful not to think ahead to the precarious moment that was fast approaching, when they would stand at her door.

And then the moment was upon her. They faced each other.

"The evening was perfect," she said.

"Yeah, it was."

"Thank you, Jack."

"My pleasure."

"I…"

"Yeah?"

He waited, still lightly clasping her hand. She looked at his mouth. She'd been looking at his mouth all night. It was a tempting mouth. Chiseled on top, slightly fuller below.

Oh, what was the use of kidding herself? She wanted his kiss. She wanted to feel that tempting mouth against her own. Just once before they said good-night. Or goodbye.

He let go of her hand. She sighed at the loss of his touch.

But then his palm was gliding up her arm, the caress burning, teasing her through her red velvet sleeve.

"Olivia." He said it so tenderly.

She tipped her face up to his. "Jack, I know we agreed not to get personal." Her voice was more breath than sound. She made herself continue. "But there's something I have to know."

"Name it."

"Are you married, Jack?"

He shook his head very slowly.

"Engaged?"

"No."

"Living with anyone?"

"Well…"

Her heart seemed to sink right down into her red satin shoes. "Oh, Jack."

"There's this damn tomcat, see."

"What are you saying, Jack?"

"There's a tomcat. I've been calling him Buzz, because the hair on his head is so short it looks like a buzz cut, you know? He hangs around my apartment. He seems to *think* he lives with me."

Sweet relief coursed through her. It must have shown on her face because he said, "Don't look so happy. The damn cat won't get lost. I'm hoping by the time I get home he'll have given up and moved on."

She tried to look more solemn. "So your only roommate is a cat?"

"Or so the cat seems to think."

"I'm just so glad to hear that."

And she was, oh, she was! Now, there was absolutely nothing standing between her and Jack and the good-night kiss she'd been dreaming of sharing with him.

And of course Jack must want to kiss her, too. He had followed her around the casino for half the night, waiting for just the right moment to step forward and introduce himself. He'd shared a meal with her, and they'd talked for hours. He desired her. It was obvious. Why else would he be with her now?

But maybe he didn't want to push her. After all, they'd only just met.

Olivia smiled. He was probably only waiting for a little signal from her, that was all. Olivia swayed toward Jack, lifting her mouth and letting her eyelids flutter closed.

Chapter Three

Jack Roper gazed down at Olivia's soft, enticing lips. He wanted to taste them.

But there was no damn way he was going to.

Because he knew that the minute he put his mouth on hers and pulled her slim body close he would completely forget the real reason he'd spent the evening with her.

Suppressing a sigh, he stepped back.

She must have felt his withdrawal, because her cornflower blue eyes popped open. She blinked, and he watched a blush move up her slender neck and steal beneath the freckles that dusted her nose.

"Well." She twisted her hands together. "Um, thank you. For everything. And good night." She began fiddling with the small red velvet evening purse that hung from her shoulder on a silken rope.

Damn, he thought angrily. He liked her. Really liked her. She was a true innocent. She moved him, in a way he hadn't been moved in more years than he cared to count.

She moved him so much that he felt like a first-class jerk for the way he was deceiving her.

He had a moment's crazy urge to tell her everything, right now, as she frantically pawed through her little purse seeking the computerized card that would let her into her room.

But then she looked up at him, those forget-me-not eyes wide and vulnerable. She held the key card in the air. "Found it." She was striving for jauntiness but missed it by a mile.

And he heard himself saying, "If I knocked on your door at noon, would you be ready for breakfast at the greasy spoon of my choice?"

It broke the heart he didn't even know he had anymore to see the way her face changed. She looked like someone had turned on a klieg light beneath her pale skin. She glowed, brighter than a searchlight on opening night.

He wanted to grab her and shake her and tell her it was a rotten world out there. She had to protect herself, learn to cover her feelings, not let strangers see every little thing that went on inside of her.

But he didn't. He ordered his hands to stay loose at his sides and made his mouth smile an easy smile.

"I'll be ready," she said.

"Great. See you then."

Once inside her suite Olivia tossed her evening bag on the little table by the door and waltzed through the foyer into the sitting room. She danced around the love seat, whirled past the easy chair and spun into the bedroom, where she at last collapsed, giggling joyously across the king-size bed.

She noticed then that the light on her phone was blinking. She sighed. It would be her father, of course. Wanting her to call him back, no matter what time it was.

She wasn't going to do it. She simply wasn't.

But of course, even as she determined to stand her ground on this, she was picturing the way he was probably pacing the floor of his study right now, unable to sleep because of his concern for her.

It was only because she knew how he worried about her that she'd called him when she'd first arrived here in Vegas. She'd felt driven to reassure him that she was all right. But she'd also told him firmly that he was not to call her back.

With a little groan Olivia sat up and rubbed her eyes. Then she buzzed the desk to make sure the message really had been from her father.

"I show six messages here," the switchboard operator said. "All from Lawrence Larrabee—hey, is that *the* Lawrence Larrabee, as in Larrabee Lager?"

"Yes," Olivia said, sighing. "I'm afraid it is."

"Well, what do you know? Anyway, he called six times and each time left the same message. Call him back as soon as you get in."

Olivia suddenly realized she was getting a headache. "Thank you." She hung up and pondered the idea of wandering into the bathroom to see if there was a complimentary packet of pain reliever in there.

But then she decided she only needed to relax. So she kicked off her shoes and sat Indian-style on the bed. She closed her eyes and rolled her neck and chanted one of the affirmations she'd picked up in a stress-management class.

"I am in charge of my life and affairs. I am in charge of my life and affairs. I am in charge of—"

Right then the phone started ringing.

Olivia went on chanting.

The phone went on ringing.

Olivia was determined not to answer.

But somehow, around the seventh ring, her hand reached out on its own accord and snatched the darn thing from its cradle.

"What?"

"Livvy?"

"No, sorry. There's no one by that name here."

Her father let out a tired breath. "It's damn late, Livvy."

She thought of Jack, and her mood lightened marginally. "I know. So late it's practically early."

"I left several messages requesting that you call."

"Well, I told you I wouldn't."

"Are you all right?"

"Stop worrying, Dad. Let it be. I need a little time away, that's all. Can't you please understand that?"

He was quiet for a moment. She heard a murmur on the other end and knew that Mindy Long—a special lady her father had been seeing for the past year—was there with him. She also knew the things Mindy would be saying. More than once Olivia had confided in Mindy. Mindy understood Olivia's position and would be on her side.

Olivia urged, "Please, Dad. Listen to Mindy."

"I *have* been listening to Mindy. I've been listening to Mindy all night. You two women will drive me to an early grave."

"Please." She put everything she had into the word, to try to get through to him. "I love you and I know you'd do anything for me. But this is something you just *can't* do for me. I have to do it on my own."

Her father made a disgusted sound. "But what is it you're doing?"

"I'm...finding myself."

Her father swore roundly. "Fine. Find yourself in Malibu, where you belong."

"No."

"This is insane, Olivia. There is nothing in Las Vegas that will help you to *find* yourself. There are endless miles of sagebrush and cactus. And there is gambling. And that is it."

"Dad—"

"It's absurd. I want you to come home. I'm sorry about Cameron." Her father felt guilty about what had happened, because Cameron worked for him. "I never should have introduced you two, I understand that now. It was all my fault and I'll—"

"It was not your fault. Please, Dad, don't—"

"Yes, yes it was. I thought he was a nice young man."

"He *is* a nice young man, Dad. Just not a faithful one."

"He's toast in the brewing industry, I can tell you that."

"You already told me that. And I told you that he's the best salesman you've got. And I don't want you to fire him because of me. Please."

"Livvy, you are too forgiving. You have got to toughen up a little or—"

Olivia just didn't want to hear anymore, so she prepared to say what she'd been hoping she wouldn't have to say. "Dad, I want you to stop calling me."

"Livvy, I—"

"Listen. I mean this. If you don't let me work this out on my own, I'll go somewhere else."

That gave him pause. "What?"

"I said, I'll go somewhere else. And this time I won't call you to tell you I'm all right."

"Now, Livvy. Don't do anything you'll regret."

"This is the situation, Dad. You leave me alone. Stop calling me. Let me work this out for myself, or I will get in my car and drive. I'll disappear. And when I finally stop, it'll be somewhere you've never heard of. Understand?"

"Please don't do that, Livvy."

"Then stop calling me."

The ensuing silence from her father's end was hard for Olivia to bear. But she did bear it, because she had to, even though she knew that he truly did want the very best for her.

"All right," Lawrence Larrabee said at last.

He sounded so weary. Olivia ached for him. But she couldn't give him what he wanted. Not anymore. At some point she had to live her life as she chose to. She had to make her own mistakes and suffer her own consequences. She was almost thirty and she was going to have to grow up.

He asked, "Have you got enough money?"

She wanted to cry. "Of course."

"If you need anything…"

"I know. I love you, Dad."

"I never doubted that. And I love you."

"Bye."

And then he was gone.

Olivia very gently put the phone back in its cradle. And then she stared toward the far wall for a time, questioning everything—all of it, from coming here in the first place to the conversation she'd just had with her father.

She'd said she was "finding herself," and sincerely meant it at the moment. But the more she thought about it, the more she had to agree with her father. Las Vegas was an odd place to go to find oneself.

And then there was Jack, about whom she really knew nothing. Which wasn't his fault, of course. She'd been the one to suggest they remain "strangers in Las Vegas" for an evening. Tomorrow, she was sure, they would get to know each other better.

The wisdom of there even *being* a "Jack" in her life at this point made her wonder. She'd just been betrayed in the worst kind of way by one man. Perhaps that should have told her something about her judgment where men were concerned. She really hadn't had much experience in that area, to be honest. And maybe it would be advisable to stay away from men for a while.

Maybe tomorrow she should tell Jack that she'd enjoyed

their evening together more than he could ever know, but she wasn't going to have breakfast with him after all. She could explain gently and regretfully that, while he was the most incredible man she'd ever laid eyes on, the timing was all wrong. She simply had too much work to do on herself before she would be ready to share anything meaningful with a man.

"Yuck," Olivia said to the far wall.

The thought of sending Jack away was just too depressing to consider. And hadn't she come here in the first place to avoid depression? A lot of good she'd do herself if she sent Jack away in order to "find herself" and then became depressed once he was gone. Because, truthfully, the idea of not seeing Jack tomorrow left her feeling more than a little dismal.

And beyond that, there remained the fact that she really didn't know the man at all. Maybe he wouldn't even show up tomorrow. Maybe she was wasting her time sitting here worrying about whether or not she should send him away, because she was never going to see him again, anyway. Maybe he would—

"Oh, stop it," she muttered at the wall. "Stop it right now. No more thinking tonight, and that's that."

With a soft little sigh, she slid off the bed. Once she managed to undo the tiny buttons at the back of her red velvet dress, she slithered it down over her hips and stepped out of it. Then she went straight to the bathroom for a long, soothing soak in the tub.

Behind her, the expensive dress lay on the floor in a crimson puddle, right where it had fallen, next to her red satin shoes. A trail of silky underthings marked the way she had gone.

Olivia woke to the sound of knocking.

After a few grunts and groans she rolled her head and

squinted at the digital clock-radio by the bed.

Noon.

Jack was supposed to come for her at noon.

"Omigod!" She leapt from the bed. "Coming!" She looked down at herself. She was wearing black silk shorty pajamas.

"Unacceptable," she decided aloud. She was crazy about Jack, but that didn't mean she could greet him at the door wearing nothing but black silk lingerie. She scanned the room frantically, looking for something to put on over the pajamas, calling out at the same time, "Just a minute! Be right there!"

The short robe that matched the pajamas was nowhere in sight. And anyway, it was too suggestive by far.

She raced to her stack of luggage in the dressing area and plowed through the largest suitcase, which was a total mess even though she'd only been in Las Vegas since early yesterday morning. Already she was missing Constance, her live-in housekeeper at home, who kept everything in order and seemed somehow always to be able to find whatever Olivia was looking for.

"Aha!" she crowed, as she found a huge knit shirt that was supposed to be worn with stirrup pants. The stirrup pants were nowhere in sight. But the shirt was modest enough by itself. Olivia tugged it over her head and smoothed it down.

Then she rushed to the door and swung it wide.

And there was Jack, wearing chinos and a shirt with a designer logo on it. He looked as if he'd been awake for hours.

"Hi."

"Hi."

After that, she wasn't sure what to say next.

The lines around his eyes deepened with his smile. "Forgot to set the alarm, huh?"

She just stared, thinking how absurdly glad she was to see him. He looked her up and down and went on smiling.

She realized that they couldn't stand here all day, gawking at each other and grinning. "I need a few minutes." She almost invited him to wait in her sitting room, but held back. It seemed a little too intimate for right now.

"I'll be in the lobby."

"Okay. I'll be there in twenty minutes. I promise."

Jack took her to a place called Randy Jim's.

Randy Jim's was an actual railroad car parked between a Joshua tree and a saguaro cactus out on Highway 147. The sign in the window said Breakfast Served All Day. They ate biscuits and gravy and drank coffee they poured themselves from the insulated pot the waitress provided.

They were both quiet, but more because neither of them felt like talking, Olivia thought, than anything else. They looked out the window at the highway and then back at each other.

Once or twice Olivia almost broke the companionable silence to tell him that she'd lied about her name. But she was having such a lovely time that she decided she could put it off for a little while longer. She definitely would tell him by the end of the day. But for right now, even though she probably shouldn't, she was going to postpone the unpleasant task for a while and just enjoy being with him.

When they were through eating, they lingered a while, sharing a newspaper that some other customer had left behind.

At one point Olivia glanced over the top of the entertainment section she was reading. She saw the crown of Jack's head, his brown elbows and forearms and his fingers. The rest of him was hidden by the sports section.

And she had the warmest, sweetest welling of emotion within her. She didn't examine it, for fear of losing it. She only smiled to herself and went back to her own reading.

"Ready to go?" he inquired just a little while later.

On their way back to the hotel/casino, Jack asked if she'd tried the pool up on the roof yet. She admitted she hadn't.

"How about now?" he asked.

She agreed that a swim was just what she needed.

The roof pool was open to the sun, with a view of the gray outlines of the mountains that loomed in the distance. And even though it was October, the heat in the middle of the day made the air dance and shimmer.

Olivia was careful of her pale skin, slathering herself in sunscreen and then putting her chaise longue in the shade of a potted palm. Jack put his chaise beside hers, though his bronze skin looked like it could withstand a lot more sun than hers.

After a few minutes in the water they lay down side by side, and for a while neither spoke. Olivia closed her eyes and listened to the splashing and giggling from the kids who were playing in the pool. Once or twice the kids got carried away. The water would splash so high Olivia would feel the cool drops on her legs. It felt good.

She felt good.

"What are you smiling about?" Jack's voice was low and very close.

She turned her head and opened her eyes. He lay on his stomach and had rested his head on his hands at the edge of his chaise, so that his face was less than two feet from her own.

She studied him, her breath catching a little. His lashes were very thick and pale gold, like his brows.

Earlier, she'd had a chance to admire him without being too obvious about it. His body was lean, his shoulders broad, his musculature well developed, though spare. He had more than a few scars—on his arms and shoulders and on his chest. There was one on his leg that ran around the back of his calf, like a white snake against the bronze flesh. A warrior's scars, she thought, and wondered if he'd been in the military.

"Earth to Olivia," he teased softly.

"What?"

"I asked what you were smiling about."

Instead of answering, she asked a question of her own. "You were watching me, weren't you? While I had my eyes closed."

"Is that a crime? If so, I plead guilty."

"No, it's no crime."

"Good. Now, what were you smiling about?"

"I was thinking that I feel good."

The corners of his mouth curled in a lazy grin. "I suppose there are worse reasons to smile."

A word she'd been trying to think of finally occurred to her. "Obsidian," she whispered.

He lifted an eyebrow. "What?"

"Your eyes," she mused. "Like obsidian. That deep black green. Especially for a man with light hair, it's very unusual." She purposely used the word he'd employed to describe her the night before, wondering if he'd remember, if he'd come back with some clever rejoinder.

But instead of a clever reply, he only looked away. "Yeah. So I've been told."

His reaction puzzled her. "What? Did I say something?"

"Nothing. It's nothing."

"Yes, it is. I can tell."

"It's nothing, really. Someone used to say that about my eyes, that's all. But it doesn't matter. It was a long time ago."

"You mean, someone used to say that your eyes are unusual?"

"Yeah."

"Who?"

"It was a long time ago."

"Who?"

"No one. My father."

She turned over onto her stomach. Then she scooted closer, so there were only inches between their noses. She could smell him. Moisture and chlorine. Some kind of lotion or after-shave. And something else, slightly musky and very seductive to her: his body's special scent.

She put aside her pleasurable contemplation of how much he attracted her. She had another thing on her mind right then. She was thinking of how she wanted to learn all about him, but how she had no right to expect him to tell her any of his secrets when he still believed that she was someone named Loveless.

Do it. Tell him who you really are right now, an inner voice urged.

But she couldn't quite say the words.

Instead she decided to lay a little groundwork for the beginnings of trust between them.

"Jack?"

"Um?"

"I think we just broke last night's agreement."

He looked puzzled for a minute, and then he understood. "You mean because I mentioned my father?"

"Yes. You came very close to revealing something about yourself, about who you really are." She laid a hand on his arm. His skin was warm, the muscles beneath hard under her palm. "I'm glad."

"Right." The word was gruff.

"You'll tell me more."

"It looks likely."

"But not right now, is that it?"

He chuckled. And then, with a stunning economy of movement, he was on his feet and reaching for her hand. "Come on."

"What?" But even as she asked the question, she was pushing herself up and swinging her legs to the concrete.

"Time for a swim," he announced, spinning her around and scooping her up against his chest.

She understood what he planned too late. By the time she shouted, "No, Jack!" he had already strode to the edge of the pool and was tossing her in.

They tried some of the other casinos that night.

They crossed an actual moat, complete with drawbridge, to enter the Excalibur. Then they stood on the street gawking with all the other tourists in front of the Mirage, where an imitation volcano spewed real fire into the night sky every fifteen minutes. Inside, they watched Siegfried & Roy perform fantastic illusions.

When the hour grew late, they found their special place again, back at their own hotel, in the wing chairs by the potted palm.

There, as she'd been building her courage all day to do, Olivia ventured, "Jack, I, um…"

He leaned near her chair. "What?"

She swallowed. Sweet heaven, this was difficult.

She didn't even know she was twisting her hands together until he captured them and held them still in his. "Just say it." With his thumbs he idly stroked the hands he held captive. "Come on, I'm listening."

She dragged in a big breath and came out with it. "I'm not who you think I am."

He frowned. "What?"

"I said, I'm not who you think I am."

Suddenly his expression was very strange, very distant. He'd stopped his subtle stroking of her hands.

She forced herself to go on. "I lied, Jack. My name isn't Loveless. My name is Larrabee."

He tipped his head to the side. "You lied?"

She bobbed her head up and down. "Yes, I did. When I told you my name last night, I just wanted to be someone else at that moment."

"Someone else?" He was still looking strange and distant.

She hastened to make him see. "Yes. Someone other than me. Oh, I'm sure it doesn't make any sense to you—"

"I didn't say that."

"You didn't have to."

"Olivia, I—"

"No. Let me finish. Let me explain." Her words came fast, then. They tumbled over each other getting out of her mouth. "You see, I'm rich, Jack. Very rich. My father is Lawrence Larrabee, of Larrabee Brewing Company. And Jack, I hate being rich. I'm just no good at it. And all my life being Lawrence Larrabee's daughter has overshadowed everything. It cuts me off from people, it makes me different. And most of the time I never know if a person likes me for myself or for my money or what. It's very confusing to me. But with you it was different. You didn't have any idea who I was, and still you were…interested in me."

Jack had let go of her hand. She looked at him, begging him with her eyes to understand.

But he didn't seem to understand at all. Instead he was withdrawing from her, just as she had feared he might when he learned that she had pretended to be someone she wasn't.

She blundered on, willing him to forgive her deception, to understand how she'd felt. "It meant so much to me, Jack. That you didn't have a clue who I was and yet still you were following me. I couldn't stand to watch your eyes change, Jack. Because that's what always happens with people. They learn who I am and their eyes change. I'm not *me* anymore. I hate that. I...'' Her voice trailed off as Jack actually stood and turned away from her. It was obvious he couldn't bear to hear another word.

She pleaded, ''Jack? Oh, Jack. Please. I'm sorry. Forgive me.''

He turned then. ''Stop,'' he said quietly. He looked completely composed. ''There's nothing to forgive.''

She stared up at him, bewildered. What in the world could be going through his mind?

''But I *lied* to you.''

He put up a hand. ''Hey.'' His voice was so tender. Slowly he sank to his chair again.

And then he did the most wonderful thing. He reached out, hesitantly, as if he were doing something she might not allow, and he touched the side of her face. One feather-light caress, from her temple to her chin. To Olivia it was the most consuming touch she'd ever known. It burned her right down to her soul.

He whispered, ''It's okay. It's not a big deal.''

''It's not?''

''No.''

She blinked at him, bewildered. He was behaving very strangely, first seeming unable to bear what she was telling him and then suddenly turning around and saying there was nothing to forgive.

But then it came to her. Of course, he must have been hurt at first that she hadn't trusted him. And now he wanted to let it go, since he realized that there had been no malice in what she had done.

Like her, Jack only wanted the two of them to go on from here. The important thing was that he wouldn't hold it against her for pretending to be someone else.

He was smiling at her. ''It's late.''

She bit her lip, since it was trembling a little. "So late it's practically early."

He made a low sound in his throat, and she knew he remembered how they'd shared the same exchange the night before. Then, once more, he was on his feet, holding out his hand.

"Come on. I'll take you to your room."

She pushed away the vague uneasiness that kept trying to sweep over her and went with him.

Like the night before, they rode the elevator hand in hand.

However, unlike the night before, this time she was certain that he would kiss her when they reached her door.

But he didn't.

And for a moment she even thought he was going to leave without a word about seeing her again.

She couldn't let that happen.

She collected all her courage and suggested, "It's my turn to treat for breakfast. There's a café downstairs by the other pool, the indoor one? Meet me there. At noon."

He said nothing. His look was rueful.

She refused to believe that he was trying to think of a way to bow out. "Okay, okay. I know, it's hardly Randy Jim's. But what do you expect? I'm new in town."

"Olivia…"

"I promise to set my alarm. I won't stand you up." She held up her hand. "Scout's honor."

Oh, Lord. What if he said no? She didn't even have his room number.

"All right." His voice was grim. "I'll be there."

Before she could drum up the nerve to ask him what in the world was going on with him, he turned and was gone.

She stared after him for a moment, her heart so heavy it seemed to weight her feet to the floor. What had happened? She wasn't really sure.

She was only sure about one thing.

She'd seen the look in his eyes just before he turned away from her. And she knew what that look meant.

He never intended to see her again.

Chapter Four

In Jack's room the message light was blinking.

He knew who it would be. But he buzzed the switchboard anyway, just in case it might be someone else.

It wasn't.

"Lawrence Larrabee called," the switchboard operator said. "He wants you to call him back as soon as you get in."

Jack punched up the home number Larrabee had given him. It was answered on the third ring.

"Hello?"

It was the aged housekeeper, Zelda, whom Jack had met on the interview two days before, when Larrabee had hired him. Zelda was a tank of a woman, a true family retainer. Zelda did not approve of private investigators; that had been clear to Jack from the moment she'd opened the door of Larrabee's huge Bel Air mansion to him. She'd looked at him as if he were something she'd found stuck to the bottom of her shoe.

"Let me speak to Lawrence Larrabee," Jack said.

"Who is calling?"

"Jack Roper."

There was a disapproving pause, then "One moment, please."

Larrabee was on the line in seconds flat. "Roper. What the hell's going on? It's the middle of the night."

"Fine. I'll call in the morning." Jack started to hang up.

"Roper!" Lawrence Larrabee's shout came through even though the phone was nowhere near Jack's ear.

With a sigh Jack put the phone to his ear again. "Mr. Larrabee, *you* called *me*."

"You're damn right I did. I want to know what's going on."

"I'm doing my job. Keeping an eye on your daughter."

"And?"

"And what? She's fine. Having a ball."

"What do you mean *a ball?*"

"I mean, she seems to be having a great time."

"Doing what?"

"Seeing the sights. Taking in some shows. Gambling a little."

"Gambling?"

"Mr. Larrabee, she hasn't been throwing her money around, I promise you."

"I don't care about the money. It's my *daughter* I'm worried about. She's a very sensitive girl. And if she's developing a gambling problem I—"

"She's not. Forget that."

"All right. But does she seem okay? Emotionally, I mean? And mentally?"

"Look. I'm no mind reader, but she seems fine to me."

"She's recently been put through hell. I don't think I have to tell you—"

"You're right. You don't."

Larrabee had explained all about the two-timing fiancé at the interview. Jack was in no mood to hear it all again. Tonight he'd had to listen to Olivia beg him to forgive her for deceiving him about her last name. He felt like a worm. Jack didn't think he could take it if Larrabee started in again about what some other guy had done to her.

Larrabee was still running his inquisition. "She hasn't hooked up with any suspicious characters, has she?"

Nobody but me, Jack thought but didn't say. He'd yet to explain to Larrabee that *he* was the one Olivia was having a ball with, though he'd had three conversations with the man since he and Olivia had begun spending every waking moment together.

"Well, has she?" Larrabee prodded, since Jack had yet to answer him.

"Hooked up with any suspicious characters?" Jack repeated, begging the question with an obvious stall.

"That's what I asked. Come on, Roper. What do you think I'm paying you for? Give it to me straight."

Jack thought about Olivia. About how all he really wanted was to go on meeting her at noon, wandering this gaudy gambling mecca through the day and into the night together. And not parting until "it was so late, it was practically early."

Or, better yet, not parting at all.

But he knew that what he wanted was impossible.

Unlike Olivia, Jack was a realist. He knew very well that they were on a collision course with emotional disaster.

There was just nowhere this relationship could go. She was a poor little rich girl, who wore her heart on her red velvet sleeve. And he was nobody from nowhere, who'd been duping her from the moment she'd cried out "Wait! Don't go" on the street outside the casino.

And the only way to end it was to cut it clean.

"Roper?" Larrabee's voice was getting agitated.

It was the moment. Time to end this charade.

He made himself do it. "Yeah, she's been seeing a suspicious character, all right. Me."

Larrabee made a sort of wheezing, choking sound. *"What?"*

"I said she's been with me. Since last night—or is it night before last by now?"

The pause before Lawrence Larrabee spoke was a gruesome one.

But at last the older man asked in a voice of equal parts velvet and steel, "What exactly are you telling me, Roper?"

Grimly, Jack explained. "She caught me watching her."

"She *what?"*

"I think you heard me, Mr. Larrabee."

"How could she have caught you? You never get caught. You came highly recommended. You won medals as a cop. You've been in a forced recon team in the jungles of Southeast Asia. You've tracked down men no one else could find and stayed with them for days without them realizing you were watching them. You're the best in the business. I have it in writing from several different sources."

Jack rubbed the bridge of his nose. "I'm just giving you the facts here. She caught me. Twice."

Larrabee repeated the word with frank disbelief. *"Twice?"*

"Yeah, twice."

The truth was that the beer baron's daughter had been the cutest thing Jack had ever seen, sitting there at the blackjack table in that strange red dress, peeking at her cards and biting the edge of her tongue. Jack had forgotten the basic rule of the job: stay invisible.

She'd looked up and caught him gawking like some rank amateur. He'd known then that if she spotted him again, she'd have to put two and two together and realize he was following her. He would be dead meat.

But he'd been sure she would never catch him a second time. No one else ever had.

Wrong again.

Outside, she'd headed off down the street like she knew right where she was going, picking up the hem of that odd dress to keep it from trailing on the sidewalk. Her baby-fine hair, which was an intriguing color, halfway between gold and bronze, had hung in slightly bedraggled ringlets down her back.

He'd thought, *Unreal. Scarlett O'Hara in Las Vegas.*

He'd been amused by her...and he hadn't been on his toes.

She'd chosen that moment to whirl around. She was looking right at him again before he even realized he was had. He explained to Larrabee, "The second time she spotted me, I figured it was over. So I was going to walk away and call you right then, tell you I'd been seen and you'd better find someone else."

"Okay." Larrabee seemed to be speaking through clenched teeth. "And why didn't you do that?"

"Because she'd jumped to a conclusion."

"What conclusion?"

"She assumed I was following her around because I was interested."

"What do you mean, *interested?*"

"I mean *interested.* Attracted. She thought I found her—"

"Never mind. I get the idea. Go on."

"Fine. She thought I was attracted to her, and she was flattered. When I started to walk away, she asked me not to go. We struck up a conversation. I played along. We had dinner together Tuesday. And then from noon Wednesday, we've been mostly together. I just left her at her room twenty minutes ago."

Lawrence Larrabee allowed another gruesome pause to elapse. Then he softly said, "I don't like this, Roper."

Jack said nothing. What was there to say?

"Have you taken advantage of her?"

Jack groaned. "Oh, come on, Larrabee. I feel enough like a jerk already."

"You've kept hands off?"

"Yeah. I haven't even kissed her. Now, look. I've told you what's happening. And now I'm out of it. I'll send you a bill for the first day, and you can consider Wednesday on me. It was a damn great day as far as I was concerned, anyway. Fair enough?"

"No."

Now Jack was the one speaking softly. "Excuse me?"

"I said, no. It isn't *fair enough,* not by a long shot. I've explained to you that Olivia is in a very shaky emotional state right now. And if what you've described to me, this little *friendship* you two seem to have developed, is really happening—"

"Oh, come off it, Larrabee. Do you actually believe this is something I'd make up?"

Larrabee was silent again. Then he admitted, "No, I do not think you've made it up. Olivia has just had her confidence in her appeal as a woman shattered. Right now, any reasonably attractive man could—"

"Look. Let's not go on and on about this. I'm just a hired hand here, and I want out."

"Well, Mr. Roper, I'm not letting you out."

Jack said something very crude under his breath. Then he carefully inquired, "Was there some specific way you planned to stop me from getting out?"

"As a matter of fact, yes. I'll pay you—"

"Please. There are some things even a P.I. won't do for money."

"What are you saying?"

"Let me draw you a picture. Keep your money."

"Fine. Then think of Olivia."

"Damn it, I *am* thinking of Olivia."

"Roper, you are not. If you were thinking of Olivia, you would know that if you really are her friend now, then the *last* thing you should do is vanish from her life without explanation."

"*Friend* is your word, not mine."

"You're going to have to break this off more gradually, Roper. You know it. And I know it."

"If you're so worried about her, maybe you'd better come here yourself."

"I can't."

"Right. You're so damned *concerned* about her, but you can't spare the time for her."

"That's not it. She doesn't want me there. She's threatened to disappear if I don't leave her alone. Unfortunately I believe her."

Now Jack was the one muttering. "I don't like this."

"Neither do I. But it's happened. And we have to deal with it. You stay with my daughter, Roper. Understand? Keep your hands off and start figuring out a way to tell her goodbye gently. Are we clear?"

Jack swore some more.

"I'll be in touch. Call me here or at Larrabee Enterprises if anything new comes up."

Though Olivia was right on time for breakfast at the pool-side café, Jack was there ahead of her.

She saw him before he spotted her, because he already had his nose buried in the morning edition of the *Las Vegas Sun*.

She stood for a moment by the little sign that said Please Wait To Be Seated and let the gladness and gratitude wash over her.

He was here! He hadn't gone away!

All night, or what had remained of it after they'd parted, she'd tossed and turned. She'd been distressingly certain that the strange way he'd behaved before he'd left her at her door had meant the worst: she would never see him again.

Though she'd only spent two evenings and a day with him, and he'd told her nothing about who he really was, Olivia felt that she knew Jack Roper right down to his soul.

He'd never even kissed her, yet in some deep, inchoate way, she knew him intimately.

And she had been certain when he'd left her last night that he had not planned to keep their date this morning. She was also reasonably sure about what had caused his retreat from her.

It was her money. As usual.

Jack was a proud man and, she suspected now, a poor one. He had probably just lost his job or something and had come here to Las Vegas as a place to forget his troubles for a few days before he decided what to do next.

And last night, when he'd learned how wealthy she was, he'd decided it would never work out between them. He'd decided to stop seeing her.

But, thank heaven, sometime in the night he must have changed his mind. And here he was, after all.

"How many?" the hostess asked.

"I'm joining someone." Olivia gestured toward Jack. "That man over there, as a matter of fact."

Just then Jack looked up from his paper. He smiled at her.

"This way, then," the hostess said.

Jack lowered his paper as she approached. His mouth was wary, but his black eyes shone. She knew he was as glad to see her as she was to see him.

Olivia's feet hardly touched the floor. Her happiness allowed her to defy gravity.

He'd met her this morning, after all. And soon enough he would share his secrets. It was only a matter of time.

That day they visited Hoover Dam, where they looked out over the massive spillway onto Lake Mead, rode in an elevator down to the power plant for a guided tour and then watched a movie about the dam's construction. To Olivia it was all great fun to ooh and ah over what the promotional film had declared to be one of the engineering wonders of the United States.

And truthfully, as long as Jack was beside her, it didn't really matter what they did. As far as she was concerned, they could have spent the whole day in the wing chairs by the potted palm.

Jack was attentive and funny and said he was having a good time. And when he looked at her, Olivia knew that at last she'd found someone who wanted her for herself alone.

But she also knew he was troubled. She could see it in the depths of his eyes. And after they had dinner at a place called The Golden Steer, she dared to ask him what was on his mind.

He took her arm. "Let's go for a ride," he said.

She went willingly, praying that the time had come when he would reveal to her the secrets of his heart.

They drove out to the desert, out across the wide, empty flatness in the direction of the gray hump of Mount Charleston, to the northwest.

Out in the middle of nowhere, with only sagebrush and tumbleweed for company, Jack pulled off the road and drove over the cracked and bumpy desert floor until they reached a sign that said: Las Vegas, Where The Fun Never Stops.

He parked beneath the sign and turned off the engine. Behind them was the glow of the city and ahead, the shadow of the mountains. Above, the waning moon gleamed down, and the stars were so thick they all seemed to blend together in the wide, wide sky.

He turned to her, putting his arm across the back of her seat. Even through the darkness, she could see the unhappiness in his eyes.

She gave him an encouraging smile. "What is it, Jack? I've known all day that something is bothering you. Tell me what it is. Maybe I can help."

He shook his head, murmuring her name in a musing way.

And then he cupped her chin.

Olivia went on smiling, though she knew that the smile was a little wobbly. His touch affected her deeply. Her skin burned beneath the light caress of his fingers. Her heartbeat seemed faster and stronger, too.

He longed to kiss her. She could see it in his eyes, in the gentle yet hungry curve of his mouth, which was mere inches from her own. Idly he caressed her jawline, his thumb and fingers softly stroking.

She drew in a breath. It sighed into her lungs. Now her whole body was tingling, though he only touched her chin. She waited for his lips to meet hers.

When it didn't happen, she dared to softly implore, "Kiss me, Jack."

His eyes were so sad. He dropped his hand and sat back in his seat.

Disappointed and slightly mortified, Olivia retreated to her seat as well. For a while they stared out at the wide starry sky. In the distance a coyote howled.

At last Olivia knew something had to be said. "Why didn't you kiss me, Jack? You wanted to, I know you did. I don't understand."

"It would be wrong."

She looked at him. "That doesn't make sense. You said you're not committed to anyone else...and neither am I. We're both adults. What could be wrong about us sharing a kiss?"

"A lot."

"But what?"

"Olivia—"

"Is it a money problem, Jack? Are you out of a job or something? If it is, it doesn't matter to me. I swear to you, it doesn't matter at all."

"It's not money."

She wasn't sure she believed him. Still, what else could she do but ask, "Okay, then, what is it?"

"Hell" was all he said. He reached for the keys to start the car.

"Wait." She put her hand on his arm and felt him stiffen in reaction. "Let's not go yet. Please, Jack."

"Olivia, there's no point in staying here."

"Oh, but there is. There really is. We could talk a little, Jack. About ourselves. It doesn't have to be anything too fresh or too painful." She thought of Cameron and realized there was at least one thing in her life that she wouldn't be talking about right now. Around Jack she felt like a beautiful, desirable woman. She wasn't quite ready to have him learn that her ex-fiancé hadn't found her desirable at all.

She rushed on. "It could be anything. Our life stories— at least up to a point. Or maybe what growing up was like for us. I was an only child, myself."

Olivia released Jack's arm and shifted in her seat. She wanted to give him something, to reveal something of who she really was, so that maybe he would feel that he could trust her in return.

She thought of her mother and she felt the old, hollow ache inside.

Olivia had no memory of the woman who had given her life. She knew from pictures that Karyn Larrabee had been pretty, with a heart-shaped face and big blue eyes. And she knew from her father that Karyn had been kind; a gentle woman who laughed easily, who loved cats and roses and movies with Jimmy Stewart in them.

Olivia said, "My mother died when I was just a baby."

Jack looked away. "Olivia, you don't have to—"

"Yes," she said. "I want to. Please listen."

He turned to face her. Then he conceded. "All right."

She twisted her hands together, realized she was doing it and forced them to be still. "My mother was kidnapped," she said softly, "and held for ransom. My father paid. But they killed her anyway.

"It was all over the papers, maybe you heard about it. The kidnappers themselves died in a bloody shootout with the authorities. I was just a baby, way too young to remember any of it." Jack was watching her. She could feel his eyes, though she was staring out the windshield. She made herself look at him. "But sometimes I feel like I remember it, when I look in my Dad's eyes."

"Olivia—"

She put up a hand. "I miss her, you know? Still, to this day. I miss someone I never even knew." She swallowed and took in a breath. "Anyway. About my childhood—remember I suggested that we could talk about our childhoods?"

Jack nodded.

"Well, I was raised by my dad. He was a good dad. He always had time for me. I was fortunate in always having love. My earliest memories are of just the two of us, me and Dad. A family. I had nurses and companions, of course, as I was growing up. But my father was always there to pour my breakfast cereal, to teach me to ride a bike. And to chase away the boogeymen under my bed.

"But he's too protective. I suppose it's because of what happened to my mother. He was always afraid to let me out of his sight. His name is a household word. He even let the ad agency talk him into putting his picture on the bottles when they launched Lawrence Larrabee's Private Reserve five years ago. But he's always been careful to keep me out of the spotlight. I've led a very private, sheltered kind of life. So now I'm twenty-nine years old and still working on making a life of my own, even though I should have done it years ago." She sighed. "Does that make sense?"

"Yeah. It makes sense." Jack's voice was soft. He reached out and touched her hair. It was a touch of understanding, of reassurance. And yet it stirred her body, made her skin feel hot and prickly and her blood pump harder in her veins.

It was odd, Olivia thought, how strongly she was attracted to Jack physically. Until Jack, she'd thought herself pretty much a cold fish when it came to those intimate things that went on between men and women. In fact, *cold fish* were exactly the words Cameron had used at the end, when she'd caught him with Bree Haversham, his executive assistant.

"Oh, get real, Olivia," Cameron had said. *"What do you care if I have a little fun with someone else? You're a cold fish in bed, anyway, and we both know it damn well."*

"Earth to Olivia."

She felt herself blushing.

"Are you all right?"

"Yes. Yes, I'm fine."

Jack gave her a smile that was somehow both encouraging and teasing at the same time. "So. I guess it's my turn, huh? You expect to hear my life story."

Anticipation lightened her heart. Now they were getting somewhere. She squirmed in her seat a little. "Oh, yes. I do, Jack. I want to know everything about you that you're willing to tell me."

He tipped his head, as if he was wondering whether she meant what she was saying. "It's a downer of a story, really."

"Let me judge that for myself, please. You just tell it."

He still looked doubtful, but he agreed. "Okay. You asked for it." He paused, collecting his thoughts, she imagined. Then he said, "I was born in Bakersfield, an only child like you were. Until I was nine, I lived near there on a farm."

"Your parents owned a farm?"

"It was my father's farm."

"What was your father's name?"

"John Roper."

"What was he like?"

Jack rubbed his eyes.

"You're quiet. What does that mean? You had a problem with your father?"

"I guess you could say that. If he even *was* my father."

She was trying to follow this. "He *wasn't* your father?"

"I don't know. John Roper didn't believe he was my father, even though my mother, Alana, always insisted that he was."

"Your father *told* you that he didn't believe you were his son?"

"No. It was a big secret. But every once in a while, when he and my mother would have a fight, he'd let it slip in some sideways remark. And by the time I was seven or eight, I'd figured it out."

Olivia thought of what Jack had said the day before, about his father calling Jack's eyes unusual. "But you don't know for sure, do you, if he was right or not?"

"It doesn't matter." Jack's shrug was unconcerned.

Too unconcerned, Olivia thought. "Jack, come on. It must matter to you."

"Look." Jack's voice was cold. "I agreed to tell you

about my childhood. But let's not make a big deal of it, okay? It was a long time ago. And they're both dead now. My father didn't think that he was my father. My mother swore that he was. I don't know which one of them was right. Can we leave it at that.'' It wasn't a question.

Olivia said softly, ''Of course, Jack. Please go on.''

''I've forgotten where I was.'' His tone was curt.

She prompted him. ''You said that you lived on the farm until you were nine. What happened then?''

He looked at her for a moment, as if he was considering telling her he didn't want to talk anymore. She was grateful when he went on. ''My father died that year, of a massive coronary.''

''Your mother sold the farm?''

''Yeah. But the money didn't last long. Eventually Alana went back to what she had been doing before she met him. She was a cocktail waitress and sometime piano player. I lived wherever she lived until I graduated high school and struck out on my own.''

''What were you like as a teenager?''

''A borderline delinquent. I managed to avoid getting into any major scrapes with the authorities. But looking back, I don't know how I did it. When I got out of high school, I joined the service. I wanted to see the world. And I saw more than I bargained for. I spent a lot of time in the East. Southeast Asia, to be specific, special maneuvers.''

''What are those?''

He shook his head. ''Let's just say it was dangerous work, and somehow I survived with all my parts intact.''

She thought of the scars she'd seen on his body and asked without thinking, ''Is that how you got all those scars? In the service?''

His teeth flashed in a grin. ''You noticed my scars.''

She was blushing again. ''Well. Did you get them in the service?''

"Yeah. Most of them, anyway. I reupped more than once, didn't know what else to do with myself. When I got out, I was twenty-six. So I took the GI bill and went to college for a while."

"What did you study?"

"Police Science. Then I was with the L.A.P.D. for six years, but I decided to get out. It was hell on my liver, I was drinking so much. Four years ago I resigned and started my own business."

"Doing what?"

He had been looking out the windshield. Now he faced her. "Discovery and salvage."

"What's that?"

He let out a long breath.

She knew they were getting to the part he didn't want to talk about. "Oh, all right. You can stop."

He grunted. "Gee. Thanks."

"One more question."

"So you say now."

"You never mentioned a girlfriend or a wife."

"What can I say? I guess they all blur together after a while."

She punched his shoulder. "Very funny. Have you ever been married?"

"No."

"There was never anyone…special?"

"Yeah," he admitted. "There was. Once."

"What was her name?"

"Sandy Chernak. She was a cop, with L.A.P.D. like I was. She was a good woman. And a true friend. We were talking about moving in together. But then she was killed on a domestic call."

"Was that when you started drinking too much?"

"You got it."

"And was it also when you decided to get off the force?"

"Yes."

"What about your mother, Alana? Is she still alive?"

"She died a few years ago. And that was more than one question."

"Oops. Sorry." Olivia attempted to look apologetic, though inside, she was anything but. Though he hadn't exactly been eager to tell her all about himself, he had revealed a thing or two.

She felt she knew him better.

And how she ached for him. For the boy whose father had never claimed him, for the man who'd lost a lover to a violent death. She wondered about his mother. What might Alana have been like? And had she really betrayed John Roper? And if Alana had betrayed her husband, then was there an old man alive somewhere today with eyes like Jack's?

"Earth to Olivia."

She grinned at him. "Just wondering."

"I'll bet. Can we go now?"

She pretended to have to think about it.

He remarked, "You're pushing it, Ms. Larrabee."

She let out an airy sigh. "Oh, all right. We can go."

He started the car and they headed for the road.

Olivia felt wonderful the whole drive back. When they arrived at the hotel, they enjoyed their nightly ritual of sitting in the wing chairs by the trusty potted palm.

At the door to her room, he did it again.

That is, he *didn't* kiss her. But she didn't feel as bad about that as she had the night before. Last night she'd been sure she would never see him again.

But tonight, she had heard the story of most of his life. She understood him better. The kisses would come soon enough, of that she was certain.

And she was learning. She made a date for breakfast before he left and came right out and asked him for his room number, which he gave her with no hesitation at all.

The next day they tried the casinos downtown. They viewed the 100 ten-thousand-dollar bank notes in the glass display at Binion's Horseshoe, played baccarat at The Lucky Lady and yanked the one-armed bandit at The Golden Nugget.

In the afternoon they swam. And in the evening, they went to The Bacchanal in Caesar's Palace, a restaurant that resembled nothing so much as the garden of an Italian villa.

All told, it was another absolutely enchanting day, marred only by the continuing feeling Olivia had that something was bothering Jack.

But whenever she tried to get him to talk about it, she got nowhere.

And the moment came again when they stood at the door of her room to say good-night and she couldn't help wondering how long he would hide his troubles from her—not to mention if she would ever know his kiss.

"Earth to Olivia." Jack was smiling down into her eyes. He touched her hair, a breath of a touch, as if he didn't dare do more.

"Jack." She said his name with great seriousness.

He mimicked her tone. "Olivia."

"Jack, I—"

"Shh." He put his finger to her lips. "It was a great day."

His touch was magic, as usual. She wanted more. So very much more.

But she really had no idea how to *get* more. So all she said was "Good night."

"Tomorrow," he promised. "The poolside café. Noon."

"Yes." And she stood staring dreamily after him until he had disappeared beyond the turn to the elevators.

Then she shook herself and let herself into her suite. Inside, she leaned against the closed door and tried not to feel let down.

She looked around, idly deciding that she really could have invited Jack in without being embarrassed. Things didn't look as bad as they might have, given that she'd been on her own for five entire days. The maids here were kind. They stacked her clothing neatly in the dressing area, so when she came in at night, she didn't trip on her own strewn clothes.

Yes, she could have invited Jack in. But she'd missed the chance. And now it was too late.

Or was it?

Olivia straightened from the door and strode to the love seat.

She sat. Then she cradled her chin in her hand and tapped her heels on the floor, lost in thought. Soon enough, the tapping began to irritate her. So she kicked the shoes across the room and tapped with her nyloned feet.

The more she thought, the more she was positive that they couldn't go on like this. Something simply *had* to be done.

Olivia stood. She swept into the bedroom, headed right for the big walk-in closet and dressing area off the bathroom where her suitcases were. There she began tossing clothes in the air from the maid's neatly stacked pile.

Moments later she let out a triumphant little yelp.

She held up her discovery, shaking it a few times to smooth it out. It was the merest wisp of red satin, with skinny little spaghetti straps and a back that dipped to display more than most women should ever reveal.

Olivia bit her tongue, still thinking. There was a little robe to go with it, she knew there was.

More clothing flew.

And then she crowed again. "Aha!"

With the wisps of satin and lace over her arm, she returned to the bedroom, where she set the lingerie out, with great care, on the bed. Right then, she realized she was going to need something to cover the skimpy outfit when she went to Jack's room. She grinned as she thought of her sable, which Constance always packed for her to take on trips, whether Olivia needed it or not. Tonight, at least, the sinfully expensive fur would come in handy.

That settled, Olivia stared down at the short gown and robe for a time, her tongue caught between her teeth.

She was thinking, *What I am about to do is a conscious act. And I am a responsible woman.*

Though her hand shook a little, she picked up the phone anyway and pressed the button for the concierge.

Twenty minutes later, there was a discreet knock. When she opened the door, a bellman wheeled in a cart bearing champagne on ice. He also handed her a small brown bag, which she quickly set on the cart next to the champagne.

''Shall I open the champagne for you, madam?''

''No, thanks.'' Olivia shoved an enormous tip at him and ushered him out the door.

Then, right where she was standing, she unzipped the little black number she'd changed into before dinner and dropped it to the floor. Shedding underwear as she went, she marched to the bathroom where the big sunken tub and the scented bath oil were waiting.

On another floor, in a room a good deal smaller than Olivia's suite, Jack was lying on the bed, fully dressed except for his shoes. His hands were laced behind his head. He was staring at the ceiling, thinking exactly what he thought every night lately.

He was a rat. A creep. Lower than the lowest of the low. He should have found a way to tell Olivia everything by now, so he could do her the biggest favor he would ever do her: get out of her life.

Both yesterday and the day before he'd awakened firm in his purpose: somehow, before they parted for the night, he would tell her who and what he was.

But the moment he'd looked up from his morning paper and had seen her waiting a few feet away, her eyes glowing bright blue at the sight of him, he'd been done for. He'd known he would give anything for one more day.

It was a minor miracle, as far as he was concerned, that he hadn't laid a hand on her.

Or maybe it wasn't. Maybe, though he wanted her to the point of pain, he could bear the pain. As long as he could have one more day at her side.

Somehow, the excuse he'd made for himself that first night had stuck with him. As long as he didn't put his hands on her, the lie he was living remained marginally acceptable.

However, if he ever crossed that line, he would never be able to live with himself.

But he wouldn't cross that line. He knew it. He could control himself—barely.

And she would help him with her shyness and her inexperience. Because she was never going to push the issue, though he knew she felt the same longings he did. She simply wasn't the type of woman to become aggressive about something like sex.

Jack shifted on the bed a little, feeling edgy and aroused. He closed his eyes.

And there she was, on the back of his eyelids, smiling that innocently alluring smile of hers, holding up her lips in the shy hope of a kiss.

He groaned, rolled to his side and tried to call up a few arousal-reducing images. But it did no good. His body, kept so strictly under control every moment he was with her, had to make its needs felt at some point. Now, deep in the night, was the only time.

With a low moan of surrender, he allowed it to happen.

Her image came before him, in the red dress of that first evening. He saw her just as she had looked when they'd stood facing each other on the street, the dress molded against her slim body by the wind; her hair, deep gold and fine as spun silk, blowing around her face, catching on her sweet lips, so that she had to put up a hand and brush it away.

But in his fantasy they didn't stand on a street. They stood in some soft, private place, and the wind was warm, coming from some unknown source. In his fantasy nothing held him back. The last tattered shreds of his mangled integrity no longer clutched at him.

He was free. To touch and to know. To fully possess.

"Jack."

Her voice was soft in his ear as he hovered at the edge of sleep. And the red dress was sliding from her pale shoulders, revealing her slender arms, the soft rise of her breasts, the luminescence of her skin....

"Jack?"

Someone was knocking. Though he hated to leave his sweet fantasy, he opened his eyes.

"Jack?"

Jack lay very still.

"Jack, are you in there?"

It was her. Olivia. Knocking at the door.

"Jack, please."

He sat up and rubbed at his eyes.

"Jack?"

"Coming!"

He rolled off the bed, stumbled to the door and pulled it open.

Only then did he realize the magnitude of his recklessness. Because she really was there. His dream come to life. And his defenses were most definitely down.

All he could do was stare.

Her gold-and-bronze hair was loose on her shoulders. Her pale skin gleamed. She was wrapped in a coat of shining sable that fell to midcalf.

His stunned gaze strayed down the shapely bit of bare leg that could be seen beneath the hem of the fur coat. On her feet were a pair of slippers. Red backless slippers with open toes and high heels. Naughty slippers, designed purely to entice.

He could smell her. A warm, sweet beguiling smell. Like the crushed and purified essence of ten thousand rare and fragrant flowers.

In one hand, with commendable dexterity, she was managing to hold a bottle of champagne and two glasses. In the other hand she clutched a plain brown bag.

Chapter Five

Jack blinked owlishly at her.

Olivia realized she'd caught him napping, though he still had on his clothes. Luckily she'd planned what her first words would be.

"May I come in, darling?"

He muttered something like "Ugh, Olivia."

She decided she'd better take action before she lost her nerve. So, as alluringly as she could, Olivia swept into the room.

"Why don't you close the door?" she asked, low and huskily, just the way she'd practiced it while she was sitting in the tub.

Jack shut the door.

Olivia turned again and took the few remaining steps to the small table and chairs in the corner by the room's one window. There, with great care, she set down the brown bag. That left one hand free to pry the two glasses from her nervously tight fingers. She did this slowly, so as not to drop the champagne. When the glasses were free, she set them on the table not far from the bag.

That left both hands available to deal with the champagne.

Swiftly and masterfully she peeled the foil from the bottle, unwrapped the wire and eased out the cork. It came free with a soft explosion that echoed nicely in the room. A trail of vapor rose into the air.

It was expertly done. She congratulated herself, and her confidence rose a little. Opening champagne was something Olivia had always been good at.

With a flourish she lifted one of the flutes, tipped it slightly and poured. When the glass was full and the bubbles danced upward inside, she held it out.

''Champagne?''

Jack said nothing.

A slight feeling of hysteria rose inside Olivia. She was making a fool of herself.

She cut off the treacherous thought. Trying her best for a seductive sway, she approached him. Then, forcing herself to look provocatively into his eyes, she took his hand and wrapped it around the flute.

Olivia stepped back, keeping eye contact, making her lashes droop a little in a bedroom sort of way. Jack just went on staring.

Panic clutched at her. She was *positive* she was making a fool of herself now.

But it was too late to turn back.

Doing her best to move languidly, Olivia backed up until her knees touched the bed. Very slowly she allowed her sable to drop from her shoulders. She caught it before it hit the floor and tossed it across one of the chairs at the table.

Slowly Jack's gaze traveled from her head to her high-heeled red slippers and back up again. Once he'd looked her over thoroughly, he raised the glass to his lips and took a big gulp of champagne.

Oh, Olivia thought desperately. *This isn't going right at all.*

She said his name nervously. "Jack?"

Jack didn't answer.

Mostly because his throat was so dry it hurt. He took another swig of the champagne.

"Jack?" she asked again. This time her voice cracked.

Jack knew he should do something—say something. *Anything.* But the words just wouldn't come.

He wanted to reach for her.

But he couldn't do that.

If he did, he would never be able to live with himself later.

So what the hell was he going to do?

The answer came. He had to tell her.

Tonight. Right now.

He couldn't live another moment this way, looking at her, wanting her and knowing he could never touch. It was time to bust this thing open, even though he knew it would be the end once she'd heard the truth.

He knocked back the last of the champagne, set the empty glass on the television and forced himself to speak. "Olivia, I..."

Olivia saw the pained look on his face and was certain she knew exactly what it meant.

He *did* think she was ridiculous.

And he was trying to find a way to let her down easy.

Oh, it was all so clear to her now!

The reason he'd never kissed her was the most obvious one. He didn't *want* to kiss her. He wasn't attracted to her at all. Of course he wasn't. Men like Jack were never attracted to wimpy little nothings like she was. He'd enjoyed her company and wanted to be friends. She'd misunderstood his motives from the first.

Her skin, which had felt cold with her nervousness a moment ago, now flooded with mortified heat. And her eyes were burning, filling up with tears of humiliation.

Oh, this was a thousand times worse than finding Cameron and Bree Haversham doing those shocking things on Cameron's cherrywood desk. At least then she'd been calm, dry-eyed and dignified. At least then, she'd been *dressed!*

She glanced down in horror at her bare legs and the little points of her nipples that showed right through the satin and lace of her gown and skimpy robe, and then she glanced up again and into Jack's obsidian eyes.

"Olivia…"

The tears pressed, insistent, unstoppable, against her lower lids.

She had to get out. Now. Before she suffered the final humiliation and sobbed like a baby right here in front of him.

Where she found her voice, she had no idea. But somehow she managed to chirp out in a fractured soprano, "Er, um, excuse me. I see I've made a major error in judgment here. And I really must be on my way."

She grabbed her coat, shoved her arms in it and clutched it close around herself. Then, lowering her head so she wouldn't have to see his face anymore, she aimed herself at the door.

She didn't make it. He caught her arm.

"Damn it, Olivia."

"Let me go." She gave a jerk, but he held on without exerting any effort at all.

"Listen—"

"Please." The tears were rising, pushing to get out.

"Olivia, don't."

The tears started falling. She could feel them, tumbling

over the weak dam of her lids and slipping down her cheeks. She bit back a sob just as he pulled her against his hard, warm chest. "Don't cry." His voice was husky against her ear.

She struggled, moaning, as the tears kept falling. She knew they were staining his shirt. Her nose filled up.

She sniffed. "Oh please. I'm so ridiculous. You must let me go."

He didn't. Instead, he made soothing, gentle noises, and he continued to hold her close and sure against his body. "Come on, come on, it's okay."

And suddenly, with a low wail, she was throwing her arms around him, holding him as close as he was holding her. "Oh, I'm such a fool. Such a nothing."

"You're not. Don't say that. There, don't cry." Keeping her close, he took her to the side of the bed. "Come on. Sit down. It's okay. It's really okay."

He sat and gently urged her to sit beside him, which she finally did. Then he reached for the box of tissues on the nightstand and offered them to her. She yanked out several.

"Oh, Jack." She blew her nose. "I'm just not desirable to men."

"That's bull—"

"Don't. Please. Let me finish." It all came tumbling out then, between snorts at the tissues and a hiccup or two. "I thought you found me...that you wanted to, well, you know. But I can see now that it wasn't true. It's like Cameron said—"

"Cameron." He repeated the name in a grim tone.

She explained, "Cameron's my ex-fiancé."

"I see."

"No, you don't. You don't see at all. Because I've been lying to you, by not telling you."

"Telling me what?"

"Oh, Jack."

"Telling me what?" he repeated, relentlessly gentle.

She dragged in a breath. "Telling you the truth."

"And what is the truth?"

She made herself say it. "That the real reason I came here to Las Vegas was because I caught my fiancé—my *ex*-fiancé now—with another woman. In flagrante delicto, or however they say that. Making love. Having sex, you know what I mean?"

Jack made another of those understanding noises. He was stroking her back through the soft fur of her coat.

Olivia sagged against him, resting her head in the hollow of his shoulder. She sighed, swiped at her nose with a tissue again and then forced herself to go on.

"I caught him with his associate, Bree Haversham. On his desk. Can you believe it? His *desk*. And that's when he told me that I was a cold fish when it came to sex and what did I care if he made love with some other woman, since it was obvious that I hadn't any interest or ability in that department, anyway?" She let out a frantic little wail. "He actually said that to me, while Bree was trying to find her panty hose and button up her blouse. He stood there with his, um…not zipped up, and he told me that I was a terrible lover and should go home and think about how if I didn't marry him, what else was I going to do with my pointless little life."

Jack muttered something crude about Cameron under his breath.

"Oh, Jack. It was *horrible*." She cuddled up closer against his side.

He kissed the top of her head and rubbed her back some more. "Is that all?"

She sniffed a little, then confessed, "No, it isn't."

"What else?"

"Well, first of all, Cameron was pretty much right." She could feel him tense beside her and knew he was going to say that wasn't so. "No. Wait. Don't defend me. Let me finish." She gave out a shaky little sigh. "I really am lousy in bed. The two times I made love with Cameron were, well, they were grim, Jack. Really grim."

"That doesn't mean—"

"Shh." She patted his hand, which was wrapped around her shoulder. "Let me get this out. I mean it. I just want to get it all out. Okay?"

He made a low noise of agreement.

She drew in a few breaths and rubbed at her nose with the tissue again. "Thanks. Anyway, I'm lousy in bed. And I was going to marry Cameron, a man I didn't really even love, for exactly the reason he said. Because my life *is* pointless. And I thought that maybe by marrying and settling down with someone dependable, I could make my life more meaningful. Although, as it turned out, Cameron wasn't as dependable as I'd thought."

"Not by a long shot," Jack muttered.

"Oh, Jack. I only ever wanted to do one thing. To cook. I love to cook. I'm a trained chef. But I let my father talk me out of doing what *I* wanted to do. I went to work for him in this stupid figurehead job at Larrabee Brewing that means nothing to me or to the company. It's a pointless job in a pointless life."

Her hand was lying on his thigh. He took it in his, weaving their fingers together, and then lifting it to his lips for a light, comforting kiss. "Anything more?"

"Yes."

"What?" He gave her hand a squeeze, but didn't let go of it.

She held on tight, glad for the contact. "The worst part of all."

"Yeah?"

"My father."

"What about him?"

"What he did, when he heard what had happened with Cameron."

"What did he do?"

"He...he came to my beach house and said he'd fire Cameron. Cameron is president of sales for Larrabee Brewing, and he's the best salesman my father's ever had. But just like that, my father was going to fire him. I didn't want my father firing anyone for my sake, especially not the best salesman he's ever had. And then, right on top of telling me he was firing Cameron, my father said that he'd find me someone new and better in no time."

She pulled away enough to capture Jack's glance. "Can you believe it? My father actually said he'd find me someone *new*. Like a fiancé was a dress or a piece of furniture, something I could return for a refund if I wasn't satisfied. And the scary thing, the really terrifying thing is, it *could* happen. I could live the rest of my life in the house my father gave me, working in the job he made up for me, married to the man he *bought* for me."

Olivia sat a little straighter, pulling out of the circle of Jack's arm and removing her hand from his reassuring clasp. He let her go, sitting a little away himself, as if to give her the space she needed to say whatever else she needed to say.

She rubbed at her burning eyes. Her fingers came away smudged with the makeup she'd so artfully applied before coming to Jack's room. And the smudges reminded her of what a fool she'd just been.

She told him the rest. "I had to get away, Jack. I got in my car and drove all night to get here, to Las Vegas. And I met you. And the way you looked at me, I thought you...wanted me. Just because I was me. I mean, you didn't even know who I was that first night, when you saw me at the blackjack table and followed me out onto the street. And best of all, there was the way I felt when *I* looked at *you*. I thought, well, maybe my life is pointless. But Cameron was wrong. The way I feel about Jack proves I'm not a cold fish after all.''

She looked deep into Jack's eyes, which were so very dark and full of things she couldn't understand. ''But now I see the truth, Jack. You're a kind man and a good one. You've been nice to me. I don't know why. But I finally get it. You're not interested in me in any romantic way and I—''

Jack loosed a short, crude expletive.

Olivia hiccuped in surprise. ''Pardon me?''

''I said, that is baloney.''

''I don't think baloney was the word you used.''

''Don't cloud the issue. What I'm telling you is, I'm damned interested in you.''

''Oh, Jack.'' She shook her head. Then she stood and looked down at him. ''See? That's how you are. Kind. Trying to let me down easy.''

''I am *not* kind.'' His eyes were narrowed. ''If I were kind, I would let you believe this garbage you're spouting. I'd hustle you out of here and wish you well with your life—which I'm certain is far from pointless, by the way.''

''Oh, Jack. Thanks for trying. But I've already made enough of a fool of myself for one night. I've had a lovely time with you and I—''

He grabbed her hand and yanked her onto his lap.

''Jack!''

''You're going nowhere. Yet.'' He shifted her around a little, so that she was sitting sideways.

''But Jack, I—''

''Listen.'' He put his forehead against hers and spoke through gritted teeth. ''When I opened the door and found you there just now, I could hardly move. Or speak. And not because I wasn't attracted to you. Get it? But because, when you knocked on the door, I was dreaming of you, in that strange red dress you were wearing that first night I saw you. And in my dream you were taking *off* that red dress. Slowly. Very slowly.''

Olivia could hardly breathe. Somehow the surge of hope and pleasure she was feeling had cut off her air. ''Oh, Jack. Are you sure you—?''

He stopped her words with a single burning glance. ''Yes.''

''Well then, why haven't you *kissed* me, Jack? Why haven't you, um...''

''Made love with you?''

She looked down at her hands, which were twisting together. ''Yes.''

''Because I'm not who you think I am.''

She lifted her head, looked in his eyes. ''What do you mean?''

He dragged in a breath. ''I'm a—''

Olivia knew, in a burst of painful understanding, that she didn't want to hear it, not now, not tonight. ''No!'' She put her hand on his mouth. ''I've changed my mind. Don't say it.''

''But I—''

''No. Listen.'' Her voice was strong and steady, a tone so uncharacteristic of her that it shocked them both just a little. ''You listen to me.''

His eyes searched hers. And at last, with a slow nod, he agreed to her demand. He would not talk until she'd had her say.

For a moment she had no idea how to begin. But then the words came.

''Tonight,'' she said. ''Tonight, right now. This is *our* night, Jack. It's going to happen for us tonight. And nothing, not whatever you're keeping from me, or my fear that you'll find out how really horrible I am in bed—*nothing* is going to stop it from happening. *Nothing*. Do you understand?''

"But—"

"Shh." This time her voice was softer. "Please. You and me, together. In this bed. That's what I want tonight. Is it what you want too, Jack?"

Jack looked away.

She took his chin and guided him back so he had to look at her. "Is it?"

She stared into his eyes, willing him to say the words she longed to hear. "Stop thinking," she commanded. "Do you want me?"

Jack looked at her. He despised himself for what he was about to do.

But he was a starving man. And she'd laid a banquet before him.

To hell with it. He'd take what she offered.

One night of bliss.

"Yes, I want you."

"Then won't you *please* make love with me?"

"Yes." He gave her the answer before she even finished asking the question.

Chapter Six

As soon as she heard his *yes,* Olivia let out a long sigh. Then, smiling, she rested against him.

Jack wrapped both arms around her and cradled her close. She nuzzled his shirt, scenting him and loving the feel of him, the warmth and the strength.

Now that it was truly decided, a shyness came over her. She had no more to say. But he stroked her hair and caressed her back and kissed the crown of her head.

One and then the other, her naughty red slippers dropped to the floor.

"I'm trying to think logically," he murmured against her neck.

"Stop that," she chided. "There's no need for logic now."

His hand, rough, warm and large, was on her thigh, where her coat had fallen away. She looked down at it, saw that the back of it was dusted with shiny gold hair. He began rubbing her thigh, back and forth.

She let her eyes drift closed. And she simply felt his touch. It was lovely.

"Olivia."

"Um?"

"There is a need for logic in one area."

"What?"

"Contraception."

She felt very smug. "Oh, forget that. I've taken care of that."

The rogue dared to chuckle. "What? You're carrying protection around in a pocket of that fancy coat?"

"No. In a brown paper bag." She pointed at the table. "That bag, to be specific."

She could tell by how quiet he was that he was repressing more chuckling. "I see."

"I called the concierge. They sent a box, along with the champagne. A dozen. Will that be enough?"

"Hmm." He thought that over. "I suppose a dozen will just have to do."

"Well." Suddenly she felt shy again. "Good." She buried her face in his chest and found herself wondering if she really was going to be able to go through with this after all.

She'd felt so utterly sure just a moment ago. But now, the more she thought about it...

"Shh," he said against her hair. "Don't think. The time for thinking is over."

"Yes." She whispered the word. "I know that. I do."

He stroked her back and shoulders some more with one hand, while the hand on her thigh continued its wonderful massage. Then his fingers strayed.

She murmured his name and then gave a small, excited gasp as his hand slipped inside her coat and touched the red satin there. A little thrill of delight skittered through her as he began slowly to stroke upward.

"I love the feel of you, Olivia." He murmured the words

on a ragged breath, gathering her closer, into the heat and hardness of him.

It was then that she felt the bulge of his manhood, pressing at her softness. She shivered a little, both frightened and aroused.

His hand moved between the satin and the lace, up over her rib cage, until it found her breast. She gasped.

He whispered something against her temple. She didn't hear the words. And then his lips tasted her skin. He nibbled a trail over her cheekbone. His mouth sought hers.

And found it.

Olivia let out a small, grateful cry. At last. After four nights of wondering if she would ever know the feel of Jack's lips on hers, it was happening.

They were sharing their first kiss.

And it was everything she'd yearned for. And more.

His mouth played on hers, his teeth lightly nipping, his tongue pressing for entry.

On a soft exhalation, Olivia parted her lips. And his tongue was inside.

Olivia was absolutely stunned. It was wonderful. His mouth tasted hers, his arms held her close.

He broke the kiss. Olivia moaned. His lips moved to her chin, her neck, the little points of bone at the base of her throat.

He gave a low growl. Her coat was in his way. He shoved the soft fur aside, urging her to lift up a little. And then the coat was gone.

The next sound he made was a hungry one as he lowered his head and nibbled starved, hot kisses on her shoulder. As he tasted her skin, he pushed impatiently at the lace robe. He helped her free of the sleeves quickly, ruthlessly. And when the little scrap of robe no longer covered her, he tossed it away, too.

And then, for a moment, he was still.

Olivia felt her heart stop. He seemed to be studying the red satin gown, as if it were the wrapping on a very special package. Experimentally he slid a finger beneath one of the gown's slender straps. Slowly he lifted the strap and let it fall along her arm.

The left side of the gown dropped away, revealing one high, pink-tipped breast. Olivia had to hold back a moan that would also have been a plea. She wanted him to touch her breast.

"What?" he softly inquired.

"I…"

"Yes?"

"I want…"

"What?" He smiled a smile that seemed to know it all. And then his hand was straying again. Moving inexorably downward until, at last, she had her wish.

His hand swept over her breast, sending arrows of pure pleasure down to the feminine heart of her. He brushed back and forth, making her nipple into a hard, hungry nub.

In an ecstasy of sensation, Olivia let her head fall back. Jack cupped her breast, his hand so very warm and encompassing. And then he lowered his head and replaced his hand with his mouth. He licked. And then he sucked.

Olivia let out a groan that was so purely sexual she hardly knew it as her own. She shoved her hands into his hair and clutched him close, as he kissed her in a way that made her cry out for more and more of the same.

He pulled away enough to challenge silkily, "You're trembling."

"I…" Her skin flamed.

"Don't be embarrassed. It's the same for me."

"It is?"

"Don't you know what you do to me?" His hand was on her thigh again, sliding upward, until it disappeared beneath the hem of her short gown. "You turn me inside out."

"Oh, Jack."

"All I want to do is touch you, right here."

She gasped as his finger stroked the little strip of silk that covered her mound. The light teasing touch sent a shaft of liquid heat all through her. Her womanhood seemed to bloom. It was all at once hot and heavy and moist.

He must have felt the heat and moisture through the scrap of silk. He made a male sound of discovery, of satisfaction.

She let out a low moan of pleasure.

Beneath the hem of her gown, his fingers quested, rubbing her more boldly, pressing against the barrier of now-damp cloth. She squirmed and wriggled, pushing herself against his hand. And he seemed to know exactly what her body wanted, because he stretched her panties out of the way.

And then he was touching her, in her most secret place. His fingers found her and parted her.

She cried out. He muttered something low and knowing. She moved, frantic and needful, against his stroking hand.

And then it happened. Like a flower made of moist fire, she felt herself opening, expanding, pulsing out to set the rest of her aflame. She called out something that wasn't a word, but was nonetheless utterly triumphant and totally free. And then she went limp in Jack's strong arms.

"Olivia," he whispered, after several moments had gone by.

"Um?"

"Come on." Proprietarily he smoothed the strap of her gown back in place over her shoulder, covering her breast again. "Lie down."

"Um," she said again. It was the only thing she could manage right then. She felt so contented. So peaceful. Like a little boat drifting on a still summer sea.

She grumbled a bit in protest when he slid her off his lap and onto the bed. But he ignored her murmurs of complaint, as he stood and then bent to raise her feet onto the mattress and to urge her to lie with her head among the pillows.

When she was comfortable, he straightened and looked down at her. "Feel good?"

"Um." She stretched a little, pointing her toes, thoroughly enjoying the way his gaze swept over her, hot and possessive. She held up her arms.

But he didn't come down to her.

He took one of her hands and lightly kissed it. Then he went quickly to the table and returned with the brown bag. From it he took the box of condoms, which he set on the nightstand.

After that he undressed. He did it swiftly, tossing each item of clothing onto the corner chair as he removed it.

Most of his body was already familiar to her. They had shared more than one swim at the roof pool, after all. But still, to see him standing before her completely naked made the heat start to curl in her belly all over again.

She gazed on the fine musculature of his shoulders and arms, wondering again at the scars that here and there marred the bronze perfection of his skin. She let her gaze wander, following the T of golden hair that whorled around his nipples, trailed down his solar plexus and over the rock-hard planes of his abdomen. The hair grew darker near the juncture of his thighs. He was fully ready for lovemaking. She blushed a little at the sight.

With the swift and easy grace so characteristic of him, he stretched out beside her. He pressed himself along the length of her. She found herself assailed by a thousand sensations.

There was the heat of him and that manly scent that was only his. There was the corded strength of him. And the rough kiss of his body hair.

He clasped her waist. His hand slid upward. He took the straps of her gown and peeled them down, one at a time, revealing both of her round, pale breasts. He bent over her, gently, and kissed each one in turn. She gasped a little, and she felt his smile against her skin.

"Sit up."

She did as he bade. He gathered the hem of the flimsy gown.

"Raise your arms."

She did. And the gown was gone.

All that was left was her silky panties. But not for long. He whisked them away, too.

And then he urged her to stretch out again. She lay back down, compliant and brimming all through with a strange, peaceful, utterly perfect desire.

In a distant sort of way, she thought of Cameron. And the bleak experience that making love with him had been. But that all seemed very far away now. And so terribly simple.

Cameron had been the wrong man. That was all. And though her foolish mind had kept trying to tell her that she and Cameron would somehow make things work, her body had refused to be fooled.

"What is going through that mind of yours?" Jack asked.

It didn't even occur to her to dissemble. "I was just thinking that Cameron was the wrong man." She brazenly wrapped her hand around Jack's nape and pulled him closer. "And you're the right one."

His eyes clouded. He opened his mouth to speak.

She shook her head against the pillow. "Shh. No more doubts. No more hesitations, remember? Not tonight."

He lowered his head even closer to hers and nibbled her lower lip. "I remember." He nibbled some more. And then, with a low, hungry moan, he opened his mouth on hers.

Olivia gave a long, delighted sigh as her lips parted. Their tongues played together. And as he kissed her, his hand found her center once more. She lifted her body toward him.

He muttered, "You're ready. I want you. Can't wait."

He was kissing a path down her exposed neck to her breast. And then he captured that breast in his mouth and began to suck.

"Yes, yes, yes," she chanted, as she held his head close.

But he would not stay there. He kissed his way down, over her ribs to her quivering belly and then lower still.

Then his lips were there, in her most private place. And she wanted them there. She felt his mouth opening, his tongue delving, and she gave herself up to this most stunning of intimacies.

She felt her body rising, building toward fulfillment once again. And she clutched at his hard shoulders, thinking to pull him up, so he could enter her and join her this time.

But the sensations were too overwhelming. And those intimate kisses went on and on. And the hot flower of her womanhood was blooming again, opening, spreading to encompass the whole world.

Lost to everything but Jack's secret kiss, Olivia tossed her head on the pillows and found her release.

And just when the tremors began to subside, he was rising above her. She moaned and clutched at him. Swiftly, impatiently, he grappled with one of the condoms. And then it was on.

She looked up at him, into his midnight eyes, as he covered her body with his. He positioned himself. Then slowly, inexorably, he found his way home.

Oh, she thought, as her body took him in. She had been empty, empty all this time.

And now, at last, she was filled. With him. She opened wider, he pressed deeper.

"I knew," he muttered on a torn breath. "Yeah. I knew. Like silk, Olivia. You're like silk."

At last he filled her completely. There was no emptiness left. Only him.

And still he held her eyes.

Experimentally, he pulled back. She gave a low cry. And he returned. He did it again, only to come back again.

And soon enough she was pulling back and returning with him. He lowered himself fully upon her. She clutched his broad back and held on tight.

He picked up the rhythm. She followed without missing a single beat. They moved faster and faster, toward a white-hot center of absolute bliss. She lifted her legs and wrapped them around him, holding on for dear life and for their mutual ecstasy.

Again fulfillment approached, like a huge wave breaking over her, consuming her, towing her down. She welcomed it, writhing and whimpering like a wild thing.

And then she felt Jack stiffen. He cried out.

As he spilled into her, her consummation came, more powerful and complete than the two that Jack had given her before. Her cries echoed his cries. The world spun away.

Oh, how had she lived, she wondered inchoately, until this moment? Her life had been gray until this moment. And now it was a rainbow. A technicolor dream.

They lay entwined for the longest time. And then Jack rolled them both to their sides, so that they faced each other. Idly he smoothed her hair and then edged even closer to place a light kiss on her nose. Then he left her to rid himself of the condom.

He was back in no time, stretching out beside her once more.

She dared to reach out and touch his chest, to feel the hair there that was wiry over his nipples and became silky where it began its inviting trail down his abdomen. She felt one of the scars, jagged as a lightning bolt, that started in the curve of his shoulder and traveled down to his left nipple.

"Where did this come from?"

"An encounter with an angry barbwire fence, I think."

"And this one?"

"Hell, who knows?"

"The one on your leg, that curls around your calf?"

"In a bar on Alvarado Street, when I was still a cop. I tried to break up a knife fight. Two mean drunks. I got a hold of one of them and was reading him his Miranda rights, when the other one, who was supposed to be passed out on the floor, crawled up and grabbed my leg and started—"

"Never mind. I get the idea." She kissed the jagged scar he'd said he'd acquired on a barbwire fence. Then she snuggled into his shoulder with a sigh. "Maybe we could just lie here like this forever."

She could hear his smile in his voice. "Not a bad idea."

His arm was wrapped around her, his hand tracing a heart on her upper arm. Then in one long stroke, his hand slid down her arm and over the gentle curve of her hip. Her belly jumped when he caressed the little cove between her pelvic bone and her abdomen.

"Hey."

She lifted her head. He snared her glance. She watched the heat kindle in his eyes.

He touched her, opening her. She looked down, watched his hand, even as she felt the magic beginning all over again. Olivia surrendered to it utterly, wishing the night would never end.

Her wish was not granted. Though for a few enchanted hours Olivia was sure that the wonder and power of their passion could hold back the dawn.

Still, the moment came when, through the open curtains of the window, the rising sun began painting the desert sky in iridescent strokes of orange and magenta.

Olivia buried her head against Jack's chest. "It's morning," she whispered. And then she yawned.

Jack lifted up a little and looked past her shoulder at the clock, which sat on the nightstand next to the phone.

"Yeah." He shook his head when he saw the time. He lay back down and she snuggled against him as he tucked the blankets more comfortably around them.

She kissed his chin and closed her eyes. She felt herself drifting toward sleep and smiled. "Good night. Or should I say, good morning?"

"Does it matter?"

"No. Doesn't matter. Doesn't matter at all."

She felt his hand, smoothing the hair back from her neck. She felt his lips on her forehead, right between her brows, in the most tender of kisses.

With a soft sigh Olivia let sleep have its way with her.

The phone by her bed was ringing.

Olivia reached out and grabbed it from its cradle just as it shrilled out a second ring, before she remembered that it was not her phone at all, but Jack's.

"'Lo?" She murmured the word without thinking how drowsy and contented she must sound.

"Olivia?" She recognized her father's shocked voice. "Olivia, my God, is that you?"

Chapter Seven

Olivia dragged herself to a sitting position.

"Olivia, are you there? Olivia!"

She looked at Jack. He was sitting up, too, by then. He stared back at her. His face was very strange, very still. His eyes were so deep. They told her nothing.

On the phone her father kept talking to her, saying her name. But she knew that he had not called to speak with her.

It was Jack he had called for. So she held out the phone. Jack took it.

"Yeah?" he said warily into the mouthpiece.

Her father started shouting at Jack. He shouted loud enough that Olivia could make out a few of the words. Her father called Jack a bastard. And she heard him say the word *fired.*

"Fine," was all Jack said. Then he held out the phone to Olivia. "He wants to talk to you."

Olivia took the phone. Very carefully she put it to her ear.

"Livvy?" her father asked. She could hear his fear for her and his love, but she felt no response to it. She felt numb, anesthetized.

"I told you that you had to leave me alone, Dad." She spoke slowly and precisely.

"Livvy, please, I—"

"Goodbye, Dad."

"Olivia, wait! Don't—"

Olivia quietly hung up the phone.

Sitting there in the silence of harsh morning, in the bed where she had known such tender ecstasy only hours before, she stared at Jack. He stared back.

And then the phone started ringing again.

Olivia turned to it, picked it up and found the plug where the cord was connected. She pulled it out.

"There," she said calmly as the ringing stopped. She tugged the sheet up to cover her breasts and then folded her hands in her lap. "Now. I think you owe me an explanation, Jack."

Jack looked at her, at the grim set to her pretty chin and the flat deadness in her eyes. He realized that it had all happened just as he'd feared it would.

He'd done it. Tossed away his last shred of self-respect. Made love to the sweetest, most innocent woman on earth without telling her the truth about himself first.

"I'm waiting, Jack." Her voice was as dead as her expression.

There was nothing to do now but one thing. Tell her. Time, as he had always known it would, had run out.

"I'm a private investigator," he said. "Your father hired me to keep an eye on you while you were in Las Vegas."

She stared at him. "I see."

He made himself continue. "It was a simple surveillance gig, or that was all it was supposed to be."

"But then I caught you watching me."

"Right. You caught me twice. And I knew it was either give up the job or make a move."

"You made a move."

He nodded.

"So this was all a job to you."

"Olivia—"

She put up a hand. "No. Never mind. Don't explain any more. I've heard enough. More than enough." She raked her hair back from her face and stared blankly at the bedspread. Then she lifted her head and looked at him, a vacant look. "I have to go now."

And with that she tossed back the covers and swung her feet to the floor. For a moment she hovered there, on the edge of the mattress, her slim back slumped, her head hung low.

Jack's gut clenched. He hated himself. "God. Olivia." He reached out.

"Don't." There was steel in her soft voice. Her shoulders straightened. "Don't touch me. Ever again."

His insides twisted at her words. He withdrew his hand.

She bent and slid on the red slippers. Then she stood.

He watched her, wanting to stop her, knowing he wouldn't.

He remembered how young she had seemed—was it only last night? Right now she didn't seem young at all.

Her pale, slim body gleamed in the morning light. She was beautiful, the way a statue can be beautiful. He felt that if he did touch her now—which he wasn't going to do— her skin would be cold and smooth as marble under his hand.

She strode to the table, where her coat hung over a chair. He watched her round, tight buttocks, only vaguely aware that he was clutching the sheet in a death grip to keep from rising and preventing her escape.

She scooped up the coat and wrapped herself in its thick folds. She walked to the door.

She turned back to him before she went out. "Don't follow me anymore, Jack. If you do—" Her voice broke then. He saw the lost little girl inside of her. A pain shot through him, sharp and terrible. He had to look away. "If you do," she began again as he made himself face her once more, "I'll call the police."

She turned and went through the door, closing it softly behind her.

After she had gone, Jack didn't move for a while.

He was trying to convince himself that he should respect her wishes and give her what she wanted. He should leave her alone.

But then he knew he couldn't do that. After what he'd done to her, he couldn't just leave her alone out there in the big bad world. At the mercy of suspicious characters like himself.

He looked at the clock. It was seven minutes since she'd left. In her mental state she might do anything. She could just keep on walking, to the elevator, down to the lobby and right out the door.

"Please, God, don't let her do that," Jack muttered at the ceiling. He was not a religious man, but he was willing to try anything right then.

He threw back the covers, strode to his own suitcase and grabbed a pair of jeans and a sport shirt. He was packed and out the door in five minutes flat.

He needn't have hurried.

Olivia was in bad shape, but not so bad that she'd stroll out onto the Las Vegas Strip, wearing nothing but her sable and a pair of red high-heeled slippers.

She returned to her room.

When she let herself in, the phone was ringing. It would be her father, of course. She walked to the table by the love seat and unplugged it. When the extension in the bedroom kept on ringing, she marched in there and unplugged that one, too.

Then, when it was finally quiet, she sank to the side of the bed and rubbed her eyes. She looked at the clock. It wasn't even nine yet. She'd had about an hour and a half of sleep.

She felt terrible, all shaky and bewildered. But she knew that if she stretched out on the bed, the comfort of sleep would elude her. And even if she did manage to doze off for a while, she would still feel awful when she woke up.

Besides, there was her father to consider. He would be on his way here, she had no doubt. In a few hours he'd be pounding on the door.

She wasn't going to be here when Lawrence Larrabee arrived. He had meddled in her life one time too many. This thing with Jack was the last straw.

Jack.

Olivia hunched her shoulders, clutching her middle. Just thinking his name made her double over with pain. She had to stop thinking of him. She must forget him. Completely.

She made herself sit straight.

Then, shoulders back, she got to her feet and let the sable drop to the floor. She walked out of the red slippers. She went to the bathroom and stood under the shower, trying to clear her mind a little.

It didn't do much good. She got out and dried herself and tossed some more clothes on the floor, until she found some pink slacks and the big pink shirt that went with them. There was a cat's face embroidered on the shirt, a winking cat's face. It was a silly outfit, really. A silly outfit for a silly woman with a pointless life. She even found the pink flats that completed the ensemble. She'd be totally color coordinated as she ran off to Lord-knew-where.

When she was all dressed, she packed. Or she tried to pack. But she had no clue how to get her clothes back into all the suitcases and garment bags. Constance, who usually went with her whenever she traveled, always packed for her.

Finally she stuffed a few things into one of the smaller suitcases. Then she transferred her wallet and other essentials back to her shoulder bag from the evening purse she'd used last night. Slinging the shoulder bag in place, she grabbed the suitcase and her makeup case and headed for the door.

In the room she left a fortune in designer clothing, not to mention her sable. But what did she need with all those things, anyway? She was nobody, headed for nowhere. Starting fresh and traveling light.

She took State Route 95 because, when she got out on the highway, her car ended up on that road. It wasn't really important which road she took, though. As long as she wasn't headed back to L.A., any direction was fine with her.

State Route 95, as it happened, took her north and slightly west, through the high desert. She saw a lot of tall mesas and more sagebrush than she ever wanted to see again. She drove with single-minded concentration, stopping only when she had no choice, either for gas or to answer nature's call.

As morning faded into noon and noon moved along toward evening, she drove by high, stark peaks and past towns named Indian Springs, Beatty, Tonopah and Coaldale. It was nearing five and the sun was sinking toward the horizon when State Route 95 met up with Highway 80. At that interchange she switched directions a little and found herself heading straight for Reno.

Olivia reached Reno at six o'clock and left the highway briefly. Looking around in the gathering twilight, she decided that Reno was a lot like Las Vegas, only smaller. Also, it had pine trees instead of sagebrush.

She considered checking into a hotel for the night, especially since the air had the moist chill of a coming storm in it, and big dark clouds had rolled in, obscuring the early-evening sky.

But then she decided that she still wasn't ready to be cooped up inside four walls with only her own thoughts for company.

Better to keep moving.

She got back on the highway and went west, crossing into California. But then she kept seeing signs that said how far it was to Los Angeles. And she wasn't going to Los Angeles. She was going *away* from Los Angeles.

She turned off the main highway the next chance she got. By then, twilight had settled over the world. It was almost full dark. Then the rain started.

At first the rain was light. Olivia turned her wipers on low and had no problem. Occasionally a flash of lightning would bleach the angry darkness and make the tall trees on either side of the road seem to loom threateningly at the car. Then the thunder would roll.

Olivia drove on as the gathering darkness became true night, turning randomly each time she came to a crossroads. Soon enough, as the rain increased and each new road grew narrower and more twisted, she realized that she really had no idea at all where she was. Not that it mattered. She'd been headed for nowhere when she left Las Vegas, after all. And these tiny, rutted roads she was driving on made her more and more sure she was getting there.

Once she came to a crossroads that she was certain she'd been at before. The sign had the same unfamiliar places listed on it as the one she'd just seen a while back.

It came to her that she was probably driving in circles. A

small shiver of uneasiness went through her. She tried to ignore it.

But the storm was becoming a little frightening. The rain grew progressively worse. It began beating at the windshield, heavy and thick. And now it was freezing a little, becoming slushy, half snow. She had to crane her head forward and squint her eyes to see the narrow road, even with the wipers on high.

Once or twice, far behind her, she caught a glimpse of the beams of another car's headlights when the road would straighten out for a little. But ahead there was only darkness. Sometimes she thought she saw the lights of cabins or houses tucked among the trees off the road, but by the time she spotted them, she'd be rounding another bend and the reassuring glimmer of brightness would be lost to her.

She began to feel very much on her own. More than once she found herself looking in her rearview mirror for a sign of that other vehicle behind her, to prove to herself that she wasn't completely alone on an unknown road.

She tried not to give in to anxiety. She told herself not to be foolish. Of course she would find her way out of this maze sooner or later. Actually it had barely been an hour since she'd turned off the highway. It only *seemed* like the middle of the night.

She would be okay. She would be just fine. She was in charge of her life and affairs.

Right then her cute little foreign car made two small coughing noises and stopped running.

It took Olivia a moment to realize that she was slowing down and that pressing the gas pedal had no effect. As soon as she accepted that the car wasn't working, she steered to the shoulder, a maneuver made possible by the fact that she was on a slight downhill grade at the time.

It was after she'd come to a full stop that she glanced at the gas gauge. It was as far to the bottom of the reserve space as it could get. And the little red signal light was on. Obviously it had been on for quite some time now.

With a tired groan, Olivia leaned her head on the steering wheel.

Oh, why hadn't she remembered to fill up in Reno? Her mind was simply not working very well.

She was fatigued from lack of sleep. She'd been driving for eleven hours, and she was using every ounce of willpower she had at every moment not to think of Jack.

Jack.

There, she'd done it.

With a moan that was half exhaustion and half wounded grief, she let her head drop back against the seat.

Jack.

Rain beat on the car. Lightning flashed, thunder boomed and rolled away.

Jack had betrayed her. He'd done worse than betray her. He'd deceived her. The Jack she'd thought she knew didn't even exist. He'd been her father's man all along.

She had thought that what had happened with Cameron was bad.

But that was *nothing* next to this.

Jack's deception was a lance, turning in the deepest part of her.

Making love with Jack had been the one bold and dangerous thing she'd ever done in her life. And it had all been a lie.

Jack was her father's employee. He had made love to her in the line of duty. Everything they'd shared had been a sham. As Olivia herself was a sham.

A poor little rich girl.

And *girl* was the right word. There was no point in kidding herself. In all the ways that mattered she was still a girl at twenty-nine. A girl no man would want without the added attraction of her daddy's millions.

Olivia looked up. The furious rain still beat on the windshield. And a pair of high beams shone in the rear window at her.

She was about to be rescued by some kindly traveler. The car was pulling to a stop behind her.

Olivia sat up straight in the seat and raked her hair back with both hands. She felt marginally better, now that help had arrived. She might have made a mess of everything, but at least she wouldn't be stuck here alone in the freezing rain all night.

In fact, now that she thought about it, it was probably rude of her to just sit here and let her rescuer get all wet. If anyone got drenched it should be her, a girl who didn't even have enough sense to put gas in her car before leaving the main highway in a thunderstorm.

Olivia shoved open her door and stepped out into the driving, icy rain. She was soaked to the skin in ten seconds, the time it took her to close her door and turn with a grateful, if somewhat forced, smile for her deliverer.

But the smile froze into a sneer.

Because her rescuer was Jack.

Chapter Eight

Jack emerged from his car, which he'd left running, and came straight for her.

Olivia watched him approach, his tall, broad-shouldered body silhouetted in the beams from his headlights. The rain pelted her, plastering her hair to her head, gluing her silly pink outfit to her body. She felt only minimal satisfaction in noting that he was getting just as wet as she was.

"What's the problem?" he asked, when he was close enough that she could hear him without his having to shout. His breath came out as freezing mist.

She clenched her fists at her sides to keep them from scratching his eyes out. "I told you not to follow me."

"I suppose you're out of gas."

"I told you to leave me alone."

"Pop the trunk. I'll get your things."

"I don't want your help."

"Olivia, it's damn wet out here." He reached for the door latch.

She slid to the side and blocked him with her body. The rain truly was very cold. She was starting to shiver. She wrapped her arms around herself. "I won't take your help."

Lightning forked across the sky. Thunder boomed.

Jack spoke with great patience. "You don't have any choice." Water ran off his hawklike nose and over the beard stubble on his cheeks.

He hadn't shaved that morning, she realized. He must have been in a big hurry to chase after her. Her father must really be paying him a lot.

"Come on, Olivia." He sounded tired. "Get in my car and turn up the heater. I'll get your things."

"No." She shivered harder, hunching her shoulders to hoard her body's warmth, pressing herself back against the door.

He shrugged. And before she could yell at him to get his hands off her, he took her by the shoulders and moved her out of his way.

Then he pulled open her door. She watched as he yanked the keys from the ignition, popped the trunk latch and scooped up her purse, all in one fluid movement. He was very efficient, she decided. But then, her father only hired the best.

He slammed the door. "Get in my car. Now."

"No."

They looked at each other through the thick veil of the rain. Even with water running down his nose, she thought, he was the best looking, most purely masculine man she'd ever seen.

She hated him.

But hatred wasn't all of it.

Her traitorous body yearned for him.

Last night he had taught her what she was capable of feeling. It was a lesson that would be engraved on her nerve endings for the rest of her life. And right now it was fresh as a new wound.

She tore her gaze away from his, but it did no good. She only ended up slowly perusing the rest of him. His black knit shirt was stuck to the hard muscles of his torso. His jeans were shiny, slick with the rain, clinging to the strong shape of his legs. He looked good in denim, she decided. More dangerous, more elemental, even more rawly masculine than he did in his suits or his sports clothes.

"Olivia." His voice was rough and husky. It seemed to ignite her already-taut nerves. She realized what she was doing, looking him over with blatant sensual intent. Her head snapped up.

And she was staring right into his eyes again. She read the message in those eyes. She saw that he was thinking exactly what she was thinking.

About last night. About the two of them. About their separate bodies joined and moving as one.

Another javelin of lightning blazed across the sky. The thunder that came after was like giant sheets snapping in a gale-force wind.

"Jack." She barely mouthed his name. She was captured, held by his eyes. All she wanted right then was to throw herself against him, feel his arms close around her and lift her mouth for his kiss.

Her own desire shocked her. She wanted him. Right now. Here, in this wild, unknown place in the driving rain. Even after what he had done, after the way he had betrayed her. Next to the physical need she was feeling, his deception suddenly seemed a paltry thing.

"No." Her voice was low and husky, not convincing at all.

"Olivia."

"No." With a sharp cry she broke the seductive hold of his gaze. She spun on her heel and began walking away, down the narrow road between the tall rows of evergreens, not caring that there was really nowhere to go, only knowing that if she stayed near him for one second longer, she would be begging for his kiss.

Behind her she heard him swear. She waited for him to catch up to her, to dare to touch her. Because she was going to fight him. She was going to kick and scratch and bite to get away from him. He had no right to touch her now. And she would show him that was so.

But he didn't follow. Instead, after a moment or two, she heard her trunk slam. She kept walking, fast as she could, head down, clutching her middle, trying to press her teeth together hard enough that they would stop chattering. Her pink flats were full of water. They squished disgustingly with every step.

But she doggedly put one foot in front of the other, even after she realized that Jack had climbed back in his car and pulled out onto the road again. At first she thought he was going to leave her there, do exactly what she'd ordered him to do. And right at that moment she was glad he was going, even though she had no idea what she would do once his car had disappeared around the next bend.

But she never had to confront that problem. She saw soon enough that he wasn't going anywhere. He only eased in alongside her and drove at a snail's pace to keep even with her.

She walked faster, shivering so hard she almost felt nauseous. But walking faster was a silly and ineffectual gesture, of course. Because he only sped up from three miles an hour to four and stayed with her.

The road took an uphill turn. Head into the wind, she began climbing. The rain beat at her unmercifully. She slogged along.

In ten minutes or so she reached the top of that grade. Ahead of her, by the light of Jack's high beams, she could see that the road twisted down and then vanished around a bend into the trees.

She bent her head again, which kept the worst of the rain off her face, and started down.

She got about five steps before the futility of it all came crashing in on her. She stopped there, on the side of the road, next to a yellow sign with a picture of a leaping deer on it.

Jack, riding slowly and patiently at her side, stopped as well. He leaned across the seat and pushed the passenger door open. With a sigh of resignation she slid into the seat.

She pulled the door closed, her body immediately grateful for the warmth of the heater that was blasting around her freezing bare ankles.

"Here." Jack reached over the seat. "Wrap this around you." It was a thick plaid blanket. She took it from him without comment, wrapping herself in its heavy folds and then huddling against the door.

She closed her eyes as Jack backed the car onto the shoulder and skillfully turned it around. Once they were pointed back the way they'd come, he smoothly depressed the accelerator, and the car picked up speed.

She stayed hugging the door in grim dread. She was sure that once they were really moving, he would start talking. Lecturing her for being a fool. Or perhaps taunting her for the way he knew she felt about him. But he didn't. He was a cipher behind the wheel.

And she was grateful. She wasn't in the mood to listen to a single word from him.

She wasn't in the mood for anything but wallowing in her own despondency. She'd thought she'd hit rock bottom back in Las Vegas. But this was a new low altogether.

Slowly her spasmodic shivers faded. Her hair was still sopping wet, and her clothes clung, damp and uncomfortable, to her body. Her pink shoes felt like wet cardboard against her toes, and she seemed to be enveloped in a musty, humid smell, like wet wool. But at least she didn't feel like she was going to throw up from being so cold.

They reached Highway 80 again in less than twenty minutes. Olivia's depression deepened when she saw how ridiculously close she had been to civilization all the time. She *had* been driving in circles.

And Jack, who had been following her, knew that she'd managed to get herself lost just a few miles from the freeway. It was one more humiliation on top of all the others.

She was leaning against the passenger door pondering this most recent disgrace when Jack spoke. "We'll stop there and get a room." She glanced his way in time to see the sign he was gesturing at.

Gas Food Lodging
TRUCK PLAZA
NEXT RIGHT

"You need to get out of those wet clothes," he added, sounding defensive. "And I want to change, too. And a good night's sleep wouldn't hurt either of us."

She didn't answer, only looked out the windshield at the pounding sheets of slushy rain.

"Olivia, you'll feel better in the morning. Then you can decide what you want to do next."

She leaned against the door again and closed her eyes. She knew very well what would happen in the morning. He would inform her that now that she was rested, she was ready to go back to Daddy where she belonged.

"Olivia." He swore, low and feelingly. "Okay, I'll take your silence for agreement." He turned the wheel toward the off ramp.

When he pulled to a stop, she sat up and looked around. They were parked before the lobby doors of the Highway

Haven Motel. Out the windshield she could see the coffee shop and truck stop, which branched off the motel in an L. Out her side window she spied a few cars and pickups, looking small and lost in the pouring rain. Beyond the cars and pickups loomed a row of big rigs.

"I'll be able to see you from inside the lobby," Jack said.

She let out a tired breath of air. "What's that supposed to mean?"

"It means if you get any more crazy ideas about running off, I'll see you go."

She leaned her elbow on the door and rested her head on her hand. "Jack, this may come as a shock to you, but I'm a grown adult. And this is the United States of America. You have no right to stop me from going anywhere I want to go."

"I didn't say I'd stop you. I won't stop you. But I won't let you wander off alone, either."

"You mean you'd follow me."

"You got it. So stay here."

She shook her head.

"What does that mean?" he demanded.

She slanted him a look. "It means I'm too tired to fight with you right now."

"You'll stay here, then?"

She made a low noise of disgust. "Sure."

"Do I have your word?"

She made the same noise again. "Sure." She gave him a direct look. "I promise I'll stay here."

He stared at her for a moment. Then he seemed to decide her word was something he could trust.

"Good," he said. "I'll be right back." He got out of the car and went in through the glass doors. He glanced at her once before turning his back to her and enlisting the night clerk to check him into a room.

Olivia watched him, sitting very still. After thirty seconds it was clear that he'd decided she was too beaten and dejected to try any more crazy stunts tonight.

Good, she thought grimly. Because she wasn't quite as beaten as she'd led Jack to believe. And right then he should have known that her word could not be trusted.

She knew she didn't have much time. A minute or two at the most, before he either turned around again or finished at the check-in desk.

She looked around for her purse, but it wasn't on the front seat. He'd either put it in the back seat or tossed it in his trunk.

Well, too bad. She'd do without it. This was a point of honor as far as Olivia was concerned. She had to get away before Jack returned her to her father as if she were some naughty, runaway little girl with no power at all over her own destiny.

Olivia tossed the blanket off her shoulders, leaned on her door and swung her feet to the pavement. Hunched over, not daring the slightest glance back, she shoved the door closed and made a beeline through the rain for the row of huge trucks that stood so tall and proud at the edge of the lot.

She slipped between them. Then she crouched against the nearest one, the rain pelting her. She was listening for Jack's pursuit. But what she heard instead was the sound of a truck's powerful engine starting up. It wasn't the one she crouched against, but the one right next to it, a shiny maroon affair with a huge picture of a pretty blond woman painted on the trailer. She was just staring into the wide brown eyes of the bigger-than-life-size blonde when she saw and heard the driver's door of the maroon rig swing open.

Her own swiftness astounded her. She was around the back of the maroon rig before its driver jumped to the pavement. She bent down and watched the man's booted feet under the truck as they went the way she had come. As he moved toward the back, she inched forward, past another giant-size rendering of the same pretty blonde that adorned the other side of the trailer. She found herself at the front of the truck just as its driver reached the back. She heard him fool with something back there, probably checking to see that the big doors were firmly shut.

The driver's door was still open, the engine still running at a low, smooth idle. Not daring a glance at the motel, where Jack was probably discovering right now that she wasn't where she was supposed to be, Olivia darted past the nose of the truck and reached the driver's side. With a low grunt she hoisted herself up and into the cab. Then she saw the curtains behind the seat and knew they must lead to that little area behind the cab where the truck driver could sleep during long-distance rides.

Praying the driver wouldn't notice the extra water in his truck, since he himself was probably pretty wet by now, she slithered up over the seat and through the curtains.

She found herself on a bed that was surprisingly comfortable. Swiftly she scooted around to make sure the curtains were in place. Then she froze, hardly daring to breathe, as she heard the driver climb back into the cab.

The cab door slammed. The driver turned on the radio, and country music played. She heard the massive gears shifting. And the truck was moving.

She couldn't believe it. They were driving away. She had actually escaped from Jack.

She closed her eyes, feeling a lovely surge of self-righteous triumph. And then the triumph faded.

Now what was she going to do with herself?

And, now that she had a minute to think about it, what about Jack? Leaving him in his room at a Las Vegas hotel had been one thing. But escaping him here, at a truck stop on Highway 80 after dark, was something else altogether.

He would be worried sick. Even if he'd made love to her

under false pretenses, she knew he still felt responsible for her. And her disappearing like this would not be easy for him to take.

Olivia rolled over on the bed and contemplated the nearby ceiling. Oh, what was the matter with her? That Jack Roper might experience a little emotional distress when he found she was gone was the least of her problems right now.

And, anyway, what else could she have done? She wasn't about to return to her father. Never again. Not until she was a grown woman in more than just years.

Olivia realized she was shivering again. Now that the adrenaline rush of running from Jack had passed, her whole body ached and shook with cold. Luckily the bed had blankets.

In fact, now that her eyes were adjusted to the dimness, she could see that this cozy sleeping place was quite nicely appointed. There was a little square of floor, a narrow door that would allow exit without going over the seat of the cab, some cupboards and even a microwave. She gave a little sigh and knew she could have done much worse than having to spend a few hours in this snug portable room.

If she was lucky, she might even manage to slip out when the truck stopped, without the driver even knowing she'd been there. It would be one less embarrassing moment that she'd have to live through.

Gently she slid off her soggy flats and set them in the corner by the pillow, against the cab, where they wouldn't fall off onto the tiny floor and alert the driver that he wasn't traveling alone. She slipped under the blankets and pulled them gratefully up around her chin.

The bed was comfortable, really comfortable, she decided. Her eyes drooped closed.

Sleep came like stepping off a cliff, a quick drop into the waiting arms of oblivion.

* * *

"All right, Mr. Roper, we've got the description. We can keep an eye out for her."

"In case she turns up dead in a ditch, you mean," Jack supplied grimly.

The deputy gave him a wounded look. "There's only so much we can do. You gotta know that. Without signs of a struggle or any evidence of foul play, all we've got is an adult female who decided she didn't want to stay where she was."

Jack knew the deputy was right. He stood. "Fine. Well, you have the description. I'll be at the Highway Haven Motel until morning. And I'll call here before I move on."

"Sounds good. Sorry we can't do more."

"Yeah, I know. Thanks, anyway." Jack turned with a wave and left the sheriff's small station.

Outside, the rain was still coming down heavily. He stood in the shelter of the overhanging portico and stared out at the darkness and the storm.

He'd been a damned idiot, just as he'd always been when it came to the beer baron's daughter. He'd been sure she was finished, too worn-out to try any more funny stuff. And he'd taken her word that she would stay where he'd left her. He'd turned his back on her for two full minutes. And she'd used that time to get away.

She'd vanished into nowhere.

God. Where was she now? Please, let her be all right.

He'd checked every inch of the damn parking lot, gone through the coffee shop from end to end, including both rest rooms. She was nowhere to be found. Then he'd driven up and down the frontage road. Nothing.

He even took the ramp onto the highway and headed for the next exit, at which he'd turned around and gone back the other way, making a loop in both directions for a distance of fifteen miles.

Now, he was reasonably certain she'd managed to hitch

a ride during that crucial two minutes when he'd been signing into the room. She hadn't even taken her purse with her, the little fool. What did she think she was going to do with herself without even a quarter for a phone call, wandering around in a freezing rainstorm wearing only a pair of cotton slacks and a big pink shirt with a cat's face on it?

He prayed that whoever had picked her up was a decent human being. And he swore that when he found her, he would wring her pretty white neck.

Because he would find her. There was no question of that. He'd found more than one person who'd tried to disappear. That was what he was best at: hunting down the missing, whether they wanted to be found or not.

Something wasn't the same.

Slowly Olivia opened her eyes. She saw the ceiling, close enough to touch.

Where was she?

She remembered. The big truck with the woman's face painted on the side. She'd crawled into the sleeping compartment, and the truck had driven away from the Highway Haven Motel. And from Jack.

But she wasn't going to think about Jack. Not right now. She had to figure out what wasn't the same.

Then it came to her. The truck had stopped.

Olivia lay very still, listening for sounds that would tell her the driver was still in the cab. She heard nothing but the steady drone of rain on the roof.

Cautiously she pushed the warm cocoon of covers back and dared a peek into the cab. There was no one there.

Shy as a turtle she withdrew her head from between the curtains. She groped for her shoes, found them and slid them on, though they felt as sodden and squishy as water-logged newspaper.

She slid off the edge of the bed onto the floor. The sudden

movement caused a mild bout of dizziness. She paused a moment for the dizziness to pass. Once her equilibrium had returned, she patted at her damp, tangled hair and pressed the pads of her fingers against her eyes. She straightened her soggy pink slacks and smoothed her wrinkled shirt.

Then she drew in a deep breath and grasped the latch of the little door. It swung out. She jumped to the ground, right into a huge puddle.

Dejected, she looked down at herself. Now she was not only wrinkled and soggy, she was splattered with mud. The rain, steady and hard as it had been for what must have been hours now, poured down on her head, soaking her damp hair all over again.

Olivia shoved the door of the sleeper shut. It looked as if the truck was parked on the street of some small town or other. She was only a few steps from an old-fashioned covered sidewalk, so she took those steps.

She was out of the rain. And that was good. She was also standing by some sort of quaint store. The window by the door was painted with a rainbow. Over the rainbow, it said, Santino's BB & V. Below the rainbow, in smaller letters there was the explanation: Barber, Beauty And Variety: For All Your Household Needs.

Olivia walked on, shivering, wrapping her arms around herself, to the next door up, which belonged to Lily's Café. The sign said Homemade Eats. Breakfast Served All Day.

Both businesses were closed. She turned, now that the big truck no longer blocked the view, and looked up at the heavens. They were gray and angry and showed no stars or moon. In the distance a rim of hills touched the sky. The hills were covered with the dark, spiked shadows of evergreen trees.

Shivering harder, she turned and began walking the other way, down the street, past the café and the store called Santino's and another store that was named Fletcher Gold Sales.

She was looking for a light or some sign that someone in this place was awake. As she walked, though she despised herself for doing it, she longed for Jack. She also wished that she could just crawl into a hole and pull the hole in after her.

The minute she cleared the big rig on the other end, she saw a business that was still open. It was the town tavern, across and a few doors down the street. The lights were on there. Music and laughter came from inside.

Even through the heavy numbness of her misery, she was drawn to the light and the voices like a hungry animal to the smell of food. She slogged out into the rain and trudged across the street.

The name of the place was written in lariat script on the window and over the door: The Hole in the Wall.

Olivia shivered even harder when she saw that. She was feeling so strange and dizzy, and she had wished for a hole to crawl into. And here it was.

Maybe she was dreaming. Maybe none of this was real. Maybe, in a few moments, she would wake beside Jack in his room in Las Vegas. He would wrap his arms around her and kiss her on the tip of her nose, and she would be so grateful because none of the awful things that had happened since this morning would have been true. It would all have been one long, distressingly vivid bad dream.

She could tell her crazy dream to Jack, and Jack would hold her close and rub her back and say she mustn't worry. It was only a nightmare. And now it was over. He would tip her chin up and look deeply into her eyes and she would sigh and offer her mouth eagerly for his kiss.

Olivia closed her eyes. She shook her head. She waited for the nightmare to end.

But when she opened her eyes again, she was still standing on the strange small-town street in front of a bar called the Hole in the Wall.

With a little moan she moved forward onto the sidewalk. Then she took the few steps to the double doors. She reached out both hands and pushed the doors open, slipping between them before they swung shut again. The moment she was inside, she shrank back into the shadows to the side of the doors.

Warmth. And smoke. And music and laughter.

There were a lot of people in this place. And they seemed to be having some kind of a party. Crepe paper streamers hung from the light fixtures, and there were balloons everywhere. There was a banner over the bar that read Happy Seventy-Seventh, Oggie.

In the center of the room an old man with his back to her was sitting in front of a cake. A very pregnant woman with strawberry hair bent near, lighting the candles, *a lot* of candles.

"Hey, Jared. 'Nother round down here," a voice called from the other end of the long bar to her left.

"Coming right up."

Olivia glanced toward the bartender when she heard his voice. He was a tall, dark man dressed all in black. His body was hard looking and lean, like Jack's, and he—

Olivia gasped as the man turned in her direction and she got a good look at his face. Oh, Lord. He looked like Jack. So much like Jack it was frightening.

The bartender must have heard her gasp. His eyes found her in the shadows. His eyes were gray eyes, not Jack's eyes at all. Olivia's heart slowed down a little.

"Can I help you, miss?" the bartender asked.

"I, uh…"

All at once everyone began to sing "Happy Birthday" to Oggie. There was much stomping and whistling and several catcalls.

"Settle down, you hooligans," the old man groused. "I

got a lot of candles here. This is going to be some job."
Slowly the old man pushed himself to his feet.

"Miss?" the bartender asked again.

Olivia hardly heard him. Absently she waved away his
question. She was noticing more individual faces now. And
there were several in the circle closest to the old man that
reminded her of Jack. And there was a blond woman. A
blond woman who looked just like the painting on the side
of the truck that had brought Olivia to this unknown place.

Olivia trembled. Her heart raced. Could she be hallucinating? It was surely possible after all she'd been through.

The old man drew in a huge breath and blew. He got half
the candles. He blew again. "That does it," he declared.
"Cut the damn thing, will you, Eden?"

"Miss?" It was the bartender again. Somehow he'd come
around the bar and was at her side without her even noticing
that he'd moved. "Are you all right?"

She waved him away again and began to move, like a
sleepwalker, toward the people and the cake and the old
man.

"Get her a stiff one, Jared," a man's voice wryly suggested. "She looks like she needs it."

The tall, pregnant redhead looked up then from cutting
the first slice of birthday cake. She drew in a sharp breath.

"Oh, my God." The pregnant woman set down her knife.
"Jared, she's drenched. Get a blanket from the back room.
Now." The pregnant woman moved then, pushing through
the press of people. She had a beautiful, kind face with a
wide mouth and big dark eyes.

Olivia watched the pregnant woman coming, until a
movement from the old man distracted her. She blinked and
shifted her gaze to him as he slowly turned to look her way.

Olivia heard a tiny, mewling cry and didn't even know it
was coming from her own mouth.

It wasn't possible. It must be a dream. But the old man's

eyes—small, beady eyes—reminded her quite forcefully of Jack. It made no sense. They weren't like Jack's eyes at all. Except for the color.

Obsidian.

Yes, obsidian eyes. And the set of the old man's jaw, the shape of his mouth. So much about him. Like Jack.

It was too much for Olivia. Slowly, and then faster and faster, the room began to spin.

Suddenly all the people were converging on her. Their concerned expressions and exclamations of surprise overwhelmed her.

She sank into unconsciousness, her last awareness that of strong, unseen arms catching her before she hit the floor.

Chapter Nine

"There. She's coming around," a man's voice said.

Cautiously Olivia opened her eyes. A man was bending over her. "Can you hear me?" the man asked.

Olivia managed a nod as she became aware that someone had put a pillow under her head and tucked a warm blanket around her body. "What happened?"

"You fainted." The man smiled. "I'm Will Bacon. I run the local medical clinic. We were just trying to decide whether to call for the ambulance or not."

Olivia struggled to sit up. Gently the man eased her back down. "Relax. Don't push yourself."

Olivia blinked and shifted her glance from the man's kind face. She drew in a sharp breath when she saw that there were people all around, looking down at her.

"Step back everyone," Will Bacon said. "Don't crowd her."

The ring of faces receded a little.

"Find out who she is," another man whispered.

"Let's not worry about that now," a woman said. Olivia sought the voice. It was the pregnant redhead from her strange dream—the dream that seemed not to have ended, after all. "She appears to be thoroughly exhausted more than anything. What do you think, Will?"

"Yes, I'd say that's exactly her problem," Will Bacon agreed. "What she probably needs most right now is a good night's sleep in a warm, dry place."

"Sam and I have plenty of room," a small, voluptuous black-haired woman offered. "She can spend the night with us."

Olivia stared at the black-haired woman. She was one of the people who resembled Jack.

"Well, what do you say?" Will asked. "We can call the ambulance, if you want. Or you can spend the night at Delilah's house."

Olivia looked around at all the curious and concerned faces. She felt an instinctive trust for these people. Even if half of them did look like Jack.

Or perhaps *because* half of them looked like Jack.

"It's up to you," Will prompted softly. "Would you like to go to the hospital, or stay at Sam and Delilah's?"

"Sam and Delilah's, please," Olivia said.

"Good enough." Will looked up. "Patrick, why don't you carry her out to your four-by-four?"

"Sure."

A man came and bent beside her. His hair was brown and his eyes were blue. But he had Jack's chin. Olivia closed her eyes.

With great care, the man, Patrick, slid his arms beneath her and hoisted her, still wrapped in the warm blanket, against his chest. Then Patrick stood and carried her out into the rain and the darkness and gently slid her into the front seat of a vehicle.

The drive to Sam and Delilah's house was a short one. To Olivia it seemed that they'd barely started and they were there. The man named Patrick carried her in the front door. Inside, the black-haired woman, Delilah, took charge.

"This way, carefully." Delilah led the way up a flight of stairs. "I have the bed turned down."

They took her into a large, blue room and eased her onto a firm double bed.

In the doorway the old man with the obsidian eyes was watching, leaning on a cane. "Hell. She's a cute little thing, ain't she?"

"Forget it, Father," Delilah said. "You're out of sons to match her up with. And you and Patrick may go. We want to get her out of those wet things."

Grumbling, the old man turned and stumped off down the hall. Patrick followed. Olivia was left with four women: Delilah, a fine-boned brunette, the pregnant red-haired woman and the blonde whose likeness had been painted on the side of the truck.

The brunette was at Olivia's feet, sliding off her soggy shoes. "Your feet are like ice." Her warm, soft hands rubbed them in a wonderful massage.

Olivia sighed in pleasure as her poor toes grew warmer at last.

"Can you sit up?" the blonde asked. "We've got to get these wet clothes off."

"Come on," the redhead clucked. "We'll be gentle." They eased Olivia to a sitting position and carefully helped her to remove her mud-stained clothes.

"Here we go." Delilah held out a white cotton night-gown. "Lift up your arms."

Feeling like a child with four tender mothers, Olivia obediently held her hands high. The soft fabric whispered over her head and was smoothed down her tired body by gentle hands.

"Now, her hair." The brunette was ready with a big, fluffy towel. She dried Olivia's hair with the towel, and then the blonde appeared with a brush. Olivia received a hundred strokes.

"Now you can lie down," the redhead said.

Olivia gratefully stretched out once more.

Delilah tucked the covers snugly around her.

"Rest now," the brunette murmured, smoothing Olivia's hair back as if she were a child.

"Thank you."

"You are most welcome."

Olivia watched as the women went to the door. "Good night," she said.

They whispered four good-nights in turn and then they left her, switching off the light and closing the door very softly behind them.

Once she was alone, Olivia stared at the closed door through the darkness for a long while as a lovely feeling of peace stole over her. A smile took form on her lips.

She'd made a terrible mess of things, she knew. And yet, some deep instinct told her that all was not lost.

She'd divested herself of all her worldly possessions save the clothes on her back. She'd wandered, lost and alone in a rainstorm until she reached the end of nowhere.

And the people there had taken her in. She had the peculiar sense that she was exactly where she belonged at last. Simple human kindness surrounded her. It did a lot to heal her wounded heart.

Thinking of her heart, she thought of Jack.

Oddly enough, her thoughts were tender.

She was beginning to forgive him, she realized. Now, safe in a warm bed, due to the kindness of strangers, she could let herself remember the real concern on his face when he picked her up on that deserted road. She could allow herself to recall that she'd heard her father fire him on the phone, which meant that when Jack came after her, he'd most likely done it on his own.

Poor Jack. The more she thought about him, the guiltier she felt. He was probably going out of his mind with worry. And her father. Oh, Lord. Olivia couldn't even bear to *think* about what her father was doing now.

Yes, she'd made a mess of things, all right. She had no idea at all how she was going to go about righting all the wrong she'd done.

But she would work it out. Somehow tomorrow she would deal with it all. But for now she was simply too worn-out.

Olivia turned on her side and rested her cheek on her hand. Her eyelids drooped closed. With a sigh, she surrendered to her tired body's need for sleep.

Jack wasn't so lucky.

He sat on his bed in his room at the Highway Haven and watched the blinking of the motel sign reflected in the windshield of a truck across the parking lot.

He was thinking of forget-me-not eyes. And the dusting of freckles across a certain pert nose.

He was *willing* Olivia to be all right.

With a low, crude oath, he looked at his watch. Past eleven.

He thought of Lawrence Larrabee, who was probably in Las Vegas by now. And going insane with worry over Olivia, just as Jack was.

It would only be asking for more abuse to call the man and tell him what was going on. It was the last thing Jack should do.

But still, he picked up the phone and got the number of the Vegas hotel where he and Olivia had stayed. He punched up the number, calling himself a fool after each digit.

When the hotel operator answered, he asked for Lawrence Larrabee's room.

"I'll connect you," the operator said.

Larrabee picked up before the first ring had stopped. "Hello, this is Lawrence Larrabee."

Jack dragged in a breath. "This is Jack Roper."

A barrage of heated epithets erupted from the phone. Jack waited until they petered out a little, then asked, "Do you want to know what's going on or not?"

"Of course I do, you lowlife. How is she? Where is she? Is she all right?"

"Settle down, Lawrence." Jack waited.

After a moment, in a very controlled voice, Larrabee said, "All right. I'm calm. Tell me everything. From this morning on."

"Okay. She left the hotel there at 9:30 a.m."

"You followed?"

"Yeah. I tailed her up through Tonopah and Reno. Then she crossed back into California. She got off the main highway and drove in circles on side roads until she ran out of gas. I picked her up. That was around seven-thirty tonight." He digressed enough to tell Larrabee exactly where they'd left Olivia's car.

Larrabee said he'd have the car taken care of. "What happened next?"

"I brought her back here."

"Where's *here?*"

Jack gave the general location of the Highway Haven, but nothing specific. The last thing he wanted was Lawrence Larrabee showing up there. "We were both beat. I was planning that we'd spend the night here and probably head for L.A. tomorrow."

"So she's with you now."

"Well—"

"Let me talk to her."

Now came the unpleasant part. Jack confessed, "That isn't possible."

Larrabee was silent again, as if keeping himself carefully reined. Then he inquired, "Why not?"

"She isn't here."

"What?"

"She disappeared when I went to get the room. I've been to the police, and I've combed the area. Nothing. So far."

There was another lengthy silence. Larrabee talked to someone on his end. Then he asked, "Are you saying that my daughter has vanished into the Northern California woods somewhere?"

"For now, yes."

Jack heard a woman's voice from Larrabee's end. Probably the girlfriend, Mindy Long. The voice was making those soothing sounds women make when their men are about to go through the roof.

Larrabee said, "Consider yourself fired, Roper."

Jack gave a wry chuckle. "Get current, Lawrence. You already fired me this morning, remember?"

Larrabee sputtered and huffed a little, then he asked, "Well then, why are you still out there, if you know you're not getting paid?"

"None of your damn business," Jack said. "But I'm on my own time with this, and if I tell you what's going on, it's only because I think that somewhere in that pompous, overly possessive heart of yours, you love your daughter and want the best for her."

"Well, of course I love my daughter, you—"

"Save it, Lawrence. I'll call you when I've got more to tell you."

Jack found it very satisfying to hang up on Larrabee for a change.

And after that, not knowing what else to do, he kicked

off his shoes, stretched out on the bed and grimly waited for sleep.

Near dawn, Jack sat bolt upright.

He'd dreamed of the motel sign, blinking in the windshield of a big truck. In his dream the truck had pulled out and driven away. He'd watched it go.

It was a fancy rig, glossy maroon in color, with a giant painting of a big-eyed blonde on the trailer. A rig just like the one that had been pulling out of the lot when Jack turned around and saw that Olivia was no longer in his car.

"Damn," Jack muttered under his breath. It was a long shot. But right about now, it was the only shot he had.

He got up and pulled on his clothes.

Then he went to the coffee shop and ordered breakfast.

There, for five long hours, he made a complete nuisance of himself, asking question after question of anyone who would talk to him.

Finally, around eleven in the morning, after he'd drunk so much coffee his molars felt as if they were floating, he described the maroon rig to a trucker, who answered, "You must mean the Sweet Amy."

Jack's heart, already speeding from all the caffeine, raced a little faster. But he tried to keep his voice calm. "The truck has a name?"

"It sure does. The owner, Brendan, named it after his wife."

"Brendan who?"

Now the trucker became wary. "Brendan's a good man. I wouldn't want to be sendin' no trouble his way."

"Look." Jack did his best to make his expression sincere. "I don't even know the man. And this has nothing to do with him, really. It's only that I think he might have picked up a hitchhiker here last night."

"You're after the hitcher?"

"Yeah."

"Woman or man?"

"Woman."

"Yours?"

Jack made a quick decision to play this for sympathy. He nodded. And then he looked away.

The trucker, as Jack had suspected from a certain sensitivity in his bleary eyes, had a soft heart. "Hey. You'll work it out. Me and my wife, we have our battles. But we come back around. We get through it."

Jack stared at the dusty plastic flower in the bud vase at the end of the table, as if he couldn't trust his own emotions. And then, as if he had to force himself to do it, he looked the trucker in the eye. "I have to *find* her first. Before we can work this out."

"Hell." The other man took a swig from his coffee mug. "Okay. The trucker you're lookin' for is Brendan Jones. Out of North Magdalene. That's about twenty miles above Nevada City on Highway 49."

When she woke, it took Olivia a moment to remember where she was.

And then it came to her. The blue room. In the home of some people named Sam and Delilah.

Though the room was dim, she could see that it was sunny outside. There was a rim of bright light around the shades.

Olivia pulled herself to a sitting position and was just rearranging the covers a little when the door opened a crack.

"Ah. I see you're awake at last." Delilah bustled in. She went to the window and ran up the shades.

Bright midday sun poured into the room. Olivia squinted and looked away. But her eyes adjusted swiftly to the light, and then she turned back to look out the window. She could see the top of a maple tree, whose leaves had turned the browns and oranges of fall. The sky was a clear, pristine blue.

"The rain," Delilah said, gazing out the window. "It does wonders. Makes everything seem new." She turned to Olivia, a smile on her rather exotic face. "Last night it seemed more important to get you warm and dry and rested than to make introductions. I never told you my name."

Olivia gave the other woman a shy smile. "Your name was mentioned though, I think. Delilah, right?"

Delilah nodded. "Delilah Fletcher. I'm a teacher. My husband, Sam, owns Fletcher Gold Sales on Main Street." Delilah came and sat on the edge of the bed.

Olivia knew Delilah was waiting for her to introduce herself. Instead, she asked, "What town is this?"

"North Magdalene."

"In California?"

"Yes."

"And what time is it?"

Delilah shrugged. "After noon. How are you feeling?"

"Much better."

Right then the brunette from the night before appeared in the doorway. She was carrying a tray.

"Here's your breakfast," Delilah said and stood so that the brunette could set the tray across Olivia's legs.

Olivia looked down at raisin toast, two nicely poached eggs and a mug of coffee. The coffee smelled wonderful. "I'm starving. Thank you."

"You're welcome," the brunette said. "What do you take in your coffee?"

"Black is fine."

The brunette stood, backing up until she was beside Delilah. The two of them watched, smiling, as Olivia sipped her coffee and started to work on the eggs. After a moment the brunette volunteered, "I'm Regina Jones." She gestured at Delilah. "Delilah's brother, Patrick, is my husband."

Olivia nodded. "I remember Patrick drove me here last night." She took a bite of toast. The simple food tasted like heaven. It occurred to her that she hadn't eaten at all yesterday.

Right then the doorbell rang.

"That'll be Amy or Eden," Delilah said, and left to answer.

"They're both here," Delilah announced a few moments later. She introduced the blonde as Amy. And the redhead was named Eden. They were the Jones women, Regina explained with a wry grin. Except for Delilah, who'd been born a Jones, each of them had married one of the Jones men. The old man whose birthday party she'd interrupted was named Oggie Jones. He lived here with Delilah and Sam—in the back bedroom downstairs. He was the patriarch of the Jones clan.

Now they'd introduced themselves, the four women looked at Olivia expectantly.

Finally Regina pointed out in her gentle voice, "You haven't told us *your* name yet."

Olivia looked from one face to the next. She had no idea why she was holding back. These people had been so kind to her. She certainly owed them an explanation.

She swallowed the last bite of egg and said, "I'm Olivia Larrabee. As in Larrabee Brewing?"

"The beer company?" Amy asked.

"Yes. That's my father's company."

The women nodded.

"Ah."

"Yes."

"We see."

"But what brings you here, to North Magdalene?" Regina wondered.

Olivia confessed. "I'm on the run."

The women nodded and clucked among themselves some more.

Then Delilah asked, "From whom?"

"From everything."

"Everything?" Regina repeated.

"Yes, everything."

"What is *everything*, specifically?" Amy asked.

"Everything," Olivia said once more with an expansive gesture. "Everything includes my father, who loves me a lot but won't let me lead my own life. And my father's money, which I never earned. And also my completely pointless life. And last but not least, a man named Jack."

"Ah." The women nodded to each other.

"A man."

"Yes."

"Of course, a man."

"Look." Olivia pushed the tray away. "Can we talk?"

"Certainly." Regina took the tray and set it on the dresser by the door.

"Talk," Delilah said.

Amy added, "Please do."

And Eden chimed in. "Get it all out."

Which is precisely what Olivia did.

For well over an hour she talked.

She poured her heart out. She told them everything, from her overbearing father's loving domination to her unfulfilled dream of becoming a chef, to her ex-fiancé's betrayal, to the sad and tender story of her brief, heartbreaking affair with Jack.

The women listened and clucked their tongues. They nodded and shook their heads at all the right places. Olivia felt that for the first time in her life she was fully understood.

And when at last she said, "So that's how I ended up at Oggie Jones's seventy-seventh birthday party last night." Her heart seemed to be purified and her soul felt cleansed.

For a few minutes, once the story was told, everyone was quiet. Amy patted Olivia's hand and Regina gave her a sympathetic smile. And then Eden looked at Amy, who glanced at Regina, who gave a nod to Delilah.

Delilah said gently, "Well, then. I suppose that the question you have to ask yourself next is..."

"Yes?" Olivia wondered eagerly.

"What are you going to do now?"

Chapter Ten

An hour and a half after the trucker told him where to look for Brendan Jones, Jack parked his car on Main Street in front of Lily's Café.

Experience had taught him that the best places to go for information were bars and coffee shops. In North Magdalene, he found one of each. He'd passed the bar just a moment ago. It was across and down the street right next to a restaurant called the Mercantile Grill. He would try asking questions there as soon as he was through in the café.

He got out of the car and stretched a little, working out the kinks from the drive. Then he headed for the café.

He was just about to pull the door open when it opened from inside. Two older women came out. Both were tall. One was very thin and the other was big boned and deep breasted. They wore dark-colored dresses with little white collars and looked like what they probably were: two good Christian ladies who'd just enjoyed a leisurely Sunday lunch after spending a pious morning in church.

They came out chattering together. And then they saw Jack.

They both snapped their mouths shut and stared. It would have been comical, Jack thought, if it wasn't so strange.

The thin one muttered, "Oh no. Linda Lou, it can't be. Not *another* one."

And then the big one seemed to shake herself. "Come along, Nellie," she intoned. "The resemblance is only coincidental, I'm sure. And it's rude to stare." She took the skinny one's hand and pulled her off down the street.

Jack watched them go, wondering what the hell *that* was all about. Then he shrugged and went inside.

He took a seat at the counter, ignoring the sudden hush that seemed to settle over the room as one and then another of the customers glanced his way.

"Do you want to see a menu?" the young waitress asked. Jack looked in her eyes and wondered where he'd seen her before. There was something vaguely familiar about her. "Coffee?" she prompted.

He shook his head. She seemed to be studying him, looking him over closely. He sensed that she found him familiar, too.

Well, so what? He had to find Olivia. Whether or not he and this waitress had met before was unimportant.

"I'm looking for a man," he said. "A trucker, name of Brendan Jones. You know him?"

The waitress turned and set down the coffeepot on a burner. Then she faced him again. "I'm Heather. But folks call me Sunshine. Who are you?"

In the second before Jack replied, the café was eerily silent. Jack felt as if all the eyes in the place were focused on his back, as if they all waited, holding their breaths, to hear who he was.

He told them. "My name's Roper. Jack Roper."

Was it only his imagination, or did he hear them all start breathing once again?

The waitress took the pencil from behind her ear, looked at it and then stuck it back in. "I've never heard of you."

Jack shrugged and kept to his objective. "How about Brendan Jones? Have you heard of him?"

The waitress didn't answer. She just looked at him, eye to eye. Then she said, "Wait a minute. I'll be right back."

She disappeared through a door at the end of the counter—to make a phone call, he assumed. It was a long five minutes before she returned.

When she marched over and faced him again, he took the initiative. "Well? *Now* do you know Brendan Jones?"

The waitress gave him a bright smile. "Yes. He's my uncle." Before he could demand to know more, she instructed, "You go on over to the Hole in the Wall. That's the bar, down the street and on the other side. Ask for Oggie Jones."

"What about *Brendan* Jones?"

"You ask Oggie. He'll tell you what you need to know."

The Hole in the Wall was dark and cool and very well kept.

The same thing happened there as had happened at the café. The few customers at the bar all turned and stared when Jack pushed through the double doors.

"Hell," one man muttered. "If that ain't a Jones, then I'll swear off drinkin'."

"Don't make promises you'll never keep, Rocky," the handsome young bartender advised with a show of even white teeth.

Jack decided to ignore the remarks. He wasn't going to get sidetracked from his goal.

"Oggie Jones?" he asked the bartender.

The bartender flipped a thumb over his shoulder toward a curtain that was strung across one wall. ''Through there.''

When he went through the curtain, Jack found himself in a windowless alcove, the bar's back room. There was a round table, covered with a green felt cloth, and a number of bentwood chairs. The light came from a cone-shaded light bulb suspended from the ceiling.

At the table sat an old man. He was idly shuffling a deck of cards.

The old guy looked up.

And that weird feeling came over Jack again, that feeling of familiarity, the same as with the waitress at the café. Jack had never seen the old guy before. He was sure of it. And yet there was something about him that made Jack positive they'd met in the past.

And Jack could have sworn that the old fellow was thinking just the same about him—only more so. The man looked as if he'd seen a ghost.

But then the shock in the beady eyes passed. ''I'm Oggie,'' the old man said in a voice of gravel and dust. ''Park your butt right there, son.'' He pointed at a chair.

Jack gave a brief shake of his head. ''No, thanks. I'll stand.''

''Suit yourself.'' Oggie Jones pushed the deck of cards to the center of the table and sat back. ''What can I do for you?''

''I'm looking for a trucker named Brendan Jones.''

''So I've been told. What d'you want with my boy?''

''This Brendan's your son?''

''Yep.'' Oggie pulled a cigar from his breast pocket. ''Smoke, Mr....?''

''Roper. No, thanks.''

''Ah, yes. Roper. That's right. Sunshine told me the name. But I'm seventy-seven yesterday. The memory fails.''

Looking into the crafty dark eyes, Jack didn't believe the

memory had failed one bit. He explained, ''I think your son may have taken on a hitchhiker at a truck stop up near Donner Summit last night.''

''What makes you think that?''

''Timing. I turned my back and this person disappeared. Right at that moment your son's truck was pulling out of the parking lot where it happened.''

''This person. Is it a man?''

''No, a woman. A woman named Olivia Larrabee.'' Jack took out the snapshot Larrabee had given him when Jack took the job of tailing Olivia. It showed Olivia in front of a Malibu restaurant with Cameron Cain. Jack handed the picture to the old man.

Oggie studied it closely. When he looked up again, his road map of a face revealed nothing. ''She your woman?''

The word ''Yeah'' was out of Jack's mouth before he even stopped to remind himself that he was getting out of Olivia's life just as soon as he made sure she was okay.

Oggie took a moment to bite the end off his cigar and light up. Then he asked, ''She a good woman?''

Jack didn't like the direction of this. ''What do you mean, a good woman?''

The old coot did some puffing. At last he elaborated, ''I mean the kind of woman a man wants to hang on to. A woman of heart and intestinal fortitude.''

Jack grunted. ''Intestinal—?''

''Has she got guts, son? Guts.''

Jack thought of Olivia, of how fanciful and frail she was. Not someone a man would describe as having ''guts,'' not by a long shot. But even if she didn't have ''intestinal fortitude,'' she *was* good. ''Yeah,'' he said, ruing the slight huskiness that crept into his voice, a huskiness that the shrewd old man would be sure to note. ''She's a good woman.''

Oggie looked at the snapshot again. "The fellow in this picture don't look like you."

"It isn't."

"Hmm." Oggie returned the photograph, then sat back in his chair and fiddled with the grimy suspenders he wore. He pondered aloud, "It ain't you in the picture."

"So what?"

"So, you *say* she's your woman."

"She is."

"You say she's a *good* woman."

"She's that, too."

"But somehow, you let her get away from you."

Jack felt his patience slipping dangerously. "Where the hell are you going with this, old man?"

Oggie Jones let out a nerve-flaying cackle of laughter. "Well, I gotta tell ya, son. For a man to lose a good woman is the worst kind of carelessness. A good woman is what it's all about. Ask any of my boys, they'll tell you about the importance of a woman who can—"

Jack chopped the air with his hand, a short gesture of starkly controlled violence. Oggie, who was not a fool, fell silent.

"Look," Jack said very quietly. "When can I talk to Brendan Jones?"

"A week, maybe two."

Jack stared. "What the hell do you mean?"

"I mean he's on a cross-country run. Left early this morning. Won't be back for a while."

Jack murmured the crudest phrase he could think of. But then he realized what the old man had just said. "He left *here* early this morning?"

"Yep."

"Then I take it he did come back here last night?"

"Yep." The old man grinned a crafty grin and puffed on

his cigar. "He came in special, for his old man's birthday party."

"So you saw him last night?"

"Damn straight. It was *my* party I'm talkin' about."

Jack slapped the photograph with the back of his hand. "Was the woman in this picture with him?"

Oggie seemed to ponder deeply. "No, son. I can't say as she was."

Impatience curled like a fist in Jack's stomach. He quelled it and pressed on. "Did he say anything about picking up a hitchhiker?"

"No, he didn't say a thing about a hitchhiker as far as I can recall."

The old man was so transparent, it was an insult. He was holding something back, and he didn't care if Jack knew it. Jack asked very carefully, pointing to the picture, "Have you seen this woman?"

Oggie scrunched up his wrinkled face. He looked from the picture to Jack and back again. "Son—"

"Stop calling me son."

"Sorry, er, Mr. Roper."

"Answer my question. Have you seen this woman?"

Oggie looked torn. But at last he said, "I just can't see my way clear to answerin' that question right now."

"So you *have* seen her."

"I ain't sayin' that. I ain't sayin' anything."

"Do you know where she is?"

With some stiffness, Oggie Jones got to his feet. "For right now, Mr. Roper, I'm through talkin' to you." He turned to collect the cane that was leaning against the wall. "But I'm sure we'll be communicatin' in the future."

Jack's hands itched to close around the old rogue's wattled neck. "You're damn right we will. I'm not leaving this town until I find her."

The old rascal let out another of those ugly-sounding

cackles. "I ain't surprised. When a man is damn fool enough to lose a good woman, the least he can do is give it all he's got to get her back."

Jack, who'd always prided himself on his iron control, felt that control slipping. "Who the hell do you think you are, old man?"

Oggie cackled again. "I don't believe you really want to know—at least not right now, anyway."

Jack almost asked *What the hell is that supposed to mean?* But he stopped himself. The old man was right. He *didn't* want to know. He had more important things to think about, like finding Olivia and making sure she was all right.

He reiterated, "I won't leave this town until I find her."

Oggie gave a nod. "You told me that. Gotta go." He sidled around Jack.

Jack held himself back, though the urge to violence was a hot, clawing thing inside him. He wanted to grab the old coot and shake him until the truth fell out. But he didn't. Mostly because he knew it would do no good. Oggie Jones was tough as old boots, that much was obvious. Jack knew he would get nothing out of him that he didn't want to reveal. So Jack watched, still and silent, as Oggie pushed the curtain aside and hobbled through it, vanishing from sight.

When she heard the shouting from downstairs, Olivia was in the guest bathroom enjoying a long soak in the tub.

"Where is that gal? I gotta see her right away." The voice was unmistakable: the old man, Oggie Jones.

Faintly, Olivia heard a chorus of feminine voices raised in protest, though she couldn't quite make out the words that the women said.

Oggie's reply, however, came through loud and clear. "It can't wait. I gotta talk to her now."

"But, Father—"

Olivia heard the sound of stomping on the stairs.

And then more feminine protestations, one voice after another. "Give her a few minutes."

"She's relaxing in a nice, hot bath."

"You can't—"

"Watch me." Oggie sounded resolute.

"She's been through so much, she needs a little peace."

"Peace?" Oggie snorted. "She wanted peace, she never shoulda showed up around here."

Olivia sat up straight in the tub as Oggie began pounding on the door. "I gotta talk to you, gal. Get decent and get out here."

"All right," she called back. "Give me five minutes."

"You got 'em. But no more."

Olivia heard the sound of retreating footsteps, the stumping of Oggie and his cane, followed by the lighter tread of the Jones women. Quickly she reached for a towel.

Four and a half minutes later, she emerged from the bathroom dressed in clothes borrowed from Delilah. At the bottom of the stairs, Delilah was waiting.

"He's in the study." Delilah pointed to a room right off the entrance foyer. "Be careful."

Olivia shot her a puzzled look. "What do you mean?"

"Just what I said. I don't know what he's up to. Watch your step with him. He comes up with these schemes sometimes. You have to watch him, that's all."

"What kind of schemes?"

Delilah rolled her eyes and shook her head. "Got a month? I'll tell you a few of them. You'll understand, the longer you know him. But for right now, just watch yourself. And watch him."

"Okay."

"Now go on. He's waiting."

Cautiously Olivia approached the open door of the study. She peered around the doorframe and saw Oggie, sitting in a leather swivel chair, an unlit cigar clamped between his teeth.

"It's about time. Come in. And shut the damn door."

Olivia did as she was told.

"Sit down."

She sat.

Oggie chewed on his cigar, then took it out of his mouth and looked at it. He stuck it back between his teeth unlit. "You're feeling better, I see."

Olivia cleared her throat. "Um. Yes. Much. Thank you."

"My whole damn family's taken a real shine to you."

"I'm glad. I feel the same about them."

"Yeah. It's odd, ain't it? I mean, you show up here outta nowhere, and all the women want to mother you and the men want to protect you."

"Your family is kind."

"It's more than that."

"What do you mean?"

"I think you know." His eyes bored through her. Then he shrugged and explained, "It's you, gal. They all sense your need, sense the rightness of your being here. It was the same for me. I was thirty-five when I first came here. And the minute I set foot on Main Street, I knew I was home. I met the woman I would marry that first day, and I knew she was the one. And she knew it, too. And so did her people, the Rileys. I believe you're like me. And like Eden and Sam, too."

"Eden and Sam?"

"Yeah. They came here seekin' their place. And they stayed. You been lookin', ain't you?"

"Looking?"

"For your place." The rough voice was a little impatient now. "For the place where you belong. And now you're beginnin' to realize that North Magdalene might be it. Am I right?"

Olivia didn't know quite what to say. This whole conversation was exceedingly odd, especially considering the decisions she'd just made with the help of the Jones women.

"Well?" The old man's eyes were full of secrets. "Am I right?"

"Yes." Olivia swallowed. "As a matter of fact, you are."

"'Course I am." Oggie sat back in his chair and fiddled with his suspenders a little, chortling to himself. Then he craned forward once more. "Now, I got some news for you."

"You do?"

"You bet. Your man's tracked you down."

Olivia blinked. "Excuse me?"

"Your man. Jack Roper. He's in town."

Olivia's mouth dropped open. Deep in her heart she'd always known he'd find her. But she'd imagined it would take a little longer than this. "Already? But that's impossible. How could he have found out where I went?"

Oggie waved a gnarled hand. "I ain't got a clue how. All I'm tellin' you is, he's here. He's flashin' a picture of you and askin' a lot of questions."

"You've talked to him?"

"I have."

"Did you tell him—?"

"Nothin'."

"Oh." Olivia forced herself to take a few deep breaths. A thousand emotions warred within her. Apprehension. Fear. Defiance. Anticipation. And longing.

"In this town," Oggie said, "he'll find you soon enough. We got a lot of real talkative types around here, folks that can't keep a secret even if you staple their lips shut."

Olivia pondered this information and realized that it didn't upset her as much as it probably should have.

Now that she'd enjoyed a long sleep and a good heart-to-heart talk with four sympathetic women, she felt much more able to cope. And she'd made a few plans now. She knew she wasn't going to be running anymore. She fully intended to call her father as soon as this impromptu interview with Oggie Jones was concluded. She was going to tell Lawrence Larrabee of the new plans she'd made, and she was going to carry out those plans, no matter what her father said.

Facing Jack would be harder. But she'd do it, somehow.

"It's okay," she told Oggie.

Oggie was studying her. "What do you mean, 'It's okay'?"

She drew in a breath. "I mean, you've all been wonderful. But I'm not hiding. At least not anymore. If Jack asks you again where I am, you just tell him. All right?"

Oggie looked doubtful. "That man is one tough character. And he ain't in a good mood. You know what I'm sayin'?"

Olivia sighed. "Yes. I'm afraid I do. And thanks for the warning. But I mean it. Just tell him where I am. I'll talk to him. I'll straighten things out."

"If you say so."

"I do." Olivia stood. "And now, if that's all, I'm going to call my father and—"

"Sit back down, gal."

"What?"

"It ain't all." The old man's voice was flat.

Olivia sank slowly back into the chair. "What? What's the matter?"

The old man looked at her, a piercing look. Then he turned his gaze out the window at a birch tree there. He watched the little gold leaves flicker in the gentle wind. A few blew off and floated to the ground before he admitted, "This is the hard part. And I'm at a damn loss."

Olivia said nothing. She had a feeling that being at a loss was a rare thing for Oggie Jones.

"You seen my oldest son, Jared?" Oggie asked, suddenly. "He's Eden's man. He was tendin' the bar last night."

Olivia recalled the tall, gray-eyed bartender. The one who had looked so much like a dark-haired version of Jack that she'd imagined she was hallucinating when she saw him. "Yes. I remember him."

"Jared looks just like my own father." Oggie spoke in a musing tone. "Got that tall, lean, hungry look. You know the look I mean?"

Olivia knew. It was the same look Jack had. She nodded.

"My father wasn't much of a man, to tell you true. Oh, he was tough enough and mean enough. But he had no heart. He died in a brawl when I was thirteen years old. That was back in Mission, Kansas. A long time ago."

Oggie chewed on his unlit cigar a little. His eyes were faraway. Olivia had a pretty good idea what was coming. Anticipation made her shiver a little, but she knew enough not to try to rush the old man over something as important as this.

Oggie continued. "My father had strong blood, though. His look is in all my kids. And in their kids. Some more than others." Oggie turned his beady black eyes on Olivia now. She felt he could see into her mind. "It's the look of your man, Jack. Did you notice?"

"Yes. I noticed." Olivia's voice was barely a whisper.

"You know your man's history?"

"Some of it."

"You know his mama's name?"

"Yes."

There was a long silence. The old man sighed deeply. Then he said, "I want to tell you a little story, gal."

"Yes. I want to hear it."

"But you got to promise me—"

"Anything."

"You won't go pushin' the truth on that man. You'll let him come to it in his own time."

"What?"

"You heard what I said."

She'd heard, all right. But she didn't like it. She tried to protest. "But the truth is important. He should know it."

The old man waved her argument away. "He doesn't want to know it right now. You gotta let him find his way to it in his own time."

Olivia captured her tongue between her teeth, the way she always did when she was pondering heavily.

"Well?" Oggie prompted.

"But I—"

"No buts. You keep your mouth shut, or this little talk stops now."

Olivia mustered up a glare and aimed it at the old man. "I think he should know."

"He will know. When *he's* ready." Oggie folded his hands over his paunch. "I'm waiting."

"This isn't fair."

"You're damn right."

Olivia threw up her hands. "Oh, all right. I won't say a word."

The old man beamed. "Attagirl."

"Now tell me." Olivia leaned forward eagerly. "Tell me all of it."

Oggie glanced at the door to see that it was firmly shut. Then, in a low, intense voice, he began to tell his story.

Chapter Eleven

Less than an hour after he'd confronted Oggie Jones at the Hole in the Wall, Jack found one of those people who couldn't keep a secret if you stapled their lips together.

His name was Ben Quail and he was eighty-three—or so he told Jack. His lined face was wide and his false teeth clicked together when he talked. He had two gray wisps of hair on his head, which he'd combed carefully over his crown. Jack found him sitting on a bench in front of the North Magdalene Grocery.

The first thing Ben said was, "You look like a Jones to me." The second was, "You hear about the big commotion over at the Hole in the Wall last night? Some woman came in out of the rain just when Oggie was blowing out the candles. It was Oggie Jones's birthday, see? Anyway, this woman was soaked to the skin. She took a look around the place and fainted dead away."

"No kidding. What happened next?"

"She came to, soon enough. And they took her over to Delilah's for the night."

"And where does Delilah live?"

"With her husband, Sam. Down Bullfinch Lane. Big, new house on the left, near the end. Can't miss it."

"Thank you, Ben."

"Don't mention it—you sure you aren't a Jones?"

In less than ten minutes Jack was ringing the doorbell at the house Ben Quail had described. It was opened by a petite dark-eyed woman with large breasts, a stubborn chin and a lot of glossy black hair around her face.

Jack and the woman stared at each other for a moment before either spoke. Once again, with another stranger, he had to fight down that disorienting feeling of familiarity.

"Yes?" The woman eyed him as warily as he was eyeing her.

"Hell." It was Oggie Jones's voice. "It's him. Better let him in."

Jack looked beyond the woman's shoulder and through the small foyer into the living room. He spied the old coot, stretched out in a fat easy chair, his feet propped on an ottoman.

"Where is she?" Jack demanded of the old man.

"Now, just a minute here," the gypsy-haired woman warned.

Oggie waved a hand. "Let him in, Delilah."

"I don't like his attitude."

"Delilah. Let him in."

Delilah turned enough to look over her shoulder at Oggie. They glared at each other for a moment. Then she turned back to Jack and stepped aside. "All right. Come in."

"Thank you," Jack replied, laying on the sarcasm.

He walked right by Delilah and into the living room, which was a very pleasant room with high ceilings, filled with books and comfortable-looking furniture. He saw Oggie and a big man with red gold hair combed back into a short ponytail.

But he didn't see Olivia.

"Where is she?" he demanded again.

Oggie chortled. "Allow me to introduce you folks. This is my daughter, Delilah, and her husband, Sam Fletcher. Sam and Delilah, meet Jack Roper."

"Where is she?"

"You got a one-track mind, there, son."

"Don't call me—"

"Jack."

Jack turned at the sweet sound of her voice.

She was standing on the landing at the top of the stairway, to his right. Her tawny hair was a halo around her pale face, and her eyes were soft and wide. She was wearing jeans that were a little too short for her and a shirt that was made for more generous curves. Her tender mouth trembled a little, but she appeared neither ill nor injured. She was the most adorable sight he had ever beheld in his life.

And she was all right. Every cell in his body screamed with relief.

"Olivia." He said her name, and that was all he could say. Something had temporarily cut off his air. His heart was doing the most disturbing things inside his chest.

"Oh, Jack…"

"Damn it, Olivia. You scared me to death."

In his easy chair, Oggie cackled.

Delilah said, "You don't have to deal with him now, Olivia, if you're not up to it."

Sam grunted. "Stay out of it, Lilah."

"But, Sam…" Delilah's voice trailed off. A quick glance in their direction showed Jack that Sam had put his arm around his wife. The couple shared a look that managed to be both mutual challenge—and agreement.

Jack decided he had a lot of respect for Sam Fletcher, to be able to silence the bossy Delilah with a few words and a look.

Sam volunteered, "You two can go in the study, if you need some privacy."

"Thanks, Sam." Olivia was smiling, a wistful little smile that had Jack's heart acting up all over again. "But I think Jack and I will go for a walk." She gave Jack a questioning glance. "All right, Jack?"

"Fine." He made his voice flat, in order to reveal none of the jarring tumble of emotions that roiled inside of him.

She came down the stairs. He stepped back when she reached the bottom. Right then he didn't trust himself to be too close to her.

"I'll be back soon," she told the others as she turned toward the door. "Let's go, Jack." She led the way out. He followed, keeping back.

Behind them, Oggie couldn't resist a parting shot. "You give a holler, gal, if he bothers you!"

Jack shut the door before Olivia could answer the old scoundrel.

When they reached the street, she turned to him. "I think there's a river that way." She pointed the opposite direction from the way he had come. "I saw it from one of the upstairs windows."

"So?" He felt edgy. He wanted to touch her—to pull her against him and breathe in the scent of her. But of course, he wasn't going to do that. He wasn't going to do that ever again. He was here to see that she was all right. And that was all.

"So, shall we walk that way?"

He shrugged. "Fine."

She started off down the street. He fell in beside her, but not too close. Within minutes the paved road ended, and they walked on a rutted road of red dirt lightly blanketed with pine needles. The red dirt was soft and muddy, and the ruts were full of water after last night's rain. To avoid the puddles, Jack fell in behind Olivia, who seemed quite sure of where she was going. He tried not to watch the taut curve of her buttocks as she walked. He looked up, around, anywhere but at her slim back.

From the trees a blue jay scolded them. Some distance off he could hear the honking of geese. The sky overhead, which he could glimpse through the lacy fanwork of the pine branches, was a pure blue, like Olivia's eyes.

Soon enough the needle-blanketed road came to a dead end. Olivia didn't hesitate. She walked on to where the ground dropped off. Jack followed and saw the path she'd found that cut downward to the river's edge.

They descended. When they reached the bottom, the river lay crystalline in the afternoon sun. A little to the right of the trail was a rocky point, splashed with sunlight. Olivia went out and sat on it.

Jack stood in the shadow of a big, gnarled oak for a moment, watching the way the sun glinted on her hair. And then, with a low curse, he went to her and crouched a few feet away.

He looked out over the moving water, because he couldn't quite trust himself to look at her. He was fighting that urge to touch her again.

Hell, he always wanted to touch her. He feared he would be longing to touch her when they laid him in his grave.

And he wanted to shout at her that he hadn't slept more than an hour last night for worrying about her, for picturing her lost and injured or the victim of some unsavory character or other.

Instead he made his voice level and spoke of practical matters. "I've talked to your father."

She surprised him. "So have I. Just a few minute ago."

"You called him, in Vegas?"

"Yes." She lifted her chin. The fine curve of her white throat taunted him.

He looked away. "Did you tell him where you were?"

"Yes, I did."

He shook his head. "So he's on his way here now, I suppose."

"No. He's not coming here now."

He shot her a glance. "You seem pretty sure of that."

"I am." Her voice was so calm, so assured. He realized he believed her. "It's finally happened, Jack."

"What?"

"I've finally managed to convince my father that I have to lead my own life." She shifted a little on the rock and drew her legs up, hugging them. "I guess I really scared him last night. He says he stayed up all night, talking to Mindy—you know who Mindy is?"

"Yeah."

"Well, the two of them talked all night. And he's decided to let me alone for a while. I mean *really* alone. He won't be sending anyone to, um, track me down, this time."

"Good." He edged a little closer, though he knew he should stay back. "You don't seem so angry at me anymore."

She looked at him, her expression gentle and unbearably sweet. Then she curled her legs to the side and leaned his way. "I'm not, Jack. I've had a little time to think it all over. I realize now that you were as trapped by the whole situation as I was."

Conflicting emotions warred inside him. "You're too forgiving."

"Not in this case."

"I should have walked away the second time you caught me watching you, out in front of the casino, that first night."

"My father would only have sent someone else."

"Someone who wouldn't have hurt you."

She made a soft little sound in her throat. "You never wanted to hurt me, Jack. I know that." He looked at her freckles and her slightly parted lips.

He was leaning toward her, just as she leaned toward him. He knew he should get back. But he didn't get back.

He was thinking that if he leaned forward just a little bit more, his lips could brush hers. And now he was close enough that he picked up her scent. A warm, sweet, fresh-scrubbed scent.

"I should have walked away," he repeated and leaned closer still.

Her lips now curved in the most tender of smiles. "I'm glad you didn't. If you had walked away, our beautiful time together never would have happened." She blushed a little. He watched the warm color pinken the skin beneath her freckles. It was a thoroughly enchanting sight.

"Olivia." He said her name and nothing more. It was as if her name was the only word he knew.

"Yes?" She tilted her head a bit, lifting her mouth, offering it up to him, like she'd done all those nights in Vegas when he'd left her at her door.

But the difference between those nights and now was that now he knew what her lips felt like. He knew the honeyed taste of her. And he craved more.

He leaned that crucial fraction closer.

Like the brush of a butterfly's silken wing, her lips grazed his.

That did it.

With a low oath, he shot to his feet.

He heard her disappointed little sigh but ignored it.

He stared out over the sun-shimmered water and waited for the embarrassing physical signs of his arousal to fade.

When he thought he could trust himself to look at her, he turned and met her eyes. Her expression was quite calm, which irked him to no end.

"It was all a mistake between us," he said gruffly.

"No." Her voice was firm.

"I never should have made love with you."

"Please don't say that."

"It's the truth."

"No, it's not."

"It's over." He spoke through gritted teeth. "It never should have happened in the first place, and it will never happen again. You'll go back to your life, and I'll go back to mine. Understand?"

She said nothing. For the first time since he'd met her, he found he couldn't read her thoughts in her eyes.

As they looked at each other, a slight wind came up. The trees sighed, a sad, whispering sound. Olivia shivered a little in her thin, borrowed shirt.

Jack decided he should get on with this, so he broke the silence between them by offering, "Listen. I suppose you'll be ready to go home pretty soon. I'll be glad to drive you there. Or to take you to the airport in Sacramento so you can catch a flight."

She smiled up at him. It was an enigmatic smile, one he didn't think he liked. "No, Jack. I'm going nowhere. I'm staying right here. My father's going to have Constance, my housekeeper, close up the beach house. Then she'll go and work for him. Zelda, my father's housekeeper, is retiring next spring, and so it'll all work out just fine."

Jack wondered what she was babbling about. "You're what?"

"I said I'm not returning to Malibu. I'm staying here."

He stared at her, trying to fathom what in the world she was up to now. "What for?"

"I'm going to live here."

"But why?"

"I like it here. And Eden—one of Oggie's daughters-in-law?—has offered me a job."

Jack mentally counted to ten before asking quietly, "A job doing what?"

"Cooking. I told you I could cook, didn't I?"

This was getting worse and worse. "Cooking where?"

"At the Mercantile Grill, the restaurant adjacent to the Hole in the Wall saloon."

"You're going to be a cook...at a *restaurant?*"

"Yes, Jack. I am. I told you, if you'll only remember, that cooking is what I've wanted to do all my life. And I am trained as a chef, after all."

"But this is insane. You work for your father."

"I *worked* for my father. Past tense." In one graceful motion, she stood. "Now I work for Eden Jones." She brushed off the back of her borrowed jeans.

"You don't even know these people. You can't just—"

She put up a hand. "Yes, I can, Jack." Her expression was utterly composed. "And I *do* know these people. I know this place. I know it in my heart." She touched her breast and looked up at him, her eyes bright as stars. "This is the place and these are the people I've been seeking all my life."

Jack looked at her and shook his head. It all was becoming painfully clear to him now. After all, he'd studied psychology in college.

She had not recovered from the series of crushing emotional blows that Cameron Cain, her father and then Jack himself had inflicted on her. She was mentally disturbed. There was no other word for it.

She'd driven out of Vegas going nowhere and ended up in this bend-in-the-road burg. And then, in a desperate attempt to create some kind of order in the chaos of her life, she'd convinced herself that fate had brought her here. And now she was unwilling to leave.

Which meant, of course, that he wasn't going to be able to leave, either. He felt too responsible.

He made himself ask in a reasonable tone, "You plan to live with the Fletchers, is that it?"

"No." For a woman who was mentally unbalanced, she sounded annoyingly decisive. "Delilah owns another house, over on Rambling Lane. She lived there until she married Sam. It's vacant now and fully furnished. She's going to rent it to me."

Jack looked at her, trying to push down his feeling of irritation with her, trying not to grab her and kiss her, trying to remember that she was mentally a few cards short of a full deck and thus deserved to be treated with careful consideration.

But for all his good intentions, when he spoke, his exasperation came through loud and clear. "You sure as hell have got everything worked out in a damn short period of time."

Olivia lifted her chin proudly, a Mona Lisa smile curving her sweet mouth. "That's how it is, when fate takes a hand."

Jack felt his blood pressure rising. He wanted to grab her and shake her and make her confront the hard truth right now, this very moment. He wanted to force her to admit that there was no such thing as fate, to compel her to see that she'd slipped into some netherworld of delusion.

But somehow he controlled himself. He kept his mouth shut and his hands to himself. He didn't have the right to make her face anything. He'd done way too much to her already.

It was a time for patience, he knew. He must wait. Eventually she'd be willing to look at the harsh realities that were what life was really about. She'd give up her crazy fantasy that there was something special about these infuriating people and this nowhere town.

"Oh, Jack." She was looking at him so sympathetically, as if he were the one who required patience and understanding. For a moment, that spurred his irritation. But when she went on gazing at him so tenderly, his exasperation melted.

Damn. She was one of a kind, even in her deluded state. After all he'd done to her, she could look at him with tenderness.

Though he knew he shouldn't, he touched the side of her face. It was like silk, as he'd known it would be, only warmer. "Olivia, I..."

"Yes, Jack?"

Suddenly he felt as tongue-tied as a boy with a big crush. "I'm sorry, about everything."

She caught his hand and kissed the knuckles one by one. His skin burned where her lips touched. Then she held his hand to her cheek and met his eyes. "Oh, no, Jack. You mustn't be sorry. It's all working out just as it should."

God, he thought, she's really lost it.

And yet her appeal for him, even in her state of mental confusion, was as strong as ever. It took every shred of willpower he possessed not to hook his hand around her nape and ravage her mouth with his. Hell, it was worse than ever now, with the memory of their one night branded forever in his brain.

Swiftly, before he could do the unpardonable, he stepped back from her and pulled his hand free of her tender grasp. "Look. I'll be in town for a while."

Her face showed frank delight. "Oh. I'm so glad."

He had to clear his throat before continuing. "Yeah, well..." He collected his thoughts. "I passed a motel at the foot of Main Street. Swan's, I think it's called. I'll check in there. If you need me, just call me."

"All right." That Mona Lisa smile was on her mouth again. "If you say so."

"Yeah." He was backing up. Because he knew that if he didn't back up, he'd be moving toward her. She was like a human magnet for him. He had to get far enough back to get out of her force field. "Listen, let's go. I'll walk you back to the Fletchers' house."

Still smiling, she shook her head. "It's beautiful here. I think I'll stay a while." She looked at him from under her lashes. "You could stay, too."

"No. I have to check in at the motel."

She gave a little wave. "All right, then. See you later."

"Yeah. See you later." He kept backing up, until he stumbled against the old oak tree. Then he turned and forged up the path away from her, not daring to look back.

If he had, he would have seen that she was still smiling that enigmatic smile.

Chapter Twelve

Swan's Motel sat at the foot of Main Street, the first sight to greet the weary traveler when he or she arrived in town. It consisted of two box-shaped buildings that faced each other across a tarred parking lot.

The office was paneled in knotty pine and furnished in overstuffed plaid. Above the plaid couch to the side of the check-in desk was a nicely framed colored-chalk drawing of a very pretty blonde. The blonde was looking over her shoulder and smiling a come-hither smile.

"I'd like a room," Jack said to the man behind the counter.

The man, who was reading a magazine, looked up and gasped. A fiftyish fellow, he bore a faint resemblance to the coy blonde in the drawing over the couch.

"What the hell?" the man exclaimed.

"A room," Jack said slowly. "I'd like a room."

The man backed toward the far wall, his hands up as if Jack held a gun on him. "Look. I don't want any trouble."

"Neither do I. Just a room. That's all."

"Fine. Fine." The man smoothed his thinning hair. "For how long?"

A nameplate nearby read Chuck Swan. Jack said, "One night at a time, Chuck."

Chuck coughed, then ventured, "You get a better rate if you pay for a week."

"One night at a time."

"Sure, sure." Chuck's hands were up again. "Whatever you say."

"Have you got a room at the back, on the second floor, away from traffic?"

"You bet." Chuck gestured over his shoulder at a pegboard with the room keys on it. "Room 203 or 206 is what you're after."

"Either one, then."

"Great." Chuck spun the registration book around and pointed at a blank line. "Sign here. Address, phone and license plate number, too."

Jack handed him a credit card and filled in the blanks in the book. He'd barely finished when Chuck twirled the register back around and peered at what he'd written. Chuck looked up. "Roper? I never heard of you. I thought you were one of the—"

Jack didn't want to hear the name Jones. He cut in. "I never heard of you, either, Chuck. Would you give me my key...and my credit card, too?"

"Yeah. Sure. Right." Chuck quickly took an impression of Jack's card and handed it over. Then he turned, grabbed the key to 203 off the pegboard and tossed it in the air.

Jack caught it neatly. "Thanks."

"Sure. All right. No problem."

Over the pegboard there was a stuffed deer head. The deer had big brown glass eyes and a wide rack of antlers.

Somebody had stuck a cigarette between its lips. Jack saluted the deer and went out to get his bag from the car.

When he opened the trunk, he saw the bags he'd taken from Olivia's car last night. Damn. He'd forgotten all about them. Jack stood for a moment staring into the trunk, remembering Olivia in her ill-fitting borrowed clothes. The nice thing to do would be to drive back over to the Fletchers' house right now and deliver her bags to her.

But Jack Roper wasn't nice.

And he didn't feel like dealing with Olivia again right this minute. He'd had enough for one day. She might be the most adorable woman on earth, but she was also disturbed and refused to admit it. In fact, she acted as if she thought *he* was the one with the problem.

And besides, she knew where he was. If she needed her things right away, she could get in touch with him. Otherwise, he'd get them to her when he was damn good and ready to play delivery boy.

That decided, he shouldered his own bag and went to his room, which he discovered had been done up just like the office—in knotty pine and plaid, but minus the deer head and the flirty blonde. He put his bag on the rack in the tiny closet. Then he stripped down and showered, after which he stretched out on the bed.

When he woke it was growing dark outside and he was hungry.

In a town the size of North Magdalene, his options for dining were limited. He could choose between the Mercantile Grill and Lily's Café.

It wasn't much of a choice. Both places would no doubt be infested with people named Jones, or at the very least, crawling with people who were related to people named Jones. Right then, he didn't care much for Joneses.

After a few minutes of consideration, he decided he'd eat his dinner at Lily's.

However, when he got to the café, he saw that they closed at five on Sundays. He was too late.

Grimly he turned for the Mercantile Grill.

The first thing he heard when he entered the restaurant was Olivia's laughter. It was only a short trill of sound, but he recognized it, muffled by the wall that divided the kitchen from the main part of the restaurant. He deduced that she'd started right in at her new job.

He asked for a secluded table and got one. For a few moments after he was seated, he kept listening to hear Olivia's laugh again. But then he realized what he was doing.

He was here to fill his growling stomach, not to moon over a woman that he was soon going to have to learn to forget. To take his mind off her, he concentrated on his surroundings.

The restaurant, surprisingly, was a nice one. The walls were warm looking, exposed brick, the carpet a deep forest green. He ordered steak, potatoes and a salad.

The food was good. He ate undisturbed. By the time he got to that final cup of coffee, he was actually beginning to imagine he might get fed and get out without having to talk to anyone named Jones.

But then, just as he was signing his credit card slip, Oggie Jones hobbled in from the Hole in the Wall next door.

"Well, what have we here?"

Jack stood. "I was just leaving."

"No, you don't. Not so fast."

"Listen—"

"You play poker?"

Jack looked at the old man, a chilling look, and didn't answer.

Oggie blithely continued. "You come on next door. They got a good game going. It's just a friendly game. They never play for big stakes. Ask anyone.'' The old fool chortled to himself, as if he'd told some hugely funny joke.

''No.''

''Aw, come on. What else you gonna do with yourself tonight? This here's North Magdalene. We ain't got a movie house, there's no place to go dancin' and the only stage show we get around here is when the school puts on *Arsenic and Old Lace*. That's comin' up in a month or so.'' There was more chortling. ''But not tonight.''

Jack couldn't believe this. The old man refused to get the message. ''Look. No, thanks. I've got to—''

''You gotta nothin'. Come with me.''

The old geezer had a hold of his arm. Jack couldn't shake him loose without being rough about it. And he didn't really feel like being rough.

What the hell, he thought. Tonight the old man didn't seem much worse than cordial. There were no strange looks or cryptic remarks.

What harm could it do to go next door and have a beer or two? Especially when the alternative was four knotty-pine-paneled walls and a lumpy bed. He'd end up there soon enough.

Oggie started pulling him toward an interior door, which Jack assumed led to the Hole in the Wall. Jack shrugged and went along.

Four hours later and two hundred dollars richer, Jack headed for Swan's Motel. He was weaving a little as he went. He'd had a beer or two more than he should have.

But all told, he felt pretty good. The night air had a real bite to it; it cleared his foggy mind a little. He stood beneath a street lamp and looked up at the sky and the rim of mountains all around and decided that this was a pretty nice little town, after all. He wondered woozily what it would be like to live in a place like this, where everyone knew everyone, and as a general rule people were open and friendly, willing to give a stranger a chance.

Even a nobody from nowhere. A professional hunter of other people's lost loved ones, with no loved ones of his own and no place to call home.

Jack leaned against the lamppost and chuckled at himself. Nothing like a few too many beers to give a man an excuse for a little self-pity.

He hugged the lamppost for a while, pondering the friendliness of people in small towns, reaching no particular conclusion. Then with a grunt he straightened, aimed himself at the motel and started moving. He didn't stop until he reached his room.

He was snoring before his head hit the pillow.

The next morning, after swallowing a couple of aspirin for his mild hangover, he had breakfast at Lily's. The waitress called Sunshine wouldn't give him his coffee until he drank his tomato juice. He grumbled that where he came from, waitresses didn't tell their customers what to eat.

She only beamed. "Aren't you glad you're *here,* then?" Next, she breezily informed him that his girlfriend was moving into her new house today. "You'll be there to help, I guess."

He wanted to ask her where she'd heard that Olivia was his girlfriend—and what help Olivia could possibly need moving into a furnished house with nothing but the borrowed clothes on her back to take with her? But he didn't. He knew he'd only be asking for more bright smiles and another volley of impertinent questions.

With breakfast over, Jack began to spare a thought or two for his business in L.A.

Roper, Inc., was a very simple operation. It consisted of Jack and an answering machine. He hooked up with clients

through an ad in the yellow pages and, more frequently,
referral.

Jack returned to his room. He intended to pick up
messages from the machine at his apartment and then
back any potential clients to explain that he was curre
tied up. It was a chore he didn't relish. While Lawre
Larrabee had been paying him big money for a simple j
it had made sense to put any other work on hold. But n
he was on his own time. Being unavailable was throw
money away, pure and simple.

However, there was no sense crying over it. What
left of his common decency demanded that he stay here u
Olivia emerged from her mental fog and agreed to ret
home.

He saw he had a problem when he got back to the roo
Swan's Motel was a long way from the cutting edge wl
it came to the amenities. Not only was the mattress lum
the phone was an old rotary model—and he had no do
all the calls would have to be channeled through Chuck
front, anyway. He needed a touch tone and a direct line
get through to his answering machine.

He ended up standing at the kiosk by the grocery stc
scribbling his messages on a notepad while Ben Quail
nearby and pretended he wasn't listening. Before Jack h
up, he taped a referral to Swan's Motel into his messa
thinking that it might be somewhat appeasing to impati
clients if they had another number to call.

That done, he decided he'd go back to his room a
phone the few prospects who'd left messages with the ne
that he wasn't available right now. Then he'd sign on
another day's lodging at Swan's Motel. And after that h
take Olivia her suitcases, a chore he didn't relish, but wh
had to be done sooner or later.

He asked Ben Quail where the house on Rambling L
was, the one Delilah Fletcher had lived in before she

married. Obliging as ever, Ben told Jack what the house looked like and how to get there.

The house was a tidy little clapboard structure. White with green trim, it had a small, sloping lawn and rose bushes in front of the porch.

Jack could hear a vacuum cleaner going, which meant Olivia was probably inside. No doubt Delilah, the dragon lady, would be there, too.

Grimly he pounded on the door. But the vacuum cleaner kept running. He rang the bell. No one came and the vacuum cleaner went on roaring.

He turned the door handle, and the door swung inward. He stepped beyond the threshold, calling out, "Hello?"

The house was as neat and simple inside as out. The front door opened directly into the living room. Right on the other side of the living room, through an arch, was the kitchen. To his right, a cheery fire burned in a potbellied stove. Beyond the stove was another arch. The roaring of the vacuum cleaner came through there. Hesitantly he followed the sound.

In one of the two bedrooms he found Olivia. She wore the same clothes she'd worn yesterday. Her hair was tied back with a scarf and her tongue was caught between her teeth. She was pushing a big, ancient-looking, upright vacuum cleaner back and forth on the small strip of beige carpet between a low, mirrored dresser and a double bed.

The sight was so appealing that Jack leaned on the doorjamb and watched.

Since she was thoroughly absorbed in her task, it took Olivia several seconds to realize she had a visitor. But when she at last noticed him, her face lit up in a delighted smile. Jack couldn't help but smile back.

With more than a little maneuvering, she managed to switch off the machine and snap it into an upright position.

"Jack. Hello." She gestured at the vacuum cleaner, her smile turning proud. "Just cleaning up a little." She blushed charmingly. "It's my first time."

He gave her a questioning look.

"With a vacuum cleaner," she explained. "I found it in the closet. I've never used one before."

He bit the inside of his mouth to keep from chuckling.

"Don't you dare laugh."

"I wasn't."

"Right." She wrinkled her nose at him, then stepped around the vacuum cleaner. "Come on. I'll give you a tour of my new house. It won't take long, I guarantee." She spread her arms. "This is the master bedroom."

He made a great show of looking around. "Very nice."

"I think so. Step this way." She edged around him at the door. He caught the smell of her, just a taunting whiff of soap and sweetness, and she was past him.

"This is the bath." She stood in the tiny hall and pointed at the pink-tiled room.

"The master bath?" he teased.

"The only bath."

He pretended to think deeply. "Very efficient."

"My sentiments exactly. This way to the back bedroom." She turned around and pointed.

He looked in. "Charming."

"Thank you." She gestured some more. "Here's a storage closet, and there are the stairs to the attic. It's a real attic, complete with spiderwebs, a few spare bed frames and a dusty dollhouse."

"Fascinating."

"This house belonged to Delilah's mother."

"I see. Speaking of Delilah," he wryly remarked, "where is she?"

"At work. She's a teacher, you know. And it's a school day."

He was still suspicious. "Then where are the rest of them?"

"The rest of them?"

"The Joneses. I expected to find them all here, helping you to get settled in."

She shrugged and held out her arms to encompass the whole small, neat house. "What's to settle? There's a little bit of dust, but I need the practice wiping it up myself. Otherwise, the place is ready to use."

She went on to explain. "When Delilah and Sam combined their households, they took the best stuff to his house, where they live. Everything else they store here. They let visiting, out-of-town relatives stay here sometimes. Very tidy relatives, from the way the place looks. So there's nothing to do but buy food."

"I see." He was leaning against the doorjamb of the back bedroom now, thinking that he loved to watch her talk, to watch the different expressions flit across her face, to see the way her hands moved when she wanted to punctuate a thought.

"Jack?"

"Yeah?"

"Would you like to go into the living room and sit down?"

The minute the words were out of her mouth, he wondered what the hell was wrong with him. The sight of her pushing that vacuum cleaner had disarmed him. He'd been behaving as if this were a social call.

He straightened from the doorjamb. "No." He made his voice flat. "I brought your things."

She looked away, the movement a transparent masking of her disappointment that he wouldn't stay. When she looked back, she was smiling again. "Of course. I was going to call you about that. Thanks for bringing them."

"It's nothing. I'll get them."

When he returned with the small suitcase, the makeup case and the shoulder purse, she was waiting in the living room.

"You can just put them down there."

He did as she instructed. Then he backed away. It was time to go.

"Listen, Jack..." Nervously she licked her lips.

"Yeah?"

"I do hate to impose on you any more than I already have, but I—"

His heart rose, though he denied the sensation. After all, if she needed something, what else could he do but help? "What? Ask."

"I haven't decided what to do yet about getting a car."

"Yeah?"

"And I wonder—"

"What?"

"I need to shop for food. And from what I understand, the local grocery store is a little limited in what it can provide. Delilah says that for major shopping most people in town drive down to Grass Valley to one of the supermarkets there and—"

"You want me to take you."

"Yes. Would you?"

"When?"

She hesitated. "Well, now would be fine. If you don't have other plans."

"I don't."

"You mean you will?"

"Yeah. Let's go."

"Well, gee." She was all smiles again. "That's great." She pulled off the scarf that held back her hair and tossed it onto a chair. Then she shook her head, so the honey gold curls fell, vibrant and silky, around her shoulders. She grabbed her purse. "Can you wait just a second and let me at least put on some lipstick?"

"You don't need lipstick." He despised the huskiness that he heard in his voice.

She laughed, a light, happy sound that caused a flaring of heat in his belly. "Oh, Jack. Of course I don't need lipstick. Anymore than I need to wear clothes. But I feel a lot better if I have it on."

"Hell."

"Please?"

"Make it quick."

"I will." She started to turn. Then she seemed to remember something. "Oh, one thing."

"What?"

"Let me cook you dinner tonight, since you're doing this for me."

The idea held definite appeal. Too much appeal. "Don't you have to work?"

"No. It's Monday. The Grill and the Hole in the Wall are both closed Mondays."

He said nothing for a moment, thinking that he should say no. Yet he couldn't help imagining the evening he'd have instead—a sandwich at the café and then off to his room and his lumpy bed. Maybe he'd stop in at the grocery store and buy a magazine to read. Or perhaps there'd be an old Western movie on the late show.

"Please, Jack." Her eyes were full of sweet appeal. "Let me do this for you. After all you've done for me."

"All I've done for you?" His voice was harsher than he meant it to be. "I've brought you nothing but grief, and you damn well know it."

She shook her head. Her eyes were shining. "That's not true, Jack. You brought me the most joy I've ever known. You know you did."

Swiftly he turned away. "Go put on your lipstick."

"What about dinner, Jack?"

"All right." He growled the words, still turned away. "Now get a move on."

At the big supermarket on Sutton Way, they filled three carts with staples and produce and all the sundry articles Olivia needed to set up housekeeping. When they reached the check-out line, Olivia flipped out a credit card to pay for everything.

After they'd loaded the groceries into the car and were started on the half-hour drive back to North Magdalene, she gave Jack a sheepish look.

"Today, Eden asked me if I had enough cash."

"Who's Eden?"

"She's my new boss at the Mercantile Grill, remember? Oggie's daughter-in-law."

"Oh. Right." Jack shot her a swift glance and then took his gaze back to the road. "So Eden asked you if you had enough cash?"

"Yes."

"And what did you say?"

"We had a long talk. I explained how I was thinking maybe I should make a totally new start here, that I should refuse to spend any money I hadn't earned from my new job."

"What did Eden say to that?"

"She laughed. She said if I was rich, I should learn to live with it. But on my own terms. She said money was only a tool, anyway.

"She's really something, you know? When she came here a year and a half ago, the Mercantile Grill was nothing but an empty building and the Hole in the Wall was a rundown saloon where brawls broke out every other night. Eden changed all that. She's worked in bars and restaurants since she was in her teens. She really knows her stuff. People come from all over to eat at the Grill, did you know that?"

He grunted, thinking of the good meal he'd had last night. "I can believe it. So what are you telling me? That you were considering throwing all your money away, but now you've changed your mind?"

"Yes. That's exactly it. I'm going to use it frugally. I'll buy only what I need to be comfortable. Soon enough I'll be able to live on what I make at the Grill. And then eventually I plan to use the money I've inherited in places where it's needed. I don't know exactly where, yet. But I will know, when the time comes."

Jack paid strict attention to the road. This sounded a little like what she'd told him yesterday, all that weird talk about "fate" and what was "meant to be." But it also made a strange kind of sense.

And that disturbed him. Because it led to an obvious question. Could it be that his poor little rich girl really was coming to grips with her life, after all?

If that was so, then he was holing up at Swan's Motel amid the plaid and knotty pine for no reason at all, while at home his phone kept ringing with job offers he could ill afford to pass up.

"Jack?"

"What?"

"Are you all right?"

He reminded himself that it was way too soon to know for sure what was going on with her. He needed to keep an eye on her for a while.

"*Jack?*"

"Huh?"

"I asked if you're all right?"

"Me? Yeah. I'm fine. Just fine."

He was amazed at the meal she cooked him. There were little lamb chops that she'd marinated and then charred in

a cast-iron skillet, new potatoes with parsley and bu[
greens that had been steamed in some kind of tart broth,
bread and a salad with more strange types of lettuce i
than he'd ever seen before.

She'd threatened to serve him Brussels sprouts and l
almost believed her when he'd seen her buy them at
supermarket. But in the end she hadn't done it.

Instead, it was all perfection, right down to the can
and the Bordeaux. And yet she made it seem so easy.

As she cooked and served him the meal, he saw a wh
new side of her. In the kitchen she was utterly at home
completely self-assured. Her bags still sat in the living ro
waiting to be unpacked. But all the groceries and cook
utensils she'd bought were put away.

She kept the talk light and companionable. When the
finished eating and were sharing more wine, she explai
all about her new job.

"I'll start out doing mostly prep work," she said, "
that's fine with me. I can chop, slice and dice with the l
of them. But Eden says I can run things Tuesday
Wednesday nights if I work out. And by the time the b
season starts next summer, well, who knows what mi
happen."

"Yeah," he muttered wryly, "who knows?"

"You know Eden's pregnant, don't you?" She laugh
He watched her, thinking that her skin had a soft radia
to it in the light from the candles that flickered betw
them. "I mean, it's pretty hard to miss, if you've seen I
She's due in a few weeks."

He finished off his fourth glass of wine and confes
he'd yet to meet the wondrous Eden.

"Well, you'll know her when you see her. Tall and g
geous, with strawberry hair and a stomach out to here." S
held her hand away from her body to show what she me

"Sounds memorable."

"Oh, she is. She is." Olivia leaned in a little and pitched her voice to a volume suitable for sharing secrets. "But the real story is that Regina's pregnant, too."

"Who's Regina?" Jack helped himself to more wine.

"She's Patrick's wife. Patrick is Oggie's second son. Regina and Patrick have been married about three months and she's only two months along. So they're kind of keeping it just in the family, for now."

Jack sat back in his chair, thinking that the wine and the good food had produced a pleasant glow. He should probably be leaving soon, but he was reluctant to break the mellow mood.

Olivia picked up her wineglass and sipped from it. "So tell me, how are the accommodations at Swan's Motel?"

He gave her a patient look.

"What?" She batted her eyelashes. "Not deluxe?"

"No. Not deluxe." He realized she didn't have his room number. "By the way, I'm in room 203. Just in case."

She repeated it. "Room 203. Thanks." They stared at each other for a few moments. Then he remembered himself and looked away.

Brightly she asked, "You know about Chloe Swan, don't you?"

He glanced at her once more. "Who's Chloe Swan?"

She fiddled with her glass. "She's the town scandal."

"Well fine, but who is she?" He raised his own wineglass to his lips.

"She used to run the motel where you're staying. But now she's going to prison. So her uncle, Chuck Swan, has taken over."

"I've met Chuck. But why is this Chloe Swan going to prison?" Jack drained his wineglass once more.

"Well, Chloe always loved Patrick—you know, Regina's husband, Oggie's middle son?"

"Got it." Jack set down his glass.

Olivia filled Jack's glass for him. "Chloe's very beaut[
I understand. She's got pale blond hair and a terrific fi[
and men really go for her."

Jack remembered the drawing of the come-hither blc
over the couch in the motel office and realized who
probably was.

Olivia was still talking. "But Chloe's always been [
sessed with Patrick. And then, this summer, Patrick mar
Regina. And Chloe went over the edge."

"You mean she went crazy?"

"Exactly. She lost it. Completely." Olivia went on to
a long, involved story that ended with Patrick Jones b[
shot.

When she finished, Jack refilled his wineglass again [
asked, "Is this for real?"

Olivia solemnly crossed her heart. "It's the truth, I sw[
And now Chloe will be doing time. And her poor U[
Chuck has to run the motel, which he's been doing for [
a year, anyway, because Chloe had run off with a stra[
previously and been gone for fourteen months."

"Who told you all this?"

"Eden and Amy, mostly. Amy's Brendan's wife. B[
dan's the one who—"

"I remember who Brendan is."

She chattered on. "And I've talked a lot with Regina [
Delilah, too. Do you know Delilah grew up despising [
brothers and her father?"

"That I can understand."

Olivia clucked her tongue. "Oh come on, the Jones [
are great."

"Right. They're great. Just great." He toasted her [
his wineglass, drank and set it down.

She put her hand over his. "Oh, Jack. You'd like [
Joneses if you gave them half a chance."

Jack watched her mouth move. Suddenly he was having trouble making out her words. Right then all he could think about was the feel of her soft palm on the back of his hand.

Her touch was light. She probably meant it as no more than a companionable gesture.

But for Jack her touch could never be merely companionable. Not when a bolt of heat shot up his arm and his heart started thudding a deep, needful rhythm inside his chest. Not when forbidden memories assailed him, and his defenses were down from too much wine.

''Jack?''

He couldn't speak.

''Jack?''

He wanted her closer.

Slowly he turned his hand over and captured her wrist. He gave a tug.

She rose, pliant and so sweetly willing, and dropped into his lap almost before he realized she was on her way.

The soft weight of her was a miracle. She smelled of wine and coffee and that fresh, indefinable something that was only hers.

''You're so damn cute.'' The mundane words seemed ripped up from the depths of him.

She looked at him, her eyes luminous as the twin candles in the center of the table.

What was it she did to him? It was the strangest thing that had ever happened to him. It was desire, and yet so much more. In her sky-colored eyes he seemed to see a fresh chance. She made the world new again.

It was only a fantasy; he knew it. But when he looked at her it seemed real. With her, somehow, he could almost believe he would find what he was missing.

Even with Sandy Chernak, the policewoman who had loved him and been good to him and whose death had nearly broken him, he'd been more careful, more guarded, mo prisoner inside himself.

But Olivia was different. He had known it from the firs when she'd looked up from that blackjack table and t eyes had met and locked.

Olivia cracked him wide open. She looked right d into his soul.

And he let her do that. He *liked* it when she did that

She lifted her arms and set them on his shoulders. "k me, Jack."

It was agony, this need he had for her.

"Kiss me, please."

With a low, urgent moan he captured her sweet mou

Chapter Thirteen

He was like a starving man.

And Olivia was utterly content to ease his hunger. A joyful groan escaped her. She pressed herself against him, opening her lips for him, so his tongue could enter and have its way with hers. She clutched his shoulders, loving the good, hard feel of them, kissing him back with everything that was in her.

His mouth wandered. He kissed a searing trail down her throat. She held him close.

"Oh, Jack." The words she'd longed to say were on her lips. She let them take form. "I love you so."

And that was when he froze, became a statue in her arms.

"Oh, no. Oh, Jack." She clutched at him, begging him with all of herself not to pull away.

But he only took her hands and held them, craning back from her, staring hard into her eyes. Soon enough, beneath his harsh regard, she stilled. Then, very gently, he lifted her and set her on her feet.

He stood. "Thank you for the dinner. There's no
about it. You can cook."

And then he turned and headed for the door. She wa
him go, out of the kitchen and across the living room
"Jack."

He stopped with his hand on the doorknob, his big
ders held stiffly, as if whatever she might say next
be a knife in the back.

She moved swiftly into the living room, halting just
feet from him.

"I meant what I said, Jack. I love you."

He flinched. "You don't. You're confused."

"No, Jack. I'm not the one who's confused."

He pulled open the door. Outside, the night was co
the sky was full of stars. "Good night, Olivia."

She stood in the doorway and watched him go.

After that, Jack didn't trust himself to get too cl
Olivia. Though he watched over her, as he'd sworn
he also kept his distance.

He heard from Ben Quail that she'd had her
hooked up. Ben's grandson was the technician who'd
the job. He also learned from Sunshine that Olivia w
ing just fine at the Mercantile Grill, catching on quick
already beginning to make useful suggestions.

Sunshine knew all about Olivia's progress in her ne
because Sunshine was Jared Jones's daughter by a pr
marriage, which made Eden Jones her stepmother.
time Jack went to Lily's Café for a meal, Sunshin
ready to make him eat his vegetables and to fill him
how Olivia was faring at the Grill.

Nights generally found him at the Hole in the W
was a good place to keep an eye on Olivia. And wha
was he going to do with himself in a town this size, an
The only real drawback to visiting the Hole in the

was that Oggie Jones hung around there, too. Once or twice, Jack caught Oggie staring at him. It was a watchful look, a waiting look. A look that sent cold fingers of dread slithering up Jack's spine. Jack would turn away.

And when he would glance over again, the old coot would be cackling with his cronies over some traveling salesman joke, paying no attention to Jack at all.

It wasn't a big deal, Jack decided. The old codger could send him all the significant looks he wanted. Jack would simply ignore him.

Beyond ignoring Oggie, Jack monitored his own alcohol consumption. He was careful to nurse one or two beers through the evening. The last thing he needed was to end every night drunk.

As one day faded into another, he found he began honestly looking forward to his evenings at the bar. The people were always friendly. The regulars—like Rocky Collins, Tim Brown and Owen Beardsly—could usually be talked into a game of pool or poker, which Jack sometimes won and sometimes lost. In the end he figured he just about broke even.

Even Jared Jones, who tended the bar most nights, was okay. Once Jack overcame that spooky feeling that he experienced with all the Joneses—that feeling of having known them before—he found he actually liked Jared. There was a sense of inner peace about Jared Jones that Jack couldn't help but respect.

On the bench in front of the grocery store one afternoon, when Jack had been in town almost a week, Ben Quail tried to tell Jack that until Jared Jones married Eden Parker, he'd been the worst brawler and troublemaker of the whole Jones gang, a man with a chip the size of Alaska on his shoulder.

"I don't believe it," Jack said flatly.

"Believe it or not, it's the absolute, unvarnished truth."

Right then, two little boys came running at them from

across the street. Breathless, they asked Jack if he'd b[
few candy bars to help them raise money for their so[
team. Jack forked over ten bucks while Ben looked on
approvingly.

"What're you gonna do with ten candy bars?"
wanted to know.

"It's not your problem. Have an Almond Delight." J
handed the old man one of the candy bars in his lap.

"You're getting a reputation." Ben began peeling off
wrapper.

"As what?"

"An easy mark." Ben took a big bite. False teeth c[
ing, he inquired as he chewed, "How many candy bars
gift subscriptions have you bought in the six days yo[
been here?"

"That's my business." Jack looked up the street, a[
from Ben. Maybe he had bought more from the local [
than he should have. But the little suckers were damned [
to resist. Most of them were polite and enthusiastic. He li[
to see that in kids. He liked to see kids with dreams
shining in their eyes.

"So tell me, Jack. You on vacation, or what?"

"You're a nosy man, Ben."

"Never said I wasn't. And I've been wondering w[
you're doing around here. Not that I don't like your c[
pany. I do. But this isn't tourist season. Don't you ha[
job you should be going to?"

"Yeah. I've got a job. But I've got a...responsibi[
too."

Ben snorted. "We're talking about that new woma[
town, am I right?"

Jack didn't reply.

Ben lifted his stooped shoulders in a shrug. "Hey.
all know she's your woman."

"Who's *we?*"

"The whole town. Get used to it. Around here the word *privacy* doesn't exist. What do you do for a living, anyway, Jack?"

"Is this any of your business?"

"Of course not." Ben grinned broadly, displaying those huge artificial teeth. "But tell me, anyway."

Jack stood. "See you later, Ben."

Ben called after him. "You might as well tell me yourself. I'll only ask around. I'll know by tomorrow, you see if I don't."

Jack avoided the old meddler for two days. But when he sat down beside him the following Monday morning, shortly after breakfast, the first words out of Ben's mouth were, "Well, if it isn't our local private eye."

Jack said nothing, only shook his head.

"Gal, we gotta talk." Leaning on his cane, Oggie stood on Olivia's porch. Behind him on the street, the old Cadillac he drove sat like a galleon at anchor. "Can I come in?"

"Of course."

As Oggie hobbled over the threshold, Olivia ran around the room, grabbing up various articles of clothing that Delilah and Eden had loaned her. Somehow she was always forgetting to hang up her clothes. She was working hard to be a better housekeeper. But Rome wasn't built in a day, after all.

"Have a seat." Her arms full of outerwear, Olivia gestured awkwardly at the couch.

"Don't mind if I do."

Oggie stumped over to the most comfortable chair and dropped into it as Olivia darted to the back bedroom, tossed the sweaters and scarves inside and shut the door.

"Can I get you anything?" Olivia asked politely, when she joined Oggie once more.

"Cup of coffee, four sugars. And an ashtray." waved one of his cigars.

"Fine. I'll be right back." Olivia hurried into the ki poured the coffee, ladled sugar into it and found a c saucer that would have to pass as an ashtray. She q returned to the living room with her offerings.

Oggie was already puffing away. He tossed his ma the makeshift ashtray almost before Olivia could s thing beside him.

She handed him the coffee. "Here you go."

He took it and sipped. "Ah. That's good." He s mug down beside the cracked saucer. "Eden tells me father's coming for a visit."

Olivia smiled. "News travels fast around here."

"That it does, that it does."

Olivia had called her father and invited him and N only that morning, and she'd spoken to Eden just ar before.

"I want to have a special dinner, while my father's I hope you'll come."

"Gal, you couldn't keep me away if you locked the county jail and swallowed the key."

"Good. Then I'll plan on you."

There was a silence. Then Oggie asked, "Now. Yo any clue why I'm here?"

Olivia sighed. "It has something to do with Jack, I ine."

"Damn right. He ain't comin' around, is he?"

She shook her head sadly. "No. He isn't."

"But then again, he ain't left town, either. So t hope."

"I'm glad you think so." Olivia tried not to sou discouraged as she had begun to feel.

Oggie slurped up some coffee and then spoke gently. "He's been avoiding you, ain't he?"

Olivia felt ashamed, as if she was letting everyone down somehow. "Yes."

"You can't let that go on."

She threw up her hands. "What am I supposed to do? I've already been completely shameless. You have no idea."

The old man cackled.

Olivia blushed. From the Jones women, she'd heard a lot about Oggie and the things he'd done in his life. "Okay, maybe you do have an idea."

Oggie did some more cackling. "Maybe I do, maybe I do."

Olivia stared at the old man for a moment, considering. She remembered Delilah's warning, to watch out for Oggie's schemes. But she was starting to feel desperate. She would take any help she could get. She prompted, "Really, Oggie. What should I do?"

Oggie looked pleased. "Well, I am flattered you've asked me. I truly am. Even though if you hadn't, I'd have told you, anyway. But you didn't doubt that, did you?"

"No. Now tell me."

"All right, all right." Oggie sat back. He drank from his coffee and puffed on his cigar. Then he sagely announced, "You need more time with him."

Olivia groaned. "Well, I know that."

"But you ain't makin' it happen, are you?"

"It's pretty hard to spend more time with a man who won't come near me."

"You got to *make* him come near you."

"I know that. But how?"

"Well, let's see." Oggie rubbed his gray-stubbled chin. "What we need to do is to give him a reason to get closer, to be around you more."

"What kind of reason?"

"Maybe something to protect you from."

"But what?"

"Don't rush me, gal. I'm thinkin'. I'm thinkin'...."

The next morning Sunshine was waiting for Jack when he took his seat at the counter at Lily's. There was a worried look on her smooth young face. "Have you heard about the mountain lion?"

"What mountain lion?"

"The one Olivia saw last night."

"When?"

"Near the cabin my father owns."

"Your father is Jared Jones?" Jack was still having trouble keeping all the relationships straight. Everybody seemed to be related to everyone else.

Sunshine looked pained. "Right. Jared Jones is my dad."

"Fine. So Olivia met a mountain lion near the cabin—"

"Where my father and Eden live. Olivia was over there for dinner, since it was the night they all have off. She left late and decided to take a shortcut back to her place. She met the lion on the trail she found that cut across to Main Street."

"She met it? It introduced itself?"

Sunshine rolled her eyes. "You want to hear about this or not?"

"I want to hear."

"Good. Then don't get sarcastic."

"All right. Tell me."

"Fine. She wasn't hurt. The mountain lion only appeared on the path in front of her, growled at her and then walked off into the trees." Sunshine turned and poured Jack a tomato juice, which she then set before him. "Grandpa Oggie doesn't like it. He says the cougars are taking over, now a man can't shoot them anymore." She set out a napkin for Jack and put flatware on top of it. "My father and Sam Fletcher are talking about seeing if they can get a depredation permit so they can track it down and get rid of it. But it'll never happen. Not unless the cougar actually kills somebody's dog or attacks a kid or something.'' She looked up. ''You want the usual, right?''

Jack was already turning for the street.

''Hey, what about your breakfast?'' Sunshine called after him.

He gave her a wave and said nothing. He had more important things to deal with than bacon and eggs.

Since Olivia had been reasonably sure Jack would be paying her a visit, she should have been prepared for the sight of him. But she wasn't.

When she pulled open the door and saw him standing on her porch, her heart seemed to stop for a moment. She had to remind herself to speak.

''Jack! How nice to see you. Come in.''

He stayed where he was. ''I heard about the cougar.''

''You did?''

''Yeah. I don't like it.''

''Yes, it was pretty frightening, but I—''

''When are you getting a car?''

She blinked. This was not how she'd imagined this conversation would go. She did her best to keep up with him. ''A car?''

''Yeah. When are you getting one?''

''Well, as a matter of fact, I'm doing all right without one so far.'' The truth was that as soon as she had a vehicle, she'd no longer have a reason to ask Jack to drive her anywhere.

''You can't go on without a car forever. When will you buy one?''

''Oh, I don't know. My father and Mindy are coming for a visit next weekend. Maybe I'll think about finding a car then. My father said he would help me choose one.''

Jack looked at her measuringly. "So your father
ing, huh?"

"Yes."

"You think you're ready to see him?"

"Yes. I think I am."

He studied her, his midnight eyes unreadable.
good for you," he said at last. There was honest adm
in his voice.

Olivia should have been pleased. But she wasn
heart sank to her toes.

She really was ready to see her father. She'd come
way in a short time. But she sensed that what kept
town was his feeling of responsibility for her. Thu
new proof that she was dealing with her problems
Jack that much closer to deciding she was fully cap
taking care of herself. She knew what would happe
He would walk out of her life forever.

He demanded, "Now, what about the car?"

She tried again. "Jack? Won't you come in?"

"No. Answer me about the car."

She sighed. "Well, as I said, maybe I'll take care
ting transportation when my father comes. He's me
that we could drive down to Auburn together and I
something."

"Good. Do it. Until then, stay out of the wood
until you do get a car, I'll meet you at the Mercanti
after your shift every night, to drive you home."

One of the many bits of advice Oggie had given
that she should put up enough resistance to Jack's pl
he wouldn't become suspicious of a setup. So she
"But I like walking home. It's not very far and I—

"Fine. As long as the weather's good, I'll wa
home."

She allowed herself to smile again. "Well, all rigl
would be very nice."

"And I mean it. Don't go wandering around the woods alone."

"Jack, this is the mountains. There are wild animals in the mountains. That's the way it is." Since there had been no cougar, except in Oggie's imagination, this was easy for her to say.

Jack was not impressed with her fearlessness. "Fine. Stay out of the woods. Do you work tonight?"

"Yes. Every night but Sunday and Monday."

"I'll be there when you get off."

"All right."

He turned to leave.

She remembered another bit of advice from Oggie: "Don't you miss a single opportunity to be near that man, understand?"

"Wait. Jack?"

He faced her again. His expression was not encouraging. "What?"

"I'm sorry to impose on you any more than I already have. I really am. But I'm out of food and I wonder if—"

"No problem. I'll get myself some breakfast and come back for you. About an hour. Good enough?"

"Thanks. But listen. I was just ready to fix my own breakfast and it would be no problem to fix some for you, too."

She knew he was remembering what had happened the last time she'd cooked for him. She could see it in his eyes.

"No, thanks. One hour. Be ready."

"But—"

He turned and ran down the steps away from her so fast that an uninformed observer might have wondered what was chasing him.

Chapter Fourteen

The trip to Grass Valley got Olivia the groceries she needed and that was all.

With Jack she got nowhere. He sat behind the wheel, not speaking unless spoken to, his face a stern mask. He pushed the cart for her in the supermarket, never cracking so much as a smile.

When they drove up in front of her house at a little after one in the afternoon, he helped her lug the bags of food and sundries into the house.

"What time are you off tonight?" he asked when all the bags were inside.

"I'll be through by ten-thirty."

"Fine. I'll be waiting for you."

Before she could even thank him for his help with the groceries, he was out the door.

It was the same that night. He met her as he'd said he would, walked beside her to her house and then stood on the sidewalk and watched to see that she was safely inside.

The next night was no different. Olivia began to wonder if she would ever break through the wall of silence he'd thrown up to keep her at a distance.

On the third night, Thursday, the situation improved a little. But only because a pretty little calico cat that Olivia had recently befriended was waiting on the porch when they arrived.

"What is that?" Jack surprised her by breaking the silence between them. "You've got a cat now?"

She jumped at the chance to exchange a few sentences. "No, not really. She's the neighbors' cat. But she comes over sometimes. Just to visit. She's a very social cat."

He grunted. She could see in his eyes that he was on the verge of leaving again. She cast about frantically for some way to extend this pitiful attempt at conversation.

"I'll bet you're worried about..." She groped for the name of the tomcat he'd once said hung around the apartment where he lived. It came to her. "Buzz. I'll bet you miss Buzz."

He actually chuckled at that, though the sound held no humor. "No, Olivia. I do not miss Buzz. And I'll lay you a dime to a dollar that when I get back, Buzz will be long gone."

"How can you be so sure?"

"Buzz is an alley cat. He's used to taking life as he finds it. He's not one of those domesticated animals who'll hang around, sad and forlorn, waiting for some human to return."

Olivia looked at him through the darkness, wondering if he was talking about more than just a cat. "I don't agree," she said. "I have faith in Buzz."

"You don't even know Buzz." He looked away. "And besides, it's just a cat."

She dared a knowing grin. "I'll bet he's there waiting at your apartment for you to return."

Jack made a low, scoffing sound. "It would be a f
bet. You'd lose."

Her grin widened. "Fifty bucks says he's there
now."

Jack groaned. "And how are you going to prove th

She considered. "I'll ask my father to find out. Will
take my father's word?"

"Olivia, this is stupid. I'm telling you, that cat is
tory."

"Fifty bucks, Jack."

"No."

"See? You know you'll lose."

"What do you mean? I'm saving you money."

"What for? I'm rich, remember?"

"It's a stupid bet."

"Then take it. Make an easy fifty."

"You're asking for it."

"Good." She lifted her chin. "So give it to me."

There was a silence. A lengthy one, while all that
unspoken—and forbidden—arced in the cold night ai
tween them.

"Fine," Jack said at last. "You're on."

"You'll have to tell me your address."

He looked at her suspiciously, but then muttered, "C
pen?"

She dug one out of her purse and gave it to him. He
a business card from his pocket and scribbled on it,
handed the card and the pen to her. At the bottom,
written an address.

Olivia met Jack's eyes once more. "Good. I'll cal
father tomorrow and ask him to check. He'll be her
Saturday. Is that early enough to find out who wins
fifty?"

"How long will your father be staying?"

"Till Monday."

"Then we can settle this harebrained bet Tuesday, when I meet you after work."

"Tuesday it is, then." She stuck out her hand. He hesitated, but at last he reached out and took it. His grip was warm and firm. Longing filled her. He gave her hand one pump and then dropped it.

"Good night, Olivia."

"Good night, Jack."

The next night she told him that she wouldn't be working Saturday.

"Eden's given me the night off, since my father and Mindy will be here. So you won't need to walk me home."

"Fine."

As always, lately, she tried to keep the meager conversation limping along. "I'm looking forward to showing them around."

He grunted. "And introducing them to all the Joneses, too, I'll bet."

She nodded. "That, too. Jack?"

"What?"

"Tomorrow night, I'm cooking a big dinner. For Mindy and my father and Oggie and Delilah and Sam and Delilah's brothers and their wives. It'll be quite a squeeze in my little house. But Delilah's arranged for me to borrow a couple of folding tables and some chairs from the community church. I'm going to seat everyone in the living room and I, well, I'd really like it if you would come, too."

His dark eyes were fathoms deep. And very sad. She knew he wanted to go. And that he wouldn't go.

"No."

"But Jack…"

"Thanks for the invitation. But no." He turned and left her there, by her front walk.

She knew she should call him back and ask him to drive

her to Grass Valley again early tomorrow morning t‹
the food for the dinner that night. After all, she wa›
supposed to waste any opportunity to be near him. B‹
just didn't have the heart to do it, to make him driv
around to get everything for a party he wouldn't be a‹
ing. One of the Joneses would take her or lend her a ve›
All she had to do was ask.

With a dejected little sigh, she headed for her door

Lawrence Larrabee and Mindy Long arrived at e›
Saturday morning, just after Olivia had returned from ‹
Valley with the groceries for that night's feast.

Olivia saw the rental car drive up and jumped fro›
chair at the window where she'd been watching. Sh›
out the door and down the front steps with her arms s›
wide.

Her father emerged from behind the wheel. Olivia
herself against his tall, stooped body. He hugged her
She breathed in the reassuring scents that for her had a›
meant security, the smells of spicy after-shave and woo
the wintergreen mints he favored.

"It's good to see you, Dad," she whispered int
jacket.

"Good to be here, Livvy," he whispered back. "‹
to be here."

After a moment she stepped back and wiped her eyes
the heel of her hand. And then she turned to Mind
another hello hug.

"And what's this?" Olivia asked when she and M›
broke apart. She lifted Mindy's left hand, on which a
gagement diamond gleamed. "It's beautiful." She s›
into Mindy's hazel eyes. "I'm so glad."

"So are we," her father said, and put his arm aroun›
wife-to-be.

"When's the big day?"

"At Christmastime." Mindy smiled fondly up at Lawrence. "Probably during the week before Christmas Day. And then we're flying to Gstaad for an extended stay." Mindy turned to Olivia. "You'll come for the ceremony, won't you?"

"I wouldn't miss it for anything."

"Wonderful."

The two women beamed at each other, then Olivia remembered her manners. "But let's not stand out here all day. Let's get your bags and go on inside."

Olivia turned to the rental car. A long, pitiful wail came at her from the back seat.

She saw the animal carrier and stepped back. "Oh, I don't believe it. You *found* him!"

"Aside from being half-wild, that cat is not a happy traveler," her father remarked rather grimly. "He yowled through the entire flight. We were smart to take the Cessna. We probably would have been thrown off a commercial flight."

Olivia was already yanking the door wide so she could peek inside the carrier and see what Buzz looked like.

A pair of crossed amber eyes stared back at her.

"Hello, Buzz."

The cat made a sound that was not quite a growl, but almost.

"It's so nice to meet you."

The cat made another unfriendly little noise.

"Oh, come on, you're going to love it here."

The cat glared at her and even dared a warning hiss. Olivia shrugged and looked him over.

He was not an impressive sight. His hair was short and mottled gray. There was so little of it on his head that he really did look like someone had given him a flattop haircut. His face was scarred, one side of his mouth cut so he showed the world a grisly grin. One ear was split, no doubt torn in some long-ago fight. He was scrawny to the point of emaciation.

"He's the ugliest damn thing I've ever seen," Lawrence remarked from behind her.

"Shh." Olivia turned and shot her father a chiding frown. "You'll hurt his feelings."

Lawrence grunted. Buzz let out another long yowl.

"Let's get the cat—and everything else—inside, shall we?" Mindy suggested.

Olivia reached for the carrier while her father went around to collect the bags from the trunk.

They left Buzz in the living room, still in the carrier, while Olivia showed her guests the spare room. She didn't miss the glance they exchanged over the narrowness of the twin beds, but nothing was said. She left them to freshen up.

While Mindy and Lawrence took turns in the bathroom, Olivia found the bags of cat supplies they had bought and set about making a place for Buzz on the back service porch. Then she took the carrier out there and opened the door. Buzz pressed himself back into the rear of the carrier and hissed.

"Fine," she told him. "When you're ready, you come on out. But you'll have to stay in the house for a few days, I'm afraid. Until you become acclimated."

The cat glared at her, a silly-looking glare, since his eyes were crossed. Olivia left him there on the service porch, closing the door to the main part of the house to contain him.

Once they were settled in, Olivia led her guests on a tour of the town, which took no time at all, since North Magdalene's population was less than two hundred and fifty, and almost every building of note was on Main Street. They had lunch at Lily's Café after the tour and then went back to the house where Olivia began preparations for the dinner party that night.

All things considered, the party was a great success, though Olivia didn't miss the frantic looks that darted between her father and Mindy when they were first introduced to Oggie Jones. But Olivia had been prepared for that. She kept the champagne flowing.

By the end of the evening, her father and Oggie had discovered their mutual affection for the verses of Robert Service. They took turns reciting *The Cremation of Sam McGee,* toasting each other after every line.

When the party broke up around midnight, Lawrence, who had never been much of a drinker, staggered in and fell across his narrow bed. Mindy helped Olivia to clean up the house.

Once the dishes were put away, Olivia went out to the service porch to check on Buzz. He wasn't there. She had no idea how he might have escaped, but he was not behind the washer or the dryer, and there was no place else in the small space for him to hide. She and Mindy searched the house, to no avail.

Then Olivia went outside and called for a while. But there was no sign of the tom. At last she gave up and went in, feeling terrible and trying not to think about mountain lions and bears, doing her best to reassure herself that he would turn up tomorrow.

The next morning the first thing Olivia did was go outside and call, "Here, kitty, kitty, here Buzz," over and over again.

But if Buzz heard, he chose not to respond. After fifteen minutes of cat calling, she gave up and turned for the house.

She was in the kitchen sipping a solitary cup of coffee, castigating herself for shanghaiing poor Buzz from the alleys he called home and dragging him off to the woods where he didn't know his way around, when the phone rang.

Before she even had time to say hello, Jack's deep voice was grumbling in her ear. "I said your father could check and see if the damn cat was still at my place. I did *not* say he could bring the cat up here."

Warmth flooded through her at the sound of his voice…and at what his words meant. "Oh, Jack. You mean Buzz? Buzz is all right?"

"As all right as a cockeyed cat with a bad attitude can ever be."

"He got away from me last night. I was so worried."

"You can stop worrying. Just come and get him."

She almost agreed, but then reconsidered. "Jack. It's pretty obvious he wants to be with you."

"Great." Jack muttered something low and uncouth.

"Give Chuck Swan a little something extra, and I'm sure he'll let you keep Buzz in your room."

"I don't *want* Buzz in my room."

"Oh, stop fighting it, Jack. Buzz has chosen you. Accept your fate."

"I hate that word."

"I've got a litter box and lots of cat food here, if you want to drop by and pick it up."

"I'm making do."

"Well, it's all here if you want it."

"Thanks."

She sensed he was about to hang up, so she quickly added, "We missed you last night."

"I'll bet."

"Everyone said the food was superb. And the company was…interesting."

"I have no doubts about the food."

"Thank you. Oh, and don't forget. You owe me fifty dollars."

"*Minus* whatever I have to fork over to Chuck to keep a cat in my room."

She pretended to have to think that over. "Well. All right. You can deduct Buzz's expenses, but nothing else."

"I'm so grateful."

"Good."

"You have a nice time with your father," he muttered darkly.

"Thank you. I will."

She heard the click from his end before she could find something else to say to keep him on the line. She sighed. And then she hugged the receiver and stared dreamily out the window over the breakfast table. All right, it hadn't exactly been a tender tête-à-tête, but at least he had called.

About then her father stumbled in wanting to know where she kept the aspirin. She was forced to hang up the phone and hunt down the pain reliever.

Olivia made German pancakes for breakfast. Later she and her guests walked the wooded paths near the house together. They talked of ordinary things. Her father asked her if perhaps she'd like to go shopping for that four-by-four she'd mentioned she needed. Olivia thanked him but refused.

That night she took her guests to dinner at the Mercantile Grill. They complimented the food and the service, and she knew they meant what they said. The Grill was a fine place to eat. Later, back at the house, they played Hearts with a deck of cards that Olivia had found in the hall closet.

Monday it rained. But still Mindy decided to borrow one of the umbrellas Olivia had found in the attic and walk over to Main Street. Olivia and Lawrence were left alone in the house, sitting in the two easy chairs in the living room by the cozy fire in the stove.

Olivia knew what was coming. Mindy had been transparent in her efforts to give father and daughter some time alone.

"What happened to the cat?" her father asked, after a few moments of companionable silence had passed. He was staring at the friendly flames through the little window in the stove.

"He went looking for Jack."

"And found him?"

"Yes."

"Is that good?"

"I think so."

Her father shifted in his chair a little. "Is this serious, then, between you and Roper?"

Olivia spoke with quiet conviction. "Yes, it is. Very serious. It's also momentous, wonderful, scary and sad."

Her father let out a long breath. "Whew. That about says it all."

"Yes."

"You love this man?"

"Yes."

"You know, you never told me you loved Cameron."

Olivia only looked at him and then looked away.

"I didn't fire him," her father said softly.

"You mean Cameron? I'm glad."

"He quit. He said he felt the working conditions would be too difficult, after what had happened. He's found something else already, of course."

"I'm not surprised. He's a great salesman."

Her father took out one of his wintergreen mints, but didn't unwrap it. "Livvy, I..."

Olivia waited, giving him time to frame his words.

"Are you happy, Livvy?"

She thought before answering, taking time to tuck her legs up beside her and lean on the armrest of her chair. "In most everything, yes. This town is just the place for me.

And you know I always wanted to cook for a living. I feel that I'm just where I should be, doing just what I should be doing.''

"But?"

Olivia picked at a worn place on the chair arm and then stopped herself. She decided she didn't want to talk about Jack right then. She said gently, "It's my problem, Dad."

Her father looked out the window. Olivia watched his Adam's apple work as he swallowed. "You were always such a sensitive girl. I wanted to protect you from the world, from all the cruel things out there."

"I know."

"I still want to protect you."

"But you can't."

He hung his head. "I know. At last, I know. I was terrified when you disappeared. It reminded me…"

"Of my mother?"

Her father looked at her. His eyes were haunted. "Yes." Again, as she had a thousand times, she ached for him and the horror he must have known all those years ago, when her mother was kidnapped.

Olivia felt the sting of guilt. "I'm so sorry that I ran off like that, Dad. I can understand what you must have felt. If I had it to do again, I'd do it differently."

He forced a smile. "But if you'd done it differently, would you have ended up here, in this town you say is just the place for you?"

She leaned her head on her hand and felt a musing smile lifting the corners of her mouth. "You know, I believe that I would have. I believe that somehow I would have found my way here. I believe that some things are meant to be."

Her father looked at her and shook his head. "You always were a fanciful girl."

"Hmm. Still fanciful, maybe. But not a girl anymore."

Quietly he said, "Your Jack Roper bears a striking resemblance to most of the members of the Jones family."

She took in a breath and let it out. "You've noticed."

"Has *he* noticed?"

"Not that he's admitted to me."

"Oh, Livvy. I hope you know what you're doing with a man like that."

She reached across and patted his hand. "Dad, it's my life, remember? I get to create my own successes. And make my mistakes for myself."

"I know. I keep telling myself that."

"And I appreciate that you're finally letting me work things out for myself."

"If you need anything, or even if you just want to talk, you know I'm here."

"I know, Dad. And thank you." She watched fondly as he unwrapped the mint he was still holding in his hand.

Lawrence and Mindy left at three Monday afternoon for the forty-five-minute drive to Marysville where Lawrence's plane waited. Olivia hugged them both in turn and then stood on the porch out of the drizzly rain, waving as they drove away.

Her small house seemed very empty after they'd gone. She sat close to the fire and tried to read for a while.

Then she thought of calling Eden, who spent more time at home now that she was so close to her delivery day. Or maybe she could visit Amy or Regina. They'd each be glad to see her. Even Delilah would probably be home from school by now.

But in the end she did what she knew she probably shouldn't do. She put all the cat supplies from the back porch into two plastic bags, grabbed an umbrella and headed for Swan's Motel.

Unfortunately the drizzle had turned to a downpour. And

a wind had come up, so the umbrella didn't do much good. By the time she reached Jack's room, she was as drenched as she'd been the night he'd followed her from Las Vegas and picked her up on that lonely, twisting mountain road.

Since it wasn't serving any purpose, anyway, she collapsed the umbrella and then, bravely, she used the handle to knock on the door.

Jack answered within seconds. Her heart did that silly flip-flop it always performed when she saw him. He was wearing jeans and a blue chambray shirt. His feet were bare and the shirt was unbuttoned. He looked so good, he broke her heart. Behind him she could hear the drone of a TV.

She didn't miss the quick flash of gladness that lit his face nor the way he turned the gladness into a scowl.

"What the hell are you doing here?"

She held up the plastic bags and tried to display a degree of savoir faire, even though her eye makeup was probably running down her cheeks and she knew her hair was plastered to her head. "I brought the cat supplies."

He reached out and dragged her into the room, then shut the door. She was aware of a lot of plaid and pine—pine-paneled walls, a pine dresser, table, chairs and nightstand. From the unmade plaid-covered bed, Buzz granted her a sleepy cross-eyed glance.

Jack strode to the television, which was suspended from the ceiling in the corner by the door to the bathroom. He switched it off. The rain outside was suddenly a low, steady roar.

He turned and confronted her, planting a fist on his hip in a blatant display of male displeasure. "You're soaking wet."

"Very observant," she muttered, and took the few steps to the table, where she set down the bags and the dripping umbrella. She began to peel off her soaked outerwear.

"Don't take those off."

"Why not?"

"You're not staying."

She shrugged and took them off, anyway, pulling a chair over by the ancient-looking wall heater and hanging the wet things there in hopes that, by the time she left, they would be at least somewhat drier. That done, she marched right past him to the bathroom, where she grabbed a towel off the rack and dried her hair a little.

He stood in the doorway, watching her, a muscle in his jaw working furiously. She pretended to be utterly unconcerned, though her heart was racing and her skin felt prickly and warm.

She saw in the bathroom mirror that her eye makeup *was* a mess. She bore a faint resemblance to a waterlogged raccoon. Since there were no tissues that she could see near the cracked sink, she rolled off a few sheets of toilet paper and blotted up the mess around her eyes as best she could.

"Don't ever do this again," he warned, leaning in the doorway and crossing his arms over his beautiful scarred chest.

She locked glances with him in the streaked mirror above the sink. "Do what?"

"Don't come here."

"Why not?"

Suddenly he seemed unable to remain still. He left the doorway, turning for the main room. "Just don't." He muttered the words over his shoulder.

Olivia tossed her smudged makeshift tissues into the open commode and threw the towel she'd used across the sink. She went to the doorway herself and leaned in it.

"I asked you why not?" Her tone was blatantly hostile. He shot her a sharp glance, probably wondering why she was suddenly showing antagonism. She hadn't uttered an angry word around him in two weeks. Since the day he'd found her here in North Magdalene, she'd been all sweetness and light.

But something inside her had cracked. She had come here only to make another gentle, good-natured attempt to get closer to him.

But it just wasn't working. She was tired of answering his surly looks and muttered commands with sweet smiles.

It had finally happened. She was fed up with him. Jack dropped to the end of the bed.

Buzz, jostled, let out a meow of complaint and then yawned hugely, exhibiting a multitude of sharp yellow teeth.

Jack rested his elbows on his knees and looked her up and down. "You didn't get that wet running from your new car to the door of this room. You *walked* over here." It was an accusation.

She refused to be intimidated. "I'll ask you again. Why don't you want me to come here?"

Again, he didn't answer, only fired more questions at her. "What are you doing walking over here in a downpour like this? Where's that new car of yours?"

She bit her tongue and looked away.

"Answer me. Where is it?"

She made herself look back at him, square in the eye. "There is no new car. I didn't buy one."

"You said—"

"I lied."

That gave him pause. He eyed her sideways. "What do you mean, you lied?"

"I mean, I never intended to buy a vehicle this weekend. I never intended to buy a vehicle at all. Not for a while, anyway."

"Why not?"

She let out a little puff of air. "Think about it."

He raked his hair back with a hand. "I don't know what you're talking about."

"Oh, yes you do. You know. We both know. But we're supposed to pretend we *don't* know."

"You're making no sense."

"You say that. But you know it's not true. I'm making perfect sense." She kicked away from the doorway and marched over to him.

Hands on her hips, she glared at him. Then, with a low groan of frustration, she turned away. She went to the window that faced the landing. Lifting the plaid curtain, she looked out through the gray mist and driving rain at the box-shaped building across the way.

She heard him rise, though he made no sound. She felt his approach and the warmth of him so near behind her.

She didn't turn, only continued to look out at the rain. Neither spoke for a time, then she told him, "I can't take much more of this, Jack. It hurts too much. You're going to have to decide whether to stay or to go."

"I have decided." His voice was rough and low. "I'll be going. As soon as I'm sure..."

She dropped the curtain and whirled on him. "Sure of what?"

"That you'll be all right."

"You're telling me that you're still here because you feel responsible for me?"

"Yes."

"Liar."

He flinched, but recovered. One side of his mouth lifted in a threatening sneer. "Watch yourself."

"Liar."

"Don't—"

"Liar."

The third time was the charm. He took her by the arms and hauled her tight against his chest. He looked into her upturned face. "Stop this. Stop it now."

"No."

"Why are you doing this?"

"I love you, Jack."

"Shut up."

"Kiss me." Brazen, shameless as she'd always been with him, she stood on tiptoe, so her mouth was only inches from his. "Kiss me," she whispered, feeling his breath caress her lips. "It's what you want to do. What you always want to do."

"No."

"Liar."

"Shut up."

"Kiss me."

"I ought to..."

"Yes. Yes. Do it. Kiss me now."

Within the sound of the pounding rain and the angry wind, there was a silence, a moment of absolute stillness. Olivia looked into Jack's eyes. She saw the heat there. She felt his heart pounding in time with hers.

His mouth descended those final crucial millimeters. She sighed, a sigh of longing and hope.

But the kiss never happened. Instead he straightened his arms and very gently pushed her away from him. He dropped his arms.

They looked at each other. Outside the rain droned on.

He said, "I'm no good for you. We both know it."

She bit her lip and shook her head.

"I'm a guy who makes his living by keeping on the move. I'm not the right man for you. I'm...I'm useless to you as a partner in life."

"You are so wrong."

"You say that now."

"I'll say it forever if you give me a chance."

"Olivia..."

"I'm tired of playing games with you, Jack. Of going along with you so you won't decide there's nothing more to keep you here. If you're leaving, you're leaving. We can at least have honesty between us when you go.''

''What do you mean?'' His eyes were wary.

''I mean there was no cougar.''

He blinked. ''No cougar?''

''Right. No cougar. No scary animal in the woods at all. Oggie and I cooked that up to get you to come to my rescue, since you were avoiding me completely at the time.'' She sucked in a breath and told the rest. ''And I never planned to get a car until things were worked out between you and me. If I bought a car, then how would I talk you into driving me to Grass Valley to buy groceries?'' Raising her chin, she looked at him as proudly as she could. ''So now you know how I've lied to you just for the chance to be near you.''

''Olivia—''

''I'm not through. I said I lied. And I did. But at least I knew exactly what I was doing. But you're telling the worst kind of lies, Jack. You're lying to yourself. You're here for more reasons than because you feel responsible for me. I know it. Oggie knows it. Everyone in town knows it. Except you, apparently.'' Swiftly she strode to the chair and grabbed her wet things. Then she snatched up the umbrella. ''And I just hope you get honest with yourself before it's too late.''

With that she turned for the door, flung it wide and walked out into the storm.

She didn't get far. Jack caught up with her in his car just as she reached the turn from Pine Street to Rambling Lane. He rolled up beside her, leaned across to the passenger door and pushed it open.

She stopped, turned and looked at him as the rain poured down on her and the wind whipped at her clothing. Here she was, all over again, being rescued from a rainstorm by Jack.

"Get in."

She slid into the seat and pulled the door closed. He turned from the curb and drove straight to her house. As soon as the car stopped, she leaned on her door. But he reached across and held her there.

She looked straight ahead. "What is it, Jack?"

He said nothing.

She faced him. "You don't know what to say, do you? Because there's nothing to say. Until you make up your mind."

"I have made up my mind."

This was the same impasse they'd reached in his room. She'd had enough of it. "Let me go, Jack."

He released her. She slid from the car, ran up the steps and into the house.

Chapter Fifteen

Jack drove back to his room knowing the time had come to leave. As Olivia had so forthrightly confessed, there was no cougar and she could buy a vehicle anytime she wanted one.

And there was more. He'd seen it in the proud, high set to her shoulders, in the uncompromising glint in her eye. Somehow, during the brief time she had been in this small mountain town, Olivia had come into her own as a grown woman at last.

"R-rrreow?" Buzz was waiting by the door when Jack let himself into the room.

Jack shrugged out of his jacket. Then he bent and picked up the cat. As he idly rubbed Buzz's stubby head, he noticed that the message light on the phone was blinking.

The call was from a lawyer friend, Del Goldwaite.

"He wants you to call him back as soon as you can," Chuck said when Jack checked for the message. "He'll be at his office if it's before six. After that you should call him at his house.''

It was quarter of six, so Jack tried the law firm where Del was a partner. The receptionist put him on hold and then came back to say Del was on another line and would call him back in five minutes.

Jack waited ten minutes and then the phone rang.

''Roper here.''

''Jack, old buddy.''

''Del. What's the deal?''

''It's like this. A client of mine called me. His wife's run off, cleaned out their joint bank accounts and disappeared with her hairdresser—or so the client thinks, anyway. The man is out of his mind. He has reason to believe the woman's in Mexico, and he wants to hire a man to go down there and find her. He wants the best. I said I'd do what I could and I thought of you.''

''Okay.''

''But there's a glitch.''

''Yeah?''

''Since I couldn't reach you right away, the man's found someone else. I just got off the phone with him. I was pitching you like crazy. So now he says he'd like to talk to you before making a final decision. How soon can you get here?''

Jack considered. The job itself didn't thrill him, doing the footwork for a jilted husband who probably had revenge on his mind.

''Jack? You with me there?''

''What kind of money are we talking about, Del?''

Del told him.

Jack whistled under his breath and then did some fast calculating. Money like that could put him back in the black. He had to get real here. He'd just given himself what amounted to an extended vacation, looking out for a woman who didn't need looking out for anymore—if she ever really had. It was past time to get back to the real world.

"Jack? How long until you can get here?" Del was starting to sound impatient.

"Assuming I can get a flight right away, maybe three or four hours."

"Where are you, Jack?"

"Northern California. About eighty miles northeast of Sacramento."

"No." Jack knew his friend was shaking his head. "It won't work. I was thinking an hour, two, max. The man is angry. He wants action now. He won't wait, even for the best."

"But Del—"

"Look. Sorry. It's a no-go. But maybe in a few days, if the competition doesn't deliver. In the meantime, get back here to the city, so I can pull you out of a hat at the crucial moment. Understand?"

Jack understood. "Yeah. I'll be back in town by tomorrow."

"That should do it. Don't let any moss grow on it."

"I hear you. See you then." Jack hung up.

"R-r-reow?" Buzz, who'd made himself comfortable in an easy chair, paused in the bath he was giving himself to look up at Jack with cross-eyed curiosity.

Jack made his decision. Whatever had kept him hanging on here wasn't going to keep him any longer. If he didn't get back soon, he'd have no business left when he returned.

"The time has come, Buzz, my man. We're heading out."

Buzz appeared unconcerned by the news.

Jack suddenly felt charged with nervous energy. He began pacing up and down on the strip of carpet at the foot of the bed. He rubbed the back of his neck.

He had to talk to Olivia, to say goodbye. And then that was it. He was out of here.

"You're leaving," she said softly, when she opened her door and looked in his eyes.

He nodded, tipping his collar up. It was growing colder now that night was approaching. The rain had eased off. It was a steady drizzle again. It dripped from the eaves of the porch all around him.

She stepped back a little. He could feel the warm air from the fire behind her. It looked cozy in there. "Will you come in?"

"No." He held out his hand. "Here."

She took what he offered, a fifty-dollar bill.

"I didn't forget," he said, shoving his hands back into his pockets for warmth.

She set the bill on the little table by the door, then came outside, pulling the door shut behind her. She wrapped her arms around herself to keep warmer and huddled with her back against the door. "I didn't care about the bet." She looked away, as if collecting herself, and then she faced him again. "The money never mattered, Jack."

"It isn't the money."

He watched her eyes fill. They glittered like sapphires in the fading light of day. "I guess I know that." She bit the inside of her lip. He could see she was willing the tears back.

"Olivia, I..." He didn't quite know how to continue.

"What? Say it. What?"

He took in a breath, which came out as mist when he spoke. "I know this is for the best."

She looked down at her shoes. "Oh, great. That's great to hear. I'll get a lot of comfort from that—and so will you."

He ached for her, so much that he forgot himself for a

moment. He pulled his hand from his pocket and reached out. "Olivia—"

She batted his hand away. "No."

He stepped back, shoved his hands in his pockets again, looked down at the porch boards, over at the rain dripping from the eaves. Anywhere. Anywhere at all but at her stricken face.

He tried to think of the right thing to say. But all that came out was, "In a few months, you'll forget all about me."

She let out a tight little sound. He made himself look at her. Her eyes were still glittering, but with anger now, not tears.

"You're a fool, Jack Roper. A cross-eyed tomcat has more sense than you. A scrawny old alley cat knows enough to take his chance when it comes to him."

"I'm not Buzz, Olivia." He spoke quietly, feeling proud of how reasonable he sounded. "Buzz is a cat."

"Right." She looked away again. "Right. Sure." And then her eyes were pinning him. "You're not a cat. You're a man. And that gives you an excuse to let what happened to you when you were just a boy ruin your chances of ever finding love."

He felt his whole body stiffen, as something like panic stabbed through his outer calm. "I don't know what you're talking about."

"Oh, yes you do." She glared at him. She was shivering from the cold. "You know. You know very well."

"Look—"

"No, *you* look. I love you. With all my heart. And I honestly believe that you love me. But I've done all I can to get you to see what we could have together. There's nothing more I can do without your meeting me halfway. I only hope you wise up and change your mind about this before I get tired of waiting for you."

"Olivia—"

"Goodbye, Jack."

She turned, pushed open the door and went back inside, closing it firmly in his face.

There was nothing more to do. Jack knew it. He returned to his room to gather up his few belongings.

The phone rang just as he finished packing.

Olivia, he thought, despising himself for the way his heart was suddenly racing and his chest felt tight.

He reached over and picked up the receiver on the second ring. "Roper here."

"So, you're leavin' town, eh?"

Jack knew the voice. Oggie Jones. Dread curled like a small, cold snake in his stomach, though why that should be, Jack swore he didn't know.

"Hey. You there?"

Jack made himself speak. "I'm here. And yeah, I'm leaving town."

"Then listen. The Hole in the Wall's closed today. But Eden's got the boys running in and out all the time, polishing bottles and checking stock. By midnight, though, the place'll be completely deserted. Meet me there then. Go in the back way. I'll leave it open for you."

"Look, there's no reason for—"

The old man grunted. "You're outta time, boy. You put me off until the end. And this is it. You ain't gettin' away from me without hearin' the things I intend to say. Midnight. Be there."

"Listen, old man—"

But Oggie had already hung up.

Jack hung up his end, swearing to himself that he wasn't putting off leaving, not for anybody, and especially not for some crazy old coot like Oggie Jones.

"Damned old fool," he muttered to himself.

Buzz, from a nest of covers he'd made on one side of the bed, lifted his head and blinked at Jack.

Jack saw the cat staring at him.

"We're leaving. Now," he said.

Buzz yawned. The animal looked way too knowing for a cat whose eyes didn't even focus right.

"I'm not meeting that crazy old man. That's all there is to it."

Buzz said nothing, only continued to regard his master with that irritating cockeyed stare.

Chapter Sixteen

By midnight the rain had stopped.

The back door to the Hole in the Wall was unlatched, just as the old man had promised.

Jack went in and tugged the door shut behind him. He found himself in a dim hallway, which was lit with one meager fixture halfway down toward the main part of the tavern. Jack started walking.

When the hall opened up into the main room and he was a few feet from the bar, he could see the light coming through the curtains to the back room. He went through the curtains and there was Oggie, in the same chair he'd been sitting in that first day, when Jack came looking for Brendan Jones. The old man was reading the local newspaper. The smoke from his cigar curled up toward the hooded fixture over his head.

Oggie looked over the top of the paper. Jack met his eyes. Slowly Oggie folded the paper and dropped it beside his chair. Then, his cigar in the corner of his mouth, he put his hands over his belly and stared at Jack long and hard. Jack stared back, thinking that the old rogue looked a thousand years old, his eyes red and watery, smoke swirling around him, the light from above casting every wrinkle on his face into road map relief.

Jack waited what seemed like forever for Oggie Jones to speak. When Oggie remained silent, Jack prompted coldly, "Okay, I'm here. Whatever it is, say it now."

Oggie coughed, then puffed on his cigar some more. At last he suggested, "Have a seat."

"I'll stand. Talk."

Oggie fiddled with his suspenders. He studied the glass ashtray on the green felt cloth that covered the table. Finally he said, "I got a story to tell you."

"A story about what?"

"About a cardsharp named Oggie Jones." Oggie reached out and idly spun the ashtray. "And about the cardsharp's lady, Alana Dukes."

The sound of his mother's maiden name on the old man's lips hit Jack like a freezing wind. He wanted to turn and run back out the way he had come.

But he didn't. What point was there in that now? He'd heard just enough that he wasn't going to be able to hide from the truth anymore. He might as well hear the rest.

"You sure you won't sit down?" The rough voice actually held a note of concern.

Jack decided maybe the suggestion was a good one, after all. He yanked out a seat and dropped into it. "All right. I'm listening."

Oggie moved in his chair, settling in, getting as comfortable as his old bones would allow him to be. He crossed his legs, then uncrossed them, grimacing a little with the effort.

Jack waited, uncomplaining. He was feeling a little numb,

suddenly. A little sick. And whether the old man told the story fast or slow didn't matter much, anyway.

Oggie sat back with a long exhalation of breath. "I met Alana in Saint Louis at a little place called the Red Garter. It was after the second great war. The country was prospering."

The old man scratched the side of his face, his black eyes narrowing. "It wasn't love. Back then, I didn't believe there was such a thing as love. But it was close to love. As close as a drifter like me had ever come to it, anyway. We respected each other, Alana and me. And we suited each other, too."

The old man tipped his head and stared at the ceiling, pensively rubbing his chin, as if he saw the face of Alana Dukes up there in the shadows and smoke. "Ah, she was a beauty, white-blond hair and big green eyes. Kept the suckers goin', she did, smilin' and flirtin', while I raked in the winnings. We were a hell of a team." Oggie shook his head, bent forward with a grunt and stubbed out his cigar in the ashtray. Then he was looking straight ahead again, though his eyes were still decades away.

"We lasted five years together, Alana and me. We prospered like this great land. A pair of entrepreneurs, that's how we thought of ourselves, doin' well off the extra cash in other people's pockets. Movin' West, we were. Carryin' our nest egg in one of Alana's nylon stockings.

"But then we hit Bakersfield." The old man took a minute for the ritual of lighting a fresh cigar, spitting the end on the floor and putting the match to it, puffing until it glowed red.

"And?" It was Jack's voice, though it sounded so ragged he hardly recognized it as his own.

Oggie examined the red coal at the end of his new cigar. "And Alana fell in love with another man. It happened overnight. One night she was sleepin' with me, like always.

And the next night she was gone. She'd met him because she loved apricots, she told me. She'd stopped at this little roadside stand—*his* roadside stand, it turned out, to buy some apricots. And there he was. A farmer. John Roper. A real upstandin' guy, John Roper was. He claimed he was willin' to forgive Alana's checkered past as long as she married him and put her wild life behind her for good.'' Oggie cleared his throat. ''She came to me and told me she was leavin'.''

''What did you do?''

''What the hell could I do? It was her life. I wished her well. We split the nest egg. Then I went out and got good and drunk and gambled my half of our savings away in one night.'' The gnarled hand tapped the cigar on the edge of the ashtray. Jack watched the cinders drop. ''I was sulkin', see? But hell. I could see she'd found her man. I'd thought we had it good together, but after seeing the look in her eyes when she talked about Roper, I realized I didn't have a clue what *good* was. And eventually I had to admit to myself that things had been fadin' between the two of us for a while anyway.''

''And then?''

Oggie's shrug said it all.

''You left.''

''You bet. I went on my way, with nothin' in my pockets and no prospects to speak of. I came here, to North Magdalene. And I met Bathsheba.'' At the mention of the strange, biblical name, the old man's face changed. It seemed to glow from within. ''We married within a month of our meeting, and had a son within the year.''

''Jared.''

''Yeah.'' The old man's eyes were on Jack. They burned right through him. ''I thought,'' Oggie said quietly, ''that Jared was my firstborn. But now—''

It was enough. Jack's chest felt so tight he could hardly draw breath. "Look. I get the point."

"Do you?"

"Yeah."

Gently Oggie said, "I didn't know you existed, son."

Jack looked away, then made himself look into those wise eyes once more. "I understand. And it doesn't matter."

"That ain't true."

"Yes, it is. You didn't know about me. It wasn't your fault. It just happened."

"Naw, it didn't. Didn't your mother ever—"

Jack cut him off. "Look. It was like you said. She loved John Roper. She wanted to believe I was his. She swore I was his."

"But you weren't. And John Roper knew it, too, didn't he?"

"I think so. I don't know. And what's the point in speculating? I'm a grown man now. This is ancient history."

"No, son. You live it now. You live it every day of your life."

"No."

"Yes." Oggie waved a hand. His eyes were like broken shards of black glass. He went on, his sandpaper voice growing urgent. "It *is* important. It's made you what you are today. When John Roper realized you weren't his blood son, he turned away from you. He was your dad, and he turned away. That's what happened, ain't it? He turned away from you *and* your mama. And your mama blamed you, didn't she? Your mama never loved you right, either, because she couldn't forgive you for being born and losing her the man she loved. You grew up belonging nowhere, claimed by no one."

"Stop." Jack squeezed the word out past the knot in his throat. He sucked in air. "I already said it doesn't matter."

The old man was relentless. "Yeah, it does. A man needs

to know his people—and his place. Or else he wanders. He lives outside the circle of life. He can't give himself to anything. A place. A woman. The raising of a child.''

"No.''

Oggie went on as if Jack hadn't spoken. ''But now, I'm here to tell you I know you're mine. And I do claim you, son. Hell, I woulda claimed you way back then if I'da known.''

It was too much. Jack stood, shoving his chair away so violently that it hit the curtain and fell on its side behind him. ''I said stop this.'' He leaned across the table. ''Let it be, you crazy old fool.''

"No.'' Oggie looked up at Jack, unflinching. His rheumy gaze was so intense it raised the short hairs on the back of Jack's neck. He calmly explained, ''A Jones don't never stop. And I'm a Jones. Just like you're a Jones, no matter what damn name you go by.''

"No."

"Yeah.'' Oggie pushed himself painfully to his feet, his knotted knuckles white on the green tablecloth. ''You're mine.'' He craned toward Jack so that not more than a foot of charged air separated the two of them. ''I knew you were mine the minute I set my eyes on you that day you came lookin' for that lost woman of yours. *Mine,* Jack Roper. One of my kids. As much a part of me as Jared or Patrick, Delilah or Brendan.''

Jack hit the table with his fist and spoke through teeth so tightly clenched that they ached. ''I don't even *know* you, old man.''

"You will, if you just let yourself.''

"No.''

"Yes.''

Jack swore, a short, dark oath. He turned. And then, kicking aside the chair that lay across his path, he shoved through the curtain and got the hell out of there.

"Run if you want!" The old man called after him. "But you'll never get away. A man is what he is, and he never finds peace until he looks in the mirror and understands what he sees. Son! Son, you listen to me!"

Once he reached the back parking lot, Jack leaned against the old Cadillac that belonged to Oggie and gulped in air like a man just saved from drowning. When at last he began to believe that maybe his rubbery legs would hold him upright, he straightened. Then he headed for Swan's Motel.

But his feet didn't take him there. Instead they turned on Pine Street and then again on Rambling Lane. He broke into a run. He pounded up the long, twisting street toward the little white house with the green trim. He was breathing hard when he mounted the porch.

The light was off. The house was dark. He imagined she was sleeping. He had no right to hope she would welcome him. But right then his need was so great that he knocked anyway.

The porch light came on, blinding him in a cold spill of brightness. He felt naked. And then she peeked through the curtain of the window beside the door.

Her sweet face was pale, scrubbed clean of makeup. They stared at each other. He knew he should turn and leave. He prayed she'd let him in.

She dropped the curtain. Then he heard the lock being turned. She pulled the door open and stepped back.

He went in.

She closed the door behind him and turned to face him, clutching her robe at the neck. "You talked to Oggie."

He stared at her, then accused, "You know."

She nodded. "Oggie made me promise not to tell you. He said you didn't want to know."

Jack heard a laugh. It came from his own mouth. It sounded a lot like a groan. "He was right. But deep down,

I *did* know. I think I knew the minute I saw him, that
day I came looking for you. But I could pretend I d
know. As long as no one told it straight-out to my fac
long as no one mentioned names. Places. Details. Bu
old bastard just couldn't let it be.''

"Oh, Jack." Her eyes were full of love. Of unders
ing. He hated her right then, almost as much as he ye
for her. "He wants another chance," she said. "He
to be your father."

"Damn it, Olivia. I'm forty-one years old. I am w
am. It's a little late now."

"No, Jack. It's not. It's never too late."

"Yeah, it is. Knowing the truth doesn't change who
It just makes it all…sadder, more pathetic, somehow.'

"Only because you let it be that way."

"You're a damn dreamer. You always did live in a
tasy world."

"No, Jack. I don't live in a fantasy world. Not anyr
I live in the real world, a world I'm creating. Day by d

Her pretty chin was held high, her blue eyes shone
wanted to grab her and shake her until she admitted he
right, that her head was full of pointless fantasies, w
she insisted on calling dreams.

He also wanted her to reach out her hand and pull
out of the darkness in which he suffered and into the
that seemed to glow all around her.

He knew that neither of those two things would hap
He knew that there was a hard shell around his heart. C
was the only one who'd seen through the shell, down
the depths of him. But she couldn't break the shell. No
could do that. It was too much a part of him.

She asked the question. "Why are you here, Jack?"

He gave her the brutal truth. "Because I want you
always want you. And I couldn't stay away. Not ton
not after listening to all those things I never wanted to

But I'm leaving at daylight, just as I planned." He looked at her, at all of her, from the tangle of sleep-mussed gold curls to the bare pink toes that peeked out beneath her robe. He said roughly, "I want to be inside you. One more time."

Three steps separated them. She bridged them without seeming to move.

"All right." Her little chin was still high. But her tender mouth quivered. Two bright spots of color stained her cheeks.

Shame flooded through him, tempering his anger, his pain...and his desire. He hung his head. "Get smart. Don't let me use you. Send me away."

"Shh. I love you."

The words pierced him. He hadn't known how he had wanted to hear them until she had uttered them.

"Say it again." His voice was like the sound of something tearing.

"I love you."

"Again."

"I love you, love you, love you..."

Her soft hand framed the side of his face. She came up on tiptoe and pressed her lips to his. His mouth burned at the contact. His body was on fire with need of her. Yet he forced his hands to stay at his sides. He let her do the kissing.

She did a damn fine job of it, too. She nibbled and tasted, licked and caressed. Her scent, that scent of flowers and freshness, swam all around him. He was hard, achingly hard. He could feel his manhood, pushing at the placket of his jeans, wanting to be out and inside of her, where it was safe and warm, where heaven was.

With a groan, though he kept his hands to himself, he pressed his hips against her. She sighed and pressed back. He thought he would die—and be happy to go.

Still kissing him, cradling his face in her tender hands,

she lifted her hips and rubbed boldly against the ridge of him. He groaned again.

She stepped back then.

Stunned, starved for her, he opened his eyes. If she refused him now—

But she wasn't refusing him. "Take off your jacket."

He did as she asked, tossing it across a chair.

She was holding out her hand. "Come on. Let's go to bed." When they reached the bedroom, Olivia let go of Jack's hand. Then she crossed the room and turned on the little lamp on the nightstand.

She was very frightened. But absolutely sure that she was doing the right thing. She loved this man. And if tonight was the last one they'd have together, it was better than no last night at all.

She had condoms, which she removed from the drawer in the stand and set beside the lamp. A wave a sadness washed over her, as she thought of how she had bought them two weeks ago, so certain that she and Jack would work out their problems soon, wanting to be prepared when their moment of tender reunion came.

Well, she was prepared, all right. But the reunion, it seemed, would never be. This was more in the nature of an intimate farewell.

She knew he was looking at the condoms, and she gave a little shrug. "Okay, I admit it. I want you, too." She forced a smile. "I always will. And this is a better way to end it than me calling you a fool and closing the door in your face, don't you think?"

From the shadows she could feel his eyes caressing her with heat and hunger. "Yeah. Take off the robe."

Her body responded instantly to his command. She felt her nipples grow to hard little nubs. Down there, the luxurious heaviness, the warmth and the wetness had begun.

"Take it off."

She bit her lip. The robe was of thick, pink chenille, hardly the type of thing one wore when one planned a seduction. Regina had given it to her. And Jack wanted her to take it off.

She did, not daring to look at him across the room. She paid great attention to her task as she untied the belt and dropped it to the ground. Then, one shoulder at a time, she shrugged out of the sleeves. It dropped in a pink pile at her feet. She looked down at it, as if wondering how it got there.

Now she wore only a pink flannel nightgown, which was also a hand-me-down from Regina.

"Come here." Jack's voice was gruff.

She looked up then, into his eyes. And she was captured. She couldn't look away. Slowly, like a sleepwalker, she approached him. And when she stood right before him, he reached out, cupped her face and brought her mouth to his.

The kiss was hot and consuming, as purely carnal a caress as she had ever known. His tongue swept her mouth, claiming it, leaving no room for anything there but the taste, the feel, the reality of him.

His hands slid down her neck, out over her shoulders, rubbing, pressing. And then, swift and knowing, they were at her hips, bunching her modest nightgown, sliding it up her legs and holding it at her waist.

She wore no panties. From the waist down, she was bare. He touched her, touched the womanly heart of her, as he went on kissing her in that total, consuming way. He felt her wetness, her readiness, and he groaned into her mouth.

She might have been embarrassed. But there was no space, no time, for such a trifling emotion. His need was on him, and she was ready for him.

His mouth still locked with hers, he took her shoulders and slowly, inexorably, pushed her back, toward the bed and the nightstand and the pool of light the lamp made in the night-dark room. When they reached the bed, his hands left her, though his mouth went on tormenting hers. He fumbled with his jeans, ripping them open, shoving them out of the way, surging against her, so she felt his hardness touch her belly through the fleecy fabric of her gown.

He fumbled on the table, still kissing her, seeming to drink her very being from her mouth. He found one of the condoms and tore it open, tossing the little foil package away. He slid the condom in place.

"Now," he said into her mouth. "Inside you. Now."

He took the gown and gathered it up, out of his way. Then he pushed her down, back across the bed, mouth still locked with hers. He nudged her legs apart and positioned himself between them.

And then, in one long, deep stroke, he was inside.

Her body opened to him easily. It was so good to feel herself expanding to take him, to have him inside, to hold him there, for as long as he would stay.

Until daylight.

Not long enough. But better than not at all.

He sighed, a sigh of relief that seemed to border on pain. The sigh trailed across her cheek as he released her mouth and buried his head in the curve of her shoulder.

"No one like you. Ever."

She whispered, "Please…"

He vowed, "Soon. Soon."

And yet he didn't move.

And suddenly it didn't matter. Because her completion happened, anyway, so suddenly it was as if it spun into being out of nothingness. Olivia cried aloud, pressing herself up, feeling the sparks inside, like stars bursting, sending light flooding out to every limb. He stiffened, pressing into her so hard and deep. She knew he'd reached his release as well. Their bodies moved apart, limp. They both were breathing hard.

But then, all at once, he was kissing her again in the soft

hollow of her throat. And down over her breasts, her belly. Into the bronze nest of curls. He parted her and tasted her.

She moaned. She clutched his head. He looked up, his face cruel, ruthless with desire.

"I must remember."

"Never forget."

Until daylight.

She encircled him with her hand. He threw his head back, sent a feral cry to heaven. She stroked, faster and faster. He spilled, hot and quick, across her hand.

They rested.

And it started again.

She dared to recall her vain hope from their night in Las Vegas. Maybe she would win out over time at last. Maybe daylight would never come. Maybe they could go on forever, in the velvet heart of midnight. Rising and falling. Resting. Then reaching out once again.

He filled her, a long, gentle slide inside. He moved slowly within her. She thought of the movements of the sea, far from shore, an extended, heaving rise and fall. When fulfillment came it was like an expansion, like something that grew and increased until she could no longer contain it. It overflowed the frail vessel of her body and set the night afire in a river of flame.

Later she lay tucked against him. His leg between hers, his arms tight around her. He reached down and found the covers, pulled them up.

"Jack?"

"Shh. Rest now."

"One thing."

"Shh."

"Don't leave me when I'm asleep. Promise."

"I promise."

"You'll wake me?"

"I will." He tucked the covers around them.

"It's late," she said.

He gave her the answer. "So late, it's practically early."

They both closed their eyes. Sleep embraced them as one.

They were together.

Until dawn.

But in the back room of the Hole in the Wall, Oggie sat alone. He knew he should go home to his warm bed at his daughter's house. But he hadn't the energy.

He was tired. The plans and schemes that usually filled his mind were gone. For the first time, besides being old, he felt old.

His eyes drifted closed.

A sad dream engulfed him. Slowly one lone tear slid over the wrinkles on his cheek and plopped onto his gnarled hands.

His dream turned cruel. He shuddered, and his lighted cigar dropped from his lips onto the folded newspaper that lay on the old plank floor.

For a while the coal at the end of the cigar only smoldered, slowly scorching a black hole in the center of the front page. But then a tiny tongue of fire rose up. It flickered, died, then rose again.

Soon enough it danced up strong and then forked out, to claim the shadows and snake in blazing ribbons along the tinder-dry floor. By the time the old man coughed and looked up, the curtain to the main room was a wall of flame.

Chapter Seventeen

Olivia heard the church bell clanging madly. The long wail of a siren joined in.

"What?" She woke fully. Jack was already rolling from the bed. "What is it?"

He shoved his feet into his jeans, pulled them up, buttoned them. "I don't know. A fire, maybe. Or an accident." He sat down and yanked on his socks and boots.

Olivia threw back the covers.

"Stay here. I'll see what it is," Jack urged.

"No way." She grabbed for a pair of jeans of her own, as well as a sweater, shimmying into them swiftly, then reaching for a pair of socks.

He was already dressed, anxious to be gone.

"Just a minute more," she told him as she found her socks and shoes. She jerked them on, fast as she could, then stood. "Okay. Let's go."

She grabbed a heavy cardigan off the coatrack in the hall.

Jack took his jacket from the chair in the front room. They ran out into the night, where the church bell clanged louder and another siren had joined the first one.

Jack pointed. "Look. See the smoke. It looks like a fire. Probably on Main Street."

She glanced around for his car.

He seemed to know her thoughts. "I didn't bring it. Come on. If you're coming, let's run for it."

He held out his hand. She put hers inside it. They ran, the night air cold in their lungs, their breath emerging as fog into the darkness.

Each house they passed had a light on inside. People stood on their porches. And some ran, with them, toward Main Street. They turned onto Pine, Jack ahead, towing Olivia along. She had a stitch in her side and nursed it. But she did her best to keep up. She wanted to see what had happened, to help if she could.

They reached Main Street.

They saw the source of all the furor at the same time.

"My God! The Hole in the Wall."

There were fire trucks, with the big canvas hoses already unrolled. There were four-by-fours with racks of red-and-blue lights on top. And there were people everywhere.

Olivia forgot the stitch in her side. She ran with Jack to the section of street right in front of the bar.

There, the night was bright as day. The heat from the flames pushed back the autumn coolness. The faces all around were lit with eerie reflected light, the expressions stunned and awed. Above, a forest service helicopter circled, blades beating.

"I'll see if I can help." Jack left her, making his way over to where the volunteer fire crew, which included the Jones men, held the hoses and aimed them through the broken windows. The hoses spewed fat shafts of water. The water sizzled as it hit the flames. But the fire was well along, and the Hole in the Wall was aged, dry wood. They were trying for containment. Even Olivia could see that.

"It's spread to the Mercantile, look there," someone said.

Olivia looked and saw the garish light inside the brick building that meant there were flames inside of it, too.

"Must have gone through that center hall," someone else said.

"Please. Keep back." It was Eden's voice. Olivia looked and saw her, her bathrobe barely meeting around her huge stomach. "Keep back. Don't worry. It's only a building. We have insurance, after all."

"There's no one inside, then?" Nellie Anderson, who practically ran the community church, wanted to know.

"No one. They all went home hours ago," Eden soothed.

"Thank the Lord." Linda Lou Beardsly, Nellie's friend, clasped her hands together and tipped her head toward the sky.

But then Delilah ran up, her black hair loose and flying. "Have you seen my father? Has anyone seen my father? He's not in his bed. I can't find my—"

Olivia knew, with a sudden sick lurch in the pit of her stomach, where the old man must be. After all, he and Jack had met only hours before. The Hole in the Wall would have been the perfect place that time of night for a man to tell the hardest truths to his son. Quiet. Deserted. A place where no one else would hear the things they said.

"Oh, no…" The words escaped her lips as she turned to look for Jack. He stood by the other men. And he had heard Delilah's cries.

Jack saw Olivia. Their eyes locked. And she knew what he was going to do.

He spoke to Jared. Jared shook his head. But Jack grabbed the other man and muttered something low and intense, as he pointed toward the place where Eden stood. Olivia knew the gist of what Jack was saying.

You've got a wife and baby. You can't risk it. But I've got nobody. I'm going in....

Right then, Delilah grabbed Olivia's arm. "Olivia. Have you seen him? My father, do you know where he is?"

But Olivia didn't answer. She was watching Jack and Jared. She saw Jared nod. Jared picked up a bucket that stood near his feet and doused Jack with its contents. Then he shrugged out of his heavy fire-resistant jacket and handed it over. Jack slipped it on. Jared set his hard hat on Jack's head.

"No! Jack, no!" Olivia yanked her arm from Delilah's grasp and shoved her way through the crowd.

But she wasn't fast enough. Jack was already disappearing into the roiling smoke beyond the double doors, as Jared shouted orders to the other men. "Keep the hoses going in the windows, wet it down!"

"Jack! No! Don't do it!" Olivia ran for the doors, thinking wildly that if he was going into that inferno, he was going to have to drag her right along with him.

But then, in midflight, she felt a hand close over her arm. She was yanked backward. Another hand grabbed her other arm.

She kicked, she screamed. "Let me go! Don't you see? He'll die in there, don't you see?"

But the strong hands held her fast. "Easy, Olivia, settle down." Jared spoke gently. But his grip was firm. She knew he wasn't going to let her go.

Jared shouted more orders. "Patrick, go around back. See if any of the guys back there have seen a sign of Dad."

Patrick shot around the back of the building.

Olivia forced herself to speak reasonably. "Jared, please. I'm all right. You can let me go now."

Jared only shook his head and held on.

Jack could hardly see. The smoke was too thick. All around him was the hissing of water hitting fire, the roar of hungry, undoused flames, the crackling of boiling pitch and the creaking of burned beams about to give.

Smoke clogged his lungs, stinging. It burned to draw breath. He yanked his shirt over his mouth. The shirt was wet, thanks to Jared. It helped a little to screen out the acrid smoke. But not much.

To his left there was the sound of bottles exploding behind the bar. Then a long, whiplike *snap*—the big mirror cracking from the heat. Next, a tinkling like a thousand tiny bells as the mirror disintegrated and collapsed onto the floor.

Jack peered through slitted eyes, trying to get his bearings, to see his way to the back room. He looked from side to side. Jets of water from the hoses shot by through the windows behind him. He had to be careful not to stumble into them. Their pressure was great enough to knock him off his feet and push him into the blaze that raged all around.

He coughed, swiped at his burning eyes, then peered toward where he thought the back room should be. He saw a hole there, where the curtain had hung. And beyond it, a fire storm. It looked like the whole back room was alive with flame.

He heard an ominous crack, like a gunshot in the roar and whisper of the fire. And he watched, stunned and sickened, as the ceiling in the back room crashed down to meet the floor.

If Oggie was still in there, he'd been burned alive. And now the charred old bones were crushed as well.

Jack tried to see if there might be a way through the fire, out the back hall through which he'd entered earlier that night. But the back hall looked like a tunnel of flame.

Jack dropped to the floor, starving for air. He sucked it in, smoky, but at least breathable this low down. Over behind the bar more bottles exploded, more glass rained down.

He looked around again and saw that the support beams

in the middle of the floor were afire. The flames licked and ate at them.

Overhead the ceiling seemed to be moaning.

Jack knew there was no time. He knew that if the old man wasn't outside somewhere right now, he was dead. If Jack wanted to save himself, it was time to get out.

And yet he didn't move.

He thought of the people he had saved in his life.

He'd dragged a buddy, half-dead, through a jungle on the other side of the world. The buddy had lived.

He'd pulled a baby from a burning hut. The baby had lain so still, he'd thought life had left it. But when he put his mouth on the tiny blue lips and gave the gift of breath, the baby coughed and puckered up its little face and let out an angry cry.

He'd tracked a little girl to a mine shaft where her kidnappers had left her to die. She was so weak she couldn't hold on to him. She lay limp, her head lolling, as Jack carried her out. After a few days in the hospital she'd been fine.

But Oggie Jones was not going to be fine. Jack's own father, and he'd come too late to save him.

Jack's eyes were full, burning, wet. And it wasn't just the smoke. Something was breaking inside of him, like a wall going, a shell cracking.

"Oggie! Damn you, Oggie, are you here?" he shouted, knowing it was useless, knowing the old man was dead.

But what had it been for, all those people he had saved, all the women and the children, the buddies and the babies? He knew what for. To give them a chance to return to what Jack had never known: a home and a family. A place that mattered and people who cared.

And this time? This time was different. He didn't want to admit it. He fought admitting it. But this was for *him*.

He'd been a fool to turn away from the old man. He could see that clearly, now that it was too late.

He wanted the old man alive. He wanted a chance with him. He *wanted* the family he had never known....

Overhead the ceiling gave an ominous, extended moan. Not more than a minute—two, at the most—and it would come crashing down.

"Oggie!" Jack shouted one more time. And then, after a short fit of coughing, he screamed, "Father! Father, where the hell are you?"

More bottles exploded. The water from the hoses hissed and popped in a futile effort to douse the conflagration.

Jack's body, which had learned the habit of survival in a thousand different trials, pushed to go on living. He began to crawl backward.

He was almost to the door when he heard the groan.

It sounded human.

He froze, peering to his right, where he thought he'd heard the sound. Smoke eddied and swirled. Then he saw it. Sticking out from the overturned table not five feet away. An arm and a gnarled, aged, human hand.

With a cry like an animal in pain, Jack slithered closer. The arm disappeared beneath the overturned table. Somehow Oggie had made it this far.

Jack shoved the table up and over. It fell into the nearby flames with a muffled crash. The old man rolled his head and groaned once more, unconscious, but definitely alive.

Jack lifted himself to a crouch, pulled the limp body up by an arm and positioned himself.

In the middle of the room, one of the support beams collapsed. It broke in the middle and gave. Sparks showered. The ceiling cracked and groaned. Jack could hear it beginning to go.

With a yank that made the unconscious man moan, Jack pulled his father onto his back. Then he rolled to his feet, still crouching beneath his load, and aimed himself at the door.

"Everybody back!" Jared shouted, taking his own advice and pulling Olivia along with him. "The roof's going!"

Olivia, numb by then, staggered back because she was pulled that way. She stared, awestruck, broken inside, as the Hole in the Wall saloon caved in upon itself. She heard the groaning, the cracking, and then the center gave, pulling the rest in with it.

Sparks shot up to heaven. The red glow inside peeled open to expose itself to the night. It was savagely beautiful.

And it meant Jack was dead.

And just as she allowed her mind to frame her loss, it happened.

A bent, distorted figure burst through the double doors.

Chapter Eighteen

"Look!" someone shouted.

"Woo-ee, lookee there!"

"Do you believe it?"

"It's Roper."

"He's got Oggie."

"He's saved the old man!"

Olivia blinked. And joy shot through her, sharp as a lance, painfully sweet. "Jack!" She yanked against Jared's restraining hands. This time he released her.

Olivia ran. It wasn't far.

But she wasn't quite fast enough. There were others ahead of her. They'd already formed a circle around Jack and his burden. So she stood on tiptoe behind Rocky Collins, peering over his shoulder, trying to see what was happening in the center of the circle where Jack was.

Olivia glanced from face to face. Brendan was there. And Amy. Delilah. Patrick. Regina. Eden. All of them. All the

Joneses. Even Jared managed to slip past the outside of the circle to get to his father's side. Except for the men who had to stay with the fire, everyone crowded around Oggie Jones.

Carefully Jack knelt and laid the old man on the ground.

Delilah knelt beside Jack. "My sweet Lord." Delilah looked at Jack. There were tears in her dark eyes and a warm, exultant gratitude. "You did it. You brought him out."

"Come on now, folks, let us through. Let us see to this." It was the calm voice of Will Bacon, the practical nurse who ran the local medical clinic. People moved aside for Will, who was followed by Bertha Potts. Bertha drove the ambulance and assisted Will at the clinic.

Will crouched beside Oggie, who was coughing and coming around.

"Just take it easy, Oggie," Will said. "Looks like you're going to be all right."

Oggie coughed some more and tried to speak, but another bout of coughing racked him.

"You just lie down. Bertha, a pillow, please. And bring the oxygen tank."

But Oggie shoved the pillow away and sat up. "Let a man get his breath, will you, Will Bacon?"

"All right, all right."

"What happened, Oggie?" someone asked.

Bertha tersely instructed, "Don't bother him with questions now. Can't you see the man can hardly breathe?"

Oggie coughed some more. But all eyes were on him. He wasn't passing up an opportunity like that. He shoved away the oxygen mask that Bertha was trying to put over his mouth. "I woke up from a little nap. The damn place was alive with flames. I couldn't find my cane. I staggered out through the burnin' curtain, into the main room. I made it almost to the door. And then I tripped. Grabbed on to a table, and it came down over me. It's the last thing I remember—until I heard someone calling me." Oggie hacked and spat.

"It was that cigar of yours, wasn't it, Father?" Delilah's tears had already passed. Now she was looking more herself.

Oggie grumbled and hacked some more. "Don't get on me, Delilah, damn it. Can't you see I almost died?"

"But if I've told you once, I've told you a hundred times—"

"Shh, sweetheart," Sam Fletcher said gently, behind his wife.

Delilah looked up at him. "But Sam—"

Sam shook his head. Delilah said no more.

And now Oggie was looking at Jack's soot-smeared face. "It was you, wasn't it? You were callin' me." Oggie grabbed Jack's hand. "You pulled me out, didn't you, son?"

Jack nodded.

"You called me *Father*...."

Jack nodded again.

Will Bacon shook his head. "Can you folks go into all this later and let me and Bertha do our job? Oggie, you've got one heck of a goose egg here. And you've got several burns that need attention."

"Well, I told you, I fell down and hit my head. And I was just pulled from a burnin' buildin'. It makes sense I got burned. But right now I'm tryin' to talk to my son here. This is important. This is priority number one, you hear what I'm tellin' you, Will?"

"Take it easy. Bertha, let's get him into the ambulance."

"What the hell's the matter with you, Will?" Oggie demanded to know. "Can't you see what's happenin' here?"

"Settle down," Jack soothed. "Settle down. Will's right. You need care. And we can talk about this later." Jack smiled.

"You hear that?" Oggie gave in to another coughing fit. But as soon as it passed, he went on, "You all hear that? He's gonna talk to me. We got a lot to say to each other. 'Cause, you see, I'm his dad."

Delilah grunted. "Oh, well. What a surprise," she muttered, not sounding surprised at all.

Jack blinked and stared at his half sister, while those nearby in the crowd whispered knowingly among themselves.

Delilah rolled her eyes. "Oh, please. It was so obvious, right from the first. I grew up with three other brothers just like you, after all." She put her hand on Jack's shoulder and stared into his eyes. Suddenly she was looking emotional again. "And I'm glad we've found you...." She sniffed a little. "Though I admit, I'd like to hear you tell me that my father never cheated on my mother. That's the one thing I've always respected about my brothers and my father. They drive the rest of us crazy, but they never cheat."

"He didn't," Jack said gruffly.

"Damn straight I didn't," Oggie groused. And then he yelled at Bertha. "Hey, easy there. Can't you see I'm old?"

"Quit your bellyaching," Bertha advised. By then Oggie was on the gurney.

"Everyone, clear the way."

The crowd cleared a path as they wheeled the old man toward the ambulance.

Jack watched them take his father away. And then he handed Jared back his hard hat and jacket and turned to scan the crowd.

Olivia waved. He saw her. She smiled at him. He pushed through the crowd until he reached her side. He held out his hand.

She took it.

Right then, in the circle where Oggie had been, Eden groaned and clutched her huge stomach.

"Eden, honey?" Jared's usually stern face was a portrait of stark fear. "Is it—?"

"Yes." Eden's contorted expression slowly relaxed. "There. Got through that one."

"Oh, my God."

"Jared, it's okay."

But Jared was already shouting. "Hey, I need help! Bertha, Will, get the hell over here. Eden's having the baby now!"

"Jared. Jared, settle down." Eden reached for her husband's hand and brought it to her lips. "I'm fine. And anyway, first babies take a while." She glanced at the Mercantile Grill, which was still ablaze inside. She sighed. "Well, it could be worse. The Mercantile building is brick. They'll be able to save the structure at least."

Right then the front wall of the bar gave way. It collapsed inward like a toy stepped on by a thoughtless child.

Rocky Collins, who practically lived at the Hole in the Wall, stared at the disintegrating building as if he were losing his best friend.

Tim Brown, another Hole in the Wall regular, patted Rocky on the back. "Don't worry, Rock. You know Eden. She'll have them rebuilding in no time flat."

"Yeah. Sure. You're right, Tim." Rocky tried to keep his chin up. "Somehow, I'll get by till the Hole in the Wall's standin' again."

By that time Will Bacon was at Eden's side. "I think you'd better ride along with us to the hospital, don't you?"

Eden cried out as another contraction gripped her. When it eased, she agreed. "Yes, I think you're right."

Jared helped his wife into the ambulance, where Oggie was already waiting. "I'll follow in the truck," he told Will Bacon. Patrick and Brendan promised they'd watch over things until the fire had burned down to nothing and everyone went home. The ambulance pulled away. As soon as it disappeared around a bend, everyone turned back to watch the burning buildings and the relentless efforts of the volunteer firemen.

At last, as the sky to the east began to turn pale, the fire was declared contained. A few random threads of smoke still spiraled up from the ruins, but nothing was left burning. The Mercantile stood gutted, a black shell. The Hole in the Wall was no more.

Slowly, in groups of twos and threes, the townspeople left the scene and trudged back to their beds.

Except for Olivia and Jack.

They stood side by side, holding hands, until the last fire fighter had gone home. Then, together, they turned to face the eastern mountains where a new day was being born.

Olivia watched the thread of gold that was the sun as it strove to breach the crest of the highest hill. She was thinking that only a few hours before, she'd wanted to hold back the dawn.

Now she smiled in welcome, as morning claimed the world. "You understand now. Don't you, Jack?" she asked him quietly.

He nodded. Then he lifted her hand and pressed it to his lips.

She looked at him, into those beautiful obsidian eyes. "And we're staying here, we're living here."

"All right." They were only two little words. But they meant everything to her.

But Jack was still a realist. He tipped his head toward the burned-out Mercantile. "I want to point out, however, that we're both unemployed, as of now."

"We'll find something. The family will help. And I'm rich, after all."

She didn't say which family. He knew. The Joneses. The

family that had taken her in and helped her to find the incredible woman inside herself. The family that seemed to have been his all along.

"I won't live off your money."

"Of course you won't. But this is our place, Jack." Her face glowed in the new light of day. "The place we really found each other. The place we're meant to be, where our children will grow up. It's going to be a great life we'll have, Jack. I know it. I feel it in my bones."

The sun broke above the mountains. Jack Roper reached for the woman he loved. They kissed, there in the middle of Main Street, with the dawn on one side and the burned-out buildings on the other. Then, hand in hand, they turned for the little house on Rambling Lane.

They made only one stop on the way, at Swan's Motel, where they let Buzz out of Jack's room. The cat followed behind them, loyal as a dog, all the way to the white house with green trim.

Inside they undressed and showered quickly, together. Then they climbed wearily into bed.

He gathered her into his arms. "I love you."

"I know. And I'm so glad you're willing to say it at last."

"We're getting married. As soon as we can get a license. Today. Tomorrow, at the latest."

"Can we get some sleep first?"

"All right. But as soon as we wake up, we're looking for the nearest justice of the peace."

"Absolutely." She yawned and snuggled up close.

Jack nuzzled her damp hair. She smelled, as always, of soap and of sweetness.

Her breath was even, her body limp. She was already asleep.

Jack lay holding her, thinking about the shell, vanished now, that had for so long encased his heart. Olivia had seen beyond it. She'd led him to this town where his family waited.

And then she and the town and a crazy old man had set to work on him, to crack open the shell.

Jack Roper was a realist. He didn't believe in fate. Yet, somehow, while hunting down a poor little rich girl, he had found everything that had been missing in his life: a family, a life's mate and a true home at last.

In his arms Olivia stirred. "Jack?"

"Umm?"

"Stop thinking, Jack. Get some rest."

"I think we should be married in Vegas."

"Great idea." She yawned. "Now please. Rest."

He kissed the crown of her head. "Shh. All right."

At the foot of the bed, Buzz lay purring. Jack Roper, home at last, closed his eyes and went to sleep.

Epilogue

Jack and Olivia were married in Las Vegas the next day.
When they called to tell the family about it, they learned
that Eden Jones had delivered a baby girl, Sally Louise.

In the following spring Regina Jones had a daughter.
They named her Anthea Jane.

Also in the spring, the calico cat that Olivia had befriended produced four kittens. Two of them bore a startling
resemblance to Buzz.

The Hole in the Wall and the Mercantile Grill reopened
eighteen months after the fire. Six months after that, Olivia
became head chef there.

Jack found a job at the local sheriff's station as a deputy.
When the county sheriff retired, Jack ran for his job and
won.

At one hundred and three years old Oggie Jones was in-
terviewed by a reporter from the *Sacramento Bee*.

"To what do you attribute your long life, Mr. Jones?"
the reporter inquired at the end of the interview.

"Fortitude, orneriness and having known the love of a good woman—not necessarily in that order. Anythin' else you want to know?"

"No, Mr. Jones," the reporter replied. "I think that just about says it all."

* * * * *

Award-winning, bestselling authors

Christine Rimmer & Laurie Paige

are known for their heartwarming, emotional stories of
family, children and the connections that grow between
couples. Here are two compelling stories about
marriages of convenience....

DOUBLE DARE

They'd known each other forever and Casey and Joanna
married to keep custody of his nephew. But sharing a life, a
family...a *bed*...wasn't like anything they'd ever expected....

MOLLY DARLING

He knew his tiny daughter needed a mother—and that
Molly would shower Lass with tender care. But what
happened when Sam realized he wanted Molly's love,
tenderness and *passion* for himself?

Come see how

Convenient Vows **become anything but**
convenient in May 2001.

Available wherever Silhouette books are sold!

Silhouette®
Where love comes alive™

If you enjoyed what you just read,
then we've got an offer you can't resist!

Take 2
bestselling novels FREE!
Plus get a FREE surprise gift!

Beloved author
❤ *Sherryl Woods*

is back with a brand-new miniseries

The Calamity Janes

**Five women. Five Dreams.
A lifetime of friendship....**

On Sale May 2001—DO YOU TAKE THIS REBEL?
Silhouette Special Edition

On Sale August 2001—COURTING THE ENEMY
Silhouette Special Edition

On Sale September 2001—TO CATCH A THIEF
Silhouette Special Edition

On Sale October 2001—THE CALAMITY JANES
Silhouette Single Title

On Sale November 2001—WRANGLING THE REDHEAD
Silhouette Special Edition

"Sherryl Woods is an author who writes with a very
special warmth, wit, charm and intelligence."
—*New York Times* bestselling author
Heather Graham Pozzessere

Available at your favorite retail outlet.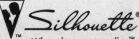

▼ *Silhouette*®
Where love comes alive™

Visit Silhouette at www.eHarlequin.com
SSETCJ

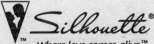

LINDSAY McKENNA

continues her most popular series with a
brand-new, longer-length book.

And it's the story you've been waiting for....

Morgan's Mercenaries:
Heart of Stone

They had met before. Battled before. And
Captain Maya Stevenson had never again
wanted to lay eyes on Major Dane York—
the man who once tried to destroy
her military career! But on their latest
mission together, Maya discovered that beneath
the fury in Dane's eyes lay a raging passion. Now she
struggled against dangerous desire, as Dane's command
over her seemed greater still. For this time, he laid claim
to her heart....

Only from Lindsay McKenna and Silhouette Books!

> "When it comes to action and romance,
> nobody does it better than Ms. McKenna."
> —*Romantic Times Magazine*

Available in March at your favorite retail outlet.

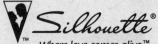